# Historical Adventures: 1

# Historical Adventures: 1

The Brethren

★

Red Eve

**H. Rider Haggard**

*Historical Adventures: 1*
*The Brethren & Red Eve*
by H. Rider Haggard

Leonaur is an imprint of Oakpast Ltd



ISBN: 978-1-84677-994-7 (hardcover)
ISBN: 978-1-84677-993-0 (softcover)

**http://www.leonaur.com**

**Publisher's Notes**

The views expressed in this book are not necessarily those of the publisher.

# Contents

# The Brethren

# Dedication

R.M.S. *Mongolia*

12th May, 1904

Mayhap, Ella, here too distance lends its enchantment, and these gallant brethren would have quarrelled over Rosamund, or even had their long swords at each other's throat. Mayhap that Princess and heroine might have failed in the hour of her trial and never earned her saintly crown. Mayhap the good horse "Smoke" would have fallen on the Narrow Way, leaving false Lozelle a victor, and Masouda, the royal-hearted, would have offered up a strangely different sacrifice upon the altars of her passionate desire.

Still, let us hold otherwise, though we grow grey and know the world for what it is. Let us for a little time think as we thought while we were young; when faith knew no fears for anything and death had not knocked upon our doors; when you opened also to my childish eyes that gate of ivory and pearl which leads to the blessed kingdom of Romance.

At the least I am sure, and I believe that you, my sister, will agree with me, that, above and beyond its terrors and its pitfalls, Imagination has few finer qualities, and none, perhaps, more helpful to our hearts, than those which enable us for an hour to dream that men and women, their fortunes and their fate, are as we would fashion them.

*H. Rider Haggard*

To Mrs. Maddison Green

*Two lovers by the maiden sate,*
*Without a glance of jealous hate;*
*The maid her lovers sat between,*
*With open brow and equal mien;—*
*It is a sight but rarely spied,*
*Thanks to man's wrath and woman's pride.*

Scott

# Author's Note

Standing a while ago upon the flower-clad plain above Tiberius, by the Lake of Galilee, the writer gazed at the double peaks of the Hill of Hattin. Here, or so tradition says, Christ preached the Sermon on the Mount—that perfect rule of gentleness and peace. Here, too—and this is certain—after nearly twelve centuries had gone by, Yusuf Salah-ed-din, whom we know as the Sultan Saladin, crushed the Christian power in Palestine in perhaps the most terrible battle which that land of blood has known. Thus the Mount of the Beatitudes became the Mount of Massacre.

Whilst musing on these strangely-contrasted scenes enacted in one place there arose in his mind a desire to weave, as best he might, a tale wherein any who are drawn to the romance of that pregnant and mysterious epoch, when men by thousands were glad to lay down their lives for visions and spiritual hopes, could find a picture, however faint and broken, of the long war between Cross and Crescent waged among the Syrian plains and deserts. Of Christian knights and ladies also, and their loves and sufferings in England and the East; of the fearful lord of the Assassins whom the Franks called Old Man of the Mountain, and his fortress city, Masyaf. Of the great-hearted, if at times cruel Saladin and his fierce Saracens; of the rout at Hattin itself, on whose rocky height the Holy Rood was set up as a standard and captured, to be seen no more by Christian eyes; and of the last surrender, whereby the Crusaders lost Jerusalem forever.

Of that desire this story is the fruit.

# Prologue

Salah-ed-din, Commander of the Faithful, the king Strong to Aid, Sovereign of the East, sat at night in his palace at Damascus and brooded on the wonderful ways of God, by Whom he had been lifted to his high estate. He remembered how, when he was but small in the eyes of men, Nour-ed-din, king of Syria, forced him to accompany his uncle, Shirkuh, to Egypt, whither he went, "like one driven to his death," and how, against his own will, there he rose to greatness. He thought of his father, the wise Ayoub, and the brethren with whom he was brought up, all of them dead now save one; and of his sisters, whom he had cherished. Most of all did he think of her, Zobeide, who had been stolen away by the knight whom she loved even to the loss of her own soul—yes, by the English friend of his youth, his father's prisoner, Sir Andrew D'Arcy, who, led astray by passion, had done him and his house this grievous wrong. He had sworn, he remembered, that he would bring her back even from England, and already had planned to kill her husband and capture her when he learned her death. She had left a child, or so his spies told him, who, if she still lived, must be a woman now—his own niece, though half of noble English blood.

Then his mind wandered from this old, half-forgotten story to the woe and blood in which his days were set, and to the last great struggle between the followers of the prophets Jesus and Mahomet, that Jihad [Holy War] for which he made ready—and he sighed. For he was a merciful man, who loved not slaughter, although his fierce faith drove him from war to war.

Salah-ed-din slept and dreamed of peace. In his dream a maiden stood before him. Presently, when she lifted her veil, he saw that she was beautiful, with features like his own, but fairer, and knew her surely for the daughter of his sister who had fled with the English knight. Now he wondered why she visited him thus, and in his vision prayed Allah to make the matter clear. Then of a sudden he saw this same woman standing before him on a Syrian plain, and on either side of her a countless host of Saracens and Franks, of whom thousands and tens of thousands were appointed to death. Lo! he, Salah-ed-din, charged at the head of his squadrons, scimitar aloft, but she held up her hand and stayed him.

"What do you hear, my niece?" he asked.

"I am come to save the lives of men through you," she answered; "therefore was I born of your blood, and therefore I am sent to you. Put up your sword, King, and spare them."

"Say, maiden, what ransom do you bring to buy this multitude from doom? What ransom, and what gift?"

"The ransom of my own blood freely offered, and Heaven's gift of peace to your sinful soul, O King." And with that outstretched hand she drew down his keen-edged scimitar until it rested on her breast.

Salah-ed-din awoke, and marvelled on his dream, but said nothing of it to any man. The next night it returned to him, and the memory of it went with him all the day that followed, but still he said nothing.

When on the third night he dreamed it yet again, even more vividly, then he was sure that this thing was from God, and summoned his holy Imauns and his Diviners, and took counsel with them. These, after they had listened, prayed and consulted, spoke thus:

"O Sultan, Allah has warned you in shadows that the woman, your niece, who dwells far away in England, shall by her own nobleness and sacrifice, in some time to come, save you from shedding a sea of blood, and bring rest upon the land. We charge you, therefore, draw this lady to your court, and keep her ever by your side, since if she escape you, her peace goes with her."

Salah-ed-din said that this interpretation was wise and true, for thus also he had read his dream. Then he summoned a certain false knight who bore the Cross upon his breast, but in secret had accepted the Koran, a Frankish spy of his, who came from that country where dwelt the maiden, his niece, and from him learned about her, her father, and her home. With him and another spy who passed as a Christian palmer, by the aid of Prince Hassan, one of the greatest and most trusted of his Emirs, he made a cunning plan for the capture of the maiden if she would not come willingly, and for her bearing away to Syria.

Moreover—that in the eyes of all men her dignity might be worthy of her high blood and fate—by his decree he created her, the niece whom he had never seen, Princess of Baalbec, with great possessions—a rule that her grandfather, Ayoub, and her uncle, Izzeddin, had held before her. Also he purchased a stout galley of war, manning it with proved sailors and with chosen men-at-arms, under the command of the Prince Hassan, and wrote a letter to the English lord, Sir Andrew D'Arcy, and to his daughter, and prepared a royal gift of jewels, and sent them to the lady, his niece, far away in England, and with it the Patent of her rank. Her he commanded this company to win by peace, or force, or fraud, as best they might, but that without her not one of them should dare to look upon his face again. And with these he sent the two Frankish spies, who knew the place where the lady lived, one of whom, the false knight, was a skilled mariner and the captain of the ship.

These things did Yusuf Salah-ed-din, and waited patiently till it should please God to accomplish the vision with which God had filled his soul in sleep.

## Chapter 1

# By the Waters of Death Creek

From the sea-wall on the coast of Essex, Rosamund looked out across the ocean eastwards. To right and left, but a little behind her, like guards attending the person of their sovereign, stood her cousins, the twin brethren, Godwin and Wulf, tall and shapely men. Godwin was still as a statue, his hands folded over the hilt of the long, scabbarded sword, of which the point was set on the ground before him, but Wulf, his brother, moved restlessly, and at length yawned aloud. They were beautiful to look at, all three of them, as they appeared in the splendour of their youth and health. The imperial Rosamund, dark-haired and eyed, ivory skinned and slender-waisted, a posy of marsh flowers in her hand; the pale, stately Godwin, with his dreaming face; and the bold-fronted, blue-eyed warrior, Wulf, Saxon to his finger-tips, notwithstanding his father's Norman blood.

At the sound of that unstifled yawn, Rosamund turned her head with the slow grace which marked her every movement.

"Would you sleep already, Wulf, and the sun not yet down?" she asked in her rich, low voice, which, perhaps because of its foreign accent, seemed quite different to that of any other woman.

"I think so, Rosamund," he answered. "It would serve to pass the time, and now that you have finished gathering those yellow flowers which we rode so far to seek, the time—is somewhat long."

"Shame on you, Wulf," she said, smiling. "Look upon yonder sea and sky, at that sheet of bloom all gold and purple—"

"I have looked for hard on half an hour, Cousin Rosamund; also at your back and at Godwin's left arm and side-face, till in truth I thought myself kneeling in Stangate Priory staring at my father's effigy upon his tomb, while Prior John pattered the Mass. Why, if you stood it on its feet, it is Godwin, the same crossed hands resting on the sword, the same cold, silent face staring at the sky."

"Godwin as Godwin will no doubt one day be, or so he hopes—that is, if the saints give him grace to do such deeds as did our sire," interrupted his brother.

Wulf looked at him, and a curious flash of inspiration shone in his blue eyes.

"No, I think not," he answered; "the deeds you may do, and greater, but surely you will lie wrapped not in a shirt of mail, but with a monk's cowl at the last—unless a woman robs you of it and the quickest road to heaven. Tell me now, what are you thinking of, you two—for I have been wondering in my dull way, and am curious to learn how far I stand from truth? Rosamund, speak first. Nay, not all the truth—a maid's thoughts are her own—but just the cream of it, that which rises to the top and should be skimmed."

Rosamund sighed. "I? I was thinking of the East, where the sun shines ever and the seas are blue as my girdle stones, and men are full of strange learning—"

"And women are men's slaves!" interrupted Wulf. "Still, it is natural that you should think of the East who have that blood in your veins, and high blood, if all tales be true. Say, Princess"—and he bowed the knee to her with an affectation of mockery which could not hide his earnest reverence—"say, Princess, my cousin, granddaughter of Ayoub and niece of the mighty monarch, Yusuf Salah-ed-din, do you wish to leave this pale land and visit your dominions in Egypt and in Syria?"

She listened, and at his words her eyes seemed to take fire, the stately form to erect itself, the breast to heave, and the thin nostrils to grow wider as though they scented some sweet, remembered perfume. Indeed, at that moment, standing there on the promontory above the seas, Rosamund looked a very queen.

Presently she answered him with another question.

"And how would they greet me there, Wulf, who am a Norman D'Arcy and a Christian maid?"

"The first they would forgive you, since that blood is none so ill either, and for the second—why, faiths can be changed."

Then it was that Godwin spoke for the first time.

"Wulf, Wulf," he said sternly, "keep watch upon your tongue, for there are things that should not be said even as a silly jest. See you, I love my cousin here better than aught else upon the earth—"

"There, at least, we agree," broke in Wulf.

"Better than aught else on the earth," repeated Godwin; "but, by the Holy Blood and by St. Peter, at whose shrine we are, I would kill her with my own hand before her lips kissed the book of the false prophet."

"Or any of his followers," muttered Wulf to himself, but fortunately, perhaps, too low for either of his companions to hear. Aloud he said, "You understand, Rosamund, you must be careful, for Godwin ever keeps his word, and that would be but a poor end for so much birth and beauty and wisdom."

"Oh, cease mocking, Wulf," she answered, laying her hand lightly on the tunic that hid his shirt of mail. "Cease mocking, and pray St. Chad, the builder of this church, that no such dreadful choice may ever be forced upon you, or me, or your beloved brother—who, indeed, in such a case would do right to slay me."

"Well, if it were," answered Wulf, and his fair face flushed as he spoke, "I trust that we should know how to meet it. After all, is it so very hard to choose between death and duty?"

"I know not," she replied; "but oft-times sacrifice seems easy when seen from far away; also, things may be lost that are more prized than life."

"What things? Do you mean place, or wealth, or—love?"

"Tell me," said Rosamund, changing her tone, "what is that boat rowing round the river's mouth? A while ago it hung upon its oars as though those within it watched us."

"Fisher-folk," answered Wulf carelessly. "I saw their nets."

"Yes; but beneath them something gleamed bright, like swords."

"Fish," said Wulf; "we are at peace in Essex." Although Rosamund did not look convinced, he went on: "Now for Godwin's thoughts—what were they?"

"Brother, if you would know, of the East also—the East and its wars."

"Which have brought us no great luck," answered Wulf, "seeing that our sire was slain in them and naught of him came home again save his heart, which lies at Stangate yonder."

"How better could he die," asked Godwin, "than fighting for the Cross of Christ? Is not that death of his at Harenc told of to this day? By our Lady, I pray for one but half as glorious!"

"Aye, he died well—he died well," said Wulf, his blue eyes flashing and his hand creeping to his sword hilt. "But, brother, there is peace at Jerusalem, as in Essex."

"Peace? Yes; but soon there will be war again. The monk Peter—he whom we saw at Stangate last Sunday, and who left Syria but six months gone—told me that it was coming fast. Even now the Sultan Saladin, sitting at Damascus, summons his hosts from far and wide, while his priests preach battle amongst the tribes and barons of the East. And when it comes, brother, shall we not be there to share it, as were our grandfather, our father, our uncle, and so many of our kin? Shall we rot here in this dull land, as by our uncle's wish we have done these many years, yes, ever since we were home from the Scottish war, and count the kine and plough the fields like peasants, while our peers are charging on the pagan, and the banners wave, and the blood runs red upon the holy sands of Palestine?"

Now it was Wulf's turn to take fire.

"By our Lady in Heaven, and our lady here!"—and he looked at Rosamund, who was watching the pair of them with her quiet thoughtful eyes—"go when you will, Godwin, and I go with you, and as our birth was one birth, so, if it is decreed, let our death be one death." And suddenly his hand that had been playing with the sword-hilt gripped it fast, and tore the long, lean blade from its scabbard and cast it high into the air, flashing in the sunlight, to catch it as it fell again, while in a voice that caused the wild fowl to rise in thunder from the Saltings beneath, Wulf shouted the old war-cry that had rung on so many a field—"A D'Arcy! a D'Arcy! Meet D'Arcy, meet Death!" Then he sheathed his sword again and added in a shamed voice, "Are we children that we fight where no foe is? Still, brother, may we find him soon!"

Godwin smiled grimly, but answered nothing; only Rosamund said:

"So, my cousins, you would be away, perhaps to return no more, and that will part us. But"—and her voice broke somewhat—"such is the woman's lot, since men like you ever love the bare sword best of all, nor should I think well of you were it otherwise. Yet, cousins, I know not why"—and she shivered a little—"it comes into my heart that Heaven often answers such prayers swiftly. Oh, Wulf! your sword looked very red in the sunlight but now: I say that it looked very red in the sunlight. I am afraid—of I know not what. Well, we must be going, for we have nine miles to ride, and the dark is not so far away. But first, my cousins, come with me into this shrine, and let us pray St. Peter and St. Chad to guard us on our journey home."

"Our journey?" said Wulf anxiously. "What is there for you to fear in a nine-mile ride along the shores of the Blackwater?"

"I said our journey home Wulf; and home is not in the hall at Steeple, but yonder," and she pointed to the quiet, brooding sky.

"Well answered," said Godwin, "in this ancient place, whence so many have journeyed home; all the Romans who are dead, when it was their fortress, and the Saxons who came after them, and others without count."

Then they turned and entered the old church—one of the first that ever was in Britain, rough-built of Roman stone by the very hands of Chad, the Saxon saint, more than five hundred years before their day. Here they knelt a while at the rude altar and prayed, each of them in his or her own fashion, then crossed themselves, and rose to seek their horses, which were tied in the shed hard by.

Now there were two roads, or rather tracks, back to the Hall at Steeple—one a mile or so inland, that ran through the village of Bradwell, and the other, the shorter way, along the edge of the Saltings to the narrow water known as Death Creek, at the head of which the traveller to Steeple must strike inland, leaving the Priory of Stangate on his right. It was this latter path they chose, since at low tide the going there is good for horses—which, even in the summer, that of the inland track was not. Also they wished to be at home by supper-time, lest the old knight, Sir Andrew D'Arcy, the father of Rosamund and the uncle of the orphan brethren, should grow anxious, and perhaps come out to seek them.

For the half of an hour or more they rode along the edge of the Saltings, for the most part in silence that was broken only by the cry of curlew and the lap of the turning tide. No human being did they see, indeed, for this place was very desolate and unvisited, save now and again by fishermen. At length, just as the sun began to sink, they approached the shore of Death Creek—a sheet of tidal water which ran a mile or more inland, growing ever narrower, but was here some three hundred yards in breadth. They were well mounted, all three of them. Indeed, Rosamund's horse, a great grey, her father's gift to her, was famous in that country-side for its swiftness and power, also because it was so docile that a child could ride it; while those of the brethren were heavy-built but well-trained war steeds, taught to stand where they were left, and to charge when they were urged, without fear of shouting men or flashing steel.

Now the ground lay thus. Some seventy yards from the shore of Death Creek and parallel to it, a tongue of land, covered with scrub and a few oaks, ran down into the Saltings, its point ending on their path, beyond which were a swamp and the broad river. Between this tongue and the shore of the creek the track wended its way to the uplands. It was an ancient track; indeed the reason of its existence was that here the Romans or some other long dead hands had built a narrow mole or quay of rough stone, forty or fifty yards in length, out into the water of the creek, doubtless to serve as a convenience for fisher boats, which could lie alongside of it even at low tide. This mole had been much destroyed by centuries of washing, so that the end of it lay below water, although the landward part was still almost sound and level.

Coming over the little rise at the top of the wooded tongue, the quick eyes of Wulf, who rode first—for here the path along the border of the swamp was so narrow that they must go in single file—caught sight of a large, empty boat moored to an iron ring set in the wall of the mole.

"Your fishermen have landed, Rosamund," he said, "and doubtless gone up to Bradwell."

"That is strange," she answered anxiously, "since here no fishermen ever come." And she checked her horse as though to turn.

"Whether they come or not, certainly they have gone," said Godwin, craning forward to look about him; "so, as we have nothing to fear from an empty boat, let us push on."

On they rode accordingly, until they came to the root of the stone quay or pier, when a sound behind them caused them to look back. Then they saw a sight that sent the blood to their hearts, for there behind them, leaping down one by one on to that narrow footway, were men armed with naked swords, six or eight of them, all of whom, they noted, had strips of linen pierced with eyelet holes tied beneath their helms or leather caps, so as to conceal their faces.

"A snare! a snare!" cried Wulf, drawing his sword. "Swift! follow me up the Bradwell path!" and he struck the spurs into his horse. It bounded forward, to be dragged next second with all the weight of his powerful arm almost to its haunches. "God's mercy!" he cried, "there are more of them!" And more there were, for another band of men armed and linen-hooded like the first, had leapt down on to that Bradwell path, amongst them a stout man, who seemed to be unarmed, except for a long, crooked knife at his girdle and a coat of ringed mail, which showed through the opening of his loose tunic.

"To the boat!" shouted Godwin, whereat the stout man laughed—a light, penetrating laugh, which even then all three of them heard and noted.

Along the quay they rode, since there was nowhere else that they could go, with both paths barred, and swamp and water on one side of them, and a steep, wooded bank upon the other. When they reached it, they found why the man had laughed, for the boat was made fast with a strong chain that could not be cut; more, her sail and oars were gone.

"Get into it," mocked a voice; "or, at least, let the lady get in; it will save us the trouble of carrying her there."

Now Rosamund turned very pale, while the face of Wulf went red and white, and he gripped his sword-hilt. But Godwin, calm as ever, rode forward a few paces, and said quietly:

"Of your courtesy, say what you need of us. If it be money, we have none—nothing but our arms and horses, which I think may cost you dear."

Now the man with the crooked knife advanced a little, accompanied by another man, a tall, supple-looking knave, into whose ear he whispered.

"My master says," answered the tall man, "that you have with you that which is of more value than all the king's gold—a very fair lady, of whom someone has urgent need. Give her up now, and go your way with your arms and horses, for you are gallant young men, whose blood we do not wish to shed."

At this it was the turn of the brethren to laugh, which both of them did together.

"Give her up," answered Godwin, "and go our ways dishonoured? Aye, with our breath, but not before. Who then has such urgent need of the lady Rosamund?"

Again there was whispering between the pair.

"My master says," was the answer, "he thinks that all who see her will have need of her, since such loveliness is rare. But if you wish a name, well, one comes into his mind; the name of the knight Lozelle."

"The knight Lozelle!" murmured Rosamund, turning even paler than before, as well she might. For this Lozelle was a powerful man and Essex-born. He owned ships of whose doings upon the seas and in the East evil tales were told, and once had sought Rosamund's hand in marriage, but being rejected, uttered threats for which Godwin, as the elder of the twins, had fought and wounded him. Then he vanished—none knew where.

"Is Sir Hugh Lozelle here then?" asked Godwin, "masked like you common cowards? If so, I desire to meet him, to finish the work I began in the snow last Christmas twelvemonths."

"Find that out if you can," answered the tall man. But Wulf said, speaking low between his clenched teeth:

"Brother, I see but one chance. We must place Rosamund between us and charge them."

The captain of the band seemed to read their thoughts, for again he whispered into the ear of his companion, who called out:

"My master says that if you try to charge, you will be fools, since we shall stab and ham-string your horses, which are too good to waste, and take you quite easily as you fall. Come then, yield, as you can do without shame, seeing there is no escape, and that two men, however brave, cannot stand against a crowd. He gives you one minute to surrender."

Now Rosamund spoke for the first time.

"My cousins," she said, "I pray you not to let me fall living into the hands of Sir Hugh Lozelle, or of yonder men, to be taken to what fate I know not. Let Godwin kill me, then, to save my honour, as but now he said he would to save my soul, and strive to cut your way through, and live to avenge me."

The brethren made no answer, only they looked at the water and then at one another, and nodded. It was Godwin who spoke again, for now that it had come to this struggle for life and their lady, Wulf, whose tongue was commonly so ready, had grown strangely silent, and fierce-faced also.

"Listen, Rosamund, and do not turn your eyes," said Godwin. "There is but one chance for you, and, poor as it is, you must choose between it and capture, since we cannot kill you. The grey horse you ride is strong and true. Turn him now, and spur into the water of Death Creek and swim it. It is broad, but the incoming tide will help you, and perchance you will not drown."

Rosamund listened and moved her head backwards towards the boat. Then Wulf spoke—few words and sharp: "Begone, girl! we guard the boat."

She heard, and her dark eyes filled with tears, and her stately head sank for a moment almost to her horse's mane.

"Oh, my knights! my knights! And would you die for me? Well, if God wills it, so it must be. But I swear that if you die, that no man shall be aught to me who have your memory, and if you live—" And she looked at them confusedly, then stopped.

"Bless us, and begone," said Godwin.

So she blessed them in words low and holy; then of a sudden wheeled round the great grey horse, and striking the spur into its flank, drove straight at the deep water. A moment the stallion hung, then from the low quay-end sprang out wide and clear. Deep it sank, but not for long, for presently its rider's head rose above the water, and regaining the saddle, from which she had floated, Rosamund sat firm and headed the horse straight for the distant bank. Now a shout of wonderment went up from the woman thieves, for this was a deed that they had never thought a girl would dare. But the brethren laughed as they saw that the grey swam well, and, leaping from their saddles, ran forward a few paces—eight or ten—along the mole to where it was narrowest, as they went tearing the cloaks from their shoulders, and, since they had none, throwing them over their left arms to serve as bucklers.

The band cursed sullenly, only their captain gave an order to his spokesman, who cried aloud:

"Cut them down, and to the boat! We shall take her before she reaches shore or drowns."

For a moment they wavered, for the tall twin warriors who barred the way had eyes that told of wounds and death. Then with a rush they came, scrambling over the rough stones. But here the causeway was so narrow that while their strength lasted, two men were as good as twenty, nor, because of the mud and water, could they be got at from either side. So after all it was but two to two, and the brethren were the better two. Their long swords flashed and smote, and when Wulf's was lifted again, once more it shone red as it had been when he tossed it high in the sunlight, and a man fell with a heavy splash into the waters of the creek, and wallowed there till he died. Godwin's foe was down also, and, as it seemed, sped.

Then, at a muttered word, not waiting to be attacked by others, the brethren sprang forward. The huddled mob in front of them saw them come, and shrank back, but before they had gone a yard, the swords were at work behind. They swore strange oaths, they caught their feet among the rocks, and rolled upon their faces. In their confusion three of them were pushed into the water, where two sank in the mud and were drowned, the third only dragging himself ashore, while the rest made good their escape from the causeway. But two had been cut down, and three had fallen, for whom there was no escape. They strove to rise and fight, but the linen masks flapped about their eyes, so that their blows went wide, while the long swords of the brothers smote and smote again upon their helms and harness as the hammers of smiths smite upon an anvil, until they rolled over silent and stirless.

"Back!" said Godwin; "for here the road is wide; and they will get behind us."

So back they moved slowly, with their faces to the foe, stopping just in front of the first man whom Godwin had seemed to kill, and who lay face upwards with arms outstretched.

"So far we have done well," said Wulf, with a short laugh. "Are you hurt?"

"Nay," answered his brother, "but do not boast till the battle is over, for many are left and they will come on thus no more. Pray God they have no spears or bows."

Then he turned and looked behind him, and there, far from the shore now, swam the grey horse steadily, and there upon its back sat Rosamund. Yes, and she had seen, since the horse must swim somewhat sideways with the tide, for look, she took the kerchief from her throat and waved it to them. Then the brethren knew that she was proud of their great deeds, and thanked the saints that they had lived to do even so much as this for her dear sake.

Godwin was right. Although their leader commanded them in a stern voice, the band sank from the reach of those awful swords, and, instead, sought for stones to hurl at them. But here lay more mud than pebbles, and the rocks of which the causeway was built were too heavy for them to lift, so that they found but few, which when thrown either missed the brethren or did them little hurt. Now, after some while, the man called "master" spoke through his lieutenant, and certain of them ran into the thorn thicket, and thence appeared again bearing the long oars of the boat.

"Their counsel is to batter us down with the oars. What shall we do now, brother?" asked Godwin.

"What we can," answered Wulf. "It matters little if Rosamund is spared by the waters, for they will scarcely take her now, who must loose the boat and man it after we are dead."

As he spoke Wulf heard a sound behind him, and of a sudden Godwin threw up his arms and sank to his knees. Round he sprang, and there upon his feet stood that man whom they had thought dead, and in his hand a bloody sword. At him leapt Wulf, and so fierce were the blows he smote that the first severed his sword arm and the second shore through cloak and mail deep into the thief's side; so that this time he fell, never to stir again. Then he looked at his brother and saw that the blood was running down his face and blinding him.

"Save yourself, Wulf, for I am sped," murmured Godwin.

"Nay, or you could not speak." And he cast his arm round him and kissed him on the brow.

Then a thought came into his mind, and lifting Godwin as though he were a child, he ran back to where the horses stood, and heaved him onto the saddle.

"Hold fast!" he cried, "by mane and pommel. Keep your mind, and hold fast, and I will save you yet."

Passing the reins over his left arm, Wulf leapt upon the back of his own horse, and turned it. Ten seconds more, and the pirates, who were gathering with the oars where the paths joined at the root of the causeway, saw the two great horses thundering down upon them. On one a sore wounded man, his bright hair dabbled with blood, his hands gripping mane and saddle, and on the other the warrior Wulf, with starting eyes and a face like the face of a flame, shaking his red sword, and for the second time that day shouting aloud: *"A D'Arcy! a D'Arcy! Contre D'Arcy, contre Mort!"*

They saw, they shouted, they massed themselves together and held up the oars to meet them. But Wulf spurred fiercely, and, short as was the way, the heavy horses, trained to tourney, gathered their speed. Now they were on them. The oars were swept aside like reeds; all round them flashed the swords, and Wulf felt that he was hurt, he knew not where. But his sword flashed also, one blow—there was no time for more—yet the man beneath it sank like an empty sack.

By St. Peter! They were through, and Godwin still swayed upon the saddle, and yonder, nearing the further shore, the grey horse with its burden still battled in the tide. They were through! they were through! while to Wulf's eyes the air swam red, and the earth seemed as though it rose up to meet them, and everywhere was flaming fire.

But the shouts had died away behind them, and the only sound was the sound of the galloping of their horses' hoofs. Then that also grew faint and died away, and silence and darkness fell upon the mind of Wulf.

## Chapter 2

# Sir Andew D'Arcy

Godwin dreamed that he was dead, and that beneath him floated the world, a glowing ball, while he was borne to and fro through the blackness, stretched upon a couch of ebony. There were bright watchers by his couch also, watchers twain, and he knew them for his guardian angels, given him at birth. Moreover, now and again presences would come and question the watchers who sat at his head and foot. One asked:

"Has this soul sinned?" And the angel at his head answered:

"It has sinned."

Again the voice asked: "Did it die shriven of its sins?"

The angel answered: "It died unshriven, red sword aloft, fighting a good fight."

"Fighting for the Cross of Christ?"

"Nay; fighting for a woman."

"Alas! poor soul, sinful and unshriven, who died fighting for a woman's love. How shall such a one find mercy?" wailed the questioning voice, growing ever fainter, till it was lost far, far away.

Now came another visitor. It was his father—the warrior sire whom he had never seen, who fell in Syria. Godwin knew him well, for the face was the face carven on the tomb in Stangate church, and he wore the blood-red cross upon his mail, and the D'Arcy Death's-head was on his shield, and in his hand shone a naked sword.

"Is this the soul of my son?" he asked of the white robed watchers. "If so, how died he?"

Then the angel at his foot answered: "He died, red sword aloft, fighting a good fight."

"Fighting for the Cross of Christ?"

"Nay; fighting for a woman."

"Fighting for a woman's love who should have fallen in the Holy

War? Alas! poor son; alas! poor son! Alas! that we must part again forever!" and his voice, too, passed away.

Lo! a Glory advanced through the blackness, and the angels at head and foot stood up and saluted with their flaming spears.

"How died this child of God?" asked a voice, speaking out of the Glory, a low and awful voice.

"He died by the sword," answered the angel.

"By the sword of the children of the enemy, fighting in the war of Heaven?"

Then the angels were silent.

"What has Heaven to do with him, if he fought not for Heaven?" asked the voice again.

"Let him be spared," pleaded the guardians, "who was young and brave, and knew not. Send him back to earth, there to retrieve his sins and be our charge once more."

"So be it," said the voice. "Knight, live on, but live as a knight of Heaven if thou wouldst win Heaven."

"Must he then put the woman from him?" asked the angels.

"It was not said," answered the voice speaking from the Glory. And all that wild vision vanished.

Then a space of oblivion, and Godwin awoke to hear other voices around him, voices human, well-beloved, remembered; and to see a face bending over him—a face most human, most well-beloved, most remembered—that of his cousin Rosamund. He babbled some questions, but they brought him food, and told him to sleep, so he slept. Thus it went on, waking and sleep, sleep and waking, till at length one morning he woke up truly in the little room that opened out of the solar or sitting place of the Hall of Steeple, where he and Wulf had slept since their uncle took them to his home as infants. More, on the trestle bed opposite to him, his leg and arm bandaged, and a crutch by his side, sat Wulf himself, somewhat paler and thinner than of yore, but the same jovial, careless, yet at times fierce-faced Wulf.

"Do I still dream, my brother, or is it you indeed?"

A happy smile spread upon the face of Wulf, for now he knew that Godwin was himself again.

"Me sure enough," he answered. "Dream-folk don't have lame legs; they are the gifts of swords and men."

"And Rosamund? What of Rosamund? Did the grey horse swim the creek, and how came we here? Tell me quick—I faint for news!"

"She shall tell you herself." And hobbling to the curtained door, he called, "Rosamund, my—nay, our—cousin Rosamund, Godwin is himself again. Hear you, Godwin is himself again, and would speak with you!"

There was a swift rustle of robes and a sound of quick feet among the rushes that strewed the floor, and then—Rosamund herself, lovely as ever, but all her stateliness forgot in joy. She saw him, the gaunt Godwin sitting up upon the pallet, his grey eyes shining in the white and sunken face. For Godwin's eyes were grey, while Wulf's were blue, the only difference between them which a stranger would note, although in truth Wulf's lips were fuller than Godwin's, and his chin more marked; also he was a larger man. She saw him, and with a little cry of delight ran and cast her arms about him, and kissed him on the brow.

"Be careful," said Wulf roughly, turning his head aside, "or, Rosamund, you will loose the bandages, and bring his trouble back again; he has had enough of blood-letting."

"Then I will kiss him on the hand—the hand that saved me," she said, and did so. More, she pressed that poor, pale hand against her heart.

"Mine had something to do with that business also but I don't remember that you kissed it, Rosamund. Well, I will kiss him too, and oh! God be praised, and the holy Virgin, and the holy Peter, and the holy Chad, and all the other holy dead folk whose names I can't recall, who between them, with the help of Rosamund here, and the prayers of the Prior John and brethren at Stangate, and of Matthew, the village priest, have given you back to us, my brother, my most beloved brother." And he hopped to the bedside, and throwing his long, sinewy arms about Godwin embraced him again and again.

"Be careful," said Rosamund drily, "or, Wulf, you will disturb the bandages, and he has had enough of blood-letting."

Then before he could answer, which he seemed minded to do, there came the sound of a slow step, and swinging the curtain aside, a tall and noble-looking knight entered the little place. The man was old, but looked older than he was, for sorrow and sickness had wasted him. His snow-white hair hung upon his shoulders, his face was pale, and his features were pinched but finely-chiselled, and notwithstanding the difference of their years, wonderfully like to those of the daughter Rosamund. For this was her father, the famous lord, Sir Andrew D'Arcy.

Rosamund turned and bent the knee to him with a strange and Eastern grace, while Wulf bowed his head, and Godwin, since his neck was too stiff to stir, held up his hand in greeting. The old man looked at him, and there was pride in his eye.

"So you will live after all, my nephew," he said, "and for that I thank the giver of life and death, since by God, you are a gallant man—a worthy child of the bloods of the Norman D'Arcy and of Uluin the Saxon. Yes, one of the best of them."

"Speak not so, my uncle," said Godwin; "or at least, here is a worthier,"—and he patted the hand of Wulf with his lean fingers. "It was Wulf who bore me through. Oh, I remember as much as that—how he lifted me onto the black horse and bade me to cling fast to mane and pommel. Ay, and I remember the charge, and his cry of *'Contre D'Arcy, contre Mort!'* and the flashing of swords about us, and after that—nothing."

"Would that I had been there to help in that fight," said Sir Andrew D'Arcy, tossing his white hair. "Oh, my children, it is hard to be sick and old. A log am I—naught but a rotting log. Still, had I only known—"

"Father, father," said Rosamund, casting her white arm about his neck. "You should not speak thus. You have done your share."

"Yes, my share; but I should like to do more. Oh, St. Andrew, ask it for me that I may die with sword aloft and my grandsire's cry upon my lips. Yes, yes; thus, not like a worn-out war-horse in his stall. There, pardon me; but in truth, my children, I am jealous of you. Why, when I found you lying in each other's arms I could have wept for rage to think that such a fray had been within a league of my own doors and I not in it."

"I know nothing of all that story," said Godwin.

"No, in truth, how can you, who have been senseless this month or more? But Rosamund knows, and she shall tell it you. Speak on, Rosamund. Lay you back, Godwin, and listen."

"The tale is yours, my cousins, and not mine," said Rosamund. "You bade me take the water, and into it I spurred the grey horse, and we sank deep, so that the waves closed above my head. Then up we came, I floating from the saddle, but I regained it, and the horse answered to my voice and bridle, and swam out for the further shore. On it swam, somewhat slantwise with the tide, so that by turning my head I could see all that passed upon the mole. I saw them come at you, and men fall before your swords; I saw you charge them, and run back again. Lastly, after what seemed a very long while, when I was far away, I saw Wulf lift Godwin into the saddle—I knew it must be Godwin, because he set him on the black horse—and the pair of you galloped down the quay and vanished.

"By then I was near the home shore, and the grey grew very weary and sank deep in the water. But I cheered it on with my voice, and although twice its head went beneath the waves, in the end it found a footing, though a soft one. After resting awhile, it plunged forward with short rushes through the mud, and so at length came safe to land, where it stood shaking with fear and weariness. So soon as the horse got its breath again, I pressed on, for I saw them loosing the boat, and came home here as the dark closed in, to meet your uncle watching for me at the gate. Now, father, do you take up the tale."

"There is little more to tell," said Sir Andrew. "You will remember, nephews, that I was against this ride of Rosamund's to seek flowers, or I know not what, at St. Peter's shrine, nine miles away, but as the maid had set her heart on it, and there are but few pleasures here, why, I let her go with the pair of you for escort. You will mind also that you were starting without your mail, and how foolish you thought me when I called you back and made you gird it on. Well, my patron saint—or yours—put it into my head to do so, for had it not been for those same shirts of mail, you were both of you dead men to-day. But that morning I had been thinking of Sir Hugh Lozelle—if such a false, pirate rogue can be called a knight, not but that he is stout and brave enough—and his threats after he recovered from the wound you gave him, Godwin; how that he would come back and take your cousin for all we could do to stay him. True, we heard that he had sailed for the East to war against Saladin—or with him, for he was ever a traitor—but even if this were so, men return from the East. Therefore I bade you arm, having some foresight of what was to come, for doubtless this onslaught must have been planned by him."

"I think so," said Wulf, "for, as Rosamund here knows, the tall knave who interpreted for the foreigner whom he called his master, gave us the name of the knight Lozelle as the man who sought to carry her off."

"Was this master a Saracen?" asked Sir Andrew, anxiously.

"Nay, uncle, how can I tell, seeing that his face was masked like the rest and he spoke through an interpreter? But I pray you go on with the story, which Godwin has not heard."

"It is short. When Rosamund told her tale of which I could make little, for the girl was crazed with grief and cold and fear, save that you had been attacked upon the old quay, and she had escaped by swimming Death Creek—which seemed a thing incredible—I got together what men I could. Then bidding her stay behind, with some of them to guard her, and nurse herself, which she was loth to do, I set out to find you or your bodies. It was dark, but we rode hard, having lanterns with us, as we went rousing men at every stead, until we came to where the roads join at Moats. There we found a black horse—your horse, Godwin—so badly wounded that he could travel no further, and I groaned, thinking that you were dead. Still we went on, till we heard another horse whinny, and presently found the roan also riderless, standing by the path-side with his head down.

"'A man on the ground holds him!' cried one, and I sprang from the saddle to see who it might be, to find that it was you, the pair of you, locked in each other's arms and senseless, if not dead, as well you might be from your wounds. I bade the country-folk cover you up and carry you home, and others to run to Stangate and pray the Prior and the monk Stephen, who is a doctor, come at once to tend you, while we pressed onwards to take vengeance if we could. We reached the quay upon the creek, but there we found nothing save some bloodstains and—this is strange—your sword, Godwin, the hilt set between two stones, and on the point a writing."

"What was the writing?" asked Godwin.

"Here it is," answered his uncle, drawing a piece of parchment from his robe. "Read it, one of you, since all of you are scholars and my eyes are bad."

Rosamund took it and read what was written, hurriedly but in a clerkly hand, and in the French tongue. It ran thus: "The sword of a brave man. Bury it with him if he be dead, and give it back to him if he lives, as I hope. My master would wish me to do this honour to a gallant foe whom in that case he still may meet. (Signed) Hugh Lozelle, or Another."

"Another, then; not Hugh Lozelle," said Godwin, "since he cannot write, and if he could, would never pen words so knightly."

"The words may be knightly, but the writer's deeds were base enough," replied Sir Andrew; "nor, in truth do I understand this scroll."

"The interpreter spoke of the short man as his master," suggested Wulf.

"Ay, nephew; but him you met. This writing speaks of a master whom Godwin may meet, and who would wish the writer to pay him a certain honour."

"Perhaps he wrote thus to blind us."

"Perchance, perchance. The matter puzzles me. Moreover, of whom these men were I have been able to learn nothing. A boat was seen passing towards Bradwell—indeed, it seems that you saw it, and that night a boat was seen sailing southwards down St. Peter's sands towards a ship that had anchored off Foulness Point. But what that ship was, whence she came, and whither she went, none know, though the tidings of this fray have made some stir."

"Well," said Wulf, "at the least we have seen the last of her crew of women-thieves. Had they meant more mischief, they would have shown themselves again ere now."

Sir Andrew looked grave as he answered.

"So I trust, but all the tale is very strange. How came they to know that you and Rosamund were riding that day to St. Peter's-on-the-Wall, and so were able to waylay you? Surely some spy must have warned them, since that they were no common pirates is evident, for they spoke of Lozelle, and bade you two begone unharmed, as it was Rosamund whom they needed. Also, there is the matter of the sword that fell from the hand of Godwin when he was hurt, which was returned in so strange a fashion. I have known many such deeds of chivalry done in the East by Paynim men—"

"Well, Rosamund is half an Eastern," broke in Wulf carelessly; "and perhaps that had something to do with it all."

Sir Andrew started, and the colour rose to his pale face. Then in a tone in which he showed he wished to speak no more of this matter, he said:

"Enough, enough. Godwin is very weak, and grows weary, and before I leave him I have a word to say that it may please you both to hear. Young men, you are of my blood, the nearest to it except Rosamund—the sons of that noble knight, my brother. I have ever loved you well, and been proud of you, but if this was so in the past, how much more is it thus to-day, when you have done such high service to my house? Moreover, that deed was brave and great; nothing more knightly has been told of in Essex this many a year, and those who wrought it should no longer be simple gentlemen, but very knights. This boon it is in my power to grant to you according to the ancient custom. Still, that none may question it, while you lay sick, but after it was believed that Godwin would live, which at first we scarcely dared to hope, I journeyed to London and sought audience of our lord the king. Having told him this tale, I prayed him that he would be pleased to grant me his command in writing that I should name you knights.

"My nephews, he was so pleased, and here I have the brief sealed with the royal signet, commanding that in his name and my own I should give you the accolade publicly in the church of the Priory at Stangate at such season as may be convenient. Therefore, Godwin, the squire, haste you to get well that you may become Sir Godwin the knight; for you, Wulf, save for the hurt to your leg, are well enough already."

Now Godwin's white face went red with pride, and Wulf dropped his bold eyes and looked modest as a girl.

"Speak you," he said to his brother, "for my tongue is blunt and awkward."

"Sir," said Godwin in a weak voice, "we do not know how to thank you for so great an honour, that we never thought to win till we had done more famous deeds than the beating off of a band of robbers. Sir, we have no more to say, save that while we live we will strive to be worthy of our name and of you."

"Well spoken," said his uncle, adding as though to himself, "this man is courtly as he is brave."

Wulf looked up, a flash of merriment upon his open face.

"I, my uncle, whose speech is, I fear me, not courtly, thank you also. I will add that I think our lady cousin here should be knighted too, if such a thing were possible for a woman, seeing that to swim a horse across Death Creek was a greater deed than to fight some rascals on its quay."

"Rosamund?" answered the old man in the same dreamy voice. "Her rank is high enough—too high, far too high for safety." And turning, he left the little chamber.

"Well, cousin," said Wulf, "if you cannot be a knight, at least you can lessen all this dangerous rank of yours by becoming a knight's wife." Whereat Rosamund looked at him with indignation which struggled with a smile in her dark eyes, and murmuring that she must see to the making of Godwin's broth, followed her father from the place.

"It would have been kinder had she told us that she was glad," said Wulf when she was gone.

"Perhaps she would," answered his brother, "had it not been for your rough jests, Wulf, which might have a meaning in them."

"Nay, I had no meaning. Why should she not become a knight's wife?"

"Ay, but what knight's? Would it please either of us, brother, if, as may well chance, he should be some stranger?"

Now Wulf swore a great oath, then flushed to the roots of his fair hair, and was silent.

"Ah!" said Godwin; "you do not think before you speak, which it is always well to do."

"She swore upon the quay yonder"—broke in Wulf.

"Forget what she swore. Words uttered in such an hour should not be remembered against a maid."

"God's truth, brother, you are right, as ever! My tongue runs away with me, but still I can't put those words out of my mind, though which of us—"

"Wulf!"

"I mean to say that we are in Fortune's path to-day, Godwin. Oh, that was a lucky ride! Such fighting as I have never seen or dreamed of. We won it too! And now both of us are alive, and a knighthood for each!"

"Yes, both of us alive, thanks to you, Wulf—nay, it is so, though you would never have done less. But as for Fortune's path, it is one that has many rough turns, and perhaps before all is done she may lead us round some of them."

"You talk like a priest, not like a squire who is to be knighted at the cost of a scar on his head. For my part I will kiss Fortune while I may, and if she jilts me afterwards—"

"Wulf," called Rosamund from without the curtain, "cease talking of kissing at the top of your voice, I pray you, and leave Godwin to sleep, for he needs it." And she entered the little chamber, bearing a bowl of broth in her hand.

Thereon, saying that ladies should not listen to what did not concern them, Wulf seized his crutch and hobbled from the place.

## Chapter 3

# The Knighting of the Brethren

Another month had gone by, and though Godwin was still somewhat weak and suffered from a headache at times, the brethren had recovered from their wounds. On the last day of November, about two o'clock in the afternoon, a great procession might have been seen wending its way from the old Hall at Steeple. In it rode many knights fully armed, before whom were borne their banners. These went first. Then came old Sir Andrew D'Arcy, also fully armed, attended by squires and retainers. He was accompanied by his lovely daughter, the lady Rosamund, clad in beautiful apparel under her cloak of fur, who rode at his right hand on that same horse which had swum Death Creek. Next appeared the brethren, modestly arrayed as simple gentlemen, followed each of them by his squire, scions of the noble houses of Salcote and of Dengie. After them rode yet more knights, squires, tenants of various degree, and servants, surrounded by a great number of peasantry and *villeins*, who walked and ran with their women folk and children.

Following the road through the village, the procession turned to the left at the great arch which marked the boundary of the monk's lands, and headed for Stangate Abbey, some two miles away, by the path that ran between the arable land and the Salt marshes, which are flooded at high tide. At length they came to the stone gate of the Abbey, that gave the place its name of Stangate. Here they were met by a company of the Cluniac monks, who dwelt in this wild and lonely spot upon the water's edge, headed by their prior, John Fitz Brien. He was a venerable, white-haired man, clad in wide-sleeved, black robes, and preceded by a priest carrying a silver cross. Now the procession separated, Godwin and Wulf, with certain of the knights and their esquires, being led to the Priory, while the main body of it entered the church, or stood about outside its door.

Arrived in the house, the two knights elect were taken to a room where their hair was cut and their chins were shaved by a barber who awaited them. Then, under the guidance of two old knights named Sir Anthony de Mandeville and Sir Roger de Merci, they were conducted to baths surrounded with rich cloths. Into these, having been undressed by the squires, they entered and bathed themselves, while Sir Anthony and Sir Roger spoke to them through the cloths of the high duties of their vocation, ending by pouring water over them, and signing their bare bodies with the sign of the Cross. Next they were dressed again, and preceded by minstrels, led to the church, at the porch of which they and their esquires were given wine to drink.

Here, in the presence of all the company, they were clothed first in white tunics, to signify the whiteness of their hearts; next in red robes, symbolical of the blood they might be called upon to shed for Christ; and lastly, in long black cloaks, emblems of the death that must be endured by all. This done, their armour was brought in and piled before them upon the steps of the altar, and the congregation departed homeward, leaving them with their esquires and the priest to spend the long winter night in orisons and prayers.

Long, indeed, it was, in that lonesome, holy place, lit only by a lamp which swung before the altar. Wulf prayed and prayed until he could pray no more, then fell into a half dreamful state that was haunted by the face of Rosamund, where even her face should have been forgotten. Godwin, his elbow resting against the tomb that hid his father's heart, prayed also, until even his earnestness was outworn, and he began to wonder about many things.

That dream of his, for instance, in his sickness, when he had seemed to be dead, and what might be the true duty of man. To be brave and upright? Surely. To fight for the Cross of Christ against the Saracen? Surely, if the chance came his way. What more? To abandon the world and to spend his life muttering prayers like those priests in the darkness behind him? Could that be needful or of service to God or man? To man, perhaps, because such folk tended the sick and fed the poor. But to God? Was he not sent into the world to bear his part in the world—to live his full life? This would mean a half-life—one into which no woman might enter, to which no child might be added, since to monks and even to certain brotherhoods, all these things, which Nature decreed and Heaven had sanctified, were deadly sin.

It would mean, for instance, that he must think no more of Rosamund. Could he do this for the sake of the welfare of his soul in some future state?

Why, at the thought of it even, in that solemn place and hour of dedication, his spirit reeled, for then and there for the first time it was borne in upon him that he loved this woman more than all the world beside—more than his life, more, perhaps, than his soul. He loved her with all his pure young heart—so much that it would be a joy to him to die for her, not only in the heat of battle, as lately had almost chanced on the Death Creek quay, but in cold blood, of set purpose, if there came need. He loved her with body and with spirit, and, after God, here to her he consecrated his body and his spirit. But what value would she put upon the gift? What if some other man—?

By his side, his elbows resting on the altar rails, his eyes fixed upon the beaming armour that he would wear in battle, knelt Wulf, his brother—a mighty man, a knight of knights, fearless, noble, open-hearted; such a one as any woman might well love. And he also loved Rosamund. Of this Godwin was sure. And, oh! did not Rosamund love Wulf? Bitter jealousy seized upon his vitals. Yes; even then and there, black envy got hold of Godwin, and rent him so sore that, cold as was the place, the sweat poured from his brow and body.

Should he abandon hope? Should he fly the battle for fear that he might be defeated? Nay; he would fight on in all honesty and honour, and if he were overcome, would meet his fate as a brave knight should—without bitterness, but without shame. Let destiny direct the matter. It was in the hands of destiny, and stretching out his arm, he threw it around the neck of his brother, who knelt beside him, and let it rest there, until the head of the weary Wulf sank sleepily upon his shoulder, like the head of an infant upon its mother's breast.

*"Oh Jesu,"* Godwin moaned in his poor heart, "give me strength to fight against this sinful passion that would lead me to hate the brother whom I love. *Oh Jesu*, give me strength to bear it if he should be preferred before me. Make me a perfect knight—strong to suffer and endure, and, if need be, to rejoice even in the joy of my supplanter."

At length the grey dawn broke, and the sunlight, passing through the eastern window, like a golden spear, pierced the dusk of the long church, which was built to the shape of a cross, so that only its transepts remained in shadow. Then came a sound of chanting, and at the western door entered the Prior, wearing all his robes, attended by the monks and acolytes, who swung censers. In the centre of the nave he halted and passed to the confessional, calling on Godwin to follow. So he went and knelt before the holy man, and there poured out all his heart. He confessed his sins. They were but few. He told him of the vision of his sickness, on which the Prior pondered long; of his deep love, his hopes, his fears, and his desire to be a warrior who once, as a lad, had wished to be a monk, not that he might shed blood, but to fight for the Cross of Christ against the Paynim, ending with a cry of—

"Give me counsel, O my father. Give me counsel."

"Your own heart is your best counsellor," was the priest's answer. "Go as it guides you, knowing that, through it, it is God who guides. Nor fear that you will fail. But if love and the joys of life should leave you, then come back, and we will talk again. Go on, pure knight of Christ, fearing nothing and sure of the reward, and take with you the blessing of Christ and of his Church."

"What penance must I bear, father?"

"Such souls as yours inflict their own penance. The saints forbid that I should add to it," was the gentle answer.

Then with a lightened heart Godwin returned to the altar rails, while his brother Wulf was summoned to take his place in the confessional. Of the sins that he had to tell we need not speak. They were such as are common to young men, and none of them very grievous. Still, before he gave him absolution, the good Prior admonished him to think less of his body and more of his spirit; less of the glory of feats of arms and more of the true ends to which he should enter on them. He bade him, moreover, to take his brother Godwin as an earthly guide and example, since there lived no better or wiser man of his years, and finally dismissed him, prophesying that if he would heed these counsels, he would come to great glory on earth and in heaven.

"Father, I will do my best," answered Wulf humbly; "but there cannot be two Godwins; and, father, sometimes I fear me that our paths will cross, since two men cannot win one woman."

"I know the trouble," answered the Prior anxiously, "and with less noble-natured men it might be grave. But if it should come to this, then must the lady judge according to the wishes of her own heart, and he who loses her must be loyal in sorrow as in joy. Be sure that you take no base advantage of your brother in the hour of temptation, and bear him no bitterness should he win the bride."

"I think I can be sure of that," said Wulf; "also that we, who have loved each other from birth, would die before we betrayed each other."

"I think so also," answered the Prior; "but Satan is very strong."

Then Wulf also returned to the altar rails, and the full Mass was sung, and the Sacrament received by the two neophytes, and the offerings made all in their appointed order. Next they were led back to the Priory to rest and eat a little after their long night's vigil in the cold church, and here they abode awhile, thinking their own thoughts, seated alone in the Prior's chamber. At length Wulf, who seemed to be ill at ease, rose and laid his hand upon his brother's shoulder, saying:

"I can be silent no more; it was ever thus: that which is in my mind must out of it. I have words to say to you."

"Speak on, Wulf," said Godwin.

Wulf sat himself down again upon his stool, and for a while stared hard at nothing, for he did not seem to find it easy to begin this talk. Now Godwin could read his brother's mind like a book, but Wulf could not always read Godwin's, although, being twins who had been together from birth, their hearts were for the most part open to each other without the need of words.

"It is of our cousin Rosamund, is it not?" asked Godwin presently.

"Ay. Who else?"

"And you would tell me that you love her, and that now you are a knight—almost—and hard on five-and twenty years of age, you would ask her to become your affianced wife?"

"Yes, Godwin; it came into my heart when she rode the grey horse into the water, there upon the pier, and I thought that I should never see her any more. I tell you it came into my heart that life was not worth living nor death worth dying without her."

"Then, Wulf," answered Godwin slowly, "what more is there to say? Ask on, and prosper. Why not? We have some lands, if not many, and Rosamund will not lack for them. Nor do I think that our uncle would forbid you, if she wills it, seeing that you are the properest man and the bravest in all this country side."

"Except my brother Godwin, who is all these things, and good and learned to boot, which I am not," replied Wulf musingly. Then there was silence for a while, which he broke.

"Godwin, our ill-luck is that you love her also, and that you thought the same thoughts which I did yonder on the quay-head."

Godwin flushed a little, and his long fingers tightened their grip upon his knee.

"It is so," he said quietly. "To my grief it is so. But Rosamund knows nothing of this, and should never know it if you will keep a watch upon your tongue. Moreover, you need not be jealous of me, before marriage or after."

"What, then, would you have me do?" asked Wulf hotly. "Seek her heart, and perchance—though this I doubt—let her yield it to me, she thinking that you care naught for her?"

"Why not?" asked Godwin again, with a sigh; "it might save her some pain and you some doubt, and make my own path clearer. Marriage is more to you than to me, Wulf, who think sometimes that my sword should be my spouse and duty my only aim."

"Who think, having a heart of gold, that even in such a thing as this you will not bar the path of the brother whom you love. Nay, Godwin, as I am a sinful man, and as I desire her above all things on earth, I will play no such coward's game, nor conquer one who will not lift his sword lest he should hurt me. Sooner would I bid you all farewell, and go to seek fortune or death in the wars without word spoken."

"Leaving Rosamund to pine, perchance. Oh, could we be sure that she had no mind toward either of us, that would be best—to begone together. But, Wulf, we cannot be sure, since at times, to be honest, I have thought she loves you."

"And at times, to be honest, Godwin, I have been sure that she loves you, although I should like to try my luck and hear it from her lips, which on such terms I will not do."

"What, then, is your plan, Wulf?"

"My plan is that if our uncle gives us leave, we should both speak to her—you first, as the elder, setting out your case as best you can, and asking her to think of it and give you your answer within a day. Then, before that day is done I also should speak, so that she may know all the story, and play her part in it with opened eyes, not deeming, as otherwise she might, that we know each other's minds, and that you ask because I have no will that way."

"It is very fair," replied Godwin; "and worthy of you, who are the most honest of men. Yet, Wulf, I am troubled. See you, my brother, have ever brethren loved each other as we do? And now must the shadow of a woman fall upon and blight that love which is so fair and precious?"

"Why so?" asked Wulf. "Come, Godwin, let us make a pact that it shall not be thus, and keep it by the help of heaven. Let us show the world that two men can love one woman and still love each other, not knowing as yet which of them she will choose—if, indeed, she chooses either. For, Godwin, we are not the only gentlemen whose eyes have turned, or yet may turn, towards the high-born, rich, and lovely lady Rosamund. Is it your will that we should make such a pact?"

Godwin thought a little, then answered:

"Yes; but if so, it must be one so strong that for her sake and for both our sakes we cannot break it and live with honour."

"So be it," said Wulf; "this is man's work, not child's make-believe."

Then Godwin rose, and going to the door, bade his squire, who watched without, pray the Prior John to come to them as they sought his counsel in a matter. So he came, and, standing before him with downcast head, Godwin told him all the tale, which, indeed, he who knew so much already, was quick to understand, and of their purpose also; while at a question from the prior, Wulf answered that it was well and truly said, nothing having been kept back. Then they asked him if it was lawful that they should take such an oath, to which he replied that he thought it not only lawful, but very good.

So in the end, kneeling together hand in hand before the Rood that stood in the chamber, they repeated this oath after him, both of them together.

"We brethren, Godwin and Wulf D'Arcy, do swear by the holy Cross of Christ, and by the patron saint of this place, St. Mary Magdalene, and our own patron saints, St. Peter and St. Chad, standing in the presence of God, of our guardian angels, and of you, John, that being both of us enamoured of our cousin, Rosamund D'Arcy, we will ask her to wife in the manner we have agreed, and no other. That we will abide by her decision, should she choose either of us, nor seek to alter it by tempting her from her troth, or in any fashion overt or covert. That he of us whom she refuses will thenceforth be a brother to her and no more, however Satan may tempt his heart otherwise. That so far as may be possible to us, who are but sinful men, we will suffer neither bitterness nor jealousy to come between our love because of this woman, and that in war or peace we will remain faithful comrades and brethren. Thus we swear with a true heart and purpose, and in token thereof, knowing that he who breaks this oath will be a knight dishonoured and a vessel fit for the wrath of God, we kiss this Rood and one another."

This, then, these brethren said and did, and with light minds and joyful faces received the blessing of the Prior, who had christened them in infancy, and went down to meet the great company that had ridden forth to lead them back to Steeple, where their knighting should be done.

So to Steeple, preceded by the squires, who rode before them bareheaded, carrying their swords by the scabbarded points, with their gold spurs hanging from the hilts, they came at last. Here the hall was set for a great feast, a space having been left between the tables and the dais, to which the brethren were conducted. Then came forward Sir Anthony de Mandeville and Sir Roger de Merci in full armour, and presented to Sir Andrew D'Arcy, their uncle, who stood upon the edge of the dais, also in his armour, their swords and spurs, of which he gave back to them two of the latter, bidding them affix these upon the candidates' right heels. This done, the Prior John blessed the swords, after which Sir Andrew girded them about the waists of his nephews, saying:

"Take ye back the swords that you have used so well."

Next, he drew his own silver-hilted blade that had been his father's and his grandfather's, and whilst they knelt before him, smote each of them three blows upon the right shoulder, crying with a loud voice: "In the name of God, St. Michael, and St. George, I knight ye. Be ye good knights."

Thereafter came forward Rosamund as their nearest kinswoman, and, helped by other ladies, clad upon them their hauberks, or coats of mail, their helms of steel, and their kite-shaped shields, emblazoned with a skull, the cognizance of their race. This done, with the musicians marching before them, they walked to Steeple church—a distance of two hundred paces from the Hall, where they laid their swords upon the altar and took them up again, swearing to be good servants of Christ and defenders of the Church. As they left its doors, who should meet them but the cook, carrying his chopper in his hand and claiming as his fee the value of the spurs they wore, crying aloud at the same time:

"If either of you young knights should do aught in despite of your honour and of the oaths that you have sworn—from which may God and his saints prevent you!—then with my chopper will I hack these spurs from off your heels."

Thus at last the long ceremony was ended, and after it came a very great feast, for at the high table were entertained many noble knights and ladies, and below, in the hall their squires, and other gentlemen, and outside all the yeomanry and villagers, whilst the children and the aged had food and drink given to them in the nave of the church itself. When the eating at length was done, the centre of the hall was cleared, and while men drank, the minstrels made music. All were very merry with wine and strong ale, and talk arose among them as to which of these brethren—Sir Godwin or Sir Wulf—was the more brave, the more handsome, and the more learned and courteous.

Now a knight—it was Sir Surin de Salcote—seeing that the argument grew hot and might lead to blows, rose and declared that this should be decided by beauty alone, and that none could be more fitted to judge than the fair lady whom the two of them had saved from woman-thieves at the Death Creek quay. They all called, "Ay, let her settle it," and it was agreed that she would give the kerchief from her neck to the bravest, a beaker of wine to the handsomest, and a Book of Hours to the most learned.

So, seeing no help for it, since except her father, the brethren, the most of the other ladies and herself, who drank but water, gentle and simple alike, had begun to grow heated with wine, and were very urgent, Rosamund took the silk kerchief from her neck. Then coming to the edge of the dais, where they were seated in the sight of all, she stood before her cousins, not knowing, poor maid, to which of them she should offer it. But Godwin whispered a word to Wulf, and both of them stretching out their right hands, snatched an end of the kerchief which she held towards them, and rending it, twisted the severed halves round their sword hilts. The company laughed at their wit, and cried:

"The wine for the more handsome. They cannot serve that thus."

Rosamund thought a moment; then she lifted a great silver beaker, the largest on the board, and having filled it full of wine, once more came forward and held it before them as though pondering. Thereon the brethren, as though by a single movement, bent forward and each of them touched the beaker with his lips. Again a great laugh went up, and even Rosamund smiled.

"The book! the book!" cried the guests. "They dare not rend the holy book!"

So for the third time Rosamund advanced, bearing the missal.

"Knights," she said, "you have torn my kerchief and drunk my wine. Now I offer this hallowed writing—to him who can read it best."

"Give it to Godwin," said Wulf. "I am a swordsman, not a clerk."

"Well said! well said!" roared the company. "The sword for us—not the pen!" But Rosamund turned on them and answered:

"He who wields sword is brave, and he who wields pen is wise, but better is he who can handle both sword and pen—like my cousin Godwin, the brave and learned."

"Hear her! hear her!" cried the revellers, knocking their horns upon the board, while in the silence that followed a woman's voice said, "Sir Godwin's luck is great, but give me Sir Wulf's strong arms."

Then the drinking began again, and Rosamund and the ladies slipped away, as well they might—for the times were rough and coarse.

On the morrow, after most of the guests were gone, many of them with aching heads, Godwin and Wulf sought their uncle, Sir Andrew, in the solar where he sat alone, for they knew Rosamund had walked to the church hard by with two of the serving women to make it ready for the Friday's mass, after the feast of the peasants that had been held in the nave. Coming to his oaken chair by the open hearth which had a chimney to it—no common thing in those days—they knelt before him.

"What is it now, my nephews?" asked the old man, smiling. "Do you wish that I should knight you afresh?"

"No, sir," answered Godwin; "we seek a greater boon."

"Then you seek in vain, for there is none."

"Another sort of boon," broke in Wulf.

Sir Andrew pulled his beard, and looked at them. Perhaps the Prior John had spoken a word to him, and he guessed what was coming.

"Speak," he said to Godwin. "The gift is great that I would not give to either of you if it be within my power."

"Sir," said Godwin, "we seek the leave to ask your daughter's hand in marriage."

"What! the two of you?"

"Yes, sir; the two of us."

Then Sir Andrew, who seldom laughed, laughed outright.

"Truly," he said, "of all the strange things I have known, this is the strangest—that two knights should ask one wife between them."

"It seems strange, sir; but when you have heard our tale you will understand."

So he listened while they told him all that had passed between them and of the solemn oath which they had sworn.

"Noble in this as in other things," commented Sir Andrew when they had done; "but I fear that one of you may find that vow hard to keep. By all the saints, nephews, you were right when you said that you asked a great boon. Do you know, although I have told you nothing of it, that, not to speak of the knave Lozelle, already two of the greatest men in this land have sought my daughter Rosamund in marriage?"

"It may well be so," said Wulf.

"It is so, and now I will tell you why one or other of the pair is not her husband, which in some ways I would he were. A simple reason. I asked her, and she had no mind to either, and as her mother married where her heart was, so I have sworn that the daughter should do, or not at all—for better a nunnery than a loveless bridal.

"Now let us see what you have to give. You are of good blood—that of Uluin by your mother, and mine, also on one side her own. As squires to your sponsors of yesterday, the knights Sir Anthony de Mandeville and Sir Roger de Merci, you bore yourselves bravely in the Scottish War; indeed, your liege king Henry remembered it, and that is why he granted my prayer so readily. Since then, although you loved the life little, because I asked it of you, you have rested here at home with me, and done no feats of arms, save that great one of two months gone which made you knights, and, in truth, gives you some claim on Rosamund.

"For the rest, your father being the younger son, your lands are small, and you have no other gear. Outside the borders of this shire you are unknown men, with all your deeds to do—for I will not count those Scottish battles when you were but boys. And she whom you ask is one of the fairest and noblest and most learned ladies in this land, for I, who have some skill in such things, have taught her myself from childhood. Moreover, as I have no other heir, she will be wealthy. Well, what more have you to offer for all this?"

"Ourselves," answered Wulf boldly. "We are true knights of whom you know the best and worst, and we love her. We learned it for once and for all on Death Creek quay, for till then she was our sister and no more."

"Ay," added Godwin, "when she swore herself to us and blessed us, then light broke on both."

"Stand up," said Sir Andrew, "and let me look at you."

So they stood side by side in the full light of the blazing fire, for little other came through those narrow windows.

"Proper men; proper men," said the old knight; "and as like to one another as two grains of wheat from the same sample. Six feet high, each of you, and broad chested, though Wulf is larger made and the stronger of the two. Brown and waving-haired both, save for that line of white where the sword hit yours, Godwin—Godwin with grey eyes that dream and Wulf with the blue eyes that shine like swords. Ah! your grandsire had eyes like that, Wulf; and I have been told that when he leapt from the tower to the wall at the taking of Jerusalem, the Saracens did not love the light which shone in them—nor, in faith, did I, his son, when he was angry. Proper men, the pair of you; but Sir Wulf most warrior-like, and Sir Godwin most courtly."

"Now which do you think would please a woman most?"

"That, sir, depends upon the woman," answered Godwin, and straightway his eyes began to dream.

"That, sir, we seek to learn before the day is out, if you give us leave," added Wulf; "though, if you would know, I think my chance a poor one."

"Ah, well; it is a very pretty riddle. But I do not envy her who has its answering, for it might well trouble a maid's mind, neither is it certain when all is done that she will guess best for her own peace. Would it not be wiser, then, that I should forbid them to ask this riddle?" he added as though to himself and fell to thinking while they trembled, seeing that he was minded to refuse their suit.

At length he looked up again and said: "Nay, let it go as God wills Who holds the future in His hand. Nephews, because you are good knights and true, either of whom would ward her well—and she may need warding—because you are my only brother's sons, whom I have promised him to care for; and most of all because I love you both with an equal love, have your wish, and go try your fortunes at the hands of my daughter Rosamund in the fashion you have agreed. Godwin, the elder, first, as is his right; then Wulf. Nay, no thanks; but go swiftly, for I whose hours are short wish to learn the answer to this riddle."

So they bowed and went, walking side by side. At the door of the hall, Wulf stopped and said:

"Rosamund is in the church. Seek her there, and—oh! I would that I could wish you good fortune; but, Godwin, I cannot. I fear me that this may be the edge of that shadow of woman's love whereof you spoke, falling cold upon my heart."

"There is no shadow; there is light, now and always, as we have sworn that it should be," answered Godwin.

## Chapter 4
# The Letter of Saladin

'Twas past three in the afternoon, and snow clouds were fast covering up the last grey gleam of the December day, as Godwin, wishing that his road was longer, walked to Steeple church across the meadow. At the door of it he met the two serving women coming out with brooms in their hands, and bearing between them a great basket filled with broken meats and foul rushes. Of them he asked if the Lady Rosamund were still in the church, to which they answered, curtseying:

"Yes, Sir Godwin; and she bade us desire of you that you would come to lead her to the Hall when she had finished making her prayers before the altar."

"I wonder," mused Godwin, "whether I shall ever lead her from the altar to the Hall, or whether—I shall bide alone by the altar?"

Still he thought it a good omen that she had bidden him thus, though some might have read it otherwise.

Godwin entered the church, walking softly on the rushes with which its nave was strewn, and by the light of the lamp that burnt there always, saw Rosamund kneeling before a little shrine, her gracious head bowed upon her hands, praying earnestly. Of what, he wondered—of what?

Still, she did not hear him; so, coming into the chancel, he stood behind her and waited patiently. At length, with a deep sigh, Rosamund rose from her knees and turned, and he noted by the light of the lamp that there were tear-stains upon her face. Perhaps she, too, had spoken with the Prior John, who was her confessor also. Who knows? At the least, when her eyes fell upon Godwin standing like a statue before her, she started, and there broke from her lips the words:

"Oh, how swift an answer!" Then, recovering herself, added, "To my message, I mean, cousin."

"I met the women at the door," he said.

"It is kind of you to come," Rosamund went on; "but, in truth, since that day on Death Creek I fear to walk a bow-shot's length alone or in the company of women only. With you I feel safe."

"Or with Wulf?"

"Yes; or with Wulf," she repeated; "that is, when he is not thinking of wars and adventures far away."

By now they had reached the porch of the church, to find that the snow was falling fast.

"Let us bide here a minute," he said; "it is but a passing cloud."

So they stayed there in the gloom, and for a while there was silence between them. Then he spoke.

"Rosamund, my cousin and lady, I come to put a question to you, but first—why you will understand afterwards—it is my duty to ask that you will give me no answer to that question until a full day has passed."

"Surely, Godwin, that is easy to promise. But what is this wonderful question which may not be answered?"

"One short and simple. Will you give yourself to me in marriage, Rosamund?"

She leaned back against the wall of the porch.

"My father—" she began.

"Rosamund, I have his leave."

"How can I answer since you yourself forbid me?"

"Till this time to-morrow only. Meanwhile, I pray you hear me, Rosamund. I am your cousin, and we were brought up together—indeed, except when I was away at the Scottish war, we have never been apart. Therefore, we know each other well, as well as any can who are not wedded. Therefore, too, you will know that I have always loved you, first as a brother loves his sister, and now as a man loves a woman."

"Nay, Godwin, I knew it not; indeed, I thought that, as it used to be, your heart was other—where."

"Other—where? What lady—?"

"Nay, no lady; but in your dreams."

"Dreams? Dreams of what?"

"I cannot say. Perchance of things that are not here—things higher than the person of a poor maid."

"Cousin, in part you are right, for it is not only the maid whom I love, but her spirit also. Oh, in truth, you are to me a dream—a symbol of all that is noble, high and pure. In you and through you, Rosamund, I worship the heaven I hope to share with you."

"A dream? A symbol? Heaven? Are not these glittering garments to hang about a woman's shape? Why, when the truth came out you would find her but a skull in a jewelled mask, and learn to loath her for a deceit that was not her own, but yours. Godwin, such trappings as your imagination pictures could only fit an angel's face."

"They fit a face that will become an angel's."

"An angel's? How know you? I am half an Eastern; the blood runs warm in me at times. I, too, have my thoughts and visions. I think that I love power and imagery and the delights of life—a different life from this. Are you sure, Godwin, that this poor face will be an angel's?"

"I wish I were as sure of other things. At least I'll risk it."

"Think of your soul, Godwin. It might be tarnished. You would not risk that for me, would you?"

He thought. Then answered:

"No; since your soul is a part of mine, and I would not risk yours, Rosamund."

"I like you for that answer," she said. "Yes; more than for all you have said before, because I know that it is true. Indeed, you are an honourable knight, and I am proud—very proud—that you should love me, though perhaps it would have been better otherwise." And ever so little she bent the knee to him.

"Whatever chances, in life or death those words will make me happy, Rosamund."

Suddenly she caught his arm. "Whatever chances? Ah! what is about to chance? Great things, I think, for you and Wulf and me. Remember, I am half an Eastern, and we children of the East can feel the shadow of the future before it lays its hands upon us and becomes the present. I fear it, Godwin—I tell you that I fear it."

"Fear it not, Rosamund. Why should you fear? On God's knees lies the scroll of our lives, and of His purposes. The words we see and the words we guess may be terrible, but He who wrote it knows the end of the scroll, and that it is good. Do not fear, therefore, but read on with an untroubled heart, taking no thought for the morrow."

She looked at him wonderingly, and asked,

"Are these the words of a wooer or of a saint in wooer's weeds? I know not, and do you know yourself? But you say you love me and that you would wed me, and I believe it; also that the woman whom Godwin weds will be fortunate, since such men are rare. But I am forbid to answer till to-morrow. Well, then I will answer as I am given grace. So till then be what you were of old, and—the snow has ceased; guide me home, my cousin Godwin."

So home they went through the darkness and the cold, moaning wind, speaking no word, and entered the wide hall, where a great fire built in its centre roared upwards towards an opening in the roof, whence the smoke escaped, looking very pleasant and cheerful after the winter night without.

There, standing in front of the fire, also pleasant and cheerful to behold, although his brow seemed somewhat puckered, was Wulf. At the sight of him Godwin turned back through the great door, and having, as it were, stood for one moment in the light, vanished again into the darkness, closing the door behind him. But Rosamund walked on towards the fire.

"You seem cold, cousin," said Wulf, studying her. "Godwin has kept you too long to pray with him in church. Well, it is his custom, from which I myself have suffered. Be seated on this settle and warm yourself."

She obeyed without a word, and opening her fur cloak, stretched out her hands towards the flame, which played upon her dark and lovely face. Wulf looked round him.

The hall was empty. Then he looked at Rosamund.

"I am glad to find this chance of speaking with you alone, Cousin, since I have a question to ask of you; but I must pray of you to give me no answer to it until four-and-twenty hours be passed."

"Agreed," she said. "I have given one such promise; let it serve for both; now for your question."

"Ah!" replied Wulf cheerfully; "I am glad that Godwin went first, since it saves me words, at which he is better than I am."

"I do not know that, Wulf; at least, you have more of them," answered Rosamund, with a little smile.

"More perhaps, but of a different quality—that is what you mean. Well, happily here mere words are not in question."

"What, then, are in question, Wulf?"

"Hearts. Your heart and my heart—and, I suppose, Godwin's heart, if he has one—in that way."

"Why should not Godwin have a heart?"

"Why? Well, you see just now it is my business to belittle Godwin. Therefore I declare—which you, who know more about it, can believe or not as it pleases you—that Godwin's heart is like that of the old saint in the reliquary at Stangate—a thing which may have beaten once, and will perhaps beat again in heaven, but now is somewhat dead—to this world."

Rosamund smiled, and thought to herself that this dead heart had shown signs of life not long ago. But aloud she said:

"If you have no more to say to me of Godwin's heart, I will begone to read with my father, who waits for me."

"Nay, I have much more to say of my own." Then suddenly Wulf became very earnest—so earnest that his great frame shook, and when he strove to speak he could but stammer. At length it all came forth in a flood of burning words.

"I love you, Rosamund! I love you—all of you, as I have ever loved you—though I did not know it till the other day—that of the fight, and ever shall love you—and I seek you for my wife. I know that I am only a rough soldier-man, full of faults, not holy and learned like Godwin. Yet I swear that I would be a true knight to you all my life, and, if the saints give me grace and strength, do great deeds in your honour and watch you well. Oh! what more is there to say?"

"Nothing, Wulf," answered Rosamund, lifting her downcast eyes. "You do not wish that I should answer you, so I will thank you—yes, from my heart, though, in truth, I am grieved that we can be no more brother and sister, as we have been this many a year—and be going."

"Nay, Rosamund, not yet. Although you may not speak, surely you might give me some little sign, who am in torment, and thus must stay until this time to-morrow. For instance, you might let me kiss your hand—the pact said nothing about kissing."

"I know naught of this pact, Wulf," answered Rosamund sternly, although a smile crept about the corners of her mouth, "but I do know that I shall not suffer you to touch my hand."

"Then I will kiss your robe," and seizing a corner of her cloak, he pressed it to his lips.

"You are strong—I am weak, Wulf, and cannot wrench my garment from you, but I tell you that this play advantages you nothing."

He let the cloak fall.

"Your pardon. I should have remembered that Godwin would never have presumed so far."

"Godwin," she said, tapping her foot upon the ground, "if he gave a promise, would keep it in the spirit as well as in the letter."

"I suppose so. See what it is for an erring man to have a saint for a brother and a rival! Nay, be not angry with me, Rosamund, who cannot tread the path of saints."

"That I believe, but at least, Wulf, there is no need to mock those who can."

"I mock him not. I love him as well as—you do." And he watched her face.

It never changed, for in Rosamund's heart were hid the secret strength and silence of the East, which can throw a mask impenetrable over face and features.

"I am glad that you love him, Wulf. See to it that you never forget your love and duty."

"I will; yes—even if you reject me for him."

"Those are honest words, such as I looked to hear you speak," she replied in a gentle voice. "And now, dear Wulf, farewell, for I am weary—"

"To-morrow—" he broke in.

"Ay," she answered in a heavy voice. "To-morrow I must speak, and—you must listen."

The sun had run his course again, and once more it was near four o'clock in the afternoon. The brethren stood by the great fire in the hall looking at each other doubtfully—as, indeed, they had looked through all the long hours of the night, during which neither of them had closed an eye.

"It is time," said Wulf, and Godwin nodded.

As he spoke a woman was seen descending from the solar, and they knew her errand.

"Which?" asked Wulf, but Godwin shook his head.

"Sir Andrew bids me say that he would speak with you both," said the woman, and went her way.

"By the saints, I believe it's neither!" exclaimed Wulf, with a little laugh.

"It may be thus," said Godwin, "and perhaps that would be best for all."

"I don't think so," answered Wulf, as he followed him up the steps of the solar.

Now they had passed the passage and closed the door, and before them was Sir Andrew seated in his chair by the fire, but not alone, for at his side, her hand resting upon his shoulder, stood Rosamund. They noted that she was clad in her richest robes, and a bitter thought came into their minds that this might be to show them how beautiful was the woman whom both of them must lose. As they advanced they bowed first to her and then to their uncle, while, lifting her eyes from the ground, she smiled a little in greeting.

"Speak, Rosamund," said her father. "These knights are in doubt and pain."

"Now for the *coup de grace*," muttered Wulf.

"My cousins," began Rosamund in a low, quiet voice, as though she were saying a lesson, "as to the matter of which you spoke to me yesterday, I have taken counsel with my father and with my own heart.

You did me great honour, both of you, in asking me to be the wife of such worthy knights, with whom I have been brought up and have loved since childhood as a sister loves her brothers. I will be brief as I may. Alas! I can give to neither of you the answer which you wish."

"*Coup de grace* indeed," muttered Wulf, "through hauberk, gambeson, and shirt, right home to the heart."

But Godwin only turned a trifle paler and said nothing.

Now there was silence for a little space, while from beneath his bushy eyebrows the old knight watched their faces, on which the light of the tapers fell.

Then Godwin spoke: "We thank you, Cousin. Come, Wulf, we have our answer; let us be going."

"Not all of it," broke in Rosamund hastily, and they seemed to breathe again.

"Listen," she said; "for if it pleases you, I am willing to make a promise which my father has approved. Come to me this time two years, and if we all three live, should both of you still wish for me to wife, that there may be no further space of pain or waiting, I will name the man whom I shall choose, and marry him at once."

"And if one of us is dead?" asked Godwin.

"Then," replied Rosamund, "if his name be untarnished, and he has done no deed that is not knightly, will forthwith wed the other."

"Pardon me—" broke in Wulf.

She held up her hand and stopped him, saying: "You think this a strange saying, and so, perhaps, it is; but the matter is also strange, and for me the case is hard. Remember, all my life is at stake, and I may desire more time wherein to make my choice, that between two such men no maiden would find easy. We are all of us still young for marriage, for which, if God guards our lives, there will be time and to spare. Also in two years I may learn which of you is in truth the worthier knight, who to-day both seem so worthy."

"Then is neither of us more to you than the other?" asked Wulf outright.

Rosamund turned red, and her bosom heaved as she replied:

"I will not answer that question."

"And Wulf should not have asked it," said Godwin. "Brother, I read Rosamund's saying thus: Between us she finds not much to choose, or if she does in her secret heart, out of her kindness—since she is determined not to marry for a while—she will not suffer us to see it and thereby bring grief on one of us. So she says, 'Go forth, you knights, and do deeds worthy of such a lady, and perchance he who does the highest deeds shall receive the great reward.' For my part, I find this judgment wise and just, and I am content to abide its issue. Nay, I am even glad of it, since it gives us time and opportunity to show our sweet cousin here, and all our fellows, the mettle whereof we are made, and strive to outshine each other in the achievement of great feats which, as always, we shall attempt side by side."

"Well spoken," said Sir Andrew. "And you, Wulf?"

Then Wulf, feeling that Rosamund was watching his face beneath the shadow of her long eyelashes, answered:

"Before Heaven, I am content also, for whatever may be said against it, now at least there will be two years of war in which one or both of us well may fall, and for that while at least no woman can come between our brotherhood. Uncle, I crave your leave to go serve my liege in Normandy."

"And I also," said Godwin.

"In the spring; in the spring," replied Sir Andrew hastily; "when King Henry moves his power. Meanwhile, bide you here in all good fellowship, for, who knows—much may happen between now and then, and perhaps your strong arms will be needed as they were not long ago. Moreover, I look to all three of you to hear no more of this talk of love and marriage, which, in truth, disturbs my mind and house. For good or ill, the matter is now settled for two years to come, by which time it is likely I shall be in my grave and beyond all troubling.

"I do not say that things have gone altogether as I could have wished, but they are as Rosamund wishes, and that is enough for me. On which of you she looks with the more favour I do not know, and be you content to remain in ignorance of what a father does not think it wise to seek to learn. A maid's heart is her own, and her future lies in the hand of God and His saints, where let it bide, say I. Now we have done with all this business. Rosamund, dismiss your knights, and be you all three brothers and sister once more till this time two years, when those who live will find an answer to the riddle."

So Rosamund came forward, and without a word gave her right hand to Godwin and her left to Wulf, and suffered that they should press their lips upon them. So for a while this was the end of their asking of her in marriage.

The brethren left the solar side by side as they had come into it, but changed men in a sense, for now their lives were afire with a great purpose, which bade them dare and do and win. Yet they were lighter-hearted than when they entered there, since at least neither had been scorned, while both had hope, and all the future, which the young so seldom fear, lay before them.

As they descended the steps their eyes fell upon the figure of a tall man clad in a pilgrim's cape, hood and low-crowned hat, of which the front was bent upwards and laced, who carried in his hand a palmer's staff, and about his waist the scrip and water-bottle.

"What do you seek, holy palmer?" asked Godwin, coming towards him. "A night's lodging in my uncle's house?"

The man bowed; then, fixing on him a pair of beadlike brown eyes, which reminded Godwin of some he had seen, he knew not when or where, answered in the humble voice affected by his class:

"Even so, most noble knight. Shelter for man and beast, for my mule is held without. Also—a word with the lord, Sir Andrew D'Arcy, for whom I have a message."

"A mule?" said Wulf. "I thought that palmers always went afoot?"

"True, Sir Knight; but, as it chances, I have baggage. Nay, not my own, whose earthly gear is all upon my back—but a chest, that contains I know not what, which I am charged to deliver to Sir Andrew D'Arcy, the owner of this hall, or should he be dead, then to the lady Rosamund, his daughter."

"Charged? By whom?" asked Wulf.

"That, sir," said the palmer, bowing, "I will tell to Sir Andrew, who, I understand, still lives. Have I your leave to bring in the chest, and if so, will one of your servants help me, for it is heavy?"

"We will help you," said Godwin. And they went with him into the courtyard, where by the scant light of the stars they saw a fine mule in charge of one of the serving men, and bound upon its back a long-shaped package sewn over with sacking. This the palmer unloosed, and taking one end, while Wulf, after bidding the man stable the mule, took the other, they bore it into the hall, Godwin going before them to summon his uncle. Presently he came and the palmer bowed to him.

"What is your name, palmer, and whence is this box?" asked the old knight, looking at him keenly.

"My name, Sir Andrew, is Nicholas of Salisbury, and as to who sent me, with your leave I will whisper in your ear." And, leaning forward, he did so.

Sir Andrew heard and staggered back as though a dart had pierced him.

"What?" he said. "Are you, a holy palmer, the messenger of—" and he stopped suddenly.

"I was his prisoner," answered the man, "and he—who at least ever keeps his word—gave me my life—for I had been condemned to die—at the price that I brought this to you, and took back your answer, or hers, which I have sworn to do."

"Answer? To what?"

"Nay, I know nothing save that there is a writing in the chest. Its purport I am not told, who am but a messenger bound by oath to do certain things. Open the chest, lord, and meanwhile, if you have food, I have travelled far and fast."

Sir Andrew went to a door, and called to his men-servants, whom he bade give meat to the palmer and stay with him while he ate. Then he told Godwin and Wulf to lift the box and bring it to the solar, and with it hammer and chisel, in case they should be needed, which they did, setting it upon the oaken table.

"Open," said Sir Andrew. So they ripped off the canvas, two folds of it, revealing within a box of dark, foreign looking wood bound with iron bands, at which they laboured long before they could break them. At length it was done, and there within was another box beautifully made of polished ebony, and sealed at the front and ends with a strange device. This box had a lock of silver, to which was tied a silver key.

"At least it has not been tampered with," said Wulf, examining the unbroken seals, but Sir Andrew only repeated:

"Open, and be swift. Here, Godwin, take the key, for my hand shakes with cold."

The lock turned easily, and the seals being broken, the lid rose upon its hinges, while, as it did so, a scent of precious odours filled the place. Beneath, covering the contents of the chest, was an oblong piece of worked silk, and lying on it a parchment.

Sir Andrew broke the thread and seal, and unrolled the parchment. Within it was written over in strange characters. Also, there was a second unsealed roll, written in a clerkly hand in Norman French, and headed, "Translation of this letter, in case the knight, Sir Andrew D'Arcy, has forgotten the Arabic tongue, or that his daughter, the lady Rosamund, has not yet learned the same."

Sir Andrew glanced at both headings, then said:

"Nay, I have not forgotten Arabic, who, while my lady lived, spoke little else with her, and who taught it to our daughter. But the light is bad, and, Godwin, you are scholarly; read me the French. We can compare them afterwards."

At this moment Rosamund entered the solar from her chamber, and seeing the three of them so strangely employed, said:

"Is it your will that I go, father?"

"No, daughter. Since you are here, stay here. I think that this matter concerns you as well as me. Read on, Godwin."

So Godwin read:

"In the Name of God, the Merciful and Compassionate! I, Salah-ed-din, Yusuf ibn Ayoub, Commander of the Faithful, cause these words to be written, and seal them with my own hand, to the Frankish lord, Sir Andrew D'Arcy, husband of my sister by another mother, Sitt Zobeide, the beautiful and faithless, on whom Allah has taken vengeance for her sin. Or if he be dead also, then to his daughter and hers, my niece, and by blood a princess of Syria and Egypt, who among the English is named the lady Rose of the World.

"You, Sir Andrew, will remember how, many years ago, what we were friends, you, by an evil chance, became acquainted with my sister Zobeide, while you were a prisoner and sick in my father's house. How, too, Satan put it into her heart to listen to your words of love, so that she became a Cross-worshipper, and was married to you after the Frankish custom, and fled with you to England. You will remember also, although at the time we could not recapture her from your vessel, how I sent a messenger to you, saying that soon or late I would yet tear her from your arms and deal with her as we deal with faithless women. But within six years of that time sure news reached me that Allah had taken her, therefore I mourned for my sister and her fate awhile, and forgot her and you.

"Know that a certain knight named Lozelle, who dwelt in the part of England where you have your castle, has told me that Zobeide left a daughter, who is very beautiful. Now my heart, which loved her mother, goes out towards this niece whom I have never seen, for although she is your child and a Cross-worshipper at least—save in the matter of her mother's theft—you were a brave and noble knight, of good blood, as, indeed, I remember your brother was also, he who fell in the fight at Harenc.

"Learn now that, having by the will of Allah come to great estate here at Damascus and throughout the East, I desire to lift your daughter up to be a princess of my house. Therefore I invite her to journey to Damascus, and you with her, if you live. Moreover, lest you should fear some trap, on behalf of myself, my successors and councillors, I promise in the Name of God, and by the word of Salah-ed-din, which never yet was broken, that although I trust the merciful God may change her heart so that she enters it of her own will, I will not force her to accept the Faith or to bind herself in any marriage which she does not desire.

Nor will I take vengeance upon you, Sir Andrew, for what you have done in the past, or suffer others to do so, but will rather raise you to great honour and live with you in friendship as of yore.

"But if my messenger returns and tells me that my niece refuses this, my loving offer, then I warn her that my arm is long, and I will surely take her as I can.

"Therefore, within a year of the day that I receive the answer of the lady, my niece, who is named Rose of the World, my emissaries will appear wherever she may be, married or single, to lead her to me, with honour if she be willing, but still to lead her to me if she be unwilling. Meanwhile, in token of my love, I send certain gifts of precious things, and with them my patent of her title as Princess, and Lady of the City of Baalbec, which title, with its revenue and prerogatives, are registered in the archives of my empire in favour of her and her lawful heirs, and declared to be binding upon me and my successors forever.

"The bearer of this letter and of my gifts is a certain Cross-worshipper named Nicholas, to whom let your answer be handed for delivery to me. This devoir he is under oath to perform and will perform it, for he knows that if he fails therein, then that he must die.

"Signed by Salah-ed-din, Commander of the Faithful, at Damascus, and sealed with his seal, in the spring season of the year of the Hegira 581.

"Take note also that this writing having been read to me by my secretary before I set my name and seal thereunto, I perceive that you, Sir Andrew, or you, Lady Rose of the World, may think it strange that I should be at such pains and cost over a maid who is not of my religion and whom I never saw, and may therefore doubt my honesty in the matter. Know then the true reason. Since I heard that you, Lady Rose of the World, lived, I have thrice been visited by a dream sent from God concerning you, and in it I saw your face.

"Now this was the dream—that the oath I made as regards your mother is binding as regards you also; further, that in some way which is not revealed to me, your presence here will withhold me from the shedding of a sea of blood, and save the whole world much misery. Therefore it is decreed that you must come and bide in my house. That these things are so, Allah and His Prophet be my witnesses."

## Chapter 5

# The Wine Merchant

Godwin laid down the letter, and all of them stared at one another in amazement.

"Surely," said Wulf, "this is some fool's trick played off upon our uncle as an evil jest."

By way of answer Sir Andrew bade him lift the silk that hid the contents of the coffer and see what lay there. Wulf did so, and next moment threw back his head like a man whom some sudden light had blinded, as well he might, for from it came such a flare of gems as Essex had rarely seen before. Red, green and blue they sparkled; and among them were the dull glow of gold and the white sheen of pearls.

"Oh, how beautiful! how beautiful!" said Rosamund.

"Ay," muttered Godwin; "beautiful enough to maze a woman's mind till she knows not right from wrong."

Wulf said nothing, but one by one drew its treasures from the chest—coronet, necklace of pearls, breast ornaments of rubies, girdle of sapphires, jewelled anklets, and with them veil, sandals, robes and other garments of gold-embroidered purple silk. Moreover, among these, also sealed with the seals of Salah-ed-din, his viziers, officers of state, and secretaries, was that patent of which the letter spoke, setting out the full titles of the Princess of Baalbec; the extent and boundaries of her great estates, and the amount of her annual revenue, which seemed more money than they had ever heard of.

"I was wrong," said Wulf. "Even the Sultan of the East could not afford a jest so costly."

"Jest?" broke in Sir Andrew; "it is no jest, as I was sure from the first line of that letter. It breathes the very spirit of Saladin, though he be a Saracen, the greatest man on all the earth, as I, who was a friend of his youth, know well. Ay, and he is right. In a sense I sinned against him as his sister sinned, our love compelling us. Jest? Nay, no jest, but because a vision of the night, which he believes the voice of God, or perhaps some oracle of the magicians has deeply stirred that great soul of his and led him on to this wild adventure."

He paused awhile, then looked up and said, "Girl, do you know what Saladin has made of you? Why, there are queens in Europe who would be glad to own that rank and those estates in the rich lands above Damascus. I know the city and the castle of which he speaks. It is a mighty place upon the banks of Litani and Orontes, and after its military governor—for that rule he would not give a Christian—you will be first in it, beneath the seal of Saladin—the surest title in all the earth. Say, will you go and queen it there?"

Rosamund gazed at the gleaming gems and the writings that made her royal, and her eyes flashed and her breast heaved, as they had done by the church of St. Peter on the Essex coast. Thrice she looked while they watched her, then turned her head as from the bait of some great temptation and answered one word only—"Nay."

"Well spoken," said her father, who knew her blood and its longings. "At least, had the 'nay' been 'yea,' you must have gone alone. Give me ink and parchment, Godwin."

They were brought, and he wrote:

"To the Sultan Saladin, from Andrew D'Arcy and his daughter Rosamund.

"We have received your letter, and we answer that where we are there we will bide in such state as God has given us. Nevertheless, we thank you, Sultan, since we believe you honest, and we wish you well, except in your wars against the Cross. As for your threats, we will do our best to bring them to nothing. Knowing the customs of the East, we do not send back your gifts to you, since to do so would be to offer insult to one of the greatest men in all the world; but if you choose to ask for them, they are yours—not ours. Of your dream we say that it was but an empty vision of the night which a wise man should forget.—Your servant and your niece."

Then he signed, and Rosamund signed after him, and the writing was done up, wrapped in silk, and sealed.

"Now," said Sir Andrew, "hide away this wealth, since were it known that we had such treasures in the place, every thief in England would be our visitor, some of them bearing high names, I think."

So they laid the gold-embroidered robes and the priceless sets of gems back in their coffer, and having locked it, hid it away in the great iron-bound chest that stood in Sir Andrew's sleeping chamber.

When everything was finished, Sir Andrew said: "Listen now,

Rosamund, and you also, my nephews. I have never told you the true tale of how the sister of Saladin, who was known as Zobeide, daughter of Ayoub, and afterwards christened into our faith by the name of Mary, came to be my wife. Yet you should learn it, if only to show how evil returns upon a man. After the great Nur-ed-din took Damascus, Ayoub was made its governor; then some three-and-twenty years ago came the capture of Harenc, in which my brother fell. Here I was wounded and taken prisoner. They bore me to Damascus, where I was lodged in the palace of Ayoub and kindly treated. Here too it was, while I lay sick, that I made friends with the young Saladin, and with his sister Zobeide, whom I met secretly in the gardens of the palace. The rest may be guessed. Although she numbered but half my years, she loved me as I loved her, and for my sake offered to change her faith and fly with me to England if opportunity could be found, which was hard.

"Now, as it chanced, I had a friend, a dark and secret man named Jebal, the young sheik of a terrible people, whose cruel rites no Christian understands. They are the subjects of one Mahomet, in Persia, and live in castles at Masyaf, on Lebanon. This man had been in alliance with the Franks, and once in a battle I saved his life from the Saracens at the risk of my own, whereon he swore that did I summon him from the ends of the earth he would come to me if I needed help. Moreover, he gave me his signet-ring as a token, and, by virtue of it, so he said, power in his dominions equal to his own, though these I never visited. You know it," and holding up his hand, Sir Andrew showed them a heavy gold ring, in which was set a black stone, with red veins running across the stone in the exact shape of a dagger, and beneath the dagger words cut in unknown characters.

"So in my plight I bethought me of Jebal, and found means to send him a letter sealed with his ring. Nor did he forget his promise, for within twelve days Zobeide and I were galloping for Beirut on two horses so swift that all the cavalry of Ayoub could not overtake them. We reached the city, and there were married, Rosamund. There too your mother was baptised a Christian. Thence, since it was not safe for us to stay in the East, we took ship and came safe home, bearing this ring of Jebal with us, for I would not give it up, as his servants demanded that I should do, except to him alone. But before that vessel sailed, a man disguised as a fisherman brought me a message from Ayoub and his son Saladin, swearing that they would yet recapture Zobeide, the daughter of one of them and sister of the other.

"That is the story, and you see that their oath has not been forgotten, though when in after years they learned of my wife's death, they let the matter lie. But since then Saladin, who in those days was but a noble youth, has become the greatest sultan that the East has ever known, and having been told of you, Rosamund, by that traitor Lozelle, he seeks to take you in your mother's place, and, daughter, I tell you that I fear him."

"At least we have a year or longer in which to prepare ourselves, or to hide," said Rosamund. "His palmer must travel back to the East before my uncle Saladin can have our answer."

"Ay," said Sir Andrew; "perhaps we have a year."

"What of the attack on the quay?" asked Godwin, who had been thinking. "The knight Lozelle was named there. Yet if Saladin had to do with it, it seems strange that the blow should have come before the word."

Sir Andrew brooded a while, then said:

"Bring in this palmer. I will question him."

So the man Nicholas, who was found still eating as though his hunger would never be satisfied, was brought in by Wulf. He bowed low before the old knight and Rosamund, studying them the while with his sharp eyes, and the roof and the floor, and every other detail of the chamber. For those eyes of his seemed to miss nothing.

"You have brought me a letter from far away, Sir Palmer, who are named Nicholas," said Sir Andrew.

"I have brought you a chest from Damascus, Sir Knight, but of its contents I know nothing. At least you will bear me witness that it has not been tampered with," answered Nicholas.

"I find it strange," went on the old knight, "that one in your holy garb should be chosen as the messenger of Saladin, with whom Christian men have little to do."

"But Saladin has much to do with Christian men, Sir Andrew. Thus he takes them prisoner even in times of peace, as he did me."

"Did he, then, take the knight Lozelle prisoner?"

"The knight Lozelle?" repeated the palmer. "Was he a big, red-faced man, with a scar upon his forehead, who always wore a black cloak over his mail?"

"That might be he."

"Then he was not taken prisoner, but he came to visit the Sultan at Damascus while I lay in bonds there, for I saw him twice or thrice, though what his business was I do not know. Afterwards he left, and at Jaffa I heard that he had sailed for Europe three months before I did."

Now the brethren looked at each other. So Lozelle was in England. But Sir Andrew made no comment, only he said: "Tell me your story, and be careful that you speak the truth."

"Why should I not, who have nothing to hide?" answered Nicholas. "I was captured by some Arabs as I journeyed to the Jordan upon a pilgrimage, who, when they found that I had no goods to be robbed of, would have killed me. This, indeed, they were about to do, had not some of Saladin's soldiers come by and commanded them to hold their hands and give me over to them. They did so, and the soldiers took me to Damascus. There I was imprisoned, but not close, and then it was that I saw Lozelle, or, at least, a Christian man who had some such name, and, as he seemed to be in favour with the Saracens, I begged him to intercede for me. Afterwards I was brought before the court of Saladin, and having questioned me, the Sultan himself told me that I must either worship the false prophet or die, to which you can guess my answer. So they led me away, as I thought, to death, but none offered to do me hurt.

"Three days later Saladin sent for me again, and offered to spare my life if I would swear an oath, which oath was that I should take a certain package and deliver it to you, or to your daughter named the Lady Rosamund here at your hall of Steeple, in Essex, and bring back the answer to Damascus. Not wishing to die, I said that I would do this, if the Sultan passed his word, which he never breaks, that I should be set free afterwards."

"And now you are safe in England, do you purpose to return to Damascus with the answer, and, if so, why?"

"For two reasons, Sir Andrew. First, because I have sworn to do so, and I do not break my word any more than does Saladin. Secondly, because I continue to wish to live, and the Sultan promised me that if I failed in my mission, he would bring about my death wherever I might be, which I am sure he has the power to do by magic or otherwise. Well, the rest of the tale is short. The chest was handed over to me as you see it, and with it money sufficient for my faring to and fro and something to spare. Then I was escorted to Joppa, where I took passage on a ship bound to Italy, where I found another ship named the *Holy Mary* sailing for Calais, which we reached after being nearly cast away. Thence I came to Dover in a fishing boat, landing there eight days ago, and having bought a mule, joined some travellers to London, and so on here."

"And how will you return?"

The palmer shrugged his shoulders.

"As best I may, and as quickly. Is your answer ready, Sir Andrew?"

"Yes; it is here," and he handed him the roll, which Nicholas hid away in the folds of his great cloak. Then Sir Andrew added, "You say you know nothing of all the business in which you play this part?"

"Nothing; or, rather, only this—the officer who escorted me to Jaffa told me that there was a stir among the learned doctors and diviners at the court because of a certain dream which the Sultan had dreamed three times. It had to do with a lady who was half of the blood of Ayoub and half English, and they said that my mission was mixed up with this matter. Now I see that the noble lady before me has eyes strangely like those of the Sultan Saladin." And he spread out his hands and ceased.

"You seem to see a good deal, friend Nicholas."

"Sir Andrew, a poor palmer who wishes to preserve his throat unslit must keep his eyes open. Now I have eaten well, and I am weary. Is there any place where I may sleep? I must be gone at daybreak, for those who do Saladin's business dare not tarry, and I have your letter."

"There is a place," answered Sir Andrew. "Wulf, take him to it, and to-morrow, before he leaves, we will speak again. Till then, farewell, holy Nicholas."

With one more searching glance the palmer bowed and went. When the door closed behind him Sir Andrew beckoned Godwin to him, and whispered:

"To-morrow, Godwin, you must take some men and follow this Nicholas to see where he goes and what he does, for I tell you I do not trust him—ay, I fear him much! These embassies to and from Saracens are strange traffic for a Christian man. Also, though he says his life hangs on it, I think that were he honest, once safe in England here he would stop, since the first priest would absolve him of an oath forced from him by the infidel."

"Were he dishonest would he not have stolen those jewels?" asked Godwin. "They are worth some risk. What do you think, Rosamund?"

"I?" she answered. "Oh, I think there is more in this than any of us dream.

"I think," she added in a voice of distress and with an involuntary wringing motion of the hands, "that for this house and those who dwell in it time is big with death, and that sharp-eyed palmer is its midwife. How strange is the destiny that wraps us all about! And now comes the sword of Saladin to shape it, and the hand of Saladin to drag me from my peaceful state to a dignity which I do not seek; and the dreams of Saladin, of whose kin I am, to interweave my life with the bloody policies of Syria and the unending war between Cross and Crescent, that are, both of them, my heritage." Then, with a woeful gesture, Rosamund turned and left them.

Her father watched her go, and said:

"The maid is right. Great business is afoot in which all of us must bear our parts. For no little thing would Saladin stir thus—he who braces himself as I know well, for the last struggle in which Christ or Mahomet must go down. Rosamund is right. On her brow shines the crescent diadem of the house of Ayoub, and at her heart hangs the black cross of the Christian and round her struggle creeds and nations. What, Wulf, does the man sleep already?"

"Like a dog, for he seems outworn with travel."

"Like a dog with one eye open, perhaps. I do not wish that he should give us the slip during the night, as I want more talk with him and other things, of which I have spoken to Godwin."

"No fear of that, uncle. I have locked the stable door, and a sainted palmer will scarcely leave us the present of such a mule."

"Not he, if I know his tribe," answered Sir Andrew. "Now let us sup and afterwards take counsel together, for we shall need it before all is done."

An hour before the dawn next morning Godwin and Wulf were up, and with them certain trusted men who had been warned that their services would be needed. Presently Wulf, bearing a lantern in his hand, came to where his brother stood by the fire in the hall.

"Where have you been?" Godwin asked. "To wake the palmer?"

"No. To place a man to watch the road to Steeple Hill, and another at the Creek path; also to feed his mule, which is a very fine beast—too good for a palmer. Doubtless he will be stirring soon, as he said that he must be up early."

Godwin nodded, and they sat together on the bench beside the fire, for the weather was bitter, and dozed till the dawn began to break. Then Wulf rose and shook himself, saying:

"He will not think it uncourteous if we rouse him now," and walking to the far end of the hall, he drew a curtain and called out, "Awake, holy Nicholas! awake! It is time for you to say your prayers, and breakfast will soon be cooking."

But no Nicholas answered.

"Of a truth," grumbled Wulf, as he came back for his lantern, "that palmer sleeps as though Saladin had already cut his throat." Then having lit it, he returned to the guest place.

"Godwin," he called presently, "come here. The man has gone!"

"Gone?" said Godwin as he ran to the curtain. "Gone where?"

"Back to his friend Saladin, I think," answered Wulf. "Look, that is how he went." And he pointed to the shutter of the sleeping-place, that stood wide open, and to an oaken stool beneath, by means of which the sainted Nicholas had climbed up to and through the narrow window slit.

"He must be without, grooming the mule which he would never have left," said Godwin.

"Honest guests do not part from their hosts thus," answered Wulf; "but let us go and see."

So they ran to the stable and found it locked and the mule safe enough within. Nor—though they looked—could they find any trace of the palmer—not even a footstep, since the ground was frostbound. Only on examining the door of the stable they discovered that an attempt had been made to lift the lock with some sharp instrument.

"It seems that he was determined to be gone, either with or without the beast," said Wulf. "Well, perhaps we can catch him yet," and he called to the men to saddle up and ride with him to search the country.

For three hours they hunted far and wide, but nothing did they see of Nicholas.

"The knave has slipped away like a night hawk, and left as little trace," reported Wulf. "Now, my uncle, what does this mean?"

"I do not know, save that it is of a piece with the rest, and that I like it little," answered the old knight anxiously. "Here the value of the beast was of no account, that is plain. What the man held of account was that he should be gone in such a fashion that none could follow him or know whither he went. The net is about us, my nephews, and I think that Saladin draws its string."

Still less pleased would Sir Andrew have been, could he have seen the palmer Nicholas creeping round the hall while all men slept, ere he girded up his long gown and ran like a hare for London. Yet he had done this by the light of the bright stars, taking note of every window slit in it, more especially of those of the solar; of the plan of the outbuildings also, and of the path that ran to Steeple Creek some five hundred yards away.

From that day forward fear settled on the place—fear of some blow that none were able to foresee, and against which they could not guard. Sir Andrew even talked of leaving Steeple and of taking up his abode in London, where he thought that they might be safer, but such foul weather set in that it was impossible to travel the roads, and still less to sail the sea. So it was arranged that if they moved at all—

and there were many things against it, not the least of which were Sir Andrew's weak health and the lack of a house to go to—it should not be till after New Year's Day.

Thus the time went on, and nothing happened to disturb them. The friends of whom the old knight took counsel laughed at his forebodings. They said that so long as they did not wander about unguarded, there was little danger of any fresh attack upon them, and if one should by chance be made, with the aid of the men they had they could hold the Hall against a company until help was summoned. Moreover, at heart, none of them believed that Saladin or his emissaries would stir in this business before the spring, or more probably until another year had passed. Still, they always set guards at night, and, besides themselves, kept twenty men sleeping at the Hall. Also they arranged that on the lighting of a signal fire upon the tower of Steeple Church their neighbours should come to succour them.

So the time went on towards Christmas, before which the weather changed and became calm, with sharp frost.

It was on the shortest day that Prior John rode up to the Hall and told them that he was going to Southminster to buy some wine for the Christmas feast. Sir Andrew asked what wine there was at Southminster. The Prior answered that he had heard that a ship, laden amongst other things with wine of Cyprus of wonderful quality, had come into the river Crouch with her rudder broken. He added that as no shipwrights could be found in London to repair it till after Christmas, the chapman, a Cypriote, who was in charge of the wine, was selling as much as he could in Southminster and to the houses about at a cheap rate, and delivering it by means of a wain that he had hired.

Sir Andrew replied that this seemed a fair chance to get fine liquor, which was hard to come by in Essex in those times. The end of it was that he bade Wulf, whose taste in strong drink was nice, to ride with the Prior into Southminster, and if he liked the stuff to buy a few casks of it for them to make merry with at Christmas—although he himself, because of his ailments, now drank only water.

So Wulf went, nothing loth. In this dark season of the year when there was no fishing, it grew very dull loitering about the Hall, and since he did not read much, like Godwin, sitting for long hours by the fire at night watching Rosamund going to and fro upon her tasks, but not speaking with her overmuch. For notwithstanding all their pretence of forgetfulness, some sort of veil had fallen between the brethren and Rosamund, and their intercourse was not so open and familiar as of old. She could not but remember that they were no more her cousins only, but her lovers also, and that she must guard herself lest she seemed to show preference to one above the other. The brethren for their part must always bear in mind also that they were bound not to show their love, and that their cousin Rosamund was no longer a simple English lady, but also by creation, as by blood, a princess of the East, whom destiny might yet lift beyond the reach of either of them.

Moreover, as has been said, dread sat upon that rooftree like a croaking raven, nor could they escape from the shadow of its wing. Far away in the East a mighty monarch had turned his thoughts towards this English home and the maid of his royal blood who dwelt there, and who was mingled with his visions of conquest and of the triumph of his faith. Driven on by no dead oath, by no mere fancy or imperial desire, but by some spiritual hope or need, he had determined to draw her to him, by fair means if he could; if not, by foul. Already means both foul and fair had failed, for that the attack at Death Creek quay had to do with this matter they could no longer doubt. It was certain also that others would be tried again and again till his end was won or Rosamund was dead—for here, if even she would go back upon her word, marriage itself could not shield her.

So the house was sad, and saddest of all seemed the face of the old knight, Sir Andrew, oppressed as he was with sickness, with memories and fears. Therefore, Wulf could find pleasure even in an errand to Southminster to buy wine, of which, in truth, he would have been glad to drink deeply, if only to drown his thoughts awhile.

So away he rode up Steeple Hill with the Prior, laughing as he used to do before Rosamund led him to gather flowers at St. Peter's-on-the-Wall.

Asking where the foreign merchant dwelt who had wine to sell, they were directed to an inn near the minster. Here in a back room they found a short, stout man, wearing a red cloth cap, who was seated on a pillow between two kegs. In front of him stood a number of folk, gentry and others, who bargained with him for his wine and the silks and embroideries that he had to sell, giving the latter to be handled and samples of the drink to all who asked for them.

"Clean cups," he said, speaking in bad French, to the drawer who stood beside him. "Clean cups, for here come a holy man and a gallant knight who wish to taste my liquor. Nay, fellow, fill them up, for the top of Mount Trooidos in winter is not so cold as this cursed place, to say nothing of its damp, which is that of a dungeon," and he shivered, drawing his costly shawl closer round him.

"Sir Abbot, which will you taste first—the red wine or the yellow? The red is the stronger but the yellow is the more costly and a drink for saints in Paradise and abbots upon earth. The yellow from Kyrenia? Well, you are wise. They say it was my patron St. Helena's favourite vintage when she visited Cyprus, bringing with her Disma's cross."

"Are you a Christian then?" asked the Prior. "I took you for a Paynim."

"Were I not a Christian would I visit this foggy land of yours to trade in wine—a liquor forbidden to the Moslems?" answered the man, drawing aside the folds of his shawl and revealing a silver crucifix upon his broad breast. "I am a merchant of Famagusta in Cyprus, Georgios by name, and of the Greek Church which you Westerners hold to be heretical. But what do you think of that wine, holy Abbot?"

The Prior smacked his lips.

"Friend Georgios, it is indeed a drink for the saints," he answered.

"Ay, and has been a drink for sinners ere now—for this is the very tipple that Cleopatra, Queen of Egypt, drank with her Roman lover Antony, of whom you, being a learned man, may have heard. And you, Sir Knight, what say you of the black stuff—'Mavro,' we call it—not the common, but that which has been twenty years in cask?"

"I have tasted worse," said Wulf, holding out his horn to be filled again.

"Ay, and will never taste better if you live as long as the Wandering Jew. Well, sirs, may I take your orders? If you are wise you will make them large, since no such chance is likely to come your way again, and that wine, yellow or red, will keep a century."

Then the chaffering began, and it was long and keen. Indeed, at one time they nearly left the place without purchasing, but the merchant Georgios called them back and offered to come to their terms if they would take double the quantity, so as to make up a cartload between them, which he said he would deliver before Christmas Day. To this they consented at length, and departed homewards made happy by the gifts with which the chapman clinched his bargain, after the Eastern fashion. To the Prior he gave a roll of worked silk to be used as an edging to an altar cloth or banner, and to Wulf a dagger handle, quaintly carved in olive wood to the fashion of a rampant lion. Wulf thanked him, and then asked him with a somewhat shamed face if he had more embroidery for sale, whereat the Prior smiled. The quick-eyed Cypriote saw the smile, and inquired if it might be needed for a lady's wear, at which some neighbours present in the room laughed outright.

"Do not laugh at me, gentlemen," said the Eastern; "for how can I, a stranger, know this young knight's affairs, and whether he has mother, or sisters, or wife, or lover? Well here are broideries fit for any of them." Then bidding his servant bring a bale, he opened it, and began to show his goods, which, indeed, were very beautiful. In the end Wulf purchased a veil of gauze-like silk worked with golden stars as a Christmas gift for Rosamund. Afterwards, remembering that even in such a matter he must take no advantage of his brother, he added to it a tunic broidered with gold and silver flowers such as he had never seen—for they were Eastern tulips and anemones, which Godwin would give her also if he wished.

These silks were costly, and Wulf turned to the Prior to borrow money, but he had no more upon him. Georgios said, however, that it mattered nothing, as he would take a guide from the town and bring the wine in person, when he could receive payment for the broideries, of which he hoped to sell more to the ladies of the house.

He offered also to go with the Prior and Wulf to where his ship lay in the river, and show them many other goods aboard of her, which, he explained to them, were the property of a company of Cyprian merchants who had embarked upon this venture jointly with himself. This they declined, however, as the darkness was not far off; but Wulf added that he would come after Christmas with his brother to see the vessel that had made so great a voyage. Georgios replied that they would be very welcome, but if he could make shift to finish the repairs to his rudder, he was anxious to sail for London while the weather held calm, for there he looked to sell the bulk of his cargo. He added that he had expected to spend Christmas at that city, but their helm having gone wrong in the rough weather, they were driven past the mouth of the Thames, and had they not drifted into that of the Crouch, would, he thought, have foundered. So he bade them farewell for that time, but not before he had asked and received the blessing of the Prior.

Thus the pair of them departed, well pleased with their purchases and the Cypriote Georgios, whom they found a very pleasant merchant. Prior John stopped to eat at the Hall that night, when he and Wulf told of all their dealings with this man. Sir Andrew laughed at the story, showing them how they had been persuaded by the Eastern to buy a great deal more wine than they needed, so that it was he and not they who had the best of the bargain. Then he went on to tell tales of the rich island of Cyprus, where he had landed many years before and stayed awhile, and of the gorgeous court of its emperor, and of its inhabitants. These were, he said, the cunningest traders in the world—so cunning, indeed, that no Jew could overmatch them; bold sailors, also, which they had from the Phoenicians of Holy Writ, who, with the Greeks, were their forefathers, adding that what they told him of this Georgios accorded well with the character of that people.

Thus it came to pass that no suspicion of Georgios or his ship entered the mind of any one of them, which, indeed, was scarcely strange, seeing how well his tale held together, and how plain were the reasons of his presence and the purpose of his dealings in wines and silks.

## Chapter 6

# The Christmas Feast at Steeple

The fourth day after Wulf's visit to Southminster was Christmas morning, and the weather being bad, Sir Andrew and his household did not ride to Stangate, but attended mass in Steeple Church. Here, after service, according to his custom on this day, he gave a largesse to his tenants and *villeins*, and with it his good wishes and a caution that they should not become drunk at their Yuletide feast, as was the common habit of the time.

"We shall not get the chance," said Wulf, as they walked to the Hall, "since that merchant Georgios has not delivered the wine, of which I hoped to drink a cup to-night."

"Perhaps he has sold it at a better price to someone else; it would be like a Cypriote," answered Sir Andrew, smiling.

Then they went into the hall, and as had been agreed between them, together the brethren gave their Christmas gifts to Rosamund. She thanked them prettily enough, and much admired the beauty of the work. When they told her that it had not yet been paid for, she laughed and said that, however they were come by, she would wear both tunic and veil at their feast, which was to be held at nightfall.

About two o'clock in the afternoon a servant came into the hall to say that a wain drawn by three horses and accompanied by two men, one of whom led the horses, was coming down the road from Steeple village.

"Our merchant—and in time after all," said Wulf, and, followed by the others, he went out to meet them.

Georgios it was, sure enough, wrapped in a great sheepskin cloak such as Cypriotes wear in winter, and seated on the head of one of his own barrels.

"Your pardon, knights," he said as he scrambled nimbly to the ground. "The roads in this country are such that, although I have left nearly half my load at Stangate, it has taken me four long hours to come from the Abbey here, most of which time we spent in mud-holes that have wearied the horses and, as I fear, strained the wheels of this crazy wagon. Still, here we are at last, and, noble sir," he added, bowing to Sir Andrew, "here too is the wine that your son bought of me."

"My nephew," interrupted Sir Andrew.

"Once more your pardon. I thought from their likeness to you that these knights were your sons."

"Has he bought all that stuff?" asked Sir Andrew—for there were five tubs on the wagon, besides one or two smaller kegs and some packages wrapped in sheepskin.

"No, alas!" answered the Cypriote ruefully, and shrugging his shoulders. "Only two of the Mavro. The rest I took to the Abbey, for I understood the holy Prior to say he would purchase six casks, but it seems that it was but three he needed."

"He said three," put in Wulf.

"Did he, sir? Then doubtless the error was mine, who speak your tongue but ill. So I must drag the rest back again over those accursed roads," and he made another grimace. "Yet I will ask you, sir," he added to Sir Andrew, "to lighten the load a little by accepting this small keg of the old sweet vintage that grows on the slopes of Trooidos."

"I remember it well," said Sir Andrew, with a smile; "but, friend, I do not wish to take your wine for nothing."

At these words the face of Georgios beamed.

"What, noble sir," he exclaimed, "do you know my land of Cyprus? Oh, then indeed I kiss your hands, and surely you will not affront me by refusing this little present? Indeed, to be frank, I can afford to lose its price, who have done a good trade, even here in Essex."

"As you will," said Sir Andrew. "I thank you, and perhaps you have other things to sell."

"I have indeed; a few embroideries if this most gracious lady would be pleased to look at them. Some carpets also, such as the Moslems used to pray on in the name of their false prophet, Mahomet," and, turning, he spat upon the ground.

"I see that you are a Christian," said Sir Andrew. "Yet, although I fought against them, I have known many a good Mussulman. Nor do I think it necessary to spit at the name of Mahomet, who to my mind was a great man deceived by the artifice of Satan."

"Neither do I," said Godwin reflectively. "Its true servants should fight the enemies of the Cross and pray for their souls, not spit at them."

The merchant looked at them curiously, fingering the silver crucifix that hung upon his breast. "The captors of the Holy City thought otherwise," he said, "when they rode into the Mosque El Aksa up to their horses' knees in blood, and I have been taught otherwise. But the times grow liberal, and, after all, what right has a poor trader whose mind, alas! is set more on gain than on the sufferings of the blessed Son of Mary," and he crossed himself, "to form a judgment upon such high matters? Pardon me, I accept your reproof, who perhaps am bigoted."

Yet, had they but known it, this "reproof" was to save the life of many a man that night.

"May I ask help with these packages?" he went on, "as I cannot open them here, and to move the casks? Nay, the little keg I will carry myself, as I hope that you will taste of it at your Christmas feast. It must be gently handled, though I fear me that those roads of yours will not improve its quality." Then twisting the tub from the end of the wain onto his shoulder in such a fashion that it remained upright, he walked off lightly towards the open door of the hall.

"For one not tall that man is strangely strong," thought Wulf, who followed with a bale of carpets.

Then the other casks of wine were stowed away in the stone cellar beneath the hall.

Leaving his servant—a silent, stupid-looking, dark-eyed fellow named Petros—to bait the horses, Georgios entered the hall and began to unpack his carpets and embroideries with all the skill of one who had been trained in the bazaars of Cairo, Damascus, or Nicosia. Beautiful things they were which he had to show; broideries that dazzled the eye, and rugs of many hues, yet soft and bright as an otter's pelt. As Sir Andrew looked at them, remembering long dead days, his face softened.

"I will buy that rug," he said, "for of a truth it might be one on which I lay sick many a year ago in the house of Ayoub at Damascus. Nay, I haggle not at the price. I will buy it." Then he fell to thinking how, whilst lying on such a rug (indeed, although he knew it not, it was the same), looking through the rounded beads of the wooden lattice-work of his window, he had first seen his Eastern wife walking in the orange garden with her father Ayoub. Afterwards, still recalling his youth, he began to talk of Cyprus, and so time went on until the dark was falling.

Now Georgios said that he must be going, as he had sent back his guide to Southminster, where the man desired to eat his Christmas feast. So the reckoning was paid—it was a long one—and while the horses were harnessed to the wain the merchant bored holes in the little cask of wine and set spigots in them, bidding them all be sure to drink of it that night. Then calling down good fortune on them for their kindness and liberality, he made his *salaams* in the Eastern fashion, and departed, accompanied by Wulf.

Within five minutes there was a sound of shouting, and Wulf was back again saying that the wheel of the wain had broken at the first turn, so that now it was lying upon its side in the courtyard. Sir Andrew and Godwin went out to see to the matter, and there they found Georgios wringing his hands, as only an Eastern merchant can, and cursing in some foreign tongue.

"Noble knights," he said, "what am I to do? Already it is nearly dark, and how I shall find my way up yonder steep hill I know not. As for the priceless broideries, I suppose they must stay here for the night, since that wheel cannot be mended till to-morrow—"

"As you had best do also," said Sir Andrew kindly. "Come, man, do not grieve; we are used to broken axles here in Essex, and you and your servant may as well eat your Christmas dinners at Steeple as in Southminster."

"I thank you, Sir knight; I thank you. But why should I, who am but a merchant, thrust myself upon your noble company? Let me stop outside with my man, Petros, and dine with your people in that barn, where I see they are making ready their food."

"By no means," answered Sir Andrew. "Leave your servant with my people, who will look after him, and come you into the hall, and tell me some more of Cyprus till our food is ready, which will be soon. Do not fear for your goods; they shall be placed under cover."

"All unworthy as I am, I obey," answered the obsequious Georgios. "Petros, do you understand? This noble lord gives us hospitality for the night. His people will show you where to eat and sleep, and help you with your horses."

This man, who, he explained, was a Cypriote—a fisherman in summer and a muleteer in winter—bowed, and fixing his dark eyes upon those of his master, spoke in some foreign tongue.

"You hear what he says, the silly fellow?" said Georgios. "What? You do not understand Greek—only Arabic? Well, he asks me to give him money to pay for his dinner and his night's lodging. You must forgive him, for he is but a simple peasant, and cannot believe that anyone may be lodged and fed without payment. I will explain to him, the pig!" And explain he did in shrill, high notes, of which no one else could understand a word.

"There, Sir Knight, I do not think he will offend you so again. Ah! look. He is walking off—he is sulky. Well, let him alone; he will be back for his dinner, the pig! Oh, the wet and the wind! A Cypriote does not mind them in his sheepskins, in which he will sleep even in the snow."

So, Georgios still declaiming upon the shortcomings of his servant, they went back into the hall. Here the conversation soon turned upon other matters, such as the differences between the creeds of the Greek and Latin churches—a subject upon which he seemed to be an expert—and the fear of the Christians in Cyprus lest Saladin should attempt to capture that island.

At length five o'clock came, and Georgios having first been taken to the lavatory—it was but a stone trough—to wash his hands, was led to the dinner, or rather to the supper-table, which stood upon a dais in front of the entrance to the solar. Here places were laid for six—Sir Andrew, his nephews, Rosamund, the chaplain, Matthew, who celebrated masses in the church and ate at the hall on feast-days, and the Cypriote merchant, Georgios himself. Below the dais, and between it and the fire, was another table, at which were already gathered twelve guests, being the chief tenants of Sir Andrew and the reeves of his outlying lands. On most days the servants of the house, with the huntsmen, swineherds, and others, sat at a third table beyond the fire. But as nothing would stop these from growing drunken on the good ale at a feast, and though many ladies thought little of it, there was no sin that Rosamund hated so much as this, now their lord sent them to eat and drink at their ease in the barn which stood in the courtyard with its back to the moat.

When all had taken their seats, the chaplain said grace, and the meal began. It was rude but very plentiful. First, borne in by the cook on a wooden platter, came a great codfish, whereof he helped portions to each in turn, laying them on their "trenchers"—that is, large slices of bread—whence they ate them with the spoons that were given to each. After the fish appeared the meats, of which there were many sorts, served on silver spits. These included fowls, partridges, duck, and, chief of all, a great swan, that the tenants greeted by knocking their horn mugs upon the table; after which came the pastries, and with them nuts and apples. For drink, ale was served at the lower table. On the dais however, they drank some of the black wine which Wulf had bought—that is, except Sir Andrew and Rosamund, the former because he dared not, and the latter because she had always hated any drink but water—a dislike that came to her, doubtless, with her Eastern blood.

Thus they grew merry since their guest proved himself a cheerful fellow, who told them many stories of love and war, for he seemed to know much of loves, and to have been in sundry wars. At these even Sir Andrew, forgetting his ailments and forebodings, laughed well, while Rosamund, looking more beautiful than ever in the gold-starred veil and the broidered tunic which the brethren had given her, listened to them, smiling somewhat absently. At last the feast drew towards its end, when suddenly, as though struck by a sudden recollection, Georgios exclaimed:

"The wine! The liquid amber from Trooidos! I had forgotten it. Noble knight, have I your leave to draw?"

"Ay, excellent merchant," answered Sir Andrew. "Certainly you can draw your own wine."

So Georgios rose, and took a large jug and a silver tankard from the sideboard where such things were displayed. With these he went to the little keg which, it will be remembered, had been stood ready upon the trestles, and, bending over it while he drew the spigots, filled the vessels to the brim. Then he beckoned to a reeve sitting at the lower table to bring him a leather jack that stood upon the board. Having rinsed it out with wine, he filled that also, handing it with the jug to the reeve to drink their lord's health on this Yule night. The silver vessel he bore back to the high table, and with his own hand filled the horn cups of all present, Rosamund alone excepted, for she would touch none, although he pressed her hard and looked vexed at her refusal. Indeed, it was because it seemed to pain the man that Sir Andrew, ever courteous, took a little himself, although, when his back was turned, he filled the goblet up with water. At length, when all was ready, Georgios charged, or seemed to charge, his own horn, and, lifting it, said:

"Let us drink, everyone of us here, to the noble knight, Sir Andrew D'Arcy, to whom I wish, in the phrase of my own people, that he may live for ever. Drink, friends, drink deep, for never will wine such as this pass your lips again."

Then, lifting his beaker, he appeared to drain it in great gulps—an example which all followed, even Sir Andrew drinking a little from his cup, which was three parts filled with water. There followed a long murmur of satisfaction.

"Wine! It is nectar!" said Wulf.

"Ay," put in the chaplain, Matthew; "Adam might have drunk this in the Garden," while from the lower table came jovial shouts of praise of this smooth, creamlike vintage.

Certainly that wine was both rich and strong. Thus, after his sup of it, a veil as it were seemed to fall on the mind of Sir Andrew and to cover it up. It lifted again, and lo! his brain was full of memories and foresights. Circumstances which he had forgotten for many years came back to him altogether, like a crowd of children tumbling out to play. These passed, and he grew suddenly afraid. Yet what had he to fear that night? The gates across the moat were locked and guarded. Trusty men, a score or more of them, ate in his outbuildings within those gates; while others, still more trusted, sat in his hall; and on his right hand and on his left were those two strong and valiant knights, Sir Godwin and Sir Wulf. No, there was nothing to fear—and yet he felt afraid. Suddenly he heard a voice speak. It was Rosamund's; and she said:

"Why is there such silence, father? A while ago I heard the servants and bondsmen carousing in the barn; now they are still as death. Oh, and look! Are all here drunken? Godwin—"

But as she spoke Godwin's head fell forward on the board, while Wulf rose, half drew his sword, then threw his arm about the neck of the priest, and sank with him to the ground. As it was with these, so it seemed with all, for folk rocked to and fro, then sank to sleep, everyone of them, save the merchant Georgios, who rose to call another toast.

"Stranger," said Sir Andrew, in a heavy voice, "your wine is very strong."

"It would seem so, Sir Knight," he answered; "but I will wake them from their wassail." Springing from the dais lightly as a cat, he ran down the hall crying, "Air is what they need. Air!" Now coming to the door, he threw it wide open, and drawing a silver whistle from his robe, blew it long and loud. "What," he laughed, "do they still sleep? Why, then, I must give a toast that will rouse them all," and seizing a horn mug, he waved it and shouted:

"Arouse you, ye drunkards, and drink to the lady Rose of the World, princess of Baalbec, and niece to my royal master, Yusuf Salah-ed-din, who sends me to lead her to him!"

"Oh, father," shrieked Rosamund, "the wine was drugged and we are betrayed!"

As the words passed her lips there rose a sound of running feet, and through the open door at the far end of the hall burst in a score or over of armed men. Then at last Sir Andrew saw and understood.

With a roar of rage like that of a wounded lion, he seized his daughter and dragged her back with him down the passage into the solar where a fire burned and lights had been lit ready for their retiring, flinging to and bolting the door behind them.

"Swift!" he said, as he tore his gown from him, "there is no escape, but at least I can die fighting for you. Give me my mail."

She snatched his hauberk from the wall, and while they thundered at the door, did it on to him—ay, and his steel helm also, and gave him his long sword and his shield.

"Now," he said, "help me." And they thrust the oak table forward, and overset it in front of the door, throwing the chairs and stools on either side, that men might stumble on them.

"There is a bow," he said, "and you can use it as I have taught you. Get to one side and out of reach of the sword sweeps, and shoot past me as they rush; it may stay one of them. Oh, that Godwin and Wulf were here, and we would still teach these Paynim dogs a lesson!"

Rosamund made no answer but there came into her mind a vision of the agony of Godwin and of Wulf should they ever wake again to learn what had chanced to her and them. She looked round. Against the wall stood a little desk, at which Godwin was wont to write, and on it lay pen and parchment. She seized them, and as the door gave slowly inwards, scrawled:

"Follow me to Saladin. In that hope I live on.—Rosamund."

Then as the stout door at length crashed in Rosamund turned what she had written face downwards on the desk, and seizing the bow, set an arrow to its string. Now it was down and on rushed the mob up the six feet of narrow passage. At the end of it, in front of the overturned table, they halted suddenly. For there before them, skull-emblazoned, shield on arm, his long sword lifted, and a terrible wrath burning in his eyes, stood the old knight, like a wolf at bay, and by his side, bow in hand, the beauteous lady Rosamund, clad in all her festal broideries.

"Yield you!" cried a voice. By way of answer the bowstring twanged, and an arrow sped home to its feathers through the throat of the speaker, so that he went down, grabbing at it, and spoke no more for ever.

As he fell clattering to the floor, Sir Andrew cried in a great voice:

"We yield not to pagan dogs and poisoners. A D'Arcy! A D'Arcy! Meet D'Arcy, meet Death!"

Thus for the last time did old Sir Andrew utter the war-cry of his race, which he had feared would never pass his lips again. His prayer had been heard, and he was to die as he had desired.

"Down with him! seize the Princess!" said a voice. It was that of Georgios, no longer humble with a merchant's obsequious whine, but speaking in tones of cold command and in Arabic. For a moment the swarthy mob hung back, as well they might in face of that glittering sword. Then with a cry of "Salah-ed-din! Salah-ed-din!" on they surged, with flashing spears and scimitars. The overthrown table was in front of them, and one leapt upon its edge, but as he leapt, the old knight, all his years and sickness forgotten now, sprang forward and struck downwards, so heavy a blow that in the darkling mouth of the passage the sparks streamed out, and where the Saracen's head had been, appeared his heels. Back Sir Andrew stepped again to win space for his swordplay, while round the ends of the table broke two fierce-faced men. At one of them Rosamund shot with her bow, and the arrow pierced his thigh, but as he fell he struck with his keen scimitar and shore the end off the bow, so that it was useless. The second man caught his foot in the bar of the oak chair which he did not see, and went down prone, while Sir Andrew, taking no heed of him, rushed with a shout at the crowd who followed, and catching their blows upon his shield, rained down others so desperate that, being hampered by their very number, they gave before him, and staggered back along the passage.

"Guard your right, father!" cried Rosamund. He sprang round, to see the Saracen, who had fallen, on his feet again. At him he went, nor did the man wait the onset, but turned to fly, only to find his death, for the great sword caught him between neck and shoulders. Now a voice cried: "We make poor sport with this old lion, and lose men. Keep clear of his claws, and whelm him with spear casts."

But Rosamund, who understood their tongue, sprang in front of him, and answered in Arabic:

"Ay, through my breast; and go, tell that tale to Saladin!"

Then, clear and calm was heard the command of Georgios. "He who harms a hair of the Princess dies. Take them both living if you may, but lay no hand on her. Stay, let us talk."

So they ceased from their onslaught and began to consult together.

Rosamund touched her father and pointed to the man who lay upon the floor with an arrow through his thigh. He was struggling to his knee, raising the heavy scimitar in his hand. Sir Andrew lifted his sword as a husbandman lifts a stick to kill a rat, then let it fall again, saying:

"I fight not with the wounded. Drop that steel, and get you back to your own folk."

The fellow obeyed him—yes, and even touched the floor with his forehead in salaam as he crawled away, for he knew that he had been given his life, and that the deed was noble towards him who had planned a coward's stroke. Then Georgios stepped forward, no longer the same Georgios who had sold poisoned wine and Eastern broideries, but a proud-looking, high-browed Saracen clad in the mail which he wore beneath his merchant's robe, and in place of the crucifix wearing on his breast a great star-shaped jewel, the emblem of his house and rank.

"Sir Andrew," he said, "hearken to me, I pray you. Noble was that act," and he pointed to the wounded man being dragged away by his fellows, "and noble has been your defence—well worthy of your lineage and your knighthood. It is a tale that my master," and he bowed as he said the word, "will love to hear if it pleases Allah that we return to him in safety. Also you will think that I have played a knave's trick upon you, overcoming the might of those gallant knights, Sir Godwin and Sir Wulf, not with sword blows but with drugged wine, and treating all your servants in like fashion, since not one of them can shake off its fumes before to-morrow's light. So indeed it is—a very scurvy trick which I shall remember with shame to my life's end, and that perchance may yet fall back upon my head in blood and vengeance. Yet bethink you how we stand, and forgive us. We are but a little company of men in your great country, hidden, as it were, in a den of lions, who, if they saw us, would slay us without mercy. That, indeed, is a small thing, for what are our lives, of which your sword has taken tithe, and not only yours, but those of the twin brethren on the quay by the water?"

"I thought it," broke in Sir Andrew contemptuously. "Indeed, that deed was worthy of you—twenty or more men against two."

Georgios held up his hand.

"Judge us not harshly," he said, speaking slowly, who, for his own ends wished to gain time, "you who have read the letter of our lord. See you, these were my commands: To secure the lady Rose of the World as best I might, but if possible without bloodshed. Now I was reconnoitring the country with a troop of the sailors from my ship who are but poor fighters, and a few of my own people, when my spies brought me word that she had ridden out attended by only two men, and surely I thought that already she was in my hands. But the knights foiled me by strategy and strength, and you know the end of it. So afterwards my messenger presented the letter, which, indeed, should have been done at first. The letter failed also, for neither you, nor the Princess"—and he bowed to Rosamund—"could be bought. More, the whole country was awakened; you were surrounded with armed men, the knightly brethren kept watch and ward over you, and you were about to fly to London, where it would have been hard to snare you. Therefore, because I must, I—who am a prince and an emir, who also, although you remember it not, have crossed swords with you in my youth; yes, at Harenc—became a dealer in drugged wine.

"Now hearken. Yield you, Sir Andrew, who have done enough to make your name a song for generations, and accept the love of Salah-ed-din, whose word you have, the word that, as you know well, cannot be broken, which I, the lord El-Hassan—for no meaner man has been sent upon this errand—plight to you afresh. Yield you, and save your life, and live on in honour, clinging to your own faith, till Azrael takes you from the pleasant fields of Baalbec to the waters of Paradise—if such there be for infidels, however gallant.

"For know, this deed must be done. Did we return without the princess Rose of the World, we should die, every one of us, and did we offer her harm or insult, then more horribly than I can tell you. This is no fancy of a great king that drives him on to the stealing of a woman, although she be of his own high blood. The voice of God has spoken to Salah-ed-din by the mouth of his angel Sleep. Thrice has Allah spoken in dreams, telling him who is merciful, that through your daughter and her nobleness alone can countless lives be saved; therefore, sooner than she should escape him, he would lose even the half of all his empire. Outwit us, defeat us now, capture us, cause us to be tortured and destroyed, and other messengers would come to do his bidding—indeed, they are already on the way. Moreover, it is useless to shed more blood, seeing it is written in the Books that this lady, Rose of the World, must return to the East where she was begot, there to fulfil her destiny and save the lives of men."

"Then, emir El-Hassan, I shall return as a spirit," said Rosamund proudly.

"Not so, Princess," he answered, bowing, "for Allah alone has power over your life, and it is otherwise decreed. Sir Andrew, the time grows short, and I must fulfil my mission. Will you take the peace of Salah-ed-din, or force his servants to take your life?"

The old knight listened, resting on his reddened sword; then he lifted his head, and spoke:

"I am aged and near my death, wine-seller Georgios, or prince El-Hassan, whichever you may be. In my youth I swore to make no pact with Paynims, and in my eld I will not break that vow. While I can lift sword I will defend my daughter, even against the might of Saladin. Get to your coward's work again, and let things go as God has willed them."

"Then, Princess," answered El-Hassan, "bear me witness throughout the East that I am innocent of your father's blood. On his own head be it, and on yours," and for the second time he blew upon the whistle that hung around his neck.

## Chapter 7

# The Banner of Saladin

As the echoes of Hassan's whistle died away there was a crash amongst the wooden shutters of the window behind them, and down into the room leaped a long, lithe figure, holding an axe aloft. Before Sir Andrew could turn to see whence the sound came, that axe dealt him a fearful blow between the shoulders which, although the ringed mail remained unshorn, shattered his spine beneath. Down he fell, rolled on to his back, and lay there, still able to speak and without pain, but helpless as a child. For he was paralysed, and never more would move hand or foot or head.

In the silence that followed he spoke in a heavy voice, letting his eyes rest upon the man who had struck him down.

"A knightly blow, truly; one worthy of a Christian born who does murder for Paynim pay! Traitor to God and man, who have eaten my bread and now slaughter me like an ox on my hearth-stone, may your own end be even worse, and at the hands of those you serve."

The palmer Nicholas, for it was he, although he no longer wore the palmer's robe, slunk away muttering, and was lost among the crowd in the passage. Then, with a sudden and a bitter cry, Rosamund swooped forward, as a bird swoops, snatched up the sword her sire would never lift again, and setting its hilt upon the floor, cast herself forward. But its point never touched her breast, for the emir sprang swiftly and struck the steel aside; then, as she fell, caught her in his arms. "Lady," he said, loosing her very gently. "Allah does not need you yet. I have told you that it is not fated. Now will you pass me your word—for being of the blood of Salah-ed-din and D'Arcy, you, too, cannot lie—that neither now nor afterwards you will attempt to harm yourself? If not, I must bind you, which I am loth to do—it is a sacrilege to which I pray you will not force me."

"Promise, Rosamund," said the hollow voice of her father, "and go to fulfil your fate. Self-murder is a crime, and the man is right; it is decreed. I bid you promise."

"I obey and promise," said Rosamund. "It is your hour, my lord Hassan."

He bowed deeply and answered:

"I am satisfied, and henceforth we are your servants. Princess, the night air is bitter; you cannot travel thus. In which chamber are your garments?"

She pointed with her finger. A man took a taper, and, accompanied by two others, entered the place, to return presently with their arms full of all the apparel they could find. Indeed, they even brought her missal and the silver crucifix which hung above her bed and with it her leathern case of trinkets.

"Keep out the warmest cloak," said Hassan, "and tie the rest up in those carpets."

So the rugs that Sir Andrew had bought that day from the merchant Georgios were made to serve as travelling bags to hold his daughter's gear. Thus even in this hour of haste and danger thought was taken for her comfort.

"Princess," said Hassan, bowing, "my master, your uncle, sent you certain jewels of no mean value. Is it your wish that they should accompany you?"

Without lifting her eyes from her dying father's face, Rosamund answered heavily:

"Where they are, there let them bide. What have I to do with jewels?"

"Your will is my law," he said, "and others will be found for you. Princess, all is ready; we wait your pleasure."

"My pleasure? Oh, God, my pleasure?" exclaimed Rosamund in the same drear voice, still staring at her father, who lay before her on the ground.

"I cannot help it," said Hassan, answering the question in her eyes, and there was grief in his tone. "He would not come, he brought it on himself; though in truth I wish that accursed Frank had not struck so shrewdly. If you ask it, we will bear him with you; but, lady, it is idle to hide the truth—he is sped. I have studied medicine, and I know."

"Nay," said Sir Andrew from the floor, "leave me here. Daughter, we must part awhile. As I stole his child from Ayoub, so Ayoub's son steals my child from me. Daughter, cling to the faith—that we may meet again."

"To the death," she answered.

"Be comforted," said Hassan. "Has not Salah-ed-din passed his word that except her own will or that of Allah should change her heart, a Cross-worshipper she may live and die? Lady, for your own sake as well as ours, let this sad farewell be brief. Begone, my servants, taking these dead and wounded with you. There are things it is not fitting that common eyes should see."

They obeyed, and the three of them remained alone together. Then Rosamund knelt down beside her father, and they whispered into each other's ears. Hassan turned his back upon them, and threw the corner of his cloak over his head and eyes that he might neither see nor hear their voices in this dread and holy hour of parting.

It would seem that they found some kind of hope and consolation in it—at least when Rosamund kissed him for the last time, Sir Andrew smiled and said:

"Yes, yes; it may all be for the best. God will guard you, and His will be done. But I forgot. Tell me, daughter, which?"

Again she whispered into his ear, and when he had thought a moment, he answered:

"Maybe you are right. I think that is wisest for all. And now on the three of you—aye, and on your children's children's children—let my blessing rest, as rest it shall. Come hither, Emir."

Hassan heard him through his cloak, and, uncovering, came.

"Say to Saladin, your master, that he has been too strong for me, and paid me back in my own coin. Well, had it been otherwise, my daughter and I must soon have parted, for death drew near to me. At least it is the decree of God, to which I bow my head, trusting there may be truth in that dream of his, and that our sorrows, in some way unforeseen, will bring blessings to our brethren in the East. But to Saladin say also that whatever his bigot faith may teach, for Christian and for Paynim there is a meeting-place beyond the grave. Say that if aught of wrong or insult is done towards this maiden, I swear by the God who made us both that there I will hold him to account. Now, since it must be so, take her and go your way, knowing that my spirit follows after you and her; yes, and that even in this world she will find avengers."

"I hear your words, and I will deliver them," answered Hassan. "More, I believe that they are true, and for the rest you have the oath of Salah-ed-din—ay, and my oath while she is in my charge. Therefore, Sir Andrew D'Arcy, forgive us, who are but the instruments of Allah, and die in peace."

"I, who have so much to be forgiven, forgive you," answered the old knight slowly.

Then his eyes fixed themselves upon his daughter's face with one long, searching look, and closed.

"I think that he is dead," said Hassan. "May God, the Merciful and Compassionate, rest his soul!" And taking a white garment from the wall, he flung it over him, adding, "Lady, come."

Thrice Rosamund looked at the shrouded figure on the floor; once she wrung her hands and seemed about to fall. Then, as though a thought struck her, she lifted her father's sword from where it lay, and gathering her strength, drew herself up and passed like a queen down the blood-stained passage and the steps of the solar. In the hall beneath waited the band of Hassan, who bowed as she came—a vision of despairing loveliness, that held aloft a red and naked sword. There, too, lay the drugged men fallen this way and that, and among them Wulf across the table, and Godwin on the dais. Rosamund spoke.

"Are these dead or sleeping?"

"Have no fear," answered Hassan. "By my hope of paradise, they do but sleep, and will awake ere morning."

Rosamund pointed to the renegade Nicholas—he that had struck down her father from behind—who, an evil look upon his face, stood apart from the Saracens, holding in his hand a lighted torch.

"What does this man with the torch?" she asked.

"If you would know, lady," Nicholas answered with a sneer, "I wait till you are out of it to fire the hall."

"Prince Hassan," said Rosamund, "is this a deed that great Saladin would wish, to burn drugged men beneath their own roof? Now, as you shall answer to him, in the name of Saladin I, a daughter of his House, command you, strike the fire from that man's hand, and in my hearing give your order that none should even think of such an act of shame."

"What?" broke in Nicholas, "and leave knights like these, whose quality you know"—and he pointed to the brethren—"to follow in our path, and take our lives in vengeance? Why, it is madness!"

"Are you master here, traitor, or am I?" asked Hassan in cold contempt. "Let them follow if they will, and I for one shall rejoice to meet foes so brave in open battle, and there give them their revenge. Ali," he added, addressing the man who had been disguised as a merchant's underling, and who had drugged the men in the barn as his master had drugged those in the hall, and opened the moat gate to the band, "Ali, stamp upon the torch and guard that Frank till we reach the boat lest the fool should raise the country on us with his fires. Now, Princess, are you satisfied?"

"Ay, having your word," she answered. "One moment, I pray you. I would leave a token to my knights."

Then, while they watched her with wondering eyes, she unfastened the gold cross and chain that hung upon her bosom, and slipping the cross from the chain, went to where Godwin lay, and placed it on his breast. Next, with a swift movement, she wound the chain about the silver hilt of Sir Andrew's sword, and passing to Wulf, with one strong thrust, drove the point between the oak boards of the table, so that it stood before him—at once a cross, a brand of battle, and a lady's token.

"His grandsire bore it," she said in Arabic, "when he leapt on to the walls of Jerusalem. It is my last gift to him." But the Saracens muttered and turned pale at these words of evil omen.

Then taking the hand of Hassan, who stood searching her white, inscrutable face, with never a word or a backward look, she swept down the length of the long hall, and out into the night beyond.

"It would have been well to take my counsel and fire the place, or at least to cut the throats of all within it," said the man Nicholas to his guard Ali as they followed with the rest. "If I know aught of these brethren, cross and sword will soon be hard upon our track, and men's lives must pay the price of such soft folly." And he shivered as though in fear.

"It may be so, Spy," answered the Saracen, looking at him with sombre, contemptuous eyes. "It may be that your life will pay the price."

Wulf was dreaming, dreaming that he stood on his head upon a wooden plank, as once he had seen a juggler do, which turned round one way while he turned round the other, till at length some one shouted at him, and he tumbled off the board and hurt himself. Then he awoke to hear a voice shouting surely enough—the voice of Matthew, the chaplain of Steeple Church.

"Awake!" said the voice. "In God's name, I conjure you, awake!"

"What is it?" he said, lifting his head sleepily, and becoming conscious of a dull pain across his forehead.

"It is that death and the devil have been here, Sir Wulf."

"Well, they are often near together. But I thirst. Give me water."

A serving-woman, pallid, dishevelled, heavy-eyed, who was stumbling to and fro, lighting torches and tapers, for it was still dark, brought it to him in a leathern jack, from which he drank deeply.

"That is better," he said. Then his eye fell upon the bloody sword set point downwards in the wood of the table before him, and he exclaimed, "Mother of God! what is that? My uncle's silver-hilted sword, red with blood, and Rosamund's gold chain upon the hilt! Priest, where is the lady Rosamund?"

"Gone," answered the chaplain in a voice that sounded like a groan. "The women woke and found her gone, and Sir Andrew lies dead or dying in the solar—but now I have shriven him—and oh! we have all been drugged. Look at them!" and he waved his hand towards the recumbent forms. "I say that the devil has been here."

Wulf sprang to his feet with an oath.

"The devil? Ah! I have it now. You mean the Cyprian chapman Georgios. He who sold wine."

"He who sold drugged wine," echoed the chaplain, "and has stolen away the lady Rosamund."

Then Wulf seemed to go mad.

"Stolen Rosamund over our sleeping carcases! Stolen Rosamund with never a blow struck by us to save her! O, Christ, that such a thing should be! O, Christ, that I should live to hear it!" And he, the mighty man, the knight of skill and strength, broke down and wept like a very child. But not for long, for presently he shouted in a voice of thunder:

"Awake, ye drunkards! Awake, and learn what has chanced to us. Your lady Rosamund has been raped away while we were lost in sleep!"

At the sound of that great voice a tall form arose from the floor, and staggered towards him, holding a gold cross in its hand.

"What awful words are those my brother?" asked Godwin, who, pale and dull-eyed, rocked to and fro before him. Then he, too, saw the red sword and stared, first at it and next at the gold cross in his hand. "My uncle's sword, Rosamund's chain, Rosamund's cross! Where, then, is Rosamund?"

"Gone! gone! gone!" cried Wulf. "Tell him, priest."

So the chaplain told him all he knew.

"Thus have we kept our oaths," went on Wulf. "Oh, what can we do now, save die for very shame?"

"Nay," answered Godwin, dreamingly; "we can live on to save her. See, these are her tokens—the cross for me, the blood-stained sword for you, and about its hilt the chain, a symbol of her slavery. Now both of us must bear the cross; both of us must wield the sword, and both of us must cut the chain, or if we fail, then die."

"You rave," said Wulf; "and little wonder. Here, drink water. Would that we had never touched aught else, as she did, and desired that we should do. What said you of my uncle, priest? Dead, or only dying? Nay, answer not, let us see. Come, brother."

Now together they ran, or rather reeled, torch in hand, along the passage.

Wulf saw the bloodstains on the floor and laughed savagely.

"The old man made a good fight," he said, "while, like drunken brutes, we slept."

They were there, and before them, beneath the white, shroud-like cloak, lay Sir Andrew, the steel helm on his head, and his face beneath it even whiter than the cloak.

At the sound of their footsteps he opened his eyes. "At length, at length," he muttered. "Oh, how many years have I waited for you? Nay, be silent, for I do not know how long my strength will last, but listen—kneel down and listen."

So they knelt on either side of him, and in quick, fierce words he told them all—of the drugging, of the fight, of the long parley carried on to give the palmer knave time to climb to the window; of his cowardly blow, and of what chanced afterwards. Then his strength seemed to fail him, but they poured drink down his throat, and it came back again.

"Take horse swiftly," he gasped, pausing now and again to rest, "and rouse the countryside. There is still a chance. Nay, seven hours have gone by; there is no chance. Their plans were too well laid; by now they will be at sea. So hear me. Go to Palestine. There is money for your faring in my chest, but go alone, with no company, for in time of peace these would betray you. Godwin, draw off this ring from my finger, and with it as a token, find out Jebal, the black sheik of the Mountain Tribe at Masyaf on Lebanon. Bid him remember the vow he made to Andrew D'Arcy, the English knight. If any can aid you, it will be Jebal, who hates the Houses of Nur-ed-din and of Ayoub. So, I charge you, let nothing—I say nothing—turn you aside from seeking him.

"Afterwards act as God shall guide you. If they still live, kill that traitor Nicholas and Hugh Lozelle, but, save in open war, spare the Emir Hassan, who did but do his duty as an Eastern reads it, and shown some mercy, for he could have slain or burnt us all. This riddle has been hard for me; yet now, in my dying hour, I seem to see its answer. I think that Saladin did not dream in vain. Keep brave hearts, for I think also that at Masyaf you will find friends, and that things will yet go well, and our sorrows bear good fruit.

"What is that you said? She left you my father's sword, Wulf? Then wield it bravely, winning honour for our name. She left you the cross, Godwin? Wear it worthily, winning glory for the Lord, and salvation to your soul. Remember what you have sworn. Whate'er befall, bear no bitterness to one another. Be true to one another, and to her, your lady, so that when at the last you make your report to me before high Heaven, I may have no cause to be ashamed of you, my nephews, Godwin and Wulf."

For a moment the dying man was silent, until his face lit up as with a great gladness, and he cried in a loud, clear voice, "Beloved wife, I hear you! O, God, I come!"

Then though his eyes stayed open, and the smile still rested on his face, his jaw fell.

Thus died Sir Andrew D'Arcy.

Still kneeling on either side of him, the brethren watched the end, and, as his spirit passed, bowed their heads in prayer.

"We have seen a great death," said Godwin presently. "Let us learn a lesson from it, that when our time comes we may die like him."

"Ay," answered Wulf, springing to his feet, "but first let us take vengeance for it. Why, what is this? Rosamund's writing! Read it, Godwin."

Godwin took the parchment and read:

"Follow me to Saladin. In that hope I live on."

"Surely we will follow you, Rosamund," he cried aloud. "Follow you through life to death or victory."

Then he threw down the paper, and calling for the chaplain to come to watch the body, they ran into the hall. By this time about half of the folk were awake from their drugged sleep, whilst others who had been doctored by the man Ali in the barn staggered into the hall—wild-eyed, white-faced, and holding their hands to their heads and hearts. They were so sick and bewildered, indeed, that it was difficult to make them understand what had chanced, and when they learned the truth, the most of them could only groan. Still, a few were found strong enough in wit and body to grope their way through the darkness and the falling snow to Stangate Abbey, to Southminster, and to the houses of their neighbours, although of these there were none near, praying that every true man would arm and ride to help them in the hunt. Also Wulf, cursing the priest Matthew and himself that he had not thought of it before, called him from his prayers by their dead uncle, and charged him to climb the church tower as swiftly as he could, and set light to the beacon that was laid ready there.

Away he went, taking flint, steel, and tinder with him, and ten minutes later the blaze was flaring furiously above the roof of Steeple Church, warning all men of the need for help. Then they armed, saddled such horses as they had, amongst them the three that had been left there by the merchant Georgios, and gathered all of them who were not too sick to ride or run, in the courtyard of the Hall. But as yet their haste availed them little, for the moon was down. Snow fell also, and the night was still black as death—so black that a man could scarcely see the hand he held before his face. So they must wait, and wait they did, eating their hearts out with grief and rage, and bathing their aching brows in icy water.

At length the dawn began to break, and by its first grey light they saw men mounted and afoot feeling their way through the snow, shouting to each other as they came to know what dreadful thing had happened at Steeple. Quickly the tidings spread among them that Sir Andrew was slain, and the lady Rosamund snatched away by Paynims, while all who feasted in the place had been drugged with poisoned wine by a man whom they believed to be a merchant. So soon as a band was got together—perhaps thirty men in all—and there was light to stir by, they set out and began to search, though where to look they knew not, for the snow had covered up all traces of their foes.

"One thing is certain," said Godwin, "they must have come by water."

"Ay," answered Wulf, "and landed near by, since, had they far to go, they would have taken the horses, and must run the risk also of losing their path in the darkness. To the Staithe! Let us try Steeple Staithe."

So on they went across the meadow to the creek. It lay but three bow-shots distant. At first they could see nothing, for the snow covered the stones of the little pier, but presently a man cried out that the lock of the water house, in which the brethren kept their fishing-boat, was broken, and next minute, that the boat was gone.

"She was small; she would hold but six men," cried a voice. "So great a company could never have crowded into her."

"Fool!" one answered, "there may have been other boats."

So they looked again, and beneath the thin coating of rime, found a mark in the mud by the Staithe, made by the prow of a large boat, and not far from it a hole in the earth into which a peg had been driven to make her fast.

Now the thing seemed clear enough, but it was to be made yet clearer, for presently, even through the driving snow, the quick eye of Wulf caught sight of some glittering thing which hung to the edge of a clump of dead reeds. A man with a lance lifted it out at his command, and gave it to him.

"I thought so," he said in a heavy voice; "it is a fragment of that star-wrought veil which was my Christmas gift to Rosamund, and she has torn it off and left it here to show us her road. To St. Peter's-on-the-Wall! To St. Peter's, I say, for there the boats or ship must pass, and maybe that in the darkness they have not yet won out to sea."

So they turned their horses' heads, and those of them that were mounted rode for St. Peter's by the inland path that runs through Steeple St. Lawrence and Bradwell town, while those who were not, started to search along the Saltings and the river bank. On they galloped through the falling snow, Godwin and Wulf leading the way, whilst behind them thundered an ever-gathering train of knights, squires and yeomen, who had seen the beacon flare on Steeple tower, or learned the tale from messengers—yes, and even of monks from Stangate and traders from Southminster.

Hard they rode, but the lanes were heavy with fallen snow and mud beneath, and the way was far, so that an hour had gone by before Bradwell was left behind, and the shrine of St. Chad lay but half a mile in front. Now of a sudden the snow ceased, and a strong northerly wind springing up, drove the thick mist before it and left the sky hard and blue behind. Still riding in this mist, they pressed on to where the old tower loomed in front of them, then drew rein and waited.

"What is that?" said Godwin presently, pointing to a great, dim thing upon the vapour-hidden sea.

As he spoke a strong gust of wind tore away the last veils of mist, revealing the red face of the risen sun, and not a hundred yards away from them—for the tide was high—the tall masts of a galley creeping out to sea beneath her banks of oars. As they stared the wind caught her, and on the main-mast rose her bellying sail, while a shout of laughter told them that they themselves were seen. They shook their swords in the madness of their rage, knowing well who was aboard that galley; while to the fore peak ran up the yellow flag of Saladin, streaming there like gold in the golden sunlight.

Nor was this all, for on the high poop appeared the tall shape of Rosamund herself, and on one side of her, clad now in coat of mail and turban, the emir Hassan, whom they had known as the merchant Georgios, and on the other, a stout man, also clad in mail, who at that distance looked like a Christian knight. Rosamund stretched out her arms towards them. Then suddenly she sprang forward as though she would throw herself into the sea, had not Hassan caught her by the arm and held her back, whilst the other man who was watching slipped between her and the bulwark.

In his fury and despair Wulf drove his horse into the water till the waves broke about his middle, and there, since he could go no further, sat shaking his sword and shouting:

"Fear not! We follow! we follow!" in such a voice of thunder, that even through the wind and across the ever widening space of foam his words may have reached the ship. At least Rosamund seemed to hear them, for she tossed up her arms as though in token.

But Hassan, one hand pressed upon his heart and the other on his forehead, only bowed thrice in courteous farewell.

Then the great sail filled, the oars were drawn in, and the vessel swept away swiftly across the dancing waves, till at length she vanished, and they could only see the sunlight playing on the golden banner of Saladin which floated from her truck.

## Chapter 8

# The Widow Masouda

Many months had gone by since the brethren sat upon their horses that winter morning, and from the shrine of St. Peter's-on-the-Wall, at the mouth of the Blackwater in Essex, watched with anguished hearts the galley of Saladin sailing southwards; their love and cousin, Rosamund, standing a prisoner on the deck. Having no ship in which to follow her—and this, indeed, it would have been too late to do—they thanked those who had come to aid them, and returned home to Steeple, where they had matters to arrange. As they went they gathered from this man and that tidings which made the whole tale clear to them.

They learned, for instance, then and afterwards, that the galley which had been thought to be a merchantman put into the river Crouch by design, feigning an injury to her rudder, and that on Christmas eve she had moved up with the tide, and anchored in the Blackwater about three miles from its mouth. Thence a great boat, which she towed behind her, and which was afterwards found abandoned, had rowed in the dusk, keeping along the further shore to avoid observation, to the mouth of Steeple Creek, which she descended at dark, making fast to the Staithe, unseen of any. Her crew of thirty men or more, guided by the false palmer Nicholas, next hid themselves in the grove of trees about fifty yards from the house, where traces of them were found afterwards, waiting for the signal, and, if that were necessary, ready to attack and burn the Hall while all men feasted there. But it was not necessary, since the cunning scheme of the drugged wine, which only an Eastern could have devised, succeeded. So it happened that the one man they had to meet in arms was an old knight, of which doubtless they were glad, as their numbers being few, they wished to avoid a desperate battle, wherein many must fall, and, if help came, they might be all destroyed.

When it was over they led Rosamund to the boat, felt their way down the creek, towing behind them the little skiff which they had taken from the water-house—laden with their dead and wounded. This, indeed, proved the most perilous part of their adventures, since it was very dark, and came on to snow; also twice they grounded upon mud banks. Still guided by Nicholas, who had studied the river, they reached the galley before dawn, and with the first light weighed anchor, and very cautiously rowed out to sea. The rest is known.

Two days later, since there was no time to spare, Sir Andrew was buried with great pomp at Stangate Abbey, in the same tomb where lay the heart of his brother, the father of the brethren, who had fallen in the Eastern wars. After he had been laid to rest amidst much lamentation and in the presence of a great concourse of people, for the fame of these strange happenings had travelled far and wide, his will was opened. Then it was found that with the exception of certain sums of money left to his nephews, a legacy to Stangate Abbey, and another to be devoted to masses for the repose of his soul, with some gifts to his servants and the poor, all his estate was devised to his daughter Rosamund. The brethren, or the survivor of them, however, held it in trust on her behalf, with the charge that they should keep watch and ward over her, and manage her lands till she took a husband.

These lands, together with their own, the brethren placed in the hands of Prior John of Stangate, in the presence of witnesses, to administer for them subject to the provisions of the will, taking a tithe of the rents and profits for his pains. The priceless jewels also that had been sent by Saladin were given into his keeping, and a receipt with a list of the same signed in duplicate, deposited with a clerk at Southminster. This, indeed, was necessary, seeing that none save the brethren and the Prior knew of these jewels, of which, being of so great a value, it was not safe to speak. Their affairs arranged, having first made their wills in favour of each other with remainder to their heirs-at-law, since it was scarcely to be hoped that both of them would return alive from such a quest, they received the Communion, and with it his blessing from the hands of the Prior John. Then early one morning, before any were astir, they rode quietly away to London.

On the top of Steeple Hill, sending forward the servant who led the mule laden with their baggage—that same mule which had been left by the spy Nicholas—the brethren turned their horses' heads to look in farewell on their home. There to the north of them lay the Blackwater, and to the west the parish of Mayland, towards which the laden barges crept along the stream of Steeple Creek. Below was the wide, flat, plain outlined with trees, and in it, marked by the plantation where the Saracens had hid, the Hall and church of Steeple, the home in which they had grown from childhood to youth, and from youth to man's estate in the company of the fair, lost Rosamund, who was the love of both, and whom both went forth to seek. That past was all behind them, and in front a dark and troublous future, of which they could not read the mystery nor guess the end.

Would they ever look on Steeple Hall again? Were they who stood there about to match their strength and courage against all the might of Saladin, doomed to fail or gloriously to succeed?

Through the darkness that shrouded their forward path shone one bright star of love—but for which of them did that star shine, or was it perchance for neither? They knew not. How could they know aught save that the venture seemed very desperate. Indeed, the few to whom they had spoken of it thought them mad. Yet they remembered the last words of Sir Andrew, bidding them keep a high heart, since he believed that things would yet go well. It seemed to them, in truth, that they were not quite alone—as though his brave spirit companioned them on their search, guiding their feet, with ghostly counsel which they could not hear.

They remembered also their oaths to him, to one another, and to Rosamund; and in silent token that they would keep them to the death, pressed each other's hands. Then, turning their horses southwards, they rode forward with light hearts, not caring what befell, if only at the last, living or dead, Rosamund and her father should, in his own words, find no cause to be ashamed of them.

Through the hot haze of a July morning a *dromon*, as certain merchant vessels of that time were called, might have been seen drifting before a light breeze into St. George's Bay at Beirut, on the coast of Syria. Cyprus, whence she had sailed last, was not a hundred miles away, yet she had taken six days to do the journey, not on account of storms—of which there were none at this time of year, but through lack of wind to move her. Still, her captain and the motley crowd of passengers—for the most part Eastern merchants and their servants, together with a number of pilgrims of all nations—thanked God for so prosperous a voyage—for in those times he who crossed the seas without shipwreck was very fortunate.

Among these passengers were Godwin and Wulf, travelling, as their uncle had bidden them, unattended by squires or by servants. Upon the ship they passed themselves off as brothers named Peter and John of Lincoln, a town of which they knew something, having stayed there on their way to the Scottish wars; simple gentlemen of small estate, making a pilgrimage to the Holy Land in penitence for their sins and for the repose of the souls of their father and mother. At this tale their fellow-passengers, with whom they had sailed from Genoa, to which place they travelled overland, shrugged their shoulders. For these brethren looked what they were, knights of high degree; and considering their great stature, long swords, and the coats of mail they always wore beneath their gambesons, none believed them but plain gentlefolk bent on a pious errand. Indeed, they nicknamed them Sir Peter and Sir John, and as such they were known throughout the voyage.

The brethren were seated together in a little place apart in the bow of the ship, and engaged, Godwin in reading from an Arabic translation of the Gospels made by some Egyptian monk, and Wulf in following it with little ease in the Latin version. Of the former tongue, indeed, they had acquired much in their youth, since they learned it from Sir Andrew with Rosamund, although they could not talk it as she did, who had been taught to lisp it as an infant by her mother. Knowing, too, that much might hang upon a knowledge of this tongue, they occupied their long journey in studying it from such books as they could get; also in speaking it with a priest, who had spent many years in the East, and instructed them for a fee, and with certain Syrian merchants and sailors.

"Shut the book, brother," said Wulf; "there is Lebanon at last," and he pointed to the great line of mountains revealing themselves dimly through their wrappings of mist. "Glad I am to see them, who have had enough of these crooked scrolls and learnings."

"Ay," said Godwin, "the Promised Land."

"And the Land of Promise for us," answered his brother. "Well, thank God that the time has come to act, though how we are to set about it is more than I can say."

"Doubtless time will show. As our uncle bade, we will seek out this Sheik Jebal—"

"Hush!" said Wulf, for just then some merchants, and with them a number of pilgrims, their travel-worn faces full of rapture at the thought that the terrors of the voyage were done, and that they were about to set foot upon the ground their Lord had trodden, crowded forward to the bow to obtain their first view of it, and there burst into prayers and songs of thanksgiving. Indeed, one of these men—a trader known as Thomas of Ipswich—was, they found, standing close to them, and seemed as though he listened to their talk.

The brethren mingled with them while this same Thomas of Ipswich, who had visited the place before, or so it seemed, pointed out the beauties of the city, of the fertile country by which it was surrounded, and of the distant cedar-clad mountains where, as he said, Hiram, King of Tyre, had cut the timber for Solomon's Temple.

"Have you been on them?" asked Wulf.

"Ay, following my business," he answered, "so far." And he showed them a great snow-capped peak to the north. "Few ever go further."

"Why not?" asked Godwin.

"Because there begins the territory of the Sheik Al-je-bal"—and he looked at them meaningly—"whom," he added, "neither Christian nor Saracen visit without an invitation, which is seldom given."

Again they inquired why not.

"Because," answered the trader, still watching them, "most men love their lives, and that man is the lord of death and magic. Strange things are to be seen in his castle, and about it lie wonderful gardens inhabited by lovely women that are evil spirits, who bring the souls of men to ruin. Also, this Old Man of the Mountain is a great murderer, of whom even all the princes of the East are terrified, for he speaks a word to his *fedais*—or servants—who are initiated, and they go forth and bring to death any whom he hates. Young men, I like you well, and I say to you, be warned. In this Syria there are many wonders to be seen; leave those of Masyaf and its fearful lord alone if you desire to look again upon—the towers of Lincoln."

"Fear not; we will," answered Godwin, "who come to seek holy places—not haunts of devils."

"Of course we will," added Wulf. "Still, that country must be worth travelling in."

Then boats came out to greet them from the shore—for at that time Beirut was in the hands of the Franks—and in the shouting and confusion which followed they saw no more of this merchant Thomas. Nor did they seek him out again, since they thought it unwise to show themselves too curious about the Sheik Al-je-bal. Indeed, it would have been useless, since that trader was ashore two full hours before they were suffered to leave the ship, from which he departed alone in a private boat.

At length they stood in the motley Eastern crowd upon the quay, wondering where they could find an inn that was quiet and of cheap charges, since they did not wish to be considered persons of wealth or importance. As they lingered here, somewhat bewildered, a tall, veiled woman whom they had noted watching them, drew near, accompanied by a porter, who led a donkey. This man, without more ado, seized their baggage, and helped by other porters began to fasten it upon the back of the donkey with great rapidity, and when they would have forbidden him, pointed to the veiled woman.

"Your pardon," said Godwin to her at length and speaking in French, "but this man—"

"Loads up your baggage to take it to my inn. It is cheap, quiet and comfortable—things which I heard you say you required just now, did I not?" she answered in a sweet voice, also speaking in good French.

Godwin looked at Wulf, and Wulf at Godwin, and they began to discuss together what they should do. When they had agreed that it seemed not wise to trust themselves to the care of a strange woman in this fashion, they looked up to see the donkey laden with their trunks being led away by the porter.

"Too late to say no, I fear me," said the woman with a laugh, "so you must be my guests awhile if you would not lose your baggage. Come, after so long a journey you need to wash and eat. Follow me, sirs, I pray you."

Then she walked through the crowd, which, they noted, parted for her as she went, to a post where a fine mule was tied. Loosing it, she leaped to the saddle without help, and began to ride away, looking back from time to time to see that they were following her, as, indeed, they must.

"Whither go we, I wonder," said Godwin, as they trudged through the sands of Beirut, with the hot sun striking on their heads.

"Who can tell when a strange woman leads?" replied Wulf, with a laugh.

At last the woman on the mule turned through a doorway in a wall of unburnt brick, and they found themselves before the porch of a white, rambling house which stood in a large garden planted with mulberries, oranges and other fruit trees that were strange to them, and was situated on the borders of the city.

Here the woman dismounted and gave the mule to a Nubian who was waiting. Then, with a quick movement she unveiled herself, and turned towards them as though to show her beauty. Beautiful she was, of that there could be no doubt, with her graceful, swaying shape, her dark and liquid eyes, her rounded features and strangely impassive countenance. She was young also—perhaps twenty-five, no more—and very fair-skinned for an Eastern.

"My poor house is for pilgrims and merchants, not for famous knights; yet, sirs, I welcome you to it," she said presently, scanning them out of the corners of her eyes.

"We are but squires in our own country, who make the pilgrimage," replied Godwin. "For what sum each day will you give us board and a good room to sleep in?"

"These strangers," she said in Arabic to the porter, "do not speak the truth."

"What is that to you?" he answered, as he busied himself in loosening the baggage. "They will pay their score, and all sorts of mad folk come to this country, pretending to be what they are not. Also you sought them—why, I know not—not they you."

"Mad or sane, they are proper men," said the impassive woman, as though to herself, then added in French, "Sirs, I repeat, this is but a humble place, scarce fit for knights like you, but if you will honour it, the charge is—so much."

"We are satisfied," said Godwin, "especially," he added, with a bow and removing the cap from his head, "as, having brought us here without leave asked, we are sure that you will treat us who are strangers kindly."

"As kindly as you wish—I mean as you can pay for," said the woman. "Nay, I will settle with the porter; he would cheat you."

Then followed a wrangle five minutes long between this curious, handsome, still-faced woman and the porter who, after the eastern fashion, lashed himself into a frenzy over the sum she offered, and at length began to call her by ill names.

She stood looking at him quite unmoved, although Godwin, who understood all, but pretended to understand nothing, wondered at her patience. Presently, however, in a perfect foam of passion he said, or rather spat out: "No wonder, Masouda the Spy, that after hiring me to do your evil work, you take the part of these Christian dogs against a true believer, you child of Al-je-bal!"

Instantly the woman seemed to stiffen like a snake about to strike.

"Who is he?" she said coldly. "Do you mean the lord—who kills?" And she looked at him—a terrible look.

At that glance all the anger seemed to go out of the man.

"Your pardon, widow Masouda," he said. "I forgot that you are a Christian, and naturally side with Christians. The money will not pay for the wear of my ass's hoofs, but give it me, and let me go to pilgrims who will reward me better."

She gave him the sum, adding in her quiet voice: "Go; and if you love life, keep better watch over your words."

Then the porter went, and now so humble was his mien that in his dirty turban and long, tattered robe he looked, Wulf thought, more like a bundle of rags than a man mounted on the donkey's back. Also it came into his mind that their strange hostess had powers not possessed by innkeepers in England. When she had watched him through the gate, Masouda turned to them and said in French:

"Forgive me, but here in Beirut these Saracen porters are extortionate, especially towards us Christians. He was deceived by your appearance. He thought that you were knights, not simple pilgrims as you avow yourselves, who happen to be dressed and armed like knights beneath your gambesons; and," she added, fixing her eyes upon the line of white hair on Godwin's head where the sword had struck him in the fray on Death Creek quay, "show the wounds of knights, though it is true that a man might come by such in any brawl in a tavern. Well, you are to pay me a good price, and you shall have my best room while it pleases you to honour me with your company. Ah! your baggage. You do not wish to leave it. Slave, come here."

With startling suddenness the Nubian who had led away the mule appeared, and took up some of the packages. Then she led them down a passage into a large, sparsely-furnished room with high windows, in which were two beds laid on the cement floor, and asked them if it pleased them.

They said: "Yes; it will serve." Reading what passed in their minds, she added: "Have no fear for your baggage. Were you as rich as you say you are poor, and as noble as you say you are humble, both it and you are safe in the inn of the widow Masouda, O my guests—but how are you named?"

"Peter and John."

"O, my guests, Peter and John, who have come to visit the land of Peter and John and other holy founders of our faith—"

"And have been so fortunate as to be captured on its shore by the widow Masouda," answered Godwin, bowing again.

"Wait to speak of the fortune until you have done with her, Sir—is it Peter, or John?" she replied, with something like a smile upon her handsome face.

"Peter," answered Godwin. "Remember the pilgrim with the line of white hair is Peter."

"You need it to distinguish you apart, who, I suppose, are twins. Let me see—Peter has a line of white hair and grey eyes. John has blue eyes. John also is the greater warrior, if a pilgrim can be a warrior—look at his muscles; but Peter thinks the more. It would be hard for a woman to choose between Peter and John, who must both of them be hungry, so I go to prepare their food."

"A strange hostess," said Wulf, laughing, when she had left the room; "but I like her, though she netted us so finely. I wonder why? What is more, brother Godwin, she likes you, which is as well, since she may be useful. But, friend Peter, do not let it go too far, since, like that porter, I think also that she may be dangerous. Remember, he called her a spy, and probably she is one."

Godwin turned to reprove him, when the voice of the widow Masouda was heard without saying:

"Brothers Peter and John, I forgot to caution you to speak low in this house, as there is lattice-work over the doors to let in the air. Do not be afraid. I only heard the voice of John, not what he said."

"I hope not," muttered Wulf, and this time he spoke very low indeed.

Then they undid their baggage, and having taken from it clean garments, washed themselves after their long journey with the water that had been placed ready for them in great jars. This, indeed, they needed, for on that crowded *dromon* there was little chance of washing. By the time they had clothed themselves afresh, putting on their shirts of mail beneath their tunics, the Nubian came and led them to another room, large and lighted with high-set lattices, where cushions were piled upon the floor round a rug that also was laid upon the floor. Motioning them to be seated on the cushions, he went away, to return again presently, accompanied by Masouda bearing dishes upon brass platters. These she placed before them, bidding them eat. What that food was they did not know, because of the sauces with which it had been covered, until she told them that it was fish.

After the fish came flesh, and after the flesh fowls, and after the fowls cakes and sweetmeats and fruits, until, ravenous as they were, who for days had fed upon salted pork and biscuits full of worms washed down with bad water, they were forced to beg her to bring no more.

"Drink another cup of wine at least," she said, smiling and filling their mugs with the sweet vintage of Lebanon—for it seemed to please her to see them eat so heartily of her fare.

They obeyed, mixing the wine with water. While they drank she asked them suddenly what were their plans, and how long they wished to stay in Beirut. They answered that for the next few days they had none, as they needed to rest, to see the town and its neighbourhood, and to buy good horses—a matter in which perhaps she could help them. Masouda nodded again, and asked whither they wished to ride on horses.

"Out yonder," said Wulf, waving his hand towards the mountains. "We desire to look upon the cedars of Lebanon and its great hills before we go on towards Jerusalem."

"Cedars of Lebanon?" she replied. "That is scarcely safe for two men alone, for in those mountains are many wild beasts and wilder people who rob and kill. Moreover, the lord of those mountains has just now a quarrel with the Christians, and would take any whom he found prisoners."

"How is that lord named?" asked Godwin.

"Sinan," she answered, and they noted that she looked round quickly as she spoke the word.

"Oh," he said, "we thought the name was Jebal."

Now she stared at him with wide, wondering eyes, and replied:

"He is so called also; but, Sir Pilgrims, what know you of the dread lord Al-je-bal?"

"Only that he lives at a place called Masyaf, which we wish to visit."

Again she stared.

"Are you mad?" she queried, then checked herself, and clapped her hands for the slave to remove the dishes. While this was being done they said they would like to walk abroad.

"Good," answered Masouda, "the man shall accompany you—nay, it is best that you do not go alone, as you might lose your way. Also, the place is not always safe for strangers, however humble they may seem," she added with meaning. "Would you wish to visit the governor at the castle, where there are a few English knights, also some priests who give advice to pilgrims?"

"We think not," answered Godwin; "we are not worthy of such high company. But, lady, why do you look at us so strangely?"

"I am wondering, Sir Peter and Sir John, why you think it worth while to tell lies to a poor widow? Say, in your own country did you ever hear of certain twin brethren named—oh, how are they named?—Sir Godwin and Sir Wulf, of the house of D'Arcy, which has been told of in this land?"

Now Godwin's jaw dropped, but Wulf laughed out loud, and seeing that they were alone in the room, for the slave had departed, asked in his turn:

"Surely those twins would be pleased to find themselves so famous. But how did you chance to hear of them, O widowed hostess of a Syrian inn?"

"I? Oh, from a man on the *dromon* who called here while I made ready your food, and told me a strange story that he had learned in England of a band sent by Salah-ed-din—may his name be accursed!—to capture a certain lady. Of how the brethren named Godwin and Wulf fought all that band also—ay, and held them off—a very knightly deed he said it was—while the lady escaped; and of how afterwards they were taken in a snare, as those are apt to be who deal with the Sultan, and this time the lady was snatched away."

"A wild tale truly," said Godwin. "But did this man tell you further whether that lady has chanced to come to Palestine?"

She shook her head.

"Of that he told me nothing, and I have heard nothing. Now listen, my guests. You think it strange that I should know so much, but it is not strange, since here in Syria, knowledge is the business of some of us. Did you then believe, O foolish children, that two knights like you, who have played a part in a very great story, whereof already whispers run throughout the East, could travel by land and sea and not be known? Did you then think that none were left behind to watch your movements and to make report of them to that mighty one who sent out the ship of war, charged with a certain mission? Well, what he knows I know. Have I not said it is my business to know? Now, why do I tell you this? Well, perhaps because I like such knights as you are, and I like that tale of two men who stood side by side upon a pier while a woman swam the stream behind them, and afterwards, sore wounded, charged their way through a host of foes. In the East we love such deeds of chivalry. Perhaps also because I would warn you not to throw away lives so gallant by attempting to win through the guarded gates of Damascus upon the maddest of all quests.

"What, you still stare at me and doubt? Good, I have been telling you lies. I was not awaiting you upon the quay, and that porter with whom I seemed to quarrel was not charged to seize your baggage and bring it to my house. No spies watched your movements from England to Beirut. Only since you have been at dinner I visited your room and read some writings which, foolishly, you and John have left among your baggage, and opened some books in which other names than Peter and John were written, and drew a great sword from its scabbard on which was engraved a motto: 'Meet D'Arcy, meet Death!' and heard Peter call John Wulf, and John call Peter Godwin, and so forth."

"It seems," said Wulf in English, "that we are flies in a web, and that the spider is called the widow Masouda, though of what use we are to her I know not. Now, brother, what is to be done? Make friends with the spider?"

"An ill ally," answered Godwin. Then looking her straight in the face he asked, "Hostess, who know so much, tell me why, amongst other names, did that donkey driver call you 'daughter of Al-je-bal'?"

She started, and answered:

"So you understand Arabic? I thought it. Why do you ask? What does it matter to you?"

"Not much, except that, as we are going to visit Al-je-bal, of course we think ourselves fortunate to have met his daughter."

"Going to visit Al-je-bal? Yes, you hinted as much upon the ship, did you not? Perhaps that is why I came to meet you. Well, your throats will be cut before ever you reach the first of his castles."

"I think not," said Godwin, and, putting his hand into his breast, he drew thence a ring, with which he began to play carelessly.

"Whence that ring?" she said, with fear and wonder in her eyes. "It is—" and she ceased.

"From one to whom it was given and who has charged us with a message. Now, hostess, let us be plain with one another. You know a great deal about us, but although it has suited us to call ourselves the pilgrims Peter and John, in all this there is nothing of which we need be ashamed, especially as you say that our secret is no secret, which I can well believe. Now, this secret being out, I propose that we remove ourselves from your roof, and go to stay with our own people at the castle, where, I doubt not, we shall be welcome, telling them that we would bide no longer with one who is called a spy, whom we have discovered also to be a 'daughter of Al-je-bal.' After which, perhaps, you will bide no longer in Beirut, where, as we gather, spies and the 'daughters of Al-je-bal' are not welcome."

She listened with an impassive face, and answered: "Doubtless you have heard that one of us who was so named was burned here recently as a witch?"

"Yes," broke in Wulf, who now learned this fact for the first time, "we heard that."

"And think to bring a like fate upon me. Why, foolish men, I can lay you both dead before ever those words pass your lips."

"You think you can," said Godwin, "but for my part I am sure that this is not fated, and am sure also that you do not wish to harm us any more than we wish to harm you. To be plain, then, it is necessary for us to visit Al-je-bal. As chance has brought us together—if it be chance—will you aid us in this, as I think you can, or must we seek other help?"

"I do not know. I will tell you after four days. If you are not satisfied with that, go, denounce me, do your worst, and I will do mine, for which I should be sorry."

"Where is the security that you will not do it if we are satisfied?" asked Wulf bluntly.

"You must take the word of a 'daughter of Al-je-bal.' I have none other to offer," she replied.

"That may mean death," said Wulf.

"You said just now that was not fated, and although I have sought your company for my own reasons, I have no quarrel with you—as yet. Choose your own path. Still, I tell you that if you go, who, chancing to know Arabic, have learned my secret, you die, and that if you stay you are safe—at least while you are in this house. I swear it on the token of Al-je-bal," and bending forward she touched the ring in Godwin's hand, "but remember that for the future I cannot answer."

Godwin and Wulf looked at each other. Then Godwin replied:

"I think that we will trust you, and stay," words at which she smiled a little as though she were pleased, then said:

"Now, if you wish to walk abroad, guests Peter and John, I will summon the slave to guide you, and in four days we will talk more of this matter of your journey, which, until then, had best be forgotten."

So the man came, armed with a sword, and led them out, clad in their pilgrims' robes, through the streets of this Eastern town, where everything was so strange, that for awhile they forgot their troubles in studying the new life about them. They noted, moreover, that though they went into quarters where no Franks were to be seen, and where fierce-looking servants of the Prophet stared at them sourly, the presence of this slave of Masouda seemed to be sufficient to protect them from affront, since on seeing him even the turbaned Saracens nudged each other and turned aside. In due course they came to the inn again, having met no one whom they knew, except two pilgrims who had been their fellow-passengers on the *dromon*. These men were astonished when they said that they had been through the Saracen quarter of the city, where, although this town was in the hands of the Christians, it was scarcely thought safe for Franks to venture without a strong guard.

When the brethren were back in their chamber, seated at the far end of it, and speaking very low, lest they should be overheard, they consulted together long and earnestly as to what they should do. This was clear—they and something of their mission were known, and doubtless notice of their coming would soon be given to the Sultan Saladin. From the king and great Christian lords in Jerusalem they could expect little help, since to give it might be to bring about an open rupture with Saladin, such as the Franks dreaded, and for which they were ill prepared. Indeed, if they went to them, it seemed likely that they would be prevented from stirring in this dangerous search for a woman who was the niece of Saladin, and for aught they knew thrown into prison, or shipped back to Europe. True, they might try to find their way to Damascus alone, but if the Sultan was warned of their coming, would he not cause them to be killed upon the road, or cast into some dungeon where they would languish out their lives? The more they spoke of these matters the more they were perplexed, till at length Godwin said:

"Brother, our uncle bade us earnestly to seek out this Al-je-bal, and though it seems that to do so is very dangerous, I think that we had best obey him who may have been given foresight at the last. When all paths are full of thorns what matter which you tread?"

"A good saying," answered Wulf. "I am weary of doubts and troublings. Let us follow our uncle's will, and visit this Old Man of the Mountains, to do which I think the widow Masouda is the woman to help us. If we die on that journey, well, at least we shall have done our best."

## Chapter 9

# The Horses Flame and Smoke

On the following morning, when they came into the eating-room of the inn, Godwin and Wulf found they were no longer alone in the house, for sundry other guests sat there partaking of their morning meal. Among them were a grave merchant of Damascus, another from Alexandria in Egypt, a man who seemed to be an Arab chief, a Jew of Jerusalem, and none other than the English trader Thomas of Ipswich, their fellow-passenger, who greeted them warmly.

Truly they seemed a strange and motley set of men. Considering them as the young and stately widow Masouda moved from one to the other, talking to each in turn while she attended to their wants, it came into Godwin's mind that they might be spies meeting there to gain or exchange information, or even to make report to their hostess, in whose pay perhaps they were. Still if so, of this they showed no sign. Indeed, for the most part they spoke in French, which all of them understood, on general matters, such as the heat of the weather, the price of transport animals or merchandise, and the cities whither they purposed to travel.

The trader Thomas, it appeared, had intended to start for Jerusalem that morning with his goods. But the riding mule he had bought proved to be lame from a prick in the hoof, nor were all his hired camels come down from the mountains, so that he must wait a few days, or so he said.

Under these circumstances, he offered the brethren his company in their ramblings about the town. This they thought it wise not to refuse, although they felt little confidence in the man, believing that it was he who had found out their story and true names and revealed them to Masouda, either through talkativeness or with a purpose.

However these things might be, this Thomas proved of service to them, since, although he was but just landed, he seemed to know all that had passed in Syria since he left it, and all that was passing then. Thus he told them how Guy of Lusignan had just made himself king in Jerusalem on the death of the child Baldwin, and how Raymond of Tripoli refused to acknowledge him and was about to be besieged in Tiberias. How Saladin also was gathering a great host at Damascus to make war upon the Christians, and many other things, false and true.

In his company, then, and sometimes in that of the other guests—none of whom showed any curiosity concerning them, though whether this was from good manners or for other reasons they could not be sure—the brethren passed the hours profitably enough.

It was on the third morning of their stay that their hostess Masouda, with whom as yet they had no further private talk, asked them if they had not said that they wished to buy horses. On their answering "Yes," she added that she had told a certain man to bring two for them to look at, which were now in the stable beyond the garden. Thither they went, accompanied by Masouda, to find a grave Arab, wrapped in a garment of camel's hair and carrying a spear in his hand, standing at the door of the cave which served the purpose of a stable, as is common in the East where the heat is so great. As they advanced towards him, Masouda said:

"If you like the horses, leave me to bargain, and seem to understand nothing of my talk."

The Arab, who took no notice of them, saluted Masouda, and said to her in Arabic:

"Is it then for Franks that I have been ordered to bring the two priceless ones?"

"What is that to you, my Uncle, Son of the Sand?" she asked. "Let them be led forth that I may know whether they are those for which I sent."

The man turned and called into the door of the cave.

"Flame, come hither!" As he spoke, there was a sound of hoofs, and through the low archway leapt the most beautiful horse that ever their eyes had seen. It was grey in colour, with flowing mane and tail, and on its forehead was a black star; not over tall, but with a barrel-like shape of great strength, small-headed, large-eyed; wide-nostriled, big-boned, but fine beneath the knee, and round-hoofed. Out it sprang snorting; then seeing its master, the Arab, checked itself and stood still by him as though it had been turned to stone.

"Come hither, Smoke," called the Arab again, and another horse appeared and ranged itself by the first. In size and shape it was the same, but the colour was coal-black and the star upon its forehead white. Also the eye was more fiery.

"These are the horses," said the Arab, Masouda translating. "They are twins, seven years old and never backed until they were rising six, cast at a birth by the swiftest mare in Syria, and of a pedigree that can be counted for a hundred years."

"Horses indeed!" said Wulf. "Horses indeed! But what is the price of them?"

Masouda repeated the question in Arabic, whereon the man replied in the same tongue with a slight shrug of the shoulders.

"Be not foolish. You know this is no question of price, for they are beyond price. Say what you will."

"He says," said Masouda, "that it is a hundred gold pieces for the pair. Can you pay as much?"

The brethren looked at each other. The sum was large.

"Such horses have saved men's lives ere now," added Masouda, "and I do not think that I can ask him to take less, seeing that, did he but know it, in Jerusalem they could be sold for thrice as much. But if you wish, I could lend you money, since doubtless you have jewels or other articles of value you could give as security—that ring in your breast, for instance, Peter."

"We have the gold itself," answered Wulf, who would have paid to his last piece for those horses.

"They buy," said Masouda.

"They buy, but can they ride?" asked the Arab. "These horses are not for children or pilgrims. Unless they can ride well they shall not have them—no, not even if you ask it of me."

Godwin said that he thought so—at least, they would try. Then the Arab, leaving the horses standing there, went into the stable, and with the help of two of the inn servants, brought out bridles and saddles unlike any they had seen. They were but thickly-quilted pads stretching far back upon the horses' loins, with strong hide girths strapped with wool and chased stirrups fashioned like half hoofs. The bits also were only snaffles without curbs.

When all was ready and the stirrups had been let down to the length they desired, the Arab motioned to them to mount. As they prepared to do so, however, he spoke some word, and suddenly those meek, quiet horses were turned into two devils, which reared up on their hind legs and threatened them with their teeth and their front hoofs, that were shod with thin plates of iron. Godwin stood wondering, but Wulf, who was angry at the trick, got behind the horses, and watching his chance, put his hands upon the flanks of the stallion named Smoke, and with one spring leapt into the saddle. Masouda smiled, and even the Arab muttered "Good," while Smoke, feeling himself backed, came to the ground again and became quiet as a sheep. Then the Arab spoke to the horse Flame, and Godwin was allowed to vault into the saddle also.

"Where shall we go?" he asked.

Masouda said they would show them, and, accompanied by her and the Arab, they walked the horses until they were quite clear of the town, to find themselves on a road that had the sea to the left, and to the right a stretch of flat land, some of it cultivated, above which rose the steep and stony sides of hills. Here on this road the brethren trotted and cantered the horses to and fro, till they began to be at home in their strange saddles who from childhood had ridden bare-backed in the Essex marshes, and to learn what pressure on the bit was needed to check or turn them. When they came back to where the pair stood, Masouda said that if they were not afraid the seller wished to show them that the horses were both strong and swift.

"We fear no ride that he dares to take himself," answered Wulf angrily, whereon the Arab smiled grimly and said something in a low voice to Masouda. Then, placing his hand upon Smoke's flank, he leapt up behind Wulf, the horse never stirring.

"Say, Peter, are you minded to take a companion for this ride?" asked Masouda; and as she spoke a strange look came into her eyes, a wild look that was new to the brethren.

"Surely," answered Godwin, "but where is the companion?"

Her reply was to do as the Arab had done, and seating herself straddle-legged behind Godwin, to clasp him around the middle.

"Truly you look a pretty pilgrim now, brother," said Wulf, laughing aloud, while even the grave Arab smiled and Godwin muttered between his teeth the old proverb "Woman on croup, devil on bow." But aloud he said, "I am indeed honoured; yet, friend Masouda, if harm should come of this, do not blame me."

"No harm will come—to you, friend Peter; and I have been so long cooped in an inn that I, who am desert-born, wish for a gallop on the mountains with a good horse beneath me and a brave knight in front. Listen, you brethren; you say you do not fear; then leave your bridles loose, and where'er we go and whate'er we meet seek not to check or turn the horses Flame and Smoke. Now, Son of the Sand, we will test these nags of which you sing so loud a song. Away, and let the ride be fast and far!"

"On your head be it then, daughter," answered the old Arab. "Pray Allah that these Franks can sit a horse!"

Then his sombre eyes seemed to take fire, and gripping the encircling saddle girth, he uttered some word of command, at which the stallions threw up their heads and began to move at a long, swinging gallop towards the mountains a mile away. At first they went over cultivated land off which the crops had been already cut, taking two or three ditches and a low wall in their stride so smoothly that the brethren felt as though they were seated upon swallows. Then came a space of sandy sward, half a mile or more, where their pace quickened, after which they began to breast the long slope of a hill, picking their way amongst its stones like cats.

Ever steeper it grew, till in places it was so sheer that Godwin must clutch the mane of Flame, and Masouda must cling close to Godwin's middle to save themselves from slipping off behind. Yet, notwithstanding the double weights they bore, those gallant steeds never seemed to falter or to tire. At one spot they plunged through a mountain stream. Godwin noted that not fifty yards to their right this stream fell over a little precipice cutting its way between cliffs which were full eighteen feet from bank to bank, and thought to himself that had they struck it lower down, that ride must have ended. Beyond the stream lay a hundred yards or so of level ground, and above it still steeper country, up which they pushed their way through bushes, till at length they came to the top of the mountain and saw the plain they had left lying two miles or more below them.

"These horses climb hills like goats," Wulf said; "but one thing is certain: we must lead them down."

Now on the top of the mountain was a stretch of land almost flat and stoneless, over which they cantered forward, gathering speed as the horses recovered their wind till the pace grew fast. Suddenly the stallions threw themselves on to their haunches and stopped, as well they might, for they were on the verge of a chasm, at whose far foot a river brawled in foam. For a moment they stood; then, at some word from the Arab, wheeled round, and, bearing to the left, began to gallop back across the tableland, until they approached the edge of the mountainside, where the brethren thought that they would stop.

But Masouda cried to the Arab, and the Arab cried to the horses, and Wulf cried to Godwin in the English tongue, "Show no fear, brother. Where they go, we can go."

"Pray God that the girths may hold," answered Godwin, leaning back against the breast of Masouda behind him. As he spoke they began to descend the hill, slowly at first, afterwards faster and yet more fast, till they rushed downwards like a whirlwind.

How did those horses keep their footing? They never knew, and certainly none that were bred in England could have done so. Yet never falling, never stumbling even, on they sped, taking great rocks in their stride, till at length they reached the level piece of land above the stream, or rather above the cleft full eighteen feet in width at the foot of which that stream ran. Godwin saw and turned cold. Were these folk mad that they would put double-laden horses at such a jump? If they hung back, if they missed their stride, if they caught hoof or sprang short, swift death was their portion.

But the old Arab seated behind Wulf only shouted aloud, and Masouda only tightened her round arms about Godwin's middle and laughed in his ear. The horses heard the shout, and seeming to see what was before them, stretched out their long necks and rushed forward over the flat ground.

Now they were on the edge of the terrible place, and, like a man in a dream, Godwin noted the sharp, sheer lips of the cliff, the gulf between them, and the white foam of the stream a score of yards beneath. Then he felt the brave horse Flame gather itself together and next instant fly into the air like a bird. Also—and was this dream indeed, or even as they sped over that horrible pit did he feel a woman's lips pressed upon his cheek? He was not sure. Who could have been at such a time, with death beneath them? Perchance it was the wind that kissed him, or a lock of her loose hair which struck across his face.

Indeed, at the moment he thought of other things than women's lips—those of the black and yawning gulf, for instance.

They swooped through the air, the white foam vanished, they were safe. No; the hind feet of Flame had missed their footing, they fell, they were lost. A struggle. How tight those arms clung about him. How close that face was pressed against his own. Lo! it was over. They were speeding down the hill, and alongside of the grey horse Flame raced the black horse Smoke. Wulf on its back, with eyes that seemed to be starting from his head, was shouting, "A D'Arcy! A D'Arcy!" and behind him, turban gone, and white *burnous* floating like a pennon on the air, the grim-visaged Arab, who also shouted.

Swifter and yet swifter. Did ever horses gallop so fast? Swifter and yet swifter, till the air sang past them and the ground seemed to fly away beneath. The slope was done. They were on the flat; the flat was past, they were in the fields; the fields were left behind; and, behold! side by side, with hanging heads and panting flanks, the horses Smoke and Flame stood still upon the road, their sweating hides dyed red in the light of the sinking sun.

The grip loosened from about Godwin's middle. It had been close; on Masouda's round and naked arms were the prints of the steel shirt beneath his tunic, for she slipped to the ground and stood looking at them. Then she smiled one of her slow, thrilling smiles, gasped and said: "You ride well, pilgrim Peter, and pilgrim John rides well also, and these are good horses; and, oh! that ride was worth the riding, even though death had been its end. Son of the Sand, my Uncle, what say you?"

"That I grow old for such gallops—two on one horse, with nothing to win."

"Nothing to win?" said Masouda. "I am not so sure!" and she looked at Godwin. "Well, you have sold your horses to pilgrims who can ride, and they have proved them, and I have had a change from my cooking in the inn, to which I must now get me back again."

Wulf wiped the sweat from his brow, shook his head, and muttered:

"I always heard the East was full of madmen and devils; now I know that it is true."

But Godwin said nothing.

They led the horses back to the inn, where the brethren groomed them down under the direction of the Arab, that the gallant beasts might get used to them, which, after carrying them upon that fearful ride, they did readily enough. Then they fed them with chopped barley, ear and straw together, and gave them water to drink that had stood in the sun all day to warm, in which the Arab mixed flour and some white wine.

Next morning at the dawn they rose to see how Flame and Smoke fared after that journey. Entering the stable, they heard the sound of a man weeping, and hidden in the shadow, saw by the low light of the morning that it was the old Arab, who stood with his back to them, an arm around the neck of each horse, which he kissed from time to time. Moreover, he talked aloud in his own tongue to them, calling them his children, and saying that rather would he sell his wife and his sister to the Franks.

"But," he added, "she has spoken—why, I know not—and I must obey. Well, at least they are gallant men and worthy of such steeds. Half I hoped that you and the three of us and my niece Masouda, the woman with the secret face and eyes that have looked on fear, might perish in the cleft of the stream; but it was not willed of Allah. So farewell, Flame, and farewell, Smoke, children of the desert, who are swifter than arrows, for never more shall I ride you in battle. Well, at least I have others of your matchless blood."

Then Godwin touched Wulf on the shoulder, and they crept away from the stable without the Arab knowing that they had been there, for it seemed shameful to pry upon his grief. When they reached their room again Godwin asked Wulf:

"Why does this man sell us those noble steeds?"

"Because his niece Masouda has bid him so to do," he answered.

"And why has she bidden him?"

"Ah!" replied Wulf. "He called her 'the woman with the secret face and eyes that have looked on fear,' didn't he? Well, for reasons that have to do with his family perhaps, or with her secrets, or us, with whom she plays some game of which we know neither the beginning nor the end. But, Brother Godwin, you are wiser than I. Why do you ask me these riddles? For my part, I do not wish to trouble my head about them. All I know is that the game is a brave one, and I mean to go through with it, especially as I believe that this playing will lead us to Rosamund."

"May it lead us nowhere worse," answered Godwin with something like a groan, for he remembered that dream of his which he dreamed in mid-air between the edges of black rock with the bubbling foam beneath.

But to Wulf he said nothing of this dream.

When the sun was fully up they prepared to go out again, taking with them the gold to pay the Arab; but on opening the door of their room they met Masouda, apparently about to knock upon it.

"Whither go you, friends Peter and John, and so early?" she asked, looking at them with a smile upon her beautiful face that was so thrilling and seemed to hide so much mystery.

Godwin thought to himself that it was like another smile, that on the face of the woman-headed, stone sphinx which they had seen set up in the market place of Beirut.

"To visit our horses and pay your uncle, the Arab, his money," answered Wulf.

"Indeed! I thought I saw you do the first an hour ago, and as for the second, it is useless; Son of the Sand has gone."

"Gone! With the horses?"

"Nay, he has left them behind."

"Did you pay him, then, lady?" asked Godwin.

It was easy to see that Masouda was pleased at this courteous word, for her voice, which in general seemed a little hard, softened as she answered, for the first time giving him his own title.

"Why do you call me 'lady,' Sir Godwin D'Arcy, who am but an inn-keeper, for whom sometimes men find hard names? Well, perhaps

I was a lady once before I became an inn-keeper; but now I am—the widow Masouda, as you are the pilgrim Peter. Still, I thank you for this—bad guess of yours." Then stepping back a foot or two towards the door, which she had closed behind her, she made him a curtsey so full of dignity and grace that any who saw it must be sure that, wherever she might dwell, Masouda was not bred in inns.

Godwin returned the bow, doffing his cap. Their eyes met and in hers he learned that he had no treachery to fear from this woman, whatever else he might have to fear. Indeed, from that moment, however black and doubtful seemed the road, he would have trusted his life to her; for this was the message written there, a message which she meant that he should read. Yet at his heart he felt terribly afraid.

Wulf, who saw something of all this and guessed more, also was afraid. He wondered what Rosamund would have thought of it, if she had seen that strange and turbulent look in the eyes of this woman who had been a lady and was an inn-keeper; of one whom men called Spy, and daughter of Satan, and child of Al-je-bal. To his fancy that look was like a flash of lightning upon a dark night, which for a second illumines some magical, unguessed landscape, after which comes the night again, blacker than before.

Now the widow Masouda was saying in her usual somewhat hard voice:

"No; I did not pay him. At the last he would take no money; but, having passed it, neither would he break his word to knights who ride so well and boldly. So I made a bargain with him on behalf of both of you, which I expect that you will keep, since my good faith is pledged, and this Arab is a chief and my kinsman. It is this, that if you and these horses should live, and the time comes when you have no more need of them, you will cause it to be cried in the market-place of whatever town is nearest to you, by the voice of the public crier, that for six days they stand to be returned to him who lent them. Then if he comes not they can be sold, which must not be sold or given away to any one without this proclamation. Do you consent?"

"Ay," answered both of them, but Wulf added: "Only we should like to know why the Arab, Son-of-the-Sand, who is your kinsman, trusts his glorious horses to us in this fashion."

"Your breakfast is served, my guests," answered Masouda in tones that rang like the clash of metal, so steely were they. Whereon Wulf shook his head and followed her into the eating-room, which was now empty again as it had been on the afternoon of their arrival.

Most of that day they spent with their horses. In the evening, this time unaccompanied by Masouda, they rode out for a little way, though rather doubtfully, since they were not sure that these beasts which seemed to be almost human would not take the bits between their teeth and rush with them back to the desert whence they came. But although from time to time they looked about them for their master, the Arab, whinnying as they looked, this they did not do, or show vice of any kind; indeed, two ladies' palfreys could not have been more quiet. So the brethren brought them home again, groomed, fed and fondled them, while they pricked their ears, sniffing them all over, as though they knew that these were their new lords and wished to make friends of them.

The morrow was a Sunday, and, attended by Masouda's slave, without whom she would not suffer them to walk in the town, the brethren went to mass in the big church which once had been a mosque, wearing pilgrim's robes over their mail.

"Do you not accompany us, who are of the faith?" asked Wulf.

"Nay," answered Masouda, "I am in no mood to make confession. This day I count my beads at home."

So they went alone, and mingling with a crowd of humble persons at the back of the church, which was large and dim, watched the knights and priests of various nations struggling for precedence of place beneath the dome. Also they heard the bishop of the town preach a sermon from which they learnt much. He spoke at length of the great coming war with Saladin, whom he named Anti-Christ. Moreover, he prayed them all to compose their differences and prepare for that awful struggle, lest in the end the Cross of their Master should be trampled under foot of the Saracen, His soldiers slain, His fanes desecrated, and His people slaughtered or driven into the sea—words of warning that were received in heavy silence.

"Four full days have gone by. Let us ask our hostess if she has any news for us," said Wulf as they walked back to the inn.

"Ay, we will ask her," answered Godwin.

As it chanced, there was no need, for when they entered their chamber they found Masouda standing in the centre of it, apparently lost in thought.

"I have come to speak with you," she said, looking up. "Do you still wish to visit the Sheik Al-je-bal?"

They answered "Yes."

"Good. I have leave for you to go; but I counsel you not to go, since it is dangerous. Let us be open with one another. I know your object. I knew it an hour before ever you set foot upon this shore, and that is why you were brought to my house. You would seek the help of the lord Sinan against Salah-ed-din, from whom you hope to rescue a certain great lady of his blood who is your kinswoman and whom both of you—desire in marriage. You see, I have learned that also. Well, this land is full of spies, who travel to and from Europe and make report of all things to those who pay them enough. For instance—I can say it, as you will not see him again—the trader Thomas, with whom you stayed in this house, is such a spy. To him your story has been passed on by other spies in England, and he passed it on to me."

"Are then you a spy also, as the porter called you?" asked Wulf outright.

"I am what I am," she answered coldly. "Perhaps I also have sworn oaths and serve as you serve. Who my master is or why I do so is naught to you. But I like you well, and we have ridden together—a wild ride. Therefore I warn you, though perhaps I should not say so much, that the lord Al-je-bal is one who takes payment for what he gives, and that this business may cost you your lives."

"You warned us against Saladin also," said Godwin, "so what is left to us if we may dare a visit to neither?"

She shrugged her shoulders. "To take service under one of the great Frankish lords and wait a chance that will never come. Or, better still, to sew some cockle shells into your hats, go home as holy men who have made the pilgrimage, marry the richest wives that you can find, and forget Masouda the widow, and Al-je-bal and Salah-ed-din and the lady about whom he has dreamed a dream. Only then," she added in a changed voice, "remember, you must leave the horses Flame and Smoke behind you."

"We wish to ride those horses," said Wulf lightly, and Godwin turned on her with anger in his eyes.

"You seem to know our story," he said, "and the mission to which we are sworn. What sort of knights do you think us, then, that you offer us counsel which is fitter for those spies from whom you learn your tidings? You talk of our lives. Well, we hold our lives in trust, and when they are asked of us we will yield them up, having done all that we may do."

"Well spoken," answered Masouda. "Ill should I have thought of you had you said otherwise. But why would you go to Al-je-bal?"

"Because our uncle at his death bade us so to do without fail, and having no other counsel we will take that of his spirit, let come what may."

"Well spoken again! Then to Al-je-bal you shall go, and let come what come may—to all three of us!"

"To all three of us?" said Wulf. "What, then, is your part in this matter?"

"I do not know, but perhaps more than you think. At least, I must be your guide."

"Do you mean to betray us?" asked Wulf bluntly.

She drew herself up and looked him in the eyes till he grew red, then said:

"Ask your brother if he thinks that I mean to betray you. No; I mean to save you, if I can, and it comes into my mind that before all is done you will need saving, who speak so roughly to those who would befriend you. Nay, answer not; it is not strange that you should doubt. Pilgrims to the fearful shrine of Al-je-bal, if it pleases you, we will ride at nightfall. Do not trouble about food and such matters. I will make preparation, but we go alone and secretly. Take only your arms and what garments you may need; the rest I will store, and for it give you my receipt. Now I go to make things ready. See, I pray of you, that the horses Flame and Smoke are saddled by sunset."

At sundown, accordingly, the brethren stood waiting in their room. They were fully armed beneath their rough pilgrims' robes, even to the bucklers which had been hidden in their baggage. Also the saddle-bags of carpet which Masouda had given them were packed with such things as they must take, the rest having been handed over to her keeping.

Presently the door opened, and a young man stood before them clothed in the rough camel-hair garment, or *burnous*, which is common in the East.

"What do you want?" asked Godwin.

"I want you, brothers Peter and John," was the reply, and they saw that the slim young man was Masouda. "What! you English innocents, do you not know a woman through a camel-hair cloak?" she added as she led the way to the stable. "Well, so much the better, for it shows that my disguise is good. Henceforth be pleased to forget the widow Masouda and, until we reach the land of Al-je-bal, to remember that I am your servant, a half-breed from Jaffa named David, of no religion—or of all."

In the stable the horses stood saddled, and near to them another—a good Arab—and two laden Cyprian mules, but no attendant was to be seen. They brought them out and mounted, Masouda riding like a man and leading the mules, of which the head of one was tied to the tail of the other. Five minutes later they were clear of Beirut, and through the solemn twilight hush, followed the road whereon they had tried the horses, towards the Dog River, three leagues away, which Masouda said they would reach by moonrise.

Soon it grew very dark, and she rode alongside of them to show them the path, but they did not talk much. Wulf asked her who would take care of the inn while she was absent, to which she answered sharply that the inn would take care of itself, and no more. Picking their way along the stony road at a slow amble, they crossed the bed of two streams then almost dry, till at length they heard running water sounding above that of the slow wash of the sea to their left, and Masouda bade them halt. So they waited, until presently the moon rose in a clear sky, revealing a wide river in front, the pale ocean a hundred feet beneath them to the left, and to the right great mountains, along the face of which their path was cut. So bright was it that Godwin could see strange shapes carven on the sheer face of the rock, and beneath them writing which he could not read.

"What are these?" he asked Masouda.

"The tablets of kings," she answered, "whose names are written in your holy book, who ruled Syria and Egypt thousands of years ago. They were great in their day when they took this land, greater even than Salah-ed-din, and now these seals which they set upon this rock are all that is left of them."

Godwin and Wulf stared at the weather-worn sculptures, and in the silence of that moonlit place there arose in their minds a vision of the mighty armies of different tongues and peoples who had stood in their pride on this road and looked upon yonder river and the great stone wolf that guarded it, which wolf, so said the legend, howled at the approach of foes. But now he howled no more, for he lay headless beneath the waters, and there he lies to this day. Well, they were dead, everyone of them, and even their deeds were forgotten; and oh! how small the thought of it made them feel, these two young men bent upon a desperate quest in a strange and dangerous land. Masouda read what was passing in their hearts, and as they came to the brink of the river, pointed to the bubbles that chased each other towards the sea, bursting and forming again before their eyes.

"Such are we," she said briefly; "but the ocean is always yonder, and the river is always here, and of fresh bubbles there will always be a plenty. So dance on life's water while you may, in the sunlight, in the moonlight, beneath the storm, beneath the stars, for ocean calls and bubbles burst. Now follow me, for I know the ford, and at this season the stream is not deep. Pilgrim Peter, ride you at my side in case I should be washed from the saddle; and pilgrim John, come you behind, and if they hang back, prick the mules with your sword point."

Thus, then, they entered the river, which many might have feared to do at night, and, although once or twice the water rose to their saddles and the mules were stubborn in the swift stream, in the end gained the further bank in safety. Thence they pursued their path through mountains till at length the sun rose and they found themselves in a lonely land where no one was to be seen. Here they halted in a grove of oaks, off-saddled their animals, tethered and fed them with barley which they had brought upon a mule, and ate of the food that Masouda had provided. Then, having secured the beasts, they lay down to sleep, all three of them, since Masouda said that here there was nothing to fear; and being weary, slept on till the heat of noon was past, when once more they fed the horses and mules, and having dined themselves, set forward upon their way.

Now their road—if road it could be called, for they could see none—ran ever upwards through rough, mountainous country, where seemed to dwell neither man nor beast. At sunset they halted again, and at moonrise went forward till the night turned towards morning, when they came to a place where was a little cave.

Before they reached this spot of a sudden the silence of those lonely hills was broken by a sound of roaring, not very near to them, but so loud and so long that it echoed and re-echoed from the cliff. At it the horses Flame and Smoke pricked their ears and trembled, while the mules strove to break away and run back.

"What is that?" asked Wulf, who had never heard its like.

"Lions," answered Masouda. "We draw near the country where there are many of them, and therefore shall do well to halt presently, since it is best to pass through that land in daylight."

So when they came to the cave, having heard no more of the lion, or lions, they unsaddled there, purposing to put the horses into it, where they would be safe from the attack of any such ravening beast. But when they tried to do this, Smoke and Flame spread out their nostrils, and setting their feet firm before them, refused to enter the place, about which there was an evil smell.

"Perhaps jackals have been here," said Masouda. "Let us tether them all in the open."

This then they did, building a fire in front of them with dry wood that lay about in plenty, for here grew sombre cedar trees. The brethren sat by this fire; but, the night being hot, Masouda laid herself down about fifteen paces away under a cedar tree, which grew almost in front of the mouth of the cave, and slept, being tired with long riding. Wulf slept also, since Godwin had agreed to keep watch for the first part of the night.

For an hour or more he sat close by the horses, and noted that they fed uneasily and would not lie down. Soon, however, he was lost in his own thoughts, and, as he heard no more of the lions, fell to wondering over the strangeness of their journey and of what the end of it might be. He wondered also about Masouda, who she was, how she came to know so much, why she befriended them if she really was a friend, and other things—for instance, of that leap over the sunken stream; and whether—no, surely he had been mistaken, her eyes had never looked at him like that. Why, he was sleeping at his post, and the eyes in the darkness yonder were not those of a woman. Women's eyes were not green and gold; they did not grow large, then lessen and vanish away.

Godwin sprang to his feet. As he thought, they were no eyes. He had dreamed, that was all. So he took cedar boughs and threw them on to the fire, where soon they flared gloriously, which done he sat himself down again close to Wulf, who was lost in heavy slumber.

The night was very still and the silence so deep that it pressed upon him like a weight. He could bear it no longer, and rising, began to walk up and down in front of the cave, drawing his sword and holding it in his hand as sentries do. Masouda lay upon the ground, with her head pillowed on a saddle-bag, and the moonlight fell through the cedar boughs upon her face. Godwin stopped to look at it, and wondered that he had never noted before how beautiful she was. Perhaps it was but the soft and silvery light which clothed those delicate features with so much mystery and charm. She might be dead, not sleeping; but even as he thought this, life came into her face, colour stole up beneath the pale, olive-hued skin, the red lips opened, seeming to mutter some words, and she stretched out her rounded arms as though to clasp a vision of her dream.

Godwin turned aside; it seemed not right to watch her thus, although in truth he had only come to know that she was safe. He went back to the fire, and lifting a cedar bough, which blazed like a torch in his left hand, was about to lay it down again on the centre of the flame, when suddenly he heard the sharp and terrible cry of a woman in an agony of pain or fear, and at the same moment the horses and mules began to plunge and snort. In an instant, the blazing bough still in his hand, he was back by the cave, and lo! there before him, the form of Masouda, hanging from its jaws, stood a great yellow beast, which, although he had never seen its like, he knew must be a lioness. It was heading for the cave, then catching sight of him, turned and bounded away in the direction of the fire, purposing to re-enter the wood beyond.

But the woman in its mouth cumbered it, and running swiftly, Godwin came face to face with the brute just opposite the fire. He hurled the burning bough at it, whereon it dropped Masouda, and rearing itself straight upon its hind legs, stretched out its claws, and seemed about to fall on him. For this Godwin did not wait. He was afraid, indeed, who had never before fought lions, but he knew that he must do or die. Therefore he charged straight at it, and with all the strength of his strong arm drove his long sword into the yellow breast, till it seemed to him that the steel vanished and he could see nothing but the hilt.

Then a shock, a sound of furious snarling, and down he went to earth beneath a soft and heavy weight, and there his senses left him.

When they came back again something soft was still upon his face; but this proved to be only the hand of Masouda, who bathed his brow with a cloth dipped in water, while Wulf chafed his hands. Godwin sat up, and in the light of the new risen sun, saw a dead lioness lying before him, its breast still transfixed with his own sword.

"So I saved you," he said faintly.

"Yes, you saved me," answered Masouda, and kneeling down she kissed his feet; then rising again, with her long, soft hair wiped away the blood that was running from a wound in his arm.

## Chapter 10
# On Board the Galley

Rosamund was led from the Hall of Steeple across the meadow down to the quay at Steeple Creek, where a great boat waited—that of which the brethren had found the impress in the mud. In this the band embarked, placing their dead and wounded, with one or two to tend them, in the fishing skiff that had belonged to her father. This skiff having been made fast to the stern of the boat, they pushed off, and in utter silence rowed down the creek till they reached the tidal stream of the Blackwater, where they turned their bow seawards. Through the thick night and the falling snow slowly they felt their way along, sometimes rowing, sometimes drifting, while the false palmer Nicholas steered them. The journey proved dangerous, for they could scarcely see the shore, although they kept as close to it as they dared.

The end of it was that they grounded on a mud bank, and, do what they would, could not thrust themselves free. Now hope rose in the heart of Rosamund, who sat still as a statue in the middle of the boat, the prince Hassan at her side and the armed men—twenty or thirty of them—all about her. Perhaps, she thought, they would remain fast there till daybreak, and be seen and rescued when the brethren woke from their drugged sleep. But Hassan read her mind, and said to her gently enough:

"Be not deceived, lady, for I must tell you that if the worst comes to the worst, we shall place you in the little skiff and go on, leaving the rest to take their chance."

As it happened, at the full tide they floated off the bank and drifted with the ebb down towards the sea. At the first break of dawn she looked up, and there, looming large in the mist, lay a galley, anchored in the mouth of the river. Giving thanks to Allah for their safe arrival, the band brought her aboard and led her towards the cabin. On the poop stood a tall man, who was commanding the sailors that they should get up the anchor. As she came he advanced to her, bowing and saying:

"Lady Rosamund, thus you find me once more, who doubtless you never thought to see again."

She looked at him in the faint light and her blood went cold. It was the knight Lozelle.

"You here, Sir Hugh?" she gasped.

"Where you are, there I am," he answered, with a sneer upon his coarse, handsome face. "Did I not swear that it should be so, beauteous Rosamund, after your saintly cousin worsted me in the fray?"

"You here?" she repeated, "you, a Christian knight, and in the pay of Saladin!"

"In the pay of anyone who leads me to you, Rosamund." Then, seeing the emir Hassan approach, he turned to give some orders to the sailors, and she passed on to the cabin and in her agony fell upon her knees.

When Rosamund rose from them she felt that the ship was moving, and, desiring to look her last on Essex land, went out again upon the poop, where Hassan and Sir Hugh placed themselves, one upon either side of her. Then it was that she saw the tower of St. Peter's-on-the-Wall and her cousins seated on horseback in front of it, the light of the risen sun shining upon their mail. Also she saw Wulf spur his horse into the sea, and faintly heard his great cry of "Fear not! We follow, we follow!"

A thought came to her, and she sprang towards the bulwark; but they were watching and held her, so that all that she could do was to throw up her arms in token.

Now the wind caught the sail and the ship went forward swiftly, so that soon she lost sight of them. Then in her grief and rage Rosamund turned upon Sir Hugh Lozelle and beat him with bitter words till he shrank before her.

"Coward and traitor!" she said. "So it was you who planned this, knowing every secret of our home, where often you were a guest! You who for Paynim gold have murdered my father, not daring to show your face before his sword, but hanging like a thief upon the coast, ready to receive what braver men had stolen. Oh! may God avenge his blood and me on you, false knight—false to Him and me and faith and honour—as avenge He will! Heard you not what my kinsman called to me? 'We follow. We follow!' Yes, they follow, and their swords—those swords you feared to look on—shall yet pierce your heart and give up your soul to your master Satan," and she paused, trembling with her righteous wrath, while Hassan stared at her and muttered:

"By Allah, a princess indeed! So have I seen Salah-ed-din look in his rage. Yes, and she has his very eyes."

But Sir Hugh answered in a thick voice.

"Let them follow—one or both. I fear them not and out there my foot will not slip in the snow."

"Then I say that it shall slip in the sand or on a rock," she answered, and turning, fled to the cabin and cast herself down and wept till she thought that her heart would break.

Well might Rosamund weep whose beloved sire was slain, who was torn from her home to find herself in the power of a man she hated. Yet there was hope for her. Hassan, Eastern trickster as he might be, was her friend; and her uncle, Saladin, at least, would never wish that she should be shamed. Most like he knew nothing of this man Lozelle, except as one of those Christian traitors who were ever ready to betray the Cross for gold. But Saladin was far away and her home lay behind her, and her cousins and lovers were eating out their hearts upon that fading shore. And she—one woman alone—was on this ship with the evil man Lozelle, who thus had kept his promise, and there were none save Easterns to protect her, none save them—and God, Who had permitted that such things should be.

The ship swayed, she grew sick and faint. Hassan brought her food with his own hands, but she loathed it who only desired to die. The day turned to night, the night turned to day again, and always Hassan brought her food and strove to comfort her, till at length she remembered no more.

Then came a long, long sleep, and in the sleep dreams of her father standing with his face to the foe and sweeping them down with his long sword as a sickle sweeps corn—of her father felled by the pilgrim knave, dying upon the floor of his own house, and saying "God will guard you. His will be done." Dreams of Godwin and Wulf also fighting to save her, plighting their troths and swearing their oaths, and between the dreams blackness.

Rosamund awoke to feel the sun streaming warmly through the shutter of her cabin, and to see a woman who held a cup in her hand, watching her—a stout woman of middle age with a not unkindly face. She looked about her and remembered all. So she was still in the ship.

"Whence come you?" she asked the woman.

"From France, lady. This ship put in at Marseilles, and there I was hired to nurse one who lay sick, which suited me very well, as I wished to go to Jerusalem to seek my husband, and good money was offered me. Still, had I known that they were all Saracens on this ship, I am not sure that I should have come—that is, except the captain, Sir Hugh, and the palmer Nicholas; though what they, or you either, are doing in such company I cannot guess."

"What is your name?" asked Rosamund idly.

"Marie—Marie Bouchet. My husband is a fishmonger, or was, until one of those crusading priests got hold of him and took him off to kill Paynims and save his soul, much against my will. Well, I promised him that if he did not return in five years I would come to look for him. So here I am, but where he may be is another matter."

"It is brave of you to go," said Rosamund, then added by an afterthought, "How long is it since we left Marseilles?"

Marie counted on her fat fingers, and answered:

"Five—nearly six weeks. You have been wandering in your mind all that time, talking of many strange things, and we have called at three ports. I forget their names, but the last one was an island with a beautiful harbour. Now, in about twenty days, if all goes well, we should reach another island called Cyprus. But you must not talk so much, you must sleep. The Saracen called Hassan, who is a clever doctor, told me so."

So Rosamund slept, and from that time forward, floating on the calm Mediterranean sea, her strength began to come back again rapidly, who was young and strong in body and constitution. Three days later she was helped to the deck, where the first man she saw was Hassan, who came forward to greet her with many Eastern salutations and joy written on his dark, wrinkled face.

"I give thanks to Allah for your sake and my own," he said. "For yours that you still live whom I thought would die, and for myself that had you died your life would have been required at my hands by Salah-ed-din, my master."

"If so, he should have blamed Azrael, not you," answered Rosamund, smiling; then suddenly turned cold, for before her was Sir Hugh Lozelle, who also thanked Heaven that she had recovered. She listened to him coldly, and presently he went away, but soon was at her side again. Indeed, she could never be free of him, for whenever she appeared on deck he was there, nor could he be repelled, since neither silence nor rebuff would stir him. Always he sat near, talking in his false, hateful voice, and devouring her with the greedy eyes which she could feel fixed upon her face. With him often was his jackal, the false palmer Nicholas, who crawled about her like a snake and strove to flatter her, but to this man she would never speak a word.

At last she could bear it no longer, and when her health had returned to her, summoned Hassan to her cabin.

"Tell me, prince," she said, "who rules upon this vessel?"

"Three people," he answered, bowing. "The knight, Sir Hugh Lozelle, who, as a skilled navigator, is the captain and rules the sailors; I, who rule the fighting men; and you, Princess, who rule us all."

"Then I command that the rogue named Nicholas shall not be allowed to approach me. Is it to be borne that I must associate with my father's murderer?"

"I fear that in that business we all had a hand, nevertheless your order shall be obeyed. To tell you the truth, lady, I hate the fellow, who is but a common spy."

"I desire also," went on Rosamund, "to speak no more with Sir Hugh Lozelle."

"That is more difficult," said Hassan, "since he is the captain whom my master ordered me to obey in all things that have to do with the ship."

"I have nothing to do with the ship," answered Rosamund; "and surely the princess of Baalbec, if so I am, may choose her own companions. I wish to see more of you and less of Sir Hugh Lozelle."

"I am honoured," replied Hassan, "and will do my best."

For some days after this, although he was always watching her, Lozelle approached Rosamund but seldom, and whenever he did so he found Hassan at her side, or rather standing behind her like a guard.

At length, as it chanced, the prince was taken with a sickness from drinking bad water which held him to his bed for some days, and then Lozelle found his opportunity. Rosamund strove to keep her cabin to avoid him, but the heat of the summer sun in the Mediterranean drove her out of it to a place beneath an awning on the poop, where she sat with the woman Marie. Here Lozelle approached her, pretending to bring her food or to inquire after her comfort, but she would answer him nothing. At length, since Marie could understand what he said in French, he addressed her in Arabic, which he spoke well, but she feigned not to understand him. Then he used the English tongue as it was talked among the common people in Essex, and said:

"Lady, how sorely you misjudge me. What is my crime against you? I am an Essex man of good lineage, who met you in Essex and learnt to love you there. Is that a crime, in one who is not poor, who, moreover, was knighted for his deeds by no mean hand? Your father said me nay, and you said me nay, and, stung by my disappointment and his words—for he called me sea-thief and raked up old tales that are not true against me—I talked as I should not have done, swearing that I would wed you yet in spite of all. For this I was called to account with justice, and your cousin, the young knight Godwin, who was then a squire, struck me in the face. Well, he worsted and wounded me, fortune favouring him, and I departed with my vessel to the East, for that is my business, to trade between Syria and England.

"Now, as it chanced, there being peace at the time between the Sultan and the Christians, I visited Damascus to buy merchandise. Whilst I was there Saladin sent for me and asked if it were true that I belonged to a part of England called Essex. When I answered yes, he asked if I knew Sir Andrew D'Arcy and his daughter. Again I said yes, whereon he told me that strange tale of your kinship to him, of which I had heard already; also a still stranger tale of some dream that he had dreamed concerning you, which made it necessary that you should be brought to his court, where he was minded to raise you to great honour. In the end, he offered to hire my finest ship for a large sum, if I would sail it to England to fetch you; but he did not tell me that any force was to be used, and I, on my part, said that I would lift no hand against you or your father, nor indeed have I done so."

"Who remembered the swords of Godwin and Wulf," broke in Rosamund scornfully, "and preferred that braver men should face them."

"Lady," answered Lozelle, colouring, "hitherto none have accused me of a lack of courage. Of your courtesy, listen, I pray you. I did wrong to enter on this business; but lady, it was love for you that drove me to it, for the thought of this long voyage in your company was a bait I could not withstand."

"Paynim gold was the bait you could not withstand—that is what you mean. Be brief, I pray you. I weary.

"Lady, you are harsh and misjudge me, as I will show," and he looked about him cautiously. "Within a week from now, if all goes well, we cast anchor at Limazol in Cyprus, to take in food and water before we run to a secret port near Antioch, whence you are to be taken overland to Damascus, avoiding all cities of the Franks. Now, the Emperor Isaac of Cyprus is my friend, and over him Saladin has no power. Once in his court, you would be safe until such time as you found opportunity to return to England. This, then, is my plan—that you should escape from the ship at night as I can arrange."

"And what is your payment," she asked, "who are a merchant knight?"

"My payment, lady, is—yourself. In Cyprus we will be wed—oh! think before you answer. At Damascus many dangers await you; with me you will find safety and a Christian husband who loves you well—

so well that for your sake he is willing to lose his ship and, what is more, to break faith with Saladin, whose arm is long."

"Have done," she said coldly. "Sooner will I trust myself to an honest Saracen than to you, Sir Hugh, whose spurs, if you met your desert, should be hacked from your heels by scullions. Yes, sooner would I take death for my lord than you, who for your own base ends devised the plot that brought my father to his murder and me to slavery. Have done, I say, and never dare again to speak of love to me," and rising, she walked past him to her cabin.

But Lozelle looking after her muttered to himself, "Nay, fair lady, I have but begun; nor will I forget your bitter words, for which you shall pay the merchant knight in kisses."

From her cabin Rosamund sent a message to Hassan, saying that she would speak with him.

He came, still pale with illness, and asked her will, whereon she told him what had passed between Lozelle and herself, demanding his protection against this man.

Hassan's eyes flashed.

"Yonder he stands," he said, "alone. Will you come with me and speak to him?"

She bowed her head, and giving her his hand, he led her to the poop.

"Sir captain," he began, addressing Lozelle, "the Princess here tells me a strange story—that you have dared to offer your love to her, by Allah! to her, a niece of Salah-ed-din."

"What of it, Sir Saracen?" answered Lozelle, insolently. "Is not a Christian knight fit mate for the blood of an Eastern chief? Had I offered her less than marriage, you might have spoken."

"You!" answered Hassan, with rage in his low voice, "you, huckstering thief and renegade, who swear by Mahomet in Damascus and by your prophet Jesus in England—ay, deny it not, I have heard you, as I have heard that rogue, Nicholas, your servant. You, her fit mate? Why, were it not that you must guide this ship, and that my master bade me not to quarrel with you till your task was done, I would behead you now and cut from your throat the tongue that dared to speak such words," and as he spoke he gripped the handle of his scimitar.

Lozelle quailed before his fierce eyes, for well he knew Hassan, and knew also that if it came to fighting his sailors were no match for the emir and his picked Saracens.

"When our duty is done you shall answer for those words," he said, trying to look brave.

"By Allah! I hold you to the promise," replied Hassan. "Before Salah-ed-din I will answer for them when and where you will, as you shall answer to him for your treachery."

"Of what, then, am I accused?" asked Lozelle. "Of loving the lady Rosamund, as do all men—perhaps yourself, old and withered as you are, among them?"

"Ay, and for that crime I will repay you, old and withered as I am, Sir Renegade. But with Salah-ed-din you have another score to settle—that by promising her escape you tried to seduce her from this ship, where you were sworn to guard her, saying that you would find her refuge among the Greeks of Cyprus."

"Were this true," replied Lozelle, "the Sultan might have cause of complaint against me. But it is not true. Hearken, since speak I must. The lady Rosamund prayed me to do this deed, and I told her that for my honour's sake it is not possible, although it was true that I loved her now as always, and would dare much for her. Then she said that if I did but save her from you Saracens, I should not go without my reward, since she would wed me. Again, although it cost me sore, I answered that it might not be, but when once I had brought my ship to land, I was her true knight, and being freed of my oath, would do my best to save her."

"Princess, you hear," said Hassan, turning to Rosamund. "What say you?"

"I say," she answered coldly, "that this man lies to save himself. I say, moreover, that I answered to him, that sooner would I die than that he should lay a finger on me."

"I hold also that he lies," said Hassan. "Nay; unclasp that dagger if you would live to see another sun. Here, I will not fight with you, but Salah-ed-din shall learn all this case when we reach his court, and judge between the word of the princess of Baalbec and of his hired servant, the false Frank and pirate, Sir Hugh Lozelle."

"Let him learn it—when we reach his court," answered Lozelle, with meaning; then added, "Have you aught else to say to me, prince Hassan? Because if not, I must be attending to the business of my ship, which you suppose that I was about to abandon to win a lady's smile."

"Only this, that the ship is the Sultan's and not yours, for he bought it from you, and that henceforth this lady will be guarded day and night, and doubly guarded when we come to the shores of Cyprus, where it seems that you have friends. Understand and remember."

"I understand, and certainly I will remember," replied Lozelle, and so they parted.

"I think," said Rosamund, when he had gone, "that we shall be fortunate if we land safe in Syria."

"That was in my mind, also, lady. I think, too, that I have forgot my wisdom, but my heart rose against this man, and being still weak from sickness, I lost my judgment and spoke what was in my heart, who would have done better to wait. Now, perhaps, it will be best to kill him, if it were not that he alone has the skill to navigate the ship, which is a trade that he has followed from his youth. Nay, let it go as Allah wills. He is just, and will bring the matter to judgment in due time."

"Yes, but to what judgment?" asked Rosamund.

"I hope to that of the sword," answered Hassan, as he bowed and left her.

From that time forward armed men watched all the night through before Rosamund's cabin, and when she walked the deck armed men walked after her. Nor was she troubled by Lozelle, who sought to speak with her no more, or to Hassan either. Only with the man Nicholas he spoke much.

At length upon one golden evening—for Lozelle was a skilful pilot, one of the best, indeed, who sailed those seas—they came to the shores of Cyprus, and cast anchor. Before them, stretched along the beach, lay the white town of Limazol, with palm trees standing up amidst its gardens, while beyond the fertile plain rose the mighty mountain range of Trooidos. Sick and weary of the endless ocean, Rosamund gazed with rapture at this green and beauteous shore, the home of so much history, and sighed to think that on it she might set no foot. Lozelle saw her look and heard her sigh, and as he climbed into the boat which had come out to row him into the harbour, mocked her, saying:

"Will you not change your mind, lady, and come with me to visit my friend, the Emperor Isaac? I swear that his court is gay, not packed full of sour Saracens or pilgrims thinking of their souls. In Cyprus they only make pilgrimages to Paphos yonder, where Venus was born from out the foam, and has reigned since the beginning of the world—ay, and will reign until its end."

Rosamund made no answer, and Lozelle, descending into the boat, was rowed shorewards through the breakers by the dark-skinned, Cyprian oarsmen, who wore flowers in their hair and sang as they laboured at the oars.

For ten whole days they rolled off Limazol, although the weather was fair and the wind blew straight for Syria. When Rosamund asked why they bided there so long, Hassan stamped his foot and said it was because the Emperor refused to supply them with more food or water than was sufficient for their daily need, unless he, Hassan, would land and travel to an inland town called Nicosia, where his court lay, and there do homage to him. This, scenting a trap, he feared to do, nor could they put out to sea without provisions.

"Cannot Sir Hugh Lozelle see to it?" asked Rosamund.

"Doubtless, if he will," answered Hassan, grinding his teeth; "but he swears that he is powerless."

So there they bode day after day, baked by the sweltering summer sun and rocked to and fro on the long ocean rollers till their hearts grew sick within them, and their bodies also, for some of them were seized with a fever common to the shores of Cyprus, of which two died. Now and again some officer would come off from the shore with Lozelle and a little food and water, and bargain with them, saying that before their wants were supplied the prince Hassan must visit the Emperor and bring with him the fair lady who was his passenger, whom he desired to see.

Hassan would answer no, and double the guard about Rosamund, for at nights boats appeared that cruised round them. In the daytime also bands of men, fantastically dressed in silks, and with them women, could be seen riding to and fro upon the shore and staring at them, as though they were striving to make up their minds to attack the ship.

Then Hassan armed his grim Saracens and bade them stand in line upon the bulwarks, drawn scimitar in hand, a sight that seemed to frighten the Cypriotes—at least they always rode away towards the great square tower of Colossi.

At length Hassan would bear it no more. One morning Lozelle came off from Limazol, where he slept at night, bringing with him three Cyprian lords, who visited the ship—not to bargain as they pretended, but to obtain sight of the beauteous princess Rosamund. Thereon the common talk began of homage that must be paid before food was granted, failing which the Emperor would bid his seamen capture the ship. Hassan listened a while, then suddenly issued an order that the lords should be seized.

"Now," he said to Lozelle, "bid your sailors haul up the anchor, and let us begone for Syria."

"But," answered the knight, "we have neither food nor water for more than one day."

"I care not," answered Hassan, "as well die of thirst and starvation on the sea as rot here with fever. What we can bear these Cyprian gallants can bear also. Bid the sailors lift the anchor and hoist the sail, or I loose my scimitars among them."

Now Lozelle stamped and foamed, but without avail, so he turned to the three lords, who were pale with fear, and said:

"Which will you do: find food and water for this ship, or put to sea without them, which is but to die?"

They answered that they would go ashore and supply all that was needful.

"Nay," said Hassan, "you bide here until it comes."

In the end, then, this happened, for one of the lords chanced to be a nephew of the Emperor, who, when he learned that he was captive, sent supplies in plenty. Thus it came about that the Cyprian lords having been sent back with the last empty boat, within two days they were at sea again.

Now Rosamund missed the hated face of the spy, Nicholas, and told Hassan, who made inquiry, to find—or so said Lozelle—that he went ashore and vanished there on the first day of their landing in Cyprus, though whether he had been killed in some brawl, or fallen sick, or hidden himself away, he did not know. Hassan shrugged his shoulders, and Rosamund was glad enough to be rid of him, but in her heart she wondered for what evil purpose Nicholas had left the ship.

When the galley was one day out from Cyprus steering for the coast of Syria, they fell into a calm such as is common in those seas in summer. This calm lasted eight whole days, during which they made but little progress. At length, when all were weary of staring at the oil-like sea, a wind sprang up that grew gradually to a gale blowing towards Syria, and before it they fled along swiftly. Worse and stronger grew that gale, till on the evening of the second day, when they seemed in no little danger of being pooped, they saw a great mountain far away, at the sight of which Lozelle thanked God aloud.

"Are those the mountains near Antioch?" asked Hassan.

"Nay," he answered, "they are more than fifty miles south of them, between Ladikiya and Jebela. There, by the mercy of Heaven, is a good haven, for I have visited it, where we can lie till this storm is past."

"But we are steering for Darbesak, not for a haven near Jebela, which is a Frankish port," answered Hassan, angrily.

"Then put the ship about and steer there yourself," said Lozelle, "and I promise you this, that within two hours every one of you will be dead at the bottom of the sea."

Hassan considered. It was true, for then the waves would strike them broadside on, and they must fill and sink.

"On your head be it," he answered shortly.

The dark fell, and by the light of the great lantern at their prow they saw the white seas hiss past as they drove shorewards beneath bare masts. For they dared hoist no sail.

All that night they pitched and rolled, till the stoutest of them fell sick, praying God and Allah that they might have light by which to enter the harbour. At length they saw the top of the loftiest mountain grow luminous with the coming dawn, although the land itself was still lost in shadow, and saw also that it seemed to be towering almost over them.

"Take courage," cried Lozelle, "I think that we are saved," and he hoisted a second lantern at his masthead—why, they did not know.

After this the sea began to fall, only to grow rough again for a while as they crossed some bar, to find themselves in calm water, and on either side of them what appeared in the dim, uncertain light to be the bush-clad banks of a river. For a while they ran on, till Lozelle called in a loud voice to the sailors to let the anchor go, and sent a messenger to say that all might rest now, as they were safe. So they laid them down and tried to sleep.

But Rosamund could not sleep. Presently she rose, and throwing on her cloak went to the door of the cabin and looked at the beauty of the mountains, rosy with the new-born light, and at the misty surface of the harbour. It was a lonely place—at least, she could see no town or house, although they were lying not fifty yards from the tree-hidden shore. As she stood thus, she heard the sound of boats being rowed through the mist, and perceived three or four of these approaching the ship in silence, perceived also that Lozelle, who stood alone upon the deck, was watching their approach. Now the first boat made fast and a man in the prow rose up and began to speak to Lozelle in a low voice. As he did so the hood fell back from his head, and Rosamund saw the face. It was that of the spy Nicholas! For a moment she stood amazed, for they had left this man in Cyprus; then understanding came to her and she cried aloud:

"Treachery! Prince Hassan, there is treachery."

As the words left her lips fierce, wild-looking men began to scramble aboard at the low waist of the galley, to which boat after boat made fast. The Saracens also tumbled from the benches where they slept and ran aft to the deck where Rosamund was, all except one of them who was cut off in the prow of the ship. Prince Hassan appeared, too, scimitar in hand, clad in his jewelled turban and coat of mail, but without his cloak, shouting orders as he came, while the hired crew of the ship flung themselves upon their knees and begged for mercy. To him Rosamund cried out that they were betrayed and by Nicholas, whom she had seen. Then a great man, wearing a white *burnous* and holding a naked sword in his hand, stepped forward and said in Arabic:

"Yield you now, for you are outnumbered and your captain is captured," and he pointed to Lozelle, who was being held by two men while his arms were bound behind him.

"In whose name do you bid me yield?" asked the prince, glaring about him like a lion in a trap.

"In the dread name of Sinan, in the name of the lord Al-je-bal, O servant of Salah-ed-din."

At these words a groan of fear went up even from the brave Saracens, for now they learned that they had to do with the terrible chief of the Assassins.

"Is there then war between the Sultan and Sinan?" asked Hassan.

"Ay, there is always war. Moreover, you have one with you," and he pointed to Rosamund, "who is dear to Salah-ed-din, whom, therefore, my master desires as a hostage."

"How knew you that?" said Hassan, to gain time while his men formed up.

"How does the lord Sinan know all things?" was the answer; "Come, yield, and perhaps he will show you mercy."

"Through spies," hissed Hassan, "such spies as Nicholas, who has come from Cyprus before us, and that Frankish dog who is called a knight," and he pointed to Lozelle. "Nay, we yield not, and here, Assassins, you have to do not with poisons and the knife, but with bare swords and brave men. Ay, and I warn you—and your lord—that Salah-ed-din will take vengeance for this deed."

"Let him try it if he wishes to die, who hitherto has been spared," answered the tall man quietly. Then he said to his followers, "Cut them down, all save the women"—for the Frenchwoman, Marie, was now clinging to the arm of Rosamund—"and emir Hassan, whom I am commanded to bring living to Masyaf."

"Back to your cabin, lady," said Hassan, "and remember that whate'er befalls, we have done our best to save you. Ay, and tell it to my lord, that my honour may be clean in his eyes. Now, soldiers of Salah-ed-din, fight and die as he has taught you how. The gates of Paradise stand open, and no coward will enter there."

They answered with a fierce, guttural cry. Then, as Rosamund fled to the cabin, the fray began, a hideous fray. On came the Assassins with sword and dagger, striving to storm the deck. Again and again they were beaten back, till the waist seemed full of their corpses, as man by man they fell beneath the curved scimitars, and again and again they charged these men who, when their master ordered, knew neither fear nor pity. But more boatloads came from the shore, and the Saracens were but few, worn also with storm and sickness, so at last Rosamund, peeping beneath her hand, saw that the poop was gained.

Here and there a man fought on until he fell beneath the cruel knives in the midst of the circle of the dead, among them the warrior-prince Hassan. Watching him with fascinated eyes as he strove alone against a host, Rosamund was put in mind of another scene, when her father, also alone, had striven thus against that emir and his soldiers, and even then she bethought her of the justice of God.

See! his foot slipped on the blood-stained deck. He was down, and ere he could rise again they had thrown cloaks over him, these fierce, silent men, who even with their lives at stake, remembered the command of their captain, to take him living. So living they took him, with not a wound upon his skin, who when he struck them down, had never struck back at him lest the command of Sinan should be broken.

Rosamund noted it, and remembering that his command was also that she should be brought to him unharmed, knew that she had no violence to fear at the hands of these cruel murderers. From this thought, and because Hassan still lived, she took such comfort as she might.

"It is finished," said the tall man, in his cold voice. "Cast these dogs into the sea who have dared to disobey the command of Al-je-bal."

So they took them up, dead and living together, and threw them into the water, where they sank, nor did one of the wounded Saracens pray them for mercy. Then they served their own dead likewise, but those that were only wounded they took ashore. This done, the tall man advanced to the cabin and said:

"Lady, come, we are ready to start upon our journey."

Having no choice, Rosamund obeyed him, remembering as she went how from a scene of battle and bloodshed she had been brought aboard that ship to be carried she knew not whither, which now she left in a scene of battle and bloodshed to be carried she knew not whither.

"Oh!" she cried aloud, pointing to the corpses they hurled into the deep, "ill has it gone with these who stole me, and ill may it go with you also, servant of Al-je-bal."

But the tall man answered nothing, as followed by the weeping Marie and the prince Hassan, he led her to the boat.

Soon they reached the shore, and here they tore Marie from her, nor did Rosamund ever learn what became of her, or whether or no this poor woman found her husband whom she had dared so much to seek.

## CHAPTER 11

# The City of Al-Je-Bal

"I pray you have done," said Godwin, "it is but a scratch from the beast's claws. I am ashamed that you should put your hair to such vile uses. Give me a little water."

He asked it of Wulf, but Masouda rose without a word and fetched the water, in which she mingled wine. Godwin drank of it and his faintness left him, so that he was able to stand up and move his arms and legs.

"Why," he said, "it is nothing; I was only shaken. That lioness did not hurt me at all."

"But you hurt the lioness," said Wulf, with a laugh. "By St. Chad a good thrust!" and he pointed to the long sword driven up to the hilt in the brute's breast. "Why, I swear I could not have made a better myself."

"I think it was the lion that thrust," answered Godwin. "I only held the sword straight. Drag it out, brother, I am still too weak."

So Wulf set his foot upon the breast of the lion and tugged and tugged until at length he loosened the sword, saying as he strained at it:

"Oh! what an Essex hog am I, who slept through it all, never waking until Masouda seized me by the hair, and I opened my eyes to see you upon the ground with this yellow beast crouched on the top of you like a hen on a nest egg. I thought that it was alive and smote it with my sword, which, had I been fully awake, I doubt if I should have found the courage to do. Look," and he pushed the lioness's head with his foot, whereon it twisted round in such a fashion that they perceived for the first time that it only hung to the shoulders by a thread of skin.

"I am glad you did not strike a little harder," said Godwin, "or I should now be in two pieces and drowned in my own blood, instead of in that of this dead brute," and he looked ruefully at his *burnous* and hauberk, that were soaked with gore.

"Yes," said Wulf, "I never thought of that. Who would, in such a hurry?"

"Lady Masouda," asked Godwin, "when last I saw you you were hanging from those jaws. Say, are you hurt?"

"Nay," she answered, "for I wear mail like you, and the teeth glanced on it so that she held me by the cloak only. Come, let us skin the beast, and take its pelt as a present to the lord Al-je-bal."

"Good," said Godwin, "and I give you the claws for a necklace."

"Be sure that I will wear them," she answered, and helped Wulf to flay the lioness while he sat by resting. When it was done Wulf went to the little cave and walked into it, to come out again with a bound.

"Why!" he said, "there are more of them in there. I saw their eyes and heard them snarl. Now, give me a burning branch and I will show you, brother, that you are not the only one who can fight a lion."

"Let be, you foolish man," broke in Masouda. "Doubtless those are her cubs, and if you kill them, her mate will follow us for miles; but if they are left safe he will stay to feed them. Come, let us begone from this place as swiftly as we can."

So having shown them the skin of the lion, that they might know it was but a dead thing, at the sight of which they snorted and trembled, they packed it upon one of the mules and rode off slowly into a valley some five miles away, where was water but no trees. Here, since Godwin needed rest, they stopped all that day and the night which followed, seeing no more of lions, though they watched for them sharply enough. The next morning, having slept well, he was himself again, and they started forward through a broken country towards a deep cleft, on either side of which stood a tall mountain.

"This is Al-je-bal's gateway," said Masouda, "and tonight we should sleep in the gate, whence one day's ride brings us to his city."

So on they rode till at length, perched upon the sides of the cleft, they saw a castle, a great building, with high walls, to which they came at sunset. It seemed that they were expected in this place, for men hastened to meet them, who greeted Masouda and eyed the brethren curiously, especially after they had heard of the adventure with the lion. These took them, not into the castle, but to a kind of hostelry at its back, where they were furnished with food and slept the night.

Next morning they went on again to a hilly country with beautiful and fertile valleys. Through this they rode for two hours, passing on their way several villages, where sombre-eyed people were labouring in the fields. From each village, as they drew near to it, horsemen would gallop out and challenge them, whereon Masouda rode forward and spoke with the leader alone. Then he would touch his forehead with his hand and bow his head and they rode on unmolested.

"See," she said, when they had thus been stopped for the fourth time, "what chance you had of winning through to Masyaf unguarded. Why, I tell you, brethren, that you would have been dead before ever you passed the gates of the first castle."

Now they rode up a long slope, and at its crest paused to look upon a marvellous scene. Below them stretched a vast plain, full of villages, cornfields, olive-groves, and vineyards. In the centre of this plain, some fifteen miles away, rose a great mountain, which seemed to be walled all about. Within the wall was a city of which the white, flat-roofed houses climbed the slopes of the mountain, and on its crest a level space of land covered with trees and a great, many-towered castle surrounded by more houses.

"Behold the home of Al-je-bal, Lord of the Mountain," said Masouda, "where we must sleep to-night. Now, brethren, listen to me. Few strangers who enter that castle come thence living. There is still time; I can pass you back as I passed you hither. Will you go on?"

"We will go on," they answered with one breath.

"Why? What have you to gain? You seek a certain maiden. Why seek her here whom you say has been taken to Salah-ed-din? Because the Al-je-bal in bygone days swore to befriend one of your blood. But that Al-je-bal is dead, and another of his line rules who took no such oath. How do you know that he will befriend you—how that he will not enslave or kill you? I have power in this land, why or how does not matter, and I can protect you against all that dwell in it—as I swear I will, for did not one of you save my life?" and she glanced at Godwin, "except my lord Sinan, against whom I have no power, for I am his slave."

"He is the enemy of Saladin, and may help us for his hate's sake."

"Yes, he is the enemy of Salah-ed-din now more than ever. He may help you or he may not. Also," she added with meaning, "you may not wish the help he offers. Oh!" and there was a note of entreaty in her voice, "think, think! For the last time, I pray you think!"

"We have thought," answered Godwin solemnly; "and, whatever chances, we will obey the command of the dead."

She heard and bowed her head in assent, then said, looking up again:

"So be it. You are not easily turned from your purpose, and I like that spirit well. But hear my counsel. While you are in this city speak no Arabic and pretend to understand none. Also drink nothing but water, which is good here, for the lord Sinan sets strange wines before his guests, that, if they pass the lips, produce visions and a kind of waking madness in which you might do deeds whereof you were afterwards ashamed. Or you might swear oaths that would sit heavy on your souls, and yet could not be broken except at the cost of life."

"Fear not," answered Wulf. "Water shall be our drink, who have had enough of drugged wines," for he remembered the Christmas feast in the Hall at Steeple.

"You, Sir Godwin," went on Masouda, "have about your neck a certain ring which you were mad enough to show to me, a stranger—a ring with writing on it which none can read save the great men that in this land are called the dais. Well, as it chances, the secret is safe with me; but be wise; say nothing of that ring and let no eye see it."

"Why not?" asked Godwin. "It is the token of our dead uncle to the Al-je-bal."

She looked round her cautiously and replied:

"Because it is, or was once, the great Signet, and a day may come when it will save your lives. Doubtless when the lord who is dead thought it gone forever he caused another to be fashioned, so like that I who have had both in my hand could not tell the two apart. To him who holds that ring all gates are open; but to let it be known that you have its double means death. Do you understand?"

They nodded, and Masouda continued:

"Lastly—though you may think that this seems much to ask—trust me always, even if I seem to play you false, who for your sakes," and she sighed, "have broken oaths and spoken words for which the punishment is to die by torment. Nay, thank me not, for I do only what I must who am a slave—a slave."

"A slave to whom?" asked Godwin, staring at her.

"To the Lord of all the Mountains," she answered, with a smile that was sweet yet very sad; and without another word spurred on her horse.

"What does she mean," asked Godwin of Wulf, when she was out of hearing, "seeing that if she speaks truth, for our sakes, in warning us against him, Masouda is breaking her fealty to this lord?"

"I do not know, brother, and I do not seek to know. All her talk may be a part of a plot to blind us, or it may not. Let well alone and trust in fortune, say I."

"A good counsel," answered Godwin, and they rode forward in silence.

They crossed the plain, and towards evening came to the wall of the outer city, halting in front of its great gateway. Here, as at the first castle, a band of solemn-looking mounted men came out to meet them, and, having spoken a few words with Masouda, led them over the drawbridge that spanned the first rock-cut moat, and through triple gates of iron into the city. Then they passed up a street very steep and narrow, from the roofs and windows of the houses on either side of which hundreds of people—many of whom seemed to be engaged at their evening prayer—watched them go by. At the head of this street they reached another fortified gateway, on the turrets of which, so motionless that at first they took them to be statues cut in stone, stood guards wrapped in long white robes. After parley, this also was opened to them, and again they rode through triple doors.

Then they saw all the wonder of that place, for between the outer city where they stood and the castle, with its inner town which was built around and beneath it yawned a vast gulf over ninety feet in depth. Across this gulf, built of blocks of stone, quite unrailed, and not more than three paces wide, ran a causeway some two hundred yards in length, which causeway was supported upon arches reared up at intervals from the bottom of the gulf.

"Ride on and have no fear," said Masouda. "Your horses are trained to heights, and the mules and mine will follow."

So Godwin, showing nothing in his face of the doubt that he felt in his heart, patted Flame upon the neck, and, after hanging back a little, the horse started lifting its hoofs high and glancing from side to side at the terrible gulf beneath. Where Flame went Smoke knew that it could go, and came on bravely, but snorting a little, while the mules, that did not fear heights so long as the ground was firm beneath their feet, followed. Only Masouda's horse was terrified, backed, and strove to wheel round, till she drove the spur into it, when of a sudden it started and came over at a gallop.

At length they were across, and, passing under another gateway which had broad terraces on either side of it, rode up the long street beyond and entered a great courtyard, around which stood the castle, a vast and frowning fortress. Here a white-robed officer came forward, greeting them with a low bow, and with him servants who assisted them to dismount. These men took the horses to a range of stables on one side of the courtyard, whither the brethren followed to see their beasts groomed and fed. Then the officer, who had stood patiently by the while, conducted them through doorways and down passages to the guest chambers, large, stone-roofed rooms, where they found their baggage ready for them. Here Masouda said that she would see them again on the following morning, and departed in company with the officer.

Wulf looked round the great vaulted chamber, which, now that the dark had fallen, was lit by flickering lamps set in iron brackets upon the wall, and said:

"Well, for my part, I had rather pass the night in a desert among the lions than in this dismal place."

Scarcely were the words out of his lips when curtains swung aside and beautiful women entered, clad in gauzy veils and bearing dishes of food. These they placed upon the ground before them, inviting them to eat with nods and smiles, while others brought basins of scented water, which they poured over their hands. Then they sat down and ate the food that was strange to them, but very pleasant to the taste; and while they ate, women whom they could not see sang sweet songs, and played upon harps and lutes. Wine was offered to them also; but of this, remembering Masouda's words, they would not drink, asking by signs for water, which was brought after a little pause.

When their meal was done, the beautiful women bore away the dishes, and black slaves appeared. These men led them to baths such as they had never seen, where they washed first in hot water, then in cold. Afterwards they were rubbed with spicy-smelling oils, and having been wrapped in white robes, conducted back to their chamber, where they found beds spread for them. On these, being very weary, they lay down, when the strange, sweet music broke out afresh, and to the sound of it they fell asleep.

When they awoke it was to see the light streaming through the high, latticed windows.

"Did you sleep well, Godwin?" asked Wulf.

"Well enough," answered his brother, "only I dreamed that throughout the night people came and looked at me."

"I dreamed that also," said Wulf; "moreover, I think that it was not all a dream, since there is a coverlet on my bed which was not there when I went to sleep."

Godwin looked at his own, where also was another coverlet added, doubtless as the night grew colder in that high place.

"I have heard of enchanted castles," he said; "now I think that we have found one."

"Ay," replied Wulf, "and it is well enough while it lasts."

They rose and dressed themselves, putting on clean garments and their best cloaks, that they had brought with them on the mules, after which the veiled women entered the room with breakfast, and they ate. When this was finished, having nothing else to do, they made signs to one of the women that they wished for cloths wherewith to clean their armour, for, as they had been bidden, they pretended to understand no word of Arabic. She nodded, and presently returned with a companion carrying leathers and paste in a jar. Nor did they leave them, but, sitting upon the ground, whether the brethren willed it or no, took the shirts of mail and rubbed them till they shone like silver, while Godwin and Wulf polished their helms, spurs, and bucklers, cleansing their swords and daggers also, and sharpening them with a stone which they carried for that purpose.

Now as these women worked, they began to talk to each other in a low voice, and some of their talk, though not all, the brethren understood.

"A handsome pair truly," said the first. "We should be fortunate if we had such men for husbands, although they are Franks and infidels."

"Ay," answered the other; "and from their likeness they must be twins. Now which of them would you choose?"

Then for a long while they discussed them, comparing them feature by feature and limb by limb, until the brethren felt their faces grow red beneath the sunburn and scrubbed furiously at their armour to show a reason for it. At length one of the women said:

"It was cruel of the lady Masouda to bring these birds into the Master's net. She might have warned them."

"Masouda was ever cruel," answered the other, "who hates all men, which is unnatural. Yet I think if she loved a man she would love him well, and perhaps that might be worse for him than her hate."

"Are these knights spies?" asked the first.

"I suppose so," was the answer, "silly fellows who think that they can spy upon a nation of spies. They would have done better to keep to fighting, at which, doubtless, they are good enough. What will happen to them?"

"What always happens, I suppose—a pleasant time at first; then, if they can be put to no other use, a choice between the faith and the cup. Or, perhaps, as they seem men of rank, they may be imprisoned in the dungeon tower and held to ransom. Yes, yes; it was cruel of Masouda to trick them so, who may be but travellers after all, desiring to see our city."

Just then the curtain was drawn, and through it entered Masouda herself. She was dressed in a white robe that had a dagger worked in red over the left breast, and her long black hair fell upon her shoulders, although it was half hid by the veil, open in front, which hung from her head. Never had they seen her look so beautiful as she seemed thus.

"Greetings, brothers Peter and John. Is this fit work for pilgrims?" she said in French, pointing to the long swords which they were sharpening.

"Ay," answered Wulf, as they rose and bowed to her, "for pilgrims to this—holy city."

The women who were cleaning the mail bowed also, for it seemed that here Masouda was a person of importance. She took the hauberks from their hands.

"Ill cleansed," she said sharply. "I think that you girls talk better than you work. Nay, they must serve. Help these lords to don them. Fools, that is the shirt of the grey-eyed knight. Give it me; I will be his squire," and she snatched the hauberk from their hands, whereat, when her back was turned, they glanced at one another.

"Now," she said, when they were fully armed and had donned their mantles, "you brethren look as pilgrims should. Listen, I have a message for you. The Master"—and she bowed her head, as did the women, guessing of whom she spoke—"will receive you in an hour's time, till when, if it please you, we can walk in the gardens, which are worth your seeing."

So they went out with her, and as they passed towards the curtain she whispered:

"For your lives' sake, remember all that I have told you—above everything, about the wine and the ring, for if you dream the drink-dream you will be searched. Speak no word to me save of common matters."

In the passage beyond the curtain white-robed guards were standing, armed with spears, who turned and followed them without a word. First they went to the stables to visit Flame and Smoke, which whinnied as they drew near. These they found well-fed and tended—indeed, a company of grooms were gathered round them, discussing their points and beauty, who saluted as the owners of such steeds approached. Leaving the stable, they passed through an archway into the famous gardens, which were said to be the most beautiful in all the East. Beautiful they were indeed, planted with trees, shrubs, and flowers such as are seldom seen, while between fern-clad rocks flowed rills which fell over deep cliffs in waterfalls of foam. In places the shade of cedars lay so dense that the brightness of day was changed to twilight, but in others the ground was open and carpeted with flowers which filled the air with perfume. Everywhere grew roses, myrtles, and trees laden with rich fruits, while from all sides came the sound of cooing doves and the voices of many bright-winged birds which flashed from palm to palm.

On they walked, down the sand-strewn paths for a mile or more, accompanied by Masouda and the guard. At length, passing through a brake of whispering, reed-like plants, of a sudden they came to a low wall, and saw, yawning black and wide at their very feet, that vast cleft which they had crossed before they entered the castle.

"It encircles the inner city, the fortress, and its grounds," said Masouda; "and who lives to-day that could throw a bridge across it? Now come back."

So, following the gulf round, they returned to the castle by another path, and were ushered into an ante-room, where stood a watch of twelve men. Here Masouda left them in the midst of the men, who stared at them with stony eyes. Presently she returned, and beckoned to them to follow her. Walking down a long passage they came to curtains, in front of which were two sentries, who drew these curtains as they approached. Then, side by side, they entered a great hall, long as Stangate Abbey church, and passed through a number of people, all crouched upon the ground. Beyond these the hall narrowed as a chancel does.

Here sat and stood more people, fierce-eyed, turbaned men, who wore great knives in their girdles. These, as they learned afterwards, were called the *fedai*, the sworn assassins, who lived but to do the command of their lord the great Assassin. At the end of this chancel were more curtains, beyond which was a guarded door. It opened, and on its further side they found themselves in full sunlight on an unwalled terrace, surrounded by the mighty gulf into which it was built out. On the right and left edges of this terrace sat old and bearded men, twelve in number, their heads bowed humbly and their eyes fixed upon the ground. These were the dais or councillors.

At the head of the terrace, under an open and beautifully carved pavilion of wood, stood two gigantic soldiers, having the red dagger blazoned on their white robes. Between them was a black cushion, and on the cushion a black heap. At first, staring out of the bright sunlight at this heap in the shadow, the brethren wondered what it might be. Then they caught sight of the glitter of eyes, and knew that the heap was a man who wore a black turban on his head and a black, bell-shaped robe clasped at the breast with a red jewel. The weight of the man had sunk him down deep into the soft cushion, so that there was nothing of him to be seen save the folds of the bell-shaped cloak, the red jewel, and the head. He looked like a coiled-up snake; the dark and glittering eyes also were those of a snake. Of his features, in the deep shade of the canopy and of the wide black turban, they could see nothing.

The aspect of this figure was so terrible and inhuman that the brethren trembled at the sight of him. They were men and he was a man, but between that huddled, beady-eyed heap and those two tall Western warriors, clad in their gleaming mail and coloured cloaks, helm on brow, buckler on arm, and long sword at side, the contrast was that of death and life.

## CHAPTER 12

# The Lord of Death

Masouda ran forward and prostrated herself at full length, but Godwin and Wulf stared at the heap, and the heap stared at them. Then, at some motion of his chin, Masouda arose and said:

"Strangers, you stand in the presence of the Master, Sinan, Lord of Death. Kneel, and do homage to the Master."

But the brethren stiffened their backs and would not kneel. They lifted their hands to their brows in salute, but no more.

Then from between the black turban and the black cloak came a hollow voice, speaking in Arabic, and saying:

"Are these the men who brought me the lion's skin? Well, what seek ye, Franks?" They stood silent.

"Dread lord," said Masouda, "these knights are but now come from England over sea, and do not understand our tongue."

"Set out their story and their request," said Al-je-bal, "that we may judge of them."

"Dread lord," answered Masouda, "as I sent you word, they say that they are the kin of a certain knight who in battle saved the life of him who ruled before you, but is now an inhabitant of Paradise."

"I have heard that there was such a knight," said the voice. "He was named D'Arcy, and he bore the same cognizance on his shield—the sign of a skull."

"Lord, these brethren are also named D'Arcy, and now they come to ask your help against Salah-ed-din."

At that name the heap stirred as a snake stirs when it hears danger, and the head erected itself a little beneath the great turban.

"What help, and why?" asked the voice.

"Lord, Salah-ed-din has stolen a woman of their house who is his niece, and these knights, her brothers, ask you to aid them to recover her."

The beady eyes instantly became interested.

"Report has been made to me of that story," said the voice; "but what sign do these Franks show? He who went before me gave a ring, and with it certain rights in this land, to the knight D'Arcy who befriended him in danger. Where is that sacred ring, with which he parted in his foolishness?"

Masouda translated, and seeing the warning in her eyes and remembering her words, the brethren shook their heads, while Wulf answered:

"Our uncle, the knight Sir Andrew, was cut down by the soldiers of Salah-ed-din, and as he died bade us seek you out. What time had he to tell us of any ring?"

The head sank upon the breast.

"I hoped," said Sinan to Masouda, "that they had the ring, and it was for this reason, woman, that I allowed you to lead these knights hither, after you had reported of them and their quest to me from Beirut. It is not well that there should be two holy Signets in the world, and he who went before me, when he lay dying, charged me to recover his if that were possible. Let them go back to their own land and return to me with the ancient ring, and I will help them."

Masouda translated the last sentence only, and again the brethren shook their heads. This time it was Godwin who spoke.

"Our land is far away, O lord, and where shall we find this long-lost ring? Let not our journey be in vain. O mighty One, give us justice against Salah-ed-din."

"All my years have I sought justice on Salah-ed-din," answered Sinan, "and yet he prevails against me. Now I make you an offer. Go, Franks, and bring me his head, or at least put him to death as I shall show you how, and we will talk again."

When they heard this saying Wulf said to Godwin, in English:

"I think that we had best go; I do not like this company." But Godwin made no answer.

As they stood silent thus, not knowing what to say, a man entered through the door, and, throwing himself on his hands and knees, crawled towards the cushion through the double line of councillors or dais.

"Your report?" said Sinan in Arabic.

"Lord," answered the man, "I acquaint you that your will has been done in the matter of the vessel." Then he went on speaking in a low voice, so rapidly that the brethren could scarcely hear and much less understand him.

Sinan listened, then said:

"Let the *fedai* enter and make his own report, bringing with him his prisoners."

Now one of the dais, he who sat nearest the canopy, rose and pointing towards the brethren, said.

"Touching these Franks, what is your will?"

The beady eyes, which seemed to search out their souls, fixed themselves upon them and for a long while Sinan considered. They trembled, knowing that he was passing some judgment concerning them in his heart, and that on his next words much might hang—even their lives.

"Let them stay here," he said at length. "I may have questions to ask them."

For a time there was silence. Sinan, Lord of Death, seemed to be lost in thought under the black shade of his canopy; the double line of dais stared at nothingness across the passage way; the giant guards stood still as statues; Masouda watched the brethren from beneath her long eye-lashes, while the brethren watched the sharp edge of the shadow of the canopy on the marble floor. They strove to seem unconcerned, but their hearts were beating fast within them who felt that great things were about to happen, though what these might be they knew not.

So intense was the silence, so dreadful seemed that inhuman, snake-like man, so strange his aged, passionless councillors, and the place of council surrounded by a dizzy gulf, that fear took hold of them like the fear of an evil dream. Godwin wondered if Sinan could see the ring upon his breast, and what would happen to him if he did see it; while Wulf longed to shout aloud, to do anything that would break this deathly, sunlit quiet. To them those minutes seemed like hours; indeed, for aught they knew, they might have been hours.

At length there was a stir behind the brethren, and at a word from Masouda they separated, falling apart a pace or two, and stood opposite each other and sideways to Sinan. Standing thus, they saw the curtains drawn. Through them came four men, carrying a stretcher covered with a cloth, beneath which they could see the outline of a form, that lay there stirless. The four men brought the stretcher to the front of the canopy, set it on the ground, prostrated themselves, and retired, walking backwards down the length of the terrace.

Again there was silence, while the brethren wondered whose corpse it was that lay beneath the cloth, for a corpse it must surely be; though neither the Lord of the Mountain nor his dais and guards seemed to concern themselves in the matter. Again the curtains parted, and a procession advanced up the terrace. First came a great man clad in a white robe blazoned with the bleeding dagger, after whom walked a tall woman shrouded in a long veil, who was followed by a thick-set knight clad in Frankish armour and wearing a cape of which the cowl covered his head as though to keep the rays of the sun from beating on his helm. Lastly walked four guards. Up the long place they marched, through the double line of dais, while with a strange stirring in their breasts the brethren watched the shape and movements of the veiled woman who stepped forward rapidly, not seeing them, for she turned her head neither to the right nor left. The leader of the little band reached the space before the canopy, and, prostrating himself by the side of the stretcher, lay still. She who walked behind him stopped also, and, seeing the black heap upon the cushion, shuddered.

"Woman, unveil," commanded the voice of Sinan.

She hesitated, then swiftly undid some fastening, so that her drapery fell from her head. The brethren stared, rubbed their eyes, and stared again.

Before them stood Rosamund!

Yes, it was Rosamund, worn with sickness, terrors, and travel, Rosamund herself beyond all doubt. At the sight of her pale, queenly beauty the heap on the cushion stirred beneath his black cloak, and the beady eyes were filled with an evil, eager light. Even the dais seemed to wake from their contemplation, and Masouda bit her red lip, turned pale beneath her olive skin, and watched with devouring eyes, waiting to read this woman's heart.

"Rosamund!" cried the brethren with one voice.

She heard. As they sprang towards her she glanced wildly from face to face, then with a low cry flung an arm about the neck of each and would have fallen in the ecstasy of her joy had they not held her. Indeed, her knees touched the ground. As they stooped to lift her it flashed into Godwin's mind that Masouda had told Sinan that they were her brethren. The thought was followed by another. If this were so, they might be left with her, whereas otherwise that black-robed devil—

"Listen," he whispered in English; "we are not your cousins—we are your brothers, your half-brothers, and we know no Arabic."

She heard and Wulf heard, but the watchers thought that they were but welcoming each other, for Wulf began to talk also, random words in French, such as "Greeting, sister!" "Well found, sister!" and kissed her on the forehead.

Rosamund opened her eyes, which had closed, and, gaining her feet, gave one hand to each of the brethren. Then the voice of Masouda was heard interpreting the words of Sinan.

"It seems, lady, that you know these knights."

"I do—well. They are my brothers, from whom I was stolen when they were drugged and our father was killed."

"How is that, lady, seeing that you are said to be the niece of Salah-ed-din? Are these knights, then, the nephews of Salah-ed-din?"

"Nay," answered Rosamund, "they are my father's sons, but of another wife."

The answer appeared to satisfy Sinan, who fixed his eyes upon the pale beauty of Rosamund and asked no more questions. While he remained thus thinking, a noise arose at the end of the terrace, and the brethren, turning their heads, saw that the thick-set knight was striving to thrust his way through the guards who stood by the curtains and barred his path with the shafts of their spears.

Then it came into Godwin's mind that just before Rosamund unveiled he had seen this knight suddenly turn and walk down the terrace.

The lord Sinan looked up at the sound and made a sign. Thereon two of the dais sprang to their feet and ran towards the curtain, where they spoke with the knight, who turned and came back with them, though slowly, as one who is unwilling. Now his hood had fallen from his head, and Godwin and Wulf stared at him as he advanced, for surely they knew those great shoulders, those round black eyes, those thick lips, and that heavy jowl.

"Lozelle! It is Lozelle!" said Godwin.

"Ay," echoed Rosamund, "it is Lozelle, the double traitor, who betrayed me first to the soldiers of Saladin, and, because I would have none of his love, next to this lord Sinan."

Wulf heard, and, as Lozelle drew near to them, sprang forward with an oath and struck him across the face with his mailed hand. Instantly guards thrust themselves between them, and Sinan asked through Masouda:

"Why do you dare to strike this Frank in my presence?"

"Because, lord," answered Wulf, "he is a rogue who has brought all these troubles on our house. I challenge him to meet me in battle to the death."

"And I also," said Godwin.

"I am ready," shouted Lozelle, stung to fury by the blow.

"Then, dog, why did you try to run away when you saw our faces?" asked Wulf.

Masouda held up her hand and began to interpret, addressing Lozelle, and speaking in the first person as the "mouth" of Sinan.

"I thank you for your service who have served me before. Your messenger came, a Frank whom I knew in old days. As you had arranged it should be, I sent one of my *fedais* with soldiers to kill the men of Salah-ed-din on the ship and capture this lady who is his niece, all of which it seems has been done. The bargain that your messenger made was that the lady should be given over to you—"

Here Godwin and Wulf ground their teeth and glared at him.

"But these knights say that you stole her, their kinswoman, from them, and one of them has struck you and challenged you to single combat, which challenge you have accepted. I sanction the combat gladly, who have long desired to see two knights of the Franks fight in tourney according to their custom. I will set the course, and you shall be given the best horse in my kingdom; this knight shall ride his own. These are the conditions—the course shall be on the bridge between the inner and outer gates of the castle city, and the fight, which must be to the death, shall take place on the night of the full moon—that is, three days from now. If you are victor, we will talk of the matter of the lady for whom you bargained as a wife."

"My lord, my lord," answered Lozelle, "who can lay a lance on that terrible place in moonlight? Is it thus that you keep faith with me?"

"I can and will!" cried Wulf. "Dog, I would fight you in the gates of hell, with my soul on the hazard."

"Keep faith with yourself," said Sinan, "who said that you accepted the challenge of this knight and made no conditions, and when you have proved upon his body that his quarrel is not just, then speak of my faith with you. Nay, no more words; when this fight is done we will speak again, and not before. Let him be led to the outer castle and there given of our best. Let my great black horse be brought to him that he may gallop it to and fro upon the bridge, or where he will within the circuit of the walls, by day or by night; but see that he has no speech with this lady whom he has betrayed into my power, or with these knights his foes, nor suffer him to come into my presence. I will not talk with a man who has been struck in the face until he has washed away the blow in blood."

As Masouda finished translating, and before Lozelle could answer, the lord Sinan moved his head, whereon guards sprang forward and conducted Lozelle from the terrace.

"Farewell, Sir Thief," cried Wulf after him, "till we meet again upon the narrow bridge and there settle our account. You have fought Godwin, perhaps you will have better luck with Wulf."

Lozelle glared back at him, and, finding no answer, went on his way.

"Your report," said Sinan, addressing the tall *fedai* who all this while had lain upon his face before him, still as the form that was stretched upon the bier. "There should have been another prisoner, the great emir Hassan. Also, where is the Frankish spy?"

The *fedai* rose and spoke.

"Lord," he said, "I did your bidding. The knight who has gone steered the ship into the bay, as had been arranged. I attacked with the daylight. The soldiers of Salah-ed-din fought bravely, for the lady here saw us, and gave them time to gather, and we lost many men. We overcame and killed them all, except the prince Hassan, whom we took prisoner. I left some men to watch the ship. The crew we spared, as they were the servants of the Frank Lozelle, setting them loose upon the beach, together with a Frankish woman, who was the servant of the lady here, to find their way to the nearest city. This woman I would have killed, but the lady your captive begged for her life, saying she had come from the land of the Franks to seek her husband; so, having no orders, let her go. Yesterday morning we started for Masyaf, the prince Hassan riding in a litter together with that Frankish spy who was here a while ago, and told you of the coming of the ship. At night they slept in the same tent; I left the prince bound and set a guard, but in the morning when we looked we found him gone—how, I know not—and lying in the tent the Frankish spy, dead, with a knife-wound through his heart. Behold!" and withdrawing the cloth from the stretcher he revealed the stiff form of the spy Nicholas, who lay there dead, a look of terror frozen on his face.

"At least this one has come to an end he deserved," muttered Wulf to Godwin.

"So, having searched without avail, I came on here with the lady your prisoner and the Frank Lozelle. I have spoken."

Now when he had heard this report, forgetting his calm, Sinan arose from the cushion and stepped forward two paces. There he halted, with fury in his glittering eyes, looking like a man clothed in a black bell. For a moment he stroked his beard, and the brethren noted that on the first finger of his right hand was a ring so like to that which hung about the neck of Godwin that none could have told them apart.

"Man," Sinan said in a low voice, "what have you done? You have let the emir Hassan go, who is the most trusted friend and general of the Sultan of Damascus. By now he is there, or near it, and within six days we shall see the army of Salah-ed-din riding across the plain. Also you have not killed the crew and the Frankish woman, and they too will make report of the taking of the ship and the capture of this lady, who is of the house of Salah-ed-din and whom he seeks more earnestly than all the kingdom of the Franks. What have you to say?"

"Lord," answered the tall *fedai*, and his hand trembled as he spoke, "most mighty lord, I had no orders as to the killing of the crew from your lips, and the Frank Lozelle told me that he had agreed with you that they should be spared."

"Then, slave, he lied. He agreed with me through that dead spy that they should be slain, and do you not know that if I give no orders in such a case I mean death, not life? But what of the prince Hassan?"

"Lord, I have nothing to say. I think he must have bribed the spy named Nicholas"—and he pointed to the corpse—"to cut his bonds, and afterwards killed the man for vengeance sake, for by the body we found a heavy purse of gold. That he hated him as he hated yonder Lozelle I know, for he called them dogs and traitors in the boat; and since he could not strike them, his hands being bound, he spat in their faces, cursing them in the name of Allah. That is why, Lozelle being afraid to be near him, I set the spy Nicholas, who was a bold fellow, as a watch over him, and two soldiers outside the tent, while Lozelle and I watched the lady."

"Let those soldiers be brought," said Sinan, "and tell their story."

They were brought and stood by their captain, but they had no story to tell. They swore that they had not slept on guard, nor heard a sound, yet when morning came the prince was gone. Again the Lord of Death stroked his black beard. Then he held up the Signet before the eyes of the three men, saying: "You see the token. Go."

"Lord," said the *fedai*, "I have served you well for many years."

"Your service is ended. Go!" was the stern answer.

The *fedai* bowed his head in salute, stood for a moment as though lost in thought, then, turning suddenly, walked with a steady step to the edge of the abyss and leapt. For an instant the sunlight shone on his white and fluttering robe, then from the depths of that darksome place floated up the sound of a heavy fall, and all was still.

"Follow your captain to Paradise," said Sinan to the two soldiers, whereon one of them drew a knife to stab himself, but a *dai* sprang up, saying:

"Beast, would you shed blood before your lord? Do you not know the custom? Begone!"

So the poor men went, the first with a steady step, and the second, who was not so brave, reeling over the edge of the precipice as one might who is drunken.

"It is finished," said the dais, clapping their hands gently. "Dread lord, we thank thee for thy justice."

But Rosamund turned sick and faint, and even the brethren paled. This man was terrible indeed—if he were a man and not a devil—and they were in his power. How long would it be, they wondered, before they also were bidden to walk that gulf? Only Wulf swore in his heart that if he went by this road Sinan should go with him.

Then the corpse of the false palmer was borne away to be thrown to the eagles which always hovered over that house of death, and Sinan, having reseated himself upon the cushion, began to talk again through his "mouth" Masouda, in a low, quiet voice, as though nothing had happened to anger him.

"Lady," he said to Rosamund, "your story is known to me. Salah-ed-din seeks you, nor is it wonderful"—here his eyes glittered with a new and horrible light—"that he should desire to see such loveliness at his court, although the Frank Lozelle swore through yonder dead spy that you are precious in his eyes because of some vision that has come to him. Well, this heretic sultan is my enemy whom Satan protects, for even my *fedais* have failed to kill him, and perhaps there will be war on account of you. But have no fear, for the price at which you shall be delivered to him is higher than Salah-ed-din himself would care to pay, even for you. So, since this castle is impregnable, here you may dwell at peace, nor shall any desire be denied you. Speak, and your wishes are fulfilled."

"I desire," said Rosamund in a low, steady voice, "protection against Sir Hugh Lozelle and all men."

"It is yours. The Lord of the Mountain covers you with his own mantle."

"I desire," she went on, "that my brothers here may lodge with me, that I may not feel alone among strange people."

He thought awhile, and answered:

"Your brethren shall lodge near you in the guest castle. Why not, since from them you cannot need protection? They shall meet you at the feast and in the garden. But, lady, do you know it? They came here upon faith of some old tale of a promise made by him who went before me to ask my help to recover you from Salah-ed-din, unwitting that I was your host, not Salah-ed-din. That they should meet you thus is a chance which makes even my wisdom wonder, for in it I see omens. Now she whom they wished to rescue from Salah-ed-din, these tall brethren of yours might wish to rescue from Al-je-bal. Understand then, all of you, that from the Lord of Death there is but one escape. Yonder runs its path," and he pointed to the dizzy place whence his three servants had leapt to their doom.

"Knights," he went on, addressing Godwin and Wulf, "lead your sister hence. This evening I bid her, and you to my banquet. Till then, farewell. Woman," he added to Masouda, "accompany them. You know your duties; this lady is in your charge. Suffer that no strange man comes near her—above all, the Frank Lozelle. Dais take notice and let it be proclaimed—To these three is given the protection of the Signet in all things, save that they must not leave my walls except under sanction of the Signet—nay, in its very presence."

The dais rose, bowed, and seated themselves again. Then, guided by Masouda and preceded and followed by guards, the brethren and Rosamund walked down the terrace through the curtains into the chancel-like place where men crouched upon the ground; through the great hall were more men crouched upon the ground; through the ante-chamber where, at a word from Masouda, the guards saluted; through passages to that place where they had slept. Here Masouda halted and said:

"Lady Rose of the World, who are fitly so named, I go to prepare your chamber. Doubtless you will wish to speak awhile with these your—brothers. Speak on and fear not, for it shall be my care that you are left alone, if only for a little while. Yet walls have ears, so I counsel you use that English tongue which none of us understand in the land of Al-je-bal—not even I."

Then she bowed and went.

CHAPTER 13

# The Embassy

The brethren and Rosamund looked at each other, for having so much to say it seemed that they could not speak at all. Then with a low cry Rosamund said:

"Oh! let us thank God, Who, after all these black months of travel and of danger, has thus brought us together again," and, kneeling down there together in the guest-hall of the lord of Death, they gave thanks earnestly. Then, moving to the centre of the chamber where they thought that none would hear them, they began to speak in low voices and in English.

"Tell you your tale first, Rosamund," said Godwin.

She told it as shortly as she could, they listening without a word.

Then Godwin spoke and told her theirs. Rosamund heard it, and asked a question almost in a whisper.

"Why does that beautiful dark-eyed woman befriend you?"

"I do not know," answered Godwin, "unless it is because of the accident of my having saved her from the lion."

Rosamund looked at him and smiled a little, and Wulf smiled also. Then she said:

"Blessings be on that lion and all its tribe! I pray that she may not soon forget the deed, for it seems that our lives hang upon her favour. How strange is this story, and how desperate our case! How strange also that you should have come on hither against her counsel, which, seeing what we have, I think was honest?"

"We were led," answered Godwin. "Your father had wisdom at his death, and saw what we could not see."

"Ay," added Wulf, "but I would that it had been into some other place, for I fear this lord Al-je-bal at whose nod men hurl themselves to death."

"He is hateful," answered Rosamund, with a shudder; "worse even than the knight Lozelle; and when he fixes his eyes on me, my heart grows sick. Oh! that we could escape this place!"

"An eel in an osier trap has more chance of freedom," said Wulf gloomily. "Let us at least be thankful that we are caged together—for how long, I wonder?"

As he spoke Masouda appeared, attended by waiting women, and, bowing to Rosamund, said:

"It is the will of the Master, lady, that I lead you to the chambers that have been made ready for you, there to rest until the hour of the feast. Fear not; you shall meet your brethren then. You knights have leave, if it so pleases you, to exercise your horses in the gardens. They stand saddled in the courtyard, to which this woman will bring you," and she pointed to one of those two maids who had cleaned the armour, "and with them are guides and an escort."

"She means that we must go," muttered Godwin, adding aloud, "farewell, sister, until tonight."

So they parted, unwillingly enough. In the courtyard they found the horses, Flame and Smoke, as they had been told, also a mounted escort of four fierce-looking *fedais* and an officer. When they were in the saddle, this man, motioning to them to follow him, passed by an archway out of the courtyard into the gardens. Hence ran a broad road strewn with sand, along which he began to gallop. This road followed the gulf which encircled the citadel and inner town of Masyaf, that was, as it were, an island on a mountain top with a circumference of over three miles.

As they went, the gulf always on their right hand, holding in their horses to prevent their passing that of their guide, swift as it was, they saw another troop approaching them. This was also preceded by an officer of the Assassins, as these servants of Al-je-bal were called by the Franks, and behind him, mounted on a splendid coal black steed and followed by guards, rode a mail-clad Frankish knight.

"It is Lozelle," said Wulf, "upon the horse that Sinan promised him."

At the sight of the man a fury took hold of Godwin. With a shout of warning he drew his sword. Lozelle saw, and out leapt his blade in answer. Then sweeping past the officers who were with them and reining up their steeds, in a second they were face to face. Lozelle struck first and Godwin caught the stroke upon his buckler, but before he could return it the *fedais* of either party rushed between them and thrust them asunder.

"A pity," said Godwin, as they dragged his horse away. "Had they left us alone I think, brother, I might have saved you a moonlight duel."

"That I do not want to miss, but the chance at his head was good if those fellows would have let you take it," answered Wulf reflectively.

Then the horses began to gallop again, and they saw no more of Lozelle. Now, skirting the edge of the town, they came to the narrow, wall-less bridge that spanned the gulf between it and the outer gate and city. Here the officer wheeled his horse, and, beckoning to them to follow, charged it at full gallop. After him went the brethren—Godwin first, then Wulf. In the deep gateway on the further side they reined up. The captain turned, and began to gallop back faster than he had come—as fast, indeed, as his good beast would travel.

"Pass him!" cried Godwin, and shaking the reins loose upon the neck of Flame he called to it aloud.

Forward it sprang, with Smoke at its heels. Now they had overtaken the captain, and now even on that narrow way they had swept past him. Not an inch was there to spare between them and the abyss, and the man, brave as he was, expecting to be thrust to death, clung to his horse's mane with terror in his eyes. On the city side the brethren pulled up laughing among the astonished *fedais* who had waited for them there.

"By the Signet," cried the officer, thinking that the knights could not understand, "these are not men; they are devils, and their horses are goats of the mountains. I thought to frighten them, but it is I who was frightened, for they swept past me like eagles of the air."

"Gallant riders and swift, well-trained steeds," answered one of the *fedais*, with admiration in his voice. "The fight at the full moon will be worth our seeing."

Then once more they took the sand-strewn road and galloped on. Thrice they passed round the city thus, the last time by themselves, for the captain and the *fedais* were far outstripped. Indeed it was not until they had unsaddled Flame and Smoke in their stalls that these appeared, spurring their foaming horses. Taking no heed of them, the brethren thrust aside the grooms, dressed their steeds down, fed and watered them.

Then having seen them eat, there being no more to do, they walked back to the guest-house, hoping to find Rosamund. But they found no Rosamund, so sat down together and talked of the wonderful things that had befallen them, and of what might befall them in the future; of the mercy of Heaven also which had brought them all three together safe and sound, although it was in this house of hell. So the time passed on, till about the hour of sunset the women servants came and led them to the bath, where the black slaves washed and perfumed them, clothing them in fresh robes above their armour.

When they came out the sun was down, and the women, bearing torches in their hands, conducted them to a great and gorgeous hall which they had not seen before, built of fretted stone and having a carved and painted roof. Along one side of this hall, that was lit with cressets, were a number of round-headed open arches supported by elegant white columns, and beyond these a marble terrace with flights of steps which led to the gardens beneath. On the floor of this hall, each seated upon his cushion beside low tables inlaid with pearl sat the guests, a hundred or more, all dressed in white robes on which the red dagger was blazoned, and all as silent as though they were asleep.

When the brethren reached the place the women left them, and servants with gold chains round their necks escorted them to a dais in the middle of the hall where were many cushions, as yet unoccupied, arranged in a semicircle, of which the centre was a divan higher and more gorgeous than the rest.

Here places were pointed out to them opposite the divan, and they took their stand by them. They had not long to wait, for presently there was a sound of music, and, heralded by troops of singing women, the lord Sinan approached, walking slowly down the length of the great hall. It was a strange procession, for after the women came the aged, white robed dais, then the lord Al-je-bal himself, clad now in his blood-red, festal robe, and wearing jewels on his turban.

Around him marched four slaves, black as ebony, each of whom held a flaming torch on high, while behind followed the two gigantic guards who had stood sentry over him when he sat under the canopy of justice. As he advanced down the hall every man in it rose and prostrated himself, and so remained until their lord was seated, save only the two brethren, who stood erect like the survivors among the slain of a battle. Settling himself among the cushions at one end of the divan, he waved his hand, whereon the feasters, and with them Godwin and Wulf, sat themselves down.

Now there was a pause, while Sinan glanced along the hall impatiently. Soon the brethren saw why, since at the end opposite to that by which he had entered appeared more singing women, and after them, also escorted by four black torch-bearers, only these were women, walked Rosamund and, behind her, Masouda.

Rosamund it was without doubt, but Rosamund transformed, for now she seemed an Eastern queen. Round her head was a coronet of gems from which hung a veil, but not so as to hide her face. Jewelled, too, were her heavy plaits of hair, jewelled the rose-silk garments that she wore, the girdle at her waist, her naked, ivory arms and even the slippers on her feet. As she approached in her royal-looking beauty all the guests at that strange feast stared first at her and next at each other. Then as though by a single impulse they rose and bowed.

"What can this mean?" muttered Wulf to Godwin as they did likewise. But Godwin made no answer.

On came Rosamund, and now, behold! the lord Al-je-bal rose also and, giving her his hand, seated her by him on the divan.

"Show no surprise, Wulf," muttered Godwin, who had caught a warning look in the eyes of Masouda as she took up her position behind Rosamund.

Now the feast began. Slaves running to and fro, set dish after dish filled with strange and savoury meats, upon the little inlaid tables, those that were served to Sinan and his guests fashioned, all of them, of silver or of gold.

Godwin and Wulf ate, though not for hunger's sake, but of what they ate they remembered nothing who were watching Sinan and straining their ears to catch all he said without seeming to take note or listen. Although she strove to hide it and to appear indifferent, it was plain to them that Rosamund was much afraid. Again and again Sinan presented to her choice morsels of food, sometimes on the dishes and sometimes with his fingers, and these she was obliged to take. All the while also he devoured her with his fierce eyes so that she shrank away from him to the furthest limit of the divan.

Then wine, perfumed and spiced, was brought in golden cups, of which, having drunk, he offered to Rosamund. But she shook her head and asked Masouda for water, saying that she touched nothing stronger, and it was given her, cooled with snow. The brethren asked for water also, whereon Sinan looked at them suspiciously and demanded the reason. Godwin replied through Masouda that they were under an oath to touch no wine till they returned to their own country, having fulfilled their mission. To this he answered meaningly that it was good and right to keep oaths, but he feared that theirs would make them water-drinkers for the rest of their lives, a saying at which their hearts sank.

Now the wine that he had drunk took hold of Sinan, and he began to talk who without it was so silent.

"You met the Frank Lozelle to-day," he said to Godwin, through Masouda, "when riding in my gardens, and drew your sword on him. Why did you not kill him? Is he the better man?"

"It seems not, as once before I worsted him and I sit here unhurt, lord," answered Godwin. "Your servants thrust between and separated us."

"Ay," replied Sinan, "I remember; they had orders. Still, I would that you had killed him, the unbelieving dog, who has dared to lift his eyes to this Rose of Roses, your sister. Fear not," he went on, addressing Rosamund, "he shall offer you no more insult, who are henceforth under the protection of the Signet," and stretching out his thin, cruel-looking hand, on which gleamed the ring of power, he patted her on the arm.

All of these things Masouda translated, while Rosamund dropped her head to hide her face, though on it were not the blushes that he thought, but loathing and alarm.

Wulf glared at the Al-je-bal, whose head by good fortune was turned away, and so fierce was the rage swelling in his heart that a mist seemed to gather before his eyes, and through it this devilish chief of a people of murderers, clothed in his robe of flaming red, looked like a man steeped in blood. The thought came to him suddenly that he would make him what he looked, and his hand passed to his sword-hilt. But Godwin saw the terror in Masouda's eyes, saw Wulf's hand also, and guessed what was about to chance. With a swift movement of his arm he struck a golden dish from the table to the marble floor, then said, in a clear voice in French:

"Brother, be not so awkward; pick up that dish and answer the lord Sinan as is your right—I mean, touching the matter of Lozelle."

Wulf stooped to obey, and his mind cleared which had been so near to madness.

"I wish it not, lord," he said, "who, if I can, have your good leave to slay this fellow on the third night from now. If I fail, then let my brother take my place, but not before."

"Yes, I forgot," said Sinan. "So I decreed, and that will be a fight I wish to see. If he kills you then your brother shall meet him. And if he kills you both, then perhaps I, Sinan, will meet him—in my own fashion. Sweet lady, knowing where the course is laid, say, do you fear to see this fray?"

Rosamund's face paled, but she answered proudly:

"Why should I fear what my brethren do not fear? They are brave knights, bred to arms, and God, in Whose hand are all our destinies—even yours, O Lord of Death—He will guard the right."

When this speech was translated to him Sinan quailed a little. Then he answered:

"Lady, know that I am the Voice and Prophet of Allah—ay, and his sword to punish evil-doers and those who do not believe. Well, if what I hear is true, your brethren are skilled horsemen who even dared to pass my servant on the narrow bridge, so victory may rest with them. Tell me which of them do you love the least, for he shall first face the sword of Lozelle."

Now as Rosamund prepared herself to answer Masouda scanned her face through her half-closed eyes. But whatever she may have felt within, it remained calm and cold as though it were cut in stone.

"To me they are as one man," she said. "When one speaks, both speak. I love them equally."

"Then, Guest of my heart, it shall go as I have said. Brother Blue-eyes shall fight first, and if he falls then Brother Grey-eyes. The feast is ended, and it is my hour for prayer. Slaves, bid the people fill their cups. Lady, I pray of you, stand forward on the dais."

She obeyed, and at a sign the black slave-women gathered behind her with their flaming torches. Then Sinan rose also, and cried with a loud voice:

"Servants of Al-je-bal, pledge, I command you, this Flower of flowers, the high-born Princess of Baalbec, the niece of the Sultan, Salah-ed-din, whom men call the Great," and he sneered, "though he be not so great as I, this Queen of maids who soon—" Then, checking himself, he drank off his wine, and with a low bow presented the empty, jewelled cup to Rosamund. All the company drank also, and shouted till the hall rang, for her loveliness as she stood thus in the fierce light of the torches, aflame as these men were with the vision-breeding wine of Al-je-bal, moved them to madness.

"Queen! Queen!" they shouted. "Queen of our Master and of us all!"

Sinan heard and smiled. Then, motioning for silence, he took the hand of Rosamund, kissed it, and turning, passed from the hall preceded by his singing women and surrounded by the dais and guards.

Godwin and Wulf stepped forward to speak with Rosamund, but Masouda interposed herself between them, saying in a cold, clear voice:

"It is not permitted. Go, knights, and cool your brows in yonder garden, where sweet water runs. Your sister is my charge. Fear not, for she is guarded."

"Come," said Godwin to Wulf; "we had best obey."

So together they walked through the crowd of those feasters that remained, for most of them had already left the hall, who made way, not without reverence, for the brethren of this new star of beauty, on to the terrace, and from the terrace into the gardens. Here they stood awhile in the sweet freshness of the night, which was very grateful after the heated, perfume-laden air of the banquet; then began to wander up and down among the scented trees and flowers. The moon, floating in a cloudless sky, was almost at its full, and by her light they saw a wondrous scene. Under many of the trees and in tents set about here and there, rugs were spread, and to them came men who had drunk of the wine of the feast, and cast themselves down to sleep.

"Are they drunk?" asked Wulf.

"It would seem so," answered Godwin.

Yet these men appeared to be mad rather than drunk, for they walked steadily enough, but with wide-set, dreamy eyes; nor did they seem to sleep upon the rugs, but lay there staring at the sky and muttering with their lips, their faces steeped in a strange, unholy rapture. Sometimes they would rise and walk a few paces with outstretched arms, till the arms closed as though they clasped something invisible, to which they bent their heads to babble awhile. Then they walked back to their rugs again, where they remained silent.

As they lay thus, white-veiled women appeared, who crouched by the heads of these sleepers, murmuring into their ears, and when from time to time they sat up, gave them to drink from cups they carried, after partaking of which they lay down again and became quite senseless.

Only the women would move on to others and serve them likewise. Some of them approached the brethren with a slow, gliding motion, and offered them the cup; but they walked forward, taking no notice, whereupon the girls left them, laughing softly, and saying such things as "Tomorrow we shall meet," or "Soon you will be glad to drink and enter into Paradise."

"When the time comes doubtless we shall be glad, who have dwelt here," answered Godwin gravely, but as he spoke in French they did not understand him.

"Step out, brother," said Wulf, "for at the very sight of those rugs I grow sleepy, and the wine in the cups sparkles as bright as their bearers' eyes."

So they walked on towards the sound of a waterfall, and, when they came to it, drank, and bathed their faces and heads.

"This is better than their wine," said Wulf. Then, catching sight of more women flitting round them, looking like ghosts amid the moonlit glades, they pressed forward till they reached an open sward where there were no rugs, no sleepers, and no cupbearers.

"Now," said Wulf, halting, "tell me what does all this mean?"

"Are you deaf and blind?" asked Godwin. "Cannot you see that yonder fiend is in love with Rosamund, and means to take her, as he well may do?"

Wulf groaned aloud, then answered: "I swear that first I will send his soul to hell, even though our own must keep it company."

"Ay," answered Godwin, "I saw; you went near to it tonight. But remember, that is the end for all of us. Let us wait then to strike until we must—to save her from worse things."

"Who knows that we may find another chance? Meanwhile, meanwhile—" and again he groaned.

"Among those ornaments that hung about the waist of Rosamund I saw a jewelled knife," answered Godwin, sadly. "She can be trusted to use it if need be, and after that we can be trusted to do our worst. At least, I think that we should die in a fashion that would be remembered in this mountain."

As they spoke they had loitered towards the edge of the glade, and halting there stood silent, till presently from under the shadow of a cedar tree appeared a solitary, white robed woman.

"Let us be going," said Wulf; "here is another of them with her accursed cup."

But before they could turn the woman glided up to them and suddenly unveiled. It was Masouda.

"Follow me, brothers Peter and John," she said in a laughing whisper. "I have words to say to you. What! you will not drink? Well, it is wisest." And emptying the cup upon the ground she flitted ahead of them.

Silently as a wraith she went, now appearing in the open spaces, now vanishing, beneath the dense gloom of cedar boughs, till she reached a naked, lonely rock which stood almost upon the edge of the gulf. Opposite to this rock was a great mound such as ancient peoples reared over the bodies of their dead, and in the mound, cunningly hidden by growing shrubs, a massive door.

Masouda took a key from her girdle, and, having looked around to see that they were alone, unlocked it.

"Enter," she said, pushing them before her. They obeyed, and through the darkness within heard her close the door.

"Now we are safe awhile," she said with a sigh, "or, at least, so I think. But I will lead you to where there is more light."

Then, taking each of them by the hand, she went forward along a smooth incline, till presently they saw the moonlight, and by it discovered that they stood at the mouth of a cave which was fringed with bushes. Running up from the depths of the gulf below to this opening was a ridge or shoulder of rock, very steep and narrow.

"See the only road that leads from the citadel of Masyaf save that across the bridge," said Masouda.

"A bad one," answered Wulf, staring downward.

"Ay, yet horses trained to rocks can follow it. At its foot is the bottom of the gulf, and a mile or more away to the left a deep cleft which leads to the top of the mountain and to freedom. Will you not take it now? By tomorrow's dawn you might be far away."

"And where would the lady Rosamund be?" asked Wulf.

"In the harem of the lord Sinan—that is, very soon," she answered, coolly.

"Oh, say it not!" he exclaimed, clasping her arm, while Godwin leaned back against the wall of the cave.

"Why should I hide the truth? Have you no eyes to see that he is enamoured of her loveliness—like others? Listen; a while ago my master Sinan chanced to lose his queen—how, we need not ask, but it is said that she wearied him. Now, as he must by law, he mourns for her a month, from full moon to full moon. But on the day after the full moon—that is, the third morning from now—he may wed again, and I think there will be a marriage. Till then, however, your sister is as safe as though she yet sat at home in England before Salah-ed-din dreamed his dream."

"Therefore," said Godwin, "within that time she must either escape or die."

"There is a third way," answered Masouda, shrugging her shoulders. "She might stay and become the wife of Sinan."

Wulf muttered something between his teeth, then stepped towards her threateningly, saying:

"Rescue her, or—"

"Stand back, pilgrim John," she said, with a laugh. "If I rescue her, which indeed would be hard, it will not be for fear of your great sword."

"What, then, will avail, Masouda?" asked Godwin in a sad voice. "To promise you money would be useless, even if we could."

"I am glad that you spared me that insult," she replied with flashing eyes, "for then there had been an end. Yet," she added more humbly, "seeing my home and business, and what I appear to be," and she glanced at her dress and the empty cup in her hand, "it had not been strange. Now hear me, and forget no word. At present you are in favour with Sinan, who believes you to be the brothers of the lady Rosamund, not her lovers; but from the moment he learns the truth your doom is sealed. Now what the Frank Lozelle knows, that the Al-je-bal may know at any time—and will know, if these should meet.

"Meanwhile, you are free; so to-morrow, while you ride about the garden, as you will do, take note of the tall rock that stands without, and how to reach it from any point, even in the dark. To-morrow, also, when the moon is up, they will lead you to the narrow bridge, to ride your horses to and fro there, that they may learn not to fear it in that light. When you have stabled them go into the gardens and come hither unobserved, as the place being so far away you can do. The guards will let you pass, thinking only that you desire to drink a cup of wine with some fair friend, as is the custom of our guests. Enter this cave—here is the key," and she handed it to Wulf, "and if I be not there, await me. Then I will tell you my plan, if I have any, but until then I must scheme and think. Now it grows late—go."

"And you, Masouda," said Godwin, doubtfully; "how will you escape this place?"

"By a road you do not know of, for I am mistress of the secrets of this city. Still, I thank you for your thought of me. Go, I say, and lock the door behind you."

So they went in silence, doing as she bade them, and walked back through the gardens, that now seemed empty enough, to the stable-entrance of the guest-house, where the guards admitted them without question.

That night the brethren slept together in one bed, fearing that if they lay separate they might be searched in their sleep and not awake. Indeed, it seemed to them that, as before, they heard footsteps and voices in the darkness.

Next morning, when they had breakfasted, they loitered awhile, hoping to win speech with Rosamund, or sight of her, or at the least that Masouda would come to them; but they saw no Rosamund, and no Masouda came. At length an officer appeared, and beckoned to them to follow him. So they followed, and were led through the halls and passages to the terrace of justice, where Sinan, clad in his black robe, sat as before beneath a canopy in the midst of the sun-lit marble floor. There, too, beside him, also beneath the canopy and gorgeously apparelled, sat Rosamund. They strove to advance and speak with her, but guards came between them, pointing out a place where they must stand a few yards away. Only Wulf said in a loud voice, in English:

"Tell us, Rosamund, is it well with you?" Lifting her pale face, she smiled and nodded.

Then, at the bidding of Sinan, Masouda commanded them to be silent, saying that it was not lawful for them to speak to the Lord of the Mountain, or his Companion, unless they were first bidden so to do. So, having learnt what they wished to know, they were silent.

Now some of the dais drew near the canopy, and consulted with their master on what seemed to be a great matter, for their faces were troubled. Presently he gave an order, whereon they resumed their seats and messengers left the terrace. When they appeared again, in their company were three noble-looking Saracens, who were accompanied by a retinue of servants and wore green turbans, showing that they were descendants of the Prophet. These men, who seemed weary with long travel, marched up the terrace with a proud mien, not looking at the dais or any one until they saw the brethren standing side by side, at whom they stared a little. Next they caught sight of Rosamund sitting in the shadow of the canopy, and bowed to her, but of the Al-je-bal they took no notice.

"Who are you, and what is your pleasure?" asked Sinan, after he had eyed them awhile. "I am the ruler of this country. These are my ministers," and he pointed to the dais, "and here is my sceptre," and he touched the blood red dagger broidered on his robe of black.

Now that Sinan had declared himself the embassy bowed to him, courteously enough. Then their spokesman answered him.

"That sceptre we know; it has been seen afar. Twice already we have cut down its bearers even in the tent of our master. Lord of Murder, we acknowledge the emblem of murder, and we bow to you whose title is the Great Murderer. As for our mission, it is this. We are the ambassadors of Salah-ed-din, Commander of the Faithful, Sultan of the East; in these papers signed with his signet are our credentials, if you would read them."

"So," answered Sinan, "I have heard of that chief. What is his will with me?"

"This, Al-je-bal. A Frank in your pay, and a traitor, has betrayed to you a certain lady, niece of Salah-ed-din, the princess of Baalbec, whose father was a Frankish noble named D'Arcy, and who herself is named Rose of the World. The Sultan, Salah-ed-din, having been informed of this matter by his servant, the prince Hassan, who escaped from your soldiers, demands that this lady, his niece, be delivered to him forthwith, and with her the head of the Frank Lozelle."

"The head of the Frank Lozelle he may have if he will after to-morrow night. The lady I keep," snarled Sinan.

"What then?"

"Then, Al-je-bal, in the name of Salah-ed-din, we declare war on you—war till this high place of yours is pulled stone from stone; war till your tribe be dead, till the last man, woman, and child be slain, until your carcass is tossed to the crows to feed on."

Now Sinan rose in fury and rent at his beard.

"Go back," he said, "and tell that dog you name a sultan, that low as he is, the humble-born son of Ayoub, I, Al-je-bal, do him an honour that he does not observe. My queen is dead, and two days from now, when my month of mourning is expired, I shall take to wife his niece, the princess of Baalbec, who sits here beside me, my bride-elect."

At these words Rosamund, who had been listening intently, started like one who has been stung by a snake, put her hands before her face and groaned.

"Princess," said the ambassador, who was watching her, "you seem to understand our language; is this your will, to mate your noble blood with that of the heretic chief of the Assassins?"

"Nay, nay!" she cried. "It is no will of mine, who am a helpless prisoner and by faith a Christian. If my uncle Salah-ed-din is indeed as great as I have heard, then let him show his power and deliver me, and with me these my brethren, the knights Sir Godwin and Sir Wulf."

"So you speak Arabic," said Sinan. "Good; our loving converse will be easier, and for the rest—well, the whims of women change. Now, you messengers of Salah-ed-din, begone, lest I send you on a longer journey, and tell your master that if he dares to lift his standards against my walls my *fedais* shall speak with him. By day and by night, not for one moment shall he be safe. Poison shall lurk in his cup and a dagger in his bed. Let him kill a hundred of them, and another hundred shall appear. His most trusted guards shall be his executioners. The women in his harem shall bring him to his doom—ay, death shall be in the very air he breathes. If he would escape it, therefore, let him hide himself within the walls of his city of Damascus, or amuse himself with wars against the mad Cross-worshippers, and leave me to live in peace with this lady whom I have chosen."

"Great words, worthy of the Great Assassin," said the ambassador.

"Great words in truth, which shall be followed by great deeds. What chance has this lord of yours against a nation sworn to obey to the death? You smile? Then come hither you—and you." And he summoned two of his dais by name.

They rose and bowed before him.

"Now, my worthy servants," he said, "show these heretic dogs how you obey, that their master may learn the power of your master. You are old and weary of life. Begone, and await me in Paradise."

The old men bowed again, trembling a little. Then, straightening themselves, without a word they ran side by side and leapt into the abyss.

"Has Salah-ed-din servants such as these?" asked Sinan in the silence that followed. "Well, what they have done, all would do, if I bid them slay him. Back, now; and, if you will, take these Franks with you, who are my guests, that they may bear witness of what you have seen, and of the state in which you left their sister. Translate to the knights, woman."

So Masouda translated. Then Godwin answered through her.

"We understand little of this matter, who are ignorant of your tongue, but, O Al-je-bal, ere we leave your sheltering roof we have a quarrel to settle with the man Lozelle. After that, with your permission, we will go, but not before."

Now Rosamund sighed as if in relief, and Sinan answered:

"As you will; so be it," adding, "Give these envoys food and drink before they go."

But their spokesman answered: "We partake not of the bread and salt of murderers, lest we should become of their fellowship. Al-je-bal, we depart, but within a week we appear again in the company of ten thousand spears, and on one of them shall your head be set. Your safe-conduct guards us till the sunset. After that, do your worst, as we do ours. High Princess, our counsel to you is that you slay yourself and so gain immortal honour."

Then, bowing to her one by one, they turned and marched down the terrace followed by their servants.

Now Sinan waved his hand and the court broke up, Rosamund leaving it first, accompanied by Masouda and escorted by guards, after which the brethren were commanded to depart also.

So they went, talking earnestly of all these things, but save in God finding no hope at all.

## Chapter 14

# The Combat on the Bridge

"Saladin will come," said Wulf the hopeful, and from the high place where they stood he pointed to the plain beneath, across which a band of horsemen moved at full gallop. "Look; yonder goes his embassy."

"Ay," answered Godwin, "he will come, but, I fear me, too late."

"Yes, brother, unless we go to meet him. Masouda has promised."

"Masouda," sighed Godwin. "Ah! to think that so much should hang upon the faithfulness of one woman."

"It does not hang on her," said Wulf; "it hangs on Fate, who writes with her finger. Come, let us ride."

So, followed by their escort, they rode in the gardens, taking note, without seeming to do so, of the position of the tall rock, and of how it could be approached from every side. Then they went in again and waited for some sign or word of Rosamund, but in vain. That night there was no feast, and their meal was brought to them in the guest-house. While they sat at it Masouda appeared for a moment to tell them that they had leave to ride the bridge in the moonlight, and that their escort would await them at a certain hour.

The brethren asked if their sister Rosamund was not coming to dine with them. Masouda answered that as the queen-elect of the Al-je-bal it was not lawful that she should eat with any other men, even her brothers. Then as she passed out, stumbling as though by accident, she brushed against Godwin, and muttered: "Remember, to-night," and was gone.

When the moon had been up an hour the officer of their escort appeared, and led them to their horses, which were waiting, and they rode away to the castle bridge. As they approached it they saw Lozelle departing on his great black stallion, which was in a lather of foam. It seemed that he also had made trial of that perilous path, for the people, of whom there were many gathered there, clapped their hands and shouted, "Well ridden, Frank! well ridden!"

Now, Godwin leading on Flame, they faced the bridge and walked their horses over it. Nor did these hang back, although they snorted a little at the black gulf on either side. Next they returned at a trot, then over again, and yet again at a canter and a gallop, sometimes together and sometimes singly. Lastly, Wulf made Godwin halt in the middle of the bridge and galloped down upon him at speed, till within a lance's length. Then suddenly he checked his horse, and while his audience shouted, wheeled it around on its hind legs, its fore-hoofs beating the air, and galloped back again, followed by Godwin.

"All went well," Wulf said as they rode to the castle, "and nobler or more gentle horses were never crossed by men. I have good hopes for to-morrow night."

"Ay, brother, but I had no sword in my hand. Be not over confident, for Lozelle is desperate and a skilled fighter, as I know who have stood face to face with him. More over, his black stallion is well trained, and has more weight than ours. Also, yonder is a fearsome place on which to ride a course, and one of which none but that devil Sinan would have thought."

"I shall do my best," answered Wulf, "and if I fall, why, then, act upon your own counsel. At least, let him not kill both of us."

Having stabled their horses the brethren wandered into the garden, and, avoiding the cup-bearing women and the men they plied with their drugged drink, drew by a roundabout road to the tall rock. Then, finding themselves alone, they unlocked the door, and slipping through it, locked it again on the further side and groped their way to the moonlit mouth of the cave. Here they stood awhile studying the descent of the gulf as best they could in that light, till suddenly Godwin, feeling a hand upon his shoulder, started round to find himself face to face with Masouda.

"How did you come?" he asked.

"By a road in which is your only hope," she answered. "Now, Sir Godwin, waste no words, for my time is short, but if you think that you can trust me—and this is for you to judge—give me the Signet which hangs about your neck. If not, go back to the castle and do your best to save the lady Rosamund and yourselves."

Thrusting down his hand between his mail shirt and his breast, Godwin drew out the ancient ring, carved with the mysterious signs and veined with the emblem of the dagger, and handed it to Masouda.

"You trust indeed," she said with a little laugh, as, after scanning it closely by the light of the moon and touching her forehead with it, she hid it in her bosom.

"Yes, lady," he answered, "I trust you, though why you should risk so much for us I do not know."

"Why? Well, perhaps for hate's sake, for Sinan does not rule by love; perhaps because, being of a wild blood, I am willing to set my life at hazard, who care not if I win or die; perhaps because you saved me from the lioness. What is it to you, Sir Godwin, why a certain woman-spy of the Assassins, whom in your own land you would spit on, chooses to do this or that?"

She ceased and stood before him with heaving breast and flashing eyes, a mysterious white figure in the moonlight, most beautiful to see.

Godwin felt his heart stir and the blood flow to his brow, but before he could speak Wulf broke in, saying:

"You bade us spare words, lady Masouda, so tell us what we must do."

"This," she answered, becoming calm again. "Tomorrow night about this hour you fight Lozelle upon the narrow way. That is certain, for all the city talks of it, and, whatever chances, Al-je-bal will not deprive them of the spectacle of this fray to the death. Well, you may fall, though that man at heart is a coward, which you are not, for here courage alone will avail nothing, but rather skill and horsemanship and trick of war. If so, then Sir Godwin fights him, and of this business none can tell the end. Should both of you go down, then I will do my best to save your lady and take her to Salah-ed-din, with whom she will be safe, or if I cannot save her I will find her a means to save herself by death."

"You swear that?" said Wulf.

"I have said it; it is enough," she answered impatiently.

"Then I face the bridge and the knave Lozelle with a light heart," said Wulf again, and Masouda went on.

"Now if you conquer, Sir Wulf, or if your fall and your brother conquers, both of you—or one of you, as it may happen—must gallop back at full speed toward the stable gate that lies more than a mile from the castle bridge. Mounted as you are, no horse can keep pace with you, nor must you stop at the gate, but ride on, ride like the wind till you reach this place. The gardens will be empty of feasters and of cupbearers, who with every soul within the city will have gathered on the walls and on the house-tops to see the fray. There is but one fear—by then a guard may be set before this mound, seeing that Salah-ed-din has declared war upon Al-je-bal, and though yonder road is known to few, it is a road, and sentries may watch here. If so, you must cut them down or be cut down, and bring your story to an end. Sir Godwin, here is another key that you may use if you are alone. Take it."

He did so, and she continued:

"Now if both of you, or one of you, win through to this cave, enter with your horses, lock the door, bar it, and wait. It may be I will join you here with the princess. But if I do not come by the dawn and you are not discovered and overwhelmed—which should not be, seeing that one man can hold that door against many—then know that the worst has happened, and fly to Salah-ed-din and tell him of this road, by which he may take vengeance upon his foe Sinan. Only then, I pray you, doubt not that I have done my best, who if I fail must die—most horribly. Now, farewell, until we meet again or—do not meet again. Go; you know the road."

They turned to obey, but when they had gone a few paces Godwin looked round and saw Masouda watching them. The moonlight shone full upon her face, and by it he saw also that tears were running from her dark and tender eyes. Back he came again, and with him Wulf, for that sight drew them. Down he bent before her till his knee touched the ground, and, taking her hand, he kissed it, and said in his gentle voice:

"Henceforth through life, through death, we serve two ladies," and what he did Wulf did also.

"Mayhap," she answered sadly; "two ladies—but one love."

Then they went, and, creeping through the bushes to the path, wandered about awhile among the revellers and came to the guest-house safely.

Once more it was night, and high above the mountain fortress of Masyaf shone the full summer moon, lighting crag and tower as with some vast silver lamp. Forth from the guest-house gate rode the brethren, side by side upon their splendid steeds, and the moon-rays sparkled on their coats of mail, their polished bucklers, blazoned with the cognizance of a grinning skull, their close-fitting helms, and the points of the long, tough lances that had been given them. Round them rode their escort, while in front and behind went a mob of people.

The nation of the Assassins had thrown off its gloom this night, for the while it was no longer oppressed even by the fear of attack from Saladin, its mighty foe. To death it was accustomed; death was its watchword; death in many dreadful forms its daily bread. From the walls of Masyaf, day by day, *fedais* went out to murder this great one, or that great one, at the bidding of their lord Sinan.

For the most part they came not back again; they waited week by week, month by month, year by year, till the moment was ripe, then gave the poisoned cup or drove home the dagger, and escaped or were slain. Death waited them abroad, and if they failed, death waited them at home. Their dreadful caliph was himself a sword of death. At his will they hurled themselves from towers or from precipices; to satisfy his policy they sacrificed their wives and children. And their reward—in life, the drugged cup and voluptuous dreams; after it, as they believed, a still more voluptuous paradise.

All forms of human agony and doom were known to this people; but now they were promised an unfamiliar sight, that of Frankish knights slaying each other in single combat beneath the silent moon, tilting at full gallop upon a narrow place where many might hesitate to walk, and—oh, joy!—falling perchance, horse and rider together, into the depths below. So they were happy, for to them this was a night of festival, to be followed by a morrow of still greater festival, when their sultan and their god took to himself this stranger beauty as a wife. Doubtless, too, he would soon weary of her, and they would be called together to see her cast from some topmost tower and hear her frail bones break on the cruel rocks below, or—as had happened to the last queen—to watch her writhe out her life in the pangs of poison upon a charge of sorcery. It was indeed a night of festival, a night filled full of promise of rich joys to come.

On rode the brethren, with stern, impassive faces, but wondering in their hearts whether they would live to see another dawn. The shouting crowd surged round them, breaking through the circle of their guards. A hand was thrust up to Godwin; in it was a letter, which he took and read by the bright moonlight. It was written in English, and brief:

"I cannot speak with you. God be with you both, my brothers, God and the spirit of my father. Strike home, Wulf, strike home, Godwin, and fear not for me who will guard myself. Conquer or die, and in life or death, await me. To-morrow, in the flesh, or in the spirit, we will talk—Rosamund."

Godwin handed the paper to Wulf, and, as he did so, saw that the guards had caught its bearer, a withered, grey-haired woman. They asked her some questions, but she shook her head. Then they cast her down, trampled the life out of her beneath their horses' hoofs, and went on laughing. The mob laughed also.

"Tear that paper up," said Godwin. Wulf did so, saying:

"Our Rosamund has a brave heart. Well, we are of the same blood, and will not fail her."

Now they were come to the open space in front of the narrow bridge, where, tier on tier, the multitude were ranged, kept back from its centre by lines of guards. On the flat roofed houses also they were crowded thick as swarming bees, on the circling walls, and on the battlements that protected the far end of the bridge, and the houses of the outer city. Before the bridge was a low gateway, and upon its roof sat the Al-je-bal, clad in his scarlet robe of festival, and by his side, the moonlight gleaming on her jewels, Rosamund. In front, draped in a rich garment, a dagger of gems in her dark hair, stood the interpreter or "mouth" Masouda, and behind were dais and guards.

The brethren rode to the space before the arch and halted, saluting with their pennoned spears. Then from the further side advanced another procession, which, opening, revealed the knight Lozelle riding on his great black horse, and a huge man and a fierce he seemed in his armour.

"What!" he shouted, glowering at them. "Am I to fight one against two? Is this your chivalry?"

"Nay, nay, Sir Traitor," answered Wulf. "Nay, nay betrayer of Christian maids to the power of the heathen dog; you have fought Godwin, now it is the turn of Wulf. Kill Wulf and Godwin remains. Kill Godwin and God remains. Knave, you look your last upon the moon."

Lozelle heard, and seemed to go mad with rage, or fear, or both.

"Lord Sinan," he shouted in Arabic, "this is murder. Am I, who have done you so much service, to be butchered for your pleasure by the lovers of that woman, whom you would honour with the name of wife?"

Sinan heard, and stared at him with dull, angry eyes.

"Ay, you may stare," went on the maddened Lozelle, "but it is true—they are her lovers, not her brothers. Would men take so much pains for a sister's sake, think you? Would they swim into this net of yours for a sister's sake?"

Sinan held up his hand for silence.

"Let the lots be cast," he said, "for whatever these men are, this fight must go on, and it shall be fair."

So a *dai*, standing by himself, cast lots upon the ground, and having read them, announced that Lozelle must run the first course from the further side of the bridge. Then one took his bridle to lead him across. As he passed the brethren he grinned in their faces and said:

"At least this is sure, you also look your last upon the moon. I am avenged already. The bait that hooked me is a meal for yonder pike, and he will kill you both before her eyes to whet his appetite."

But the brethren answered nothing.

The black horse of Lozelle grew dim in the distance of the moonlit bridge, and vanished beneath the farther archway that led to the outer city. Then a herald cried, Masouda translating his words, which another herald echoed from beyond the gulf.

"Thrice will the trumpets blow. At the third blast of the trumpets the knights shall charge and meet in the centre of the bridge. Thenceforward they may fight as it pleases them, ahorse, or afoot, with lance, with sword, or with dagger, but to the vanquished no mercy will be shown. If he be brought living from the bridge, living he shall be cast into the gulf. Hear the decree of the Al-je-bal!"

Then Wulf's horse was led forward to the entrance of the bridge, and from the further side was led forward the horse of Lozelle.

"Good luck, brother," said Godwin, as he passed him. "Would that I rode this course instead of you."

"Your turn may come, brother," answered the grim Wulf, as he set his lance in rest.

Now from some neighbouring tower pealed out the first long blast of trumpets, and dead silence fell on all the multitude. Grooms came forward to look to girth and bridle and stirrup strap, but Wulf waved them back.

"I mind my own harness," he said.

The second blast blew, and he loosened the great sword in its scabbard, that sword which had flamed in his forbear's hand upon the turrets of Jerusalem.

"Your gift," he cried back to Rosamund, and her answer came clear and sweet:

"Bear it like your fathers, Wulf. Bear it as it was last borne in the hall at Steeple."

Then there was another silence—a silence long and deep. Wulf looked at the white and narrow ribbon of the bridge, looked at the black gulf on either side, looked at the blue sky above, in which floated the great globe of the golden moon. Then he leant forward and patted Smoke upon the neck.

For the third time the trumpets blew, and from either end of that bridge, two hundred paces long, the knights flashed towards each other like living bolts of steel. The multitude rose to watch; even Sinan rose. Only Rosamund sat still, gripping the cushions with her hands. Hollow rang the hoofs of the horses upon the stonework, swifter and swifter they flew, lower and lower bent the knights upon their saddles. Now they were near, and now they met. The spears seemed to shiver, the horses to hustle together on the narrow way and overhang its edge, then on came the black horse towards the inner city, and on sped Smoke towards the further gulf.

"They have passed! They have passed!" roared the multitude.

Look! Lozelle approached, reeling in his saddle, as well he might, for the helm was torn from his head and blood ran from his skull where the lance had grazed it.

"Too high, Wulf; too high," said Godwin sadly. "But oh! if those laces had but held!"

Soldiers caught the horse and turned it.

"Another helm!" cried Lozelle.

"Nay," answered Sinan; "yonder knight has lost his shield. New lances—that is all."

So they gave him a fresh lance, and, presently, at the blast of the trumpets again the horses were seen speeding together over the narrow way. They met, and lo! Lozelle, torn from his saddle, but still clinging to the reins, was flung backwards, far backwards, to fall on the stonework of the bridge. Down, too, beneath the mighty shock went his black horse, a huddled heap, and lay there struggling.

"Wulf will fall over him!" cried Rosamund. But Smoke did not fall; the stallion gathered itself together—the moonlight shone so clear that every watcher saw it—and since stop it could not, leapt straight over the fallen black horse—ay, and over the rider beyond—and sped on in its stride. Then the black found its feet again and galloped forward to the further gate, and Lozelle also found his feet and turned to run.

"Stand! Stand, coward!" yelled ten thousand voices, and, hearing them, he drew his sword and stood.

Within three great strides Wulf dragged his charger to its haunches, then wheeled it round.

"Charge him!" shouted the multitude; but Wulf remained seated, as though unwilling to attack a horseless man. Next he sprang from his saddle, and accompanied by the horse Smoke, which followed him as a dog follows its master, walked slowly towards Lozelle, as he walked casting away his lance and drawing the great, cross-hilted sword.

Again the silence fell, and through it rang the cry of Godwin:

"A D'Arcy! A D'Arcy!"

"A D'Arcy! A D'Arcy!" came back Wulf's answer from the bridge, and his voice echoed thin and hollow in the spaces of the gulf. Yet they rejoiced to hear it, for it told them that he was sound and strong.

Wulf had no shield and Lozelle had no helm—the fight was even. They crouched opposite each other, the swords flashed aloft in the moonlight; from far away came the distant clank of steel, a soft, continual clamour of iron on iron. A blow fell on Wulf's mail, who had nought wherewith to guard himself, and he staggered back. Another blow, another, and another, and back, still back he reeled—back to the edge of the bridge, back till he struck against the horse that stood behind him, and, resting there a moment, as it seemed, regained his balance.

Then there was a change. Look, he rushed forward, wielding the great blade in both hands. The stroke lit upon Lozelle's shield and seemed to shear it in two, for in that stillness all could hear the clang of its upper half as it fell upon the stones. Beneath the weight of it he staggered, sank to his knee, gained his feet again, and in his turn gave back. Yes, now it was Lozelle who rocked and reeled. Ay, by St. Chad! Lozelle who went down beneath that mighty blow which missed the head but fell upon his shoulder, and lay there like a log, till presently the moonlight shone upon his mailed hand stretched upward in a prayer for mercy. From house-top and terrace wall, from soaring gates and battlements, the multitude of the people of the Assassins gathered on either side the gulf broke into a roar that beat up the mountain sides like a voice of thunder. And the roar shaped itself to these words:

"Kill him! kill him! kill him!"

Sinan held up his hand, and a sudden silence fell. Then he, too, screamed in his thin voice:

"Kill him! He is conquered!"

But the great Wulf only leaned upon the cross-handle of his brand, and looked at the fallen foe. Presently he seemed to speak with him; then Lozelle lifted the blade that lay beside him and gave it to him in token of surrender. Wulf handled it awhile, shook it on high in triumph, and whirled it about his head till it shone in the moonlight. Next, with a shout he cast it from him far into the gulf, where it was seen for a moment, an arc of gleaming light, and the next was gone.

Now, taking no more heed of the conquered knight, Wulf turned and began to walk towards his horse.

Scarcely was his back towards him when Lozelle was on his feet again, a dagger in his hand.

"Look behind you!" yelled Godwin; but the spectators, pleased that the fight was not yet done, broke into a roar of cheers. Wulf heard and swung round. As he faced Lozelle the dagger struck him on the breast, and well must it have been for him that his mail was good. To use his sword he had neither space nor time, but ere the next stroke could fall Wulf's arms were about Lozelle, and the fight for life begun.

To and fro they reeled and staggered, whirling round and round, till none could tell which of them was Wulf or which his foe. Now they were on the edge of the abyss, and, in that last dread strain for mastery, seemed to stand there still as stone. Then one man began to bend down. See! his head hung over. Further and further he bent, but his arms could not be loosened.

"They will both go!" cried the multitude in their joy.

Look! A dagger flashed. Once, twice, thrice it gleamed, and those wrestlers fell apart, while from deep down in the gulf came the thud of a fallen body.

"Which—oh, which?" cried Rosamund from her battlement.

"Sir Hugh Lozelle," answered Godwin in a solemn voice.

Then the head of Rosamund fell forward on her breast, and for a while she seemed to sleep.

Wulf went to his horse, turned it about on the bridge, and throwing his arm around its neck, rested for a space. Then he mounted and walked slowly towards the inner gate. Pushing through the guard and officers, Godwin rode out to meet him.

"Bravely done, brother," he said, when they came face to face. "Say, are you hurt?"

"Bruised and shaken—no more," answered Wulf.

"A good beginning, truly. Now for the rest," said Godwin. Then he glanced over his shoulder, and added, "See, they are leading Rosamund away, but Sinan remains, to speak with you doubtless, for Masouda beckons."

"What shall we do?" asked Wulf. "Make a plan, brother, for my head swims."

"Hear what he has to say. Then, as your horse is not wounded either, ride for it when I give the signal as Masouda bade us. There is no other way. Pretend that you are wounded."

So, Godwin leading, while the multitude roared a welcome to the conquering Wulf who had borne himself so bravely for their pleasure, they rode to the mouth of the bridge and halted in the little space before the archway. There Al-je-bal spoke by Masouda.

"A noble fray," he said. "I did not think that Franks could fight so well; Say, Sir Knight, will you feast with me in my palace?"

"I thank you, lord," answered Wulf, "but I must rest while my brother tends my hurts," and he pointed to blood upon his mail. "To-morrow, if it pleases you."

Sinan stared at them and stroked his beard, while they trembled, waiting for the word of fate.

It came.

"Good. So be it. To-morrow I wed the lady Rose of Roses, and you two—her brothers—shall give her to me, as is fitting," and he sneered. "Then also you shall receive the reward of valour—a great reward, I promise you."

While he spoke Godwin, staring upward, had noted a little wandering cloud floating across the moon. Slowly it covered it, and the place grew dim.

"Now," he whispered, and bowing to the Al-je-bal, they pushed their horses through the open gate where the mob closed in on them, thus for a little while holding back the escort from following on their heels. They spoke to Flame and Smoke, and the good horses plunged onward side by side, separating the crowd as the prows of boats separate the water. In ten paces it grew thin, in thirty it was behind them, for all folk were gathered about the archway where they could see, and none beyond. Forward they cantered, till the broad road turned to the left, and in that faint light they were hidden.

"Away!" said Godwin, shaking his reins.

Forward leapt the horses at speed. Again Godwin turned, taking that road which ran round the city wall and through the gardens, leaving the guest-castle to the left, whereas their escort followed that whereby they had come, which passed along the main street of the inner town, thinking that they were ahead of them. Three minutes more and they were in the lonely gardens, in which that night no women wandered and no neophytes dreamed in the pavilions.

"Wulf," said Godwin, as they swept forward, skimming the turf like swallows, "draw your sword and be ready. Remember the secret cave may be guarded, and, if so, we must kill or be killed."

Wulf nodded, and next instant two long blades flashed in the moonlight, for the little cloud had passed away. Within a hundred paces of them rose the tall rock, but between it and the mound were two mounted guards. These heard the beating of horses' hoofs, and wheeling about, stared to see two armed knights sweeping down upon them like a whirlwind. They called to them to stop, hesitating, then rode forward a few paces, as though wondering whether this were not a vision.

In a moment the brethren were on them. The soldiers lifted their lances, but ere they could thrust the sword of Godwin had caught one between neck and shoulder and sunk to his breast bone, while the sword of Wulf, used as a spear, had pierced the other through and through, so that those men fell dead by the door of the mound, never knowing who had slain them.

The brethren pulled upon their bridles and spoke to Flame and Smoke, halting them within a score of yards. Then they wheeled round and sprang from their saddles. One of the dead guards still held his horses's reins, and the other beast stood by snorting. Godwin caught it before it stirred, then, holding all four of them, threw the key to Wulf and bade him unlock the door. Soon it was done, although he staggered at the task; then he held the horses, while one by one Godwin led them in, and that without trouble, for the beasts thought that this was but a cave-hewn stable of a kind to which they were accustomed.

"What of the dead men?" said Wulf.

"They had best keep us company," answered Godwin, and, running out, he carried in first one and then the other.

"Swift!" he said, as he threw down the second corpse. "Shut the door. I caught sight of horsemen riding through the trees. Nay, they saw nothing."

So they locked the massive door and barred it, and with beating hearts waited in the dark, expecting every moment to hear soldiers battering at its timbers. But no sound came; the searchers, if such they were, had passed on to seek elsewhere.

Now while Wulf made shift to fasten up the horses near the mouth of the cave, Godwin gathered stones as large as he could lift, and piled them up against the door, till they knew that it would take many men an hour or more to break through.

For this door was banded with iron and set fast in the living rock.

## Chapter 15

# The Flight to Emesa

Then came the weariest time of waiting the brethren had ever known, or were to know, although at first they did not feel it so long and heavy. Water trickled from the walls of this cave, and Wulf, who was parched with thirst, gathered it in his hands and drank till he was satisfied. Then he let it run upon his head to cool its aching; and Godwin bathed such of his brother's hurts and bruises as could be come at, for he did not dare to remove the hauberk, and so gave him comfort.

When this was done, and he had looked to the saddles and trappings of the horses, Wulf told of all that had passed between him and Lozelle on the bridge. How at the first onset his spear had caught in the links of and torn away the head-piece of his foe, who, if the lacings had not burst, would have been hurled to death, while that of Lozelle struck his buckler fair and shattered on it, rending it from his arm. How they pushed past each other, and for a moment the fore hoofs of Smoke hung over the abyss, so that he thought he was surely sped: How at the next course Lozelle's spear passed beneath his arm, while his, striking full upon Sir Hugh's breast, brought down the black horse and his rider as though a thunderbolt had smitten them, and how Smoke, that could not check its furious pace, leapt over them, as a horse leaps a-hunting: How he would not ride down Lozelle, but dismounted to finish the fray in knightly fashion, and, being shieldless, received the full weight of the great sword upon his mail, so that he staggered back and would have fallen had he not struck against the horse.

Then he told of the blows that followed, and of his last that wounded Lozelle, shearing through his mail and felling him as an ox is felled by the butcher: How also, when he sprang forward to kill him, this mighty and brutal man had prayed for mercy, prayed it in the name of Christ and of their own mother, whom as a child he knew in Essex: How he could not slaughter him, being helpless, but turned away, saying that he left him to be dealt with by Al-je-bal, whereupon this traitorous dog sprang up and strove to knife him. He told also of their last fearful struggle, and how, shaken as he was by the blow upon his back, although the point of the dagger had not pierced his mail, he strove with Lozelle, man to man; till at length his youth, great natural strength, and the skill he had in wrestling, learnt in many a village bout at home, enabled him to prevail, and, while they hung together on the perilous edge of the gulf, to free his right hand, draw his poniard, and make an end.

"Yet," added Wulf, "never shall I forget the look of that man's eyes as he fell backwards, or the whistling scream which came from his pierced throat."

"At least there is a rogue the less in the world, although he was a brave one in his own knavish fashion," answered Godwin. "Moreover, my brother," he added, placing his arm about Wulf's neck, "I am glad it fell to you to fight him, for at the last grip your might overcame, where I, who am not so strong, should have failed. Further, I think you did well to show mercy, as a good knight should; that thereby you have gained great honour, and that if his spirit can see through the darkness, our dead uncle is proud of you now, as I am, my brother."

"I thank you," replied Wulf simply; "but, in this hour of torment, who can think of such things as honour gained?"

Then, lest he should grow stiff, who was sorely bruised beneath his mail, they began to walk up and down the cave from where the horses stood to where the two dead Assassins lay by the door, the faint light gleaming upon their stern, dark features. Ill company they seemed in that silent, lonely place.

The time crept on; the moon sank towards the mountains.

"What if they do not come?" asked Wulf.

"Let us wait to think of it till dawn," answered Godwin.

Again they walked the length of the cave and back.

"How can they come, the door being barred?" asked Wulf.

"How did Masouda come and go?" answered Godwin. "Oh, question me no more; it is in the hand of God."

"Look," said Wulf, in a whisper. "Who stand yonder at the end of the cave—there by the dead men?"

"Their spirits, perchance," answered Godwin, drawing his sword and leaning forward. Then he looked, and true enough there stood two figures faintly outlined in the gloom. They glided towards them, and now the level moonlight shone upon their white robes and gleamed in the gems they wore.

"I cannot see them," said a voice. "Oh, those dead soldiers—what do they portend?"

"At least yonder stand their horses," answered another voice.

Now the brethren guessed the truth, and, like men in a dream, stepped forward from the shadow of the wall.

"Rosamund!" they said.

"Oh Godwin! oh Wulf!" she cried in answer. "*Oh, Jesu,* I thank Thee, I thank Thee—Thee, and this brave woman!" and, casting her arms about Masouda, she kissed her on the face.

Masouda pushed her back, and said, in a voice that was almost harsh: "It is not fitting, Princess, that your pure lips should touch the cheek of a woman of the Assassins."

But Rosamund would not be repulsed.

"It is most fitting," she sobbed, "that I should give you thanks who but for you must also have become 'a woman of the Assassins,' or an inhabitant of the House of Death."

Then Masouda kissed her back, and, thrusting her away into the arms of Wulf, said roughly:

"So, pilgrims Peter and John, your patron saints have brought you through so far; and, John, you fight right well. Nay, do not stop for our story, if you wish us to live to tell it. What! You have the soldiers' horses with your own? Well done! I did not credit you with so much wit. Now, Sir Wulf, can you walk? Yes; so much the better; it will save you a rough ride, for this place is steep, though not so steep as one you know of. Now set the princess upon Flame, for no cat is surer-footed than that horse, as you may remember, Peter. I who know the path will lead it. John, take you the other two; Peter, do you follow last of all with Smoke, and, if they hang back, prick them with your sword. Come, Flame, be not afraid, Flame. Where I go, you can come," and Masouda thrust her way through the bushes and over the edge of the cliff, talking to the snorting horse and patting its neck.

A minute more, and they were scrambling down a mountain ridge so steep that it seemed as though they must fall and be dashed to pieces at the bottom. Yet they fell not, for, made as it had been to meet such hours of need, this road was safer than it appeared, with ridges cut in the rock at the worst places.

Down they went, and down, till at length, panting, but safe, they stood at the bottom of the darksome gulf where only the starlight shone, for here the rays of the low moon could not reach.

"Mount," said Masouda. "Princess, stay you on Flame; he is the surest and the swiftest. Sir Wulf, keep your own horse Smoke; your brother and I will ride those of the soldiers. Though not very swift, doubtless they are good beasts, and accustomed to such roads." Then she leapt to the saddle as a woman born in the desert can, and pushed her horse in front.

For a mile or more Masouda led them along the rocky bottom of the gulf, where because of the stones they could only travel at a foot pace, till they came to a deep cleft on the left hand, up which they began to ride. By now the moon was quite behind the mountains, and such faint light as came from the stars began to be obscured with drifting clouds. Still, they stumbled on till they reached a little glade where water ran and grass grew.

"Halt," said Masouda. "Here we must wait till dawn for in this darkness the horses cannot keep their footing on the stones. Moreover, all about us lie precipices, over one of which we might fall."

"But they will pursue us," pleaded Rosamund.

"Not until they have light to see by," answered Masouda, "or at least we must take the risk, for to go forward would be madness. Sit down and rest a while, and let the horses drink a little and eat a mouthful of grass, holding their reins in our hands, for we and they may need all our strength before to-morrow's sun is set. Sir Wulf, say, are you much hurt?"

"But very little," he answered in a cheerful voice; "a few bruises beneath my mail—that is all, for Lozelle's sword was heavy. Tell us, I pray you, what happened after we rode away from the castle bridge."

"This, knights. The princess here, being overcome, was escorted by the slaves back to her chambers, but Sinan bade me stay with him awhile that he might speak to you through me. Do you know what was in his mind? To have you killed at once, both of you, whom Lozelle had told him were this lady's lovers, and not her brothers. Only he feared that there might be trouble with the people, who were pleased with the fighting, so held his hand. Then he bade you to the supper, whence you would not have returned; but when Sir Wulf said that he was hurt, I whispered to him that what he wished to do could best be done on the morrow at the wedding-feast when he was in his own halls, surrounded by his guards.

"'Ay,' he answered, 'these brethren shall fight with them until they are driven into the gulf. It will be a goodly sight for me and my queen to see.'"

"Oh! horrible, horrible!" said Rosamund; while Godwin muttered:

"I swear that I would have fought, not with his guards, but with Sinan only."

"So he suffered you to go, and I left him also. Before I went he spoke to me, bidding me bring the princess to him privately within two hours after we had supped, as he wished to speak to her alone about the ceremony of her marriage on the morrow, and to make her gifts. I answered aloud that his commands should be obeyed, and hurried to the guest-castle. There I found your lady recovered from her faintness, but mad with fear, and forced her to eat and drink.

"The rest is short. Before the two hours were gone a messenger came, saying that the Al-je-bal bade me do what he had commanded.

"'Return,' I answered; 'the princess adorns herself. We follow presently alone, as it is commanded.'

"Then I threw this cloak about her and bade her be brave, and, if we failed, to choose whether she would take Sinan or death for lord. Next, I took the ring you had, the Signet of the dead Al-je-bal, who gave it to your kinsman, and held it before the slaves, who bowed and let me pass. We came to the guards, and to them again I showed the ring. They bowed also, but when they saw that we turned down the passage to the left and not to the right, as we should have done to come to the doors of the inner palace, they would have stopped us.

"'Acknowledge the Signet,' I answered. 'Dogs, what is it to you which road the Signet takes?' Then they also let us pass.

"Now, following the passage, we were out of the guest house and in the gardens, and I led her to what is called the prison tower, whence runs the secret way. Here were more guards whom I bade open in the name of Sinan.

"They said: 'We obey not. This place is shut save to the Signet itself.'

"'Behold it!' I answered. The officer looked and said: 'It is the very Signet, sure enough, and there is no other.'

"Yet he paused, studying the black stone veined with the red dagger and the ancient writing on it.

"'Are you, then, weary of life?' I asked. 'Fool, the Al-je-bal himself would keep a tryst within this house, which he enters secretly from the palace. Woe to you if he does not find his lady there!'

"'It is the Signet that he must have sent, sure enough,' the captain said again, 'to disobey which is death.'

"'Yes, open, open,' whispered his companions.

"So they opened, though doubtfully, and we entered, and I barred the door behind us. Then, to be short, through the darkness of the tower basement, guiding ourselves by the wall, we crept to the entrance of that way of which I know the secret. Ay, and along all its length and through the rock door of escape at the end of which I set so that none can turn it, save skilled masons with their tools, and into the cave where we found you. It was no great matter, having the Signet, although without the Signet it had not been possible to-night, when every gate is guarded."

"No great matter!" gasped Rosamund. "Oh, Godwin and Wulf! if you could know how she thought of and made ready everything; if you could have seen how all those cruel men glared at us, searching out our very souls! If you could have heard how high she answered them, waving that ring before their eyes and bidding them to obey its presence, or to die!"

"Which they surely have done by now," broke in Masouda quietly, "though I do not pity them, who were wicked. Nay; thank me not; I have done what I promised to do, neither less nor more, and—I love danger and a high stake. Tell us your story, Sir Godwin."

So, seated there on the grass in the darkness, he told them of their mad ride and of the slaying of the guards, while Rosamund raised her hands and thanked Heaven for its mercies, and that they were without those accursed walls.

"You may be within them again before sunset," said Masouda grimly.

"Yes," answered Wulf, "but not alive. Now what plan have you? To ride for the coast towns?"

"No," replied Masouda; "at least not straight, since to do so we must pass through the country of the Assassins, who by this day's light will be warned to watch for us. We must ride through the desert mountain lands to Emesa, many miles away, and cross the Orontes there, then down into Baalbec, and so back to Beirut."

"Emesa?" said Godwin. "Why Saladin holds that place, and of Baalbec the lady Rosamund is princess."

"Which is best?" asked Masouda shortly. "That she should fall into the hands of Salah-ed-din, or back into those of the master of the Assassins? Choose which you wish."

"I choose Salah-ed-din," broke in Rosamund, "for at least he is my uncle, and will do me no wrong." Nor, knowing the case, did the others gainsay her.

Now at length the summer day began to break, and while it was still too dark to travel, Godwin and Rosamund let the horses graze, holding them by their bridles. Masouda, also, taking off the hauberk of Wulf, doctored his bruises as best she could with the crushed leaves of a bush that grew by the stream, having first washed them with water, and though the time was short, eased him much. Then, so soon as the dawn was grey, having drunk their fill and, as they had nothing else, eaten some watercress that grew in the stream, they tightened their saddle girths and started. Scarcely had they gone a hundred yards when, from the gulf beneath, that was hidden in grey mists, they heard the sound of horse's hoofs and men's voices.

"Push on," said Masouda, "Al-je-bal is on our tracks."

Upwards they climbed through the gathering light, skirting the edge of dreadful precipices which in the gloom it would have been impossible to pass, till at length they reached a great table land, that ran to the foot of some mountains a dozen miles or more away. Among those mountains soared two peaks, set close together. To these Masouda pointed, saying that their road ran between them, and that beyond lay the valley of the Orontes. While she spoke, far behind them they heard the sound of men shouting, although they could see nothing because of the dense mist.

"Push on," said Masouda; "there is no time to spare," and they went forward, but only at a hand gallop, for the ground was still rough and the light uncertain.

When they had covered some six miles of the distance between them and the mountain pass, the sun rose suddenly and sucked up the mist. This was what they saw. Before them lay a flat, sandy plain; behind, the stony ground that they had traversed, and riding over it, two miles from them, some twenty men of the Assassins.

"They cannot catch us," said Wulf; but Masouda pointed to the right, where the mist still hung, and said:

"Yonder I see spears."

Presently it thinned, and there a league away they saw a great body of mounted soldiers—perhaps there were four hundred.

"Look," she said; "they have come round during the night, as I feared they would. Now we must cross the path before them or be taken," and she struck her horse fiercely with a stick she had cut at the stream. Half a mile further on a shout from the great body of men to their right, which was answered by another shout from those behind, told them that they were seen.

"On!" said Masouda. "The race will be close." So they began to gallop their best.

Two miles were done, but although that behind was far off, the great cloud of dust to their right grew ever nearer till it seemed as though it must reach the mouth of the mountain pass before them. Then Godwin spoke:

"Wulf and Rosamund ride on. Your horses are swift and can outpace them. At the crest of the mountain pass wait a while to breathe the beasts, and see if we come. If not, ride on again, and God be with you."

"Ay," said Masouda, "ride and head for the Emesa bridge—it can be seen from far—and there yield yourselves to the officers of Salah-ed-din."

They hung back, but in a stern voice Godwin repeated:

"Ride, I command you both."

"For Rosamund's sake, so be it," answered Wulf.

Then he called to Smoke and Flame, and they stretched themselves out upon the sand and passed thence swifter than swallows. Soon Godwin and Masouda, toiling behind, saw them enter the mouth of the pass.

"Good," she said. "Except those of their own breed, there are no horses in Syria that can catch those two. They will come to Emesa, have no fear."

"Who was the man who brought them to us?" asked Godwin, as they galloped side by side, their eyes fixed upon the ever-nearing cloud of dust, in which the spear points sparkled.

"My father's brother—my uncle, as I called him," she answered. "He is a sheik of the desert, who owns the ancient breed that cannot be bought for gold."

"Then you are not of the Assassins, Masouda?"

"No; I may tell you, now that the end seems near. My father was an Arab, my mother a noble Frank, a French woman, whom he found starving in the desert after a fight, and took to his tent and made his wife. The Assassins fell upon us and killed him and her, and captured me as a child of twelve. Afterwards, when I grew older, being beautiful in those days, I was taken to the harem of Sinan, and, although in secret I had been bred up a Christian by my mother, they swore me of his accursed faith. Now you will understand why I hate him so sorely who murdered my father and my mother, and made me what I am; why I hold myself so vile also. Yes, I have been forced to serve as his spy or be killed, who, although he believed me his faithful slave, desired first to be avenged upon him."

"I do not hold you vile," panted Godwin, as he spurred his labouring steed. "I hold you most noble."

"I rejoice to hear it before we die," she answered, looking him in the eyes in such a fashion that he dropped his head before her burning gaze, "who hold you dear, Sir Godwin, for whose sake I have dared these things, although I am nought to you. Nay, speak not; the lady Rosamund has told me all that story—except its answer."

Now they were off the sand over which they had been racing side by side, and beginning to breast the mountain slope, nor was Godwin sorry that the clatter of their horses' hoofs upon the stones prevented further speech between them. So far they had outpaced the Assassins, who had a longer and a rougher road to travel; but the great cloud of dust was not seven hundred yards away, and in front of it, shaking their spears, rode some of the best mounted of their soldiers.

"These horses still have strength; they are better than I thought them," cried Masouda. "They will not gain on us across the mountains, but afterwards—"

For the next league they spoke no more, who must keep their horses from falling as they toiled up the steep path. At length they reached the crest, and there, on the very top of it, saw Wulf and Rosamund standing by Flame and Smoke.

"They rest," Godwin said, then he shouted, "Mount! mount! The foe is close."

So they climbed to their saddles again, and, all four of them together began to descend the long slope that stretched to the plain two leagues beneath. Far off across this plain ran a broad silver streak, beyond which from that height they could see the walls of a city.

"The Orontes!" cried Masouda. "Cross that, and we are safe." But Godwin looked first at his horse, then at Masouda, and shook his head.

Well might he do so, for, stout-hearted as they were, the beasts were much distressed that had galloped so far without drawing rein. Down the steep road they plunged, panting; indeed at times it was hard to keep them on their feet.

"They will reach the plain—no more," said Godwin, and Masouda nodded.

The descent was almost done, and not a mile behind them the white-robed Assassins streamed endlessly. Godwin plied his spurs and Masouda her whip, although with little hope, for they knew that the end was near. Down the last declivity they rushed, till suddenly, as they reached its foot, Masouda's horse reeled, stopped, and sank to the ground, while Godwin's pulled up beside it.

"Ride on!" he cried to Rosamund and Wulf in front; but they would not. He stormed at them, but they replied: "Nay, we will die together."

Masouda looked at the horses Flame and Smoke, which seemed but little troubled.

"So be it," she said; "they have carried double before, and must again. Mount in front of the lady, Sir Godwin; and, Sir Wulf, give me your hand, and you will learn what this breed can do."

So they mounted. Forward started Flame and Smoke with a long, swinging gallop, while from the Assassins above, who thought that they held them, went up a shout of rage and wonder.

"Their horses are also tired, and we may beat them yet," called the dauntless Masouda. But Godwin and Wulf looked sadly at the ten miles of plain between them and the river bank.

On they went, and on. A quarter of it was done. Half of it was done, but now the first of the *fedai* hung upon their flanks not two hundred yards behind. Little by little this distance lessened. At length they were scarcely fifty yards away, and one of them flung a spear. In her terror Rosamund sobbed aloud.

"Spur the horses, knights," cried Masouda, and for the first time they spurred them.

At the sting of the steel Flame and Smoke sprang forward as though they had but just left their stable door, and the gap between pursuers and pursued widened. Two more miles were done, and scarce seven furlongs from them they saw the broad mouth of the bridge, while the towers of Emesa beyond seemed so close that in this clear air they could discern the watchmen outlined against the sky. Then they descended a little valley, and lost sight of bridge and town.

At the rise of the opposing slope the strength of Flame and Smoke at last began to fail beneath their double burdens. They panted and trembled; and, save in short rushes, no longer answered to the spur. The Assassins saw, and came on with wild shouts. Nearer and nearer they drew, and the sound of their horses hoofs beating on the sand was like the sound of thunder. Now once more they were fifty yards away, and now but thirty, and again the spears began to flash, though none struck them.

Masouda screamed to the horses in Arabic, and gallantly did they struggle, plunging up the hill with slow, convulsive bounds. Godwin and Wulf looked at each other, then, at a signal, checked their speed, leapt to earth, and, turning, drew their swords.

"On!" they cried, and lightened of their weight, once more the reeling horses plunged forward.

The Assassins were upon them. Wulf struck a mighty blow and emptied the saddle of the first, then was swept to earth. As he fell from behind him he heard a scream of joy, and struggling to his knees, looked round. Lo! from over the crest of the rise rushed squadron upon squadron of turbaned cavalry, who, as they came, set their lances in rest, and shouted:

"Salah-ed-din! Salah-ed-din!"

The Assassins saw also, and turned to fly—too late!

"A horse! A horse!" screamed Godwin in Arabic; and presently—how he never knew—found himself mounted and charging with the Saracens.

To Wulf, too, a horse was brought, but he could not struggle to its saddle. Thrice he strove, then fell backwards and lay upon the sand, waving his sword and shouting where he lay, while Masouda stood by him, a dagger in her hand, and with her Rosamund upon her knees.

Now the pursuers were the pursued, and dreadful was the reckoning that they must pay. Their horses were outworn and could not fly at speed. Some of the *fedai* were cut down upon them. Some dismounted, and gathering themselves in little groups, fought bravely till they were slain, while a few were taken prisoners. Of all that great troop of men not a score won back alive to Masyaf to make report to their master of how the chase of his lost bride had ended.

A while later and Wulf from his seat upon the ground saw Godwin riding back towards him, his red sword in his hand. With him rode a sturdy, bright-eyed man gorgeously apparelled, at the sight of whom Rosamund sprang to her feet; then, as he dismounted, ran forward and with a little cry cast her arms about him.

"Hassan! Prince Hassan! Is it indeed you? Oh, God be praised!" she gasped, then, had not Masouda caught her, would have fallen.

The Emir looked at her, her long hair loose, her face stained, her veil torn, but still clad in the silk and gleaming gems with which she had been decked as the bride-elect of Al-je-bal. Then low to the earth he bent his knee, while the grave Saracens watched, and taking the hem of her garment, he kissed it.

"Allah be praised indeed!" he said. "I, His unworthy servant, thank Him from my heart, who never thought to see you living more. Soldiers, salute. Before you stands the lady Rose of the World, princess of Baalbec and niece of your lord, Salah-ed-din, Commander of the Faithful."

Then in stately salutation to this dishevelled, outworn, but still queenly woman, uprose hand, and spear, and scimitar, while Wulf cried from where he lay:

"Why, it is our merchant of the drugged wine—none other! Oh! Sir Saracen, does not the memory of that chapman's trick shame you now?"

The emir Hassan heard and grew red, muttering in his beard:

"Like you, Sir Wulf, I am the slave of Fate, and must obey. Be not bitter against me till you know all."

"I am not bitter," answered Wulf, "but I always pay for my drink, and we will settle that score yet, as I have sworn."

"Hush!" broke in Rosamund. "Although he stole me, he is also my deliverer and friend through many a peril, and, had it not been for him, by now—" and she shuddered.

"I do not know all the story, but, Princess, it seems that you should thank not me, but these goodly cousins of yours and those splendid horses," and Hassan pointed to Smoke and Flame, which stood by quivering, with hollow flanks and drooping heads.

"There is another whom I must thank also, this noble woman, as you will call her also when you hear the story," said Rosamund, flinging her arm about the neck of Masouda.

"My master will reward her," said Hassan. "But oh! lady, what must you think of me who seemed to desert you so basely? Yet I reasoned well. In the castle of that son of Satan, Sinan," and he spat upon the ground, "I could not have aided you, for there he would only have butchered me. But by escaping I thought that I might help, so I bribed the Frankish knave with the priceless Star of my House," and he touched the great jewel that he wore in his turban, "and with what money I had, to loose my bonds, and while he pouched the gold I stabbed him with his own knife and fled. But this morning I reached yonder city in command of ten thousand men, charged to rescue you if I could; if not, to avenge you, for the ambassadors of Salah-ed-din informed me of your plight. An hour ago the watchmen on the towers reported that they saw two horses galloping across the plain beneath a double burden, pursued by soldiers whom from their robes they took to be Assassins. So, as I have a quarrel with the Assassins, I crossed the bridge, formed up five hundred men in a hollow, and waited, never guessing that it was you who fled. You know the rest—and the Assassins know it also, for," he added grimly, "you have been well avenged."

"Follow it up," said Wulf, "and the vengeance shall be better, for I will show you the secret way into Masyaf—or, if I cannot, Godwin will—and there you may hurl Sinan from his own towers."

Hassan shook his head and answered:

"I should like it well, for with this magician my master also has an ancient quarrel. But he has other feuds upon his hands," and he looked meaningly at Wulf and Godwin, "and my orders were to rescue the princess and no more. Well, she has been rescued, and some hundreds of heads have paid the price of all that she has suffered. Also, that secret way of yours will be safe enough by now. So there I let the matter bide, glad enough that it has ended thus. Only I warn you all—and myself also—to walk warily, since, if I know aught of him, Sinan's *fedais* will henceforth dog the steps of every one of us, striving to bring us to our ends by murder. Now here come litters; enter them, all of you, and be borne to the city, who have ridden far enough to-day. Fear not for your horses; they shall be led in gently and saved alive, if skill and care can save them. I go to count the slain, and will join you presently in the citadel."

So the bearers came and lifted up Wulf, and helped Godwin from his horse—for now that all was over he could scarcely stand—and with him Rosamund and Masouda. Placing them in the litters, they carried them, escorted by cavalry, across the bridge of the Orontes into the city of Emesa, where they lodged them in the citadel.

Here also, after giving them a drink of barley gruel, and rubbing their backs and legs with ointment, they led the horses Smoke and Flame, slowly and with great trouble, for these could hardly stir, and laid them down on thick beds of straw, tempting them with food, which after awhile they ate. The four—Rosamund, Masouda, Godwin, and Wulf—ate also of some soup with wine in it, and after the hurts of Wulf had been tended by a skilled doctor, went to their beds, whence they did not rise again for two days.

## Chapter 16

# The Sultan Saladin

In the third morning Godwin awoke to see the ray of sunrise streaming through the latticed window.

They fell upon another bed near-by where Wulf still lay sleeping, a bandage on his head that had been hurt in the last charge against the Assassins, and other bandages about his arms and body, which were much bruised in the fight upon the dreadful bridge.

Wondrous was it to Godwin to watch him lying there sleeping healthily, notwithstanding his injuries, and to think of what they had gone through together with so little harm; to think, also, of how they had rescued Rosamund out of the very mouth of that earthly hell of which he could see the peaks through the open window-place—out of the very hands of that fiend, its ruler. Reckoning the tale day by day, he reflected on their adventures since they landed at Beirut, and saw how Heaven had guided their every step.

In face of the warnings that were given them, to visit the Al-je-bal in his stronghold had seemed a madness. Yet there, where none could have thought that she would be, they had found Rosamund. There they had been avenged upon the false knight Sir Hugh Lozelle, who had betrayed her, first to Saladin, then to Sinan, and sent him down to death and judgment; and thence they had rescued Rosamund.

Oh, how wise they had been to obey the dying words of their uncle, Sir Andrew, who doubtless was given foresight at the end! God and His saints had helped them, who could not have helped themselves, and His minister had been Masouda. But for Masouda, Rosamund would by now be lost or dead, and they, if their lives were still left to them, would be wanderers in the great land of Syria, seeking for one who never could be found.

Why had Masouda done these things, again and again putting her own life upon the hazard to save theirs and the honour of another woman? As he asked himself the question Godwin felt the red blood rise to his face. Because she hated Sinan, who had murdered her parents and degraded her, she said; and doubtless that had to do with the matter. But it was no longer possible to hide the truth. She loved him, and had loved him from the first hour when they met. He had always suspected it—in that wild trial of the horses upon the mountain side, when she sat with her arms about him and her face pressed against his face; when she kissed his feet after he had saved her from the lion, and many another time.

But as they followed Wulf and Rosamund up the mountain pass while the host of the Assassins thundered at their heels, and in broken gasps she had told him of her sad history, then it was that he grew sure. Then, too, he had said that he held her not vile, but noble, as indeed he did; and, thinking their death upon them, she had answered that she held him dear, and looked on him as a woman looks upon her only love—a message in her eyes that no man could fail to read. Yet if this were so, why had Masouda saved Rosamund, the lady to whom she knew well that he was sworn? Reared among those cruel folk who could wade to their desire through blood and think it honour, would she not have left her rival to her doom, seeing that oaths do not hold beyond the grave?

An answer came into the heart of Godwin, at the very thought of which he turned pale and trembled. His brother was also sworn to Rosamund, and she in her soul must be sworn to one of them. Was it not to Wulf, Wulf who was handsomer and more strong than he, to Wulf, the conqueror of Lozelle? Had Rosamund told Masouda this? Nay, surely not.

Yet women can read each other's hearts, piercing veils through which no man may see, and perchance Masouda had read the heart of Rosamund. She stood behind her during the dreadful duel at the gate, and watched her face when Wulf's death seemed sure; she might have heard words that broke in agony from her lips in those moments of torment.

Oh, without doubt it was so, and Masouda had protected Rosamund because she knew that her love was for Wulf and not for him. The thought was very bitter, and in its pain Godwin groaned aloud, while a fierce jealousy of the brave and handsome knight who slept at his side, dreaming, doubtless, of the fame that he had won and the reward by which it would be crowned, gripped his vitals like the icy hand of death. Then Godwin remembered the oath that they two had sworn far away in the Priory at Stangate, and the love passing the love of woman which he bore towards this brother, and the duty of a Christian warrior whereto he was vowed, and hiding his face in his pillow he prayed for strength.

It would seem that it came to him—at least, when he lifted his head again the jealousy was gone, and only the great grief remained. Fear remained also—for what of Masouda? How should he deal with her? He was certain that this was no fancy which would pass—until her life passed with it, and, beautiful as she was, and noble as she was, he did not wish her love. He could find no answer to these questions, save this—that things must go on as they were decreed. For himself, he, Godwin, would strive to do his duty, to keep his hands clean, and await the end, whatever that might be.

Wulf woke up, stretched his arms, exclaimed because that action hurt him, grumbled at the brightness of the light upon his eyes, and said that he was very hungry. Then he arose, and with the help of Godwin, dressed himself, but not in his armour. Here, with the yellow-coated soldiers of Saladin, grave-faced and watchful, pacing before their door—for night and day they were trebly guarded lest Assassins should creep in—there was no need for mail. In the fortress of Masyaf, indeed, where they were also guarded, it had been otherwise. Wulf heard the step of the sentries on the cemented pavement without, and shook his great shoulders as though he shivered.

"That sound makes my backbone cold," he said. "For a moment, as my eyes opened, I thought that we were back again in the guest chambers of Al-je-bal, where folk crept round us as we slept and murderers marched to and fro outside the curtains, fingering their knife-points. Well, whatever there is to come, thank the Saints, that is done with. I tell you, brother, I have had enough of mountains, and narrow bridges, and Assassins. Henceforth, I desire to live upon a flat with never a hill in sight, amidst honest folk as stupid as their own sheep, who go to church on Sundays and get drunk, not with *hachich*, but on brown ale, brought to them by no white-robed sorceress, but by a draggle-tailed wench in a tavern, with her musty bedstraw still sticking in her hair. Give me the Saltings of Essex with the east winds blowing over them, and the primroses abloom upon the bank, and the lanes fetlock deep in mud, and for your share you may take all the scented gardens of Sinan and the cups and jewels of his ladies, with the fightings and adventures of the golden East thrown in."

"I never sought these things, and we are a long way from Essex," answered Godwin shortly.

"No," said Wulf, "but they seem to seek you. What news of Masouda? Have you seen her while I slept, which has been long?"

"I have seen no one except the apothecary who tended you, the slaves who brought us food, and last evening the prince Hassan, who came to see how we fared. He told me that, like yourself, Rosamund and Masouda slept."

"I am glad to hear it," answered Wulf, "for certainly their rest was earned. By St. Chad! what a woman is this Masouda! A heart of fire and nerves of steel! Beautiful, too—most beautiful; and the best horsewoman that ever sat a steed. Had it not been for her—By Heaven! when I think of it I feel as though I loved her—don't you?"

"No," said Godwin, still more shortly.

"Ah, well, I daresay she can love enough for two who does nothing by halves, and, all things considered," he added, with one of his great laughs, "I am glad it is I of whom she thinks so little—yes, I who adore her as though she were my patron saint. Hark! the guards challenge," and, forgetting where he was, he snatched at his sword.

Then the door opened, and through it appeared the emir Hassan, who saluted them in the name of Allah, searching them with his quiet eyes.

"Few would judge, to look at you, Sir Knights," he said with a smile, "that you have been the guests of the Old Man of the Mountain, and left his house so hastily by the back door. Three days more and you will be as lusty as when we met beyond the seas upon the wharf by a certain creek. Oh, you are brave men, both of you, though you be infidels, from which error may the Prophet guide you; brave men, the flower of knighthood. Ay, I, Hassan, who have known many Frankish knights, say it from my heart," and, placing his hand to his turban, he bowed before them in admiration that was not feigned.

"We thank you, Prince, for your praise," said Godwin gravely, but Wulf stepped forward, took his hand, and shook it.

"That was an ill trick, Prince, which you played us yonder in England," he said, "and one that brought as good a warrior as ever drew a sword—our uncle Sir Andrew D'Arcy—to an end sad as it was glorious. Still, you obeyed your master, and because of all that has happened since, I forgive you, and call you friend, although should we ever meet in battle I still hope to pay you for that drugged wine."

Here Hassan bowed, and said softly:

"I admit that the debt is owing; also that none sorrow more for the death of the noble lord D'Arcy than I, your servant, who, by the will of God, brought it upon him. When we meet, Sir Wulf, in war—and that, I think, will be an ill hour for me—strike, and strike home; I shall not complain. Meanwhile, we are friends, and in very truth all that I have is yours. But now I come to tell you that the princess Rose of the World—Allah bless her footsteps!—is recovered from her fatigues, and desires that you should breakfast with her in an hour's time. Also the doctor waits to tend your bruises, and slaves to lead you to the bath and clothe you. Nay, leave your hauberk; here the faith of Salah-ed-din and of his servants is your best armour."

"Still, I think that we will take them," said Godwin, "for faith is a poor defence against the daggers of these Assassins, who dwell not so far away."

"True," answered Hassan; "I had forgotten." So thus they departed.

An hour later they were led to the hall, where presently came Rosamund, and with her Masouda and Hassan.

She was dressed in the rich robes of an Eastern lady, but the gems with which she had been adorned as the bride elect of Al-je-bal were gone; and when she lifted her veil the brethren saw that though her face was still somewhat pallid, her strength had come back to her, and the terror had left her eyes. She greeted them with sweet and gentle words, thanking first Godwin and then Wulf for all that they had done, and turning to Masouda, who stood by, stately, and watchful, thanked her also. Then they sat down, and ate with light hearts and a good appetite.

Before their meal was finished, the guard at the door announced that messengers had arrived from the Sultan. They entered, grey-haired men clad in the robes of secretaries, whom Hassan hastened to greet. When they were seated and had spoken with him awhile, one of them drew forth a letter, which Hassan, touching his forehead with it in token of respect, gave to Rosamund. She broke its seal, and, seeing that it was in Arabic, handed it to her cousin, saying:

"Do you read it, Godwin, who are more learned than I."

So he read aloud, translating the letter sentence by sentence. This was its purport:

"Salah-ed-din, Commander of the Faithful, the Strong-to-aid, to his niece beloved, Rose of the World, princess of Baalbec:—

"Our servant, the emir Hassan, has sent us tidings of your rescue from the power of the accursed lord of the Mountain, Sinan, and that you are now safe in our city of Emesa, guarded by many thousands of our soldiers, and with you a woman named Masouda, and your kinsmen, the two Frankish knights, by whose skill in arms and courage you were saved. Now this is to command you to come to our court at Damascus so soon as you may be fit to travel, knowing that here you will be received with love and honour. Also I invite your kinsmen to accompany you, since I knew their father, and would welcome knights who have done such great deeds, and the woman Masouda with them. Or, if they prefer it, all three of them may return to their own lands and peoples.

"Hasten, my niece, lady Rose of the World, hasten, for my spirit seeks you, and my eyes desire to look upon you. In the name of Allah, greeting."

"You have heard," said Rosamund, as Godwin finished reading the scroll. "Now, my cousins, what will you do?"

"What else but go with you, whom we have come so far to seek?" answered Wulf, and Godwin nodded his head in assent.

"And you, Masouda?"

"I, lady? Oh, I go also, since were I to return yonder," and she nodded towards the mountains, "my greeting would be one that I do not wish."

"Do you note their words, prince Hassan?" asked Rosamund.

"I expected no other," he answered with a bow. "Only, knights, you must give me a promise, for even in the midst of my army such is needful from men who can fly like birds out of the fortress of Masyaf and from the knives of the Assassins—who are mounted, moreover, on the swiftest horses in Syria that have been trained to carry a double burden," and he looked at them meaningly. "It is that upon this journey you will not attempt to escape with the princess, whom you have followed from over-sea to rescue her out of the hand of Salah-ed-din."

Godwin drew from his tunic the cross which Rosamund had left him in the hall at Steeple, and saying: "I swear upon this holy symbol that during our journey to Damascus I will attempt no escape with or without my cousin Rosamund," he kissed it.

"And I swear the same upon my sword," added Wulf, laying his hand upon the silver hilt of the great blade which had been his forefather's.

"A security that I like better," said Hassan with a smile, "but in truth, knights, your word is enough for me." Then he looked at Masouda and went on, still smiling: "Nay it is useless; for women who have dwelt yonder oaths have no meaning. Lady, we must be content to watch you, since my lord has bidden you to his city, which, fair and brave as you are, to be plain, I would not have done."

Then he turned to speak to the secretaries, and Godwin, who was noting all, saw Masouda's dark eyes follow him and in them a very strange light.

"Good," they seemed to say; "as you have written, so shall you read."

That same afternoon they started for Damascus, a great army of horsemen. In its midst, guarded by a thousand spears, Rosamund was borne in a litter. In front of her rode Hassan, with his yellow-robed bodyguard; at her side, Masouda; and behind—for, notwithstanding his hurts, Wulf would not be carried—the brethren, mounted upon ambling palfreys. After them, led by slaves, came the chargers, Flame and Smoke, recovered now, but still walking somewhat stiffly, and then rank upon rank of turbaned Saracens. Through the open curtains of her litter Rosamund beckoned to the brethren, who pushed alongside of her.

"Look," she said, pointing with her hand.

They looked, and there, bathed in the glory of the sinking sun, saw the mountains crowned far, far away with the impregnable city and fortress of Masyaf, and below it the slopes down which they had ridden for their lives. Nearer to them flashed the river bordered by the town of Emesa. Set at intervals along its walls were spears, looking like filaments against the flaming, sunset sky, and on each of them a black dot, which was the head of an Assassin, while from the turrets above, the golden banner of Saladin fluttered in the evening wind. Remembering all that she had undergone in that fearful home of devil-worshippers, and the fate from which she had been snatched, Rosamund shuddered.

"It burns like a city in hell," she said, staring at Masyaf, environed by that lurid evening light and canopied with black, smoke-like clouds. "Oh! such I think will be its doom."

"I trust so," answered Wulf fervently. "At least, in this world and the next we have done with it."

"Yes," added Godwin in his thoughtful voice; "still, out of that evil place we won good, for there we found Rosamund, and there, my brother, you conquered in such a fray as you can never hope to fight again, gaining great glory, and perhaps much more."

Then reining in his horse, Godwin fell back behind the litter, while Wulf wondered, and Rosamund watched him with dreaming eyes.

That evening they camped in the desert, and next morning, surrounded by wandering tribes of Bedouins mounted on their camels, marched on again, sleeping that night in the ancient fortress of Baalbec, whereof the garrison and people, having been warned by runners of the rank and titles of Rosamund came out to do her homage as their lady.

Hearing of it, she left her litter, and mounting a splendid horse which they had sent her as a present, rode to meet them, the brethren, in full armour and once more bestriding Flame and Smoke, beside her, and a guard of Saladin's own Mameluks behind. Solemn, turbaned men, who had been commanded so to do by messengers from the Sultan, brought her the keys of the gates on a cushion, minstrels and soldiers marched before her, whilst crowding the walls and running alongside came the citizens in their thousands. Thus she went on, through the open gates, past the towering columns of ruined temples once a home of the worship of heathen gods, through courts and vaults to the citadel surrounded by its gardens that in dead ages had been the Acropolis of forgotten Roman emperors.

Here in the portico Rosamund turned her horse, and received the salutations of the multitude as though she also were one of the world's rulers. Indeed, it seemed to the brethren watching her as she sat upon the great white horse and surveyed the shouting, bending crowd with flashing eyes, splendid in her bearing and beautiful to see, a prince at her stirrup and an army at her back, that none of those who had trod that path before her could have seemed greater or more glorious in the hour of their pride than did this English girl, who by the whim of Fate had suddenly been set so high. Truly by blood and nature she was fitted to be a queen. Yet as Rosamund sat thus the pride passed from her face, and her eyes fell.

"Of what are you thinking?" asked Godwin at her side.

"That I would we were back among the summer fields at Steeple," she answered, "for those who are lifted high fall low. Prince Hassan, give the captains and people my thanks and bid them be gone. I would rest."

Thus for the first and last time did Rosamund behold her ancient fief of Baalbec, which her grandsire, the great Ayoub, had ruled before her.

That night there was feasting in the mighty, immemorial halls, and singing and minstrelsy and the dancing of fair women and the giving of gifts. For Baalbec, where birth and beauty were ever welcome, did honour to its lady, the favoured niece of the mighty Salah-ed-din. Yet there were some who murmured that she would bring no good fortune to the Sultan or this his city, who was not all of the blood of Ayoub, but half a Frank, and a Cross worshipper, though even these praised her beauty and her royal bearing. The brethren they praised also, although these were unbelievers, and the tale of how Wulf had fought the traitor knight upon the Narrow Way, and of how they had led their kinswoman from the haunted fortress of Masyaf, was passed from mouth to mouth. At dawn the next day, on orders received from the Sultan, they left Baalbec, escorted by the army and many of the notables of the town. That afternoon they drew rein upon the heights which overlook the city of Damascus, Bride of the Earth, set amidst its seven streams and ringed about with gardens, one of the most beautiful and perhaps the most ancient city in the world. Then they rode down to the bounteous plain, and as night fell, having passed the encircling gardens, were escorted through the gates of Damascus, outside of which most of the army halted and encamped.

Along the narrow streets, bordered by yellow, flat-roofed houses, they rode slowly, looking now at the motley, many-coloured crowds, who watched them with grave interest, and now at the stately buildings, domed mosques and towering minarets, which everywhere stood out against the deep blue of the evening sky. Thus at length they came to an open space planted like a garden, beyond which was seen a huge and fantastic castle that Hassan told them was the palace of Salah-ed-din. In its courtyard they were parted, Rosamund being led away by officers of state, whilst the brethren were taken to chambers that had been prepared, where, after they had bathed, they were served with food. Scarcely had they eaten it when Hassan appeared, and bade them follow him. Passing down various passages and across a court they came to some guarded doors, where the soldiers demanded that they should give up their swords and daggers.

"It is not needful," said Hassan, and they let them go by. Next came more passages and a curtain, beyond which they found themselves in a small, domed room, lit by hanging silver lamps and paved in tesselated marbles, strewn with rich rugs and furnished with cushioned couches.

At a sign from Hassan the brethren stood still in the centre of this room, and looked about them wondering. The place was empty and very silent; they felt afraid—of what they knew not. Presently curtains upon its further side opened and through them came a man turbaned and wrapped in a dark robe, who stood awhile in the shadow, gazing at them beneath the lamps.

The man was not very tall, and slight in build, yet about him was much majesty, although his garb was such as the humblest might have worn. He came forward, lifting his head, and they saw that his features were small and finely cut; that he was bearded, and beneath his broad brow shone thoughtful yet at times piercing eyes which were brown in hue. Now the prince Hassan sank to his knees and touched the marble with his forehead, and, guessing that they were in the presence of the mighty monarch Saladin, the brethren saluted in their western fashion. Presently the Sultan spoke in a low, even voice to Hassan, to whom he motioned that he should rise, saying: "I can see that you trust these knights, Emir," and he pointed to their great swords.

"Sire," was the answer, "I trust them as I trust myself. They are brave and honourable men, although they be infidels."

The Sultan stroked his beard.

"Ay," he said, "infidels. It is a pity, yet doubtless they worship God after their own fashion. Noble to look on also, like their father, whom I remember well, and, if all I hear is true, brave indeed. Sir Knights, do you understand my language?"

"Sufficiently to speak it, lord," answered Godwin, "who have learned it since childhood, yet ill enough."

"Good. Then tell me, as soldiers to a soldier, what do you seek from Salah-ed-din?"

"Our cousin, the lady Rosamund, who, by your command, lord, was stolen from our home in England."

"Knights, she is your cousin, that I know, as surely as I know that she is my niece. Tell me now, is she aught more to you?" and he searched them with those piercing eyes.

Godwin looked at Wulf, who said in English:

"Speak the whole truth, brother. From that man nothing can be hid."

Then Godwin answered:

"Sire, we love her, and are affianced to her."

The Sultan stared at them in surprise.

"What! Both of you?" he asked.

"Yes, both."

"And does she love you both?"

"Yes," replied Godwin, "both, or so she says."

Saladin stroked his beard and considered them, while Hassan smiled a little.

"Then, knights," he said presently, "tell me, which of you does she love best?"

"That, sire, is known to her alone. When the time comes, she will say, and not before."

"I perceive," said Saladin, "that behind this riddle hides a story. If it is your good pleasure, be seated, and set it out to me."

So they sat down on the divan and obeyed, keeping nothing back from the beginning to the end, nor, although the tale was long, did the Sultan weary of listening.

"A great story, truly," he said, when at length they had finished, "and one in which I seem to see the hand of Allah. Sir Knights, you will think that I have wronged you—ay, and your uncle, Sir Andrew, who was once my friend, although an older man than I, and who, by stealing away my sister, laid the foundations of this house of love and war and woe, and perchance of happiness unforeseen.

"Now listen. The tale that those two Frankish knaves, the priest and the false knight Lozelle, told to you was true. As I wrote to your uncle in my letter, I dreamed a dream. Thrice I dreamed it; that this niece of mine lived, and that if I could bring her here to dwell at my side she should save the shedding of much blood by some noble deed of hers—ay, of the blood of tens of thousands; and in that dream I saw her face. Therefore I stretched out my arm and took her from far away. And now, through you—yes, through you—she has been snatched from the power of the great Assassin, and is safe in my court, and therefore henceforth I am your friend."

"Sire, have you seen her?" asked Godwin.

"Knights, I have seen her, and the face is the face of my dreams, and therefore I know full surely that in those dreams God spoke. Listen, Sir Godwin and Sir Wulf," Saladin went on in a changed voice, a stern, commanding voice. "Ask of me what you will, and, Franks though you are, it shall be given you for your service's sake—wealth, lands, titles, all that men desire and I can grant—but ask not of me my niece, Rose of the World, princess of Baalbec, whom Allah has brought to me for His own purposes. Know, moreover, that if you strive to steal her away you shall certainly die; and that if she escapes from me and I recapture her, then she shall die. These things I have told her already, and I swear them in the name of Allah. Here she is, and in my house she must abide until the vision be fulfilled."

Now in their dismay the brethren looked at each other, for they seemed further from their desire than they had been even in the castle of Sinan. Then a light broke upon the face of Godwin, and he stood up and answered:

"Dread lord of all the East, we hear you and we know our risk. You have given us your friendship; we accept it, and are thankful, and seek no more. God, you say, has brought our lady Rosamund to you for His own purposes, of which you have no doubt since her face is the very face of your dreams. Then let His purposes be accomplished according to His will, which may be in some way that we little guess. We abide His judgment Who has guided us in the past, and will guide us in the future."

"Well spoken," replied Saladin. "I have warned you, my guests, therefore blame me not if I keep my word; but I ask no promise from you who would not tempt noble knights to lie. Yes, Allah has set this strange riddle; by Allah let it be answered in His season."

Then he waved his hand to show that the audience was ended.

## Chapter 17

# The Brethren Depart from Damascus

At the court of Saladin Godwin and Wulf were treated with much honour. A house was given them to dwell in, and a company of servants to minister to their comfort and to guard them. Mounted on their swift horses, Flame and Smoke, they were taken out into the desert to hunt, and, had they so willed, it would have been easy for them to out-distance their retinue and companions and ride away to the nearest Christian town. Indeed, no hand would have been lifted to stay them who were free to come or go. But whither were they to go without Rosamund?

Saladin they saw often, for it pleased him to tell them tales of those days when their father and uncle were in the East, or to talk with them of England and the Franks, and even now and again to reason with Godwin on matters of religion. Moreover, to show his faith in them, he gave them the rank of officers of his own bodyguard, and when, wearying of idleness, they asked it of him, allowed them to take their share of duty in the guarding of his palace and person. This, at a time when peace still reigned between Frank and Saracen, the brethren were not ashamed to do, who received no payment for their services.

Peace reigned indeed, but Godwin and Wulf could guess that it would not reign for long. Damascus and the plain around it were one great camp, and every day new thousands of wild tribesmen poured in and took up the quarters that had been prepared for them. They asked Masouda, who knew everything, what it meant. She answered:

"It means the jihad, the Holy War, which is being preached in every mosque throughout the East. It means that the great struggle between Cross and Crescent is at hand, and then, pilgrims Peter and John, you will have to choose your standard."

"There can be little doubt about that," said Wulf.

"None," replied Masouda, with one of her smiles, "only it may pain you to have to make war upon the princess of Baalbec and her uncle, the Commander of the Faithful."

Then she went, still smiling. For this was the trouble of it: Rosamund, their cousin and their love, had in truth become the princess of Baalbec—for them. She lived in great state and freedom, as Saladin had promised that she should live in his letter to Sir Andrew D'Arcy. No insult or violence were offered to her faith; no suitor was thrust upon her. But she was in a land where women do not consort with men, especially if they be high-placed. As a princess of the empire of Saladin, she must obey its rules, even to veiling herself when she went abroad, and exchanging no private words with men. Godwin and Wulf prayed Saladin that they might be allowed to speak with her from time to time, but he only answered shortly:

"Sir Knights, our customs are our customs. Moreover, the less you see of the princess of Baalbec the better I think it will be for her, for you, whose blood I do not wish to have upon my hands, and for myself, who await the fulfilment of that dream which the angel brought."

Then the brethren left his presence sore at heart, for although they saw her from time to time at feasts and festivals, Rosamund was as far apart from them as though she sat in Steeple Hall—ay, and further. Also they came to see that of rescuing her from Damascus there was no hope at all. She dwelt in her own palace, whereof the walls were guarded night and day by a company of the Sultan's Mameluks, who knew that they were answerable for her with their lives. Within its walls, again, lived trusted eunuchs, under the command of a cunning fellow named Mesrour, and her retinue of women, all of them spies and watchful. How could two men hope to snatch her from the heart of such a host and to spirit her out of Damascus and through its encircling armies?

One comfort, however, was left to them. When she reached the court Rosamund had prayed of the Sultan that Masouda should not be separated from her, and this because of the part she had played in his niece's rescue from the power of Sinan, he had granted, though doubtfully. Moreover, Masouda, being a person of no account except for her beauty, and a heretic, was allowed to go where she would and to speak with whom she wished. So, as she wished to speak often with Godwin, they did not lack for tidings of Rosamund.

From her they learned that in a fashion the princess was happy enough—who would not be that had just escaped from Al-je-bal?—yet weary of the strange Eastern life, of the restraints upon her, and of her aimless days; vexed also that she might not mix with the brethren. Day by day she sent them her greetings, and with them warnings to attempt nothing—not even to see her—since there was no hope that they would succeed. So much afraid of them was the Sultan, Rosamund said, that both she and they were watched day and night, and of any folly their lives would pay the price. When they heard all this the brethren began to despair, and their spirits sank so low that they cared not what should happen to them.

Then it was that a chance came to them of which the issue was to make them still more admired by Saladin and to lift Masouda to honour. One hot morning they were seated in the courtyard of their house beside the fountain, staring at the passers-by through the bars of the bronze gates and at the sentries who marched to and fro before them. This house was in one of the principal thoroughfares of Damascus, and in front of it flowed continually an unending, many-coloured stream of folk.

There were white-robed Arabs of the desert, mounted on their grumbling camels; caravans of merchandise from Egypt or elsewhere; asses laden with firewood or the grey, prickly growth of the wild thyme for the bakers' ovens; water-sellers with their goatskin bags and chinking brazen cups; vendors of birds or sweetmeats; women going to the bath in closed and curtained litters, escorted by the eunuchs of their households; great lords riding on their Arab horses and preceded by their runners, who thrust the crowd asunder and beat the poor with rods; beggars, halt, maimed, and blind, beseeching alms; lepers, from whom all shrank away, who wailed their woes aloud; stately companies of soldiers, some mounted and some afoot; holy men, who gave blessings and received alms; and so forth, without number and without end.

Godwin and Wulf, seated in the shade of the painted house, watched them gloomily. They were weary of this ever-changing sameness, weary of the eternal glare and glitter of this unfamiliar life, weary of the insistent cries of the mullahs on the minarets, of the flash of the swords that would soon be red with the blood of their own people; weary, too, of the hopeless task to which they were sworn. Rosamund was one of this multitude; she was the princess of Baalbec, half an Eastern by her blood, and growing more Eastern day by day—or so they thought in their bitterness. As well might two Saracens hope to snatch the queen of England from her palace at Westminster, as they to drag the princess of Baalbec out of the power of a monarch more absolute than any king of England.

So they sat silent since they had nothing to say, and stared now at the passing crowd, and now at the thin stream of water falling continually into the marble basin.

Presently they heard voices at the gate, and, looking up, saw a woman wrapped in a long cloak, talking with the guard, who with a laugh thrust out his arm, as though to place it round her. Then a knife flashed, and the soldier stepped back, still laughing, and opened the wicket. The woman came in. It was Masouda. They rose and bowed to her, but she passed before them into the house. Thither they followed, while the soldier at the gate laughed again, and at the sound of his mockery Godwin's cheek grew red. Even in the cool, darkened room she noticed it, and said, bitterly enough:

"What does it matter? Such insults are my daily bread whom they believe—" and she stopped.

"They had best say nothing of what they believe to me," muttered Godwin.

"I thank you," Masouda answered, with a sweet, swift smile, and, throwing off her cloak, stood before them unveiled, clad in the white robes that befitted her tall and graceful form so well, and were blazoned on the breast with the cognizance of Baalbec. "Well for you," she went on, "that they hold me to be what I am not, since otherwise I should win no entry to this house."

"What of our lady Rosamund?" broke in Wulf awkwardly, for, like Godwin, he was pained.

Masouda laid her hand upon her breast as though to still its heaving, then answered:

"The princess of Baalbec, my mistress, is well and as ever, beautiful, though somewhat weary of the pomp in which she finds no joy. She sent her greetings, but did not say to which of you they should be delivered, so, pilgrims, you must share them."

Godwin winced, but Wulf asked if there were any hope of seeing her, to which Masouda answered:

"None," adding, in a low voice, "I come upon another business. Do you brethren wish to do Salah-ed-din a service?"

"I don't know. What is it?" asked Godwin gloomily.

"Only to save his life—for which he may be grateful, or may not, according to his mood."

"Speak on," said Godwin, "and tell us how we two Franks can save the life of the Sultan of the East."

"Do you still remember Sinan and his *fedais*? Yes—they are not easily forgotten, are they? Well, to-night he has plotted to murder Salah-ed-din, and afterwards to murder you if he can, and to carry away your lady Rosamund if he can, or, failing that, to murder her also. Oh! the tale is true enough. I have it from one of them under the Signet—surely that Signet has served us well—who believes, poor fool, that I am in the plot. Now, you are the officers of the bodyguard who watch in the ante-chamber to-night, are you not? Well, when the guard is changed at midnight, the eight men who should replace them at the doors of the room of Salah-ed-din will not arrive; they will be decoyed away by a false order. In their stead will come eight murderers, disguised in the robes and arms of Mameluks. They look to deceive and cut you down, kill Salah-ed-din, and escape by the further door. Can you hold your own awhile against eight men, think you?"

"We have done so before and will try," answered Wulf. "But how shall we know that they are not Mameluks?"

"Thus—they will wish to pass the door, and you will say, 'Nay, sons of Sinan,' whereon they will spring on you to kill you. Then be ready and shout aloud."

"And if they overcome us," asked Godwin, "then the Sultan would be slain?"

"Nay, for you must lock the door of the chamber of Salah-ed-din and hide away the key. The sound of the fighting will arouse the outer guard ere hurt can come to him. Or," she added, after thinking awhile, "perhaps it will be best to reveal the plot to the Sultan at once."

"No, no," answered Wulf; "let us take the chance. I weary of doing nothing here. Hassan guards the outer gate. He will come swiftly at the sound of blows."

"Good," said Masouda; "I will see that he is there and awake. Now farewell, and pray that we may meet again. I say nothing of this story to the princess Rosamund until it is done with." Then throwing her cloak about her shoulders, she turned and went.

"Is that true, think you?" asked Wulf of Godwin.

"We have never found Masouda to be a liar," was his answer. "Come; let us see to our armour, for the knives of those *fedai* are sharp."

It was near midnight, and the brethren stood in the small, domed ante-chamber, from which a door opened into the sleeping rooms of Saladin. The guard of eight Mameluks had left them, to be met by their relief in the courtyard, according to custom, but no relief had as yet appeared in the ante-chamber.

"It would seem that Masouda's tale is true," said Godwin, and going to the door he locked it, and hid the key beneath a cushion.

Then they took their stand in front of the locked door, before which hung curtains, standing in the shadow with the light from the hanging silver lamps pouring down in front of them. Here they waited awhile in silence, till at length they heard the tramp of men, and eight Mameluks, clad in yellow above their mail, marched in and saluted.

"Stand!" said Godwin, and they stood a minute, then began to edge forward.

"Stand!" said both the brethren again, but still they edged forward.

"Stand, sons of Sinan!" they said a third time, drawing their swords.

Then with a hiss of disappointed rage the *fedai* came at them.

"A D'Arcy! A D'Arcy! Help for the Sultan!" shouted the brethren, and the fray began.

Six of the men attacked them, and while they were engaged with these the other two slipped round and tried the door, only to find it fast. Then they also turned upon the brethren, thinking to take the key from off their bodies. At the first rush two of the *fedai* went down beneath the sweep of the long swords, but after that the murderers would not come close, and while some engaged them in front, others strove to pass and stab them from behind. Indeed, a blow from one of their long knives fell upon Godwin's shoulder, but the good mail turned it.

"Give way," he cried to Wulf, "or they will best us."

So suddenly they gave way before them till their backs were against the door, and there they stood, shouting for help and sweeping round them with their swords into reach of which the *fedai* dare not come. Now from without the chamber rose a cry and tumult, and the sound of heavy blows falling upon the gates that the murderers had barred behind them, while upon the further side of the door, which he could not open, was heard the voice of the Sultan demanding to know what passed.

The *fedai* heard these sounds also, and read in them their doom. Forgetting caution in their despair and rage, they hurled themselves upon the brethren, for they thought that if they could get them down they might still break through the door and slay Salah-ed-din before they themselves were slain. But for awhile the brethren stopped their rush with point and buckler, wounding two of them sorely; and when at length they closed in upon them, the gates were burst, and Hassan and the outer guard were at hand.

A minute later and, but little hurt, Godwin and Wulf were leaning on their swords, and the *fedai*, some of them dead or wounded and some of them captive, lay before them on the marble floor. Moreover, the door had been opened, and through it came the Sultan in his night-gear.

"What has chanced?" he asked, looking at them doubtfully.

"Only this, lord," answered Godwin; "these men came to kill you and we held them off till help arrived."

"Kill me! My own guard kill me?"

"They are not your guard; they are *fedai*, disguised as your guard, and sent by Al-je-bal, as he promised."

Now Salah-ed-din turned pale, for he who feared nothing else was all his life afraid of the Assassins and their lord, who thrice had striven to murder him.

"Strip the armour from those men," went on Godwin, "and I think that you will find truth in my words, or, if not, question such of them as still live."

They obeyed, and there upon the breast of one of them, burnt into his skin, was the symbol of the blood-red dagger. Now Saladin saw, and beckoned the brethren aside.

"How knew you of this?" he asked, searching them with his piercing eyes.

"Masouda, the lady Rosamund's waiting woman, warned us that you, lord, and we, were to be murdered tonight by eight men, so we made ready."

"Why, then, did you not tell me?"

"Because," answered Wulf, "we were not sure that the news was true, and did not wish to bring false tidings and be made foolish. Because, also, my brother and I thought that we could hold our own awhile against eight of Sinan's rats disguised as soldiers of Saladin."

"You have done it well, though yours was a mad counsel," answered the Sultan. Then he gave his hand first to one and next to the other, and said, simply:

"Sir Knights, Salah-ed-din owes his life to you. Should it ever come about that you owe your lives to Salah-ed-din, he will remember this."

Thus this business ended. On the morrow those of the *fedai* who remained alive were questioned, and confessing freely that they had been sent to murder Salah-ed-din who had robbed their master of his bride, the two Franks who had carried her off, and the woman Masouda who had guided them, they were put to death cruelly enough. Also many others in the city were seized and killed on suspicion, so that for awhile there was no more fear from the Assassins.

Now from that day forward Saladin held the brethren in great friendship, and pressed gifts upon them and offered them honours. But they refused them all, saying that they needed but one thing of him, and he knew what it was—an answer at which his face sank.

One morning he sent for them, and, except for the presence of prince Hassan, the most favourite of his emirs, and a famous *imaum*, or priest of his religion, received them alone.

"Listen," he said briefly, addressing Godwin. "I understand that my niece, the princess of Baalbec, is beloved by you. Good. Subscribe the Koran, and I give her to you in marriage, for thus also she may be led to the true faith, whom I have sworn not to force thereto, and I gain a great warrior and Paradise a brave soul. The *imaum* here will instruct you in the truth."

Thus he spoke, but Godwin only stared at him with eyes set wide in wonderment, and answered:

"Sire, I thank you, but I cannot change my faith to win a woman, however dearly I may love her."

"So I thought," said Saladin with a sigh, "though indeed it is sad that superstition should thus blind so brave and good a man. Now, Sir Wulf, it is your turn. What say you to my offer? Will you take the princess and her dominions with my love thrown in as a marriage portion?"

Wulf thought a moment, and as he thought there arose in his mind a vision of an autumn afternoon that seemed years and years ago, when they two and Rosamund had stood by the shrine of St. Chad on the shores of Essex, and jested of this very matter of a change of faith. Then he answered, with one of his great laughs:

"Ay, sire, but on my own terms, not on yours, for if I took these I think that my marriage would lack blessings. Nor, indeed, would Rosamund wish to wed a servant of your Prophet, who if it pleased him might take other wives."

Saladin leant his head upon his hand, and looked at them with disappointed eyes, yet not unkindly.

"The knight Lozelle was a Cross-worshipper," he said, "but you two are very different from the knight Lozelle, who accepted the Faith when it was offered to him—"

"To win your trade," said Godwin, bitterly.

"I know not," answered Saladin, "though it is true the man seems to have been a Christian among the Franks, who here was a follower of the Prophet. At least, he is dead at your hands, and though he sinned against me and betrayed my niece to Sinan, peace be with his soul. Now I have one more thing to say to you. That Frank, Prince Arnat of Karak, whom you call Reginald de Chatillon—accursed be his name!—" and he spat upon the ground, "has once more broken the peace between me and the king of Jerusalem, slaughtering my merchants, and stealing my goods. I will suffer this shame no more, and very shortly I unfurl my standards, which shall not be folded up again until they float upon the mosque of Omar and from every tower top in Palestine. Your people are doomed. I, Yusuf Salah-ed-din," and he rose as he said the words, his very beard bristling with wrath, "declare the Holy War, and will sweep them to the sea. Choose now, you brethren. Do you fight for me or against me? Or will you give up your swords and bide here as my prisoners?"

"We are the servants of the Cross," answered Godwin, "and cannot lift steel against it and thereby lose our souls." Then he spoke with Wulf, and added, "As to your second question, whether we should bide here in chains. It is one that our lady Rosamund must answer, for we are sworn to her service. We demand to see the princess of Baalbec."

"Send for her, Emir," said Saladin to the prince Hassan, who bowed and departed.

A while later Rosamund came, looking beautiful but, as they saw when she threw back her veil, very white and weary. She bowed to Saladin, and the brethren, who were not allowed to touch her hand, bowed to her, devouring her face with eager eyes.

"Greeting, my uncle," she said to the Sultan, "and to you, my cousins, greeting also. What is your pleasure with me?"

Saladin motioned to her to be seated and bade Godwin set out the case, which he did very clearly, ending:

"Is it your wish, Rosamund, that we stay in this court as prisoners, or go forth to fight with the Franks in the great war that is to be?"

Rosamund looked at them awhile, then answered:

"To whom were you sworn the first? Was it to the service of our Lord, or to the service of a woman? I have said."

"Such words as we expected from you, being what you are," exclaimed Godwin, while Wulf nodded his head in assent, and added:

"Sultan, we ask your safe conduct to Jerusalem, and leave this lady in your charge, relying on your plighted word to do no violence to her faith and to protect her person."

"My safe conduct you have," replied Saladin, "and my friendship also. Nor, indeed, should I have thought well of you had you decided otherwise. Now, henceforth we are enemies in the eyes of all men, and I shall strive to slay you as you will strive to slay me. But as regards this lady, have no fear. What I have promised shall be fulfilled. Bid her farewell, whom you will see no more."

"Who taught your lips to say such words, O Sultan?" asked Godwin. "Is it given to you to read the future and the decrees of God?"

"I should have said," answered Saladin, "'Whom you will see no more if I am able to keep you apart.' Can you complain who, both of you, have refused to take her as a wife?"

Here Rosamund looked up wondering, and Wulf broke in:

"Tell her the price. Tell her that she was asked to wed either of us who would bow the knee to Mahomet, and to be the head of his harem, and I think that she will not blame us."

"Never would I have spoken again to him who answered otherwise," exclaimed Rosamund, and Saladin frowned at the words. "Oh! my uncle," she went on, "you have been kind to me and raised me high, but I do not seek this greatness, nor are your ways my ways, who am of a faith that you call accursed. Let me go, I beseech you, in care of these my kinsmen."

"And your lovers," said Saladin bitterly. "Niece, it cannot be. I love you well, but did I know even that your life must pay the price of your sojourn here, here you still should stay, since, as my dream told me, on you hang the lives of thousands, and I believe that dream. What, then, is your life, or the lives of these knights, or even my life, that any or all of them should turn the scale against those of thousands. Oh! everything that my empire can give is at your feet, but here you stay until the dream be accomplished, and," he added, looking at the brethren, "death shall be the portion of any who would steal you from my hand."

"Until the dream be accomplished?" said Rosamund catching at the words. "Then, when it is accomplished, shall I be free?"

"Ay," answered the Sultan; "free to come or to go, unless you attempt escape, for then you know your certain doom."

"It is a decree. Take note, my cousins, it is a decree. And you, prince Hassan, remember it also. Oh! I pray with all my soul I pray, that it was no lying spirit who brought you that dream, my uncle, though how I shall bring peace, who hitherto have brought nothing except war and bloodshed, I know not. Now go, my cousins but, if you will, leave me Masouda, who has no other friends. Go, and take my love and blessing with you, ay, and the blessing of Jesu and His saints which shall protect you in the hour of battle, and bring us together again."

So spoke Rosamund and threw her veil before her face that she might hide her tears.

Then Godwin and Wulf stepped to where she stood by the throne of Saladin, bent the knee before her, and, taking her hand, kissed it in farewell, nor did the Sultan say them nay. But when she was gone and the brethren were gone, he turned to the emir Hassan and to the great *imaum* who had sat silent all this while, and said:

"Now tell me, you who are old and wise, which of those men does the lady love? Speak, Hassan, you who know her well."

But Hassan shook his head. "One or the other. Both or neither—I know not," he answered. "Her counsel is too close for me."

Then Saladin turned to the *imaum*—a cunning, silent man.

"When both the infidels are about to die before her face, as I still hope to see them do, we may learn the answer. But unless she wills it, never before," he replied, and the Sultan noted his saying.

Next morning, having been warned that they would pass there by Masouda, Rosamund, watching through the lattice of one of her palace windows, saw the brethren go by. They were fully armed and, mounted on their splendid chargers Flame and Smoke, looked glorious men as, followed by their escort of swarthy, turbaned Mameluks, they rode proudly side by side, the sunlight glinting on their mail. Opposite to her house they halted awhile, and, knowing that Rosamund watched, although they could not see her, drew their swords and lifted them in salute. Then sheathing them again, they rode forward in silence, and soon were lost to sight.

Little did Rosamund guess how different they would appear when they three met again. Indeed, she scarcely dared to hope that they would ever meet, for she knew well that even if the war went in favour of the Christians she would be hurried away to some place where they would never find her. She knew well also that from Damascus her rescue was impossible, and that although Saladin loved them, as he loved all who were honest and brave, he would receive them no more as friends, for fear lest they should rob him of her, whom he hoped in some way unforeseen would enable him to end his days in peace. Moreover, the struggle between Cross and Crescent would be fierce and to the death, and she was sure that where was the closest fighting there in the midst of it would be found Godwin and Wulf. Well might it chance, therefore, that her eyes had looked their last upon them.

Oh! she was great. Gold was hers, with gems more than she could count, and few were the weeks that did not bring her added wealth or gifts. She had palaces to dwell in—alone; gardens to wander in—alone; eunuchs and slaves to rule over—alone. But never a friend had she, save the woman of the Assassins, to whom she clung because she, Masouda, had saved her from Sinan, and who clung to her, why, Rosamund could not be sure, for there was a veil between their spirits.

They were gone—they were gone! Even the sound of their horses' hoofs had died away, and she was desolate as a child lost in a city full of folk. Oh! and her heart was filled with fears for them, and most of all for one of them. If he should not come back into it, what would her life be?

Rosamund bowed her head and wept; then, hearing a sound behind her, turned to see that Masouda was weeping also.

"Why do you weep?" she asked.

"The maid should copy her mistress," answered Masouda with a hard laugh; "but, lady, why do you weep? At least you are beloved, and, come what may, nothing can take that from you. You are not of less value than the good horse between the rider's knees, or the faithful hound that runs at his side."

A thought rose in Rosamund's mind—a new and terrible thought. The eyes of the two women met, and those of Rosamund asked, "Which?" anxiously as once in the moonlight she had asked it with her voice from the gate above the Narrow Way. Between them stood a table inlaid with ivory and pearl, whereon the dust from the street had gathered through the open lattice. Masouda leaned over, and with her forefinger wrote a single Arabic letter in the dust upon the table, then passed her hand across it.

Rosamund's breast heaved twice or thrice and was still. Then she asked: "Why did not you who are free go with him?"

"Because he prayed me to bide here and watch over the lady whom he loved. So to the death—I watch."

Slowly Masouda spoke, and the heavy words seemed like blood dropping from a death wound. Then she sank forward into the arms of Rosamund.

## CHAPTER 18

# Wulf Pays for the Drugged Wine

Many a day had gone by since the brethren bade farewell to Rosamund at Damascus. Now, one burning July night, they sat upon their horses, the moonlight gleaming on their mail. Still as statues they sat, looking out from a rocky mountain top across that grey and arid plain which stretches from near Nazareth to the lip of the hills at whose foot lies Tiberias on the Sea of Galilee. Beneath them, camped around the fountain of Seffurieh, were spread the hosts of the Franks to which they did sentinel; thirteen hundred knights, twenty thousand foot, and hordes of Turcopoles—that is, natives of the country, armed after the fashion of the Saracens. Two miles away to the southeast glimmered the white houses of Nazareth, set in the lap of the mountains. Nazareth, the holy city, where for thirty years lived and toiled the Saviour of the world. Doubtless, thought Godwin, His feet had often trod that mountain whereon they stood, and in the watered vales below His hands had sped the plough or reaped the corn. Long, long had His voice been silent, yet to Godwin's ears it still seemed to speak in the murmur of the vast camp, and to echo from the slopes of the Galilean hills, and the words it said were: "I bring not peace, but a sword."

To-morrow they were to advance, so rumour said, across yonder desert plain and give battle to Saladin, who lay with all his power by Hattin, above Tiberias.

Godwin and his brother thought that it was a madness; for they had seen the might of the Saracens and ridden across that thirsty plain beneath the summer sun. But who were they, two wandering, unattended knights, that they should dare to lift up their voices against those of the lords of the land, skilled from their birth in desert warfare? Yet Godwin's heart was troubled and fear took hold of him, not for himself, but for all the countless army that lay asleep yonder, and for the cause of Christendom, which staked its last throw upon this battle.

"I go to watch yonder; bide you here," he said to Wulf, and, turning the head of Flame, rode some sixty yards over a shoulder of the rock to the further edge of the mountain which looked towards the north. Here he could see neither the camp, nor Wulf, nor any living thing, but indeed was utterly alone. Dismounting, and bidding the horse stand, which it would do like a dog, he walked forward a few steps to where there was a rock, and, kneeling down, began to pray with all the strength of his pure, warrior heart.

"O Lord," he prayed, "Who once wast man and a dweller in these mountains, and knowest what is in man, hear me. I am afraid for all the thousands who sleep round Nazareth; not for myself, who care nothing for my life, but for all those, Thy servants and my brethren. Yes, and for the Cross upon which Thou didst hang, and for the faith itself throughout the East. Oh! give me light! Oh! let me hear and see, that I may warn them, unless my fears are vain!"

So he murmured to Heaven above and beat his hands against his brow, praying, ever praying, as he had never prayed before, that wisdom and vision might be given to his soul.

It seemed to Godwin that a sleep fell on him—at least, his mind grew clouded and confused. Then it cleared again, slowly, as stirred water clears, till it was bright and still; yet another mind to that which was his servant day by day which never could see or hear those things he saw and heard in that strange hour. Lo! he heard the spirits pass, whispering as they went; whispering, and, as it seemed to him, weeping also for some great woe which was to be; weeping yonder over Nazareth. Then like curtains the veils were lifted from his eyes, and as they swung aside he saw further, and yet further.

He saw the king of the Franks in his tent beneath, and about him the council of his captains, among them the fierce-eyed master of the Templars, and a man whom he had seen in Jerusalem where they had been dwelling, and knew for Count Raymond of Tripoli, the lord of Tiberias. They were reasoning together, till, presently, in a rage, the Master of the Templars drew his sword and dashed it down upon the table.

Another veil was lifted, and lo! he saw the camp of Saladin, the mighty, endless camp, with its ten thousand tents, amongst which the Saracens cried to Allah through all the watches of the night. He saw the royal pavilion, and in it the Sultan walked to and fro alone—none of his emirs, not even his son, were with him. He was lost in thought, and Godwin read his thought.

It was: "Behind me the Jordan and the Sea of Galilee, into which, if my flanks were turned, I should be driven, I and all my host. In front the territories of the Franks, where I have no friend; and by Nazareth their great army. Allah alone can help me. If they sit still and force me to advance across the desert and attack them before my army melts away, then I am lost. If they advance upon me round the Mountain Tabor and by the watered land, I may be lost. But if—oh! if Allah should make them mad, and they should strike straight across the desert—then, then they are lost, and the reign of the Cross in Syria is forever at an end. I will wait here. I will wait here. . ."

Look! near to the pavilion of Saladin stood another tent, closely guarded, and in it on a cushioned bed lay two women. One was Rosamund, but she slept sound; and the other was Masouda, and she was waking, for her eyes met his in the darkness.

The last veil was withdrawn, and now Godwin saw a sight at which his soul shivered. A fire-blackened plain, and above it a frowning mountain, and that mountain thick, thick with dead, thousands and thousands and thousands of dead, among which the hyenas wandered and the night-birds screamed. He could see their faces, many of them he knew again as those of living men whom he had met in Jerusalem and elsewhere, or had noted with the army. He could hear also the moanings of the few who were yet alive.

About that field—yes, and in the camp of Saladin, where lay more dead—his body seemed to wander searching for something, he knew not what, till it came to him that it was the corpse of Wulf for which he sought and found it not—nay, nor his own either. Then once more he heard the spirits pass—a very great company, for to them were gathered all those dead—heard them pass away, wailing, ever more faintly wailing for the lost cause of Christ, wailing over Nazareth.

Godwin awoke from his dream trembling, mounted his horse, and rode back to Wulf. Beneath, as before, lay the sleeping camp, yonder stretched the brown desert, and there sat Wulf watching both.

"Tell me," asked Godwin, "how long is it since I left you?"

"Some few minutes—ten perhaps," answered his brother.

"A short while to have seen so much," replied Godwin. Then Wulf looked at him curiously and asked:

"What have you seen?"

"If I told you, Wulf, you would not believe."

"Tell me, and I will say."

So Godwin told him all, and at the end asked him, "What think you?"

Wulf considered awhile, and answered:

"Well, brother, you have touched no wine to-day, so you are

not drunk, and you have done nothing foolish, so you are not mad. Therefore it would seem that the saints have been talking to you, or, at least, so I should think of any other man whom I knew to be as good as you are. Yet it is folk like you that see visions, and those visions are not always true, for sometimes, I believe, the devil is their showman. Our watch is ended, for I hear the horses of the knights who come to relieve us. Listen; this is my counsel. In the camp yonder is our friend with whom we travelled from Jerusalem, Egbert, the bishop of Nazareth, who marches with the host. Let us go to him and lay this matter before him, for he is a holy man and learned; no false, self-seeking priest."

Godwin nodded in assent, and presently, when the other knights were come and they had made their report to them, they rode off together to the tent of Egbert, and, leaving their horses in charge of a servant, entered.

Egbert was an Englishman who had spent more than thirty years of his life in the East, whereof the suns had tanned his wrinkled face to the hue of bronze, that seemed the darker in contrast with his blue eyes and snow-white hair and beard. Entering the tent, they found him at his prayers before a little image of the Virgin, and stood with bowed heads until he had finished. Presently he rose, and greeting them with a blessing, asked them what they needed.

"Your counsel, holy father," answered Wulf. "Godwin, set out your tale."

So, having seen that the tent flap was closed and that none lingered near, Godwin told him his dream.

The old man listened patiently, nor did he seem surprised at this strange story, since in those days men saw—or thought they saw—many such visions, which were accepted by the Church as true.

When he had finished Godwin asked of him as he had asked of Wulf: "What think you, holy father? Is this a dream, or is it a message? And if so, from whom comes the message?"

"Godwin D'Arcy," he answered, "in my youth I knew your father. It was I who shrove him when he lay dying of his wounds, and a nobler soul never passed from earth to heaven. After you had left Damascus, when you were the guest of Saladin, we dwelt together in the same lodging in Jerusalem, and together we travelled here, during all which time I learned to know you also as the worthy son of a worthy sire—no dissolute knight, but a true servant of the Church. It well may be that to such a one as you foresight has been given, that through you those who rule us may be warned, and all Christendom saved from great sorrow and disgrace. Come; let us go to the king, and tell this story, for he still sits in council yonder."

So they went out together and rode to the royal tent. Here the bishop was admitted, leaving them without.

Presently he returned and beckoned to them, and as they passed, the guards whispered to them:

"A strange council, sirs, and a fateful!"

Already it was near midnight, but still the great pavilion was crowded with barons and chief captains who sat in groups, or sat round a narrow table made of boards placed upon trestles. At the head of that table sat the king, Guy of Lusignan, a weak-faced man, clad in splendid armour. On his right was the white-haired Count Raymond of Tripoli, and on his left the black-bearded, frowning Master of the Templars, clad in his white mantle on the left breast of which the red cross was blazoned.

Words had been running high, their faces showed it, but just then a silence reigned as though the disputants were weary, and the king leaned back in his chair, passing his hand to and fro across his forehead. He looked up, and seeing the bishop, asked peevishly:

"What is it now? Oh! I remember, some tale from those tall twin knights. Well, bring them forward and speak it out, for we have no time to lose."

So the three of them came forward and at Godwin's prayer the bishop Egbert told of the vision that had come to him not more than an hour ago while he kept watch upon the mountain top. At first one or two of the barons seemed disposed to laugh, but when they looked at Godwin's high and spiritual face, their laughter died away, for it did not seem wonderful to them that such a man should see visions. Indeed, as the tale of the rocky hill and the dead who were stretched upon it went on, they grew white with fear, and whitest of them all was the king, Guy of Lusignan.

"Is all this true, Sir Godwin?" he asked, when the bishop had finished.

"It is true, my lord king," answered Godwin.

"His word is not enough," broke in the Master of the Templars. "Let him swear to it on the Holy Rood, knowing that if he lies it will blast his soul to all eternity." And the council muttered, "Ay, let him swear."

Now there was an annexe to the tent, rudely furnished as a chapel, and at the end of this annexe a tall, veiled object. Rufinus, the bishop of Acre, who was clad in the armour of a knight, went to the object, and drawing the veil, revealed a broken, blackened cross, set around with jewels, that stood about the height of a man above the ground, for all the lower part was gone.

At the sight of it Godwin and every man present there fell upon his knees, for since St. Helena found it, over seven centuries before, this had been accounted the most precious relic in all Christendom; the very wood upon which the Saviour suffered, as, indeed, it may have been.

Millions had worshipped it, tens of thousands had died for it, and now, in the hour of this great struggle between Christ and the false prophet it was brought from its shrine that the host which escorted it might prove invincible in battle. Soldiers who fought around the very Cross could not be defeated, they said, for, if need were, legions of angels would come to aid them.

Godwin and Wulf stared at the relic with wonder, fear, and adoration. There were the nail marks, there was the place where the scroll of Pilate had been affixed above the holy head—almost could they seem to see that Form divine and dying.

"Now," broke in the voice of the Master of the Templars, "let Sir Godwin D'Arcy swear to the truth of his tale upon this Rood."

Rising from his knees Godwin advanced to the Cross, and laying his hand upon the wood, said: "Upon the very Rood I swear that not much more than an hour ago I saw the vision which has been told to the king's highness and to all; that I believe this vision was sent to me in answer to my prayer to preserve our host and the holy city from the power of the Saracen, and that it is a true foreshadowing of what will come about should we advance upon the Sultan. I can say no more. I swear, knowing that if I lie eternal damnation is my doom."

The bishop drew back the covering over the Cross, and in silence the council took their seats again about the table. Now the king was very pale, and fearful; indeed a gloom lay upon all of them.

"It would seem," he said, "that here a messenger has been sent to us from heaven. Dare we disobey his message?"

The Grand Templar lifted his rugged, frowning face. "A messenger from heaven, said you, king? To me he seems more like a messenger from Saladin. Tell us, Sir Godwin, were not you and your brother once the Sultan's guests at Damascus?"

"That is so, my lord Templar. We left before the war was declared."

"And," went on the Master, "were you not officers of the Sultan's bodyguard?"

Now all looked intently at Godwin, who hesitated a little, foreseeing how his answer would be read, whereon Wulf spoke in his loud voice:

"Ay, we acted as such for awhile, and—doubtless you have heard the story—saved Saladin's life when he was attacked by the Assassins."

"Oh!" said the Templar with bitter sarcasm, "you saved Saladin's life, did you? I can well believe it. You, being Christians, who above everything should desire the death of Saladin, saved his life! Now, Sir Knights, answer me one more question—"

"Sir Templar, with my tongue or with my sword?" broke in Wulf, but the king held up his hand and bade him be silent.

"A truce to your tavern ruffling, young sir, and answer," went on the Templar. "Or, rather, do you answer, Sir Godwin. Is your cousin, Rosamund, the daughter of Sir Andrew D'Arcy, a niece of Saladin, and has she been created by him princess of Baalbec, and is she at this moment in his city of Damascus?"

"She is his niece," answered Godwin quietly; "she is the princess of Baalbec, but at this moment she is not in Damascus."

"How do you know that, Sir Godwin?"

"I know it because in the vision of which you have been told I saw her sleeping in a tent in the camp of Saladin."

Now the council began to laugh, but Godwin, with a set, white face, went on: "Ay, my lord Templar, and near that very blazoned tent I saw scores of the Templars and of the Hospitallers lying dead. Remember it when the dreadful hour comes and you see them also."

Now the laughter died away, and a murmur of fear ran round the board, mixed with such words as "Wizardry." "He has learnt it from the Paynims." "A black sorcerer, without doubt."

Only the Templar, who feared neither man nor spirit, laughed, and gave him the lie with his eyes.

"You do not believe me," said Godwin, "nor will you believe me when I say that while I was on guard on yonder hill-top I saw you wrangling with the Count of Tripoli—ay, and draw your sword and dash it down in front of him upon this very table."

Now again the council stared and muttered, for they too had seen this thing; but the Master answered:

"He may have learnt it otherwise than from an angel. Folk have been in and out of this tent. My lord king, have we more time to waste upon these visions of a knight of whom all we know for certain is, that like his brother, he has been in the service of Saladin, which they left, he says, in order to fight against him in this war. It may be so; it is not for us to judge; though were the times different I would inform against Sir Godwin D'Arcy as a sorcerer, and one who has been in traitorous communication with our common foe."

"And I would thrust the lie down your throat with my sword's point!" shouted Wulf.

But Godwin only shrugged: his shoulders and said nothing, and the Master went on, taking no heed.

"King, we await your word, and it must be spoken soon, for in four hours it will be dawn. Do we march against Saladin like bold, Christian men, or do we bide here like cowards?"

Then Count Raymond of Tripoli rose, and said:

"Before you answer, king, hear me, if it be for the last time, who am old in war and know the Saracens. My town of Tiberias is sacked; my vassals have been put to the sword by thousands; my wife is imprisoned in her citadel, and soon must yield, if she be not rescued. Yet I say to you, and to the barons here assembled, better so than that you should advance across the desert to attack Saladin. Leave Tiberias to its fate and my wife with it, and save your army, which is the last hope of the Christians of the East. Christ has no more soldiers in these lands, Jerusalem has no other shield. The army of the Sultan is larger than yours; his cavalry are more skilled. Turn his flank—or, better still, bide here and await his attack, and victory will be to the soldiers of the Cross. Advance and the vision of that knight at whom you scoff will come true, and the cause of Christendom be lost in Syria. I have spoken, and for the last time."

"Like his friend the knight of Visions," sneered the Grand Master, "the count Raymond is an old ally of Saladin. Will you take such coward council? On—on! and smite these heathen dogs, or be forever shamed. On, in the name of the Cross! The Cross is with us!"

"Ay," answered Raymond, "for the last time."

Then there arose a tumult through which every man shouted to his fellow, some saying one thing and some another, while the king sat at the head of the board, his face hidden in his hands. Presently he lifted it, and said:

"I command that we march at dawn. If the count Raymond and these brethren think the words unwise, let them leave us and remain here under guard until the issue be known."

Now followed a great silence, for all there knew that the words were fateful, in the midst of which Count Raymond said:

"Nay, I go with you," while Godwin echoed, "And we go also to show whether or not we are the spies of Saladin."

Of these speeches none of them seemed to take heed, for all were lost in their own thoughts. One by one they rose, bowed to the king, and left the tent to give their commands and rest awhile, before it was time to ride. Godwin and Wulf went also, and with them the bishop of Nazareth, who wrung his hands and seemed ill at ease. But Wulf comforted him, saying:

"Grieve no more, father; let us think of the joy of battle, not of the sorrow by which it may be followed."

"I find no joy in battles," answered the holy Egbert.

When they had slept awhile, Godwin and Wulf rose and fed their horses. After they had washed and groomed them, they tested and did on their armour, then took them down to the spring to drink their fill, as their masters did. Also Wulf, who was cunning in war, brought with him four large wineskins which he had provided against this hour, and filling them with pure water, fastened two of them with thongs behind the saddle of Godwin and two behind his own. Further, he filled the water-bottles at their saddle-bows, saying:

"At least we will be among the last to die of thirst."

Then they went back and watched the host break its camp, which it did with no light heart, for many of them knew of the danger in which they stood; moreover, the tale of Godwin's vision had been spread abroad. Not knowing where to go, they and Egbert, the bishop of Nazareth—who was unarmed and rode upon a mule, for stay behind he would not—joined themselves to the great body of knights who followed the king. As they did so, the Templars, five hundred strong, came up, a fierce and gallant band, and the Master, who was at their head, saw the brethren and called out, pointing to the wineskins which were hung behind their saddles:

"What do these water-carriers here among brave knights who trust in God alone?"

Wulf would have answered, but Godwin bade him be silent, saying: "Fall back; we will find less ill-omened company."

So they stood on one side and bowed themselves as the Cross went by, guarded by the mailed bishop of Acre. Then came Reginald of Chatillon, Saladin's enemy, the cause of all this woe, who saw them and cried:

"Sir Knights, whatever they may say, I know you for brave men, for I have heard the tale of your doings among the Assassins. There is room for you among my suite—follow me."

"As well him as another," said Godwin. "Let us go where we are led." So they followed him.

By the time that the army reached Kenna, where once the water was made wine, the July sun was already hot, and the spring was so soon drunk dry that many men could get no water. On they pushed into the desert lands below, which lay between them and Tiberias, and were bordered on the right and left by hills. Now clouds of dust were seen moving across the plains, and in the heart of them bodies of Saracen horsemen, which continually attacked the vanguard under Count Raymond, and as continually retreated before they could be crushed, slaying many with their spears and arrows. Also these came round behind them, and charged the rearguard, where marched the Templars and the light-armed troops named Turcopoles, and the band of Reginald de Chatillon, with which rode the brethren.

From noon till near sundown the long harassed line, broken now into fragments, struggled forward across the rough, stony plain, the burning heat beating upon their armour till the air danced about it as it does before a fire. Towards evening men and horses became exhausted, and the soldiers cried to their captains to lead them to water. But in that place there was no water. The rearguard fell behind, worn out with constant attacks that must be repelled in the burning heat, so that there was a great gap between it and the king who marched in the centre. Messages reached them to push on, but they could not, and at length camp was pitched in the desert near a place called Marescalcia, and upon this camp Raymond and his vanguard were forced back. As Godwin and Wulf rode up, they saw him come in bringing his wounded with him, and heard him pray the king to push on and at all hazards to cut his way through to the lake, where they might drink—ay, and heard the king say that he could not, since the soldiers would march no more that day. Then Raymond wrung his hands in despair and rode back to his men, crying aloud:

"Alas! alas! Oh! Lord God, alas! We are dead, and Thy Kingdom is lost."

That night none slept, for all were athirst, and who can sleep with a burning throat? Now also Godwin and Wulf were no longer laughed at because of the water-skins they carried on their horses. Rather did great nobles come to them, and almost on their knees crave for the boon of a single cup. Having watered their horses sparingly from a bowl, they gave what they could, till at length only two skins remained, and one of these was spilt by a thief, who crept up and slashed it with his knife that he might drink while the water ran to waste. After this the brethren drew their swords and watched, swearing that they would kill any man who so much as touched the skin which was left. All that long night through there arose a confused clamour from the camp, of which the burden seemed to be, "Water! Give us water!" while from without came the shouts of the Saracens calling upon Allah. Here, too, the hot ground was covered with scrub dried to tinder by the summer drought, and to this the Saracens set fire so that the smoke rolled down on the Christian host and choked them, and the place became a hell.

Day dawned at last; and the army was formed up in order of battle, its two wings being thrown forward. Thus they struggled on, those of them that were not too weak to stir, who were slaughtered as they lay. Nor as yet did the Saracens attack them, since they knew that the sun was stronger than all their spears. On they laboured towards the northern wells, till about mid-day the battle began with a flight of arrows so thick that for awhile it hid the heavens.

After this came charge and counter-charge, attack and repulse, and always above the noise of war that dreadful cry for water. What chanced Godwin and Wulf never knew, for the smoke and dust blinded them so that they could see but a little way. At length there was a last furious charge, and the knights with whom they were clove the dense mass of Saracens like a serpent of steel, leaving a broad trail of dead behind them. When they pulled rein and wiped the sweat from their eyes it was to find themselves with thousands of others upon the top of a steep hill, of which the sides were thick with dry grass and bush that already was being fired.

"The Rood! The Rood! Rally round the Rood!" said a voice, and looking behind them they saw the black and jewelled fragment of the true Cross set upon a rock, and by it the bishop of Acre. Then the smoke of the burning grass rose up and hid it from their sight.

Now began one of the most hideous fights that is told of in the history of the world. Again and again the Saracens attacked in thousands, and again and again they were driven back by the desperate valour of the Franks, who fought on, their jaws agape with thirst. A black-bearded man stumbled up to the brethren, his tongue protruding from his lips, and they knew him for the Master of the Templars.

"For the love of Christ, give me to drink," he said, recognizing them as the knights at whom he had mocked as water-carriers.

They gave him of the little they had left, and while they and their horses drank the rest themselves, saw him rush down the hill refreshed, shaking his red sword. Then came a pause, and they heard the voice of the bishop of Nazareth, who had clung to them all this while, saying, as though to himself:

"And here it was that the Saviour preached the Sermon on the Mount. Yes, He preached the words of peace upon this very spot. Oh! it cannot be that He will desert us—it cannot be."

While the Saracens held off, the soldiers began to put up the king's pavilion, and with it other tents, around the rock on which stood the Cross.

"Do they mean to camp here?" asked Wulf bitterly.

"Peace," answered Godwin; "they hope to make a wall about the Rood. But it is of no avail, for this is the place of my dream."

Wulf shrugged his shoulders. "At least, let us die well," he said.

Then the last attack began. Up the hillside rose dense volumes of smoke, and with the smoke came the Saracens. Thrice they were driven back; thrice they came on. At the fourth onset few of the Franks could fight more, for thirst had conquered them on this waterless hill of Hattin. They lay down upon the dry grass with gaping jaws and protruding tongues, and let themselves be slain or taken prisoners. A great company of Saracen horsemen broke through the ring and rushed at the scarlet tent. It rocked to and fro, then down it fell in a red heap, entangling the king in its folds.

At the foot of the Cross, Rufinus, the bishop of Acre, still fought on bravely. Suddenly an arrow struck him in the throat, and throwing his arms wide, he fell to earth. Then the Saracens hurled themselves upon the Rood, tore it from its place, and with mockery and spittings bore it down the hill towards their camp, as ants may be seen carrying a little stick into their nest, while all who were left alive of the Christian army stared upwards, as though they awaited some miracle from Heaven. But no angels appeared in the brazen sky, and knowing that God had deserted them, they groaned aloud in their shame and wretchedness.

"Come," said Godwin to Wulf in a strange, quiet voice. "We have seen enough. It is time to die. Look! yonder below us are the Mameluks, our old regiment, and amongst them Saladin, for I see his banner. Having had water, we and our horses are still fresh and strong. Now, let us make an end of which they will tell in Essex yonder. Charge for the flag of Saladin!"

Wulf nodded, and side by side they sped down the hill. Scimitars flashed at them, arrows struck upon their mail and the shields blazoned with the Death's-head D'Arcy crest. Through it all they went unscathed, and while the army of the Saracens stared, at the foot of the Horn of Hattin turned their horses' heads straight for the royal standard of Saladin. On they struggled, felling or riding down a foe at every stride. On, still on, although Flame and Smoke bled from a score of wounds.

They were among the Mameluks, where their line was thin; by

Heaven! they were through them, and riding straight at the well-known figure of the Sultan, mounted on his white horse with his young son and his emir, the prince Hassan, at his side.

"Saladin for you, Hassan for me," shouted Wulf.

Then they met, and all the host of Islam cried out in dismay as they saw the Commander of the Faithful and his horse borne to the earth before the last despairing charge of these mad Christian knights. Another instant, and the Sultan was on his feet again, and a score of scimitars were striking at Godwin. His horse Flame sank down dying, but he sprang from the saddle, swinging the long sword. Now Saladin recognized the crest upon his buckler, and cried out:

"Yield you, Sir Godwin! You have done well—yield you!"

But Godwin, who would not yield, answered:

"When I am dead—not before."

Thereupon Saladin spoke a word, and while certain of his Mameluks engaged Godwin in front, keeping out of reach of that red and terrible sword, others crept up behind, and springing on him, seized his arms and dragged him to the ground, where they bound him fast.

Meanwhile Wulf had fared otherwise, for it was his horse Smoke, already stabbed to the vitals, that fell as he plunged on prince Hassan. Yet he also arose but little hurt, and cried out:

"Thus, Hassan, old foe and friend, we meet at last in war. Come, I would pay the debt I owe you for that drugged wine, man to man and sword to sword."

"Indeed, it is due, Sir Wulf," answered the prince, laughing. "Guards, touch not this brave knight who has dared so much to reach me. Sultan, I ask a boon. Between Sir Wulf and me there is an ancient quarrel that can only be washed away in blood. Let it be decided here and now, and let this be your decree—that if I fall in fair fight, none shall set upon my conqueror, and no vengeance shall be taken for my blood."

"Good," said Saladin. "Then Sir Wulf shall be my prisoner and no more, as his brother is already. I owe it to the men who saved my life when we were friends. Give the Frank to drink that the fight may be fair."

So they gave Wulf a cup of which he drank, and when he had done it was handed to Godwin. For even the Mameluks knew and loved these brethren who had been their officers, and praised the fierce charge that they had dared to make alone.

Hassan sprang to the ground, saying:

"Your horse is dead, Sir Wulf, so we must fight afoot."

"Generous as ever," laughed Wulf. "Even the poisoned wine was a gift!"

"If so, for the last time, I fear me," answered Hassan with a smile.

Then they faced each other, and oh! the scene was strange. Up on the slopes of Hattin the fight still raged. There amidst the smoke and fires of the burning grass little companies of soldiers stood back to back while the Saracens wheeled round them, thrusting and cutting at them till they fell. Here and there knights charged singly or in groups, and so came to death or capture. About the plain hundreds of foot soldiers were being slaughtered, while their officers were taken prisoners. Towards the camp of Saladin a company advanced with sounds of triumph, carrying aloft a black stump which was the holy Rood, while others drove or led mobs of prisoners, among them the king and his chosen knights.

The wilderness was red with blood, the air was rent with shouts of victory and cries of agony or despair. And there, in the midst of it all, ringed round with grave, courteous Saracens, stood the emir, clad above his mail in his white robe and jewelled turban, facing the great Christian knight, with harness hacked and reddened, the light of battle shining in his fierce eyes, and a smile upon his stained features.

For those who watched the battle was forgotten—or, rather, its interest was centred on this point.

"It will be a good fight," said one of them to Godwin, whom they had suffered to rise, "for though your brother is the younger and the heavier man, he is hurt and weary, whereas the emir is fresh and unwounded. Ah! they are at it!"

Hassan had struck first and the blow went home. Falling upon the point of Wulf's steel helm, the heavy, razor-edged scimitar glanced from it and shore away the links from the flap which hung upon his shoulder, causing the Frank to stagger. Again he struck, this time upon the shield, and so heavily that Wulf came to his knees.

"Your brother is sped," said the Saracen captain to Godwin, but Godwin only answered:

"Wait."

As he spoke Wulf twisted his body out of reach of a third blow, and while Hassan staggered forward with the weight of the missed stroke, placed his hand upon the ground, and springing to his feet, ran backwards six or eight paces.

"He flies!" cried the Saracens; but again Godwin said, "Wait." Nor was there long to wait.

For now, throwing aside his buckler and grasping the great sword in both his hands, with a shout of "A D'Arcy! A D'Arcy!" Wulf leapt at Hassan as a wounded lion leaps. The sword wheeled and fell, and lo!

the shield of the Saracen was severed in two. Again it fell, and his turbaned helm was cloven. A third time, and the right arm and shoulder with the scimitar that grasped it seemed to spring from his body, and Hassan sank dying to the ground.

Wulf stood and looked at him, while a murmur of grief went up from those who watched, for they loved this emir. Hassan beckoned to the victor with his left hand, and throwing down his sword to show that he feared no treachery, Wulf came to him and knelt beside him.

"A good stroke," Hassan said faintly, "that could shear the double links of Damascus steel as though it were silk. Well, as I told you long ago, I knew that the hour of our meeting in war would be an ill hour for me, and my debt is paid. Farewell, brave knight. Would I could hope that we should meet in Paradise! Take that star jewel, the badge of my House, from my turban and wear it in memory of me. Long, long and happy be your days."

Then, while Wulf held him in his arms, Saladin came up and spoke to him, till he fell back and was dead.

Thus died Hassan, and thus ended the battle of Hattin, which broke the power of the Christians in the East.

## Chapter 19

# Before the Walls of Ascalon

When Hassan was dead, at a sign from Saladin a captain of the Mameluks named Abdullah unfastened the jewel from the emir's turban and handed it to Wulf. It was a glorious star-shaped thing, made of great emeralds set round with diamonds, and the captain Abdullah, who like all Easterns loved such ornaments, looked at it greedily, and muttered:

"Alas! that an unbeliever should wear the enchanted Star, the ancient Luck of the House of Hassan!" a saying that Wulf remembered.

He took the jewel, then turned to Saladin and said, pointing to the dead body of Hassan:

"Have I your peace, Sultan, after such a deed?"

"Did I not give you and your brother to drink?" asked Saladin with meaning. "Whoever dies, you are safe. There is but one sin which I will not pardon you—you know what it is," and he looked at them. "As for Hassan, he was my beloved friend and servant, but you slew him in fair fight, and his soul is now in Paradise. None in my army will raise a blood feud against you on that score."

Then dismissing the matter with a wave of his hand, he turned to receive a great body of Christian prisoners that, panting and stumbling like over-driven sheep, were being thrust on towards the camp with curses, blows and mockery by the victorious Saracens.

Among them the brethren rejoiced to see Egbert, the gentle and holy bishop of Nazareth, whom they had thought dead. Also, wounded in many places, his hacked harness hanging about him like a beggar's rags, there was the black-browed Master of the Templars, who even now could be fierce and insolent.

"So I was right," he mocked in a husky voice, "and here you are, safe with your friends the Saracens, Sir Knights of the visions and the water-skins—"

"From which you were glad enough to drink just now," said Godwin. "Also," he added sadly, "all the vision is not done." And turning, he looked towards a blazoned tent which with the Sultan's great pavilion, and not far behind it, was being pitched by the Arab camp-setters. The Master saw and remembered Godwin's vision of the dead Templars.

"Is it there that you mean to murder me, traitor and wizard?" he asked.

Then rage took hold of Godwin and he answered him:

"Were it not for your plight, here and now I would thrust those words down your throat, as, should we both live, I yet shall hope to do. You call us traitors. Is it the work of traitors to have charged alone through all this host until our horses died beneath us?"—he pointed to where Smoke and Flame lay with glazing eyes—"to have unhorsed Saladin and to have slain this prince in single combat?" and he turned to the body of the emir Hassan, which his servants were carrying away.

"You speak of me as wizard and murderer," he went on, "because some angel brought me a vision which, had you believed it, Templar, would have saved tens of thousands from a bloody death, the Christian kingdom from destruction, and yonder holy thing from mockery," and with a shudder he glanced at the Rood which its captors had set up upon a rock not far away with a dead knight tied to its black arms. "You, Sir Templar, are the murderer who by your madness and ambition have brought ruin on the cause of Christ, as was foretold by the count Raymond."

"That other traitor who also has escaped," snarled the Master.

Then Saracen guards dragged him away, and they were parted.

By now the pavilion was up and Saladin entered it, saying:

"Bring before me the king of the Franks and prince Arnat, he who is called Reginald of Chatillon."

Then a thought struck him, and he called to Godwin and Wulf, saying:

"Sir Knights, you know our tongue; give up your swords to the officer—they shall be returned to you—and come, be my interpreters."

So the brethren followed him into the tent, where presently were brought the wretched king and the grey-haired Reginald de Chatillon, and with them a few other great knights who, even in the midst of their misery, stared at Godwin and Wulf in wonderment. Saladin read the look, and explained lest their presence should be misunderstood:

"King and nobles, be not mistaken. These knights are my prisoners, as you are, and none have shown themselves braver to-day, or done me and mine more damage. Indeed, had it not been for my guards, within the hour I should have fallen beneath the sword of Sir Godwin. But as they know Arabic, I have asked them to render my words into your tongue. Do you accept them as interpreters? If not, others must be found."

When they had translated this, the king said that he accepted them, adding to Godwin:

"Would that I had also accepted you two nights gone as an interpreter of the will of Heaven!"

The Sultan bade his captains be seated, and seeing their terrible thirst, commanded slaves to bring a great bowl of sherbet made of rose-water cooled with snow, and with his own hand gave it to king Guy. He drank in great gulps, then passed the bowl to Reginald de Chatillon, whereon Saladin cried out to Godwin:

"Say to the king it is he and not I who gives this man to drink. There is no bond of salt between me and the prince Arnat."

Godwin translated, sorrowfully enough, and Reginald, who knew the habits of the Saracens, answered:

"No need to explain, Sir Knight, those words are my death-warrant. Well, I never expected less."

Then Saladin spoke again.

"Prince Arnat, you strove to take the holy city of Mecca and to desecrate the tomb of the Prophet, and then I swore to kill you. Again, when in a time of peace a caravan came from Egypt and passed by Esh-Shobek, where you were, forgetting your oath, you fell upon them and slew them. They asked for mercy in the name of Allah, saying that there was truce between Saracen and Frank. But you mocked them, telling them to seek aid from Mahomet, in whom they trusted. Then for the second time I swore to kill you. Yet I give you one more chance. Will you subscribe the Koran and embrace the faith of Islam? Or will you die?"

Now the lips of Reginald turned pale, and for a moment he swayed upon his seat. Then his courage came back to him, and he answered in a strong voice:

"Sultan, I will have none of your mercy at such a price, nor do I bow the knee to your dog of a false prophet, who perish in the faith of Christ, and, being weary of the world, am content to go to Him."

Saladin sprang to his feet, his very beard bristling with wrath, and drawing his sabre, shouted aloud:

"You scorn Mahomet! Behold! I avenge Mahomet upon you! Take him away!" And he struck him with the flat of his scimitar.

Then Mameluks leapt upon the prince. Dragging him to the entrance of the tent, they forced him to his knees and there beheaded him in sight of the soldiers and of the other prisoners.

Thus, bravely enough, died Reginald de Chatillon, whom the Saracens called prince Arnat. In the hush that followed this terrible deed king Guy said to Godwin:

"Ask the Sultan if it is my turn next."

"Nay," answered Saladin; "kings do not kill kings, but that truce-breaker has met with no more than his deserts."

Then came a scene still more dreadful. Saladin went to the door of his tent, and standing over the body of Reginald, bade them parade the captive Templars and Hospitallers before him. They were brought to the number of over two hundred, for it was easy to distinguish them by the red and white crosses on their breasts.

"These also are faith-breakers," he shouted, "and of their unclean tribes will I rid the world. Ho! my emirs and doctors of the law," and he turned to the great crowd of his captains about him, "take each of you one of them and kill him."

Now the emirs hung back, for though fanatics they were brave, and loved not this slaughter of defenceless men, and even the Mameluks murmured aloud.

But Saladin cried again:

"They are worthy of death, and he who disobeys my command shall himself be slain."

"Sultan," said Godwin, "we cannot witness such a crime; we ask that we may die with them."

"Nay," he answered; "you have eaten of my salt, and to kill you would be murder. Get you to the tent of the princess of Baalbec yonder, for there you will see nothing of the death of these Franks, your fellow-worshippers."

So the brethren turned, and led by a Mameluk, fled aghast for the first time in their lives, past the long lines of Templars and Hospitallers, who in the last red light of the dying day knelt upon the sand and prayed, while the emirs came up to kill them.

They entered the tent, none forbidding them, and at the end of it saw two women crouched together on some cushions, who rose, clinging to each other. Then the women saw also and sprang forward with a cry of joy, saying:

"So you live—you live!"

"Ay, Rosamund," answered Godwin, "to see this shame—would God that we did not—whilst others die. They murder the knights of the holy Orders. To your knees and pray for their passing souls."

So they knelt down and prayed till the tumult died away, and they knew that all was done.

"Oh, my cousins," said Rosamund, as she staggered to her feet at length, "what a hell of wickedness and bloodshed is this in which we dwell! Save me from it if you love me—I beseech you save me!"

"We will do our best," they answered; "but let us talk no more of these things which are the decree of God—lest we should go mad. Tell us your story."

But Rosamund had little to tell, except that she had been well treated, and always kept by the person of the Sultan, marching to and fro with his army, for he awaited the fulfilment of his dream concerning her. Then they told her all that had chanced to them; also of the vision of Godwin and its dreadful accomplishment, and of the death of Hassan beneath the sword of Wulf. At that story Rosamund wept and shrank from him a little, for though it was this prince who had stolen her from her home, she loved Hassan. Yet when Wulf said humbly:

"The fault is not mine; it was so fated. Would that I had died instead of this Saracen!"

Rosamund answered: "No, no; I am proud that you should have conquered."

But Wulf shook his head, and said:

"I am not proud. Although weary with that awful battle, I was still the younger and stronger man, though at first he well-nigh mastered me by his skill and quickness. At least we parted friends. Look, he gave me this," and he showed her the great emerald badge which the dying prince had given him.

Masouda, who all this while had sat very quiet, came forward and looked at it.

"Do you know," she asked, "that this jewel is very famous, not only for its value, but because it is said to have belonged to one of the children of the prophet, and to bring good fortune to its owner?"

Wulf smiled.

"It brought little to poor Hassan but now, when my grandsire's sword shore the Damascus steel as though it were wet clay."

"And sent him swift to Paradise, where he would be, at the hands of a gallant foe," answered Masouda. "Nay, all his life this emir was happy and beloved, by his sovereign, his wives, his fellows and his servants, nor do I think that he would have desired another end whose wish was to die in battle with the Franks. At least there is scarce a soldier in the Sultan's army who would not give all he has for yonder trinket, which is known throughout the land as the Star of Hassan. So beware, Sir Wulf, lest you be robbed or murdered, although you have eaten the salt of Salah-ed-din."

"I remember the captain Abdullah looking at it greedily and lamenting that the Luck of the House of Hassan should pass to an unbeliever," said Wulf. "Well, enough of this jewel and its dangers; I think Godwin has words to say."

"Yes," said Godwin. "We are here in your tent through the kindness of Saladin, who did not wish us to witness the death of our comrades, but to-morrow we shall be separated again. Now if you are to escape—"

"I will escape! I must escape, even if I am recaptured and die for it," broke in Rosamund passionately.

"Speak low," said Masouda. "I saw the eunuch Mesrour pass the door of the tent, and he is a spy—they all are spies."

"If you are to escape," repeated Godwin in a whisper, "it must be within the next few weeks while the army is on the march. The risk is great to all of us—even to you, and we have no plan. But, Masouda, you are clever; make one, and tell it to us."

She lifted her head to speak, when suddenly a shadow fell upon them. It was that of the head eunuch, Mesrour, a fat, cunning-faced man, with a cringing air. Low he bowed before them, saying:

"Your pardon, O Princess. A messenger has come from Salah-ed-din demanding the presence of these knights at the banquet that he has made ready for his noble prisoners."

"We obey," said Godwin, and rising they bowed to Rosamund and to Masouda, then turned to go, leaving the star jewel where they had been seated.

Very skilfully Mesrour covered it with a fold of his robe, and under shelter of the fold slipped down his hand and grasped it, not knowing that although she seemed to be turned away, Masouda was watching him out of the corner of her eye. Waiting till the brethren reached the tent door, she called out: "Sir Wulf, are you already weary of the enchanted Star of Fortune, or would you bequeath it to us?"

Now Wulf came back, saying heavily:

"I forgot the thing—who would not at such a time? Where is it? I left it on the cushion."

"Try the hand of Mesrour," said Masouda, whereat with a very crooked smile the eunuch produced it, and said:

"I wished to show you, Sir Knight, that you must be careful with such gems as these, especially in a camp where there are many dishonest persons."

"I thank you," answered Wulf as he took it; "you have shown me." Then, followed by the sound of Masouda's mocking laughter, they left the tent.

The Sultan's messenger led them forward, across ground strewn with the bodies of the murdered Templars and Hospitallers, lying as Godwin had seen them in his dream on the mountain top near Nazareth. Over one of these corpses Godwin stumbled in the gloom, so heavily, that he fell to his knees. He searched the face in the starlight, to find it was that of a knight of the Hospitallers of whom he had made a friend at Jerusalem—a very good and gentle Frenchman, who had abandoned high station and large lands to join the order for the love of Christ and charity. Such was his reward on earth—to be struck down in cold blood, like an ox by its butcher. Then, muttering a prayer for the repose of this knight's soul, Godwin rose and, filled with horror, followed on to the royal pavilion, wondering why such things were.

Of all the strange feasts that they ever ate the brethren found this the strangest and the most sad. Saladin was seated at the head of the table with guards and officers standing behind him, and as each dish was brought he tasted it and no more, to show that it was not poisoned. Not far from him sat the king of Jerusalem and his brother, and all down the board great captive nobles, to the number of fifty or more. Sorry spectacles were these gallant knights in their hewn and blood-stained armour, pale-faced, too, with eyes set wide in horror at the dread deeds they had just seen done. Yet they ate, and ate ravenously, for now that their thirst was satisfied, they were mad with hunger. Thirty thousand Christians lay dead on the Horn and plain of Hattin; the kingdom of Jerusalem was destroyed, and its king a prisoner. The holy Rood was taken as a trophy. Two hundred knights of the sacred Orders lay within a few score of yards of them, butchered cruelly by those very emirs and doctors of the law who stood grave and silent behind their master's seat, at the express command of that merciless master. Defeated, shamed, bereaved—yet they ate, and, being human, could take comfort from the thought that having eaten, by the law of the Arabs, at least their lives were safe.

Saladin called Godwin and Wulf to him that they might interpret for him, and gave them food, and they also ate who were compelled to it by hunger.

"Have you seen your cousin, the princess?" he asked; "and how found you her?" he asked presently.

Then, remembering over what he had fallen outside her tent, and looking at those miserable feasters, anger took hold of Godwin, and he answered boldly:

"Sire, we found her sick with the sights and sounds of war and murder; shamed to know also that her uncle, the conquering sovereign of the East, had slaughtered two hundred unarmed men."

Wulf trembled at his words, but Saladin listened and showed no anger.

"Doubtless," he answered, "she thinks me cruel, and you also think me cruel—a despot who delights in the death of his enemies. Yet it is not so, for I desire peace and to save life, not to destroy it. It is you Christians who for hard upon a hundred years have drenched these sands with blood, because you say that you wish to possess the land where your prophet lived and died more than eleven centuries ago. How many Saracens have you slain? Hundreds of thousands of them. Moreover, with you peace is no peace. Those Orders that I destroyed tonight have broken it a score of times. Well, I will bear no more. Allah has given me and my army the victory, and I will take your cities and drive the Franks back into the sea. Let them seek their own lands and worship God there after their own fashion, and leave the East in quiet.

"Now, Sir Godwin, tell these captives for me that tomorrow I send those of them who are unwounded to Damascus, there to await ransom while I besiege Jerusalem and the other Christian cities. Let them have no fear; I have emptied the cup of my anger; no more of them shall die, and a priest of their faith, the bishop of Nazareth, shall stay with their sick in my army to minister to them after their own rites."

So Godwin rose and told them, and they answered not a word, who had lost all hope and courage.

Afterwards he asked whether he and his brother were also to be sent to Damascus.

Saladin replied, "No; he would keep them for awhile to interpret, then they might go their ways without ransom."

On the morrow, accordingly, the captives were sent to Damascus, and that day Saladin took the castle of Tiberias, setting at liberty Eschiva, the wife of Raymond, and her children. Then he moved on to Acre, which he took, relieving four thousand Moslem captives, and so on to other towns, all of which fell before him, till at length he came to Ascalon, which he besieged in form, setting up his *mangonels* against its walls.

The night was dark outside of Ascalon, save when the flashes of lightning in the storm that rolled down from the mountains to the sea lit it up, showing the thousands of white tents set round the city, the walls and the sentries who watched upon them, the feathery palms that stood against the sky, the mighty, snow-crowned range of Lebanon, and encircling all the black breast of the troubled ocean. In a little open space of the garden of an empty house that stood without the walls, a man and a woman were talking, both of them wrapped in dark cloaks. They were Godwin and Masouda.

"Well," said Godwin eagerly, "is all ready?"

She nodded and answered:

"At length, all. To-morrow afternoon an assault will be made upon Ascalon, but even if it is taken the camp will not be moved that night. There will be great confusion, and Abdullah, who is somewhat sick, will be the captain of the guard over the princess's tent. He will allow the soldiers to slip away to assist in the sack of the city, nor will they betray him. At sunset but one eunuch will be on watch—Mesrour; and I will find means to put him to sleep. Abdullah will bring the princess to this garden disguised as his young son, and there you two and I shall meet them."

"What then?" asked Godwin.

"Do you remember the old Arab who brought you the horses Flame and Smoke, and took no payment for them, he who was named Son of the Sand? Well, as you know, he is my uncle, and he has more horses of that breed. I have seen him, and he is well pleased at the tale of Flame and Smoke and the knights who rode them, and more particularly at the way in which they came to their end, which he says has brought credit to their ancient blood. At the foot of this garden is a cave, which was once a sepulchre. There we shall find the horses—four of them—and with them my uncle, Son of the Sand, and by the morning light we will be a hundred miles away and lie hid with his tribe until we can slip to the coast and board a Christian ship. Does it please you?"

"Very well; but what is Abdullah's price?"

"One only—the enchanted star, the Luck of the House of Hassan; for nothing else will he take such risks. Will Sir Wulf give it?"

"Surely," answered Godwin with a laugh.

"Good. Then it must be done to-night. When I return I will send Abdullah to your tent. Fear not; if he takes the jewel he will give the price, since otherwise he thinks it will bring him ill fortune."

"Does the lady Rosamund know?" asked Godwin again.

She shook her head.

"Nay, she is mad to escape; she thinks of little else all day long. But what is the use of telling her till the time comes? The fewer in such a plot the better, and if anything goes wrong, it is well that she should be innocent, for then—"

"Then death, and farewell to all things," said Godwin; "nor indeed should I grieve to say them good-bye. But, Masouda, you run great peril. Tell me now, honestly, why do you do this?"

As he spoke the lightning flashed and showed her face as she stood there against a background of green leaves and red lily flowers. There was a strange look upon it—a look that made Godwin feel afraid, he knew not of what.

"Why did I take you into my inn yonder in Beirut when you were the pilgrims Peter and John? Why did I find you the best horses in Syria and guide you to the Al-je-bal? Why did I often dare death by torment for you there? Why did I save the three of you? And why, for all this weary while, have I—who, after all, am nobly born—become the mock of soldiers and the tire-woman of the princess of Baalbec?

"Shall I answer?" she went on, laughing. "Doubtless in the beginning because I was the agent of Sinan, charged to betray such knights as you are into his hands, and afterwards because my heart was filled with pity and love for—the lady Rosamund."

Again the lightning flashed, and this time that strange look had spread from Masouda's face to the face of Godwin.

"Masouda," he said in a whisper, "oh! think me no vain fool, but since it is best perhaps that both should know full surely, tell me, is it as I have sometimes—"

"Feared?" broke in Masouda with her little mocking laugh. "Sir Godwin, it is so. What does your faith teach—the faith in which I was bred, and lost, but that now is mine again—because it is yours? That men and women are free, or so some read it. Well, it or they are wrong. We are not free. Was I free when first I saw your eyes in Beirut, the eyes for which I had been watching all my life, and something came from you to me, and I—the cast-off plaything of Sinan—loved you, loved you, loved you—to my own doom? Yes, and rejoiced that it was so, and still rejoice that it is so, and would choose no other fate, because in that love I learned that there is a meaning in this life, and that there is an answer to it in lives to be, otherwhere if not here. Nay, speak not. I know your oath, nor would I tempt you to its breaking. But, Sir Godwin, a woman such as the lady Rosamund cannot love two men," and as she spoke Masouda strove to search his face while the shaft went home.

But Godwin showed neither surprise nor pain.

"So you know what I have known for long," he said, "so long that my sorrow is lost in the hope of my brother's joy. Moreover, it is well that she should have chosen the better knight."

"Sometimes," said Masouda reflectively, "sometimes I have watched the lady Rosamund, and said to myself, 'What do you lack? You are beautiful, you are highborn, you are learned, you are brave, and you are good.' Then I have answered, 'You lack wisdom and true sight, else you would not have chosen Wulf when you might have taken Godwin. Or perchance your eyes are blinded also.'"

"Speak not thus of one who is my better in all things, I pray you," said Godwin in a vexed voice.

"By which you mean, whose arm is perhaps a little stronger, and who at a pinch could cut down a few more Saracens. Well, it takes more than strength to make a man—you must add spirit."

"Masouda," went on Godwin, taking no note of her words, "although we may guess her mind, our lady has said nothing yet. Also Wulf may fall, and then I fill his place as best I can. I am no free man, Masouda."

"The love-sick are never free," she answered.

"I have no right to love the woman who loves my brother; to her are due my friendship and my reverence—no more."

"She has not declared that she loves your brother; we may guess wrongly in this matter. They are your words—not mine."

"And we may guess rightly. What then?"

"Then," answered Masouda, "there are many knightly Orders, or monasteries, for those who desire such places—as you do in your heart. Nay, talk no more of all these things that may or may not be. Back to your tent, Sir Godwin, where I will send Abdullah to you to receive the jewel. So, farewell, farewell."

He took her outstretched hand, hesitated a moment, then lifted it to his lips, and went. It was cold as that of a corpse, and fell against her side again like the hand of a corpse. Masouda shrank back among the flowers of the garden as though to hide herself from him and all the world. When he had gone a few paces, eight or ten perhaps, Godwin turned and glanced behind him, and at that moment there came a great blaze of lightning. In its fierce and fiery glare he saw Masouda standing with outstretched arms, pale, upturned face, closed eyes, and parted lips. Illumined by the ghastly sheen of the *levin* her face looked like that of one new dead, and the tall red lilies which climbed up her dark, pall-like robe to her throat—yes, they looked like streams of fresh-shed blood.

Godwin shuddered a little and went his way, but as she slid thence into the black, embracing night, Masouda said to herself:

"Had I played a little more upon his gentleness and pity, I think that he would have offered me his heart—after Rosamund had done with it and in payment for my services. Nay, not his heart, for he has none on earth, but his hand and loyalty. And, being honourable, he would have kept his promise, and I, who have passed through the harem of Al-je-bal, might yet have become the lady D'Arcy, and so lived out my life and nursed his babes. Nay, Sir Godwin; when you love me—not before; and you will never love me—until I am dead."

Snatching a bloom of the lilies into her hand, the hand that he had kissed, Masouda pressed it convulsively against her breast, till the red juice ran from the crushed flower and stained her like a wound. Then she glided away, and was lost in the storm and the darkness.

## Chapter 20
# The Luck of the Star of Hassan

An hour later the captain Abdullah might have been seen walking carelessly towards the tent where the brethren slept. Also, had there been any who cared to watch, something else might have been seen in that low moonlight, for now the storm and the heavy rain which followed it had passed. Namely, the fat shape of the eunuch Mesrour, slipping after him wrapped in a dark camel-hair cloak, such as was commonly worn by camp followers, and taking shelter cunningly behind every rock and shrub and rise of the ground. Hidden among some picketed dromedaries, he saw Abdullah enter the tent of the brethren, then, waiting till a cloud crossed the moon, Mesrour ran to it unseen, and throwing himself down on its shadowed side, lay there like a drunken man, and listened with all his ears. But the thick canvas was heavy with wet, nor would the ropes and the trench that was dug around permit him, who did not love to lie in the water, to place his head against it. Also, those within spoke low, and he could only hear single words, such as "garden," "the star," "princess."

So important did these seem to him, however, that at length Mesrour crept under the cords, and although he shuddered at its cold, drew his body into the trench of water, and with the sharp point of his knife cut a little slit in the taut canvas. To this he set his eye, only to find that it served him nothing, for there was no light in the tent. Still, men were there who talked in the darkness.

"Good," said a voice—it was that of one of the brethren, but which he could not tell, for even to those who knew them best they seemed to be the same. "Good; then it is settled. To-morrow, at the hour arranged, you bring the princess to the place agreed upon, disguised as you have said. In payment for this service I hand you the Luck of Hassan which you covet. Take it; here it is, and swear to do your part, since otherwise it will bring no luck to you, for I will kill you the first time we meet—yes, and the other also."

"I swear it by Allah and his prophet," answered Abdullah in a hoarse, trembling voice.

"It is enough; see that you keep the oath. And now away; it is not safe that you should tarry here."

Then came the sound of a man leaving the tent. Passing round it cautiously, he halted, and opening his hand, looked at its contents to make sure that no trick had been played upon him in the darkness. Mesrour screwed his head round to look also, and saw the light gleam faintly on the surface of the splendid jewel, which he, too, desired so eagerly. In so doing his foot struck a stone, and instantly Abdullah glanced down to see a dead or drunken man lying almost at his feet. With a swift movement he hid the jewel and started to walk away. Then bethinking him that it would be well to make sure that this fellow was dead or sleeping, he turned and kicked the prostrate Mesrour upon the back and with all his strength. Indeed, he did this thrice, putting the eunuch to the greatest agony.

"I thought I saw him move," Abdullah muttered after the third kick; "it is best to make sure," and he drew his knife.

Now, had not terror paralysed him, Mesrour would have cried out, but fortunately for himself, before he found his voice Abdullah had buried the knife three inches deep in his fat thigh. With an effort Mesrour bore this also, knowing that if he showed signs of life the next stroke would be in his heart. Then, satisfied that this fellow, whoever he might be, was either a corpse or insensible, Abdullah drew out the knife, wiped it on his victim's robe, and departed.

Not long afterwards Mesrour departed also, towards the Sultan's house, bellowing with rage and pain and vowing vengeance.

It was not long delayed.

That very night Abdullah was seized and put to the question. In his suffering he confessed that he had been to the tent of the brethren and received from one of them the jewel which was found upon him, as a bribe to bring the princess to a certain garden outside the camp. But he named the wrong garden. Further, when they asked which of the brethren it was who bribed him, he said he did not know, as their voices were alike, and their tent was in darkness; moreover, that he believed there was only one man in it—at least he heard or saw no other. He added that he was summoned to the tent by an Arab man whom he had never seen before, but who told him that if he wished for what he most desired and good fortune, he was to be there at a certain hour after sunset. Then he fainted, and was put back in prison till the morning by the command of Saladin.

When the morning came Abdullah was dead, who desired no more torments with doom at the end of them, having made shift to strangle himself with his robe. But first he had scrawled upon the wall with a piece of charcoal:

"May that accursed Star of Hassan which tempted me bring better luck to others, and may hell receive the soul of Mesrour."

Thus died Abdullah, as faithful as he could be in such sore straits, since he had betrayed neither Masouda nor his son, both of whom were in the plot, and said that only one of the brethren was present in the tent, whereas he knew well that the two of them were there and which of these spoke and gave him the jewel.

Very early that morning the brethren, who were lying wakeful, heard sounds without their tent, and looking out saw that it was surrounded by Mameluks.

"The plot is discovered," said Godwin to Wulf quietly, but with despair in his face. "Now, my brother, admit nothing, even under torture, lest others perish with us."

"Shall we fight?" asked Wulf as they threw on their mail.

But Godwin answered:

"Nay, it would serve us nothing to kill a few brave men."

Then an officer entered the tent, and commanded them to give up their swords and to follow him to Saladin to answer a charge that had been laid against them both, nor would he say any more. So they went as prisoners, and after waiting awhile, were ushered into a large room of the house where Saladin lodged, which was arranged as a court with a dais at one end. Before this they were stood, till presently the Sultan entered through the further door, and with him certain of his emirs and secretaries. Also Rosamund, who looked very pale, was brought there, and in attendance on her Masouda, calm-faced as ever.

The brethren bowed to them, but Saladin, whose eyes were full of rage, took no notice of their salutation. For a moment there was silence, then Saladin bade a secretary read the charge, which was brief. It was that they had conspired to steal away the princess of Baalbec.

"Where is the evidence against us?" asked Godwin boldly. "The Sultan is just, and convicts no man save on testimony."

Again Saladin motioned to the secretary, who read the words that had been taken down from the lips of the captain Abdullah. They demanded to be allowed to examine the captain Abdullah, and learned that he was already dead. Then the eunuch Mesrour was carried forward, for walk he could not, owing to the wound that Abdullah had given him, and told all his tale, how he had suspected Abdullah, and, following him, had heard him and one of the brethren speaking in the tent, and the words that passed, and afterwards seen Abdullah with the jewel in his hand.

When he had finished Godwin asked which of them he had heard speaking with Abdullah, and he answered that he could not say, as their voices were so alike, but one voice only had spoken.

Then Rosamund was ordered to give her testimony, and said, truly enough, that she knew nothing of the plot and had not thought of this flight. Masouda also swore that she now heard of it for the first time. After this the secretary announced that there was no more evidence, and prayed of the Sultan to give judgment in the matter.

"Against which of us," asked Godwin, "seeing that both the dead and the living witness declared they heard but one voice, and whose that voice was they did not know? According to your own law, you cannot condemn a man against whom there is no good testimony."

"There is testimony against one of you," answered Saladin sternly, "that of two witnesses, as is required, and, as I have warned you long ago, that man shall die. Indeed, both of you should die, for I am sure that both are guilty. Still, you have been put upon your trial according to the law, and as a just judge I will not strain the law against you. Let the guilty one die by beheading at sundown, the hour at which he planned to commit his crime. The other may go free with the citizens of Jerusalem who depart to-night, bearing my message to the Frankish leaders in that holy town."

"Which of us, then, is to die, and which to go free?" asked Godwin. "Tell us, that he who is doomed may prepare his soul."

"Say you, who know the truth," answered Saladin.

"We admit nothing," said Godwin; "yet, if one of us must die, I as the elder claim that right."

"And I claim it as the younger. The jewel was Hassan's gift to me; who else could give it to Abdullah?" added Wulf, speaking for the first time, whereat all the Saracens there assembled, brave men who loved a knightly deed, murmured in admiration, and even Saladin said:

"Well spoken, both of you. So it seems that both must die."

Then Rosamund stepped forward and threw herself upon her knees before him, exclaiming:

"Sire, my uncle, such is not your justice, that two should be slain for the offence of one, if offence there be. If you know not which is guilty, spare them both, I beseech you."

He stretched out his hand and raised her from her knees: then thought awhile, and said:

"Nay, plead not with me, for however much you love him the guilty man must suffer, as he deserves. But of this matter Allah alone knows the truth, therefore let it be decided by Allah," and he rested his head upon his hand, looking at Wulf and Godwin as though to read their souls.

Now behind Saladin stood that old and famous *imaum* who had been with him and Hassan when he commanded the brethren to depart from Damascus, who all this while had listened to everything that passed with a sour smile. Leaning forward, he whispered in his master's ear, who considered a moment, then answered him:

"It is good. Do so."

So the *imaum* left the court, and returned presently carrying two small boxes of sandalwood tied with silk and sealed, so like each other that none could tell them apart, which boxes he passed continually from his right hand to his left and from his left hand to his right, then gave them to Saladin.

"In one of these," said the Sultan, "is that jewel known as the enchanted Star and the Luck of the House of Hassan, which the prince presented to his conqueror on the day of Hattin, and for the desire of which my captain Abdullah became a traitor and was brought to death. In the other is a pebble of the same weight. Come, my niece, take you these boxes and give them to your kinsmen, to each the box you will. The jewel that is called the Star of Hassan is magical, and has virtue, so they say. Let it choose, therefore, which of these knights is ripe for death, and let him perish in whose box the Star is found."

"Now," muttered the *imaum* into the ear of his master, "now at length we shall learn which it is of these two men that the lady loves."

"That is what I seek to know," answered Saladin in the same low voice.

As she heard this decree Rosamund looked round wildly and pleaded: "Oh! be not so cruel. I beseech you spare me this task. Let it be another hand that is chosen to deal death to one of those of my own blood with whom I have dwelt since childhood. Let me not be the blind sword of fate that frees his spirit, lest it should haunt my dreams and turn all my world to woe. Spare me, I beseech you."

But Saladin looked at her very sternly and answered:

"Princess, you know why I have brought you to the East and raised you to great honour here, why also I have made you my companion in these wars. It is for my dream's sake, the dream which told me that by some noble act of yours you should save the lives of thousands. Yet I am sure that you desire to escape, and plots are made to take you from me, though of these plots you say that you and your woman"—and he looked darkly at Masouda—"know nothing. But these men know, and it is right that you, for whose sake if not by whose command the thing was done, should mete out its reward, and that the blood of him whom you appoint, which is spilt for you, should be on your and no other head. Now do my bidding."

For a moment Rosamund stared at the boxes, then suddenly she closed her eyes, and taking them up at hazard, stretched out her arms, leaning forward over the edge of the dais. Thereon, calmly enough the brethren took, each of them, the box that was nearest to him, that in Rosamund's left hand falling to Godwin and that in her right to Wulf. Then she opened her eyes again, stood still, and watched.

"Cousin," said Godwin, "before we break this cord that is our chain of doom, know well that, whatever chances, we blame you not at all. It is God Who acts through you, and you are as innocent of the death of either of us as of that plot whereof we stand accused."

Then he began to unknot the silk which was bound about his box. Wulf, knowing that it would tell all the tale, did not trouble himself as yet, but looked around the room, thinking that, whether he lived or died, never would he see a stranger sight. Every eye in it was fixed upon the box in Godwin's hand; even Saladin stared as though it held his own destiny. No; not every one, for those of the old *imaum* were fixed upon the face of Rosamund, which was piteous to see, for all its beauty had left it, and even her parted lips were ashy. Masouda alone still stood upright and unmoved, as though she watched some play, but he noted that her rich-hued cheek grew pale and that beneath her robe her hand was pressed upon her heart. The silence also was intense, and broken only by the little grating noise of Godwin's nails as, having no knife to cut it, he patiently untied the silk.

"Trouble enough about one man's life in a land where lives are cheap!" exclaimed Wulf, thinking aloud, and at the sound of his voice all men started, as though it had thundered suddenly in a summer sky. Then with a laugh he tore the silk about his box asunder with his strong fingers, and breaking the seal, shook out its contents. Lo! there on the floor before him, gleaming green and white with emerald and diamond, lay the enchanted Star of Hassan.

Masouda saw, and the colour crept back to her cheek. Rosamund saw also, and nature was too strong for her, for in one bitter cry the truth broke from her lips at last:

"Not Wulf! Not Wulf!" she wailed, and sank back senseless into Masouda's arms.

"Now, sire," said the old *imaum* with a chuckle, "you know which of those two the lady loves. Being a woman, as usual she chooses badly, for the other has the finer spirit."

"Yes, I know now," said Saladin, "and I am glad to know, for the matter has vexed me much."

But Wulf, who had paled for a moment, flushed with joy as the truth came home to him, and he understood the end of all their doubts.

"This Star is well named 'The Luck,'" he said, as bending down he took it from the floor and fastened it to his cloak above his heart, "nor do I hold it dearly earned." Then he turned to his brother, who stood by him white and still, saying:

"Forgive me, Godwin, but such is the fortune of love and war. Grudge it not to me, for when I am sped tonight this Luck—and all that hangs to it—will be yours."

So that strange scene ended.

The afternoon drew towards evening, and Godwin stood before Saladin in his private chamber.

"What seek you now?" said the Sultan sternly.

"A boon," answered Godwin. "My brother is doomed to die before nightfall. I ask to die instead of him."

"Why, Sir Godwin?"

"For two reasons, sire. As you learned to-day, at length the riddle is answered. It is Wulf who is beloved of the lady Rosamund, and therefore to kill him would be a crime. Further, it is I and not he whom the eunuch heard bargaining with the captain Abdullah in the tent—I swear it. Take your vengeance upon me, and let him go to fulfil his fate."

Saladin pulled at his beard, then answered:

"If this is to be so, time is short, Sir Godwin. What farewells have you to make? You say that you would speak with my niece Rosamund? Nay, the princess you shall not see, and indeed cannot, for she lies swooning in her chamber. Do you desire to meet your brother for the last time?"

"No, sire, for then he might learn the truth and—"

"Refuse this sacrifice, Sir Godwin, which perchance will be scarcely to his liking."

"I wish to say good-bye to Masouda, she who is waiting woman to the princess."

"That you cannot do, for, know, I mistrust this Masouda, and believe that she was at the bottom of your plot. I have dismissed her from the person of the princess and from my camp, which she is to leave—

if she has not already left—with some Arabs who are her kin. Had it not been for her services in the land of the Assassins and afterwards, I should have put her to death."

"Then," said Godwin with a sigh, "I desire only to see Egbert the bishop, that he may shrive me according to our faith and make note of my last wishes."

"Good; he shall be sent to you. I accept your statement that you are the guilty man and not Sir Wulf, and take your life for his. Leave me now, who have greater matters on my mind. The guard will seek you at the appointed time."

Godwin bowed and walked away with a steady step while Saladin, looking after him, muttered:

"The world could ill spare so brave and good a man."

Two hours later guards summoned Godwin from the place where he was prisoned, and, accompanied by the old bishop who had shriven him, he passed its door with a happy countenance, such as a bridegroom might have worn. In a fashion, indeed, he was happy, whose troubles were done with, who had few sins to mourn, whose faith was the faith of a child, and who laid down his life for his friend and brother. They took him to a vault of the great house where Saladin was lodged—a large, rough place, lit with torches, in which waited the headsman and his assistants. Presently Saladin entered, and, looking at him curiously, said: "Are you still of the same mind, Sir Godwin?"

"I am."

"Good. Yet I have changed mine. You shall say farewell to your cousin, as you desired. Let the princess of Baalbec be brought hither, sick or well, that she may see her work. Let her come alone."

"Sire," pleaded Godwin, "spare her such a sight."

But he pleaded in vain, for Saladin answered only, "I have said."

A while passed, and Godwin, hearing the sweep of robes, looked up, and saw the tall shape of a veiled woman standing in the corner of the vault where the shadow was so deep that the torchlight only glimmered faintly upon her royal ornaments.

"They told me that you were sick, princess, sick with sorrow, as well you may be, because the man you love was about to die for you," said Saladin in a slow voice. "Now I have had pity on your grief, and his life has been bought with another life, that of the knight who stands yonder."

The veiled form started wildly, then sank back against the wall.

"Rosamund," broke in Godwin, speaking in French, "I beseech you, be silent and do not unman me with words or tears. It is best thus, and you know that it is best. Wulf you love as he loves you, and I believe that in time you will be brought together. Me you do not love, save as a friend, and never have. Moreover, I tell you this that it may ease your pain and my conscience; I no longer seek you as my wife, whose bride is death. I pray you, give to Wulf my love and blessing, and to Masouda, that truest and most sweet woman, say, or write, that I offer her the homage of my heart; that I thought of her in my last moments, and that my prayer is we may meet again where all crooked paths are straightened. Rosamund, farewell; peace and joy go with you through many years, ay, and with your children's children. Of Godwin I only ask you to remember this, that he lived serving you, and so died."

She heard and stretched out her arms, and, none forbidding him, Godwin walked to where she stood. Without lifting her veil she bent forward and kissed him, first upon the brow and next upon the lips; then with a low, moaning cry, she turned and fled from that gloomy place, nor did Saladin seek to stay her. Only to himself the Sultan wondered how it came about that if it was Wulf whom Rosamund loved, she still kissed Godwin thus upon the lips.

As he walked back to the death-place Godwin wondered also, first that Rosamund should have spoken no single word, and secondly because she had kissed him thus, even in that hour. Why or wherefore he did not know, but there rose in his mind a memory of that wild ride down the mountain steeps at Beirut, and of lips which then had touched his cheek, and of the odour of hair that then was blown about his breast. With a sigh he thrust the thought aside, blushing to think that such memories should come to him who had done with earth and its delights, knelt down before the headsman, and, turning to the bishop, said:

"Bless me, father, and bid them strike."

Then it was that he heard a well-known footstep, and looked up to see Wulf staring at him.

"What do you here, Godwin?" asked Wulf. "Has yonder fox snared both of us?" and he nodded at Saladin.

"Let the fox speak," said the Sultan with a smile. "Know, Sir Wulf, that your brother was about to die in your place, and of his own wish. But I refuse such sacrifice who yet have made use of it to teach my niece, the princess, that should she continue in her plottings to escape, or allow you to continue in them, certainly it will bring you to your deaths, and, if need be, her also. Knights, you are brave men whom I prefer to kill in war. Good horses stand without; take them as my gift, and ride with these foolish citizens of Jerusalem. We may meet again within its streets. Nay, thank me not. I thank you who have taught Salah-ed-din how perfect a thing can be the love of brothers."

The brethren stood awhile bewildered, for it is a strange thing thus to come back from death to life. Each of them had made sure that he must die within some few minutes, and pass through the blackness which walls man in, to find he knew not what. And now, behold! the road that led to that blackness turned again at its very edge, and ran forward through the familiar things of earth to some end unknown. They were brave, both of them, and accustomed to face death daily, as in such a place and time all men must be; moreover, they had been shriven, and looked to see the gates of Paradise open on their newborn sight.

Yet, since no man loves that journey, it was very sweet to know it done with for a while, and that they still might hope to dwell in this world for many years. Little wonder, then, that their brains swam, and their eyes grew dim, as they passed from the shadow to the light again. It was Wulf who spoke the first.

"A noble deed, Godwin, yet one for which I should not have thanked you had it been accomplished, who then must have lived on by grace of your sacrifice. Sultan, we are grateful for your boon of life, though had you shed this innocent blood surely it would have stained your soul. May we bid farewell to our cousin Rosamund before we ride?"

"Nay," answered Saladin; "Sir Godwin has done that already—let it serve for both. To-morrow she shall learn the truth of the story. Now go, and return no more."

"That must be as fate wills," answered Godwin, and they bowed and went.

Outside that gloomy place of death their swords were given them, and two good horses, which they mounted. Hence guides led them to the embassy from Jerusalem that was already in the saddle, who were very glad to welcome two such knights to their company. Then, having bid farewell to the bishop Egbert, who wept for joy at their escape, escorted for a while by Saladin's soldiers, they rode away from Ascalon at the fall of night.

Soon they had told each other all there was to tell. When he heard of the woe of Rosamund Wulf well-nigh shed tears.

"We have our lives," he said, "but how shall we save her? While Masouda stayed with her there was some hope, but now I can see none."

"There is none, except in God," answered Godwin, "Who can

do all things—even free Rosamund and make her your wife. Also, if Masouda is at liberty, we shall hear from her ere long; so let us keep a good heart."

But though he spoke thus, the soul of Godwin was oppressed with a fear which he could not understand. It seemed as though some great terror came very close to him, or to one who was near and dear. Deeper and deeper he sank into that pit of dread of he knew not what, until at length he could have cried aloud, and his brow was bathed with a sweat of anguish. Wulf saw his face in the moonlight, and asked:

"What ails you, Godwin? Have you some secret wound?"

"Yes, brother," he answered, "a wound in my spirit. Ill fortune threatens us—great ill fortune."

"That is no new thing," said Wulf, "in this land of blood and sorrows. Let us meet it as we have met the rest."

"Alas! brother," exclaimed Godwin, "I fear that Rosamund is in sore danger—Rosamund or another."

"Then," answered Wulf, turning pale, "since we cannot, let us pray that some angel may deliver her."

"Ay," said Godwin, and as they rode through the desert sands beneath the silent stars, they prayed to the Blessed Mother, and to their saints, St. Peter and St. Chad—prayed with all their strength. Yet the prayer availed not. Sharper and sharper grew Godwin's agony, till, as the slow hours went by, his very soul reeled beneath this spiritual pain, and the death which he had escaped seemed a thing desirable.

The dawn was breaking, and at its first sign the escort of Saladin's soldiers had turned and left them, saying that now they were safe in their own country. All night they had ridden fast and far. The plain was behind them, and their road ran among hills. Suddenly it turned, and in the flaming lights of the new-born day showed them a sight so beautiful that for a moment all that little company drew rein to gaze. For yonder before them, though far away as yet, throned upon her hills, stood the holy city of Jerusalem. There were her walls and towers, and there, stained red as though with the blood of its worshippers, soared the great cross upon the mosque of Omar—that cross which was so soon to fall.

Yes, yonder was the city for which throughout the ages men had died by tens and hundreds of thousands, and still must die until the doom was done. Saladin had offered to spare her citizens if they consented to surrender, but they would not. This embassy had told him that they had sworn to perish with the holy Places, and now, looking at it in its splendour, they knew that the hour was near, and groaned aloud.

Godwin groaned also, but not for Jerusalem. Oh! now the last terror was upon him. Blackness surged round him, and in the blackness swords, and a sound as of a woman's voice murmuring his name. Clutching the pommel of his saddle, he swayed to and fro, till suddenly the anguish passed. A strange wind seemed to blow about him and lift his hair; a deep, unearthly peace sank into his spirit; the world seemed far away and heaven very near.

"It is over," he said to Wulf. "I fear that Rosamund is dead."

"If so, we must make haste to follow her," answered Wulf with a sob.

## Chapter 21

# What Befell Godwin

At the village of Bittir, some seven miles from Jerusalem, the embassy dismounted to rest, then again they pressed forward down the valley in the hope of reaching the Zion Gate before the mid-day heat was upon them. At the end of this valley swelled the shoulder of a hill whence the eye could command its length, and on the crest of that shoulder appeared suddenly a man and a woman, seated on beautiful horses. The company halted, fearing lest these might herald some attack and that the woman was a man disguised to deceive them. While they waited thus irresolute, the pair upon the hill turned their horses' heads, and notwithstanding its steepness, began to gallop towards them very swiftly. Wulf looked at them curiously and said to Godwin:

"Now I am put in mind of a certain ride which once we took outside the walls of Beirut. Almost could I think that yonder Arab was he who sat behind my saddle, and yonder woman she who rode with you, and that those two horses were Flame and Smoke reborn. Note their whirlwind pace, and strength, and stride."

Almost as he finished speaking the strangers pulled up their steeds in front of the company, to whom the man bowed his salutations. Then Godwin saw his face, and knew him at once as the old Arab called Son of the Sand, who had given them the horses Flame and Smoke.

"Sir," said the Arab to the leader of the embassy, "I have come to ask a favour of yonder knights who travel with you, which I think that they, who have ridden my horses, will not refuse me. This woman," and he pointed to the closely-veiled shape of his companion, "is a relative of mine whom I desire to deliver to friends in Jerusalem, but dare not do so myself because the hill dwellers between here and there are hostile to my tribe. She is of the Christian faith and no spy, but cannot speak your language. Within the south gate she will be met by her relatives. I have spoken."

"Let the knights settle it," said the commander, shrugging his shoulders impatiently and spurring his horse.

"Surely we will take her," said Godwin, "though what we shall do with her if her friends are wanting I do not know. Come, lady, ride between us."

She turned her head to the Arab as though in question, and he repeated the words, whereon she fell into the place that was shown to her between and a little behind the brethren.

"Perhaps," went on the Arab to Godwin, "by now you have learned more of our tongue than you knew when we met in past days at Beirut, and rode the mountain side on the good horses Flame and Smoke. Still, if so, I pray you of your knightly courtesy disturb not this woman with your words, nor ask her to unveil her face, since such is not the custom of her people. It is but an hour's journey to the city gate during which you will be troubled with her. This is the payment that I ask of you for the two good horses which, as I am told, bore you none so ill upon the Narrow Way and across plain and mountain when you fled from Sinan, also on the evil day of Hattin when you unhorsed Salah-ed-din and slew Hassan."

"It shall be as you wish," said Godwin; "and, Son of the Sand, we thank you for those horses."

"Good. When you want more, let it be known in the market places that you seek me," and he began to turn his horse's head.

"Stay," said Godwin. "What do you know of Masouda, your niece? Is she with you?"

"Nay," answered the Arab in a low voice, "but she bade me be in a certain garden of which you have heard, near Ascalon, at an appointed hour, to take her away, as she is leaving the camp of Salah-ed-din. So thither I go. Farewell." Then with a reverence to the veiled lady, he shook his reins and departed like an arrow by the road along which they had come.

Godwin gave a sigh of relief. If Masouda had appointed to meet her uncle the Arab, at least she must be safe. So it was no voice of hers which seemed to whisper his name in the darkness of the night when terror had ahold of him—terror, born perhaps of all that he had endured and the shadow of death through which he had so lately passed. Then he looked up, to find Wulf staring back at the woman behind him, and reproved him, saying that he must keep to the spirit of the bargain as well as to the letter, and that if he might not speak he must not look either.

"That is a pity," answered Wulf, "for though she is so tied up, she must be a tall and noble lady by the way she sits her horse. The horse, too, is noble, own cousin or brother to Smoke, I think. Perhaps she will sell it when we get to Jerusalem."

Then they rode on, and because they thought their honour in it, neither spoke nor looked more at the companion of this adventure, though, had they known it, she looked hard enough at them.

At length they reached the gate of Jerusalem, which was crowded with folk awaiting the return of their ambassadors. They all passed through, and the embassy was escorted thence by the chief people, most of the multitude following them to know if they brought peace or war.

Now Godwin and Wulf stared at each other, wondering whither they were to go and where to find the relatives of their veiled companion, of whom they saw nothing. Out of the street opened an archway, and beyond this archway was a garden, which seemed to be deserted. They rode into it to take counsel, and their companion followed, but, as always, a little behind them.

"Jerusalem is reached, and we must speak to her now," said Wulf, "if only to ask her whither she wishes to be taken."

Godwin nodded, and they wheeled their horses round.

"Lady," he said in Arabic, "we have fulfilled our charge. Be pleased to tell us where are those kindred to whom we must lead you."

"Here," answered a soft voice.

They stared about the deserted garden in which stones and sacks of earth had been stored ready for a siege, and finding no one, said:

"We do not see them."

Then the lady let slip her cloak, though not her veil revealing the robe beneath.

"By St. Peter!" said Godwin. "I know the broidery on that dress. Masouda! Say, is it you, Masouda?"

As he spoke the veil fell also, and lo! before them was a woman like to Masouda and yet not Masouda. The hair was dressed like hers; the ornaments and the necklace made of the claws of the lion which Godwin killed were hers; the skin was of the same rich hue; there even was the tiny mole upon her cheek, but as the head was bent they could not see her eyes. Suddenly, with a little moan she lifted it, and looked at them.

"Rosamund! It is Rosamund herself!" gasped Wulf. "Rosamund disguised as Masouda!"

And he fell rather than leapt from his saddle and ran to her, murmuring, "God! I thank Thee!"

Now she seemed to faint and slid from her horse into his arms, and lay there a moment, while Godwin turned aside his head.

"Yes," said Rosamund, freeing herself, "it is I and no other, yet I rode with you all this way and neither of you knew me."

"Have we eyes that can pierce veils and woollen garments?" asked Wulf indignantly; but Godwin said in a strange, strained voice:

"You are Rosamund disguised as Masouda. Who, then, was that woman to whom I bade farewell before Saladin while the headsman awaited me; a veiled woman who wore the robes and gems of Rosamund?"

"I know not, Godwin," she answered, "unless it were Masouda clad in my garments as I left her. Nor do I know anything of this story of the headsman who awaited you. I thought—I thought it was for Wulf that he waited—oh! Heaven, I thought that."

"Tell us your tale," said Godwin hoarsely.

"It is short," she answered. "After the casting of the lot, of which I shall dream till my death-day, I fainted. When I found my senses again I thought that I must be mad, for there before me stood a woman dressed in my garments, whose face seemed like my face, yet not the same.

"'Have no fear,' she said; 'I am Masouda, who, amongst many other things, have learned how to play a part. Listen; there is no time to lose. I have been ordered to leave the camp; even now my uncle the Arab waits without, with two swift horses. You, Princess, will leave in my place. Look, you wear my robes and my face—almost; and are of my height, and the man who guides you will know no difference. I have seen to that, for although a soldier of Salah-ed-din, he is of my tribe. I will go with you to the door, and there bid you farewell before the eunuchs and the guards with weeping, and who will guess that Masouda is the princess of Baalbec and that the princess of Baalbec is Masouda?'

"'And whither shall I go?' I asked.

"'My uncle, Son of the Sand, will give you over to the embassy which rides to Jerusalem, or failing that, will take you to the city, or failing that, will hide you in the mountains among his own people. See, here is a letter that he must read; I place it in your breast.'

"'And what of you, Masouda?' I asked again.

"'Of me? Oh! it is all planned, a plan that cannot fail,' she answered. 'Fear not; I escape to-night—I have no time to tell you how—and will join you in a day or two. Also, I think that you will find Sir Godwin, who will bring you home to England.'

"'But Wulf? What of Wulf?' I asked again. 'He is doomed to die, and I will not leave him.'

"'The living and the dead can keep no company,' she answered. 'Moreover, I have seen him, and all this is done by his most urgent order. If you love him, he bids that you will obey.'"

"I never saw Masouda! I never spoke such words! I knew nothing of this plot!" exclaimed Wulf, and the brethren looked at each other with white faces.

"Speak on," said Godwin; "afterwards we can debate."

"Moreover," continued Rosamund, bowing her head, "Masouda added these words, 'I think that Sir Wulf will escape his doom. If you would see him again, obey his word, for unless you obey you can never hope to look upon him living. Go, now, before we are both discovered, which would mean your death and mine, who, if you go, am safe.'"

"How knew she that I should escape?" asked Wulf.

"She did not know it. She only said she knew to force Rosamund away," answered Godwin in the same strained voice. "And then?"

"And then—oh! having Wulf's express commands, then I went, like one in a dream. I remember little of it. At the door we kissed and parted weeping, and while the guard bowed before her, she blessed me beneath her breath. A soldier stepped forward and said, 'Follow me, daughter of Sinan,' and I followed him, none taking any note, for at that hour, although perhaps you did not see it in your prisons, a strange shadow passed across the sun, of which all folk were afraid, thinking that it portended evil, either to Saladin or Ascalon.[1]

"In the gloom we came to a place, where was an old Arab among some trees, and with him two led horses. The soldier spoke to the Arab, and I gave him Masouda's letter, which he read. Then he put me on one of the led horses and the soldier mounted the other, and we departed at a gallop. All that evening and last night we rode hard, but in the darkness the soldier left us, and I do not know whither he went. At length we came to that mountain shoulder and waited there, resting the horses and eating food which the Arab had with him, till we saw the embassy, and among them two tall knights.

"'See,' said the old Arab, 'yonder come the brethren whom you seek. See and give thanks to Allah and to Masouda, who has not lied to you, and to whom I must now return.'

"Oh! my heart wept as though it would burst, and I wept in my joy—wept and blessed God and Masouda. But the Arab, Son of the Sand, told me that for my life's sake I must be silent and keep myself close veiled and disguised even from you until we reached Jerusalem,

1. The eclipse, which overshadowed Palestine and caused much terror at Jerusalem on 4th September, 1187, the day of the surrender of Ascalon.-*Author*

lest perhaps if they knew me the embassy might refuse escort to the princess of Baalbec and niece of Saladin, or even give me up to him.

"Then I promised and asked, 'What of Masouda?' He said that he rode back at speed to save her also, as had been arranged, and that was why he did not take me to Jerusalem himself. But how that was to be done he was not sure as yet; only he was sure that she was hidden away safely, and would find a way of escape when she wished it. And—and—you know the rest, and here, by the grace of God, we three are together again."

"Ay," said Godwin, "but where is Masouda, and what will happen to her who has dared to venture such a plot as this? Oh! know you what this woman did? I was condemned to die in place of Wulf—how, does not matter; you will learn it afterwards—and the princess of Baalbec was brought to say me farewell. There, under the very eyes of Saladin, Masouda played her part and mimicked you so well that the Sultan was deceived, and I, even I, was deceived. Yes, when for the first and last time I embraced her, I was deceived, although, it is true, I wondered. Also since then a great fear has been with me, although here again I was deceived, for I thought I feared—for you.

"Now, hark you, Wulf; take Rosamund and lodge her with some lady in this city, or, better still, place her in sanctuary with the nuns of the Holy Cross, whence none will dare to drag her, and let her don their habit. The abbess may remember you, for we have met her, and at least she will not refuse Rosamund a refuge."

"Yes, yes; I mind me she asked us news of folk in England. But you? Where do you go, Godwin?" said his brother.

"I? I ride back to Ascalon to find Masouda."

"Why?" asked Wulf. "Cannot Masouda save herself, as she told her uncle, the Arab, she would do? And has he not returned thither to take her away?"

"I do not know," answered Godwin; "but this I do know, that for the sake of Rosamund, and perhaps for my sake also, Masouda has run a fearful risk. Bethink you, what will be the mood of Saladin when at length he finds that she upon whom he had built such hopes has gone, leaving a waiting woman decked out in her attire."

"Oh!" broke in Rosamund. "I feared it, but I awoke to find myself disguised, and she persuaded me that all was well; also that this was done by the will of Wulf, whom she thought would escape."

"That is the worst of if," said Godwin. "To carry out her plan she held it necessary to lie, as I think she lied when she said that she believed we should both escape, though it is true that so it came about. I will tell you why she lied. It was that she might give her life to set you free to join me in Jerusalem."

Now Rosamund, who knew the secret of Masouda's heart, looked at him strangely, wondering within herself how it came about that, thinking Wulf dead or about to die, she should sacrifice herself that she, Rosamund, might be sent to the care of Godwin. Surely it could not be for love of her, although they loved each other well. From love of Godwin then? How strange a way to show it!

Yet now she began to understand. So true and high was this great love of Masouda's that for Godwin's sake she was ready to hide herself in death, leaving him—now that, as she thought, his rival was removed—to live on with the lady whom he loved; ay, and at the price of her own life giving that lady to his arms. Oh! how noble must she be who could thus plan and act, and, whatever her past had been, how pure and high of soul! Surely, if she lived, earth had no grander woman; and if she were dead, heaven had won a saint indeed.

Rosamund looked at Godwin, and Godwin looked at Rosamund, and there was understanding in their eyes, for now both of them saw the truth in all its glory and all its horror.

"I think that I should go back also," said Rosamund.

"That shall not be," answered Wulf. "Saladin would kill you for this flight, as he has sworn."

"That cannot be," added Godwin. "Shall the sacrifice of blood be offered in vain? Moreover it is our duty to prevent you."

Rosamund looked at him again and stammered:

"If—if—that dreadful thing has happened, Godwin—if the sacrifice—oh! what will it serve?"

"Rosamund, I know not what has chanced; I go to see. I care not what may chance; I go to meet it. Through life, through death, and if there be need, through all the fires of hell, I ride on till I find Masouda, and kneel to her in homage—"

"And in love," exclaimed Rosamund, as though the words broke from her lips against her will.

"Mayhap," Godwin answered, speaking more to himself than to her.

Then seeing the look upon his face, the set mouth and the flashing eyes, neither of them sought to stay him further.

"Farewell, my liege-lady and cousin Rosamund," Godwin said; "my part is played. Now I leave you in the keeping of God in heaven and of Wulf on earth. Should we meet no more, my counsel is that you two wed here in Jerusalem and travel back to Steeple, there to live in peace, if it may be so. Brother Wulf, fare you well also. We part to-day for the first time, who from our birth have lived together and loved together and done many a deed together, some of which we can look back upon without shame. Go on your course rejoicing, taking the love and gladness that Heaven has given you and living a good and Christian knight, mindful of the end which draws on apace, and of eternity beyond."

"Oh! Godwin, speak not thus," said Wulf, "for in truth it breaks my heart to hear such fateful words. Moreover, we do not part thus easily. Our lady here will be safe enough among the nuns—more safe than I can keep her. Give me an hour, and I will set her there and join you. Both of us owe a debt to Masouda, and it is not right that it should be paid by you alone."

"Nay," answered Godwin; "look upon Rosamund, and think what is about to befall this city. Can you leave her at such a time?"

Then Wulf dropped his head, and trusting himself to speak no more words, Godwin mounted his horse, and, without so much as looking back, rode into the narrow street and out through the gateway, till presently he was lost in the distance and the desert.

Wulf and Rosamund watched him go in silence, for they were choked with tears.

"Little did I look to part with my brother thus," said Wulf at length in a thick and angry voice. "By God's Wounds! I had more gladly died at his side in battle than leave him to meet his doom alone."

"And leave me to meet my doom alone," murmured Rosamund; then added, "Oh! I would that I were dead who have lived to bring all this woe upon you both, and upon that great heart, Masouda. I say, Wulf, I would that I were dead."

"Like enough the wish will be fulfilled before all is done," answered Wulf wearily, "only then I pray that I may be dead with you, for now, Rosamund, Godwin has gone, forever as I fear, and you alone are left to me. Come; let us cease complaining, since to dwell upon these griefs cannot help us, and be thankful that for a while, at least, we are free. Follow me, Rosamund, and we will ride to this nunnery to find you shelter, if we may."

So they rode on through the narrow streets that were crowded with scared people, for now the news was spread that the embassy had rejected the terms of Saladin. He had offered to give the city food and to suffer its inhabitants to fortify the walls, and to hold them till the following Whitsuntide if, should no help reach them, they would swear to surrender then. But they had answered that while they had life they would never abandon the place where their God had died.

So now war was before them—war to the end; and who were they that must bear its brunt? Their leaders were slain or captive, their king a prisoner, their soldiers skeletons on the field of Hattin. Only the women and children, the sick, the old, and the wounded remained—perhaps eighty thousand souls in all—but few of whom could bear arms. Yet these few must defend Jerusalem against the might of the victorious Saracen. Little wonder that they wailed in the streets till the cry of their despair went up to heaven, for in their hearts all of them knew that the holy place was doomed and their lives were forfeited.

Pushing their path through this sad multitude, who took little note of them, at length they came to the nunnery on the sacred Via Dolorosa, which Wulf had seen when Godwin and he were in Jerusalem after they had been dismissed by Saladin from Damascus. Its door stood in the shadow of that arch where the Roman Pilate had uttered to all generations the words "Behold the man!"

Here the porter told him that the nuns were at prayer in their chapel. Wulf replied that he must see the lady abbess upon a matter which would not delay, and they were shown into a cool and lofty room. Presently the door opened, and through it came the abbess in her white robes—a tall and stately Englishwoman, of middle age, who looked at them curiously.

"Lady Abbess," said Wulf, bowing low, "my name is Wulf D'Arcy. Do you remember me?"

"Yes. We met in Jerusalem—before the battle of Hattin," she answered. "Also I know something of your story in this land—a very strange one."

"This lady," went on Wulf, "is the daughter and heiress of Sir Andrew D'Arcy, my dead uncle, and in Syria the princess of Baalbec and the niece of Saladin."

The abbess started, and asked: "Is she, then, of their accursed faith, as her garb would seem to show?"

"Nay, mother," said Rosamund, "I am a Christian, if a sinful one, and I come here to seek sanctuary, lest when they know who I am and he clamours at their gates, my fellow Christians may surrender me to my uncle, the Sultan."

"Tell me the story," said the abbess; and they told her briefly, while she listened, amazed. When they had finished, she said:

"Alas! my daughter, how can we save you, whose own lives are at stake? That belongs to God alone. Still, what we can we will do gladly, and here, at least, you may rest for some short while. At the most holy altar of our chapel you shall be given sanctuary, after which no Christian man dare lay a hand upon you, since to do so is a sacrilege that would cost him his soul. Moreover, I counsel that you be enrolled upon our books as a novice, and don our garb. Nay," she added with a smile, noting the look of alarm on the face of Wulf, "the lady Rosamund need not wear it always, unless such should be her wish. Not every novice proceeds to the final vows."

"Long have I been decked in gold-embroidered silks and priceless gems," answered Rosamund, "and now I seem to desire that white robe of yours more than anything on earth."

So they led Rosamund to the chapel, and in sight of all their order and of priests who had been summoned, at the altar there, upon that holy spot where they said that once Christ had answered Pilate, they placed her hand and gave her sanctuary, and threw over her tired head the white veil of a novice. There, too, Wulf left her, and riding away, reported himself to Balian of Ibelin, the elected commander of the city, who was glad enough to welcome so stout a knight where knights were few.

Oh! weary, weary was that ride of Godwin's beneath the sun, beneath the stars. Behind him, the brother who had been his companion and closest friend, and the woman whom he had loved in vain; and in front, he knew not what. What went he forth to seek? Another woman, who had risked her life for them all because she loved him. And if he found her, what then? Must he wed her, and did he wish this? Nay, he desired no woman on the earth; yet what was right that he would do. And if he found her not, what then? Well, at least he would give himself up to Saladin, who must think ill of them by whom he had dealt well, and tell him that of this plot they had no knowledge. Indeed, to him he would go first, if it were but to beg forgiveness for Masouda should she still be in his hands. Then—for he could not hope to be believed or pardoned a second time—then let death come, and he would welcome it, who greatly longed for peace.

It was evening, and Godwin's tired horse stumbled slowly through the great camp of the Saracens without the walls of fallen Ascalon. None hindered him, for having been so long a prisoner he was known by many, while others thought that he was but one of the surrendered Christian knights. So he came to the great house where Saladin lodged, and bade the guard take his name to the Sultan, saying that he craved audience of him. Presently he was admitted, and found Saladin seated in council among his ministers.

"Sir Godwin," he said sternly, "seeing how you have dealt by me, what brings you back into my camp? I gave you brethren your lives, and you have robbed me of one whom I would not lose."

"We did not rob you, sire," answered Godwin, "who knew nothing of this plot. Nevertheless, as I was sure that you would think thus, I am come from Jerusalem, leaving the princess and my brother there, to tell the truth and to surrender myself to you, that I may bear in her place any punishment which you think fit to inflict upon the woman Masouda."

"Why should you bear it?" asked Saladin.

"Because, Sultan," answered Godwin sadly, and with bent head, "whatever she did, she did for love of me, though without my knowledge. Tell me, is she still here, or has she fled?"

"She is still here," answered Saladin shortly. "Would you wish to see her?"

Godwin breathed a sigh of relief. At least, Masouda still lived, and the terror that had struck him in the night was but an evil dream born of his own fears and sufferings.

"I do," he answered, "once, if no more. I have words to say to her."

"Doubtless she will be glad to learn how her plot prospered," said Saladin, with a grim smile. "In truth it was well laid and boldly executed."

Calling to one of his council, that same old *imaum* who had planned the casting of the lots, the Sultan spoke with him aside. Then he said:

"Let this knight be led to the woman Masouda. Tomorrow we will judge him."

Taking a silver lamp from the wall, the *imaum* beckoned to Godwin, who bowed to the Sultan and followed. As he passed wearily through the throng in the audience room, it seemed to Godwin that the emirs and captains gathered there looked at him with pity in their eyes. So strong was this feeling in him that he halted in his walk, and asked:

"Tell me, lord, do I go to my death?"

"All of us go thither," answered Saladin in the silence, "but Allah has not written that death is yours to-night."

They passed down long passages; they came to a door which the *imaum*, who hobbled in front, unlocked.

"She is under ward then?" said Godwin.

"Ay," was the answer, "under ward. Enter," and he handed him the lamp. "I remain without."

"Perchance she sleeps, and I shall disturb her," said Godwin, as he hesitated upon the threshold.

"Did you not say she loved you? Then doubtless, even if she

sleeps, she, who has dwelt at Masyaf will not take your visit ill, who have ridden so far to find her," said the *imaum* with a sneering laugh. "Enter, I say."

So Godwin took the lamp and went in, and the door was shut behind him. Surely the place was familiar to him? He knew that arched roof and these rough, stone walls. Why, it was here that he had been brought to die, and through that very door the false Rosamund had come to bid him farewell, who now returned to greet her in this same darksome den. Well, it was empty—doubtless she would soon come, and he waited, looking at the door. It did not stir; he heard no footsteps; nothing broke that utter silence. He turned again and stared about him. Something glinted on the ground yonder, towards the end of the vault, just where he had knelt before the executioner. A shape lay there; doubtless it was Masouda, imprisoned and asleep.

"Masouda," he said, and the sounding echoes from the arched walls answered back, "Masouda!"

He must awaken her; there was no choice. Yes, it was she, asleep, and she still wore the royal robes of Rosamund, and a clasp of Rosamund's still glittered on her breast.

How sound Masouda slept! Would she never wake? He knelt down beside her and put out his hand to lift the long hair that hid her face.

Now it touched her, and lo! the head fell over.

Then, with horror in his heart, Godwin held down the lamp and looked. Oh! those robes were red, and those lips were ashen. It was Masouda, whose spirit had passed him in the desert; Masouda, slain by the headsman's sword! This was the evil jest that had been played upon him, and thus—thus they met again.

Godwin rose to his feet and stood over her still shape as a man stands in a dream, while words broke from his lips and a fountain in his heart was unsealed.

"Masouda," he whispered, "I know now that I love you and you only, henceforth and forever, O woman with a royal heart. Wait for me, Masouda, wherever you may dwell."

While the whispered words left his lips, it seemed to Godwin that once more, as when he rode with Wulf from Ascalon, the strange wind blew about his brow, bringing with it the presence of Masouda, and that once more the unearthly peace sank into his soul.

Then all was past and over, and he turned to see the old *imaum* standing at his side.

"Did I not tell you that you would find her sleeping?" he said, with his bitter, chuckling laugh. "Call on her, Sir Knight; call on her! Love, they say, can bridge great gulfs—even that between severed neck and bosom."

With the silver lamp in his hand Godwin smote, and the man went down like a felled ox, leaving him once more in silence and in darkness.

For a moment Godwin stood thus, till his brain was filled with fire, and he too fell—fell across the corpse of Masouda, and there lay still.

## CHAPTER 22

# At Jerusalem

Godwin knew that he lay sick, but save that Masouda seemed to tend him in his sickness he knew no more, for all the past had gone from him. There she was always, clad in a white robe, and looking at him with eyes full of ineffable calm and love, and he noted that round her neck ran a thin, red line, and wondered how it came there.

He knew also that he travelled while he was ill, for at dawn he would hear the camp break up with a mighty noise, and feel his litter lifted by slaves who bore him along for hours across the burning sand, till at length the evening came, and with a humming sound, like the sound of hiving bees, the great army set its bivouac. Then came the night and the pale moon floating like a boat upon the azure sea above, and everywhere the bright, eternal stars, to which went up the constant cry of *"Allahu Akbar! Allahu Akbar!* God is the greatest, there is none but He."

"It is a false god," he would say. "Tell them to cry upon the Saviour of the World."

Then the voice of Masouda would seem to answer:

"Judge not. No god whom men worship with a pure and single heart is wholly false. Many be the ladders that lead to heaven. Judge not, you Christian knight."

At length that journey was done, and there arose new noises as of the roar of battle. Orders were given and men marched out in thousands; then rose that roar, and they marched back again, mourning their dead.

At last came a day when, opening his eyes, Godwin turned to rest them on Masouda, and lo! she was gone, and in her accustomed place there sat a man whom he knew well—Egbert, once bishop of Nazareth, who gave him to drink of sherbet cooled with snow. Yes, the Woman had departed and the Priest was there.

"Where am I?" he asked.

"Outside the walls of Jerusalem, my son, a prisoner in the camp of Saladin," was the answer.

"And where is Masouda, who has sat by me all these days?"

"In heaven, as I trust," came the gentle answer, "for she was a brave lady. It is I who have sat by you."

"Nay," said Godwin obstinately, "it was Masouda."

"If so," answered the bishop again, "it was her spirit, for I shrove her and have prayed over her open grave—her spirit, which came to visit you from heaven, and has gone back to heaven now that you are of the earth again."

Then Godwin remembered the truth, and groaning, fell asleep. Afterwards, as he grew stronger, Egbert told him all the story. He learned that when he was found lying senseless on the body of Masouda the emirs wished Saladin to kill him, if for no other reason because he had dashed out the eye of the holy *imaum* with a lamp. But the Sultan, who had discovered the truth, would not, for he said that it was unworthy of the *imaum* to have mocked his grief, and that Sir Godwin had dealt with him as he deserved. Also, that this Frank was one of the bravest of knights, who had returned to bear the punishment of a sin which he did not commit, and that, although he was a Christian, he loved him as a friend.

So the *imaum* lost both his eye and his vengeance.

Thus it had come about that the bishop Egbert was ordered to nurse him, and, if possible to save his life; and when at last they marched upon Jerusalem, soldiers were told off to bear his litter, and a good tent was set apart to cover him. Now the siege of the holy city had begun, and there was much slaughter on both sides.

"Will it fall?" asked Godwin.

"I fear so, unless the saints help them," answered Egbert. "Alas! I fear so."

"Will not Saladin be merciful?" he asked again.

"Why should he be merciful, my son, since they have refused his terms and defied him? Nay, he has sworn that as Godfrey took the place nigh upon a hundred years ago and slaughtered the Mussulmen who dwelt there by thousands, men, women, and children together, so will he do to the Christians. Oh! why should he spare them? They must die! They must die!" and wringing his hands Egbert left the tent.

Godwin lay still, wondering what the answer to this riddle might be. He could think of one, and one only. In Jerusalem was Rosamund, the Sultan's niece, whom he must desire to recapture, above all things, not only because she was of his blood, but since he feared that if he did not do so his vision concerning her would come to nothing.

Now what was this vision? That through Rosamund much slaughter should be spared. Well, if Jerusalem were saved, would not tens of thousands of Moslem and Christian lives be saved also? Oh! surely here was the answer, and some angel had put it into his heart, and now he prayed for strength to plant it in the heart of Saladin, for strength and opportunity.

This very day Godwin found the opportunity. As he lay dozing in his tent that evening, being still too weak to rise, a shadow fell upon him, and opening his eyes he saw the Sultan himself standing alone by his bedside. Now he strove to rise to salute him, but in a kind voice Saladin bade him lie still, and seating himself, began to talk.

"Sir Godwin," he said, "I am come to ask your pardon. When I sent you to visit that dead woman, who had suffered justly for her crime, I did an act unworthy of a king. But my heart was bitter against her and you, and the *imaum*, he whom you smote, put into my mind the trick that cost him his eye and almost cost a worn-out and sorrowful man his life. I have spoken."

"I thank you, sire, who were always noble," answered Godwin.

"You say so. Yet I have done things to you and yours that you can scarcely hold as noble," said Saladin. "I stole your cousin from her home, as her mother had been stolen from mine, paying back ill with ill, which is against the law, and in his own hall my servants slew her father and your uncle, who was once my friend. Well, these things I did because a fate drove me on—the fate of a dream, the fate of a dream. Say, Sir Godwin, is that story which they tell in the camps true, that a vision came to you before the battle of Hattin, and that you warned the leaders of the Franks not to advance against me?"

"Yes, it is true," answered Godwin, and he told the vision, and of how he had sworn to it on the Rood.

"And what did they say to you?"

"They laughed at me, and hinted that I was a sorcerer, or a traitor in your pay, or both."

"Blind fools, who would not hear the truth when it was sent to them by the pure mouth of a prophet," muttered Saladin. "Well, they paid the price, and I and my faith are the gainers. Do you wonder, then, Sir Godwin, that I also believe my vision which came to me thrice in the night season, bringing with it the picture of the very face of my niece, the princess of Baalbec?"

"I do not wonder," answered Godwin.

"Do you wonder also that I was mad with rage when I learned that at last yonder brave dead woman had outwitted me and all my spies and guards, and this after I had spared your lives? Do you wonder that I am still so wroth, believing as I do that a great occasion has been taken from me?"

"I do not wonder. But, Sultan, I who have seen a vision speak to you who also have seen a vision—a prophet to a prophet. And I tell you that the occasion has not been taken—it has been brought, yes, to your very door, and that all these things have happened that it might thus be brought."

"Say on," said Saladin, gazing at him earnestly.

"See now, Salah-ed-din, the princess Rosamund is in Jerusalem. She has been led to Jerusalem that you may spare it for her sake, and thus make an end of bloodshed and save the lives of folk uncounted."

"Never!" said the Sultan, springing up. "They have rejected my mercy, and I have sworn to sweep them away, man, woman, and child, and be avenged upon all their unclean and faithless race."

"Is Rosamund unclean that you would be avenged upon her? Will her dead body bring you peace? If Jerusalem is put to the sword, she must perish also."

"I will give orders that she is to be saved—that she may be judged for her crime by me," he added grimly.

"How can she be saved when the stormers are drunk with slaughter, and she but one disguised woman among ten thousand others?"

"Then," he answered, stamping his foot, "she shall be brought or dragged out of Jerusalem before the slaughter begins."

"That, I think, will not happen while Wulf is there to protect her," said Godwin quietly.

"Yet I say that it must be so—it shall be so."

Then, without more words, Saladin left the tent with a troubled brow.

Within Jerusalem all was misery, all was despair. There were crowded thousands and tens of thousands of fugitives, women and children, many of them, whose husbands and fathers had been slain at Hattin or elsewhere. The fighting men who were left had few commanders, and thus it came about that soon Wulf found himself the captain of very many of them.

First Saladin attacked from the west between the gates of Sts. Stephen and of David, but here stood strong fortresses called the Castle of the Pisans and the Tower of Tancred, whence the defenders made sallies upon him, driving back his stormers. So he determined to change his ground, and moved his army to the east, camping it near the valley of the Kedron. When they saw the tents being struck the Christians thought that he was abandoning the siege, and gave thanks to God in all their churches; but lo! next morning the white array of these appeared again on the east, and they knew that their doom was sealed.

There were in the city many who desired to surrender to the Sultan, and fierce grew the debates between them and those who swore that they would rather die. At length it was agreed that an embassy should be sent. So it came under safe conduct, and was received by Saladin in presence of his emirs and counsellors. He asked them what was their wish, and they replied that they had come to discuss terms. Then he answered thus:

"In Jerusalem is a certain lady, my niece, known among us as the princess of Baalbec, and among the Christians as Rosamund D'Arcy, who escaped thither a while ago in the company of the knight, Sir Wulf D'Arcy, whom I have seen fighting bravely among your warriors. Let her be surrendered to me that I may deal with her as she deserves, and we will talk again. Till then I have no more to say."

Now most of the embassy knew nothing of this lady, but one or two said they thought that they had heard of her, but had no knowledge of where she was hidden.

"Then return and search her out," said Saladin, and so dismissed them.

Back came the envoys to the council and told what Saladin had said.

"At least," exclaimed Heraclius the Patriarch, "in this matter it is easy to satisfy the Sultan. Let his niece be found and delivered to him. Where is she?"

Now one declared that was known by the knight, Sir Wulf D'Arcy, with whom she had entered the city. So he was sent for, and came with armour rent and red sword in hand, for he had just beaten back an attack upon the barbican, and asked what was their pleasure.

"We desire to know, Sir Wulf," said the patriarch, "where you have hidden away the lady known as the princess of Baalbec, whom you stole from the Sultan?"

"What is that to your Holiness?" asked Wulf shortly.

"A great deal, to me and to all, seeing that Saladin will not even treat with us until she is delivered to him."

"Does this council, then, propose to hand over a Christian lady to the Saracens against her will?" asked Wulf sternly.

"We must," answered Heraclius. "Moreover, she belongs to them."

"She does not belong," answered Wulf. "She was kidnapped by Saladin in England, and ever since has striven to escape from him."

"Waste not our time," exclaimed the patriarch impatiently. "We understand that you are this woman's lover, but however that may be, Saladin demands her, and to Saladin she must go. So tell us where she is without more ado, Sir Wulf."

"Discover that for yourself, Sir Patriarch," replied Wulf in fury. "Or, if you cannot, send one of your own women in her place."

Now there was a murmur in the council, but of wonder at his boldness rather than of indignation, for this patriarch was a very evil liver.

"I care not if I speak the truth," went on Wulf, "for it is known to all. Moreover, I tell this man that it is well for him that he is a priest, however shameful, for otherwise I would cleave his head in two who has dared to call the lady Rosamund my lover." Then, still shaking with wrath, the great knight turned and stalked from the council chamber.

"A dangerous man," said Heraclius, who was white to the lips; "a very dangerous man. I propose that he should be imprisoned."

"Ay," answered the lord Balian of Ibelin, who was in supreme command of the city, "a very dangerous man—to his foes, as I can testify. I saw him and his brother charge through the hosts of the Saracens at the battle of Hattin, and I have seen him in the breach upon the wall. Would that we had more such dangerous men just now!"

"But he has insulted me," shouted the patriarch, "me and my holy office."

"The truth should be no insult," answered Balian with meaning. "At least, it is a private matter between you and him on account of which we cannot spare one of our few captains. Now as regards this lady, I like not the business—"

As he spoke a messenger entered the room and said that the hiding-place of Rosamund had been discovered. She had been admitted a novice into the community of the Virgins of the Holy Cross, who had their house by the arch on the Via Dolorosa.

"Now I like it still less," Balian went on, "for to touch her would be sacrilege."

"His Holiness, Heraclius, will give us absolution," said a mocking voice.

Then another leader rose—he was one of the party who desired peace—and pointed out that this was no time to stand on scruples, for the Sultan would not listen to them in their sore plight unless the lady were delivered to him to be judged for her offence. Perhaps, being his own niece, she would, in fact, suffer no harm at his hands, and whether this were so or not, it was better that one should endure wrong, or even death, than many.

With such words he over-persuaded the most of them, so that in the end they rose and went to the convent of the Holy Cross, where the patriarch demanded admission for them, which, indeed, could not be refused. The stately abbess received them in the refectory, and asked their pleasure.

"Daughter," said the patriarch, "you have in your keeping a lady named Rosamund D'Arcy, with whom we desire to speak. Where is she?"

"The novice Rosamund," answered the abbess, "prays by the holy altar in the chapel."

Now one murmured, "She has taken sanctuary," but the patriarch said:

"Tell us, daughter, does she pray alone?"

"A knight guards her prayers," was the answer.

"Ah! as I thought, he has been beforehand with us. Also, daughter, surely your discipline is somewhat lax if you suffer knights thus to invade your chapel. But lead us thither."

"The dangers of the times and of the lady must answer for it," the abbess replied boldly, as she obeyed.

Presently they were in the great, dim place, where the lamps burned day and night. There by the altar, built, it was said, upon the spot where the Lord stood to receive judgment, they saw a kneeling woman, who, clad in the robe of a novice, grasped the stonework with her hands. Without the rails, also kneeling, was the knight Wulf, still as a statue on a sepulchre. Hearing them, he rose, turned him about, and drew his great sword.

"Sheathe that sword," commanded Heraclius.

"When I became a knight," answered Wulf, "I swore to defend the innocent from harm and the altars of God from sacrilege at the hands of wicked men. Therefore I sheathe not my sword."

"Take no heed of him," said one; and Heraclius, standing back in the aisle, addressed Rosamund:

"Daughter," he cried, "with bitter grief we are come to ask of you a sacrifice, that you should give yourself for the people, as our Master gave Himself for the people. Saladin demands you as a fugitive of his blood, and until you are delivered to him he will not treat with us for the saving of the city. Come forth, then, we pray you."

Now Rosamund rose and faced them, with her hand resting upon the altar.

"I risked my life and I believe another gave her life," she said, "that

I might escape from the power of the Moslems. I will not come forth to return to them."

"Then, our need being sore, we must take you," answered Heraclius sullenly.

"What!" she cried. "You, the patriarch of this sacred city, would tear me from the sanctuary of its holiest altar? Oh! then, indeed shall the curse fall upon it and you. Hence, they say, our sweet Lord was haled to sacrifice by the command of an unjust judge, and thereafter Jerusalem was taken by the sword. Must I too be dragged from the spot that His feet have hallowed, and even in these weeds"—and she pointed to her white robe—"thrown as an offering to your foes, who mayhap will bid me choose between death and the Koran? If so, I say assuredly that offering will be made in vain, and assuredly your streets shall run red with the blood of those who tore me from my sanctuary."

Now they consulted together, some taking one side and some the other, but the most of them declared that she must be given up to Saladin.

"Come of your own will, I pray you," said the patriarch, "since we would not take you by force."

"By force only will you take me," answered Rosamund.

Then the abbess spoke.

"Sirs, will you commit so great a crime? Then I tell you that it cannot go without its punishment. With this lady I say"—and she drew up her tall shape—"that it shall be paid for in your blood, and mayhap in the blood of all of us. Remember my words when the Saracens have won the city, and are putting its children to the sword."

"I absolve you from the sin," shouted the patriarch, "if sin it is."

"Absolve yourself," broke in Wulf sternly, "and know this. I am but one man, but I have some strength and skill. If you seek but to lay a hand upon the novice Rosamund to hale her away to be slain by Saladin, as he has sworn that he would do should she dare to fly from him, before I die there are those among you who have looked the last upon the light."

Then, standing there before the altar rails, he lifted his great blade and settled the skull-blazoned shield upon his arm.

Now the patriarch raved and stormed, and one among them cried that they would fetch bows and shoot Wulf down from a distance.

"And thus," broke in Rosamund, "add murder to sacrilege! Oh! sirs, bethink what you do—ay, and remember this, that you do it all in vain. Saladin has promised you nothing, except that if you deliver me to him, he will talk with you, and then you may find that you have sinned for nothing. Have pity on me and go your ways, leaving the issue in the hand of God."

"That is true," cried some. "Saladin made no promises."

Now Balian, the guardian of the city, who had followed them to the chapel and standing in the background heard what passed there, stepped forward and said:

"My lord Patriarch, I pray you let this thing be, since from such a crime no good could come to us or any. That altar is the holiest and most noted place of sanctuary in all Jerusalem. Will you dare to tear a maiden from it whose only sin is that she, a Christian, has escaped the Saracens by whom she was stolen? Do you dare to give her back to them and death, for such will be her doom at the hands of Saladin? Surely that would be the act of cowards, and bring upon us the fate of cowards. Sir Wulf, put up your sword and fear nothing. If there is any safety in Jerusalem, your lady is safe. Abbess, lead her to her cell."

"Nay," answered the abbess with fine sarcasm, "it is not fitting that we should leave this place before his Holiness."

"Then you have not long to wait," shouted the patriarch in fury. "Is this a time for scruples about altars? Is this a time to listen to the prayers of a girl or to threats of a single knight, or the doubts of a superstitious captain? Well, take your way and let your lives pay its cost. Yet I say that if Saladin asked for half the noble maidens in the city, it would be cheap to let him have them in payment for the blood of eighty thousand folk," and he stalked towards the door.

So they went away, all except Wulf, who stayed to make sure that they were gone, and the abbess, who came to Rosamund and embraced her, saying that for the while the danger was past, and she might rest quiet.

"Yes, mother," answered Rosamund with a sob, "but oh! have I done right? Should I not have surrendered myself to the wrath of Saladin if the lives of so many hang upon it? Perhaps, after all, he would forget his oath and spare my life, though at best I should never be suffered to escape again while there is a castle in Baalbec or a guarded harem in Damascus. Moreover, it is hard to bid farewell to all one loves forever," and she glanced towards Wulf, who stood out of hearing.

"Yes," answered the abbess, "it is hard, as we nuns know well. But, daughter, that sore choice has not yet been thrust upon you. When Saladin says that he sets you against the lives of all this cityful, then you must judge."

"Ay," repeated Rosamund, "then I—must judge."

The siege went on; from terror to terror it went on. The *mangonels* hurled their stones unceasingly, the arrows flew in clouds so that none could stand upon the walls. Thousands of the cavalry of Saladin hovered round St. Stephen's Gate, while the engines poured fire and bolts upon the doomed town, and the Saracen miners worked their way beneath the barbican and the wall. The soldiers within could not sally because of the multitude of the watching horsemen; they could not show themselves, since he who did so was at once destroyed by a thousand darts, and they could not build up the breaches of the crumbling wall. As day was added to day, the despair grew ever deeper. In every street might be met long processions of monks bearing crosses and chanting penitential psalms and prayers, while in the house-doors women wailed to Christ for mercy, and held to their breasts the children which must so soon be given to death, or torn from them to deck some Mussulman harem.

The commander Balian called the knights together in council, and showed them that Jerusalem was doomed.

"Then," said one of the leaders, "let us sally out and die fighting in the midst of foes."

"Ay," added Heraclius, "and leave our children and our women to death and dishonour. Then that surrender is better, since there is no hope of succour."

"Nay," answered Balian, "we will not surrender. While God lives, there is hope."

"He lived on the day of Hattin, and suffered it," said Heraclius; and the council broke up, having decided nothing.

That afternoon Balian stood once more before Saladin and implored him to spare the city.

Saladin led him to the door of the tent and pointed to his yellow banners floating here and there upon the wall, and to one that at this moment rose upon the breach itself.

"Why should I spare what I have already conquered, and what I have sworn to destroy?" he asked. "When I offered you mercy you would have none of it. Why do you ask it now?"

Then Balian answered him in those words that will ring through history forever.

"For this reason, Sultan. Before God, if die we must, we will first slaughter our women and our little children, leaving you neither male nor female to enslave. We will burn the city and its wealth; we will grind the holy Rock to powder and make of the mosque el-Aksa, and the other sacred places, a heap of ruins. We will cut the throats of the five thousand followers of the Prophet who are in our power, and then, every man of us who can bear arms, we will sally out into the midst of you and fight on till we fall. So I think Jerusalem shall cost you dear."

The Sultan stared at him and stroked his beard.

"Eighty thousand lives," he muttered; "eighty thousand lives, besides those of my soldiers whom you will slay. A great slaughter—and the holy city destroyed forever. Oh! it was of such a massacre as this that once I dreamed."

Then Saladin sat still and thought a while, his head bowed upon his breast.

## Chapter 23

# Saint Rosamund

From the day when he saw Saladin Godwin began to grow strong again, and as his health came back, so he fell to thinking. Rosamund was lost to him and Masouda was dead, and at times he wished that he were dead also. What more had he to do with his life, which had been so full of sorrow, struggle and bloodshed? Go back to England to live there upon his lands, and wait until old age and death overtook him? The prospect would have pleased many, but it did not please Godwin, who felt that his days were not given to him for this purpose, and that while he lived he must also labour.

As he sat thinking thus, and was very unhappy, the aged bishop Egbert, who had nursed him so well, entered his tent, and, noting his face, asked:

"What ails you, my son?"

"Would you wish to hear?" said Godwin.

"Am I not your confessor, with a right to hear?" answered the gentle old man. "Show me your trouble."

So Godwin began at the beginning and told it all—how as a lad he had secretly desired to enter the Church; how the old prior of the abbey at Stangate counselled him that he was too young to judge; how then the love of Rosamund had entered into his life with his manhood, and he had thought no more of religion. He told him also of the dream that he had dreamed when he lay wounded after the fight on Death Creek; of the vows which he and Wulf had vowed at the time of their knighting, and of how by degrees he had learned that Rosamund's love was not for him. Lastly, he told him of Masouda, but of her Egbert, who had shriven her, knew already.

The bishop listened in silence till he had finished. Then he looked up, saying:

"And now?"

"Now," answered Godwin, "I know not. Yet it seems to me that I hear the sound of my own feet walking upon cloister stones, and of my own voice lifted up in prayer before the altar."

"You are still young to talk thus, and though Rosamund be lost to you and Masouda dead, there are other women in the world," said Egbert.

Godwin shook his head.

"Not for me, my father."

"Then there are the knightly Orders, in which you might rise high."

Again he shook his head.

"The Templars and the Hospitallers are crushed. Moreover, I watched them in Jerusalem and the field, and love them not. Should they change their ways, or should I be needed to fight against the Infidel, I can join them by dispensation in days to come. But counsel me—what shall I do now?"

"Oh! my son," the old bishop said, his face lighting up, "if God calls you, come to God. I will show you the road."

"Yes, I will come," Godwin answered quietly. "I will come, and, unless the Cross should once more call me to follow it in war, I will strive to spend the time that is left to me in His service and that of men. For I think, my father, that to this end I was born."

Three days later Godwin was ordained a priest, there in the camp of Saladin, by the hand of the bishop Egbert, while around his tent the servants of Mahomet, triumphant at the approaching downfall of the Cross, shouted that God is great and Mahomet His only prophet.

********

Saladin lifted his head and looked at Balian.

"Tell me," he said, "what of the princess of Baalbec, whom you know as the lady Rosamund D'Arcy? I told you that I would speak no more with you of the safety of Jerusalem until she was delivered to me for judgment. Yet I see her not."

"Sultan," answered Balian, "we found this lady in the convent of the Holy Cross, wearing the robe of a novice of that order. She had taken the sanctuary there by the altar which we deem so sacred and inviolable, and refused to come."

Saladin laughed.

"Cannot all your men-at-arms drag one maiden from an altar stone?—unless, indeed, the great knight Wulf stood before it with sword aloft," he added.

"So he stood," answered Balian, "but it was not of him that we thought, though assuredly he would have slain some of us. To do this thing would have been an awful crime, which we were sure must bring down the vengeance of our God upon us and upon the city."

"What of the vengeance of Salah-ed-din?"

"Sore as is our case, Sultan, we still fear God more than Saladin."

"Ay, Sir Balian, but Salah-ed-din may be a sword in the hand of God."

"Which sword, Sultan, would have fallen swiftly had we done this deed."

"I think that it is about to fall," said Saladin, and again was silent and stroked his beard.

"Listen, now," he said at length. "Let the princess, my niece, come to me and ask it of my grace, and I think that I will grant you terms for which, in your plight, you may be thankful."

"Then we must dare the great sin and take her," answered Balian sadly, "having first slain the knight Wulf, who will not let her go while he is alive."

"Nay, Sir Balian, for that I should be sorry, nor will I suffer it, for though a Christian he is a man after my own heart. This time I said 'Let her come to me,' not 'Let her be brought.' Ay, come of her own free will, to answer to me for her sin against me, understanding that I promise her nothing, who in the old days promised her much, and kept my word. Then she was the princess of Baalbec, with all the rights belonging to that great rank, to whom I had sworn that no husband should be forced upon her, nor any change of faith. Now I take back these oaths, and if she comes, she comes as an escaped Cross-worshipping slave, to whom I offer only the choice of Islam or of a shameful death."

"What high-born lady would take such terms?" asked Balian in dismay. "Rather, I think, would she choose to die by her own hand than by that of your hangman, since she can never abjure her faith."

"And thereby doom eighty thousand of her fellow Christians, who must accompany her to that death," answered Saladin sternly. "Know, Sir Balian, I swear it before Allah and for the last time, that if my niece Rosamund does not come, of her own free will, unforced by any, Jerusalem shall be put to sack."

"Then the fate of the holy city and all its inhabitants hangs upon the nobleness of a single woman?" stammered Balian.

"Ay, upon the nobleness of a single woman, as my vision told me it should be. If her spirit is high enough, Jerusalem may yet be saved. If it be baser than I thought, as well may chance, then assuredly with her it is doomed. I have no more to say, but my envoys shall ride with you bearing a letter, which with their own hands they must present to my niece, the princess of Baalbec. Then she can return with them to me, or she can bide where she is, when I shall know that I saw but a lying vision of peace and mercy flowing from her hands, and will press on this war to its bloody end."

Within an hour Balian rode to the city under safe conduct, taking with him the envoys of Saladin and the letter, which they were charged to deliver to Rosamund.

It was night, and in their lamp-lit chapel the Virgins of the Holy Cross upon bended knees chanted the slow and solemn *Miserere*. From their hearts they sang, to whom death and dishonour were so near, praying their Lord and the merciful Mother of God to have pity, and to spare them and the inhabitants of the hallowed town where He had dwelt and suffered, and to lead them safe through the shadow of a fate as awful as His own. They knew that the end was near, that the walls were tottering to their fall, that the defenders were exhausted, and that soon the wild soldiers of Saladin would be surging through the narrow streets.

Then would come the sack and the slaughter, either by the sword of the Saracens, or, perchance, if these found time and they were not forgotten, more mercifully at the hands of Christian men, who thus would save them from the worst.

Their dirge ended, the abbess rose and addressed them. Her bearing was still proud, but her voice quavered.

"My daughters in the Lord," she said, "the doom is almost at our door, and we must brace our hearts to meet it. If the commanders of the city do what they have promised, they will send some here to behead us at the last, and so we shall pass happily to glory and be ever with the Lord. But perchance they will forget us, who are but a few among eighty thousand souls, of whom some fifty thousand must thus be killed. Or their arms may grow weary, or themselves they may fall before ever they reach this house—and what, my daughters, shall we do then?"

Now some of the nuns clung together and sobbed in their affright, and some were silent. Only Rosamund drew herself to her full height, and spoke proudly.

"My Mother," she said, "I am a newcomer among you, but I have seen the slaughter of Hattin, and I know what befalls Christian women and children among the unbelievers. Therefore I ask your leave to say my say."

"Speak," said the abbess.

"This is my counsel," went on Rosamund, "and it is short and plain. When we know that the Saracens are in the city, let us set fire to this convent and get us to our knees and so perish."

"Well spoken; it is best," muttered several. But the abbess answered with a sad smile:

"High counsel indeed, such as might be looked for from high blood. Yet it may not be taken, since self-slaughter is a deadly sin."

"I see little difference between it," said Rosamund, "and the stretching out of our necks to the swords of friends. Yet, although for others I cannot judge, for myself I do judge who am bound by no final vows. I tell you that rather than fall into the hands of the Paynims, I will dare that sin and leave them nothing but the vile mould which once held the spirit of a woman."

And she laid her hand upon the dagger hilt that was hidden in her robe.

Then again the abbess spoke.

"To you, daughter, I cannot forbid the deed, but to those who have fully sworn to obey me I do forbid it, and to them I show another if a more piteous way of escape from the last shame of womanhood. Some of us are old and withered, and have naught to fear but death, but others are still young and fair. To these I say, when the end is nigh, let them take steel and score face and bosom and seat themselves here in this chapel, red with their own blood and made loathsome to the sight of man. Then will the end come upon them quickly, and they will pass hence unstained to be the brides of Heaven."

Now a great groan of horror went up from those miserable women, who already saw themselves seated in stained robes, and hideous to behold, there in the carved chairs of their choir, awaiting death by the swords of furious and savage men, as in a day to come their sisters of the Faith were to await it in the doomed convent of the Virgins of St. Clare at Acre.[1]

Yet one by one, except the aged among them, they came up to the abbess and swore that they would obey her in this as in everything, while the abbess said that herself she would lead them down that dreadful road of pain and mutilation. Yes, save Rosamund, who declared that she would die undisfigured as God had made her, and two other novices, they swore it one by one, laying their hands upon the altar.

Then again they got them to their knees and sang the *Miserere*.

1. Those who are curious to know the story of the end of those holy heroines, the Virgins of St. Clare, I think in the year 1291, may read it in my book, *A Winter Pilgrimage*, pp. 270 and 271—*Author.*]

Presently, above their mournful chant, the sound of loud, insistent knockings echoed down the vaulted roofs. They sprang up screaming:

"The Saracens are here! Give us knives! Give us knives!"

Rosamund drew the dagger from its sheath.

"Wait awhile," cried the abbess. "These may be friends, not foes. Sister Ursula, go to the door and seek tidings."

The sister, an aged woman, obeyed with tottering steps, and, reaching the massive portal, undid the *guichet*, or lattice, and asked with a quavering voice:

"Who are you that knock?" while the nuns within held their breath and strained their ears to catch the answer.

Presently it came, in a woman's silvery tones, that sounded strangely still and small in the spaces of that tomb-like church.

"I am the Queen Sybilla, with her ladies."

"And what would you with us, O Queen? The right of sanctuary?"

"Nay; I bring with me some envoys from Saladin, who would have speech with the lady named Rosamund D'Arcy, who is among you."

Now at these words Rosamund fled to the altar, and stood there, still holding the naked dagger in her hand.

"Let her not fear," went on the silvery voice, "for no harm shall come to her against her will. Admit us, holy Abbess, we beseech you in the name of Christ."

Then the abbess said, "Let us receive the queen with such dignity as we may." Motioning to the nuns to take their appointed seats. in the choir she placed herself in the great chair at the head of them, whilst behind her at the raised altar stood Rosamund, the bare knife in her hand.

The door was opened, and through it swept a strange procession. First came the beauteous queen wearing her insignia of royalty, but with a black veil upon her head. Next followed ladies of her court—twelve of them—trembling with fright but splendidly apparelled, and after these three stern and turbaned Saracens clad in mail, their jewelled scimitars at their sides. Then appeared a procession of women, most of them draped in mourning, and leading scared children by the hand; the wives, sisters, and widows of nobles, knights and burgesses of Jerusalem. Last of all marched a hundred or more of captains and warriors, among them Wulf, headed by Sir Balian and ended by the patriarch Heraclius in his gorgeous robes, with his attendant priests and acolytes.

On swept the queen, up the length of the long church, and as she came the abbess and her nuns rose and bowed to her, while one offered her the chair of state that was set apart to be used by the bishop in his visitations. But she would have none of it.

"Nay," said the queen, "mock me with no honourable seat who come here as a humble suppliant, and will make my prayer upon my knees."

So down she went upon the marble floor, with all her ladies and the following women, while the solemn Saracens looked at her wondering and the knights and nobles massed themselves behind.

"What can we give you, O Queen," asked the abbess, "who have nothing left save our treasure, to which you are most welcome, our honour, and our lives?"

"Alas!" answered the royal lady. "Alas, that I must say it! I come to ask the life of one of you."

"Of whom, O Queen?"

Sybilla lifted her head, and with her outstretched arm pointed to Rosamund, who stood above them all by the high altar.

For a moment Rosamund turned pale, then spoke in a steady voice:

"Say, what service can my poor life be to you, O Queen, and by whom is it sought?"

Thrice Sybilla strove to answer, and at last murmured:

"I cannot. Let the envoys give her the letter, if she is able to read their tongue."

"I am able," answered Rosamund, and a Saracen emir drew forth a roll and laid it against his forehead, then gave it to the abbess, who brought it to Rosamund. With her dagger blade she cut its silk, opened it, and read aloud, always in the same quiet voice, translating as she read:

"In the name of Allah the One, the All-merciful, to my niece, aforetime the princess of Baalbec, Rosamund D'Arcy by name, now a fugitive hidden in a convent of the Franks in the city el-Kuds Esh-sherif, the holy city of Jerusalem:

"Niece,—All my promises to you I have performed, and more, since for your sake I spared the lives of your cousins, the twin knights. But you have repaid me with ingratitude and trickery, after the manner of those of your false and accursed faith, and have fled from me. I promised you also, again and yet again, that if you attempted this thing, death should be your portion. No longer, therefore, are you the princess of Baalbec, but only an escaped Christian slave, and as such doomed to die whenever my sword reaches you.

"Of my vision concerning you, which caused me to bring you to the East from England, you know well. Repeat it in your heart before you answer. That vision told me that by your nobleness and sacrifice you should save the lives of many. I demanded that you should be brought back to me, and the request was refused—why, it matters not. Now I understand the reason—that this was so ordained. I demand no more that force should be used to you. I demand that you shall come of your own free will, to suffer the bitter and shameful reward of your sin. Or, if you so desire, bide where you are of your own free will, and be dealt with as God shall decree. This hangs upon your judgment. If you come and ask it of me, I will consider the question of the sparing of Jerusalem and its inhabitants. If you refuse to come, I will certainly put every one of them to the sword, save such of the women and children as may be kept for slaves. Decide, then, Niece, and quickly, whether you will return with my envoys, or bide where they find you.—

"Yusuf Salah-ed-din."

Rosamund finished reading, and the letter fluttered from her hand down to the marble floor.

Then the queen said:

"Lady, we ask this sacrifice of you in the name of these and all their fellows," and she pointed to the women and the children behind her.

"And my life?" mused Rosamund aloud. "It is all I have. When I have paid it away I shall be beggared," and her eyes wandered to where the tall shape of Wulf stood by a pillar of the church.

"Perchance Saladin will be merciful," hazarded the queen.

"Why should he be merciful," answered Rosamund, "who has always warned me that if I escaped from him and was recaptured, certainly I must die? Nay, he will offer me Islam, or death, which means—death by the rope—or in some worse fashion."

"But if you stay here you must die," pleaded the queen, "or at best fall into the hands of the soldiers. Oh! lady, your life is but one life, and with it you can buy those of eighty thousand souls."

"Is that so sure?" asked Rosamund. "The Sultan has made no promise; he says only that, if I pray it of him, he will consider the question of the sparing of Jerusalem."

"But—but," went on the queen, "he says also that if you do not come he will surely put Jerusalem to the sword, and to Sir Balian he said that if you gave yourself up he thought he might grant terms which we should be glad to take. Therefore we dare to ask of you to give your life in payment for such a hope. Think, think what otherwise must be the lot of these"—and again she pointed to the women and children—"ay, and your own sisterhood and of all of us. Whereas, if you die, it will be with much honour, and your name shall be worshipped as a saint and martyr in every church in Christendom.

"Oh! refuse not our prayer, but show that you indeed are great enough to step forward to meet the death which comes to every one of us, and thereby earn the blessings of half the world and make sure your place in heaven, nigh to Him Who also died for men. Plead with her, my sisters—plead with her!"

Then the women and the children threw themselves down before her, and with tears and sobbing prayed her that she would give up her life for theirs. Rosamund looked at them and smiled, then said in a clear voice:

"What say you, my cousin and betrothed, Sir Wulf D'Arcy? Come hither, and, as is fitting in this strait, give me your counsel."

So the grey-eyed, war-worn Wulf strode up the aisle, and, standing by the altar rails, saluted her.

"You have heard," said Rosamund. "Your counsel. Would you have me die?"

"Alas!" he answered in a hoarse voice. "It is hard to speak. Yet, they are many—you are but one."

Now there was a murmur of applause. For it was known that this knight loved his lady dearly, and that but the other day he had stood there to defend her to the death against those who would give her up to Saladin.

Now Rosamund laughed out, and the sweet sound of her laughter was strange in that solemn place and hour.

"Ah, Wulf!" she said. "Wulf, who must ever speak the truth, even when it costs him dear. Well, I would not have it otherwise. Queen, and all you foolish people, I did but try your tempers. Could you, then, think me so base that I would spare to spend this poor life of mine, and to forego such few joys as God might have in store for me on earth, when those of tens of thousands may hang upon the issue? Nay, nay; it is far otherwise."

Then Rosamund sheathed the dagger that all this while she had held in her hand, and, lifting the letter from the floor, touched her brow with it in signal of obedience, saying in Arabic to the envoys:

"I am the slave of Salah-ed-din, Commander of the Faithful. I am the small dust beneath his feet. Take notice, Emirs, that in presence of all here gathered, of my own free will I, Rosamund D'Arcy, aforetime princess and sovereign lady of Baalbec, determine to accompany you to the Sultan's camp, there to make prayer for the sparing of the lives of the citizens of Jerusalem, and afterwards to suffer the punishment of death in payment of my flight, according to my royal uncle's high decree. One request I make only, if he be pleased to grant it—that my body be brought back to Jerusalem for burial before this altar, where of my own act I lay down my life. Emirs, I am ready."

Now the envoys bowed before her in grave admiration, and the air grew thick with blessings. As Rosamund stepped down from the altar the queen threw her arms about her neck and kissed her, while lords and knights, women and children, pressed their lips upon her hands, upon the hem of her white robe, and even on her feet, calling her "Saint" and "Deliverer."

"Alas!" she answered, waving them back. "As yet I am neither of these things, though the latter of them I hope to be. Come; let us be going."

"Ay," echoed Wulf, stepping to her side, "let us be going."

Rosamund started at the words, and all there stared. "Listen, Queen, Emirs, and People," he went on. "I am this lady's kinsman and her betrothed knight, sworn to serve her to the end. If she be guilty of a crime against the Sultan, I am more guilty, and on me also shall fall his vengeance. Let us be going."

"Wulf, Wulf," she said, "it shall not be. One life is asked—not both."

"Yet, lady, both shall be given that the measure of atonement may run over, and Saladin moved to mercy. Nay, forbid me not. I have lived for you, and for you I die. Yes, if they hold me by force, still I die, if need be, on my own sword. When I counselled you just now, I counselled myself also. Surely you never dreamed that I would suffer you to go alone, when by sharing it I could make your doom easier."

"Oh, Wulf!" she cried. "You will but make it harder."

"No, no; faced hand in hand, death loses half its terrors. Moreover, Saladin is my friend, and I also would plead with him for the people of Jerusalem."

Then he whispered in her ear, "Sweet Rosamund, deny me not, lest you should drive me to madness and self-murder, who will have no more of earth without you."

Now, her eyes full of tears and shining with love, Rosamund murmured back:

"You are too strong for me. Let it befall as God wills."

Nor did the others attempt to stay him any more.

Going to the abbess, Rosamund would have knelt before her, but it was the abbess who knelt and called her blessed, and kissed her. The sisters also kissed her one by one in farewell. Then a priest was brought—not the patriarch, of whom she would have none, but another, a holy man.

To him apart at the altar, first Rosamund and then Wulf made confession of their sins, receiving absolution and the sacrament in that form in which it was given to the dying; while, save the emirs, all in the church knelt and prayed as for souls that pass.

The solemn ritual was ended. They rose, and, followed by two of the envoys—for already the third had departed under escort to the court of Saladin to give him warning—the queen, her ladies and all the company, walked from the church and through the convent halls out into the narrow Street of Woe. Here Wulf, as her kinsman, took Rosamund by the hand, leading her as a man leads his sister to her bridal. Without it was bright moonlight, moonlight clear as day, and by now tidings of this strange story had spread through all Jerusalem, so that its narrow streets were crowded with spectators, who stood also upon every roof and at every window.

"The lady Rosamund!" they shouted. "The blessed Rosamund, who goes to a martyr's death to save us. The pure Saint Rosamund and her brave knight Wulf!" And they tore flowers and green leaves from the gardens and threw them in their path.

Down the long, winding streets, with bent heads and humble mien, companioned ever by the multitude, through which soldiers cleared the way, they walked thus, while women held up their children to touch the robe of Rosamund or to look upon her face. At length the gate was reached, and while it was unbarred they halted. Then came forward Sir Balian of Ibelin, bareheaded, and said:

"Lady, on behalf of the people of Jerusalem and of the whole of Christendom, I give you honour and thanks, and to you also, Sir Wulf D'Arcy, the bravest and most faithful of all knights."

A company of priests also, headed by a bishop, advanced chanting and swinging censers, and blessed them solemnly in the name of the Church and of Christ its Master.

"Give us not praise and thanks, but prayers," answered Rosamund; "prayers that we may succeed in our mission, to which we gladly offer up our lives, and afterwards, when we are dead, prayers for the welfare of our sinful souls. But should we fail, as it may chance, then remember of us only that we did our best. Oh! good people, great sorrows have come upon this land, and the Cross of Christ is veiled with shame. Yet it shall shine forth once more, and to it through the ages shall all men bow the knee. Oh! may you live! May no more death come among you! It is our last petition, and with it, this—that when at length you die we may meet again in heaven! Now fare you well."

Then they passed through the gate, and as the envoys declared that none might accompany them further, walked forward followed by the sound of the weeping of the multitude towards the camp of Saladin, two strange and lonesome figures in the moonlight.

At last these lamentations could be heard no more, and there, on the outskirts of the Moslem lines, an escort met them, and bearers with a litter.

But into this Rosamund would not enter, so they walked onwards up the hill, till they came to the great square in the centre of the camp upon the Mount of Olives, beyond the grey trees of the Garden of Gethsemane. There, awaiting them at the head of the square, sat Saladin in state, while all about, rank upon rank, in thousands and tens of thousands, was gathered his vast army, who watched them pass in silence.

Thus they came into the presence of the Sultan and knelt before him, Rosamund in her novice's white robe, and Wulf in his battered mail.

## CHAPTER 24

# The Dregs of the Cup

Saladin looked at them, but gave them no greeting. Then he spoke:

"Woman, you have had my message. You know that your rank is taken from you, and that with it my promises are at an end; you know also that you come hither to suffer the death of faithless women. Is it so?"

"I know all these things, great Salah-ed-din," answered Rosamund.

"Tell me, then, do you come of your own free will, unforced by any, and why does the knight Sir Wulf, whose life I spared and do not seek, kneel at your side?"

"I come of my own free will, Salah-ed-din, as your emirs can tell you; ask them. For the rest, my kinsman must answer for himself."

"Sultan," said Wulf, "I counselled the lady Rosamund that she should come—not that she needed such counsel—and, having given it, I accompanied her by right of blood and of Justice, since her offence against you is mine also. Her fate is my fate."

"I have no quarrel against you whom I forgave, therefore you must take your own way to follow the path she goes."

"Doubtless," answered Wulf, "being a Christian among many sons of the Prophet, it will not be hard to find a friendly scimitar to help me on that road. I ask of your goodness that her fate may be my fate."

"What!" said Saladin. "You are ready to die with her, although you are young and strong, and there are so many other women in the world?"

Wulf smiled and nodded his head.

"Good. Who am I that I should stand between a fool and his folly? I grant the boon. Your fate shall be her fate; Wulf D'Arcy, you shall drink of the cup of my slave Rosamund to its last bitterest dregs."

"I desire no less," said Wulf coolly.

Now Saladin looked at Rosamund and asked,

"Woman, why have you come here to brave my vengeance? Speak on if you have aught to ask."

Then Rosamund rose from her knees, and, standing before him, said:

"I am come, O my mighty lord, to plead for the people of Jerusalem, because it was told me that you would listen to no other voice than that of this your slave. See, many moons ago, you had a vision concerning me. Thrice you dreamed in the night that I, the niece whom you had never seen, by some act of mine should be the means of saving much life and a way of peace. Therefore you tore me from my home and brought my father to a bloody death, as you are about to bring his daughter; and after much suffering and danger I fell into your power, and was treated with great honour. Still I, who am a Christian, and who grew sick with the sight of the daily slaughter and outrage of my kin, strove to escape from you, although you had warned me that the price of this crime was death; and in the end, through the wit and sacrifice of another woman, I did escape.

"Now I return to pay that price, and behold! your vision is fulfilled—or, at the least, you can fulfil it if God should touch your heart with grace, seeing that of my own will I am come to pray you, Salah-ed-din, to spare the city, and for its blood to accept mine as a token and an offering.

"Oh, my lord! as you are great, be merciful. What will it avail you in the day of your own judgment that you have added another eighty thousand to the tally of your slain, and with them many more thousands of your own folk, since the warriors of Jerusalem will not die unavenged? Give them their lives and let them go free, and win thereby the gratitude of mankind and the forgiveness of God above."

So Rosamund spoke, and stretching out her arms towards him, was silent.

"These things I offered to them, and they were refused," answered Saladin. "Why should I grant them now that they are conquered?"

"My lord, Strong-to-Aid," said Rosamund, "do you, who are so brave, blame yonder knights and soldiers because they fought on against desperate odds? Would you not have called them cowards if they had yielded up the city where their Saviour died and struck no blow to save it? Oh! I am outworn! I can say no more; but once again, most humbly and on my knees, I beseech you speak the word of mercy, and let not your triumph be dyed red with the blood of women and of little children."

Then casting herself upon her face, Rosamund clasped the hem of his royal robe with her hands, and pressed it to her forehead.

So for a while she lay there in the shimmering moonlight, while utter silence fell upon all that vast multitude of armed men as they waited for the decree of fate to be uttered by the conqueror's lips. But Saladin sat still as a statue, gazing at the domes and towers of Jerusalem outlined against the deep blue sky.

"Rise," he said at length, "and know, niece, that you have played your part in a fashion worthy of my race, and that I, Salah-ed-din, am proud of you. Know also that I will weigh your prayer as I have weighed that of none other who breathes upon the earth. Now I must take counsel with my own heart, and to-morrow it shall be granted—or refused. To you, who are doomed to die, and to the knight who chooses to die with you, according to the ancient law and custom, I offer the choice of Islam, and with it life and honour."

"We refuse," answered Rosamund and Wulf with one voice. The Sultan bowed his head as though he expected no other answer, and glanced round, as all thought to order the executioners to do their office. But he said only to a captain of his Mameluks:

"Take them; keep them under guard and separate them, till my word of death comes to you. Your life shall answer for their safety. Give them food and drink, and let no harm touch them until I bid you."

The Mameluk bowed and advanced with his company of soldiers. As they prepared to go with them, Rosamund asked:

"Tell me of your grace, what of Masouda, my friend?"

"She died for you; seek her beyond the grave," answered Saladin, whereat Rosamund hid her face with her hands and sighed.

"And what of Godwin, my brother?" cried Wulf; but no answer was given him.

Now Rosamund turned; stretching out her arms towards Wulf, she fell upon his breast. There, then, in the presence of that countless army, they kissed their kiss of betrothal and farewell. They spoke no word, only ere she went Rosamund lifted her hand and pointed upwards to the sky.

Then a murmur rose from the multitude, and the sound of it seemed to shape itself into one word: "Mercy!"

Still Saladin made no sign, and they were led away to their prisons.

Among the thousands who watched this strange and most thrilling scene were two men wrapped in long cloaks, Godwin and the bishop Egbert. Thrice did Godwin strive to approach the throne. But it seemed that the soldiers about him had their commands, for they would not suffer him to stir or speak; and when, as Rosamund passed, he strove to break a way to her, they seized and held him. Yet as she went by he cried:

"The blessing of Heaven be upon you, pure saint of God—on you and your true knight."

Catching the tones of that voice above the tumult, Rosamund stopped and looked around her, but saw no one, for the guard hemmed her in. So she went on, wondering if perchance it was Godwin's voice which she had heard, or whether an angel, or only some Frankish prisoner had spoken.

Godwin stood wringing his hands while the bishop strove to comfort him, saying that he should not grieve, since such deaths as those of Rosamund and Wulf were most glorious, and more to be desired than a hundred lives.

"Ay, ay," answered Godwin, "would that I could go with them!"

"Their work is done, but not yours," said the bishop gently. "Come to our tent and let us to our knees. God is more powerful than the Sultan, and mayhap He will yet find a way to save them. If they are still alive tomorrow at the dawn we will seek audience of Saladin to plead with him."

So they entered the tent and prayed there, as the inhabitants of Jerusalem prayed behind their shattered walls, that the heart of Saladin might be moved to spare them all. While they knelt thus the curtain of the tent was drawn aside, and an emir stood before them.

"Rise," he said, "both of you, and follow me. The Sultan commands your presence."

Egbert and Godwin went, wondering, and were led through the pavilion to the royal sleeping place, which guards closed behind them. On a silken couch reclined Saladin, the light from the lamp falling on his bronzed and thoughtful face.

"I have sent for you two Franks," he said, "that you may bear a message from me to Sir Balian of Ibelin and the inhabitants of Jerusalem. This is the message:—Let the holy city surrender to-morrow and all its population acknowledge themselves my prisoners. Then for forty days I will hold them to ransom, during which time none shall be harmed. Every man who pays ten pieces of gold shall go free, and two women or ten children shall be counted as one man at a like price. Of the poor, seven thousand shall be set free also, on payment of thirty thousand bezants. Such who remain or have no money for their ransom—and there is still much gold in Jerusalem—shall become my slaves. These are my terms, which I grant at the dying prayer of my niece, the lady Rosamund, and to her prayer alone. Deliver them to Sir Balian, and bid him wait on me at the dawn with his chief notables, and answer whether he is willing to accept them on behalf of the people. If not, the assault goes on until the city is a heap of ruins covering the bones of its children."

"We bless you for this mercy," said the bishop Egbert, "and we hasten to obey. But tell us, Sultan, what shall we do? Return to the camp with Sir Balian?"

"If he accepts my terms, nay, for in Jerusalem you will be safe, and I give you your freedom without ransom."

"Sire," said Godwin, "ere I go, grant me leave to bid farewell to my brother and my cousin Rosamund."

"That for the third time you may plot their escape from my vengeance?" said Saladin. "Nay, bide in Jerusalem and await my word; you shall meet them at the last, no more."

"Sire," pleaded Godwin, "of your mercy spare them, for they have played a noble part. It is hard that they should die who love each other and are so young and fair and brave."

"Ay," answered Saladin, "a noble part; never have I seen one more noble. Well, it fits them the better for heaven, if Cross-worshippers enter there. Have done; their doom is written and my purpose cannot be turned, nor shall you see them till the last, as I have said. But if it pleases you to write them a letter of farewell and to send it back by the embassy, it shall be delivered to them. Now go, for greater matters are afoot than this punishment of a pair of lovers. A guard awaits you."

So they went, and within an hour stood before Sir Balian and gave him the message of Saladin, whereat he rose and blessed the name of Rosamund. While he called his counsellors from their sleep and bade his servants saddle horses, Godwin found pen and parchment, and wrote hurriedly:

> To Wulf, my brother, and Rosamund, my cousin and his betrothed,—I live, though well-nigh I died by dead Masouda—Jesus rest her gallant and most beloved soul! Saladin will not suffer me to see you, though he has promised that I shall be with you at the last, so watch for me then. I still dare to hope that it may please God to change the Sultan's heart and spare you. If so, this is my prayer and desire—that you two should wed as soon as may be, and get home to England, where, if I live, I hope to visit you in years to come. Till then seek me not, who would be lonely a while. But if it should be fated otherwise, then when my sins are purged I will seek you among the saints, you who by your noble deed have earned the sure grace of God.
>
> The embassy rides. I have no time for more, though there is much to say. Farewell.
>
> *Godwin*

The terms of Saladin had been accepted. With rejoicing because their lives were spared, but with woe and lamentation because the holy city had fallen again into the hands of the Moslem, the people of Jerusalem made ready to leave the streets and seek new homes elsewhere. The great golden cross was torn from the mosque el-Aksa, and on every tower and wall floated the yellow banners of Saladin. All who had money paid their ransoms, and those who had none begged and borrowed it as they could, and if they could not, gave themselves over to despair and slavery. Only the patriarch Heraclius, forgetting the misery of these wretched ones, carried off his own great wealth and the gold plate of the churches.

Then Saladin showed his mercy, for he freed all the aged without charge, and from his own treasure paid the ransom of hundreds of ladies whose husbands and fathers had fallen in battle, or lay in prison in other cities.

So for forty days, headed by Queen Sybilla and her ladies, that sad procession of the vanquished marched through the gates, and there were many of them who, as they passed the conqueror seated in state, halted to make a prayer to him for those who were left behind. A few also who remembered Rosamund, and that it was because of her sacrifice that they continued to look upon the sun, implored him that if they were not already dead, he would spare her and her brave knight.

At length it was over, and Saladin took possession of the city. Having purged the Great Mosque, washing it with rose-water, he worshipped in it after his own fashion, and distributed the remnant of the people who could pay no ransom as slaves among his emirs and followers. Thus did the Crescent triumph aver the Cross in Jerusalem, not in a sea of blood, as ninety years before the Cross had triumphed over the Crescent within its walls, but with what in those days passed for gentleness, peace, and mercy.

For it was left to the Saracens to teach something of their own doctrines to the followers of Christ.

During all those forty days Rosamund and Wulf lay in their separate prisons, awaiting their doom of death. The letter of Godwin was brought to Wulf, who read it and rejoiced to learn that his brother lived. Then it was taken from him to Rosamund, who, although she rejoiced also, wept over it, and wondered a little what it might mean. Of one thing she was sure from its wording—that they had no hope of life.

They knew that Jerusalem had fallen, for they heard the shouts of triumph of the Moslems, and from far away, through their prison bars could see the endless multitude of fugitives passing the ancient gates laden with baggage, and leading their children by the hand, to seek refuge in the cities of the coast. At this sight, although it was so sad, Rosamund was happy, knowing also that now she would not suffer in vain.

At length the camp broke up, Saladin and many of the soldiers entering Jerusalem; but still the pair were left languishing in their dismal cells, which were fashioned from old tombs. One evening, while Rosamund was kneeling; at prayer before she sought her bed, the door of the place was opened, and there appeared a glittering captain and a guard of soldiers, who saluted her and bade her follow him.

"Is it the end?" she asked.

"Lady," he answered, "it is the end." So she bowed her head meekly and followed. Without a litter was ready, in which they placed her and bore her through the bright moonlight into the city of Jerusalem and along the Way of Sorrow, till they halted at a great door, which she knew again, for by it stood the ancient arch.

"They have brought me back to the Convent of the Holy Cross to kill me where I asked that I might be buried," she murmured to herself as she descended from the litter.

Then the doors were thrown open, and she entered the great courtyard of the convent, and saw that it was decorated as though for a festival, for about it and in the cloisters round hung many lamps. More; these cloisters and the space in front of them were crowded with Saracen lords, wearing their robes of state, while yonder sat Saladin and his court.

"They would make a brave show of my death," thought Rosamund again. Then a little cry broke from her lips, for there, in front of the throne of Saladin, the moonlight and the lamp-blaze shining on his armour, stood a tall Christian knight. At that cry he turned his head, and she grew sure that it was Wulf, wasted somewhat and grown pale, but still Wulf.

"So we are to die together," she whispered to herself, then walked forward with a proud step amidst the deep silence, and, having bowed to Saladin, took the hand of Wulf and held it.

The Sultan looked at them and said:

"However long it may be delayed, the day of fate must break at last. Say, Franks, are you prepared to drink the dregs of that cup I promised you?"

"We are prepared," they answered with one voice.

"Do you grieve now that you laid down your lives to save those of all Jerusalem?" he asked again.

"Nay," Rosamund answered, glancing at Wulf's face; "we rejoice exceedingly that God has been so good to us."

"I too rejoice," said Saladin; "and I too thank Allah Who in bygone days sent me that vision which has given me back the holy city of Jerusalem without bloodshed. Now all is accomplished as it was fated. Lead them away."

For a moment they clung together, then emirs took Wulf to the right and Rosamund to the left, and she went with a pale face and high head to meet her executioner, wondering if she would see Godwin ere she died. They led her to a chamber where women waited but no swordsman that she could see, and shut the door upon her.

"Perchance I am to be strangled by these women," thought Rosamund, as they came towards her, "so that the blood royal may not be shed."

Yet it was not so, for with gentle hands, but in silence, they unrobed her, and washed her with scented waters and braided her hair, twisting it up with pearls and gems. Then they clad her in fine linen, and put over it gorgeous, broidered garments, and a royal mantle of purple, and her own jewels which she had worn in bygone days, and with them others still more splendid, and threw about her head a gauzy veil worked with golden stars. It was just such a veil as Wulf's gift which she had worn on the night when Hassan dragged her from her home at Steeple. She noted it and smiled at the sad omen, then said:

"Ladies, why should I mock my doom with these bright garments?"

"It is the Sultan's will," they answered; "nor shall you rest to-night less happily because of them."

Now all was ready, and the door opened and she stepped through it, a radiant thing, glittering in the lamplight. Then trumpets blew and a herald cried: "Way! Way there! Way for the high sovereign lady and princess of Baalbec!"

Thus followed by the train of honourable women who attended her, Rosamund glided forward to the courtyard, and once more bent the knee to Saladin, then stood still, lost in wonder.

Again the trumpets blew, and on the right a herald cried, "Way! Way there! Way for the brave and noble Frankish knight, Sir Wulf D'Arcy!"

Lo! attended by emirs and notables, Wulf came forth, clad in splendid armour inlaid with gold, wearing on his shoulder a mantel set with gems and on his breast the gleaming Star of the Luck of Hassan. To Rosamund he strode and stood by her, his hands resting on the hilt of his long sword.

"Princess," said Saladin, "I give you back your rank and titles, because you have shown a noble heart; and you, Sir Wulf, I honour also as best I may, but to my decree I hold. Let them go together to the drinking of the cup of their destiny as to a bridal bed."

Again the trumpets blew and the heralds called, and they led them to the doors of the chapel, which at their knocking were thrown wide. From within came the sound of women's voices singing, but it was no sad song they sang.

"The sisters of the Order are still there," said Rosamund to Wulf, "and would cheer us on our road to heaven."

"Perchance," he answered. "I know not. I am amazed."

At the door the company of Moslems left them, but they crowded round the entrance as though to watch what passed. Now down the long aisle walked a single white robed figure. It was the abbess.

"What shall we do, Mother?" said Rosamund to her.

"Follow me, both of you," she said, and they followed her through the nave to the altar rails, and at a sign from her knelt down.

Now they saw that on either side of the altar stood a Christian priest. The priest to the right—it was the bishop Egbert—came forward and began to read over them the marriage service of their faith.

"They'd wed us ere we die," whispered Rosamund to Wulf.

"So be it," he answered; "I am glad."

"And I also, beloved," she whispered back.

The service went on—as in a dream, the service went on, while the white-robed sisters sat in their carven chairs and watched. The rings that were handed to them had been interchanged; Wulf had taken Rosamund to wife, Rosamund had taken Wulf to husband, till death did them part.

Then the old bishop withdrew to the altar, and another hooded monk came forward and uttered over them the benediction in a deep and sonorous voice, which stirred their hearts most strangely, as though some echo reached them from beyond the grave. He held his hands above them in blessing and looked upwards, so that his hood fell back, and the light of the altar lamp fell upon his face.

It was the face of Godwin, and on his head was the tonsure of a monk. Once more they stood before Saladin, and now their train was swelled by the abbess and sisters of the Holy Cross.

"Sir Wulf D'Arcy," said the Sultan, "and you, Rosamund, my niece, princess of Baalbec, the dregs of your cup, sweet or bitter, or bitter-sweet, are drunk; the doom which I decreed for you is accomplished, and, according to your own rites, you are man and wife till Allah sends upon you that death which I withhold. Because you showed mercy upon those doomed to die and were the means of mercy, I also give you mercy, and with it my love and honour. Now bide here if you will in my freedom, and enjoy your rank and wealth, or go hence if you will, and live out your lives across the sea. The blessing of Allah be upon you, and turn your souls light. This is the decree of Yusuf Salah-ed-din, Commander of the Faithful, Conqueror and Caliph of the East."

Trembling, full of joy and wonder, they knelt before him and kissed his hand. Then, after a few swift words between them, Rosamund spoke.

"Sire, that God whom you have invoked, the God of Christian and of Moslem, the God of all the world, though the world worship Him in many ways and shapes, bless and reward you for this royal deed. Yet listen to our petition. It may be that many of our faith still lie unransomed in Jerusalem. Take my lands and gems, and let them be valued, and their price given to pay for the liberty of some poor slaves. It is our marriage offering. As for us, we will get us to our own country."

"So be it," answered Saladin. "The lands I will take and devote the sum of them as you desire—yes, to the last bezant. The jewels also shall be valued, but I give them back to you as my wedding dower. To these nuns further I grant permission to bide here in Jerusalem to nurse the Christian sick, unharmed and unmolested, if so they will, and this because they sheltered you. Ho! minstrels and heralds lead this new-wed pair to the place that has been prepared for them."

Still trembling and bewildered, they turned to go, when lo! Godwin stood before them smiling, and kissed them both upon the cheek, calling them "Beloved brother and sister."

"And you, Godwin?" stammered Rosamund.

"I, Rosamund, have also found my bride, and she is named the Church of Christ."

"Do you, then, return to England, brother?" asked Wulf.

"Nay," Godwin answered, in a fierce whisper and with flashing eyes, "the Cross is down, but not forever. That Cross has Richard of England and many another servant beyond the seas, and they will come at the Church's call. Here, brother, before all is done, we may meet again in war. Till then, farewell."

So spoke Godwin and then was gone.

# Red Eve

# Dedication

Ditchingham
May 27, 1911
*My dear Jehu*
For five long but not unhappy years, seated or journeying side by side, we have striven as Royal Commissioners to find a means whereby our coasts may be protected from "the outrageous flowing surges of the sea" (I quote the jurists of centuries ago), the idle swamps turned to fertility and the barren hills clothed with forest; also, with small success, how "foreshore" may be best defined!

What will result from all these labours I do not know, nor whether grave geologists ever read romance save that which the pen of Time inscribes upon the rocks. Still, in memory of our fellowship in them I offer to you this story, written in their intervals, of Red Eve, the dauntless, and of Murgh, Gateway of the Gods, whose dreadful galley still sails from East to West and from West to East, yes, and evermore shall sail.
Your friend and colleague,
*H. Rider Haggard*
To Dr. Jehu, F.G.S.,
St. Andrews, N.B.

# Murgh the Death

They knew nothing of it in England or all the Western countries in those days before Crecy was fought, when the third Edward sat upon the throne. There was none to tell them of the doom that the East, whence come light and life, death and the decrees of God, had loosed upon the world. Not one in a multitude in Europe had ever even heard of those vast lands of far Cathay peopled with hundreds of millions of cold-faced yellow men, lands which had grown very old before our own familiar states and empires were carved out of mountain, of forest, and of savage-haunted plain. Yet if their eyes had been open so that they could see, well might they have trembled. King, prince, priest, merchant, captain, citizen and poor labouring hind, well might they all have trembled when the East sent forth her gifts!

Look across the world beyond that curtain of thick darkness. Behold! A vast city of fantastic houses half buried in winter snows and reddened by the lurid sunset breaking through a saw-toothed canopy of cloud. Everywhere upon the temple squares and open spaces great fires burning a strange fuel—the bodies of thousands of mankind. Pestilence was king of that city, a pestilence hitherto unknown. Innumerable hordes had died and were dying, yet innumerable hordes remained. All the patient East bore forth those still shapes that had been theirs to love or hate, and, their task done, turned to the banks of the mighty river and watched.

********

Down the broad street which ran between the fantastic houses advanced a procession toward the brown, ice-flecked river. First marched a company of priests clad in black robes, and carrying on poles lanterns of black paper, lighted, although the sun still shone. Behind marched another company of priests clad in white robes, and bearing white lanterns, also lighted. But at these none looked, nor did they listen to the dirges that they sang, for all eyes were fixed upon him who filled the centre space and upon his two companions.

The first companion was a lovely woman, jewel-hung, wearing false flowers in her streaming hair, and beneath her bared breasts a kirtle of white silk. Life and love embodied in radiance and beauty, she danced in front, looking about her with alluring eyes, and scattering petals of dead roses from a basket which she bore. Different was the second companion, who stalked behind; so thin, so sexless that none could say if the shape were that of man or woman. Dry, streaming locks of iron-grey, an ashen countenance, deep-set, hollow eyes, a beetling, parchment-covered brow; lean shanks half hidden with a rotting rag, claw-like hands which clutched miserably at the air. Such was its awful fashion, that of new death in all its terrors.

Between them, touched of neither, went a man, naked save for a red girdle and a long red cloak that was fastened round his throat and hung down from his broad shoulders. There was nothing strange about this man, unless it were perhaps the strength that seemed to flow from him and the glance of his icy eyes. He was just a burly yellow man, whose age none could tell, for the hood of the red cloak hid his hair; one who seemed to be far removed from youth, and yet untouched by time. He walked on steadily, intently, his face immovable, taking no heed.

Only now and again he turned those long eyes of his upon one of the multitude who watched him pass crouched upon their knees in solemn silence, always upon one, whether it were man, woman, or child, with a glance meant for that one and no other. And ever the one upon whom it fell rose from the knee, made obeisance, and departed as though filled with some inspired purpose.

Down to the quay went the black priests, the white priests, and the red-cloaked man, preceded by rose life, followed by ashen death. Through the funeral fires they wended, and the lurid sunset shone upon them all.

To the pillars of this quay was fastened a strange, high-pooped ship with crimson sails set upon her masts. The white priests and the black priests formed lines upon either side of the broad gangway of that ship and bowed as the red-cloaked man walked over it between them quite alone, for now she with the dead roses and she of the ashen countenance had fallen back. As the sun sank, standing on the lofty stern, he cried aloud:

"Here the work is done. Now I, the Eating Fire, I the Messenger, get me to the West. Among you for a while I cease to burn; yet remember me, for I shall come again."

As he spoke the ropes of the ship were loosened, the wind caught her crimson sails, and she departed into the night, one blood-red spot against its blackness.

The multitude watched until they could see her no longer. Then they flamed up with mingled joy and rage. They laughed madly. They cursed him who had departed.

"We live, we live, we live!" they cried. "Murgh is gone! Murgh is gone! Kill his priests! Make sacrifice of his Shadows. Murgh is gone bearing the curse of the East into the bosom of the West. Look, it follows him!" and they pointed to a cloud of smoke or vapour, in which terrible shapes seemed to move dimly, that trailed after the departing, red-sailed ship.

The black priests and the white priests heard. Without struggle, without complaint, as though they were but taking part in some set ceremony, they kneeled down in lines upon the snow. Naked from the waist up, executioners with great swords appeared. They advanced upon the kneeling lines without haste, without wrath, and, letting fall the heavy swords upon the patient, outstretched necks, did their grim office till all were dead. Then they turned to find her of the flowers who had danced before, and her of the tattered weeds who had followed after, purposing to cast them to the funeral flames. But these were gone, though none had seen them go. Only out of the gathering darkness from some temple or pagoda-top a voice spoke like a moaning wind.

"Fools," wailed the voice, "still with you is Murgh, the second Thing created; Murgh, who was made to be man's minister. Murgh the Messenger shall reappear from beyond the setting sun. Ye cannot kill, ye cannot spare. Those priests you seemed to slay he had summoned to be his officers afar. Fools! Ye do but serve as serves Murgh, Gateway of the Gods. Life and death are not in your hands or in his. They are in the hands of the Master of Murgh, Helper of man, of that Lord whom no eye hath seen, but whose behests all who are born obey—yes, even the mighty Murgh, Looser of burdens, whom in your foolishness ye fear."

********

So spoke this voice out of the darkness, and that night the sword of the great pestilence was lifted from the Eastern land, and there the funeral fires flared no more.

## CHAPTER 1

# The Trysting-Place

On the very day when Murgh the Messenger sailed forth into that uttermost sea, a young man and a maiden met together at the Blythburgh marshes, near to Dunwich, on the eastern coast of England. In this, the month of February of the year 1346, hard and bitter frost held Suffolk in its grip. The muddy stream of Blyth, it is true, was frozen only in places, since the tide, flowing up from the Southwold harbour, where it runs into the sea between that ancient town and the hamlet of Walberswick, had broken up the ice. But all else was set hard and fast, and now toward sunset the cold was bitter.

Stark and naked stood the tall, dry reeds. The blackbirds and starlings perched upon the willows seemed swollen into feathery balls, the fur started on the backs of hares, and a four-horse wain could travel in safety over swamps where at any other time a schoolboy dared not set his foot.

On such an eve, with snow threatening, the great marsh was utterly desolate, and this was why these two had chosen it for their meeting place.

To look on they were a goodly pair—the girl, who was clothed in the red she always wore, tall, dark, well shaped, with large black eyes and a determined face, one who would make a very stately woman; the man broad shouldered, with grey eyes that were quick and almost fierce, long limbed, hard, agile, and healthy, one who had never known sickness, who looked as though the world were his own to master. He was young, but three-and-twenty that day, and his simple dress, a tunic of thick wool fastened round him with a leathern belt, to which hung a short sword, showed that his degree was modest.

The girl, although she seemed his elder, in fact was only in her twentieth year. Yet from her who had been reared in the hard school of that cruel age childhood had long departed, leaving her a ripened woman before her time.

This pair stood looking at each other.

"Well, Cousin Eve Clavering," said the man, in his clear voice, "why did your message bid me meet you in this cold place?"

"Because I had a word to say to you, Cousin Hugh de Cressi," she answered boldly; "and the marsh being so cold and so lonesome I thought it suited to my purpose. Does Grey Dick watch yonder?"

"Ay, behind those willows, arrow on string, and God help him on whom Dick draws! But what was that word, Eve?"

"One easy to understand," she replied, looking him in the eyes—"Farewell!"

He shivered as though with the cold, and his face changed.

"An ill birthday greeting, yet I feared it," he muttered huskily, "but why more now than at any other time?"

"Would you know, Hugh? Well, the story is short, so I'll let it out. Our great-grandmother, the heiress of the de Cheneys, married twice, did she not, and from the first husband came the de Cressis, and from the second the Claverings. But in this way or in that we Claverings got the lands, or most of them, and you de Cressis, the nobler stock, took to merchandise. Now since those days you have grown rich with your fishing fleets, your wool mart, and your ferry dues at Walberswick and Southwold. We, too, are rich in manors and land, counting our acres by the thousand, but yet poor, lacking your gold, though yonder manor"—and she pointed to some towers which rose far away above the trees upon the high land—"has many mouths to feed. Also the sea has robbed us at Dunwich, where I was born, taking our great house and sundry streets that paid us rent, and your market of Southwold has starved out ours at Blythburgh."

"Well, what has all this to do with you and me, Eve?"

"Much, Hugh, as you should know who have been bred to trade," and she glanced at his merchant's dress. "Between de Cressi and Clavering there has been rivalry and feud for three long generations. When we were children it abated for a while, since your father lent money to mine, and that is why they suffered us to grow up side by side. But then they quarrelled about the ferry that we had set in pawn, and your father asked his gold back again, and, not getting it, took the ferry, which I have always held a foolish and strife-breeding deed, since from that day forward the war was open. Therefore, Hugh, if we meet at all it must be in these frozen reeds or behind the cover of a thicket, like a village slut and her man."

"I know that well enough, Eve, who have spoken with you but twice in nine months." And he devoured her beautiful face with hungry eyes. "But of that word, 'Farewell'—"

"Of that ill word, this, Hugh: I have a new suitor up yonder, a fine French suitor, a very great lord indeed, whose wealth, I am told, none can number. From his mother he has the Valley of the Waveney up to Bungay town—ay, and beyond—and from his father, a whole county in Normandy. Five French knights ride behind his banner, and with them ten squires and I know not how many men-at-arms. There is feasting yonder at the manor, I can tell you. Ere his train leaves us our winter provender will be done, and we'll have to drink small beer till the wine ships come from France in spring."

"And what is this lord's name?"

"God's truth, he has several," she answered. "Sir Edmund Acour in England, and in France the high and puissant Count of Noyon, and in Italy, near to the city of Venice—for there, too, he has possessions which came to him through his grandmother—the Seigneur of Cattrina."

"And having so much, does he want you, too, as I have heard, Eve? And if so, why?"

"So he swears," she answered slowly; "and as for the reason, why, I suppose you must seek it in my face, which by ill-fortune has pleased his lordship since first he saw it a month ago. At the least he has asked me in marriage of my father, who jumped at him like a winter pike, and so I'm betrothed."

"And do you want him, Eve?"

"Ay, I want him as far as the sun is from the moon or the world from either. I want him in heaven or beneath the earth, or anywhere away from me."

At these words a light shone in Hugh's keen grey eyes.

"I'm glad of that, Eve, for I've been told much of this fine fellow—amongst other things that he is a traitor come here to spy on England. But should I be a match for him, man to man, Eve?" he asked after a little pause.

She looked him up and down; then answered:

"I think so, though he is no weakling; but not for him and the five knights and the ten squires, and my noble father, and my brother, and the rest. Oh, Hugh, Hugh!" she added bitterly, "cannot you understand that you are but a merchant's lad, though your blood be as noble as any in this realm—a merchant's lad, the last of five brothers? Why were you not born the first of them if you wished for Eve Clavering, for then your red gold might have bought me."

"Ask that of those who begot me," said Hugh. "Come now, what's in your mind? You're not one to be sold like a heifer at a faring and go whimpering to the altar, and I am not one to see you led there while I stand upon my feet. We are made of a clay too stiff for a French lord's fingers, Eve, though it is true that they may drag you whither you would not walk."

"No," she answered, "I think I shall take some marrying against my wish. Moreover, I am Dunwich born."

"What of that, Eve?"

"Go ask your godsire and my friend, Sir Andrew Arnold, the old priest. In the library of the Temple there he showed me an ancient roll, a copy of the charter granted by John and other kings of England to the citizens of Dunwich."

"What said this writing, Eve?"

"It said, among other things, that no man or maid of Dunwich can be forced to marry against their will, even in the lifetime of their parents."

"But will it hold to-day?"

"Ay, I think so. I think that is why the holy Sir Andrew showed it to me, knowing something of our case, for he is my confessor when I can get to him."

"Then, sweet, you are safe!" exclaimed Hugh, with a sigh of relief.

"Ay, so safe that to-morrow Father Nicholas, the French chaplain in his train, has been warned to wed me to my lord Acour—that is, if I'm there to wed."

"And if this Acour is here, I'll seek him out to-night and challenge him, Eve," and Hugh laid hand upon his sword.

"Doubtless," she replied sarcastically, "Sir Edmund Acour, Count of Noyon, Seigneur of Cattrina, will find it honour to accept the challenge of Hugh de Cressi, the merchant's youngest son. Oh, Hugh, Hugh! are your wits frozen like this winter marsh? Not thus can you save me."

The young man thought a while, staring at the ground and biting his lips. Then he looked up suddenly and said:

"How much do you love me, Eve?"

With a slow smile, she opened her arms, and next moment they were kissing each other as heartily as ever man and maid have kissed since the world began, so heartily, indeed, that when at length she pushed him from her, her lovely face was as red as the cloak she wore.

"You know well that I love you, to my sorrow and undoing," she said, in a broken voice. "From childhood it has been so between us, and till the grave takes one or both it will be so, and for my part beyond it, if the priests speak true. For, whatever may be your case, I am not one to change my fancy. When I give, I give all, though it be of little worth. In truth, Hugh, if I could I would marry you to-night, though you are naught but a merchant's son, or even—" And she paused, wiping her eyes with the back of her slim, strong hand.

"I thank you," he answered, trembling with joy. "So it is with me. For you and no other woman I live and die; and though I am so humble I'll be worthy of you yet. If God keeps me in breath you shall not blush for your man, Eve. Well, I am not great at words, so let us come to deeds. Will you away with me now? I think that Father Arnold would find you lodging for the night and an altar to be wed at, and to-morrow our ship sails for Flanders and for France."

"Yes, but would your father give us passage in it, Hugh?"

"Why not? It could not deepen the feud between our Houses, which already has no bottom, and if he refused, we would take one, for the captain is my friend. And I have some little store set by; it came to me from my mother."

"You ask much," she said; "all a woman has, my life, perchance, as well. Yet there it is; I'll go because I'm a fool, Hugh; and, as it chances, you are more to me than aught, and I hate this fine French lord. I tell you I sicken at his glance and shiver when he touches me. Why, if he came too near I should murder him and be hanged. I'll go, though God alone knows the end of it."

"Our purpose being honest, the end will be good, Eve, though perhaps before all is done we may often think it evil. And now let's away, though I wish that you were dressed in another colour."

"Red Eve they name me, and red is my badge, because it suits my dark face best. Cavil not at my robe, Hugh, for it is the only dowry you will get with Eve Clavering. How shall we go? By the Walberswick ferry? You have no horses."

"Nay, but I have a skiff hidden in the reeds five miles furlongs off. We must keep to the heath above Walberswick, for there they might know your red cloak even after dark, and I would not have you seen till we are safe with Sir Arnold in the Preceptory. Mother of Heaven! what is that?"

"A peewit, no more," she answered indifferently.

"Nay, it is my man Dick, calling like a peewit. That is his sign when trouble is afoot. Ah, here he comes."

As he spoke a tall, gaunt man appeared, advancing towards them. His gait was a shambling trot that seemed slow, although, in truth, he was covering the ground with extraordinary swiftness. Moreover, he moved so silently that even on the frost-held soil his step could not be heard, and so carefully that not a reed stirred as he threaded in and out among their clumps like an otter, his head crouched down and his long bow pointed before him as though it were a spear. Half a minute more, and he was before them—a very strange man to see. His years were not so many, thirty perhaps, and yet his face looked quite old because of its lack of colouring, its thinness, and the hard lines that marked where the muscles ran down to the tight, straight mouth and up to the big forehead, over which hung hair so light that at a little distance he seemed ashen-grey. Only in this cold, rocky face, set very far apart, were two pale-blue eyes, which just now, when he chose to lift their lids that generally kept near together, as though he were half asleep, were full of fire and quick cunning.

Reaching the pair, this strange fellow dropped to his knee and raised his cap to Eve, the great lady of the Claverings—Red Eve, as they called her through that country-side. Then he spoke, in a low, husky voice:

"They're coming, master! You and your mistress must to earth unless you mean to face them in the open," and the pale eyes glittered as he tapped his great black bow.

"Who are coming, Dick? Be plain, man!"

"Sir John Clavering, my lady's father; young John, my lady's brother; the fine French lord who wears a white swan for a crest; three of the nights, his companions; and six—no seven—men-at-arms. Also from the other side of the grieve, Thomas of Kessland, and with him his marsh men and verderers."

"And what are they coming for?" he asked again. "Have they hounds, and hawk on wrist?"

"Nay, but they have swords and knife on thigh," and he let his pale eyes fall on Eve.

"Oh, have done!" she broke in. "They come to take me, and I'll not be taken! They come to kill you, and I'll not see you slain and live. I had words with my father this morning about the Frenchman and, I fear, let out the truth. He told me then that ere the Dunwich roses bloomed again she who loved you would have naught but bones to kiss. Dick, you know the fen; where can we hide till nightfall?"

"Follow me," said the man, "and keep low!"

Plunging into the dense brake of reeds, through which he glided like a polecat, Dick led them over ground whereon, save in times of hard frost, no man could tread, heading toward the river bank. For two hundred paces or more they went thus, till, quite near to the lip of the stream, they came to a patch of reeds higher and thicker than the rest, in the centre of which was a little mound hid in a tangle of scrub and rushes. Once, perhaps a hundred or a thousand years before, some old marsh dweller had lived upon this mound, or been buried in it. At any rate, on its southern side, hidden by reeds and a withered willow, was a cavity of which the mouth could not be seen that might have been a chamber for the living or the dead.

Thrusting aside the growths that masked it, Dick bade them enter and lie still.

"None will find us here," he said as he lifted up the reeds behind them, "unless they chance to have hounds, which I did not see. Hist! be still; they come!"

## Chapter 2
# The Fight by the River

For a while Hugh and Eve heard nothing, but Grey Dick's ears were sharper than theirs, quick as these might be. About half a minute later, however, they caught the sound of horses' hoofs ringing on the hard earth, followed by that of voices and the crackle of breaking reeds.

Two of the speakers appeared and pulled up their horses near by in a dry hollow that lay between them and the river bank. Peeping between the reeds that grew about the mouth of the earth-dwelling, Eve saw them.

"My father and the Frenchman," she whispered. "Look!" And she slid back a little so that Hugh might see.

Peering through the stems of the undergrowth, set as it were in a little frame against the red and ominous sky, the eyes of Hugh de Cressi fell upon Sir Edmund Acour, a gallant, even a splendid-looking knight—that was his first impression of him. Broad shouldered, graceful, in age neither young nor old, clean featured, quick eyed, with a mobile mouth and a little, square-cut beard, soft and languid voiced, black haired, richly dressed in a fur robe, and mounted on a fine black horse, such was the man.

Staring at Acour, and remembering that he, too, loved Red Eve, Hugh grew suddenly ashamed. How could a mere merchant compare himself with this magnificent lord, this high-bred, many-titled favourite of courts and of fortune? How could he rival him, he who had never yet travelled a hundred miles from the place where he was born, save once, when he sailed on a trading voyage to Calais? As well might a hooded crow try to match a peregrine that swooped to snatch away the dove from beneath its claws. Yes, he, Hugh, was the grey crow, Eve was the dove whom he had captured, and yonder shifty-eyed Count was the fleet, fierce peregrine who soon would tear out his heart and bear the quarry far away. Hugh shivered a little as the thought struck him, not with fear for himself, but at the dread of that great and close bereavement.

The girl at his side felt the shiver, and her mind, quickened by love and peril, guessed its purport. She said nothing, for words were dangerous; only turning her beautiful face she pressed her lips upon her lover's hand. It was her message to him; thereby, as he knew well, humble as he might be, she acknowledged him her lord forever. I am with you, said that kiss. Have no fear; in life or in death none shall divide us. He looked at her with grateful eyes, and would have spoken had she not placed her hand upon his mouth and pointed.

Acour was speaking in English, which he used with a strong French accent.

"Well, we do not find your beautiful runaway, Sir John," he said, in a clear and cultivated voice; "and although I am not vain, for my part I cannot believe that she has come to such a place as this to meet a merchant's clerk, she who should company with kings."

"Yet I fear it is so, Sir Edmund," answered Sir John Clavering, a stout, dark man of middle age. "This girl of mine is very heady, as I give warning you will find out when she is your wife. For years she has set her fancy upon Hugh de Cressi; yes, since they were boy and girl together, as I think, and while he lives I doubt she'll never change it."

"While he lives—then why should he continue to live, Sir John?" asked the Count indifferently. "Surely the world will not miss a chapman's son!"

"The de Cressis are my kin, although I hate them, Sir Edmund. Also they are rich and powerful, and have many friends in high places. If this young man died by my command it would start a blood feud of which none can tell the end, for, after all, he is nobly born."

"Then, Sir John, he shall die by mine. No, not at my own hands, since I do not fight with traders. But I have those about me who are pretty swordsmen and know how to pick a quarrel. Before a week is out there will be a funeral in Dunwich."

"I know nothing of your men, and do not want to hear of their quarrels, past or future," said Sir John testily.

"Of course not," answered the Count. "I pray you, forget my words. Name of God! what an accursed and ill-omened spot is this. I feel as though I were standing by my own grave—it came upon me suddenly." And he shivered and turned pale.

Dick lifted his bow, but Hugh knocked the arrow aside ere he could loose it.

"To those who talk of death, death often draws near," replied Clavering, crossing himself, "though I find the place well enough, seeing the hour and season."

"Do you—do you, Sir John? Look at that sky; look at the river beneath which has turned to blood. Hark to the howl of the wind in the reeds and the cry of the birds we cannot see. Ay, and look at our shadows on the snow. Mine lies flat by a great hole, and yours rising against yonder bank is that of a hooded man with hollow eyes—Death himself as I should limn him! There, it is gone! What a fool am I, or how strong is that wine of yours! Shall we be going also?"

"Nay, here comes my son with tidings. Well, Jack, have you found your sister?" he added, addressing a dark and somewhat saturnine young man who now rode up to them from over the crest of the hollow.

"No, sir, though we have beat the marsh through and through, so that scarce an otter could have escaped us. And yet she's here, for Thomas of Kessland caught sight of her red cloak among the reeds, and what's more, Hugh de Cressi is with her, and Grey Dick too, for both were seen."

"I am glad there's a third," said Sir John drily, "though God save me from his arrows! This Grey Dick," he added to the Count, "is a wild, homeless half-wit whom they call Hugh de Cressi's shadow, but the finest archer in Suffolk, with Norfolk thrown in; one who can put a shaft through every button on your doublet at fifty paces—ay, and bring down wild geese on the wing twice out of four times, for I have seen him do it with that black bow of his."

"Indeed? Then I should like to see him shoot—at somebody else," answered Acour, for in those days such skill was of interest to all soldiers. "Kill Hugh de Cressi if you will, friend, but spare Grey Dick; he might be useful."

"Ay, Sir Edmund," broke in the young man furiously, "I'll kill him if I can catch him, the dog who dares to bring scandal on my sister's name. Let the Saints but give me five minutes face to face with him alone, with none to help either of us, and I'll beat him to a pulp, and hang what's left of him upon the nearest tree to be a warning to all such puppies."

"I note the challenge," said Sir Edmund, "and should the chance come my way will keep the lists for you with pleasure, since whatever this Hugh may be I doubt that from his blood he'll prove no coward. But, young sir, you must catch your puppy ere you hang him, and if he is in this marsh he must have gone to ground."

"I think so, too, Sir Edmund; but, if so, we'll soon start the badger. Look yonder." And he pointed to smoke rising at several spots half a mile or more away.

"What have you done, son?" asked Sir John anxiously.

"Fired the reeds," he said with a savage laugh, "and set men to watch that the game does not break back. Oh, have no fear, father! Red Eve will take no harm. The girl ever loved fire. Moreover, if she is there she will run to the water before it, and be caught."

"Fool," thundered Sir John, "do you know your sister so little? As like as not she'll stay and burn, and then I'll lose my girl, who, when all is said, is worth ten of you! Well, what is done cannot be undone, but if death comes of this mad trick it is on your head, not mine! To the bank, and watch with me, Sir Edmund, for we can do no more."

********

Ten minutes later, and the fugitives in the mound, peeping out from their hole, saw clouds of smoke floating above them.

"You should have let me shoot, Master Hugh," said Grey Dick, in his hard, dry whisper. "I'd have had these three, at least, and they'd have been good company on the road to hell, which now we must walk alone."

"Nay," answered Hugh sternly, "I'll murder none, though they strive to murder us, and these least of all," and he glanced at Eve, who sat staring out of the mouth of the hole, her chin resting on her hand. "You had best give in, sweetheart," he said hoarsely. "Fire is worse than foes, and it draws near."

"I fear it less," she answered. "Moreover, marriage is worse than either—sometimes."

Hugh took counsel with Grey Dick.

"This place will burn like tinder," he said, pointing to the dry reeds which grew thickly all about them, and to the masses of brushwood and other rubbish that had drifted against the side of the little mound in times of flood. "If the fire reaches us we must perish of flame, or smoke, or both."

"Ay," answered Dick, "like old witch Sarah when they burned her in her house. She screeched a lot, though some say it was her cat that screeched and she died mum."

"If we could get into the water now, Dick?"

He shook his ash-hued head.

"The pools are frozen. Moreover, as well die of heat as cold; I love not ice-water."

"What counsel, then, Dick?"

"You'll not take the best, master—to loose my bow upon them. That fine fellow did well to be afraid, for had you not knocked up my hand there'd be an arrow sticking in his throat by now. He was right, Death walked near to him."

"It must not be, Dick, unless they strike first. What else?"

"Perchance, when the smoke begins to trouble them, which it must soon, they'll move. Then we will run for the river; 'tis but fifty yards. The Lady Eve can swim like a duck, and so can you. The tide has turned, and will bear you to the point, and I'll hold the bank against any who try to follow, and take my chance. What say you of that plan, lady?"

"That it is good as another, or as bad," she answered indifferently. "Let's bide where we are and do what we must when we must. Nay, waste no more breath, Hugh. I'll not yield and go home like a naughty child to be married. It was you who snatched away Grey Dick's shaft, not I; and now I'll save myself."

"Red Eve!—that's Red Eve!" muttered the henchman, with a dry chuckle of admiration. "The dead trouble neither man nor woman. Ah, she knows, she knows!"

After this there was silence for a while, save for the roar of the fire that ever drew more near.

Eve held her cloak pressed against her mouth to filter the smoke, which grew thick.

"It is time to move," said Hugh, coughing as he spoke. "By Heaven's grace, we are too late! Look!"

As he spoke, suddenly in the broad belt of reeds which lay between them and the river bank fire appeared in several places, caused doubtless by the flaming flakes which the strong wind had carried from behind the mound. Moreover, these new fires, burning up briskly and joining themselves together, began to advance toward the three in the hole.

"The wind has turned," said Dick. "Now it is fire, or water if you can get there. How do you choose to die?" and as he spoke he unstrung his bow and slipped it into its leathern case.

"Neither one way nor the other," answered Eve. "Some may die to-night, but we shall not."

Hugh leapt up and took command.

"Cover your faces to the eyes, and run for it," he said. "I'll go first, then you, Eve, and Dick behind. Make for the point and leap—the water is deep there."

They sprang to their feet and forward into the reeds. When they were almost at the edge of the fire a shout told them that they had been seen. Eve, the swift of foot, outpaced Hugh, and was the first to leap into that circle of tall flames. She was through it! They were all through it, scorched but unharmed. Thirty paces away was the little point of land where nothing grew, for the spring tides washed it, that jutted out into the waters of the Blythe, and, perhaps a hundred to their right, the Claverings poured down on them, foot and horse together.

Hugh caught his foot in a willow root and fell. Eve and Grey Dick sped onward unknowing. They reached the point above the water, turned, and saw. Dick slipped his bow from its case, strung it, and set an arrow on the string. Hugh had gained his feet, but a man who had come up sprang, and cast his arms about him. Hugh threw him to the ground, for he was very strong, and shook himself free. Then he drew the short and heavy sword that he wore, and, shouting out, "Make way!" to those who stood between him and the little promontory, started to run again.

These opened to the right and left to let him pass, for they feared the look in his eyes and the steel in his hand. Only young John Clavering, who had leapt from his horse, would not budge. As Hugh tried to push past him, he struck him in the face, calling out:

"We have caught the de Cressi thief! Take him and hang him!"

At the insult of the blow and words, Hugh stopped dead and turned quite white, whereupon the men, thinking that he was afraid, closed in upon him. Then in the silence the harsh, croaking voice of Grey Dick was heard saying:

"Sir John of Clavering, bid your people let my master go, or I will send an arrow through your heart!" and he lifted the long bow and drew it.

Sir John muttered something, thinking that this was a poor way to die, and again the men fell back, except one French knight, who, perhaps, did not catch or understand his words.

This man stretched out his hand to seize Hugh, but before ever it fell upon his shoulder the bow twanged and Acour's retainer was seen whirling round and round, cursing with pain. In the palm of his hand was an arrow that had sunk through it to the feathers.

"You are right; that knave shoots well," said the Count to Sir John, who made no answer.

Now again all fell back, so that Hugh might have run for it if he would. But his blood was up, and he did not stir.

"John Clavering," he said, addressing the young man, "just now, when

I lay hid in yonder hole, I heard you say that if you had five minutes with me alone you'd beat me to a pulp and hang what was left of me on the nearest tree. Well, here I stand, and there's a tree. Having first tried to burn me and your sister, you have struck me in the face. Will you make good your words, or shall I strike *you* in the face and go my way? Nay, keep your dogs off me! Grey Dick yonder has more arrows."

Now a tumult rose, some saying one thing and some another, but all keeping an eye upon Grey Dick and his bent bow. At last Sir Edmund Acour rode forward, and in his polished, stately way said to John:

"Young sir, this merchant is in the right, and whatever his trade may be, his blood is as good as your own. After your brave words, either you should fight him or take back the blow you gave."

Then he leaned down and whispered into John's ear:

"Your sword is longer than his. Make an end of him and of all his trouble, lest men should laugh at you as an empty boaster."

Now John, who was brave and needed but little urging, turned to his father and said:

"Have I your leave to whip this fellow, sir?"

"You should have asked that before you struck him in the face," replied the knight. "You are a man grown. Do as best pleases you. Only if you take the blow, begone from Blythburgh."

Then Eve, who all this time had been listening, called out from where she stood above the river.

"Brother John, if you fight your cousin Hugh, who is my affianced husband, and fall, on your own head be it, for know, your blood shall not stand between him and me, since it was you who struck him, and not he you. Be warned, John, and let him go, lest he should send you farther than you wish to travel. And to you, Hugh, I say, though it is much to ask, if he throws down his sword, forget that unknightly blow and come thither."

"You hear," said Hugh shortly to John. "Now, because she is your sister, if it's your will I'll begone in peace."

"Ay," answered John, setting his thin lips, "because you are a coward, woman-thief, and seek to live that you may bring shame upon our House. Well, that will pass when you die presently!"

"John, John, boast not," cried Eve. "Who has shown you where you will sleep to-night?"

"Whether I shall live or die, God knows alone," said Hugh solemnly. "But what I seek to know is, should it chance to be your lot to die, whether your people or this Frenchman will set on me, or raise a blood-feud against me. Tell me now, Sir John Clavering."

"If you kill my son in combat *à outrance*, he being the challenger," answered the knight, "none shall lift hand against you for that deed if I can hold them back. But know that I have other cause of quarrel against you"—and he pointed to his daughter—"and that if you meddle more with her, who is not for you, certainly you shall die."

"And, young sir," broke in Sir Edmund, "I pray you to understand that this Lady Eve to-morrow becomes my wife with the will of her father and her kin; and that if you try to stand between us, although I may not fight you, seeing what I am and what you are, I'll kill you like a rat when and where I get the chance! Yes," he added, in a savage snarl, "I pledge my knightly honour that I will kill you like a rat, if I must follow you across the world to do so!"

"You will not have need to travel far if I have my will," answered the young man sternly, "since Red Eve is mine, not yours, and, living or dead, mine she will remain. As for your fine knightly honour, Sir Edmund Acour, Count de Noyon, Seigneur of Cattrina, what has a traitor to his King to do with honour, one who is here as a spy of Philip of France, as the poor merchant's lad knows well? Oh, take you hand from your sword, of which you say I am not worthy, and, since you say also that I have so many enemies, let me begin with a squire of my own degree."

Now at these bold words arose a clamour of voices speaking in French and English.

"What say you to this, Sir Edmund?" shouted Sir John Clavering above them all. "You are a great lord and a wealthy, beloved by me also as the affianced of my daughter, but I am a loyal Englishman who have no truck with traitors to my King."

"What say I?" asked Sir Edmund calmly. "I say that if this fellow can fight as well as he can lie, your son has but a poor chance with him. As you know well, I came hither from France to visit my estates, not to learn what strength his Grace of England, my liege lord, gathers for the new war with Philip."

"Enough," said Sir John; "though this is the first I have heard of such a war, for it would seem that you know more of King Edward's mind than I do. The light begins to fail, there is no time for talk. Stand clear, all men, and let these two settle it."

"Ay," croaked Grey Dick, "stand clear, all men, while my master cuts the throat of his cousin Clavering, since he who stands not clear shall presently lie straight!" and he tapped his terrible bow with his right hand, then instantly seized the string again.

The two were face to face. Round them on horse and on foot, at a distance perhaps of twenty paces, were gathered the Clavering men and the French Count's troop; for now all had come up from the far parts of the marsh. Only toward the river side the ring was open, whether because those who made it feared Grey Dick's arrows, or in order that he and Red Eve might see everything that chanced.

The pair were well matched, for though Hugh was the taller, John, his senior by a year, was thicker set and better trained in arms. But the sword of John was longer by a hand's breadth than that Hugh carried as a merchant, which was heavy, of such a make as the ancient Romans used, and sharpened on either edge. Neither of them wore armour, since Hugh had no right to do so, and John had not come out to fight.

They stood still for a moment in the midst of a breathless silence, the red light of the stormy sunset striking across them both. Everything was red, the smoke-clouds rising from the sullen, burning marsh, into which the fire was still eating far away; the waters of the Blythe brimful with the tide that had just turned toward the sea, the snow and ice itself. Even the triangle of wild swans brought by the hard weather from the northern lands looked red as they pursued their heavy and majestic flight toward the south, heedless of man and his affairs beneath.

Not long did these remain heedless, however, since, either to show his skill or for some other purpose of his own, Grey Dick lifted his bow and loosed an arrow, almost, it seemed, at hazard. Yet that arrow pierced the leader of the flock, so that down it came in wide circles, and in a last struggle hovered for a moment over the group of men, then fell among them with a thud, the blood from its pierced breast bespattering Sir Edmund Acour and John Clavering's black hair.

"An ill omen for those two, and especially for him who wears a white swan for a crest," said a voice. But at the moment none took much notice, except Grey Dick, who chuckled at the success of his shot, since all were intent on greater matters—namely, which of those two young men should die.

Sir John, the father, rode forward and addressed them.

"To the death without mercy to the fallen," he said grimly.

They bent their heads in answer.

"Now!" he cried, and reined back his horse.

"The first home thrust wins," whispered Acour to him, as he wiped the blood of the swan off his sleeve. "Thank God, your son's sword is the longer!"

Perhaps the pair heard this whisper, or, perhaps, being without mail, they knew that it was so. At least for a while they circled round and round each other, but out of reach.

Then at length John Clavering rushed in and thrust. Hugh sprang back before his point. Again he rushed and thrust and again Hugh sprang back. A third time and Hugh fairly ran, whereon a shout went up from the Claverings.

"The chapman's afraid!" cried one. "Give him a yard measure," shouted another; "he cannot handle steel!"

Eve turned her face, and her very eyes were sick with doubt.

"Is it true?" she gasped.

"Ay," answered Dick the Archer, "it's true that he draws him to the river bank! Those who wait will learn why. Oh, the swan! He sees not the swan!"

As he spoke, Hugh, in his retreat before another of John Clavering's rushes, struck his foot against the great dead bird, and staggered. John leapt upon him, and he went down.

"Is he pierced?" muttered Eve.

"Nay, missed," answered Dick, "by half an inch. Ah, I thought so!"

As the words left his lips Clavering fell sprawling on his back, for Hugh had caught his leg with his left arm and thrown him, so that they lay both together on the ground.

There they closed, rolling over each other, but too close to stab.

"Now good-night, John," said Dick, with his hoarse chuckle. "Throat him, master—throat him!"

The flurry in the snow was at an end. John lay on his back, de Cressi knelt on him and lifted his short sword.

"Do you yield?" men heard him say.

"Nay," answered Clavering. Then suddenly Hugh rose and suffered his adversary to do likewise.

"I'll not stick you like a hog!" he said, and some cried, "Well done!" for the act seemed noble. Only Acour muttered, "Fool!"

Next instant they were at it again, but this time it was Hugh who attacked and John who gave back right to the river's edge, for skill and courage seemed to fail him at once.

"Turn your head, lady," said Dick, "for now one must die." But Eve could not.

The swords flashed for the last time in the red light, then that of de Cressi vanished. Clavering threw his arms wide, and fell backward. A splash as of a great stone thrown into water, and all was done.

Hugh stood a moment on the river's bank, staring at the stream beneath; then he turned and began to walk slowly toward the dead swan.

Ere ever he reached it Sir John Clavering fell from his horse in a swoon, and a shout of rage went up from all his people.

"Kill him!" they yelled, and leapt forward.

Now Hugh understood, and ran for the point of land. One man, a Frenchman, got in front of him. He cut him down, and sped on.

"What now?" said Eve, as he joined them.

He did not answer, only pointed first to the Clavering folk and next to the water, showing that she must choose between the two.

"Swim for it!" growled Grey Dick. "I'll hold them back a while and then join you," and as he spoke his bow twanged.

For an instant Eve paused, then threw off her scarlet cloak.

"Remember, I slew your brother!" said Hugh hoarsely.

"I remember that he would have slain you," she answered; and leapt straight from the point into the icy flood, beneath which her head sank. When it rose again there was another head beside it, that of dead John, who appeared for one moment, to be seen no more for ever, since ere morning the ocean had him.

Now Hugh leapt after her, and presently the pair of them were swimming side by side to the river's further shore. Then, as now, it was but a narrow stream. Yet they did not reach it easily, for, cumbered as they were with clothes, and numbed by the ice-cold water, the fierce tide caught them and carried them beyond the bend. There they were lost in the gathering darkness, so that most of those who watched believed that they had sunk and drowned. But it was not so, for after a long struggle they came safe to shore near to a clump of willows, and clambered over the frozen mud to the heath beyond.

"First fire, then water," said Hugh, in a mazed voice.

"You have missed out love and death," answered the girl—"a full feast for a day that is not done. But whither now?"

"To take sanctuary at the Preceptory and raise my kin. Forward, Eve, ere you freeze."

"I think there is that in me which will not freeze," she answered; and broke into a run.

Now night closed in, and the snow which had been threatening all day began to fall, making their path over the heath difficult.

"We need Grey Dick to guide us; but alack, I fear he is dead!" muttered Hugh.

"I think others will be dead, not Dick," she answered.

Just then they heard a footstep behind them.

Hugh wheeled round and drew his sword, but almost before it had left the scabbard a long figure glided out of the snow, and said:

"More to the left, master, more to the left, unless you would make your peace on Blythburgh bridge, where some would be glad to meet you."

"How went it?" asked Hugh shortly.

"Not well. I shot thrice and slew three men, two of the French knights, and Thomas of Kessland, against whom I had a score that now is settled. But the fourth time I missed."

"Who?" asked Eve between her teeth as she ran beside him.

"The Frenchman who means to marry you. When the others fell back he came at me on his horse as I was setting a fresh arrow, thinking to get me. I had to shoot quick, and aimed low for his heart, because in that light I could not make certain of his face. He saw, and jerked up the horses head, so that the shaft took it in the throat and killed the beast without hurting its rider. He was off in an instant and at me, with others, before I could draw again. So I thought it time to go, which I did, backward, as he thrust. Perhaps he thinks he killed me, as I meant he should, only when he looks at his sword he'll find it clean. That's all."

And again Grey Dick chuckled.

## Chapter 3

# Father Andrew

None were abroad in the streets of Dunwich on that bitter winter night when these three trudged wearily down Middlegate Street through the driving snow to the door of the grey Preceptory of the Knights Templar. In a window above the porch a light burned dimly, the only one to be seen in any of the houses round about, for by now all men were abed.

"'Tis Father Arnold's room," said Eve. "He sits there at his books. I'll knock and call him, but do you two go lay hold of the ring of the church door," and she nodded toward a grey pile that stood near by. "Then none can touch you, and how know we who may be in this house?"

"I'll go no step further," answered Hugh sullenly. "All this Temple ground is sanctuary, or at least we will risk it." And, seizing the knocker, he hammered at the door.

The light in the window vanished, and presently they heard a sound of creaking bolts. Then the door opened, revealing a tall man, white-bearded, ancient, and clad in a frayed, furred robe worn over a priest's cassock, who held a lantern in his hand.

"Who knocks?" he asked. "Does some soul pass that you disturb me after curfew?"

"Ay, Father Andrew," answered Hugh, "souls have passed, and souls are near to passing. Let us in, and we will tell you all."

Without waiting for an answer he entered with the others, pushed to the massive door and bolted it again.

"What's this? A woman?" said the old priest. "Eve of Clavering, by the Saints!"

"Yes," she answered calmly, though her teeth chattered; "Eve of Clavering, Eve the Red, this time with the blood of men, soaked with the waters of the Blythe, frozen with the snows of Dunwich Heath, where she has lain hid for hours with a furze bush for shelter. Eve who seeks shriving, a dry rag for her back, a morsel for her lips, and fire to warm her, which in the Name of Christ and of charity she prays you will not refuse to her."

So she spoke, and laughed recklessly.

Almost before she had finished her wild words the old man, who looked what he was, a knight arrayed in priestly robes, had run to a door at the end of the hall and was calling through it, "Mother Agnes! Mother Agnes!"

"Be not so hasty, Sir Andrew," answered a shrill voice. "A *posset* must have time to boil. It is meet now that you wear a tonsure that you who are no longer a centurion should forget these 'Come, and he cometh,' ways. When the water's hot—"

The rest of that speech was lost, for Father Arnold, muttering some word belonging to his "centurion" days, dived into the kitchen, to reappear presently dragging a little withered old woman after him who was dressed in a robe of conventual make.

"Peace, Mother Agnes, peace!" he said. "Take this lady, dry her, array her in your best gown, give her food, warm her, and bring her back to me. Short? What care I if the robe be short? Obey, or it will not be come, and he cometh, but go and she goeth, and then who will shelter one who talks so much?"

He thrust the pair of them through the kitchen door and, returning, led Hugh and Grey Dick up a broad oak stair to what had been the guest-hall of the Preceptory on its first floor.

It was a very great chamber where, before their Order was dispersed, all the Knights Templar had been wont to dine with those who visited them at times of festival. Tattered banners still hung among the cobwebs of the ancient roof, the shields of past masters with stately blazonings were carved in stone upon the walls. But of all this departed splendour but little could be seen, since the place was lit only by a single lamp of whale's oil and a fire that burned upon the wide stone hearth, a great fire, since Father Arnold, who had spent many years of his life in the East, loved warmth.

"Now, Hugh de Cressi," he said, "what have you done?"

"Slain my cousin, John of Clavering, Father, and perhaps another man."

"In fair fight, very fair fight," croaked Grey Dick.

"Who doubts it? Can a de Cressi be a murderer?" asked the priest. "And you, Richard the Archer, what have you done?"

"Shot a good horse and three bad men dead with arrows—at

least they should be dead—and another through the hand, standing one against twenty."

"A gallant—I mean—an evil deed," broke in the old warrior priest, "though once it happened to me in a place called Damascus—but you both are wet, also. Come into my chamber; I can furnish you with garments of a sort. And, Richard, set that black bow of yours near the fire, but not too fire. As you should know well, a damp string is ill to draw with. Nay, fear not to leave it; this is sanctuary, and to make sure I will lock the doors."

********

Half an hour was gone by, and a very strange company had gathered round the big fire in the guest-chamber of the Temple, eating with appetite of such food as its scanty larder could provide for them. First there was Red Eve in a woollen garment, the Sunday wear of Mother Agnes for twenty years past and more, which reached but little below her knees, and was shaped like a sack. On her feet were no shoes, and for sole adornment her curling black hair fell about her shoulders, for so she had arranged it because the gown would not meet across her bosom. Yet, odd as it might be, in this costume Eve looked wonderfully beautiful, perhaps because it was so scant and the leathern strap about her waist caused it to cling close to her shapely form.

By her stood Hugh, wearing a splendid suit of chain armour. It had been Sir Andrew Arnold's in his warlike years, and now he lent it to his godson Hugh because, as he said, he had nothing else. Also, it may have crossed the minds of both of them that such mail as this which the Saracens had forged, if somewhat out of fashion, could still turn sword-cuts.

Then there was Grey Dick, whose garments seemed to consist of a sack with holes in it tied round him with a rope, his quiver of arrows slung over it for ornament. He sat by the fire on a stool, oiling his black bow with a rind of the fat bacon that he had been eating.

All the tale had been told, and Father Arnold looked very grave indeed.

"I have known strange and dreadful stories in my time," he said, "but never, I think, one stranger or more dreadful. What would you do now, godson?"

"Take sanctuary for myself and Grey Dick because of the slaying of John Clavering and others, and afterward be married by you to Eve."

"Be married to the sister with the brother's blood upon your hands without absolution from the Church or pardon from the King; and you but a merchant's younger son and she to-night one of the greatest heiresses in East Anglia! Why, how may that be?"

"I blame him not," broke in Eve. "John, whom I never loved, strove to smoke us out like rats because he was in the pay of the Norman, my Lord of Acour. John struck Hugh in the face with his hand and slandered him with his tongue. John was given his life once, and afterwards slain in fair fight. Oh, I say, I blame him not, nor shall John's blood rise between him and me!"

"Yet the world will blame him, and you, too, Eve; yes, even those who love you both. A while must go by, say a year. At least I'll not marry you at once, and cannot, if I would, with both your fathers living and unadvised, and the sheriff waiting at the gate. Tell me now, do any know that you have entered here?"

"Nay," said Dick, looking up from his bow. "The hunt came after us, but I hid these two in a bush and led it away past Hinton to the Ipswich road, keeping but just ahead in the snow and talking in three voices. Then I gave them the slip and returned. They'll not guess that we have come to Dunwich for a while."

"And when they do even the boldest will not enter this holy sanctuary while the Church has terrors for men's souls. Yet, here you must not stay for long, lest in this way or in that your lives pay the price of it, or a bloody feud break out between the Claverings of Blythburgh and the de Cressis of Dunwich. Daughter Eve, get you to bed with old Agnes. You are so weary that you will not mind her snores. To-morrow ere the dawn I'll talk with you, and, meanwhile, I have words for Hugh. Nay, have no fear, the windows are all barred, and Archer Dick shall watch the door."

Eve went, unwillingly enough, although she could scarcely walk, flashing a good-night to her lover with her fine eyes. Presently Grey Dick also went to sleep, like a dog with one eye open, in the little ante-chamber, near to the great door.

"Now, Hugh," said Father Arnold, when they were left alone, "your case is desperate, for if you stay here certainly these Claverings will have your blood. Yet, if you can be got away safely, there is still a shaft that you may shoot more deadly than any that ever left Grey Dick's quiver. But yesterday I told you for your comfort—when we spoke of his wooing of Red Eve—that this Norman, for such he is, although his mother was English and he was English born, is a traitor to King Edward, whom he pretends to serve."

"Ay, and I said as much to him this afternoon when he prated to me of his knightly honour, and, though I had no time to take note of faces, I thought he liked it little who answered hotly that I was a liar."

"I am sorry, Hugh; it may put him on his guard, or perhaps he'll pay no heed. At least the words are said, and there's an end. Now hearken. I told neither you nor any one all the blackness of his treachery. Have you guessed what this Acour is here to do?"

"Spy out the King's power in these parts, I suppose."

"More than that"—and he dropped his voice to a whisper—"spy out a safe landing-place for fifty thousand Normans upon our Suffolk coast. They are to sail hither this coming summer and set the crown of England upon their Duke John, who will hold it as vassal to his sire, Philip of France."

"God's name! Is that true?"

"Ay, though in such a devil's business that Name is best left out. Look you, lad, I had warning from overseas, where, although I am now nothing but a poor old priest of a broken Order, I still have friends in high places. Therefore I watched and found that messengers were passing between Acour and France. One of these messengers, a priest, came a week ago to Dunwich, and spent the night in a tavern waiting for his ship to sail in the morning. The good wife who keeps that tavern—ask not her name—would go far to serve me. That night this priest slept sound, and while he slept a letter was cut from the lining of his cassock, and another without writing sewn there in place of it, so that he'll never know the difference till he reaches John of Normandy, and then not where he lost it. Stay, you shall see," and he went to the wall and from some secret place behind the hangings produced a writing, which he handed to Hugh, who looked at it, then gave it back to him, saying:

"Read it to me, Father, English I can spell out, but this French puzzles my eyes."

So he read, Hugh listening eagerly to every word:

My Lord Duke:

This by a faithful hand that you know to tell you all goes well with your Grace's business, and with that of your royal father. While pretending to hunt or hawk I have found three places along this seaboard at any one of which the army can land next summer with little resistance to fear, for though the land is rich in cattle and corn, the people are few.

These places of which I have made survey have deep water up to the beach. I will tell you of them more particularly when I return. Meanwhile I linger here for sundry reasons, which you know, hoping to draw those of whom you speak to me to your cause, which, God aiding me, I shall do, since he of England has wronged one of them and slighted the others, so that they are bitter against him, and ready to listen to the promises which I make in your name.

As an excuse for my long stay that has caused doubts in some quarters, I speak of my Suffolk lands which need my care. Also I court the daughter of my host here, the Knight of Clavering, a stubborn Englishman who cannot be won, but a man of great power and repute. This courtship, which began in jest, has ended in earnest, since the girl is very haughty and beautiful, and as she will not be played with I propose, with your good leave, to make her my wife. Her father accepts my suit, and when he and the brother are out of the way, as doubtless may happen after your army comes, she will have great possessions.

I thank your Grace for the promise of the wide English lands of which I spoke to you, and the title that goes with them. These I will do my best to earn, nor will I ask for them till I kneel before you when you are crowned King of England at Westminster, as I doubt not God will bring about before this year is out. I have made a map of the road by which your army should march on London after landing, and of the towns to be sacked upon the way thither. This, however, I keep, since although not one in ten thousand of these English swine can read French, or any other tongue, should it chance to be lost, all can understand a map. Not that there is any fear of loss, for who will meddle with a priest who carries credentials signed by his Holiness himself.

I do homage to your Grace. This written with my hand from Blythburgh, in Suffolk, on the twentieth day of February, 1346.

Edmund of Noyon.

Father Arnold ceased reading, and Hugh gasped out:

"What a fool is this knave-Count!"

"Most men are, my son, in this way or in that, and the few wise profit by their folly. Thus this letter, which he thought so safe, will save England to Edward and his race, you from many dangers, your betrothed from a marriage which she hates—that is, if you can get safe away with it from Dunwich."

"Where to, Father?"

"To King Edward in London, with another that I will write for you ere the dawn."

"But is it safe, Father, to trust so precious a thing to me, who have bitter enemies awaiting me, and may as like as not be crow's meat by to-morrow?"

Father Arnold looked at him with his soft and dreamy eyes, then said: "I think the crow's not hatched that will pick your bones, Hugh, though at the last there be crows, or worms, for all of us."

"Why not, Father? Doubtless, this morning young John of Clavering thought as much, and now he is in the stake-nets, or food for fishes."

"Would you like to hear, Hugh, and will you keep it to yourself, even from Eve?"

"Ay, that I would and will."

"He'll think me mad!" muttered the old priest to himself, then went on aloud as one who takes a sudden resolution. "Well, I'll tell you, leaving you to make what you will of a story that till now has been heard by no living man."

"Far in the East is the great country that we call Cathay, though in truth it has many other names, and I alone of all who breathe in England have visited that land."

"How did you get there?" asked Hugh, amazed, for though he knew dimly that Father Arnold had travelled much in his youth, he never dreamed that he had reached the mystic territories of Cathay, or indeed that such a place really was except in fable.

"It would take from now till morning to tell, son, nor even then would you understand the road. It is enough to say that I went on a pilgrimage to Jerusalem, where our blessed Saviour died. That was the beginning. Thence I travelled with Arabs to the Red Sea, where wild men made a slave of me, and we were blown across the Indian Ocean to a beauteous island named Ceylon, in which all the folk are black.

"From this place I escaped in a vessel called a junk, that brought me to the town of Singapore. Thence at last, following my star, I came to Cathay after two years of journeyings. There I dwelt in honour for three more years, moving from place to place, since never before had its inhabitants seen a Western man, and they made much of me, always sending me forward to new cities. So at length I reached the greatest of them all, which is called Kambaluc, or Peking, and there was the guest of its Emperor, Timur.

"All the story of my life and adventures yonder I have written down, and any who will may read it after I am dead. But of these I have no time to speak, nor have they anything to do with you. Whilst I dwelt in Kambaluc as the guest of the Emperor Timur, I made study of the religion of this mighty people, who, I was told, worshipped gods in the shape of men. I visited a shrine called the Temple of Heaven, hoping that there I should see such a god who was named Tien, but found in it nothing but splendid emptiness.

"Then I asked if there was no god that I could see with my eyes, whereon the Emperor laughed at me and said there was such a god, but he counselled me not to visit him. I prayed him to suffer me to do so, since I, who worshipped the only true God, feared no other. Whereon, growing angry, he commanded some of his servants to 'take this fool to the house of Murgh and let him see whether his God could protect him against Murgh.' Having said this he bade me farewell, adding that though every man must meet Murgh once, few met him twice, and therefore he did not think that he should see me again.

"Now, in my heart I grew afraid, but none would tell me more of this Murgh or what was likely to happen to me at his hands. Still, I would not show any fear, and; strong in the faith of Christ, I determined to look upon this idol, for such I expected him to be.

"That night the servants ofTimur bore me out of the city in a litter, and by the starlight I saw that we travelled toward a hill through great graveyards, where people were burying their dead. At the foot of the hill they set me down upon a road, and told me to walk up it, and that at dawn I should see the House of Murgh, whereof the gates were always open, and could enter there if I wished. I asked if they would wait for my return, whereon they answered, smiling, that if I so desired they would do so till evening, but that it seemed scarcely needful, since they did not suppose that I should return.

"'Do yonder pilgrims to the House of Murgh return?' asked their captain, pointing towards those graveyards which we had passed.

"I made no answer, but walked forward up a broad and easy road, unchallenged of any, till I came to what, even in that dim light, I could see was a great and frowning gateway, whereof the doors appeared to be open. Now, at first I thought I would pass this gateway at once and see what lay beyond. But from this I was held back by some great fear, for which I could find no cause, unless it were bred of what the Emperor and his servants had said to me. So I remembered their words—namely, that I should tarry till dawn to enter the house.

"There, then, I tarried, seated on the ground before the gateway, and feeling as though, yet alive, I had descended among the dead. Indeed, the silence was that of the dead. No voice spoke, no hound barked, no leaf stirred. Only far above me I heard a continual soughing, as though winged souls passed to and fro. Never in my life had I felt so much alone, never so much afraid.

"At length the dawn broke, and oh, glad was I to see its light, for fear lest I should die in darkness! Now I saw that I was on a hilltop where grew great groves of cedar trees, and that set amid them was a black-tiled temple, surrounded by a wall built of black brick.

"It was not a great place, although the gateway, which was surmounted by two black dragons of stone or iron, was very great, so great that a tall ship could have sailed through it and left its arch untouched.

"I kneeled down and prayed to the blessed Saints and the guardian angels to protect me. Then I arose, crossed myself to scare off all evil things by that holy sign, and set forward toward the mighty gateway. Oh, never, never till that hour had I understood how lowly a thing is man! On that broad road, travelling toward the awful, dragon-guarded arch, beyond which lay I knew not what, it seemed to me that I was the only man left in the world, I, whose hour had come to enter the portals of destruction.

"I passed into the cold shadow of the gateway, unchallenged by any watchman, and found myself in a courtyard surrounded by a wall also built of black brick, which had doors in it that seemed to be of dark stone or iron. Whither these doors led I do not know, since the wall cut off the sight of any buildings that may have lain beyond. In the centre of this courtyard was a pool of still, black water, and at the head of the pool a chair of black marble."

Sir Andrew paused, and Hugh said:

"A plain place for a temple, Father, without adornments or images. But perhaps this was the outer court, and the temple stood within."

"Ay, son, the plainest temple that ever I saw, who have seen many in all lands, though what was beyond it I do not know. And yet—terrible, terrible, terrible!—I tell you that those black walls and that black water were more fearsome to look on than any churchyard vault grim with bones, or a torture-pit where victims quiver out their souls midst shrieks and groanings. And yet I could see nothing of which to be afraid, and hear nothing save that soughing of invisible wings whereof I have spoken. An empty chair, a pool of water, some walls and doors, and, above, the quiet sky. What was there to fear in such things as these? Still, so greatly did I fear that I sank to my knees and began to pray once more, this time to the blessed Saviour himself, since I was sure that none else could help me.

"When I looked up again the chair was no longer empty. Hugh, a man sat in it, of whom I thought at first only one thing—that he must be very strong, though not bigger than other men. Strength seemed to flow from him. I should not have wondered if he had placed his hands upon the massive sides of that stone chair and torn it asunder."

"What was he like, Father? Samson or Goliath?"

"I never saw either, son, so cannot say. But what was he like? Oh, I cannot say that either, although still I see him in my heart. My mortal lips will not tell the likeness of that man, perhaps because he seemed to be like all men, and yet different from all. He had an iron brow, beneath which shone deep, cold eyes. He was clean-shaven, or perchance his face grew no hair. His lips were thick and still and his features did not change like those of other men. He looked as though he could not change; as though he had been thus for infinite ages, and yet remained neither young nor old. As for his dress, he wore a cloak of flaming red, such a cloak as your Eve loves to wear, and white sandals on his feet. There was no covering on his shaven head, which gleamed like a skull. His breast was naked, but across it hung one row of black jewels. From the sheen of them I think they must have been pearls, which are sometimes found of that colour in the East. He had no weapon nor staff, and his hands hung down on either side of the chair.

"For a long while I watched him, but if he saw me he took no note. As I watched I perceived that birds were coming to and leaving him in countless numbers, and thought that it must be their wings which made the constant soughing sound that filled all the still and dreadful air."

"What kind of birds were they, Father?"

"I am not sure, but I think doves; at least, their flight was straight and swift like to that of doves. Yet of this I am not sure either, since I saw each of them for but a second. As they reached the man they appeared out of nothingness. They were of two colours, snow-white and coal-black. The white appeared upon his right side, the black upon his left side. Each bird in those never-ceasing streams hovered for an instant by his head, the white over his right shoulder, the black over his left shoulder, as though they whispered a message to his ear, and having whispered were gone upon their errand."

"What was that errand, Father?"

"How can I know, as no one ever told me? Yet I will hazard a guess that it had to do with the mystery of life and death. Souls that were born into the world, and souls departing from the world, perchance, making report to one of God's ministers clothed in flesh. But who can say? At least I watched those magic fowls till my eyes grew dizzy, and a sort of slumber began to creep into my brain.

"How long I stayed thus I do not remember, for I had lost all sense of time. In the end, however, I was awakened by a cold, soft voice, the sound of which seemed to flow through my veins like ice, that addressed me in our own rough English tongue, spoken as you and I learned it at our nurses' knees.

"'To what god were you praying just now, Andrew Arnold?'

"'Oh, sir,' I answered, 'how do you, who dwell in Cathay, where I am a stranger, know my language and my name?'

"He lifted his cold eyes and looked at me, and I felt them pierce into the depths of my soul. 'In the same way that I know your heart,' he said. 'But do not ask questions. Answer them, that I may learn whether you are a true man or a liar.'

"'I was praying to Christ,' I faltered, 'the Saviour of us all.'

"'A great God, Andrew Arnold, and a pure, though His followers are few in the world as yet. But do you think that He can save you from Me, as you were asking Him to do?'

"'He can save my soul,' I replied, plucking up courage, who would not deny the Lord even in a devil's den.

"'Ah! your soul. Well, I have nothing to do with souls, except to count them as they pass through my dominion, and you are quite right to pray to one of the lords of that into which you go. Now, man, what is your business with me, and why do you visit one of whom you are so much afraid?'

"'O Murgh!' I began, then ceased, for I knew not what to answer.

"'So they have told you my name? Now I will tell you one of its meanings. It is "Gate of the Gods." Why did you dare to visit Gate of the Gods? You fear to answer. Listen! You came forth to see some painted idol, or some bedizened priest muttering rites he does not understand to that which is not; and lo! you have found that which is behind all idols and all priests. You sought an incensed and a golden shrine and you have found only the black and iron portals which every man must pass but which few desire to enter until they are called. Well, you are young and strong, come try a fall with Murgh, and when he has thrown you, rise and choose which of those ways you will,' and he swept his hand toward the doors around him. 'Then forget this world and enter into that which you have chosen.'

"Now, because I could not help myself, I rose from my knees and advanced, or was drawn toward that dreadful man. As I came he, too, rose from his chair, stretching out his arms as a wrestler does, and I knew that within the circle of those arms lay my death. Still I, who in my youth was held brave, went on and rushed, striving to clasp him. Next moment, before ever I touched him—oh, well was it for me that I touched him not!—some strength seized me and whirled me round and round as a dead leaf is whirled by the wind, and tossed me up and cast me down and left me prone and nerveless.

"'Rise,' said the cold voice above me, 'for you are unhurt.'

"So I rose, and felt even then that I who thought that every bone in my body must be broken, was stronger than I had ever been before. It was as though the lamp which had burnt low was filled suddenly with a new and purer oil.

"'Man,' said mine adversary, and I thought that in his cold eyes there was something like a smile, 'did you think to touch Murgh and live? Did you think to wrestle with him as in a book of one of your prophets a certain Jacob wrestled with an angel, and conquered—until it was his turn to pass the Gate of the Gods?'

"Now I stared at this dweller in Cathay, who spoke my tongue and knew the tale of Jacob in the ancient Book, then answered:

"'Sir Murgh, or Sir Gate, or whatever your name may be, I thought to do nothing. You drew me to you, you challenged me and, since by the rule of my Order I may refuse no challenge from one who is not a Christian, I came on to do my best. But before ever I laid hand on you I was cast down by a wind. That is all the story, save that it has pleased you to let me live, who evidently could have slain me, for which I thank you.'

"'You are wrong, Sir Andrew,' he answered, 'I did not draw you to me. Men come to Murgh at their appointed hour; Murgh does not come to them. You sought him before your hour, and therefore he refused you. Yet you will meet him again, as all flesh must when its hour comes, and because you are bold and have not cringed before my strength, for your comfort I will show you when and how. Stand by me, but lay no hand on me or my robe, and look into my glass while for a moment, for your sake, I stay the stream of time and show you what lies beneath its foam that blinds the eyes of men.'

"He waved his arms and the black doves and the white doves ceased to appear and disappear, and the eternal soughings of their wings was silent. He pointed to the water at his feet and I saw, not a picture, but a scene so real that I could have sworn it was alive about me. Yes, those who took part in it stood in front of me as though the pool were solid ground that their feet pressed. *You* were one of them, son, *you* were one of them," and the old knight paused, supporting himself against the mantel-shelf as though that recollection overcame him.

"What did you see?" whispered Hugh.

"By God's holy name, I saw the Blythburgh Marshes deep in snow that was red, blood-red with the light of sunrise. Oh! I could not be mistook, and there ran the wintry river, there the church tower soared, there were the frowning, tree-clad banks. There was the rough moorland over which the east wind piped, for the dead bracken bent before it, and not twenty paces from me leaped a hare, disturbed suddenly from its form by a hungry fox, whose red head peeped through the reeds. Yes, yes, I saw the brute's white teeth gleam as it licked its disappointed lips, and I felt glad that its prey had beaten it! When you look upon that scene, Hugh, as one day you shall, remember the hare and the head of the hungry fox, and by these judge my truth."

"A fox and a hare!" broke in Hugh. "I'd show you such to-morrow; was there no more?"

"Ay, much. For instance, a hollow in the Marsh, an open grave, and an axe; yes, an axe that had delved it where the bog was soft beneath the snow. Grey Dick held the axe in one hand and his black bow in the other, while Red Eve, your Eve, stood at its edge and stared into it like one in a dream. Then at the head of the grave an old, old man clad in mail beneath his priestly robes, and that man *myself*, Hugh, grown very ancient, but still myself, and no other.

"And at the foot of the grave *you*, Hugh de Cressi, you and no other, wayworn and fierce, but also clad in mail, and wearing a knight's crest upon your shield. You with drawn sword in hand, and facing you, also with drawn sword, rage and despair on his dark face, a stately, foreign-looking man, whom mine eyes have never seen, but whom I should know again midst a million, a man who, I think, was doomed to fill the grave.

"Lastly, standing on a little mound near to the bank of the swirling river, where jagged sheets of ice ground against each other like the teeth of the wicked in hell, strangely capped and clad in black, his arms crossed upon his breast and a light smile in his cold eyes, he who was called Murgh in Cathay, he who named himself Gateway of the Gods!

"For a moment I saw, then all was gone, and I found myself—I know not why—walking toward the mighty arch whereon sat the iron dragons. In its shadow I turned and looked back. There at the head of the pool the man was seated in his chair, and to right and to left of him came the black doves and the white doves in countless multitudes, all the thousands of them that had been stayed in their flight pouring down upon him at once—or so I thought. They wheeled about his head, they hid his face from me, and I—I departed into the shadow of the arch, and I saw him and them no more."

## Chapter 4

# The Penance

The tale was done, and these two stood staring at one another from each side of the glowing hearth, whose red light illumined their faces. At length the heavy silence was broken by Sir Andrew.

"I read your heart, Hugh," he said, "as Murgh read mine, for I think that he gave me not only strength, but something of his wisdom also, whereby I was able to win safe back to England and to this hour to walk unharmed by many a pit. I read your heart, and in its book is written that you think me mad, one who pleases his old age with tales of marvel that others told him, or which his own brain fashioned."

"Not so, Father," answered Hugh uneasily, for in truth some such thoughts were passing through his mind. "Only—only the thing is very strange, and it happened so long ago, before Eve and I were born, before those that begot us were born either, perchance."

"Yes; more than fifty years ago—it may be sixty—I forget. In sixty years the memory plays strange tricks with men, no doubt, so how can I blame you if you believe—what you do believe? And yet, Hugh," he went on after a pause, and speaking with passion, "this was no dream of which I tell you. Why do you suppose that among all those that have grown up about me I have chosen you out to love, you and your Eve? Not because a chance made me your godsire and her my pupil. I say that from your infancy your faces haunted me. Ay, and when you had turned childhood's corner and once I met the pair of you walking hand in hand, then of a sudden I knew that it was you two and no others whom that god or devil had showed to me standing by the open grave upon the banks of Blythe. I knew it of Dick the Archer also, and can I be mistaken of such a man as that who has no fellow in England? But you think I dreamed it all, and perhaps I should not have spoken, though something made me speak. Well, in a day to come you may change your mind, since whatever dangers threaten you will not die yet, Hugh. Tell me now, what is this Frenchman like who would marry Eve? I have never seen him."

Hugh, who was glad to get back to the things of earth, described Acour as best he could.

"Ah!" said Sir Andrew. "Much such a man as stood face to face with you by the grave while Murgh watched; and you are not likely to be friends, are you? But I forgot. You have determined that it was but a dream and now you are wondering how he who is called Gate of the Gods in Cathay could come to Blythburgh. Well, I think that all the world is his garden, given to him by God, but doubtless that's only another face of my dream whereof we'll speak no more—at present. Now for your troubles, which are no dream. Lie you down to sleep on the skin of that striped beast. I killed it in Cathay—in my day of dreams, and now it shall serve for yours, from which may the dead eyes of John Clavering be absent! I go forth to seek your father and to arrange certain matters. With Grey Dick at the door you'll be safe for a while, I think. If not, here's a cupboard where you may hide." And, drawing aside the arras, he showed him a certain secret place large enough to hold a man, then left the room.

Hugh laid himself upon the skin of the beast, which had been a tiger, though he did not know it by that name. So weary was he that not all he had gone through that day or even the old warrior-priest's marvellous tale, in which he and Eve played so wonderful a part, could keep his eyes from closing. Presently he was fast asleep, and so remained until, four hours later, something disturbed him, and he awoke to see Sir Andrew writing at a desk.

"Rise, my son," said the old priest without looking up from his paper. "Early as it is you must be stirring if you would be clear of Dunwich by daybreak and keep a whole skin. I have set a taper in my sleeping-closet yonder, and there you'll find water to wash with and a stool to kneel on for your prayers, neither of which neglect, since you have blood on your hands and great need for Heaven's help."

So Hugh arose, yawning, and stumbled heavily to the chamber, for he was still faint with sleep, which would not leave him till he had plunged his head into a basin of icy water. This done, he knelt and prayed as he had been bidden, with a very earnest heart, and afterward came back to the guest-hall.

Seeing folk gathered there as he entered he laid hand on sword, not his own with which he had killed his cousin, but a long and knightly weapon that Sir Andrew had given him with the armour. Drawing it, he advanced boldly, for he thought that his enemies might have found him out, and that his best safety lay in courage. Thus he appeared in the ring of the lamplight clad in gleaming steel and with raised weapon.

"What, son!" asked a testy voice which he knew for that of his own father, "is it not enough to have killed your cousin? Would you fall on your brothers and me also, that you come at us clad in mail and with bare steel in hand?"

Hearing these words Hugh sheathed the sword, and, advancing toward the speaker, a handsome, portly man, who wore a merchant's robe lined with rich fur, sank to his knee before him.

"Your pardon, my father," he said. "Sir Andrew here will have told you the story; also that I am not to blame for this blood-shedding."

"I think you need to ask it," replied Master de Cressi, "and if you and that lean henchman of yours are not to blame, then say who is?"

Now a tall, slim figure glided up to them. It was Eve, clothed in her own robe again, and beautiful as ever after her short rest.

"Sir, I am to blame," she said in her full, low voice. "My need was sore and I sent a messenger to Hugh bidding him meet me in the Blythburgh Marsh. There we were set on, and there John Clavering, my brother, smote Hugh in the face. Would you, a de Cressi, have had him take the blow and yield me up to the Frenchman?"

"By God and my forefathers, no! least of all from one of your stock—saving your presence," answered the merchant. "In truth, had he done so, dead or living from that day I would have called him no son of mine. Yet, Red Eve, you and he and your love-makings have brought much trouble on me and my House. Look now what it means. A feud to the death between our families of which no man can foresee the end. Moreover, how can you marry, seeing that a brother's blood runs between you?"

"It is on John's head," she answered sadly, "not on Hugh's hand. I warned him, and Hugh spared him once. What more could we do?"

"I know not, Eve; I only know what you have done, you and Hugh and Grey Dick. Four dead and two wounded, that's the bill I must discharge as best I may. Doubtless too soon there will be more to follow, whether they be Claverings or de Cressis. Well, we must take things as God sends them, and leave Him to balance the account.

"But there is no time to lose if Hugh's neck is to escape a halter. Speak you, Father Andrew, who are wise and old, and have this matter in hand. Oh! Hugh, Hugh, you were born a fighter, not a merchant like your brethren," and he pointed to three young men who all this while had stood silently behind him looking upon their youngest brother with grave disapproval. "Yes, the old Norman blood comes out in you, and the Norman mail suits you well," he added with a flash of pride, "and so there's an end—or a beginning. Now, Sir Andrew, speak."

"Master de Cressi," said the old priest, "your son Hugh rides to London on an errand of mine which I think will save his neck from that halter whereof you spoke but now. Are those four mounted men that you promised me ready to companion him?"

"They will be within an hour, Father, but not before, since six good horses cannot be laid hands on in the dead of night, being stabled without the gates. But what is this message of yours, and to whom does Hugh go?"

"To his Grace Edward the King, none less, Geoffrey de Cressi, with that which shall earn pardon for him and Dick the Archer, or so I believe. As for what it is I may not tell you or any man. It has to do with great matters of State that are for the King's ear alone; and I charge you, every one, on your honour and your safety, to make no mention of this mission without these walls. Do you swear, Geoffrey de Cressi, and you, his sons?"

Then one by one they swore to be secret as the grave; and Eve swore also, though of her he had sought no promise. When this was finished Sir Andrew asked if any of his brothers accompanied Hugh, saying that if so they must arm.

"No," answered Master de Cressi, "one of the family is enough to risk as well as four of our best servants. My sons bide here with me, who may need their help, though they are not trained to arms."

"Perhaps it is as well," said Sir Andrew drily, "though were I their age—well, let that be. Now, son Hugh, before you eat do you and Eve come with me into the church."

At these words Hugh flushed red with joy, and opened his lips to speak.

"Nay, nay," broke in Sir Andrew, with a frown; "for a different purpose to that which is in your mind. Man, is this a time for marrying and giving in marriage? And if it were, could I marry you who are stained with new-shed blood? 'Tis that you both may be absolved from the guilt of that blood and learn the penance which God decrees to you through the mouth of me, His unworthy minister, in payment of its shedding. Thus you, son, may go forth upon your great adventure with a clean heart, and you, daughter, may await what shall befall with a quiet mind. Say, are you willing?"

Now they bowed their heads and answered that they were, though Eve whispered to Hugh that she misdoubted her of this talk of penance.

"So do I," he replied, beneath his breath, "but he is a merciful confessor and loves us. From some it might be harder."

They passed down the stairs, followed by Master de Cressi and his sons, into the entrance hall, where Grey Dick stood watching by the door.

"Whither go they?" he asked of Sir Andrew, "for their road is mine."

"To confession at God's altar," answered the old priest. "Do you come also, Richard?"

"Oh!" he replied, "I hoped it had been to breakfast. As for confession I have naught upon my soul save that I shot too low at the Frenchman."

"Bide where you are, O man of blood," said Sir Andrew sternly: "and pray that a better mood be given to you before it is too late."

"Ay, Father," he answered unabashed. "I'll pray, and it is as well that one should wait to watch the door lest you should all presently become men of blood against your will."

Turning to the right, Sir Andrew led them down steps to a passage underground that joined the Temple to the Church of the Holy Virgin and St. John. It was but short, and at the end of it they found a massive door which he unbolted, and, passing this door, entered the great building, whereof the silence and the icy cold struck them like blows. They had but two lanterns between them, one of which Master de Cressi and his elder sons took with them to the nave of the church. Bearing the other, Sir Andrew departed into the vestry, leaving Hugh and Eve seated together in the darkness of the chancel stalls.

Presently his light reappeared in the confessional, where he sat robed, and thither at his summons went first Hugh and then Eve. When their tales were told, those who watched in the nave of the splendid building—which, reared by the Knights Templar, was already following that great Order to decay and ruin—saw the star of light he bore ascend to the high altar. Here he set it down, and, advancing to the rail, addressed the two shadowy figures that knelt before him.

"Son and daughter," he said, "you have made confession with contrite hearts, and the Church has given you absolution for your sins. Yet penance remains, and because those sins, though grievous in themselves, were not altogether of your own making, it shall be light. Hugh de Cressi and Eve Clavering, who are bound together by lawful love between man and woman and the solemn oath of betrothal which you here renew before God, this is the penance that I lay upon you by virtue of the authority in me vested as a priest of Christ: Because between you runs the blood of John Clavering, the cousin of one of you and the brother of the other, slain by you, Hugh de Cressi, in mortal combat but yester eve, I decree and enjoin that for a full year from this day you shall not be bound together as man and wife in the holy bonds of matrimony, nor converse after the fashion of affianced lovers. If you obey this her command, faithfully, then by my mouth the Church declares that after the year has gone by you may lawfully be wed where and when you will. Moreover, she pronounces her solemn blessing on you both and her dreadful curse upon any and upon all who shall dare to sunder you against your desires, and of this blessing and this curse let all the congregation take notice."

Now Hugh and Eve rose and vanished into the darkness. When they had gone the priest celebrated a short mass, but two or three prayers and a blessing, which done, all of them returned to the Preceptory as they had come.

Here food was waiting for them, prepared by the old Sister Agnes. It was a somewhat silent meal of which no one ate very much except Grey Dick, who remarked aloud that as this might be his last breakfast it should be plentiful, since, shriven or unshriven, it was better to die upon a full stomach.

Master de Cressi called him an impious knave. Then he asked him if he had plenty of arrows, because if not he would find four dozen of the best that could be made in Norwich done up in a cloak on the grey horse he was to ride, and a spare bow also.

"I thank you for the arrows, Master, but as for the bow, I use none but my own, the black bow which the sea brought to me and death alone shall part from me. Perchance both will be wanted, since the Claverings will scarcely let us out of the sanctuary if they can help it. Still, it is true they may not know where we lie hid, and that is our best chance of eating more good breakfasts this side the grave."

"A pest on your evil talk," said de Cressi with an uneasy laugh, for he loved Hugh best of all his sons and was afraid of him. "Get through safely, man, and though I like not your grim face and bloody ways you shall lose little by it. I promise you," he added in a whisper, "that if you bring my boy safe home again, you shall not want for all your life; ay, and if there is need, I'll pay your blood-scot for you."

"Thank you, master, thank you. I'll remember, and for my part promise you this, that if he does not return safe, Dick the Archer never will. But I think I'll live to shoot more than your four dozen of arrows."

As he spoke there came a knock upon the outer door and every one sprang up.

"Fear not," said Sir Andrew; "doubtless it will be the men with the horses. I'll go look. Come you with me, Richard."

Presently he returned, saying that it was so, and that Master de Cressi's servants were waiting with the beasts in the courtyard. Also that they brought tidings that some of the Clavering party were now at the Mayor's house, rousing him from his sleep, doubtless to lay information of the slayings and ask for warrant to take those who wrought them, should they be in the borough.

"Then we had best be going," said Hugh, "since soon they will be here with or without their warrant."

"Ay," answered Sir Andrew. "Here are the papers. Take them, Hugh, and hide them well; and if any accident should befall you, try to pass them on to Richard that they may be delivered into the King's hands at Westminster. Say that Sir Andrew Arnold sends you on business that has to do with his Grace's safety, and neither of you will be refused a hearing. Then act as he may command you, and maybe ere long we shall see you back at Dunwich pardoned."

"I think it is the Claverings and their French lord who need pardon, not I," said Hugh. "But be that as it may, what of Eve?"

"Fear not for Eve, son, for here she bides in sanctuary until the Frenchman is out of England, or perchance," he added grimly, "under English soil."

"Ay, ay, we'll guard the maid," broke in Master de Cressi. "Come! to saddle ere you be trapped."

So they descended to a back entrance, and through it into the courtyard, where the four armed men waited with six good horses, one of them Hugh's own. Here he bade farewell to his brothers, to his father, who kissed him on the brow, and to Sir Andrew, who stretched his hand above his head in blessing. Then he turned to Eve and was about to embrace her even before that company, when Sir Andrew looked at him, and, remembering the penance that had been laid upon him, he but pressed her hand, whispering: "God be with you, sweetheart!"

"He is with us all, but I would that you could be with me also," she answered in the same low voice. "Still, man must forth to battle and woman must wait and watch, for that is the world's way. Whate'er befalls, remember that dead or living I'll be wife to no man but you. Begone now ere my heart fails me, and guard yourself well, remembering that you bear in your breast not one life, but two."

Then Hugh swung himself to the saddle of which Grey Dick had already tested the girths and stirrup leathers. In another minute the six of them were clattering over the stones of Middlegate Street, while the burgesses of Dunwich peeped from their window places, wondering what knight with armed men rode through their town thus early.

Just as the grey dawn broke they passed the gate, which, there being peace in the land, was already open. Fifteen minutes later they were on the lonely Westleton Heath, where for a while naught was to be heard save the scream of the curlew and the rush of the wings of the wild-duck passing landward from the sea. Presently, however, another sound reached their ears, that of horses galloping behind them. Grey Dick pulled rein and listened.

"Seven, I think, not more," he said. "Now, master, do you stand or run, for these will be Clavering horses?"

Hugh thought for a moment. His aim was not to fight, but to get through to London. Yet if he fled the pursuers would raise the country on them as they came, so that in the end they must be taken, since those who followed would find fresh horses.

"It seems best to stand," he said.

"So say I," answered Grey Dick; and led the way to a little hillock by the roadside on which grew some wind-bent firs.

Here they dismounted and gave their horses into the keeping of one man, while Grey Dick and the others drew their bows from the cases and strung them. Scarcely had they done so when the mist, lifting in the morning breeze, showed them their pursuers—seven of them, as Dick had said—headed by one of the French knights, and riding scattered, between two and three hundred yards away. At the same moment a shout told them that they had been seen.

"Hark now all!" said Hugh. "I would shed no more blood if it may be so, who have earned enough of penance. Therefore shoot at the horses, not at the riders, who without them will be helpless. And let no man harm a Clavering unless it be to save his own life."

"Poor sport!" grunted Grey Dick.

Nevertheless, when the Norman knight who led came within two hundred yards, shouting to them in French to surrender, Dick lifted his great bow, drew and loosed carelessly, as though he shot at hazard, the others holding their bows till the Claverings were nearer. Yet there was little of hazard when Grey Dick shot, save to that at which he aimed. Away rushed the arrow, rising high and, as it seemed, bearing somewhat to the left of the knight. Yet when it drew near to that knight the wind told on it and bent it inward, as he knew it would. Fair and full it struck upon the horse's chest, piercing through to the heart, so that down the poor beast came, throwing its rider to the ground.

"A good shot enough," grumbled Grey Dick. "Still, it is a shame to slay nags of such a breed and let the rogues who ride them go."

But his companions only stared at him almost in awe, while the other Clavering men rode on. Before they had covered fifty paces, again the great bow twanged, and again a horse was seen to rear itself up, shaking the rider from its back, and then plunge away to die. Now Hugh's serving-men also lifted their bows, but Grey Dick hissed:

"Leave them to me! This is fine work, and you'd muddle it!"

Ere the words had ceased to echo another horse was down.

Then, as those who remained still came on, urged by the knight who ran shouting behind them, all loosed, and though some arrows went wide, the end of it was that ere they reached the little mound every Clavering horse was dead or sore wounded, while on the heath stood or lay seven helpless men.

"Now," said Grey Dick, "let us go and talk with these foot-soldiers."

So they went out, all of them, except he who had the horses, and Hugh called aloud that the first man of the Claverings who lifted a bow or drew a sword should die without mercy. And he pointed to Grey Dick, who stood beside him, arrow on string.

The Claverings began to talk together excitedly.

"Throw down your weapons!" commanded Hugh.

Still they hesitated. Then, without further warning Dick sent an artful arrow through the cap of one of them, lifting it from his head, and instantly set another shaft to his string. After this, down went the swords and bows.

"Daggers and knives, too, if it please you, masters!"

Then these followed.

Now Hugh spoke a word to his men, who, going to the dead and dying horses, took from them the stirrup-leathers and bridle-reins and therewith bound the Claverings back to back. But the French knight, in acknowledgment of his rank, they trussed up by himself, having first relieved him of his purse by way of fine. As it chanced, however, Hugh turned and saw them in the act.

"God's truth! Would you make common thieves of us?" he said angrily. "Their weapons and harness are ours by right of war, but I'll hunt the man who steals their money out of my company."

So the purse was restored. When it was safe in the knight's pouch again Hugh saluted him, begging his pardon that it should have been touched.

"But how are you named, sir?" he added.

"Sir Pierre de la Roche is my name," replied the knight sadly, and in French.

"Then, Sir Pierre de la Roche," said Hugh, "here you and your people must bide until some come to set you free, which, as this place is lonely and little crossed in winter, may be to-day or may be to-morrow. When at length you get back to Blythburgh Manor, however, or to Dunwich town, I trust it to your honour to declare that Hugh de Cressi has dealt well with you. For whereas he might have slain you every one, as you would have slain him and his if you could, he has harmed no hair of your heads. As for your horses, these, to his sorrow, he was obliged to kill lest they should be used to ride him down. Will you do this of your courtesy?"

"Ay," answered the knight, "since to your gentleness we owe our lives. But with your leave I will add that we were overcome not by men, but by a devil"—and he nodded toward Grey Dick—"since no one who is only man can have such hellish skill in archery as we saw yesterday, and now again this morning. Moreover," he went on, contemplating Dick's ashen hair and cold eyes set wide apart in the rocky face, like to those of a Suffolk horse, "the man's air shows that he is in league with Satan."

"I'll not render your words into our English talk, Sir Pierre," replied Hugh, "lest he of whom you speak should take them amiss and send you where you might learn them false. For know, had he been what you say, the arrow that lies in your horse's heart would have nailed the breastplate to your own. Now take a message from me to your lord, Sir Edmund Acour, the traitor. Tell him that I shall return ere long, and that if he should dare to attempt ill toward the Lady Eve, who is my betrothed, or toward my father and brethren, or any of my House, I promise, in Grey Dick's name and my own, to kill him or those who may aid him as I would kill a forest wolf that had slunk into my sheepfold. Farewell! There is bracken and furze yonder where you may lie warm till some pass your way. Mount, men!"

So they rode forward, bearing all the Clavering weapons with them, which a mile or two further on Grey Dick hid in an empty fox's earth where he knew he could find them again. Only he kept the French knight's beautiful dagger that was made of Spanish steel, inlaid with gold, and used it to his life's end.

Here it may be told that it was not until thirty-six hours had gone by, as Hugh learned afterward, that a countryman brought this knight and his companions, more dead than alive, to Dunwich in his wain. As he was travelling across Westleton Heath, with a load of corn to be ground at the Dunwich mill, it seemed that he heard voices calling feebly, and guided by them found these unhappy men half buried in the snow that had fallen on that day, and so rescued them from death.

But when Sir Edmund Acour knew the story of their overthrow

and of the message that Hugh had sent to him, he raved at them, and especially at Sir Pierre de la Roche, saying that the worst of young de Cressi's crimes against him was that he had left such cowardly hounds alive upon the earth. So he went on madly till Sir John Clavering checked him, bidding him wait to revile these men until he, and not his horse, had met Grey Dick's arrows and Hugh de Cressi's sword.

"For," he added, "it may happen then that you will fare no better than they have done, or than did John, my son."

********

On the morning of the third day after they left Dunwich, having been much delayed by foul weather and fouler roads, Hugh de Cressi and his company came at length to London. They had suffered no further adventure on their way for, though the times were rough and they met many evil-looking fellows, none ventured to lift hand against six men so well armed and sturdy. Guided by one of their number who had often been to London on Master de Cressi's business, they rode straight to Westminster. Having stabled their horses at an inn near by, and cleaned the mire of the road from their mail and garments, they went up to the palace, where Hugh told his errand to an officer whom he found on duty at the gate.

"Then it is a fool's errand," said the captain, "seeing that his Grace rode yesterday to his castle at Windsor to hunt and revel, and will be gone eight days at the least."

"Then to Windsor I must follow," answered Hugh.

## Chapter 5

# Grey Dick Shows His Archery

So sorely did the horses need rest, that Hugh and his people could not ride from London till the following morning, and evening was closing in before they found themselves drawing near the gate of Windsor Castle. In the market-place of the little town they pulled rein, while one of them went to search for a good inn at which they might lie, for the place seemed to be very full of people. Suddenly, as they stood there, wondering at the mighty, new-built keep which towered above them, a trumpet was blown and from round a corner appeared a gay procession of noble-looking men, and with them some ladies, who carried hawk on wrist, all mounted on splendid horses.

Now, the people who had gathered to study the strangers or tout for their custom, took off their bonnets and bent low, saying: "The King! The King! God save him!"

"Which is his Grace?" asked Hugh of one of them, whereon the man pointed to a royal-eyed and bearded knight, still in early middle life, who rode toward him, talking to a gallant youth at his side.

Now a thought came into Hugh's mind that the present time is always the best time to strike. Leaping from his horse, he advanced bowing, and stood in the pathway of the King. Seeing this, two of the fine Court lords spurred their horses and rode straight at him, thinking to drive him back. But he held his ground, for their insolence made him angry, and, catching the bridle of one of the horses, threw it on its haunches so sharply that the knight who rode it rolled from his saddle into the mire, whereupon every one laughed. In a moment he was on his feet again, and shouting:

"Out of the road, jackanapes, dressed in your grandfather's mail, unless you would stop there in the stocks. Do you know whose path you block?"

"That of his Grace," answered Hugh, "for whom I have a message that he will be glad to hear, and, popinjay, this for yourself; were it not for his presence it is you who should stop upon the road till you were carried thence."

Now, noting this disturbance, the King spoke to the youth at his side, who came forward and said, in a pleasant, courteous voice, addressing Hugh:

"Sir, why do you make trouble in these streets, and tumble the good Sir Ambrose Lacey from his horse with such scant ceremony?"

"Sir," answered Hugh, "because the good Sir Ambrose tried to ride his horse over me for no offence save that I would deliver a message to his Grace, which he will wish to hear."

"This is scarcely a time for the giving of messages," replied the young man, "but what is your name, and who sends the message? I am the Prince Edward," he added modestly, "so you may speak to me without fear."

"My name is Hugh de Cressi, your Highness, and I am sent by the Reverend Father Sir Andrew Arnold, of Dunwich, and have followed his Grace from Westminster, whither I and my men rode first."

Now, the Prince went to the King and spoke to him, and, returning presently, said:

"My father says that he knows both the names you give well enough and holds them dear. He bids that you and your people should follow him to the castle, where you will be entertained, with your horses. Sir Ambrose," he added, "the King desires that you should forget your choler, since he saw what passed, and deems that this young stranger did well to check your horse. Follow on, Hugh de Cressi, the officers will show you where you and your men may lodge."

So Hugh obeyed, and rode with the rest of the train and his folks through the gates of Windsor Castle. Nor did they do so unobserved, since many of the Court had no love for Sir Ambrose, and were glad to see him tumbled in the mire.

After they had stabled their beasts, as Hugh, followed by Grey Dick, was advancing toward a hall which he was told that he might enter, an officer came up.

"His Grace desires your presence before you sup," he said.

Pointing to Grey Dick, at whom the officer looked doubtfully, Hugh asked that he might accompany him, as he had much to do with the message. After some argument they were led through various passages to a chamber, at the door of which the officer wished to take away Dick's bow. But he would not give it up.

"The bow and I do not part," he said, in his croaking voice, "for we are husband and wife, and live and sleep together as the married should."

As Dick spoke the door was opened, and Prince Edward appeared.

"And do you eat together also, good fellow?" he asked, having overheard the talk.

"Ay, sir, we feed full together," replied Dick grimly; "or so thought some on Blythburgh Marsh a few days gone."

"I should like to hear that tale," said the Prince. "Meanwhile, since both my father and I love archers, let him pass with his bow. Only keep his arrows lest it should happen to grow hungry here."

Then they entered the chamber, led by the Prince. It was a fine place, with a vaulted stone roof and windows of coloured glass, that looked like the chancel of a church. Only at the head of it, where the altar should have been, was a kind of dais. On this dais were set some high-backed oaken chairs with many lanterns behind them in which burned tapers that, together with a great wood fire, gave light to the chamber.

In one of these chairs sat a gracious lady, who was embroidering something silken in a frame. This was Queen Philippa, and talking to her stood the tall King, clad in a velvet robe lined with fur. Behind, seated at a little table on which lay parchments, was a man in a priest's robe, writing. There was no one else in the room.

Hugh and Dick advanced to the foot of the dais, and stood there bowing.

"Who are these?" asked the King of the Prince. "Oh, I remember, the man who overthrew Sir Ambrose and said he had a message!"

"Ay, Sire," answered the Prince; "and this dust-coloured fellow is his servant, who will not part with his bow, which he calls his wife and says he sleeps with."

"I would all Englishmen did the same," broke in the King. "Say, man, can you shoot straight?"

"I know not, Sire," replied Grey Dick, "but perhaps straighter than most, for God, Who withheld all else from me, gave me this gift. At least, if I be not made drunk overnight, I'll match myself against any man at this Court, noble or simple, and stake twenty angels on it."

"Twenty angels! Have you so much, fellow?"

"Nay, Sire, nor more than one; but as I know I shall win, what does that matter?"

"Son," said the King, "see that this man is kept sober to-night, and to-morrow we will have a shooting match. But, sirrah, if you prove yourself to be a boaster you shall be whipped round the walls, for I love not tall words and small deeds. And now, young Master de Cressi, what is this message of yours?"

Hugh thrust his hand into his bosom, and produced a sealed packet which was addressed to "His Grace King Edward of England, sent from Andrew Arnold, priest, by the hand of Hugh de Cressi."

"Can you read?" the King asked of Hugh when he had spelt out this superscription.

"Ay, Sire; at least if the writing be that of Sir Andrew Arnold, for he was my master."

"A learned one and a brave, Hugh de Cressi. Well, break seal; we listen."

Hugh obeyed, and read as follows:

"Your Grace:

"Mayhap, Sire, you will remember me, Andrew Arnold, late master of the Templars in this town of Dunwich, in whose house, by your warrant for certain services rendered to your grandsire, your sire, and to yourself, I still dwell on as a priest ordained. Sire, the bearer of this, Hugh de Cressi, my godchild, is the son of Geoffrey de Cressi, of this town, the great wool-merchant, with whom your Highness has had dealings—"

"In truth I have!" interrupted the King, with a laugh. "Also I think the account is still open—against myself. Well, it shall be paid some day, when I have conquered France. Forward!"

"Sire, this Hugh is enamoured of Eve Clavering, daughter of Sir John Clavering of Blythburgh, a cousin of his House, a very beauteous maiden, commonly known as Red Eve, and she in turn is enamoured of and betrothed to him—"

Here Queen Philippa suddenly became interested.

"Why is the lady called Red Eve, sir?" she asked in her soft voice. "Because her cheeks are red?"

"No, Madam," answered Hugh, blushing; "because she always loves to wear red garments."

"Ah, then she is dark!"

"That is so, Madam; her eyes and hair are black as ash-buds."

"God's truth! Lady," interrupted King Edward, "is this young man's message of the colour of the eyes of his mistress, which, without doubt, being in love, he describes falsely? On with the letter!"

"Out of this matter," continued Hugh, "rose a feud yesterday, during which Hugh de Cressi killed his cousin John, fighting *à outrance*, and his servant, Richard the Archer, who accompanies him, commonly known as Grey Dick, slew three men with as many arrows, two of them being Normans whose names are unknown to us, and the third a grieve to Sir John Clavering, called Thomas of Kessland. Also, he killed a horse, and when another Frenchman tried to grasp his master, sent a shaft through the palm of his hand."

"By St. George," said the King, "but here is shooting! Were they near to you, Grey Dick?"

"Not so far away, Sire. Only the light was very bad, or I should have had the fourth. I aimed low, Sire, fearing to miss his skull, and he jerked up his horse's head to take the arrow."

"A good trick! I've played it myself. Well, let us have done with the letter, and then we'll come to archery."

"Sire," read on Hugh, "I ask your royal pardon to Hugh de Cressi and Richard the Archer for these slayings, believing that when you have read these letters it will be granted."

"That remains to be seen," muttered the King.

"Sire, Sir Edmund Acour, who has lands here in Suffolk, Count de Noyon in Normandy, and Seigneur of Cattrina in Italy—"

"I know the man," exclaimed Edward to the Queen, "and so do you. A handsome knight and a pleasant, but one of whom I have always misdoubted me."

"—Is also enamoured of Eve Clavering, and with her father's will seeks to make her his wife, though she hates him, and by the charter of Dunwich, of which she is a citizen, has the right to wed whom she will."

"It is well there are not many such charters. The old story—brave men done to death for the sake of a woman who is rightly named Red Eve," mused the King.

"My Liege, I pray that you will read the letter herein enclosed. Hugh de Cressi will tell you how it came to my hand, since I lack time to write all the story. If it seems good to your Grace, I pray you scotch this snake while he is in your garden, lest he should live to sting you when you walk abroad. If it please you to give your royal warrant to the bearer of this letter, and to address the same to such of your subjects in Dunwich as you may think good, I doubt not but that men can be found to execute the same. Thus would a great and traitorous plot be brought to nothing, to your own glory and the discomfiture of your foes in France, who hope to lay their murderous hands upon the throne of England. "Your humble servant and subject,

"Andrew Arnold."

"What's this?" exclaimed the King starting from his seat. "To lay hands upon the throne of England! Quick with the other letter, man!"

"I was charged that it is for your Grace's eye alone," said Hugh as he unfolded the paper. "Is it your pleasure that I read it aloud, if I can, for it is writ in French?"

"Give it me," said the King. "Philippa, come help me with this crabbed stuff."

Then they withdrew to the side of the dais, and, standing under a lantern, spelled out Sir Edmund Acour's letter to the Duke of Normandy, word by word.

The King finished the letter, and, still holding it in his hand, stood for a minute silent. Then his rage broke out.

"'He of England,'" he quoted. "That's your husband, Edward, Lady, who is to be overthrown and killed 'that Philip's son may take his seat and be crowned King at Westminster,' which God is to bring about before this year is out. Yes; and my cities are to be sacked and my people slain, and this French dog, Edmund Acour, who has sworn fealty to me, is to be rewarded with wide English lands and high English titles. Well, by God's blood I swear that, dead or living, he shall be lifted higher than he hopes, though not by Normandy or my brother of France! Let me think! Let me think! If I send men-at-arms he'll hear of it and slip away. Did not good old Sir Andrew call him a snake? Now, where's this girl, Red Eve?"

"In sanctuary, Sire, at the Temple Church in Dunwich," answered Hugh.

"Ah, and she's a great heiress now, for you killed her brother, and Acour, although he has wide possessions in sundry lands, was ever a spendthrift and deep in debt. No, he'll not leave unless he can get the girl; and old Sir Andrew will guard her well with the power of the Church, and with his own right arm if need be, for he's still more knight than priest. So there's no hurry. Tell me all you know of this story, Hugh de Cressi, omitting nothing, however small. Nay, have no fear, if you can vouch for your fellow there, all of us in this chamber are loyal to England. Speak out, man."

So Hugh began and told of the de Cressis and the Claverings and their feud, and of how he and Eve had always loved each other. He told of their meeting in the reeds of Blythburgh Fen, and of the death of John de Clavering at his hand and of the others at the hand of Grey Dick, and of the escape of Acour from the fourth arrow. He told how he and Eve had swum the Blyth in flood though the ice cut them, and hid on the moor while Grey Dick led the Claverings astray, and came at last safe to sanctuary. He told how Acour's letter had been won from his messenger by Sir Andrew's loyal guile. He told of the penance that Sir Andrew had laid upon them because of the new-shed blood of John Clavering, of the flight from Dunwich and the shooting of the horses of the Clavering men, and of their ride to London and to Windsor. He told everything, save only the tale of what Sir Andrew had seen in the House of Murgh in far Cathay.

When at last he had finished, and though it was long none there grew weary of that story, the King turned to the clerk, and said:

"Brother Peter, make out a full pardon to Hugh de Cressi of Dunwich and Richard Archer his servant for all slayings or other deeds wrought by them contrary to our general peace. Draw it wide, and bring the same to me for execution ere I sleep to-night. Make out a commission also to the Mayor of Dunwich—nay, I'll think that matter over and instruct you further. Hugh de Cressi, you have our thanks, and if you go on as you have begun you shall have more ere long, for I need such men about me. You also, strange and death-like man named Grey Dick, shall not lack our favour if it proves that you can shoot but half as well as you have boasted, and, unless you lie, both of you, as it seems that you have done. And now to supper, though in truth this news does not kindle appetite. Son, see that this gentleman is well served, and that none mock him more about the fashion of his armour, above all Sir Ambrose, for I'll not suffer it. Plate and damascene do not make a man, and this, it seems, was borrowed from as brave, ay, and as learned, a knight as ever bestrode a horse in war. Come, Lady," and taking the Queen by the hand, he left the chamber.

That evening Hugh ate his food seated among the knights of the Household at a high table in the great hall, at the head of which, for the King supped in private, was placed the young Prince Edward. He noted that now none laughed at him about the fashion of his mail or his country ways. Indeed, when after supper Sir Ambrose Lacey came to him and asked his pardon for the talk that he had used to him in the Windsor street—he was sure that some word had been sent round that his business had brought him favour with the King and that he must be treated with all courtesy. Several of those who sat round him tried to discover what that business was. But of this he would say nothing, parrying their questions with others about the wars in France, and listening with open ears to the tales of great deeds done there.

"Ah, would that I could see such things!" he said.

To which one of them answered:

"Well, why not? There'll be chance enough ere long, and many of us would be glad of a squire built like you."

Now, at lower tables, in that vast hall, Hugh's servants, and with them Grey Dick, sat among the men-at-arms of the King's Guard, who were all chosen for their courage, and skill in archery. These soldiers, noting the strange-faced, ashen-haired fellow who ate with his bow resting on the bench beside him, inquired about him from the other Dunwich men, and soon heard enough to cause them to open their eyes. When the ale had got hold of them they opened their mouths also, and, crowding round Dick, asked if it were true that he could shoot well.

"As well as another," he answered, and would say no more.

Then they looked at his bow, and saw that it was old-fashioned, like his master's mail, and of some foreign make and wood, but a mighty weapon such as few could handle and hold straight. Lastly, they began to challenge him to a match upon the morrow, to which he answered, who also had been drinking ale and was growing angry, that he'd give the best of them five points in fifty.

Now they mocked, for among them were some famous archers, and asked at what range.

"At any ye will," answered Grey Dick, "from twelve score yards down to one score yards. Now trouble me no longer, who if I must shoot to-morrow would sleep first and drink no more of your strong ale that breeds bad humours in one reared upon dyke water."

Then, seizing his bow, he glided away in his curious stoat-like fashion to the hole where he had been shown that he should sleep.

"A braggart!" said one.

"I am not so sure," answered a grizzled captain of archers, who had fought in many wars. "Braggarts make a noise, but this fellow only spoke when we squeezed him and perhaps what came out of those thin lips was truth. At least, from his look I'd sooner not find him against me bow to bow."

Then they fell to betting which of them would beat Grey Dick by the heaviest points.

********

Next morning about nine o'clock the King sent a messenger to Hugh, bidding him and his servant Richard wait upon them. They went with this messenger, who led them to a little chamber, where his Grace sat, attended only by the clerk, Brother Peter, and a dark-browed minister, whose name he never learned.

"Hugh de Cressi and Richard Archer," said Edward, motioning to the minister to hand Hugh a parchment to which hung a great seal, "here is the pardon which I promised you. No need to stay to read it, since it is as wide as Windsor Keep, and woe betide him who lifts hand against either of you for aught you may have done or left undone in the past contrary to the laws of our realm. Yet remember well that this grace runs not to the future. Now that matter is ended, and we come to one that is greater. Because of the faith put in you by our loyal and beloved subject, Sir Andrew Arnold, your godsire, and because we like the fashion of you, Hugh de Cressi, and hold you brave and honest, it has pleased us to give you a commission under which we direct the Mayor of Dunwich and all true and lawful men of that town and hundred to aid you in the taking or, if need be, in the slaying of our subject, Sir Edmund Acour, Count of Noyon and Seigneur of Cattrina. We command you to bring this man before us alive or dead, that his cause may be judged of our courts and the truth of the matter alleged against him by the Reverend Father Sir Andrew Arnold therein determined. Nevertheless, we command you not to wound or kill the said knight unless he resists the authority of us by you conveyed and you cannot otherwise hold him safe from escaping from out this our realm. This commission you will presently go forth to execute, keeping its tenor and your aim secret until the moment comes to strike, and, as you perform your duty, of which you will return and make report to us, so shall we judge and reward you. Do you understand?"

"Sire," answered Hugh, bowing, "I understand, and I will obey to my last breath."

"Good! When the parchments are engrossed my officer here will read them to you and explain aught that may need it. Meanwhile, we have an hour or two during which your horses can eat, for there are no fresh beasts here to give you, and it is best, to avoid doubts, that you should return as you came, only showing your powers if any should attempt to arrest you. So let us have done with these heavy matters, and disport us for a while. This servant of yours has made a common boast that he will outshoot any of our picked archers, and now we are ready to go forth and put him to the proof of the butts. Let him know, however, that, notwithstanding our words of yesterday, we shall not hold him to blame if he fails, since many a man of higher degree promises more at night than he can perform in the morning."

"Sire, I'll do my best. I can no more," said Grey Dick. "Only I pray that none may be suffered to hang about or pester me at the butts, since I am a lonely man who love not company when I use my art."

"That shall be so," said the King. "And now to the sport."

"The sport!" grumbled Grey Dick, when he and Hugh were alone together. "Why, it is other sport we should be seeking, with Acour and his knaves for targets. Go to the King, master, and show him that while we linger here the Frenchman may slip away, or work more and worse treasons."

"I cannot, Dick; the parchments are not written out, and his Grace is bent upon this pleasure match. Moreover, man, all these archers here—yes, and their betters also—would say that you had fled because you were an empty boaster who dared not face the trial."

"They'd say that, would they?" snarled Grey Dick. "Yes, they'd say that, which would be bitter hearing for you and me. Well, they shall not say it. Yet I tell you, master," he added in a burst of words, "although I know not why, I'd rather bear their scorn and be away on the road to Dunwich."

"It may not be, Dick," replied Hugh, shaking his head doubtfully. "See, here they come to fetch us."

********

In a glade of the forest of Windsor situated near to the castle and measuring some twenty-five score yards of open level ground, stood Grey Dick, a strange, uncouth figure, at whom the archers of the guard laughed, nudging each other. In his bony hand, however, he held that at which they did not laugh, namely, the great black bow, six feet six inches long, which he said had come to him "from the sea," and was fashioned, not of yew, but of some heavy, close-grained wood, grown perhaps in Southern or even in far Eastern lands. Still, one of them, who had tried to draw this bow to his ear and could not, said aloud that "the Suffolk man would do naught with that clumsy pole." Whereat, Grey Dick, who heard him, grinning, showing his white teeth like an angry dog.

Near by, on horseback and on foot, were the King, the young Prince Edward, and many knights and ladies; while on the other side stood scores of soldiers and other folk from the castle, who came to see this ugly fellow well beaten at his own game.

"Dick," whispered Hugh, "shoot now as you never shot before. Teach them a lesson for the honour of Suffolk."

"Let me be, master," he grumbled. "I told you I would do my best."

Then he sat himself down on the grass and began to examine his arrows one by one, to all appearance taking no heed of anything else.

Presently came the first test. At a distance of five score yards was set a little "clout," or target, of white wood, not more than two feet square. This clout had a red mark, or eye, three inches across, painted in its centre, and stood not very high above the sward.

"Now, Richard," said the King, "three of the best archers that we have about us have been chosen to shoot against you and each other by their fellows. Say, will you draw first or last?"

"Last, Sire," he answered, "that I may know their mettle."

Then a man stepped forward, a strong and gallant looking fellow, and loosed his three arrows. The first missed the clout, the second pierced the white wood, and the third hit the red eye.

The clout having been changed, and the old one brought to the King with the arrows in it, the second man took his turn. This time all three of the arrows hit the mark, one of them being in the red. Again it was changed, and forth came the great archer of the guard, a tall and clear-eyed man named Jack Green, and whom, it was said, none had ever beaten. He drew, and the arrow went home in the red on its left edge. He drew again, and the arrow went home in the red on its right edge. He drew a third time, and the arrow went home straight in the very centre of the red, where was a little black spot.

Now a great laugh went up, since clearly the Suffolk man was beaten ere ever he began.

"Your Dick may do as well; he can do no better," said the King, when the target was brought to him.

Grey Dick looked at it.

"A boon, your Grace," said Dick. "Grant that this clout may be set up again with the arrows fast. Any may know them from mine since they are grey, whereas those I make are black, for I am a fletcher in my spare hours, and love my own handiwork."

"So be it," said the King, wondering; and the clout was replaced upon its stand.

Now Grey Dick stretched himself, looked at the clout, looked at his bow, and set a black-winged arrow on the string. Then he drew, it seemed but lightly and carelessly, as though he thought the distance small. Away flew the shaft, and sank into the red a good inch within the leftmost arrow of Jack Green.

"Ah," said the onlookers, "a lucky shot indeed!"

Again he drew, and again the arrow sank into the red, a good inch within the rightmost shot of Jack Green.

"Oh!" said the onlookers, "this man is an archer; but Jack's last he cannot best, let the devil help him how he will."

"In the devil's name, then, be silent!" wheezed Grey Dick, with a flash of his half-opened eye.

"Ay, be silent—be silent!" said the King. "We do not see such shooting every day."

Now Dick set his foot apart and, arrow on string, thrice he lifted his bow and thrice let it sink again, perhaps because he felt some breath of wind stir the still air. A fourth time he lifted, and drew, not as he had before, but straight to the ear, then loosed at once.

Away rushed the yard-long shaft, and folk noted that it scarcely seemed to rise as arrows do, or at least not half so high. It rushed, it smote, and there was silence, for none could see exactly what had happened. Then he who stood near the target to mark ran forward, and screamed out:

"By God's name, he has shattered Jack Green's centre arrow, and shot *clean through the clout!*"

Then from all sides rose the old archer cry, "*He, He! He, He!*" while the young Prince threw his cap on high, and the King said:

"Would that there were more such men as this in England! Jack Green, it seems that you are beaten."

"Nay," said Grey Dick, seating himself again upon the grass, "there is naught to choose between us in this round. What next, your Grace?"

Only Hugh, who watched him, saw the big veins swell beneath the pale skin of his forehead, as they ever did when he was moved.

"The war game," said the King; "that is, if you will, for here rough knocks may be going. Set it out, one of you."

Then a captain of the archers explained this sport. In short it was that man should stand against man clad in leather jerkins, and wearing a visor to protect the face, and shoot at each other with blunt arrows rubbed with chalk, he who first took what would have been a mortal wound to be held worsted.

"I like not blunted arrows," said Grey Dick; "or, for the matter of that, any other arrows save my own. Against how many must I play? The three?"

The captain nodded.

"Then, by your leave, I will take them all at once."

Now some said that this was not fair, but in the end Dick won his point, and those archers whom he had beaten, among them Jack Green, were placed against him, standing five yards apart, and blunted arrows served out to all. Dick set one of them on the string, and laid the two others in front of them. Then a knight rode to halfway between them, but a little to one side, and shouted: "Loose!"

As the word struck his ear Dick shot with wonderful swiftness, and almost as the arrow left the bow flung himself down, grasping another as he fell. Next instant, three shafts whistled over where he had stood. But his found its mark on the body of him at whom he had aimed, causing the man to stagger backward and throw down his bow, as he was bound to do, if hit.

Next instant Dick was up again and his second arrow flew, striking full and fair before ever he at whom it was aimed had drawn.

Now there remained Jack Green alone, and, as Dick set the third arrow, but before he could draw, Jack Green shot.

"Beat!" said Dick, and stood quite still.

At him rushed the swift shaft, and passed over his shoulder within a hairbreadth of his ear. Then came Dick's turn. On Jack Green's cap was an archer's plume.

"Mark the plume, lords," he said, and lo! the feather leapt from that cap. Now there was silence. No one spoke, but Dick drew out three more arrows.

"Tell me, captain," he said, "is your ground marked out in scores; and what is the farthest that any one of you has sent a flighting shot?"

"Ay," answered the officer, "and twenty score and one yard is the farthest, nor has that been done for many a day."

Dick steadied himself, and seemed to fill his lungs with air. Then, stretching his long arms to the full, he drew the great bow till the horns looked as though they came quite close together, and loosed. High and far flew that shaft; men's eyes could scarcely follow it, and all must wait long before a man came running to say where it had fallen.

"Twenty score and two yards!" he cried.

"Not much to win by," grunted Dick, "though enough. I have done twenty and one score once, but that was somewhat downhill."

Then, while the silence still reigned, he set the second arrow on the string, and waited, as though he knew not what to do. Presently, about fifty paces from him, a wood dove flew from out a tree and, as such birds do at the first breath of spring, for the day was mild and sunny, hovered a moment in the air ere it dipped toward a great fir where doubtless it had built for years. Never, poor fowl, was it destined to build again, for as it turned its beak downward Dick's shaft pierced it through and through and bore it onward to the earth.

Still in the midst of a great silence, Dick took up his quiver and emptied it on the ground, then gave it to the captain of the archers, saying:

"And you will, step sixty, nay, seventy paces, and set this mouth upward in the grass where a man may see it well."

The captain did so, propping the quiver straight with stones and a bit of wood. Then, having studied all things with his eyes, Dick shot upward, but softly. Making a gentle curve, the arrow turned in the air as it drew near the quiver, and fell into its mouth, striking it flat.

"Ill done," grumbled Dick; "had I shot well, it should have been pinned to earth. Well, yon shadow baulked me, and it might have been worse."

Then he unstrung his bow, and slipped it into its case.

Now, at length, the silence was broken, and in good earnest. Men, especially those of Dunwich, screamed and shouted, hurling up their caps. Jack Green, for all jealousy was forgotten at the sight of this wondrous skill, ran to Dick, clasped him in his arms, and, dragging the badge from off his breast, tried to pin it to his rough doublet. The young Prince came and clapped him on the shoulder, saying:

"Be my man! Be my man!"

But Dick only growled, "Paws off! What have I done that I have not done a score of times before with no fine folk to watch me? I shot to please my master and for the honour of Suffolk, not for you, and because some dogs keep their tails too tightly curled."

"A sulky fellow," said the Prince, "but, by heaven, I like him!"

Then the King pushed his horse through the throng, and all fell back before his Grace.

"Richard Archer," he said, "never has such marksmanship as yours been seen in England since we sat upon the throne, nor shall it go unrewarded. The twenty angels that you said you would stake last night shall be paid to you by the treasurer of our household. Moreover, here is a gift from Edward of England, the friend of archers, that you may be pleased to wear," and taking his velvet cap from off his head, the King unpinned from it a golden arrow of which the barbed head was cut from a ruby, and gave it to him.

"I thank you, Sire," said Dick, his pale skin flushing with pride and pleasure. "I'll wear it while I live, and may the sight of it mean death to many of your enemies."

"Without doubt it will, and that ere long, Richard, for know you that soon we sail again for France, whence the tempest held us back, and it is my pleasure that you sail with us. Therefore I name you one of our fletchers, with place about our person in our bodyguard of archers. Jack Green will show you your quarters, and instruct you in your duties, and soon you shall match your skill against his again, but next time with Frenchmen for your targets."

"Sire," said Dick, very slowly, "take back your arrow, for I cannot do as you will."

"Why, man? Are you a Frenchman?" asked the King, angrily, for he was not wont to have his favours thus refused.

"My mother never told me so, Sire, although I don't know for certain who my father may have been. Still, I think not, since I hate the sight of that breed as a farmer's dog hates rats. But, Sire, I have a good master, and do not wish to change him for one who, saving your presence, may prove a worse, since King's favour on Monday has been known to mean King's halter on Tuesday. Did you not promise to whip me round your walls last night unless I shot as well as I thought I could, and now do you not change your face and give me golden arrows?"

At these bold words a roar of laughter went up from all who heard them, in which the King himself joined heartily enough.

"Silence!" he cried presently. "This yeoman's tongue is as sharp as his shafts. I am pierced. Let us hear whom he will hit next."

"You again, Sire, I think," went on Dick, "because, after the fashion of kings, you are unjust. You praise me for my shooting, whereas you should praise God, seeing that it is no merit of mine, but a gift He gave me at my birth in place of much which He withheld. Moreover, my master there," and he pointed to Hugh, "who has just done you better service than hitting a clout in the red and a dow beneath the wing, you forget altogether, though I tell you he can shoot almost as well as I, for I taught him."

"Dick, Dick!" broke in Hugh in an agony of shame. Taking no heed, Dick went on imperturbably: "And is the best man with a sword in Suffolk, as the ghost of John Clavering knows to-day. Lastly, Sire, you send this master of mine upon a certain business where straight arrows may be wanted as well as sharp swords, and yet you'd keep me here whittling them out of ashwood, who, if I could have had my will, would have been on the road these two hours gone. Is that a king's wisdom?"

"By St. George!" exclaimed Edward, "I think that I should make you councillor as well as fletcher, since without doubt, man, you have a bitter wit, and, what is more rare, do not fear to speak the truth as you see it. Moreover, in this matter, you see it well. Go with Hugh de Cressi on the business which I have given him to do, and, when it is finished, should both or either of you live, neglect not our command to rejoin us here, or—if we have crossed the sea—in France. Edward of England needs the service of such a sword and such a bow."

"You shall have them both, Sire," broke in Hugh, "for what they are worth. Moreover, I pray your Grace be not angry with Grey Dick's words, for if God gave him a quick eye, He also gave him a rough tongue."

"Not I, Hugh de Cressi, for know, we love what is rough if it be also honest. It is smooth, false words of treachery that we hate, such words as are ever on the lips of one whom we send you forth to bring to his account. Now to your duty. Farewell till we meet again, whether it be here or where all men, true or traitors, must foot their bill at last."

## Chapter 6

# The Snare

About noon of the day on which Hugh and his company had ridden for London, another company entered Dunwich—namely, Sir John Clavering and many of his folk, though with him were neither Sir Edmund Acour nor any of his French train. Sir John's temper had never been of the best, for he was a man who, whatever his prosperity, found life hard and made it harder for all those about him. But seldom had he been angrier than he was this day, when his rage was mingled with real sorrow for the loss of his only son, slain in a fight brought about by the daughter of one of them and the sister of the other and urged for honour's sake by himself, the father of them both.

Moreover, the marriage on which he had set his heart between Eve and the glittering French lord whose future seemed so great had been brought to naught, and this turbulent, hot-hearted Eve had fled into sanctuary. Her lover, too, the youngest son of a merchant, had ridden away to London, doubtless upon some mission which boded no good to him or his, leaving a blood feud behind him between the wealthy de Cressis and all the Clavering kin.

There was but one drop of comfort in his cup. By now, as he hoped, Hugh and his death's-head, Grey Dick, a spawn of Satan that all the country feared, and who, men said, was a de Cressi bastard by a witch, were surely slain or taken by those who followed upon their heels.

Sir John rode to the Preceptory and hammered fiercely on its oak-en door. Presently it was opened by Sir Andrew Arnold himself, who stood in the entrance, grey and grim, a long sword girt about his loins and armour gleaming beneath his monkish robe.

"What would you, Sir John Clavering, that you knock at this holy house thus rudely?" he asked.

"My daughter, priest, who, they say, has sheltered here."

"They say well, knight, she has sheltered here beneath the wings of St. Mary and St. John. Begone and leave her in peace."

"I make no more of such wings than if they were those of farmyard geese," roared the furious man. "Bring her or I will pluck her forth."

"Do so," replied Sir Andrew, "if you live to pass this consecrated sword," and he laid his hand upon its hilt. "Take with her also the curse of the Mother of God, and His beloved Apostle, and that of the whole Church of Christ, by me declared upon your head in this world and upon your soul in the world to come. Man, this is sanctuary, and if you dare to set foot within it in violence, may your body perish and your soul scorch everlastingly in the fires of hell. And you," he added, raising his voice till it rang like a trumpet, addressing the followers of Sir John, "on you also let the curse of excommunication fall. Now slay me and enter if you will, but then every drop of blood in these veins shall find a separate tongue and cry out for vengeance on you before the judgment seat of God, where presently I summon you to meet me."

Then he crossed himself, drew the great sword, and, holding it in his left hand, stretched out his right toward them in malediction.

The Clavering men heard and saw. They looked at each other, and, as though by common consent, turned and rode away, crossing themselves also. In truth, they had no stomach for the curse of the Church when it was thundered forth from the lips of such a monk as Sir Andrew Arnold, who, they knew well, had been one of the greatest and holiest warriors of his generation, and, so said rumour, was a white wizard to boot with all the magic of the East at his command.

"Your men have gone, Sir John," said the old priest; "will you follow them or will you enter?"

Now fear drove out the knight's rage and he spoke in another voice.

"Sir Andrew, why do you bring all these wrongs upon me? My boy is dead at the hand of Hugh de Cressi, your godson, and he has robbed me of my daughter, whom I have affianced to a better and a nobler man. Now you give her sanctuary and threaten me with the curse of the Church because I would claim her, my own flesh and blood; ay, and my heiress too to-day. Tell me, as one man to another, why do you do these things?"

"And tell me, Sir John Clavering, why for the sake of pelf and of honours that you will never harvest do you seek to part those who love each other and whom God has willed to bring together? Why would you sell your child to a gilded knave whom she hates? Nay, stop me not. I'd call him that and more to his face and none have ever known me lie. Why did you suffer this Frenchman or your dead son, or both of them, to try to burn out Hugh de Cressi and Red Eve as though they were rats in rubbish?"

"Would you know, Father? Then I'll tell you. Because I wish to see my daughter set high among lords and princes and not the wife of a merchant's lad, who by law may wear cloth only and rabbit fur. Because, also, I hate him and all his kin, and if this is true of yesterday, how much more true is it now that he has killed my son, and by the arrows of that wolf-man who dogs his heels, slain my guests and my grieve. Think not I'll rest till I have vengeance of him and all his cursed House. I'll appeal to the King, and if he will not give me justice I'll take it for myself. Ay, though you are old, I tell you you shall live to see the de Cressi vault crowded with the de Cressi dead."

Sir Andrew hid his eyes for a moment with his hand, then let it fall and spoke in a changed voice.

"It comes upon me that you speak truth, Sir John, for since I met a certain great Master in the East, at times I have a gift of foresight. I think that much sorrow draws near this land; ay, and others. I think that many vaults and many churchyards, too, will ere long be filled with dead; also that the tomb of the Claverings at Blythburgh will soon be opened. Mayhap the end of this world draws near to all men, as surely it draws near to you and me. I know not—yet truth was in your lips just now, and in mine as well, I think. Oh, man, man!" he went on after a pause, "appeal not unto the world's Caesar lest Caesar render different judgment to that which you desire. Get you home, and on your knees appeal unto God to forgive you your proud, vengeance-seeking heart. Sickness draws near to you; death draws near to you, and after death, hell—or heaven. I have finished."

As he heard these words Sir John's swarthy face grew pale and for a little while his rage died down. Then it flared up again.

"Don't dream to frighten me with your spells, old wizard," he said. "I'm a hale man yet, though I do lose my breath at times when my mind is vexed with wrongs, and I'll square my own account with God without your help or counsel. So you'll not give me my daughter?"

"Nay, here she bides in sanctuary for so long as it shall please her."

"Does she in truth? Perhaps you married her to this merchant fellow ere he rode this morning."

"Nay, Sir John, they betrothed themselves before the altar and in presence of his kin, no more. Moreover, if you would know, because of your son's blood which runs between them I, after thought and prayer, speaking in the name of the Church, swore them to this penance—that for a year from yesterday they should not wed nor play the part of lovers."

"I thank you, priest, for this small grace," answered Sir John, with a bitter laugh, "and in my turn I swear this, that after the year they shall not wed, since the one of them will be clay and the other the wife of the man whom I have chosen. Now, play no tricks on me, lest I burn this sanctuary of yours about your head and throw your old carcass to roast among the flames."

Sir Andrew made no reply, only, resting his long sword on the threshold, he leant upon its hilt, and fixed his clear grey eyes upon Clavering's face. What Sir John saw in those eyes he never told, but it was something which scared him. At least that shortening of the breath of which he had spoken seemed to take a hold of him, for he swayed upon his horse as though he were about to fall, then, recovering, turned and rode straight for Blythburgh.

********

It was the second night after that day when Sir Andrew had looked John Clavering in the eyes.

Secretly and in darkness those three whom Grey Dick had killed were borne into the nave of Blythburgh church and there laid in the grave which had been made ready for them. Till now their corpses had been kept above ground in the hope that the body of John Clavering the younger might be added to their number. But search as they would upon seashore and river-bank, nothing of him was ever seen again. This funeral was celebrated in the darkness, since neither Sir John nor Acour desired that all men should see three bodies that had been slain by one archer, aided by a merchant's lad, standing alone against a score, and know, to say naught of the wounded, that there was yet another to be added to the tale. Therefore they interred them by night with no notice of the ceremony.

It was a melancholy scene. The nave of the great church, lighted only with the torches borne by the six monks of the black Augustines from the neighbouring priory of St. Osyth; the candles, little stars of light, burning far away upon the altar; the bearers of the household of the Claverings and the uncoffined corpses lying on their biers by the edge of the yawning graves; the mourners in their mail; the low voice of the celebrating priest, a Frenchman, Father Nicholas, chaplain to Acour, who hurried through the Latin service as though he wished to be done with it; the deep shadows of the groined roof whereon the rain pattered—such were the features of this interment. It was done at last, and the poor dead, but a few days before so full of vigour and of passion, were left to their last sleep in the unremembered grave. Then the mourners marched back to the manor across the Middle Marsh and sought their beds in a sad silence.

Shortly after daybreak they were called from them again by the news that those who had followed Hugh de Cressi had returned. Quickly they rose, thinking that these came back with tidings of accomplished vengeance, to find themselves face to face with seven starved and miserable men who, all their horses being dead, had walked hither from Dunwich.

The wretched story was learned at length, and then followed that violent scene, which has been told already, when Acour cursed his followers as cowards, and Clavering, sobered perhaps by the sadness of the midnight burial or by the memory of Arnold's words, reproved him. Lastly, stung by the taunts that were heaped upon them, Sir Pierre de la Roche gave Hugh's message—that if they lifted hand against his love or his House he would kill them like ravening wolves, "which I think he certainly will do, for none can conquer him and his henchman," he added shortly.

Then Sir John's rage flared up again like fire when fresh fuel is thrown on ashes. He cursed Hugh and Grey Dick; he cursed his daughter; he even cursed Acour and asked for the second time how it came about that he who had brought all this trouble on him was given the evil name of traitor.

"I know not," answered Sir Edmund fiercely, and laying his hand upon his sword, "but this I know, that you or any man will do well not to repeat it if you value life."

"Do you threaten me?" asked Sir John. "Because, if so, you will do well to begone out of this house of shame and woe lest you be borne out feet first. Nay, nay, I forgot," he added slowly, clasping his head in his hands, "you are my daughter's affianced, are you not, and will give her high place and many famous titles, and her son shall be called Clavering, that the old name may not die but be great in England, in France, and in Italy. You must bide to marry her, lest that cuckoo, Hugh de Cressi, that cuckoo with the sharp bill, should creep into my nest. I'll not be worsted by a stripling clad in merchant's cloth who slew my only son. Take not my words ill, noble Noyon, for I am overdone with grief for the past and fear for the future. You must bide to marry her by fair means or by foul. Draw her from the sanctuary and marry her whether she say you yea or nay. You have my leave, noble Noyon," and so speaking he swayed and fell prone upon the floor.

At first they thought that he was dead. But the chaplain, Nicholas, who was a leech, bled him, and he came to himself again, although he still wandered in his talk and lay abed.

Then Acour and Nicholas took counsel together.

"What is to be done?" said Sir Edmund, "for I am on fire for this maid, and all her scorn and hate do but fan my flame. Moreover, she is now very rich, for that old hot-head cannot live long. His violent humours will kill him, and, as you know, Father, although I have great possessions, my costs are large and I have still greater debts. Lastly, shall de Noyon and his knights be worsted by a wool-merchant's younger son, a mere 'prentice lad, and his henchman, a common archer of the fens? Show me how to get her, Nicholas, and I'll make an abbot of you yet. This sanctuary, now? will it hold? If we stormed the place and took her, would the Holy Father give us absolution, do you think?"

"No, my lord," answered the fox-faced Nicholas. "The Church is great because the Church is one, and what the priest does the Pope upholds, especially when that priest is no mean man. This holy monk, Sir Andrew Arnold, has reputation throughout Europe, and, though he seems so humble, because of his wisdom is in the counsel of many great men whose fathers or grandfathers were guided by him long ago. Commit what crime you will, dip yourself to the lips in blood, and you may find forgiveness, but touch not an ancient and acknowledged sanctuary of the Church, since for this offence there will be none."

"What then, Nicholas? Must I give up the chase and fly? To speak truth, things seem to threaten me. Why has that Hugh twice called me traitor? Have any of my letters fallen into strange hands, think you? I have written several, and you know my mission here."

"It is possible, lord; all things are possible, but I think not. I think that he only draws the bow at a hazard, which is more than Grey Dick does," he added with a chuckle. "These brute English hate us French, whom they know to be their masters in all that makes a man, and traitor to their fool king is the least of the words they throw at us."

"Well, priest, my mother was English, as my wife will be. Therefore stay your tongue on that matter and tell me how I am to make her my wife," answered Acour haughtily.

The chaplain cringed and bowed, rubbing his thin hands together.

"I thought you wished to speak of the English, my lord, otherwise I should not have ventured—but as to the lady Eve, something comes to me. Why does she stay in sanctuary who herself has committed no crime? Is it not, such is her madness, because she would be out of reach of you and your endearments? Now if she believed you gone far enough away, let us say to France, and knew that her father lay ill, why then—" and he paused.

"You mean that she might come out of sanctuary of her own accord?"

"Yes, lord, and we might set a *springe* to catch this bird so rare and shy, and though she'd flutter, flutter, flutter, and peck, peck, peck, what could she do when you smoothed her plumage with your loving hand, and a priest was waiting to say the word that should cause her to forget her doubts and that merchant bumpkin?"

"Ah, Nicholas, you have a good wit, and if all goes well you shall certainly be an abbot. But would her father, do you think—"

"Lord, that beef-eating knight is in such a rage that he would do anything. What did he say just before the stroke took him? That you were to marry her by fair means or by foul. Yes, and he told me an hour ago that if only he knew she was your wife, he would die happy. Oh, you have his warrant for anything you do to bring about this end. Still there is no need to tell him too much lest it should cause his good name to be aspersed by the vulgar. Many, it seems, love this Red Eve for her high spirit, and are friends to the de Cressis, an open-handed race who know how to bind folk to them. Listen how it must be done."

********

That day it was given out that Sir Edmund Acour, those of his knights who remained alive and all his following were about to leave for London and lay their cause before the King, having learned that Hugh de Cressi had gone thither to prejudice his Grace on his own behalf. It was added, moreover, that they would not return to Suffolk, but proposed when they had found justice or the promise of it, to take ship at Dover for France. Next morning, accordingly, they rode away from Blythburgh Manor and passed through Dunwich with much pomp, where the citizens of that town, who were friends of the de Cressis, stared at them with no kind eyes. Indeed, one of these as they crossed the market-place called to them to be careful not to meet Hugh de Cressi and Grey Dick upon their journey, lest there should be more midnight burials and men-at-arms turned into foot-soldiers, whereat all about him laughed rudely.

But Acour did not laugh. He ground his teeth and said into the ear of Nicholas:

"Register this vow for me, priest, that in payment for that jest I'll sack and burn Dunwich when our army comes, and give its men and children to the sword and its women to the soldiers."

"It shall be done, lord," answered the chaplain, "and should your heart soften at the appointed time I'll put you in memory of this solemn oath."

At the great house of the Mayor of Dunwich Sir Edmund drew rein and demanded to see him. Presently this Mayor, a timid, uncertain-looking man, came in his robes of office and asked anxiously what might be the cause of this message and why an armed band halted at his gate.

"For no ill purpose, sir," answered Acour, "though little of justice have I found at your hands, who, therefore, must seek it at the Court of my liege lord, King Edward. All I ask of you is that you will cause this letter to be delivered safely to the lady Eve Clavering, who lies in sanctuary at the Preceptory of St. Mary and St. John. It is one of farewell, since it seems that this lady who, by her own will and her father's, was my affianced, wishes to break troth, and I am not a man who needs an unwilling bride. I'd deliver it myself only that old knave, half priest and half knight, but neither good—"

"You'd best speak no ill of Sir Andrew Arnold here," said a voice in the crowd.

"Only the master of the Preceptory," went on Acour, changing his tone somewhat, "might take fright and think I wished to violate his sanctuary if I came there with thirty spears at my back."

"And no fool either," said the voice, "seeing that they are French spears and his is an English sanctuary."

"Therefore," continued Acour, "I pray you, deliver the letter. Perchance when we meet again, Master Mayor," he added with a venomous glance of his dark eyes, "you will have some boon to ask of me, and be sure I'll grant it—if I can."

Then without waiting for an answer, for the mob of sturdy fishermen, many of whom had served in the French wars, looked threatening, he and his following rode away through the Ipswich gate and out on to the moorlands beyond, which some of them knew but too well.

All the rest of that day they rode slowly, but when night came, having halted their horses at a farm and given it out that they meant to push on to Woodbridge, they turned up a by-track on the lonely heath, and, unseen by any, made their through the darkness to a certain empty house in the marshes not far from Beccles town. This house, called Frog Hall, was part of Acour's estate, and because of the ague prevalent there in autumn, had been long unattended. Nor did any visit it at this season of the year, when no cattle grazed upon these salt marshes.

Here, then, he and his people lay hid, cursing their fortunes, since, notwithstanding the provisions that they had conveyed thither in secret, the place was icy cold in the bitter, easterly winds which tore over it from the sea. So lonely was it, also, that the Frenchmen swore that their comrades slain by Grey Dick haunted them at nights, bidding them prepare to join the number of the dead. Indeed, had not Acour vowed that he would hang the first man who attempted to desert, some of them would have left him to make the best of their way back to France. For always as they crouched by the smoking hearth they dreamed of Grey Dick and his terrible arrows.

Sir Edmund Acour's letter came safely into the hands of Eve, brought to her by the Mayor himself. It read thus:

> *Lady,*
> You will no more of me, so however much you should live to ask it, I will have no more of you. I go hang your merchant lout, and afterward away to France, who wish to have done with your cold Suffolk, where you may buy my lands cheap if you will. Yet, should Master Hugh de Cressi chance to escape me, I counsel you to marry him, for I can wish you no worse fate, seeing what you will be, than to remember what you might have been. Meanwhile it is my duty as a Christian to tell you, in case you should desire to speak to him ere it be too late, that your father lies at the point of death from a sickness brought on by his grief at the slaying of his son and your cruel desertion of him, and calls for you in his ravings. May God forgive you, as I try to do, all the evil that you have wrought, which, perhaps, is not done with yet. Unless Fate should bring us together again, for as aught I know it may, I bid you farewell forever. Would that I had never seen your face, but well are you named Red Eve, who, like the false Helen in a story you have never heard, were born to bring brave men to their deaths. Again farewell,
> *De Noyon*

"Who is this Helen?" asked Eve of Sir Andrew when the letter had been read.

"A fair Grecian, daughter, over whom nations fought when the world was young, because of her beauty."

"Ah, well! she did not make herself beautiful, did she? and, perchance, was more sinned against than sinning, since women, having but one life to live, must follow their own hearts. But this Helen has been dead a long while, so let her rest, if rest she may. And now it seems that Acour is away and that my father lies very sick. What shall I do? Return to him?"

"First I will make sure that the Frenchman has gone, and then we will see, daughter."

So Sir Andrew sent out messengers who reported it to be true that Acour had ridden straight to London to see the King and then sail for Dover. Also they said that no Frenchmen were left at Blythburgh save those who would never leave the place again, and that Sir John Clavering lay sick in his bed at the manor.

"God fights for us!" said Sir Andrew with a little laugh. "This Acour's greeting at Court may be warmer than he thinks and at the least you and Dunwich are well rid of him. Though I had sooner that you stayed here, to-morrow, daughter, you shall ride to Blythburgh. Should your father die, as I think he will ere long, it might grieve you in the after years to remember that you had bid him no farewell. If he recovers or is harsh with you it will be easy for you to seek sanctuary again."

## Chapter 7

# The Love Philtre

So it came about that on the morrow Eve and Sir Andrew, accompanied only by a single serving man, fearing no guile since it seemed certain that the Frenchmen were so far away, rode across the moor to Blythburgh. At the manor-house they found the drawbridge up. The watchman at the gate said also that his orders were to admit none, for the Frenchmen being gone, there were but few to guard the place.

"What, good fellow," asked Eve, "not even the daughter of the house who has heard that her father lies so sick?"

"Ay, he lies sick, lady," the man replied, "but such are his orders. Yet if you will bide here a while, I'll go and learn his mind."

So he went and returned presently, saying that Sir John commanded that his daughter was to be admitted, but that if Sir Andrew attempted to enter he should be driven back by force.

"Will you go in or will you return with me?" asked her companion of Eve.

"God's truth!" she answered, "am I one to run away from my father, however bad his humour? I'll go in and set my case before him, for after all he loves me in his own fashion and when he understands will, I think, relent."

"Your heart is your best guide, daughter, and it would be an ill task for me to stand between sire and child. Enter then, for I am sure that the Saints and your own innocence will protect you from all harm. At the worst you can come or send to me for help."

So they parted, and the bridge having been lowered, Eve walked boldly to her father's sleeping chamber, where she was told he lay. As she approached the door she met several of the household leaving it with scared faces, who scarcely stayed to salute her. Among these were two servants of her dead brother John, men whom she had never liked, and a woman, the wife of one of them, whom she liked least of all.

Pushing open the door, which was shut behind her, she advanced toward Sir John, who was not, as she had thought, in bed, but clad in a furred robe and standing by the hearth, on which burnt a fire. He watched her come, but said no word, and the look of him frightened her somewhat.

"Father," she said, "I heard that you were sick and alone—"

"Ay," he broke in, "sick, very sick here," and he laid his hand upon his heart, "where grief strikes a man. Alone, too, since you and your fellow have done my only son to death, murdered my guests, and caused them to depart from so bloody a house."

Now Eve, who had come expecting to find her father at the point of death and was prepared to plead with him, at these violent words took fire as was her nature.

"You know well that you speak what is not true," she said. "You and your Frenchmen strove to burn us out of Middle Marsh; my brother John struck Hugh de Cressi as though he were a dog and used words toward him that no knave would bear, let alone one better born than we are. Moreover, afterward once he spared his life, and Grey Dick, standing alone against a crowd, did but use his skill to save us. Is it murder, then to protect our honour and to save ourselves from death? And am I wrong to refuse to marry a fine French knave when I chance to love an honest man?"

"And, pray, am I your father, girl, that you dare to scold at me thus?" shouted Sir John, growing purple with wrath. "If I choose a husband for you, by what right do you refuse him, saying that you love a Dunwich shop-boy? Down on your knees and beg my pardon, or you shall have the whipping you have earned."

Now Eve's black eyes glittered dangerously.

"Ill would it go with any man who dared to lay a hand upon me," she said, drawing herself up and grasping the dagger in her girdle. "Yes, very ill, even though he were my own father. Look at me and say am I one to threaten? Ay, and before you answer bear in mind that there are those at my call who can strike hard, and that among them I think you'll find the King of England."

She paused.

"What hellish plot is this that you hatch against me?" asked Sir John, with some note of doubt in his voice. "What have I to fear from my liege lord, the King of England?"

"Only, sir, that you consort with and would wed me to one who, although you may not know it, has, I am told, much to fear from him, so much that I wonder that he has ridden to seek his Grace's presence.

Well, you are ill and I am angered and together we are but as steel and flint, from the meeting of which comes fire that may burn us both. Therefore, since being better than I thought, you need me not and have only cruel words for greeting, I'll bid you farewell and get me back to those who are kindlier. God be with you, and give you your health again."

"Ah!" said or rather snarled Sir John, "I thought as much and am ready for the trick. You'd win back to sanctuary, would you, and the company of that old wizard, Andrew Arnold, thence to make a mock of me? Well, not one step do you take upon that road while I live," and pushing past her he opened the door and shouted aloud.

Apparently the men and woman whom Eve had met in the passage were still waiting there, for instantly they all reappeared.

"Now, fellows," said Sir John, "and you, Jane Mell, take this rebellious girl of mine to the chamber in the prisoners' tower, whence I think she'll find it hard to fly to sanctuary. There lock her fast, feeding her with the bread and water of affliction to tame her proud spirit, and suffering none to go near her save this woman, Jane Mell. Stay, give me that bodkin which she wears lest she, who has learned bloody ways of late, should do some of you or herself a mischief."

As he spoke one of the men deftly snatched the dagger from Eve's girdle and handed it to Sir John who threw it into the farthest corner of the room. Then he turned and said:

"Now, girl, will you go, or must you be dragged?"

She raised her head slowly and looked him in the eyes. Mad as he was with passion there was something in her face that frightened him.

"Can you be my father?" she said in a strained, quiet voice. "Oh! glad am I that my mother did not live to see this hour."

Then she wheeled round and addressed the men.

"Hearken, fellows. He who lays a finger on me, dies. Soon or late assuredly he dies as he would not wish to die. Yes, even if you murder me, for I have friends who will learn the truth and pay back coin for coin with interest a hundredfold. Now I'll go. Stand clear, knaves, and pray to God that never again may Red Eve cross the threshold of her prison. Pray also that never again may you look on Hugh de Cressi's sword or hear Grey Dick's arrows sing, or face the curse of old Sir Andrew."

So proud and commanding was her mien and so terrible the import of her words, that these rough hinds shrank away from her and the woman hid her face in her hands. But Sir John thundered threats and oaths at them, so that slowly and unwillingly they ringed Eve round. Then with head held high she walked thence in the midst of them.

The prisoners' chamber beneath the leads of the lofty tower was cold and unfurnished save for a stool and a truckle-bed. It had a great door of oak locked and barred on the outer side, with a grille in it through which the poor wretch within could be observed. There was no window, only high up beneath the ceiling were slits like loopholes that not a child could have passed. Such was the place to which Eve was led.

Here they left her. At nightfall the door was opened and Jane Mell entered, bearing a loaf of bread and a jug of water, which she set down upon the floor.

"Would you aught else?" she asked.

"Ay, woman," answered Eve, "my thick red woollen cloak from my chamber, and hood to match. Also water to wash me, for this place is cold and foul, and I would die warm and clean."

"First I must get leave from my lord your father," said the woman in a surly voice.

"Get it then and be swift," said Eve, "or leave it ungotten; I care little."

Mell went and within half an hour returned with the garments, the water and some other things. Setting them down without a word she departed, locking and bolting the door behind her.

While there remained a few rays of light to see by, Eve ate and drank heartily, for she needed food. Then having prayed according to her custom, she laid herself down and slept as a child sleeps, for she was very strong of will and one who had always taught herself to make the best of evil fortune. When she woke the daws were cawing around the tower and the sun shone through the loopholes. She rose refreshed and ate the remainder of her bread, then combed her hair and dressed herself as best she could.

Two or three hours later the door was opened and her father entered. Glancing at him she saw that little sleep had visited him that night, for he looked old and very weary, so weary that she motioned to him to sit upon the stool. This he did, breathing heavily and muttering something about the steepness of the tower stairs. Presently he spoke.

"Eve," he said, "is your proud spirit broken yet?"

"No," she answered, "nor ever will be, living or dead! You may kill my body, but my spirit is me, and that you will never kill. As God gave it so I will return it to Him again."

He stared at her, with something of wonder and more of admiration in his look.

"Christ's truth," he said, "how proud I could be of you, if only you'd let me! I deem your courage comes from your mother, but she never had your shape and beauty. And now you are the only one left, and you hate me with all your proud heart, you, the heiress of the Claverings!"

"Whose estate is this," she answered, pointing to the bare stone walls. "Think you, my father, that such treatment as I have met with at your hands of late would breed love in the humblest heart? What devil drives you on to deal with me as you have done?"

"No devil, girl, but a desire for your own good, and," he added with a burst of truth, "for the greatness of my House after I am gone, which will be soon. For your old wizard spoke rightly when he said that I stand near to death."

"Will marrying me to a man I hate be for my good and make your House great? I tell you, sir, it would kill me and bring the Claverings to an end. Do you desire also that your broad lands should go to patch a spendthrift Frenchman's cloak? But what matters your desire seeing that I'll not do it, who love another man worth a score of him; one, too, who will sit higher than any Count of Noyon ever stood."

*"Pish!"* he said. "'Tis but a girl's whim. You speak folly, being young and headstrong. Now, to have done with all this mummer's talk, will you swear to me by our Saviour and on the welfare of your soul to break with Hugh de Cressi once and forever? For if so I'll let you free, to leave me if you will, and dwell where it pleases you."

She opened her lips to answer, but he held up his hand, saying:

"Wait ere you speak, I have not done. If you take my offer I'll not even press Sir Edmund Acour on you; that matter shall stand the chance of time and tide. Only while you live you must have no more to do with the man who slew your brother. Now will you swear?"

"Not I," she answered. "How can I who but a few days ago before God's altar and His priest vowed myself to this same Hugh de Cressi for all his life?"

Sir John rose from the stool and walked, or, rather, tottered to the door.

"Then stay here till you rot," he said quite quietly, "for I'll give you no burial. As for this Hugh, I would have spared him, but you have signed his death-warrant."

He was gone. The heavy door shut, the bars clanged into their sockets. Thus these two parted, for when they met once more no word passed between them; and although she knew not how these things would end, Eve felt that parting to be dreadful. Turning her face to the wall, for a while she wept, then, when the woman Mell came with her bread and water, wiped away her tears and faced her calmly. After all, she could have answered no otherwise; her soul was pure of sin, and, for the rest, God must rule it. At least she would die clean and honest.

That night she was wakened from her sleep by the clatter of horses' hoofs on the courtyard stones. She could hear no more because a wind blew that drowned all sound of voices. For a while a wild hope had filled her that Hugh had come, or perchance Sir Andrew, with the Dunwich folk, but presently she remembered that this was foolish, since these would never have been admitted within the moat. So sighing sadly she turned to rest again, thinking to herself that doubtless her father had called in some of his vassal tenants from the outlying lands to guard the manor in case it should be attacked.

Next morning the woman Jane Mell brought her better garments to wear, of her best indeed, and, though she wondered why they were sent, for the lack of anything else to do she arrayed herself in them, and braided her hair with the help of a silver mirror that was among the garments. A little later this woman appeared again, bearing not bread and water, but good food and a cup of wine. The food she ate with thankfulness, but the wine she would not drink, because she knew that it was French and had heard Acour praise it.

The morning wore away to noon, and again the door opened and there stood before her—Sir Edmund Acour himself, gallantly dressed, as she noticed vaguely, in close-fitting tunic of velvet, long shoes that turned up at the toes and a cap in which was set a single nodding plume. She rose from her stool and set her back against the wall with a prayer to God in her heart, but no word upon her lips, for she felt that her best refuge was silence. He drew the cap from his head, and began to speak.

"Lady," he said, "you will wonder to see me here after my letter to you, bidding you farewell, but you will remember that in this letter I wrote that Fate might bring us together again, and it has done so through no fault or wish of mine. The truth is that when I was near to London I heard that danger awaited me there on account of certain false accusations, such danger that I must return again to Suffolk and seek a ship at some eastern port. Well, I came here last night, and learned that you were back out of sanctuary and also that you had quarrelled with your father who in his anger had imprisoned you in this poor place. An ill deed, as I think, but in truth he is so distraught with grief and racked with sickness that he scarce knows what he does."

Now he paused, but as Eve made no answer went on:

"Pity for your lot, yes, and my love for you that eats my heart out, caused me to seek your father's leave to visit you and see if perchance I could not soften your wrath against me."

Again he paused and again there was no answer.

"Moreover," he added, "I have news for you which I fear you will think sad and which, believe me, I pray you, it pains me to give, though the man was my rival and my enemy. Hugh de Cressi, to whom you held yourself affianced, is dead."

She quivered a little at the words, but still made no answer, for her will was very strong.

"I had the story," he continued, "from two of his own men, whom we met flying back to Dunwich from London. It seems that messengers from your father reached the Court of the King before this Hugh, telling him of the slaying in Blythburgh Marsh. Then came Hugh himself, whereon the King seized him and his henchman, the archer, and at once put them on their trial as the murderers of John Clavering, of my knights, and Thomas of Kessland, which they admitted boldly. Thereon his Grace, who was beside himself with rage, said that in a time of war, when every man was needed to fight the French, he was determined by a signal example to put a stop to the shedding of blood in these private feuds. So he ordered the merchant to the block, and his henchman, the archer, to the gallows, giving them but one hour to make their peace with God. Moreover," he went on, searching her cold impassive face with his eyes, "I did not escape his wrath, for he gave command that I was to be seized wherever I might be found and cast into prison till I could be put upon my trial, and my knights with me. Of your father's case he is considering since his only son has been slain and he holds him in regard. Therefore it is that I am obliged to avoid London and take refuge here."

Still Eve remained silent, and in his heart Acour cursed her stubbornness.

"Lady," he proceeded, though with somewhat less assurance—for now he must leave lies and get to pleading, and never did a suit seem more hopeless, "these things being so through no fault of mine whose hands are innocent of any share in this young man's end, I come to pray of you, the sword of death having cut all your oaths, that you will have pity on my love and take me as your husband, as is your father's wish and my heart's desire. Let not your young life be swallowed up in grief, but make it joyous in my company. I can give you greatness, I can give you wealth, but most of all I can give you such tender adoration as never woman had before. Oh! sweet Eve, your answer," and he cast himself upon the ground before her, and, snatching the hem of her robe, pressed it to his lips.

Then at length Eve spoke in a voice that rang like steel:

"Get you gone, knave, whose spurs should be hacked from your heels by scullions. Get you gone, traitor and liar, for well I know that Hugh de Cressi is not dead, who had a certain tale to tell of you to the King of England. Get you back to the Duke of Normandy and there ask the price of your betrayal of your liege lord, Edward, and show him the plans of our eastern coast and the shores where his army may land in safety."

Acour sprang to his feet and his face went white as ashes. Thrice he strove to speak but could not. Then with a curse he turned and left the chamber.

********

"The hunt's up," said Father Nicholas when he had heard all this tale a little later, "and now, lord, I think that you had better away to France, unless you desire to stop without companions in the church yonder."

"Ay, priest, I'll away, but by God's blood, I'll take that Red Eve with me! For one thing she knows too much to leave her behind. For a second I mean to pay her back, and for a third, although you may think it strange, I'm mad for her. I tell you she looked wondrous standing with her back against that wall, her marble face never wincing when I told her all the lie about young de Cressi's death—which will be holy truth when I get a chance at him—watching me out of those great, dark eyes of hers."

"Doubtless, lord, but how did she look when she called you knave and traitor? I think you said those were her wicked words. Oh!" he added with a ring of earnestness in his smooth voice, "let this Red Eve be. At bed or board she's no mate for you. Something fights at her side, be it angel or devil, or just raw chance. At the least she'll prove your ruin unless you let her be."

"Then I'll be ruined, Nicholas, for I'll not leave her, for a while, at any rate. What! de Noyon, whom they call Danger of Dames, beaten by a country girl who has never seen London or Paris! I'd sooner die."

"As well may chance if the country lad and the country archer come back with Edward's warrant in their pouch," answered the priest, shrugging his lean shoulders. "Well, lord, what is your plan?"

"To carry her off. Can't we manage nine stone of womanhood between us?"

"If she were dead it might be done, though hardly—over these Suffolk roads. But being very much alive with a voice to scream with, hands to fight with, a brain to think with and friends who know her from here to Yarmouth, or to Hull, and Monsieur Grey Dick's arrows pricking us behind perchance—well, I don't know."

"Friend," said Acour, tapping him on the shoulder meaningly, "there must be some way; there are always ways, and I pray you to hunt them out. Come, find me one, or stay here alone to explain affairs, first to this Dick whom you have so much upon the brain, and afterward to Edward of England or his officers."

Father Nicholas looked at the great Count's face. Then he looked at the ground, and, having studied it a while without result, turned his beady eyes to the heavens, where it would seem that he found inspiration.

"I am a stranger to love, thank the Saints," he said, "but, as you know, lord, I am a master leech, and amongst other things have studied certain medicines which breed that passion in the human animal."

"Love philtres?" queried Acour doubtfully.

"Yes, that kind of thing. One dose, and those who hate become enamoured, and those who are enamoured hate."

"Then in God's or Satan's name, give her one. Only be careful it is the right sort, for if you made a mistake so that she hated me any more than she does at present, I know not what would happen. Also if you kill her I'll dig a sword point through you. How would the stuff work?"

"She'll seem somewhat stupid for a while, perhaps not speak, but only smile kindly. That will last twelve hours or so, plenty of time for you to be married, and afterward, when the grosser part of the potion passes off leaving only its divine essence, why, afterward she'll love you furiously."

"A powerful medicine, truly, that can change the nature of woman. Moreover, I'd rather that she loved me—well, as happy brides do. Still I put up with the fury provided it be of the good kind. And now how is it to be done?"

"Leave that to me, lord," said Nicholas, with a cunning smile. "Give me a purse of gold, not less than ten pieces, for some is needed to melt in the mixture, and more to bribe that woman and others. For the rest, hold yourself ready to become a husband before sunset tomorrow. Go see Sir John and tell him that the lady softens. Send men on to King's Lynn also to bid them have our ship prepared to sail the minute we appear, which with good fortune should be within forty-eight hours from now. Above all, forget not that I run great risk to soul and body for your sake and that there are abbeys vacant in Normandy. Now, farewell, I must to my work, for this medicine takes much skill such as no other leech has save myself. Ay, and much prayer also, that naught may hinder its powerful working."

"Prayer to the devil, I think," said his master looking after him with a shrug of his shoulders. "God's truth! if any one had told me three months gone that de Noyon would live to seek the aid of priests and potions to win a woman's favour, I'd have named him liar to his face. What would those who have gone before her think of this story, I wonder?"

Then with a bitter laugh he turned and went about his business, which was to lie to the father as he had lied to the daughter. Only in this second case he found one more willing to listen and easier to deceive.

********

On the following morning, as it chanced, Eve had no relish for the food that was brought to her, for confinement in that narrow place had robbed her of her appetite. Also she had suffered much from grievous fear and doubt, for whatever she might say to Acour, how could she be sure that his story was not true? How could she be sure that her lover did not, in fact, now lie dead at the headsman's hands? Such things often happened when kings were wroth and would not listen. Or perhaps Acour himself had found and murdered him, or hired others to do the deed. She did not know, and, imprisoned here without a friend, what means had she of coming at the truth? Oh! if only she could escape! If only she could speak with Sir Andrew for one brief minute, she, poor fool, who had walked into this trap of her own will.

She sent away the food and bade the woman Mell bring her milk, for that would be easy to swallow and give her sustenance. After some hours it came, Mell explaining that she had been obliged to send for it to the farmsteading, as none drank milk in the manor-house. Being thirsty, Eve took the pitcher and drained it to the last drop, then threw it down, saying that the vessel was foul and made the milk taste ill.

The woman did not answer, only smiled a little as she left the chamber, and Eve wondered why she smiled.

A while later she grew very sleepy, and, as it seemed to her, had strange dreams in her sleep. She dreamed of her childhood, when she and Hugh played together upon the Dunwich shore. She dreamed of her mother, and thought dimly that she was warning her of something. She heard voices about her and thought that they were calling her to be free. Yes, and followed them readily enough, or so it seemed in her dream, followed them out of that hateful prison, for the bolts clanged behind her, down stairs and into the courtyard, where the sun's light almost blinded her and the fresh air struck her hot brow like ice. Then there were more voices, and people moving to and fro and the drone of a priest praying and a touch upon her hand from which she shrank. And oh! she wished that dream were done, for it was long, long. It wearied her, and grasped her heart with a cold clutch of fear.

## Chapter 8

# Too Late

It was past three o'clock on this same day when Eve had drunk the milk and some hours after she began to dream, that Hugh de Cressi and his men, safe and sound but weary, halted their tired horses at the door of the Preceptory of the Templars in Dunwich.

"Best go on to his worship the Mayor and serve the King's writ upon him, master," grumbled Grey Dick as they rode up Middlegate Street. "You wasted good time in a shooting bout at Windsor against my will, and now you'll waste more time in a talking match at Dunwich. And the sun grows low, and the Frenchmen may have heard and be on the wing, and who can see to lay a shaft at night?"

"Nay, man," answered Hugh testily, "first I must know how she fares."

"The lady Eve will fare neither better nor worse for your knowing about her, but one with whom you should talk may fare further, for doubtless his spies are out. But have your way and leave me to thank God that no woman ever found a chance to clog my leg, perhaps because I was not born an ass."

It is doubtful if Hugh heard these pungent and practical remarks, for ere Dick had finished speaking them, he was off his horse, and hammering at the Preceptory door. Some while passed before any answer came, for Sir Andrew was walking in the garden beyond the church, in no happy mind because of certain rumours that had reached him, and the old nun Agnes, spying armed men and not knowing who they were, was afraid to open. So it came about that fifteen minutes or more went by before at length Hugh and his godsire stood face to face.

"How is Eve and where? Why is she not with you, Father?" he burst out.

"One question at a time, son, for whose safe return I thank God. I know not how she is, and she is not with me because she is not here. She has returned to her father at Blythburgh."

"Why?" gasped Hugh. "You swore to keep her safe."

"Peace, and you shall learn," and as shortly as he could he told him.

"Is that all?" asked Hugh doubtfully, for he saw trouble in Sir Andrew's face.

"Not quite, son. Only to-day I have learned that Acour and his folk never went to London, and are back again at Blythburgh Manor."

"So much the better, Father, for now I have the King's warrant addressed to the Mayor and all his Grace's subject in Dunwich, to take these Frenchmen, living or dead."

"Ah! But I have learned also that her father holds Eve a prisoner, suffering her to speak with none, and—one lamb among those wolves—Oh! God! why didst Thou suffer my wisdom to fail me? Doubtless for some good purpose—where is my faith? Yet we must act. Hie, you there," he called to one of the men-at-arms, "go to Master de Cressi's house and bid him meet us by the market-cross mounted and armed, with all his sons and people. And, you, get out my horse. Mother Agnes, bring my armour, since I have no other squire! We'll go to the Mayor. Now, while I don my harness, tell me all that's passed, wasting no words."

Another half-hour almost had gone by before Hugh met his father, two of his brothers and some men riding into the market-place. They greeted in haste but thankfulness, and something of the tale was told while they passed on to the house of the Mayor, who, as they thought, had already been warned of their coming by messengers. But here disappointment awaited them, for this officer, a man of wealth and honour, was, as it chanced, absent on a visit to Norwich, whence it was said that he would not return for three full days.

"Now what shall we do?" asked Sir Andrew, his face falling. "It is certain that the burgesses of Dunwich will not draw sword in an unknown quarrel, except upon the direct order of their chief, for there is no time to collect them and publish the King's warrant. It would seem that we must wait till to-morrow and prepare to-night."

"Not I," answered Hugh. "The warrant is to me as well as to the Mayor. I'll leave it with his clerk, which is good delivery, and away to Blythburgh Manor on the instant with any who will follow me, or without them. Come, Dick, for night draws on and we've lost much time."

Now his father tried to dissuade him, but he would not listen, for the fear in his heart urged him forward. So the end of it was that the whole party of them—thirteen men in all, counting those that Master de Cressi brought, rode away across the heath to Blythburgh, though the horses of Hugh's party being very weary, not so fast as he could have wished.

Just as the sun sank they mounted the slope of the farther hill on the crest of which stood the manor-house backed by winds.

"The drawbridge is down, thanks be to God!" said Sir Andrew, "which shows that no attack is feared. I doubt me, son, we shall find Acour flown."

"That we shall know presently," answered Hugh.

"Now, dismount all and follow me."

They obeyed, though some of them who knew old Sir John's temper seemed not to like the business. Leaving two of their people with the horses, they crossed the bridge, thinking to themselves that the great house seemed strangely silent and deserted. Now they were in the outer court, on one side of which stood the chapel, and still there was no one to be seen. Dick tapped Hugh upon the shoulder, pointing to a window of this chapel that lay in the shadow, through which came a faint glimmering of light, as though tapers burned upon the altar.

"I think there's a burying yonder," he whispered, "at which all men gather."

Hugh blanched, for might it not be Eve whom they buried? But Sir Andrew, noting it, said:

"Nay, nay, Sir John was sick. Come, let us look."

The door of the chapel was open and they walked through it as quietly as they could, to find the place, which was not very large, filled with people. Of these they took no heed, for the last rays of the sunlight flowing through the western window, showed them a scene that held their eyes.

A priest stood before the lighted altar holding his hands in benediction over a pair who kneeled at its rail. One of these wore a red cloak down which her dark hair streamed. She leaned heavily against the rail, as a person might who is faint with sleep or with the ardour of her orisons. It was Red Eve, no other!

At her side, clad in gleaming mail, kneeled a knight. Close by Eve stood her father, looking at her with a troubled air, and behind the knight were other knights and men-at-arms. In the little nave were all the people of the manor and with them those that dwelt around, every one of them intently watching the pair before the altar.

The priest perceived them at first just as the last word of the blessing passed his lips.

"Why do armed strangers disturb God's house?" he asked in a warning voice.

The knight at the altar rails sprang up and turned round. Hugh saw that it was Acour, but even then he noted that the woman at his side, she who wore Eve's garment, never stirred from her knees.

Sir John Clavering glared down the chapel, and all the other people turned to look at them. Now Hugh and his company halted in the open space where the nave joined the chancel, and said, answering the priest:

"I come hither with my companions bearing the warrant of the King to seize Edmund Acour, Count de Noyon, and convey him to London, there to stand his trial on a charge of high treason toward his liege lord, Edward of England. Yield you, Sir Edmund Acour."

At these bold words the French knights and squires drew their swords and ringed themselves round their captain, whereon Hugh and his party also drew their swords.

"Stay," cried old Sir Andrew in his ringing voice. "Let no blood be shed in the holy house of God. You men of Suffolk, know that you harbour a foul traitor in your bosoms, one who plots to deliver you to the French. Lift no hand on his behalf, lest on you also should fall the vengeance of the King, who has issued his commands to all his officers and people, to seize Acour living or dead."

Now a silence fell upon the place, for none liked this talk of the King's warrant, and in the midst of it Hugh asked:

"Do you yield, Sir Edmund Acour, or must we and the burgesses of Dunwich who gather without seize you and your people?"

Acour turned and began to talk rapidly with the priest Nicholas, while the congregation stared at each other. Then Sir John Clavering, who all this while had been listening like a man in a dream, suddenly stepped forward.

"Hugh de Cressi," he said, "tell me, does the King's writ run against John Clavering?"

"Nay," answered Hugh, "I told his Grace that you were an honest man deceived by a knave."

"Then what do you, slayer of my son, in my house? Know that I have just married my daughter to this knight whom you name traitor, and that I here defend him to the last who is now my kin. Begone and seek elsewhere, or stay and die."

"How have you married her?" asked Hugh in a hollow voice. "Not of her own will, surely? Rise, Eve, and tell us the truth."

Eve stirred. Resting her hands upon the altar rails, slowly she raised herself to her feet and turned her white face toward him.

"Who spoke?" she said. "Was it Hugh that Acour swore is dead? Oh! where am I? Hugh, Hugh, what passes?"

"Your honour, it seems, Eve. They say you are married to this traitor."

"I married, and in this red robe! Why, that betokens blood, as blood there must be if I am wed to any man save you," and she laughed, a dreadful laugh.

"In the name of Christ," thundered old Sir Andrew, "tell me, John Clavering, what means this play? Yonder woman is no willing wife. She's drugged or mad. Man, have you doctored your own daughter?"

"Doctored my daughter? I! I! Were you not a priest I'd tear out your tongue for those words. She's married and of her own will. Else would she have stood silent at this altar?"

"It shall be inquired of later," Hugh answered coldly. "Now yield you, Sir Edmund Acour, the King's business comes first."

"Nay," shouted Clavering, springing forward and drawing his sword; "in my house my business comes first. Acour is my daughter's husband and so shall stay till death or Pope part them. Out of this, Hugh de Cressi, with all your accursed chapman tribe."

Hugh walked toward Acour, taking no heed. Then suddenly Sir John lifted his sword and smote with all his strength. The blow caught Hugh on the skull and down he fell, his mail clattering on the stones, and lay still. With a whine of rage, Grey Dick leapt at Clavering, drawing from his side the archer's axe he always wore. But old Sir Andrew caught and held him in his arms.

"Vengeance is God's, not ours," he said. "Look!"

As he spoke Sir John began to sway to and fro. He let fall his murdering sword, he pressed his hands upon his heart, he threw them high. Then suddenly his knees gave beneath him; he sank to the floor a huddled heap and sat there, resting against the altar rail over which his head hung backward, open mouthed and eyed.

The last light of the sky went out, only that of the tapers remained. Eve, awake at last, sent up shriek after shriek; Sir Andrew bending over the two fallen men, the murderer and the murdered, began to shrive them swiftly ere the last beat of life should have left their pulses. His father, brothers, and Grey Dick clustered round Hugh and lifted him. The fox-faced priest, Nicholas, whispered quick words into the ears of Acour and his knights. Acour nodded and took a step toward Eve, who just then fell swooning and was grasped by Grey Dick with his left hand, for in his right he still held the axe.

"No, no," hissed Nicholas, dragging Sir Edmund back, "life is more than any woman." Then some one overset the tapers, so that the place was plunged in gloom, and through it none saw Acour and his train creep out by the chancel door and hurry to their horses, which waited saddled in the inner yard.

The frightened congregation fled from the nave with white faces, each seeking his own place, or any other that was far from Blythburgh Manor. For did not their dead master's guilt cling to them, and would they not also be held guilty of the murder of the King's officer, and swing for it from the gallows? So it came about that when at last lights were brought Hugh's people found themselves alone.

"The Frenchmen have fled!" cried Grey Dick. "Follow me, men," and with most of them he ran out and began to search the manor, till at length they found a woman who told them that thirty minutes gone Acour and all his following had ridden through the back gates and vanished at full gallop into the darkness of the woods.

With these tidings, Dick returned to the chapel.

"Master de Cressi," said Sir Andrew when he had heard it, "back with some of your people to Dunwich and raise the burgesses, warning them that the King's wrath will be great if these traitors escape the land. Send swift messengers to all the ports; discover where Acour rides and follow him in force and if you come up with him, take him dead or living. Stop not to talk, man, begone! Nay, bide here, Richard, and those who rode with you to London, for Acour may return again and some must be left to guard the lady Eve and your master, quick or dead."

De Cressi, his two sons and servants went, and presently were riding for Dunwich faster than ever they rode before. But, as it proved, Acour was too swift for them. When at length a messenger galloped into Lynn, whither they learned that he had fled, it was to find that his ship, which awaited him with sails hoisted, had cleared the port three hours before, with a wind behind her which blew straight for Flanders.

"Ah!" said Grey Dick when he heard the news, "this is what comes of wasting arrows upon targets which should have been saved for traitors' hearts! With those three hours of daylight in hand we'd have ringed the rogues in or run them down. Well, the devil's will be done; he does but spare his own till a better day."

But when the King heard the news he was very wroth, not with Hugh de Cressi, but with the burgesses of Dunwich, whose Mayor, although he was blameless, lost his office over the matter. Nor was there any other chosen afterward in his place, as those who read the records of that ancient port may discover for themselves.

********

When Master de Cressi and his people were gone, having first searched the great manor-house and found none in it save a few serving-men and women, whom he swore to put to death if they disobeyed him, Grey Dick raised the drawbridge. Then, all being made safe, he set a watch upon the walls and saw that there was wood in the iron cradle on the topmost tower in case it should be needful to light the beacon and bring aid. But it was not, since the sun rose before any dared to draw near those walls, and then those that came proved to be friendly folk from Dunwich bearing the ill news that the Frenchmen were clean away.

About midnight the door of the chamber in which Sir Andrew knelt by a bed whereon lay Hugh de Cressi opened and the tall Eve entered, bearing a taper in her hand. For now her mind had returned to her and she knew all.

"Is he dead, Father?" she asked in a small, strange voice; then, still as any statue, awaited the answer that was more to her than life.

"Nay, daughter. Down on your knees and give thanks. God, by the skill I gained in Eastern lands, has stayed the flow of his life's blood, and I say that he will live."

Then he showed her how her father's sword had glanced from the short hood of chain-mail which he had given Hugh, stunning him, but leaving the skull unbroken. Biting into the neck below, it had severed the outer vein only. This he had tied with a thread of silk and burned with a hot iron, leaving a scar that Hugh bore to his death, but staunching the flow of blood.

"How know you that he will live?" asked Eve again, "seeing that he lies like one that is sped."

"I know it, daughter. Question me no more. As for his stillness, it is that which follows a heavy blow. Perhaps it may hold him fast many days, since certainly he will be sick for long. Yet fear nothing; he will live."

Now Eve uttered a great sigh. Her breast heaved and colour returned to her lips. She knelt down and gave thanks as the old priest-knight had bidden her. Then she rose, took his hand and kissed it.

"Yet one more question, Father," she said. "It is of myself. That knave drugged me. I drank milk, and, save some dreams, remember no more till I heard Hugh's voice calling. Now they tell me that I have stood at the altar with de Noyon, and that his priest read the mass of marriage over us, and—look! Oh! I never noted it till now—there is a ring upon my hand," and she cast it on the floor. "Tell me, Father, according to the Church's law is that man my—my husband?"

Sir Andrew's eloquent dark eyes, that ever shadowed forth the thoughts which passed within him, grew very troubled.

"I cannot tell you," he answered awkwardly after thinking a while. "This priest, Nicholas, though I hold him a foul villain, is doubtless still a priest, clothed with all the authority of our Lord Himself, since the unworthiness of the minister does not invalidate the sacrament. Were it otherwise, indeed, few would be well baptized or wed or shriven. Moreover, although I suspect that himself he mixed the draught, yet he may not have known that you were drugged, and you stood silent, and, it would appear, consenting. The ceremony, alas! was completed; I myself heard him give the benediction. Your father assisted thereat and gave you to the groom in the presence of a congregation. The drugging is a matter of surmise and evidence which may not be forthcoming, since you are the only witness, and where is the proof? I fear me, daughter, that according to the Church's law you are de Noyon's lawful wife—"

"The Church's law," she broke in; "how about God's law? There lies the only man to whom I owe a bond, and I'll die a hundred deaths before any other shall even touch my hand. Ay, if need be, I'll kill myself and reason out the case with St. Peter in the Gates."

"Hush! hush! speak not so madly. The knot that the Church ties it can unloose. This matter must to his Holiness the Pope; it shall be my business to lay it before him; yea, letters shall go to Avignon by the first safe hand. Moreover, it well may happen that God Himself will free you, by the sword of His servant Death. This lord of yours, if indeed he be your lord, is a foul traitor. The King of England seeks his life, and there is another who will seek it also ere very long," and he glanced at the senseless form of Hugh. "Fret not yourself overmuch, daughter. Be grateful rather that matters are no worse, and that you remain as you always were. Another hour and you might have been snatched away beyond our finding. What is not ended can still be mended. Now go, seek the rest you need, for I would not have two sick folk on my hands. Oh, seek it with a thankful heart, and forget not to pray for the soul of your erring father, for, after all he loved you and strove for your welfare according to his lights."

"It may be so," answered Eve, "and I'll pray for him, as is my duty. I'll pray also that I may never find such another friend as my father showed himself to me."

********

Then she bent for a moment over Hugh, stretching out her hands above him as though in blessing, and departed as silently as she had come.

Three days went by before Hugh found his mind again, and after that for two weeks he was so feeble that he must lie quite still and scarcely talk at all. Sir Andrew, who nursed him continually with the help of Grey Dick, who brought his master *possets*, bow on back and axe at side but never opened his grim mouth, told his patient that Eve was safe and sound, but that he must not see her until he grew strong again.

So Hugh strove to grow strong, and, nature helping him, not in vain. At length there came a day when he might rise from his bed, and sit on a bench in the pleasant spring sunshine by the open window. Walk he could not, however, not only on account of his weakness, but because of another hurt, now discovered for the first time, which in the end gave him more trouble than did the dreadful and dangerous blow of Clavering's sword. It seemed that when he had fallen suddenly beneath that murderous stroke all his muscles relaxed as though he were dead, and his left ankle bent up under him, wrenching its sinews in such a fashion that for the rest of his life he walked a little lame. Especially was this so in the spring season, though whether because he had received his hurt at that time or owing to the quality of the air none could ever tell him.

Yet on that happy day he thought little of these harms, who felt the life-blood running once more strongly through his veins and who awaited Eve's long-promised advent. At length she came, stately, kind and beautiful, for now her grief and terror had passed by, leaving her as she was before her woes fell upon her. She came, and in Sir Andrew's presence, for he would not leave them, the tale was told.

Hugh learned for the first time all the truth of her imprisonment and of her shameful drugging. He learned of the burying of Sir John Clavering and of her naming as sole heiress to his great estates. To these, however, Acour had not been ashamed to submit some shadowy claim, made "in right of his lawful wife, Dame Eve Acour, Countess de Noyon," which claim had been sent by him from France addressed to "all whom it might concern." He learned of the King's wrath at the escape of this same Acour, and of his Grace's seizure of that false knight's lands in Suffolk, which, however, proved to be so heavily mortgaged that no one would grow rich upon them.

Lastly he learned that King Edward, in a letter written by one of his secretaries to Sir Andrew Arnold and received only that morning, said that he held him, Hugh de Cressi, not to blame for Acour's escape. It commanded also that if he recovered from his wound, for the giving of which Sir John Clavering should have paid sharply if he had lived, he and the archer, his servant, should join him either in England or in France, whither he purposed shortly to proceed with all his host. But the Mayor and men of Dunwich he did not hold free of blame.

The letter added, moreover, that the King was advised that Edmund Acour on reaching Normandy had openly thrown off his allegiance to the crown of England and there was engaged in raising forces to make war upon him. Further, that this Acour alleged himself to be the lawfully married husband of Eve Clavering, the heiress of Sir John Clavering, a point upon which his Grace demanded information, since if this were true he purposed to escheat the Clavering lands. With this brief and stern announcement the letter ended.

"By God's mercy, Eve, tell me, are you this fellow's wife?" exclaimed Hugh.

"Not so," she answered. "Can a woman who is Dunwich born be wed without consent? And can a woman whose will is foully drugged out of her give consent to that which she hates? Why, if so there is no justice in the world."

"'Tis a rare jewel in these evil days, daughter," said Sir Andrew with a sigh. "Still fret not yourself son Hugh. A full statement of the case, drawn by skilled clerks and testified to by many witnesses, has gone forward already to his Holiness the Pope, of which statement true copies have been sent to the King and to the Bishops of Norwich and of Canterbury. Yet be warned that in such matters the law ecclesiastic moves but slowly, and then only when its wheels are greased with gold."

"Well," answered Hugh with a fierce laugh, "there remains another law which moves more swiftly and its wheels are greased with vengeance; the law of the sword. If you are married, Eve, I swear that before very long you shall be widowed or I dead. I'll not let de Noyon slip a second time even if he stands before the holiest altar in Christendom."

"I'd have killed him in the chapel yonder," muttered Grey Dick, who had entered with his master's food and not been sent away. "Only," he added looking reproachfully at Sir Andrew, "my hand was stayed by a certain holy priest's command to which, alack, I listened."

"And did well to listen, man, since otherwise by now you would be excommunicate."

"I could mock at that," said Dick sullenly, "who make confession in my own way, and do not wish to be married, and care not the worth of a horseshoe nail how and where I am buried, provided those I hate are buried first."

"Richard Archer, graceless wight that you are," said Sir Andrew, "I say you stand in danger of your soul."

"Ay, Father, and so the Frenchman, Acour, stood in danger of his body. But you saved it, so perhaps if there is need at the last, you will do as much for my soul. If not it must take its chance," and snatching at the dish-cover angrily, he turned and left the chamber.

"Well," commented Sir Andrew, shaking his head sadly, "if the fellow's heart is hard it is honest, so may he be forgiven who has something to forgive like the rest of us. Now hearken to me, son and daughter. Wrong, grievous and dreadful, has been done to you both. Yet, until death or the Church levels it, a wall that you may not climb stands between you, and when you meet it must be as friends—no more."

"Now I begin to wish that I had learned in Grey Dick's school," said Hugh. But whatever she thought, Eve set her lips and said nothing.

CHAPTER 9

# Crecy Field

It was Saturday, the 26th of August, in the year 1346. The harassed English host—but a little host, after all, retreating for its life from Paris—had forced the passage of the Somme by the ford which a forgotten traitor, Gobin Agache by name, revealed to them. Now it stood at bay upon the plain of Crecy, there to conquer or to die.

"Will the French fight to-day, what think you?" asked Hugh of Grey Dick, who had just descended from an apple-tree which grew in the garden of a burnt-out cottage. Here he had been engaged on the twofold business of surveying the disposition of the English army and in gathering a pocketful of fruit which remained upon the tree's topmost boughs.

"I think that these are very good apples," answered Dick, speaking with his mouth full. "Eat while you get the chance, master, for, who knows, the next you set your teeth in may be of the kind that grew upon the Tree of Life in a very old garden," and he handed him two of the best. Then he turned to certain archers, who clustered round with outstretched hands, saying: "Why should I give you my apples, fellows, seeing that you were too lazy to climb and get them for yourselves? None of you ever gave me anything when I was hungry, after the sack of Caen, in which my master, being squeamish, would take no part. Therefore I went to bed supperless, because, as I remember you said, I had not earned it. Still, as I don't want to fight the French with a bellyache, go scramble for them."

Then, with a quick motion, he flung the apples to a distance, all save one, which he presented to a tall man who stood near, adding:

"Take this, Jack Green, in token of fellowship, since I have nothing else to offer you. I beat you at Windsor, didn't I, when we shot a match before the King? Now show your skill and beat me and I'll say 'thank you.' Keep count of your arrows shot, Jack, and I'll keep count of mine, and when the battle is over, he who has grassed most Frenchmen shall be called the better man."

"Then I'm that already, lad," answered the great yeoman with a grin as he set his teeth in the apple. "For, look you, having served at Court I've learned how to lie, and shall swear I never wasted shaft, whereas you, being country born, may own to a miss or two for shame's sake. Or, likelier still, those French will have one or both of us in their bag. If all tales are true, there is such a countless host of them that we few English shall not see the sky for arrows."

Dick shrugged his shoulders and was about to answer when suddenly a sound of shouting deep and glad rose from the serried companies upon their left. Then the voice of an officer was heard calling:

"Line! Line! The King comes!"

Another minute and over the crest of a little rise appeared Edward of England clad in full armour. He wore a surtout embroidered with the arms of England and France, but his helm hung at his saddle-bow that all might see his face. He was mounted, not on his war steed, but on a small, white, ambling palfrey, and in his hand he bore a short baton. With him came two marshals, gaily dressed, and a slim young man clad from head to foot in plain black armour, and wearing a great ruby in his helm, whom all knew for Edward, Prince of Wales.

On he rode, acknowledging the cheering of his soldiers with smiles and courtly bows, till at length he pulled rein just in front of the triple line of archers, among whom were mingled some knights and men-at-arms, for the order of battle was not yet fully set. Just then, on the plain beneath, riding from out the shelter of some trees and, as they thought, beyond the reach of arrows, appeared four splendid French knights, and with them a few squires. There they halted, taking stock, it would seem, of the disposition of the English army.

"Who are those that wear such fine feathers?" asked the King.

"One is the Lord of Bazeilles," answered a marshal. "I can see the monk upon his crest, but the blazons of the others I cannot read. They spy upon us, Sire; may we sally out and take them?"

"Nay," answered Edward, "their horses are fresher than ours; let them go, for pray God we shall see them closer soon."

So the French knights, having stared their full, turned and rode away slowly. But one of their squires did otherwise. Dismounting from his horse, which he left with another squire to hold, he ran forward a few paces to the crest of a little knoll. Thence he made gestures of contempt and scorn toward the English army, as he did so shouting foul words, of which a few floated to them in the stillness.

"Now," said Edward, "if I had an archer who could reach that varlet, I'll swear that his name should not be forgotten in England. But alas! it may not be, for none cam make an arrow fly true so far."

Instantly Grey Dick stepped forward.

"Sire, may I try?" he asked, stringing his great black bow as he spoke.

"Who are you?" said the King, "who seem to have been rolled in ashes and wear my own gold arrow in your cap? Ah! I remember, the Suffolk man who showed us all how to shoot at Windsor, he who is called Grey Dick. Yes, try, Grey Dick, try, if you think that you can reach so far. Yet for the honour of St. George, man, do not miss, for all the host will see Fate riding on your shaft."

For one moment Dick hesitated. Such awful words seemed to shake even his iron nerve.

"I've seen you do as much, Dick," said the quiet voice of Hugh de Cressi behind him. "Still, judge you."

Then Dick ground his heels into the turf and laid his weight against the bow. While all men watched breathless, he drew it to an arc, he drew it till the string was level with his ear. He loosed, then, slewing round, straightened himself and stared down at the earth. As he said afterward, he feared to watch that arrow.

Away it sped while all men gazed. High, high it flew, the sunlight glinting on its polished barb. Down it came at length, and the King muttered "Short!" But while the word passed his lips that shaft seemed to recover itself, as though by magic, and again rushed on. He of the foul words and gestures saw it coming, and turned to fly. As he leapt forward the war arrow struck him full in the small of the back, just where the spine ends, severing it, so that he fell all of a heap like an ox beneath the axe, and lay a still and huddled shape.

From all the English right who saw this wondrous deed there went up such a shout that their comrades to the left and rear thought for a moment that battle had been joined. The King and the Prince stared amazed. Hugh flung his arms about Dick's neck, and kissed him. Jack Green cried:

"No archer, but a wizard! Mere man could not have sent a true shaft so far."

"Then would to heaven I had more such wizards," said the King. "God be with you, Grey Dick, for you have put new heart into my and all our company. Mark, each of you, that he smote him in the back, smote him running! What reward would you have, man?"

"None," answered Dick in a surly voice. "My reward is that, whatever happens, yon filthy French knave will never mock honest English folk again. Or so I think, though the arrow barely reached him. Yet, Sire," he added after a pause, "you might knight my master, Hugh de Cressi, if you will, since but for him I should have feared to risk that shot."

Then turning aside, Dick unstrung his bow, and, pulling the remains of the apple out of his pouch, began to munch it unconcernedly.

"Hugh de Cressi!" said the King. "Ah! yes, I mind me of him and of the rogue, Acour, and the maid, Red Eve. Well, Hugh, I am told you fought gallantly at Blanche-Tague two days gone and were among the last to cross the Somme. Also, we have other debts to pay you. Come hither, sir, and give me your sword."

"Your pardon, my liege," said Hugh, colouring, "but I'll not be knighted for my henchman's feats, or at all until I have done some of my own."

"Ah, well, Master Hugh," said the King, "that's a right spirit. After the battle, perhaps, if it should please God that we live to meet again in honour. De Cressi," he added musingly, "why this place is called Crecy, and here, I think, is another good omen. At Crecy shall de Cressi gain great honour for himself and for St. George of England. You are luck bringers, you two. Let them not be separated in the battle, lest the luck should leave them. See to it, if it please you, my lord of Warwick. Young de Cressi can draw a bow; let him fight amongst the archers and have liberty to join the men-at-arms when the time comes. Or stay; set them near my son the Prince, for there surely the fight will be hottest.

"And now, you men of England, whatever your degree, my brothers of England, gentle and simple, Philip rolls down upon us with all the might of France, our heritage which he has stolen, our heritage and yours. Well, well, show him to-day, or to-morrow, or whenever it may be, that Englishmen put not their faith in numbers, but in justice and their own great hearts. Oh, my brothers and my friends, let not Edward, whom you are pleased to serve as your lawful King, be whipped off the field of Crecy and out of France! Stand to your banners, stand to your King, stand to St. George and God! Die where you are if need be, as I will. Never threaten and then show your backs like that knave the archer shot but now. Look, I give my son into your keeping," and he pointed to the young Prince, who all this while sat upon his horse upright and silent. "The Hope of England shall be your leader, but if he flies, why then, cut him down, and fight without him. But he'll not fly and you'll not fly; no, you and he together will this day earn a name that shall be told of when the world is grey with age. Great is the chance that life has given you; pluck it, pluck it from the land of opportunity and, dead or living, become a song forever in the mouths of men unborn. Think not of prisoners; think not of ransoms and of wealth. Think not of me or of yourselves, but think of England's honour, and for that strike home, for England watches you to-day."

"We will, we will! Fear not, King, we will," shouted the host in answer.

With a glad smile, Edward took his young son's hand and shook it; then rode away followed by his marshals.

"De Cressi," he said, as he passed Hugh, "the knave Acour, your foe and mine, is with Philip of France. He has done me much damage, de Cressi, more than I can stop to tell. Avenge it if you can. Your luck is great, you may find the chance. God be with you and all. My lords, farewell. You have your orders. Son Edward, fare you well, also. Meet me again with honour, or never more."

It was not yet noon when King Edward spoke these words, and long hours were to go by before the battle joined. Indeed, most thought that no blow would be struck that day, since it was known that Philip had slept at Abbeville, whence for a great army the march was somewhat long. Still, when all was made ready, the English sat them down in their ranks, bows and helmets at side, ate their mid-day meal with appetite, and waited whatever fate might send them.

In obedience to the King's command Hugh and Grey Dick had been attached to the immediate person of the Prince of Wales, who had about him, besides his own knights, a small band of chosen archers and another band of men-at-arms picked for their strength and courage. These soldiers were all dismounted, since the order had gone forth that knight and squire must fight afoot, every horse having been sent to the rear, for that day the English expected to receive charges, not to make them. This, indeed, would have been impossible, seeing that all along their front the wild Welsh had laboured for hours digging pits into which horses might plunge and fall.

There then the Prince's battle sat, a small force after all, perhaps twelve hundred knights and men-at-arms, with three or four thousand archers, and to their rear, as many of the savage, knife-armed Welsh who fought that day under the banner of their country, the red Dragon of Merlin. Grey Dick's place was on the extreme left of the archer bodyguard, and Hugh's on the extreme right of that of the men-at-arms, so that they were but a few yards apart and could talk together. From time to time they spoke of sundry things, but mostly of home, for in this hour of danger through which both of them could hardly hope to live, even if one did, their thoughts turned thither, as was but natural.

"I wonder how it fares with the lady Eve," said Hugh, with a sigh, for of her no news had come to him since they had parted some months before, after he recovered from the wound which Clavering gave him.

"Well enough, doubtless. Why not?" replied Dick. "She is strong and healthy, she has many friends and servants to guard her and no enemy there to harm her, for her great foe is yonder," and he nodded towards Abbeville. "Oh, without doubt well enough. It is she who should wonder how it fares with us. Let us hope that, having naught else to do, she remembers us in her prayers, since in such a case even one woman's prayers are worth something, for does not a single feather sometimes turn the scale?"

"I think that Eve would rather fight than pray," answered Hugh, with a smile, "like old Sir Andrew, who would give half his remaining days to sit here with us this afternoon. Well, he is better where he is. Dick, that knave Acour sent only insolent words in answer to my challenge, which I despatched to him by the knight I took and spared at Caen."

"Why should he do more, master? He can find plenty of ways of dying without risking a single combat with one whom he has wronged and who is therefore very dangerous. You remember his crest, master—a silver swan painted on his shield. I knew it, and that is why I shot that poor fowl just before you killed young Clavering on the banks of Blythe, to teach him that swans are not proof against arrows. Watch for the swan crest, master, when the battle joins, and so will I, I promise you."

"Ay, I'll watch," said Hugh grimly. "God help all swans that come my way. Let us pray that this one has not taken wing, for if so I, too, must learn to fly."

Thus they talked of these and other things amongst the hum of the great camp, which was like to that of bees on a lime-tree in summer, and whilst they talked the blue August sky became suddenly overcast. Dense and heavy clouds hid up its face, a cold and fitful wind began to blow, increasing presently to a gale which caused the planted standards, blazoned with lions rampant and with *fleurs-de-lis*, and the pennons of a hundred knights set here and there among the long battle lines, first to flap and waver and then to stand out straight as though they were cut of iron.

A word of command was called from rank to rank.

"Sheath bows!" it said, and instantly thousands of slender points were lifted and sank again, vanishing into the leathern cases which the archers bore.

Scarcely were these snug when the storm broke. First fell a few heavy drops, to be followed by such a torrent that all who had cloaks were glad to wear them. From the black clouds above leapt lightnings that were succeeded by the deep and solemn roll of thunder. A darkness fell upon the field so great that men wondered what it might portend, for their minds were strained. That which at other times would have passed without remark, now became portentous. Indeed, afterward some declared that through it they had seen angels or demons in the air, and others that they had heard a voice prophesying woe and death, to whom they knew not.

"It is nothing but a harvest tempest," said Dick presently, as he shook the wet from him like a dog and looked to the covering of his quiver. "See, the clouds break."

As he spoke a single red ray from the westering sun shot through a rift in the sky and lay across the English host like a sword of light, whereof the point hung over the eastern plain. Save for this flaming sword all else was dark, and silent also, for the rain and thunder had died away. Only thousands of crows, frightened from the woods, wheeled to and fro above, their black wings turning to the redness of blood as they crossed and recrossed that splendid path of light, and their hoarse cries filling the solemn air with clamour. The sight and sounds were strange, nor did the thickest-headed fellow crouched upon Crecy's fateful plain ever forget them till his dying day.

The sky cleared by slow degrees, the multitudes of crows wheeled off toward the east and vanished, the sun shone out again in quiet glory.

"Pray God the French fight us to-day," said Hugh as he took off his cloak and rolled it up.

"Why, master?"

"Because, Dick, it is written that the rain falls on the just and the unjust; and the unjust, that is the French, or rather the Italians whom they hire, use these new-fangled cross-bows which as you know cannot be cased like ours, and therefore stretch their strings in wet."

"Master," remarked Dick, "I did not think you had so much wit—that is, since you fell in love, for before then you were sharp enough. Well, you are right, and a little matter like that may turn a battle. Not but what I had thought of it already."

Hugh was about to answer with spirit, when a sound of distant shouting broke upon their ears, a very mighty sound, and next instant some outposts were seen galloping in, calling: "Arm! Arm! The French! The French!"

Suddenly there appeared thousands of cross-bow men, in thick, wavering lines, and behind them the points of thousands of spears, whose bearers as yet were hidden by the living screen of the Italian archers. Yes, before them was the mighty host of France glittering in the splendid light of the westering sun, which shone full into their faces.

The irregular lines halted. Perhaps there was something in the aspect of those bands of Englishmen still seated in silence on the ground, with never a horse among them, that gave them pause. Then, as though at a word of command, the Genoese cross-bow men set up a terrific shout.

"Do they think to make us run at a noise, like hares?" said Hugh contemptuously.

But Grey Dick made no answer, for already his pale eyes were fixed upon the foe with a stare that Hugh thought was terrible, and his long fingers were playing with the button of his bow-case. The Genoese advanced a little way, then again stood and shouted, but still the English sat silent.

A third time they advanced and shouted more loudly than before, then began to wind up their cross-bows.

From somewhere in the English centre rose a heavy, thudding sound which was new to war. It came from the mouths of cannons now for the first time fired on a field of battle, and at the report of them the Genoese, frightened, fell back a little. Seeing that the balls fell short and did but hop toward them slowly, they took courage again and began to loose their bolts.

"You're right, master," exclaimed Grey Dick in a fierce chuckle, "their strings *are* wet," and he pointed to the quarrels that, like the cannon balls, struck short, some within fifty paces of those who shot them, so that no man was hurt.

Now came a swift command, and the English ranks rose to their feet, uncased their bows and strung them all as though with a single hand. A second command and every bow was bent. A third and with a noise that was half hiss and half moan, thousands of arrows leapt forward. Forward they leapt, and swift and terrible they fell among the ranks of the advancing Genoese. Yes, and ere ever one had found its billet, its quiver-mate was hastening on its path. Then—oh! the sunlight showed it all—the Genoese rolled over by scores, their frail armour bitten through and through by the grey English arrows. By scores that grew to hundreds, that grew till the poor, helpless men who were yet unhurt among them wailed out in their fear, and, after one short, hesitant moment, surged back upon the long lines of men-at-arms behind.

From these arose a great shout: *"Trahison! Trahison! Tuez! Tuez!"*

Next instant the appalling sight was seen of the chivalry of France falling upon their friends, whose only crime was that their bow-strings were wet, and butchering them where they stood. So awful and unexpected was this spectacle that for a little while the English archers, all except Grey Dick and a few others cast in the same iron mould, ceased to ply their bows and watched amazed.

The long shafts began to fly again, raining alike upon the slaughterers and the slaughtered. A few minutes, five perhaps, and this terrible scene was over, for of the seven thousand Genoese but a tithe remained upon their feet, and the interminable French lines, clad in sparkling steel and waving lance and sword, charged down upon the little English band.

"Now for the feast!" screamed Grey Dick. "That was but a snack to sharp the appetite," and as he said the words a gorgeous knight died with his arrow through the heart.

It came, the charge came. Nothing could stop it. Down went man and horse, line upon line of them swept to death by the pitiless English arrows, but still more rushed on. They fell in the pits that had been dug; they died beneath the shafts and the hoofs of those that followed, but still they struggled on, shouting: "Philip and St. Denis!" and waving their golden banner, the Oriflamme of France.

The charge crept up as a reluctant, outworn wave creeps to a resisting rock. It foamed upon the rock. The archers ceased to shoot and drew their axes. The men-at-arms leapt forward. The battle had joined at last! Breast to breast they wrestled now. Hugh's sword was red, and red was Grey Dick's axe. Fight as they would, the English were borne back. The young Prince waved his arm, screaming something, and at that sight the English line checked its retreat, stood still, and next plunged forward with a roar of:

"England and the Prince!"

That assault was over. Backward rolled the ride of men, those who were left living. After them went the dark Welsh. Their commanders ordered them to stand; the Earl of Warwick ordered them to stand. The Prince himself ordered them to stand, running in front of them, only to be swept aside like a straw before a draught of wind. Out they broke, grinning and gnashing their teeth, great knives in their hands.

The red Dragon of Merlin which a giant bore led them on. It sank, it fell, it rose again. The giant was down, but another had it. They scrambled over the mass of dead and dying. They got among the living beyond. With eerie screams they houghed the horses and, when the riders fell, hacked open the lacings of their helms, and, unheeding of any cries for mercy, drove the great knives home. At length all were dead, and they returned again waving those red knives and singing some fierce chant in their unknown tongue.

The battle was not over yet. Fresh horses of Frenchmen gathered out of arrow range, and charged again under the banners of Blois, Alencon, Lorraine, and Flanders. Forward they swept, and with them came one who looked like a king, for he wore a crown upon his helm. The hawk-eyed Dick noted him, and that his bridle was bound to those of the knights who rode upon his either side. On them he rained shafts from his great black bow, for Grey Dick never shot without an aim, and after the battle one of his marked arrows was found fixed in the throat of the blind king of Bohemia.

This second charge could not be stayed. Step by step the English knights were beaten back; the line of archers was broken through; his guard formed round the Prince, Hugh among them. Heavy horses swept on to them. Beneath the hoofs of one of these Hugh was felled, but, stabbing it from below, caused the poor beast to leap aside. He gained his feet again. The Prince was down, a splendid knight—it was the Count of Flanders—who had sprung from his horse, stood over him, his sword point at his throat, and called on him to yield. Up ran Robert Fitzsimmon, the standard bearer, shouting:

"To the son of the King! To the son of the King!"

He struck down a knight with the pole of his standard. Hugh sprang like a wild-cat at Louis of Flanders, and drove his sword through his throat. Richard de Beaumont flung the great banner of Wales over the Prince, hiding him till more help came to beat back the foe. Then the Prince struggled from the ground, gasping:

"I thank you, friends," and once more the French retreated. The Welsh banner rose again and that danger was over.

The Earl of Warwick ran up. Hugh noted that his armour was covered with blood.

"John of Norwich," he cried to an aged knight, who stood leaning on his sword, "take one with you, away to the King and pray him for aid. The French gather again; we are outworn with blows; the young Prince is in danger of his life or liberty. Begone!"

Old John's eyes fell on Hugh.

"Come with me, you Suffolk man," he said, and away they went.

"Now what would you give," he gasped as they ran, "to be drinking a stoup of ale with me in my tower of Mettingham as you have done before this red day dawned? What would you give, young Hugh de Cressi?"

"Nothing at all," answered Hugh. "Rather would I die upon this field in glory than drink all the ale in Suffolk for a hundred years."

"Well said, young man," grunted John. "So do I think would I, though I have never longed for a quart of liquor more."

They came to a windmill and climbed its steep stairs. On the top stage, amid the corn sacks stood Edward of England looking through the window-places.

"Your business, Sir John?" he said, scarcely turning his head.

The old knight told it shortly.

"My son is not dead and is not wounded," replied the King, "and I have none to send to his aid. Bid him win his spurs; the day shall yet be his. Look," he added, pointing through the window-place, "our banners have not given back a spear's throw, and in front of them the field is paved with dead. I tell you the French break. Back, de Norwich! Back, de Cressi, and bid the Prince to charge!"

Some one thrust a cup of wine into Hugh's hand. He swallowed it, glancing at the wild scene below, and presently was running with Sir John toward the spot where they saw the Prince's banner flying. They came to Warwick and told him the King's answer.

"My father speaks well," said the Prince. "Let none share our glory this day! My lord, form up the lines, and when my banner is lifted thrice, give the word to charge. Linger not, the dark is near, and either France or England must go down ere night."

Forward rolled the French in their last desperate onset; horse and foot mingled together. Forward they rolled almost in silence, the arrows playing on their dense host, but not as they did at first, for many a quiver was empty. Once, twice, thrice the Prince's banner bowed and lifted, and as it rose for the third time there rang out a shout of:

"Charge for St. George and Edward!"

Then England, that all these long hours had stood still, suddenly hurled herself upon the foe. Hugh, leaping over a heap of dead and dying, saw in front of him a knight who wore a helmet shaped like a wolf's head and had a wolf painted upon his shield. The wolf knight charged at him as though he sought him alone. An arrow from behind—it was Grey Dick's—sank up to the feathers in the horse's neck, and down it came. The rider shook himself clear and began to fight. Hugh was beaten to his knee beneath a heavy blow that his helm turned. He rose unhurt and rushed at the knight, who, in avoiding his onset, caught his spur on the body of a dead man and fell backward.

Hugh leapt on to him, striving to thrust his sword up beneath his gorget and make an end of him.

"Grace!" said the knight in French, "I yield me."

"We take no prisoners," answered Hugh, as he thrust again.

"Pity, then," said the knight. "You are brave, would you butcher a fallen man? If you had tripped I would have spared you. Show mercy, some day your case may be mine and it will be repaid to you."

Hugh hesitated, although now the point of his sword was through the lacing of the gorget.

"For your lady's sake, pity," gasped the knight as he felt its point.

"You know by what name to conjure," said Hugh doubtfully. "Well, get you gone if you can, and pray for one Hugh de Cressi, for he gives you your life."

The knight seemed to start, then struggled to his feet, and, seizing a loose horse by the bridle, swung himself to the saddle and galloped off into the shadows.

"Master," croaked a voice into Hugh's ear, "I've seen the swan! Follow me. My arrows are all gone, or I'd have shot him."

"God's truth! show him to me," gasped Hugh, and away they leapt together.

Soon they had outrun even the slaughtering Welsh, and found themselves mingled with fugitives from the French army. But in the gathering twilight none seemed to take any note of them. Indeed every man was engaged in saving his own life and thought that this was the purpose of these two also. Some three hundred yards away certain French knights, mounted, often two upon one horse, or afoot, were flying from that awful field, striking out to the right in order to clear themselves of the cumbering horde of fugitives. One of these knights lagged behind, evidently because his horse was wounded. He turned to look back, and a last ray from the dying sun lit upon him.

"Look," said Dick; and Hugh saw that on the knight's shield was blazoned a white swan and that he wore upon his helmet a swan for a crest. The knight, who had not seen them, spurred his horse, but it would not or could not move. Then he called to his companions for help, but they took no heed. Finding himself alone, he dismounted, hastily examined the horse's wound, and, having unbuckled a cloak from his saddle, cast down his shield in order that he might run more lightly.

"Thanks to God, he is mine," muttered Hugh. "Touch him not, Dick, unless I fall, and then do you take up the quarrel till you fall."

So speaking he leapt upon the man out of the shadow of some thorns that grew there.

"Lift your shield and fight," said Hugh, advancing on him with raised sword. "I am Hugh de Cressi."

"Then, sir, I yield myself your prisoner," answered the knight, "seeing that you are two and I but one."

"Not so. I take no prisoners, who seek vengeance, not ransom, and least of all from you. My companion shall not touch you unless I fall. Swift now, the light dies, and I would kill you fighting."

The knight picked up his shield.

"I know you," he said. "I am not he you think."

"And I know you," answered Hugh. "Now, no words, of them there have been enough between us," and he smote at him.

For two minutes or more they fought, for the armour of both was good, and one was full of rage and the other of despair. There was little fine sword-play about this desperate duel; the light was too low for it. They struck and warded, that was all, while Grey Dick stood by and watched grimly. Some more fugitives came up, but seeing that blows passed, veered off to the left, for of blows they had known enough that day. The swan knight missed a great stroke, for Hugh leapt aside; then, as the Frenchman staggered forward, struck at him with all his strength. The heavy sword, grasped in both hands, for Hugh had thrown aside his shield, caught his foe where neck joins shoulder and sank through his mail deep into the flesh beneath. Down he went. It was finished.

"Unlace his helm, Dick," grasped Hugh. "I would see his face for the last time, and if he still lives—"

Dick obeyed, cutting the lashings of the helm.

"By the Saints!" he said presently in a startled voice, "if this be Sir Edmund Acour he has strangely changed."

"I am not Acour, lord of Noyon," said the dying man in a hollow voice. "Had you given me time I would have told you so."

"Then, in Christ's name, who are you?" asked Hugh, "that wear de Noyon's cognizance?"

"I am Pierre de la Roche, one of his knights. You have seen me in England. I was with him there, and you made me prisoner on Dunwich heath. He bade me change arms with him before the battle, promising me great reward, because he knew that if he were taken, Edward of England would hang him as a traitor, whereas me they might ransom. Also, he feared your vengeance."

"Well, of a truth, you have the reward," said Dick, looking at his ghastly wound.

"Where then is Acour?" gasped Hugh.

"I know not. He fled from the battle an hour ago with the King of France, but I who was doomed would not fly. Oh, that I could find a priest to shrive me!"

"Whither does he fly?" asked Hugh again.

"I know not. He said that if the battle went against us he would seek his castle in Italy, where Edward cannot reach him."

"What armour did he wear?" asked Dick.

"Mine, mine—a wolf upon his shield, a wolf's head for crest."

Hugh reeled as though an arrow had passed through him.

"The wolf knight, Acour!" he groaned. "And I spared his life."

"A very foolish deed, for which you now pay the price," said Dick, as though to himself.

"We met in the battle and he told me," said de la Roche, speaking very slowly, for he grew weak. "Yes, he told me and laughed. Truly we are Fate's fools, all of us," and he smiled a ghastly smile and died.

Hugh hid his face in his hands and sobbed in his helpless rage.

"The innocent slain," he said, "by me, and the guilty spared—by me. Oh, God! my cup is full. Take his arms, man, that one day I may show them to Acour, and let us be going ere we share this poor knight's fate. Ah! who could have guessed it was thus that I and Sir Pierre should meet and part again."

## Chapter 10
# The King's Champion

Back over that fearful field, whereof the silence was broken only by the groans of the wounded and the dying, walked Hugh and Grey Dick. They came to the great rampart of dead men and horses that surrounded the English line, and climbed it as though it were a wall. On the further side bonfires had been lit to lighten the darkness, and by the flare of them they saw Edward of England embracing and blessing his son, the Black Prince, who, unhelmeted, bowed low before him in his bloodstained mail.

"Who were they besides, Sir Robert Fitzsimmon and Richard de Beaumont who helped you when you were down, my son?" asked the King.

The Prince looked about him.

"I know not, Sire. Many, but here is one of them," and he pointed to Hugh, who just then appeared within the circle of the firelight. "I think that he slew the Count Louis of Flanders."

"Ah!" said the King, "our young merchant of Dunwich—a gallant man. Kneel you down, merchant of Dunwich."

Hugh knelt, and the King, taking the red sword from his hand, struck him with it on the shoulder, saying:

"Rise, Sir Hugh de Cressi, for now I give you that boon which your death-faced servant asked before the battle. You have served us, or rather England well, both of you. But whose armour is that the archer carries, Sir Hugh?"

"Sir Edmund Acour's, lord de Noyon, Sire, only, alack! another man was within the armour."

"Your meaning?" said the King briefly, and in few words Hugh told the tale.

"A strange story, Sir Hugh. It would seem that God fought against you in this matter. Also I am wroth; my orders were that none of my men should sally out, though I fear me that you are not the only one who has broken them, and for your great deeds I forgive you."

"Sire," said Hugh, dropping to his knee again, "a boon. This de Noyon, your enemy and mine, has cheated and mocked me. Grant to me and my servant, Richard the archer, permission to follow after him and be avenged upon him."

"What is this you ask, Sir Hugh? That you and your brave henchman should wander off into the depths of France, there to perish in a dungeon or be hanged like felons? Nay, nay, we need good men and have none to spare for private quarrels. As for this traitor, de Noyon, and his plot, that egg is broken ere it was hatched, and we fear him no more. You follow me, Sir Hugh, and your servant with you, whom we make a captain of our archers. Until Calais is taken, leave not our person for any cause, and ask no more such boons lest you lose our favour. Nay, we have no more words for you since many others seek them. Stand back, Sir Hugh! What say you, my lord of Warwick? Ay, it is a gruesome task, but let the Welshmen out, those wounded will be well rid of their pain, and Christ have mercy on their souls. Forget not when it is finished to gather all men that they may give thanks to God for His great mercies."

********

Well nigh a year had gone, for once again the sun shone in the brazen August heavens. Calais had fallen at last. Only that day six of her noblest citizens had come forth, bearing the keys of the fortress, clad in white shirts, with ropes about their necks, and been rescued from instant death at the hands of the headsman by the prayer of Queen Philippa.

In his tent sat Hugh de Cressi, who, after so much war and hardship, looked older than his years, perhaps because of a red scar across the forehead, which he had come by during the siege. With him was his father, Master de Cressi, who had sailed across from Dunwich with a cargo of provisions, whereof, if the truth were known, he had made no small profit. For they were sold, every pound of them, before they left the ship's hold, though it is true the money remained to be collected.

"You say that Eve is well, my father?"

"Aye, well enough, son. Never saw I woman better or more beautiful, though she wears but a sad face. I asked her if she would not sail with me and visit you. But she answered: 'Nay, how can I who am another man's wife? Sir Hugh, your son, should have killed the wolf and let the poor swan go. When the wolf is dead, then, perchance, I will visit him. But, meanwhile, say to him that Red Eve's heart is where it always was, and that, like all Dunwich, she joys greatly in his fame and is honoured in his honour.' Moreover, to Grey Dick here, she sends many messages, and a present of wines and spiced foods for his stomach and of six score arrows made after his own pattern for his quiver."

"But for me no gift, father?" said Hugh.

"Nothing, son, save her love, which she said was enough. Also, in all this press of business and in my joy at finding you safe I had almost forgotten it, there is a letter from the holy Father, Sir Andrew. I have it somewhere in my pouch amid the bills of exchange," and he began to hunt through the parchments which he carried in a bag within his robe.

At length the letter was found. It ran thus:

> *To Sir Hugh de Cressi, knight, my beloved godson:*
> With what rejoicings I and another have heard of your knightly deeds through the letters that you have sent to us and from the mouths of wounded soldiers returned from the war, your honoured father will tell you. I thank God for them, and pray Him that this may find you unhurt and growing ever in glory.
>
> My son, I have no good news for you. The Pope at Avignon, having studied the matter, (if indeed it ever reached his own ears) writes by one of his secretaries to say that he will not dissolve the alleged marriage between the Count of Noyon and the lady Eve of Clavering until the parties have appeared before him and set out their cause to his face. Therefore Eve cannot come to you, nor must you come to her while de Noyon lives, unless the mind of his Holiness can be changed. Should France become more quiet, so that English folk can travel there in safety, perchance Eve and I will journey to Avignon to lay her plaint before the Holy Father. But as yet this seems scarcely possible. Moreover, I trust that the traitor, Acour, may meet his end in this way or in that, and so save us the necessity. For, as you know, such cases take long to try, and the cost of them is great. Moreover, at the Court of Avignon the cause of one of our country must indeed be good just now when the other party to it is of the blood of France.
>
> Soon I hope to write to you again, who at present have no more to say, save that notwithstanding my years I am well and strong, and would that I sat with you before the walls of Calais. God's blessing and mine be on you, and to Richard the archer,

greetings. Dunwich has heard how he shot the foul-tongued Frenchman before the great battle closed, and the townsfolk lit a bonfire on the walls and feasted all the archers in his honour.
*Andrew Arnold*

"I have found another letter," said Master de Cressi, when Hugh had finished reading, "which I remember Sir Andrew charged me to give to you also," and he handed him a paper addressed in a large, childish hand.

Hugh broke its silk eagerly, for he knew that writing.

*Hugh,*
Clement the Pope will not void my false marriage unless I appear before him, and this as yet I cannot do because of the French wars. Moreover, he sets the curse of the Church upon me and any man with whom I shall dare to re-marry until this be done. For myself I would defy the Church, but not for you or for children that might come to us. Moreover, the holy father, Sir Andrew, forbids it, saying that God will right all in His season and that we must not make Him wroth. Therefore, Hugh, lover you are, but husband you may not be while de Noyon lives or until the Pope gives his dispensation of divorce, which latter may be long in winning, for the knave de Noyon has been whispering in his ear. Hugh, this is my counsel: Get you to the King again and crave his leave to follow de Noyon, for if once you twain can come face to face I know well how the fray will end. Then, when he is dead, return to one who waits for you through this world and the next.

Hugh, I am proud of your great deeds. No longer can they mock you as 'the merchant's son,' Sir Hugh. God be with you, as are my prayers and love.
*Eve Clavering*

I forgot to tell you that Sir Andrew is disturbed in heart. He looks into a crystal which he says he brought with him from the East, and swears he sees strange sights there, pictures of woe such as have not been since the beginning of the world. Of this woe he preaches to the folk of Dunwich, warning them of judgment to come, and they listen affrighted because they know him to be a holy man who has a gift from God. Yet he says that you and I, Eve, need fear nothing. May it be so, Hugh.—*E.*

Now when he had thought awhile and hidden up Eve's letter, Hugh turned to his father and asked him what were these sermons that Sir Andrew preached.

"I heard but one of them, son," answered Master de Cressi, "though there have been three. By the Holy Mother! it frightened me so much that I needed no more of that medicine. Nor, to tell truth, when I got home again could I remember all he said, save that it was of some frightful ill which comes upon the world from the East and will leave it desolate."

"And what think folk of such talk, father?"

"Indeed, son, they know not what to think. Most say that he is mad; others say that he is inspired of God. Yet others declare that he is a wizard and that his familiar brings him tidings from Cathay, where once he dwelt, or perchance, from hell itself. These went to the bishop, who summoned Sir Andrew and was closeted with him for three hours. Afterward he called in the complainers and bade them cease their scandal of wizardry, since he was sure that what the holy Father said came from above and not from below. He added that they would do well to mend their lives and prepare to render their account, as for his part he should also, since the air was thick with doom. Then he gave his benediction to the old knight and turned away weeping, and since that hour none talk of wizardry but all of judgment. Men in Dunwich who have quarrelled from boyhood, forgive each other and sing psalms instead of swearing oaths, and I have been paid debts that have been owing to me for years, all because of these sermons."

"An awesome tale, truly," said Hugh. "Yet like this bishop I believe that what Sir Andrew says will come to pass, for I know well that he is not as other men are."

That night, by special leave, Hugh waited on the King, and with him Grey Dick, who was ever his shadow.

"What is it now, Sir Hugh de Cressi?" asked Edward.

"Sire, after the great battle, nigh upon a year ago, you told me that I must serve you till Calais fell. I have served as best I could and Calais has fallen. Now I ask your leave to go seek my enemy—and yours—Sir Edmund Acour, Count de Noyon."

"Then you must go far, Sir Hugh, for I have tidings that this rogue who was not ashamed to wear another man's armour, and so save himself from your sword, is away to Italy this six months gone, where, as the Seigneur de Cattrina, he has estates near Venice. But tell me how things stand. Doubtless that Red Eve of yours—strangely enough I thought of her at Crecy when the sky grew so wondrous at nightfall—is at the bottom of them."

"That is so, Sire," and he told him all the tale.

"A strange case truly, Sir Hugh," said the King when he had heard it out. "I'll write to Clement for you both, but I doubt me whether you and your Eve will get justice from him, being English. England and Englishmen find little favour at Avignon just now, and mayhap Philip has already written on behalf of de Noyon. At the best His Holiness will shear you close and keep you waiting while he weighs the wool. No, Red Eve is right: this is a knot soonest severed by the sword. If you should find him, de Noyon could scarce refuse to meet you, for you shall fight him as the champion of our cause as well as of your own. He's at Venice, for our Envoy there reported it to me, trying to raise a fresh force of archers for the French.

"You have leave to go, Sir Hugh, who deserve much more, having served us well," went on the King. "We'll give you letters to Sir Geoffrey Carleon, who represents us there, and through him to the Doge. Farewell to you, Sir Hugh de Cressi, and to you, Captain Richard the Archer. When all this game is played, return and make report to us of your adventures, and of how de Noyon died. The Queen will love to hear the tale, and your nuptials and Red Eve's shall be celebrated at Westminster in our presence, for you have earned no less. Master Secretary, get your tools, I will dictate the letters. After they are signed to-morrow, see them into the hands of Sir Hugh, with others that I will give him for safe carriage, for alas I have creditors at Venice. Make out an open patent also to show that he and this captain travel as our messengers, charging all that do us service to forward them upon their journey."

********

Three days later Hugh and Grey Dick, in the character of royal messengers from the King of England to the Doge of Venice, took passage in a great vessel bound for Genoa with a cargo of wool and other goods. On board this ship before he sailed Hugh handed to his father letters for Eve and for Sir Andrew Arnold. Also he received from him money in plenty for his faring, and bills of exchange upon certain merchants of Italy, which would bring him more should it be needed.

Their parting was very sad, since the prophecies of Sir Andrew had taken no small hold upon Master de Cressi's mind.

"I fear me greatly, dear son," he said, "that we part to meet no more. Well, such is the lot of parents. They breed those children that heaven decrees to them; with toil and thought and fears they rear them up from infancy, learning to love them more than their own souls, for their sakes fighting a hard world. Then the sons go forth, north and south, and the daughters find husbands and joys and sorrows of their own, and both half forget them, as is nature's way. Last of all those parents die, as also is nature's way, and the half forgetfulness becomes whole as surely as the young moon grows to full. Well, well, this is a lesson that each generation must learn in turn, as you will know ere all is done. Although you are my youngest, I'll not shame to say I have loved you best of all, Hugh. Moreover, I've made such provision as I can for you, who have raised up the old name to honour, and who, as I hope, will once more blend the de Cressis and the Claverings, the foes of three generations, into a single House."

"Speak not so, father," answered Hugh, who was moved almost to tears. "Mayhap it is I who shall die, while you live on to a green old age. At least know that I am not forgetful of your love and kindness, seeing that after Eve you are dearer to me than any on the earth."

"Ay, ay, after Eve and Eve's children. Still you'll have a kind thought for me now and then, the old merchant who so often thwarted you when you were a wayward lad—for your own good, as he held. For what more can a father hope? But let us not weep before all these stranger men. Farewell, son Hugh, of whom I am so proud. Farewell, son Hugh," and he embraced him and went across the gangway, for the sailors were already singing their shanty at the anchor.

"I never had a father than I can mind," said Grey Dick aloud to himself, after his fashion, "yet now I wish I had, for I'd like to think on his last words when there was nothing else to do. It's an ugly world as I see it, but there's beauty in such love as this. The man for the maid and the maid for the man—*pish*! they want each other. But the father and the mother—they give all and take nothing. Oh, there's beauty in such love as this, so perhaps God made it. Only, then, how did He also make Crecy Field, and Calais siege, and my black bow, and me the death who draws it?"

********

The voyage to Genoa was very long, for at this season of the year the winds were light and for the most part contrary. At length, however, Hugh and Dick came there safe and sound. Having landed and bid farewell to the captain and crew of the ship, they waited on the head of a great trading house with which Master de Cressi had dealings.

This signor, who could speak French, gave them lodging and welcomed them well, both for the sake of Hugh's father and because they came as messengers from the King of England. On the morrow of their arrival he took them to a great lord in authority, who was called a Duke. This Duke, when he learned that one was a knight and the other a captain archer of the English army and that they both had fought at Crecy, where so many of his countrymen—the Genoese bowmen—had been slain, looked on them somewhat sourly.

Had he known all the part they played in that battle, in truth his welcome would have been rough. But Hugh, with the guile of the serpent, told him that the brave Genoese had been slain, not by the English arrows, for which even with their wet strings they were quite a match (here Dick, who was standing to one side grinned faintly and stroked the case of his black bow, as though to bid it keep its memories to itself), but by the cowardly French, their allies. Indeed Hugh's tale of that horrible and treacherous slaughter was so moving that the Duke burst into tears and swore that he would cut the throat of every Frenchman on whom he could lay hands.

After this he began to extol the merits of the cross-bow as against the long arm of the English, and Hugh agreed that there was much in what he said. But Grey Dick, who was no courtier, did not agree. Indeed, of a sudden he broke in, offering in his bad French to fight any cross-bow man in Genoa at six score yards, so that the Duke might learn which was the better weapon. But Hugh trod on his foot and explained that he meant something quite different, being no master of the French tongue. So that cloud passed by.

The end of it was that this Duke, or Doge, whose name they learned was Simon Boccanera, gave them safe conduct through all his dominion, with an order for relays of horses. Also he made use of them to take a letter to the Doge of Venice, between which town and Genoa, although they hated each other bitterly, there was at the moment some kind of hollow truce. So having drunk a cup of wine with him they bade him farewell.

Next morning the horses arrived, and with them two led beasts to carry their baggage, in charge of a Genoese guide. So they departed on their long ride of something over two hundred English miles, which they hoped to cover in about a week. In fact, it took them ten days, for the roads were very rough and the pack-beasts slow. Once, too, after they had entered the territory of Venice, they were set on in a defile by four thieves, and might have met their end had not Grey Dick's eyes been so sharp. As it was he saw them coming, and, having his bow at hand, for he did not like the look of the country or its inhabitants, leaped to earth and shot two of them with as many arrows, whereon the other two ran away. Before they went, however, they shot also and killed a pack-beast, so that the Englishmen were obliged to throw away some of their gear and go on with the one that remained.

At length, on the eleventh afternoon, they saw the lovely city of Venice, sparkling like a cluster of jewels, set upon its many islands amid the blue waters of the Adriatic. Having crossed some two miles of open water by a ferry which plied for the convenience of travellers, they entered the town through the western gate, and inquired as best they could (for now they had no guide, the Genoese having left them long before) for the house of Sir Geoffrey Carleon, the English Envoy. For a long while they could make no one understand. Indeed, the whole place seemed to be asleep, perhaps because of the dreadful heat, which lay over it like a cloud and seemed to burn them to the very bones.

Perplexed and outworn, at last Hugh produced a piece of gold and held it before a number of men who were watching them idly, again explaining in French that he wished to be led to the house of the English ambassador. The sight of the money seemed to wake their wits, for two or three of the fellows ran forward quarrelling with each other, till one of them getting the mastery, seized Hugh's tired horse by the bridle and dragged it down a side street to the banks of a broad canal.

Here he called something aloud, and presently two men appeared rowing a large, flat-bottomed punt from a dock where it was hidden. Into this boat the horses and pack-beast were driven, much against their will. Hugh and Dick having followed them, the three Italians began to punt them along the canal, which was bordered with tall houses. A mile or so farther on it entered another canal, where the houses were much finer and built in a style of which they had never seen the like, with beautiful and fantastic arches supported upon pillars.

At length to their great joy they came opposite to a house over the gateway of which, stirless in the still air, hung a flag whereon were blazoned the leopards of England. Here the boatmen, pulling in their poles, save one to which they made the punt fast in mid-stream, showed by their gestures that they desired to be paid. Hugh handed the piece of gold to the man who had led them to the boat, whereon he was seized with a fit of uncontrollable fury. He swore, he raved, he took the piece of gold and cast it down on the bilge-boards, he spat on it and his two companions did likewise.

"Surely they are mad," said Hugh.

"Mad or no, I like not the looks of them," answered Dick. "Have a care, they are drawing their knives," and as he spoke one of the rogues struck him in the face; while another strove to snatch away the pouch that hung at his side.

Now Grey Dick awoke, as it were. To the man who had tried to take his pouch he dealt such a buffet that he plunged into the canal. But him who had struck him he seized by the arm and twisted it till the knife fell from his hand. Then gripping his neck in an iron grasp he forced him downward and rubbed his nose backward and forward upon the rough edge of the boat, for the Italian was but as a child to him when he put out his strength.

In vain did his victim yell for mercy. He showed him none, till at length wearying of the game, he dealt him such a kick that he also flew over the thwarts to join his fellow-bully in the water.

Then seeing how it had gone with his companions who, sorely damaged, swam to the farther side of the canal and vanished, the third man, he whom they had first met, sheathed his knife. With many bows and cringes he pulled up the pole and pushed the punt to the steps of the house over which the flag hung, where people were gathering, drawn by the clamour.

"Does Sir Geoffrey Carleon dwell here?" asked Hugh in a loud voice, whereon a gentleman with a pale face and a grizzled beard who appeared to be sick, for he was leaning on a staff, hobbled from out the porch, saying:

"Ay, ay, that is my name. Who are you that make this tumult at my gates? Another turbulent Englishman, I'll be bound."

"Ay, sir, an Englishman called Sir Hugh de Cressi, and his companion, Richard the Archer, whom these rogues have tried to rob and murder, messengers from his Grace King Edward."

Now Sir Geoffrey changed his tone.

"Your pardon if I spoke roughly, Sir Hugh, but we poor Envoys have to do with many rufflers from our own land. Enter, I pray you. My servants will see to your gear and horses. But first, what is the trouble between you and these fellows?"

Hugh told him briefly.

"Ah!" he said, "a common trick with foreigners. Well for you that night had not fallen, since otherwise they might have rowed you up some back waterway and there done you to death. The canals of Venice hide the traces of many such foul deeds. Mother of Heaven!" he added, "why, this boatman is none other than Giuseppe, the noted bravo," and he turned and in Italian bade his servants seize the man.

But Giuseppe had heard enough. Springing into the water he

swam like a duck for the farther bank of the canal, and, gaining it, ran swiftly for some alley, where he vanished.

"He's gone," said Sir Geoffrey, "and as well hunt with a lantern for a rat in a sewer as for him. Well, we have his boat, which shall be sent to the magistrate with letters of complaint. Only, Sir Hugh, be careful to wear mail when you walk about at night, lest that villain and his mates should come to collect their fare with a stiletto. Now, enter and fear not for your goods. My folk are honest. God's name! how fearful is this heat. None have known its like. Steward, give me your arm."

*********

An hour later and Hugh, clad in fresh garments of sweet linen, bathed and shaved, sat at table in a great, cool room with Sir Geoffrey and his lady, a middle-aged and anxious-faced woman, while Grey Dick ate at a lower board with certain of the Envoy's household.

"I have read the letters which concern the business of his Grace the King," said Sir Geoffrey, who was toying languidly with some Southern fruits, for he would touch no meat. "They have to do with moneys that his Grace owes to great bankers of this city but does not yet find it convenient to discharge. I have seen their like before, and to-morrow must deal with them as best I may—no pleasant business, for these usurers grow urgent," and he sighed. "But," he added, "the King says that you, Sir Hugh de Cressi, whom he names his 'brave, trusty and most well beloved knight and companion in war,'" and he bowed courteously to Hugh, "have another business which he commands me to forward by every means in my power, and that without fail. What is this business, Sir Hugh?"

"It is set out, Sir Geoffrey, in a letter from his Grace to the Doge of Venice, which I am to ask you to deliver. Here it is. Be pleased to read it, it is open."

The Envoy took the letter and read it, lifting his eyebrows as he did so.

"By St. Mark,—he's the right saint to swear by in Venice"—he exclaimed when he had finished, "this is a strange affair. You have travelled hither to offer single combat to Edmund Acour, Count of Noyon and Seigneur of Cattrina. The Doge is urged by his friendship to the throne of England to bring about this combat to the death, seeing that de Noyon has broken his oath of homage, has plotted to overthrow King Edward, has fought against him and that therefore you are his Grace's champion as well as the avenger of certain private wrongs which you will explain. That's the letter. Well, I think the Doge will listen to it, because he scarce dare do otherwise who wishes no quarrel with our country just now when it is victorious. Also this de Noyon, whom we call Cattrina here, has allied himself with certain great men of the Republic, with whom he is connected by blood, who are secret enemies to the Doge. Through them he strives to stir up trouble between Venice and England, and to raise mercenaries to serve the flag of France, as did the Genoese, to their sorrow. Therefore I think that in the Doge you will find a friend. I think also that the matter, being brought forward with such authority, the Seigneur de Cattrina will scarcely care to refuse your challenge if you can show that you have good cause for quarrel against him, since in such affairs the Venetians are punctilious. But now tell me the tale that I may judge better."

So Hugh told him all.

"A strange story and a good cause," said Sir Geoffrey when he had done. "Only this Cattrina is dangerous. Had he known you came to Venice, mayhap you had never lived to reach my house. Go armed, young knight, especially after the sun sinks. I'll away to write to the Doge, setting out the heads of the matter and asking audience. The messenger shall leave ere I sleep, if sleep I may in this heat. Bide you here and talk with my lady, if it so pleases you, for I would show you my letter ere we bid good-night, and the thing is pressing. We must catch Cattrina before he gets wind of your presence in Venice."

## Chapter 11
# The Challenge

"How long is it since you have seen England, Sir Hugh?" asked Dame Carleon languidly.

"Some eighteen months, lady, although in truth it seems more, for many things have happened to me in that time."

"Eighteen months only! Why, 'tis four long years since I looked upon the downs of Sussex, which are my home, the dear downs of Sussex, that I shall see never again."

"Why say you so, lady, you have many years of life before you?"

"Because they are done, Sir Hugh. Oh, in my heart I feel that they are done. That should not grieve me, since my only child is buried in this glittering, southern city whereof I hate the sounds and sights that men call so beautiful. Yet I would that I might have been laid at last in the kind earth of Sussex where for generations my forbears have been borne to rest," and suddenly she began to weep.

"What ails you, lady? You are not well?"

"Oh, I know not. I think it is the heat or some presage of woe to come, not to me only, but to all men. Look, nature herself is sick," and she led him to the broad balcony of the chamber and pointed to long lines of curious mist which in the bright moonlight they could see creeping toward Venice from the ocean, although what wind there was appeared to be off land.

"Those fogs are unnatural," she went on. "At this season of the year there should be none, and these come, not from the lagoons, but up from the sea where no such vapours were ever known to rise. The physicians say that they foretell sickness, whereof terrible rumours have for some time past reached us from the East, though none know whether these be true or false."

"The East is a large place, where there is always sickness, lady, or so I have heard."

"Ay, ay, it is the home of Death, and I think that he travels to us thence. And not only I, not only I; half the folk in Venice think the same, though why, they cannot tell. Listen."

As she spoke, the sound of solemn chanting broke upon Hugh's ear. Nearer it grew, and nearer, till presently there emerged from a side street a procession of black monks who bore in front of them a crucifix of white ivory. Along the narrow margin which lay between the houses and the canal they marched, followed by a great multitude of silent people.

"It is a dirge for the dead that they sing," said Dame Carleon, "and yet they bury no man. Oh! months ago I would have escaped from this city, and we had leave to go. But then came orders from the King that we must bide here because of his creditors. So here we bide for good and all. Hush! I hear my husband coming; say nothing of my talk, it angers him. Rest you well, Sir Hugh."

"Truly that lady has a cheerful mind," grumbled Grey Dick, when she had gone, leaving them alone upon the balcony. "Ten minutes more of her and I think I should go hang myself, or squat upon these stones and howl at the moon like a dog or those whimpering friars."

Hugh made no answer, for he was thinking of his father's tale of the prophecies of Sir Andrew Arnold, and how they grew sad in Dunwich also. In truth, like Lady Carleon, he found it in his heart to wish that he too were clear of Venice, which he had reached with so much toil.

"Bah!" he said presently, "this place stinks foully. It puts me in mind of some woman, most beauteous indeed, but three days dead. Let us go in."

********

On the following morning, while they sat at breakfast, there came a messenger from the Doge of Venice, whose name Hugh learned was Andrea Dandolo, bearing a letter sealed with a great seal. This letter, when opened, was found to be from some high officer. It stated that the Doge would hold a Court at noon, after which it was his pleasure to receive the English knight who came as a messenger from the mighty monarch, King Edward, and to talk with him on matters set out in the letter of Sir Geoffrey Carleon. The writing added that the Seigneur of Cattrina, who in France was known as the Count de Noyon and in England as Sir Edmund Acour, would be present at the Court and doubtless ready to answer all questions that might be put to him.

"Then at last we shall come face to face," said Hugh, with a fierce laugh.

"Yes, master," put in Dick, "but you've done that several times before and always ended back to back. Pray the Saints such may not be the finish of this meeting also."

Then he turned and went to clean his master's armour, for in this martial dress, notwithstanding the great heat, Hugh determined to appear before the Doge. It was good armour, not that, save for the sword, which Sir Arnold had given him, whereat the Court at Windsor had laughed as out of date, but mail of a newer fashion, some of it, from the bodies of knights who fell at Crecy, after which battle such wares had been cheap.

Still, Dick could have wished that it had been better for so fine an occasion, seeing that it was marked with many a battle dint and that right across the Cressi cognizance, which Hugh had painted on his shield after he was knighted—a golden star rising from an argent ocean—was a scar left by the battle-axe of a Calais man-at-arms. Moreover Hugh, or rather Dick, took with him other armour, namely, that of the knight, Sir Pierre de la Roche, whom Hugh had killed at Crecy thinking that he was Edmund Acour, whose mail Pierre wore.

For the rest, Dick clad himself in his uniform of a captain of archers of King Edward's guard, wearing a green tunic over his mail shirt, and a steel-lined cap from which rose a heron's plume, pinned thereto with his Grace's golden arrow.

All being ready they started in a painted barge, accompanied by Sir Geoffrey Carleon, who wore his velvet robe of office, and grumbled at its weight and warmth. A row of some fifteen minutes along the great canal brought them to a splendid portal upon the mole, with marble steps. Hence they were conducted by guards across a courtyard, where stood many gaily dressed people who watched them curiously, especially Grey Dick, whose pale, sinister face caused them to make a certain sign with their fingers, to avert the evil eye, as Sir Geoffrey explained to them. Leaving this courtyard they went up more steps and along great corridors into the finest apartment that they had ever seen. It was a glitter of gold and marble, and rich with paintings.

Here on a kind of throne sat the Doge Dandolo, an imperial-looking man, magnificently attired. Guards stood like statues behind him, while in front, talking together and moving from place to place, were gathered all the great nobles of Venice, with their beauteous ladies. From time to time the Doge summoned one or other of these, who was called to him by a black-robed secretary. Advancing with bows the courtier talked to him a while, then was dismissed by a gracious motion of the hand.

As the Englishmen entered this hall a herald called their names thus from a written slip of paper:

"The Cavalier Geoffrey Carleon, Ambassador of England. The Cavalier Hugh de Cressi, Messenger from the King of England, and the Captain Richard Archer, his companion."

Now all talk was hushed and every eye turned to scan these strangers of whose business, it would seem, something was already known.

"A fine man," said one lady to another of Hugh, "but why does he come here in dinted armour?"

"Oh! he is English and the English are barbarians who like to be ready to cut some one's throat," answered her companion. "But Holy Jesus! look at the long fellow with the death's head who walks behind him, and carries his luggage in a sack. His face makes my back creep."

Fortunately neither Hugh nor Dick understood these and other such sayings which Sir Geoffrey repeated to them afterward and therefore walked on with their host unconcerned. Once, however, Grey Dick nudged his master and whispered in his ear:

"Be glad, our man is here. It is he who mocks us to those popinjays. Nay, turn not to look; you will see plenty of his sweet face presently."

Now they stood before the chair of state, from which the Doge rose, and advanced two steps to greet the Ambassador of England. When these courtesies were over Sir Geoffrey presented Hugh to him, to whom he bowed, and Dick, whose salute he acknowledged with a wave of his jewelled hand. Afterward they talked, all crowding round to listen, Sir Geoffrey himself, who spoke Italian well, acting as the interpreter.

"You come hither, Cavalier de Cressi," said the Doge, "on behalf of his royal Grace, King Edward, who speaks of you in his letter in terms of which any knight may well be proud. We understand that this captain with you is your companion," and he glanced curiously at Dick out of the corners of his dark eyes, adding, "If those are gifts which he bears in that leathern sack and the long case in his hand, let our servants relieve him of them."

"Let his servants leave me alone," growled Grey Dick when this was translated. "Say to this fine lord, Sir Knight, that the gifts in the sack are not for him, and that which the case scatters he would scarcely care to have."

Sir Geoffrey made some explanation in a low voice, and with a smile the Doge waved the matter by, then said:

"Will the noble cavalier be so good as to set out his business, unless it is for our private ear alone?"

Hugh answered that it was for the public ear of all Venice, and especially for that of the lord who was called Sir Edmund Acour in England, the Count de Noyon in France, and the Seigneur of Cattrina in Italy.

"Will you pleased to point out this lord to us," said the Doge, glancing at the gorgeous throng which was gathered behind them.

"I cannot, illustrious Doge," answered Hugh, "that is, with certainty. As it chances I have seen his face but twice—once in a marsh when I had other things to think of who must watch my enemy's sword, and once at eve in the corner of a dark chapel, where he had just gone through the rite of marriage with a lady whom he had drugged, which lady was my affianced wife. Often afterward I sought to see that face, especially in the great fray of Crecy, but failed, in a case which with your leave I will narrate to you."

Now when all that company understood the meaning of these outspoken words, they swayed to and fro and whispered like reeds in an evening wind. Presently above this whispering a soft yet penetrating voice was heard to say:

"If this English knight desires to study the poor face of Acour, de Noyon, and Cattrina, he who owns it is much honoured and prays your Excellency's leave to wait upon his pleasure."

So saying a tall and noble-looking man, who wore the badge of a white swan worked in pearls upon his rich tunic, stepped forward out of the ring of courtiers and bowed, first to the Doge and next to Hugh.

De Cressi looked at his handsome face with its quick dark eyes and little, square-cut, black beard, and answered:

"I thank you, Sir Edmund Acour, for I take it you are he. Now I shall never forget you again, for though a man may shift his armour he cannot change his countenance"—a saying at which de Noyon coloured a little and looked down uneasily.

"Cavalier de Cressi, he whom you seek is before you; we ourselves vouch for his identity," said the Doge. "Now be pleased to set out your case."

"My private case I thrust to one side," answered Hugh, Sir Geoffrey interpreting all the time, "for it is a matter between this Count, a certain lady and myself, and can wait. That which I have to lay before you, Illustrious, has to do with my master the King of England, as whose champion I am here to-day. I accuse this lord of the three names of black treachery to his august liege, Edward, all details of which treason I am prepared to furnish, and on behalf of that most puissant monarch I challenge him to single combat, as I am empowered and commissioned to do."

"Why should I fight the King of England's bravoes?" inquired Acour in a languid voice of those who stood about him, a question at which they laughed.

"If the charge of treason is not sufficient," went on Hugh, "I'll add to it one of cowardice. At the battle of Crecy, as a man here will bear me witness," and he pointed to Dick, "I overcame in single combat a knight who wore upon his shield the cognizance of a wolf and on his helm a wolf's head, which were the arms of Sir Pierre de la Roche. At this knight's prayer I spared his life, for that day we took no prisoners, and let him go. Afterward I fought with another knight carrying the cognizance of a white swan, the arms of the Count de Noyon, and slew him in fair and single fight. But before he died he told me that he bore that armour by command of his lord, the Count de Noyon, and that the said Count fought that day in his mail because he feared the vengeance of the King of England and my own. Thus it came about that the Wolf who fought paid the price for the Swan who fled away, hid in the armour of his friend, whom he left to die for him."

There followed a great silence, for all those noble lords and ladies who thought little of treason, which to most of them was a very familiar thing, were not a little stirred by this tale of cowardice and false arms. The Doge said:

"Noble Cattrina, you have heard the story of the English knight. What do you answer to it?"

"Only that it is a lie, Illustrious, like everything else that he has told us," replied Acour with a shrug of his broad shoulders.

"You said that you had a witness, Cavalier de Cressi," said the Doge. "Where is he?"

"Here," answered Hugh. "Stand forward, Dick, and tell what you saw."

Dick obeyed, and in his low, rasping voice, with more detail than Hugh had given, set out the story of those two combats at Crecy, of the sparing of the wolf knight and the slaying of the swan knight.

"What say you now, noble Cattrina?" asked the Doge.

"I say that the man lies even better than his master," answered Acour coolly, and all the Court laughed.

"Illustrious," said Hugh, "doubtless you have some herald at your

Court. I pray that he may fetch his book and tell us what are the arms of de Noyon and Cattrina, with all their colourings and details."

The Doge beckoned to an officer in a broidered tabard, who with bows, without needing to fetch any book, described the crest and arms of Cattrina in full particular. He added that, to his knowledge, these were borne by no other family or man in Italy, France, or England.

"Then you would know them if you saw them?" said Hugh.

"Certainly, cavalier. On it I stake my repute as a herald."

Now while all wondered what this talk might mean, the Doge and Acour most of any, although the latter grew uneasy, fearing he knew not what, Hugh whispered to Dick. Then Dick loosed the mouth of the leather sack he carried, and out of it tumbled on to the marble floor a whole suit of blood-stained armour.

"Whence came these?" asked Hugh of Dick.

"Off the body of the night, Sir Pierre de la Roche, whom you slew at Crecy. I stripped him of them myself."

"Whose crest and cognizance are these, herald?" asked Hugh again, lifting the helm and shield and holding them on high that all might see.

The herald stepped forward and examined them.

"Without doubt," he said slowly, "they are those of the lord of Cattrina. Moreover," he added, "five years ago I limned yonder swan upon this very shield with my own hand. I did it as a favour to Cattrina there, who said that he would trust the task to none but an artist."

Now the silence grew intense, so much so that the rustle of a lady's dress sounded loud in the great hall.

"What say you now, my lord of Cattrina?" asked the Doge.

"I say that there is some mistake, Illustrious. Even if there were none," he added slowly, "for their own good and lawful purposes knights have changed armour before to-day."

"There is no mistake!" cried Hugh in a ringing voice. "This signor of so many names is a signor of many coats also, which he can change to save his skin. He wore that of Sir Pierre de la Roche to protect himself from the vengeance of the King of England and of the English squire whom he had wronged. He took mercy from the hand of that squire, who, as he knew well, would have shown him none had he guessed the truth. He left the poor knight, whom he had bribed to be his double, to die beneath that same squire's hand who thought him named de Noyon. Therefore the blood of this de la Roche is on his head. Yet these are small matters of private conduct, and one that is greater overtops them. This false lord, as Sir Edmund Acour, swore fealty to Edward of England. Yet while he was bound by that sacred oath he plotted to depose Edward and to set up on his throne the Duke of Normandy.

"The King of England learned of that plot through me, and gave me charge to kill or capture the traitor. But when we came face to face in a consecrated church where I thought it sacrilege to draw sword, he, who had just done me bitter wrong, stayed not to answer the wrong. He slunk away into the darkness, leaving me felled by a treacherous blow. Thence he fled to France and stirred up war against his liege lord under the Oriflamme of King Philip. Now that this banner is in the dust he has fled again to Venice, and here, as I have heard, broods more mischief. Once, when after the sack of Caen I sent him my challenge, he returned to me an insolent answer that he did not fight with merchants' sons—he who could take mercy from the hand of a merchant's son.

"Now that for deeds done a King has made me knight, and now that this King under his seal and sign has named me his champion, in your presence, Illustrious, and in that of all your Court, I challenge Cattrina again to single combat to the death with lance and sword and dagger. Yes, and I name him coward and scullion if he refuses this, King Edward's gage and mine," and drawing the gauntlet from his left hand, Hugh cast it clattering to the marble floor at de Noyon's feet.

A babble of talk broke out in the great hall, and with it some *vivas* and clapping of hands, for Hugh had spoken boldly and well; moreover, the spectators read truth in his grey eyes. A dark figure in priest's robe—it was that of Father Nicholas, the secretary who had brewed Red Eve's potion—glided up to Cattrina and whispered swiftly in his ear. Then the Doge lifted his hand and there was silence.

"My lord of Cattrina," he said, "Sir Hugh de Cressi, speaking as the champion of our ally, the King of England, has challenged you to single combat *à outrance*. What say you?"

"I, Illustrious?" he answered in his rich voice, drawling out his words like one who is weary. "Oh, of course, I say that if yon brawler wishes to find a grave in fair Venice, which is more than he deserves, I am not the man to thwart him, seeing that his cut-throat King—"

"As the ambassador of that King I protest," broke in Sir Geoffrey. "It is an insult that such a word should be used before me."

"I accept the protest of his Excellency, who forgot his noble presence," replied Cattrina bowing back. "Seeing that his King, who is not a cut-throat"—here a titter of laughter went through the company, though it was evident from the frown upon his face that the Doge liked the jest ill—"has chosen to make a knight of this de Cressi. Or so he says, which will show you, friends all, how hard it must be to find gentlemen in England."

Again the company tittered, though Dick's grey face turned scarlet and he bit upon his pale lip until the blood ran.

"As you accept the challenge," broke in the Doge shortly, "cease from gibes, my lord, which more befit an angry woman's mouth than that of one whose life is about to be put to hazard, and take up the gage of his Grace of England."

Cattrina looked round and bade a page who waited on his person obey the Doge's command, saying:

"Your pardon, most Illustrious, if I do not touch that glove myself, as it seems somewhat foul. I think it must have served its owner in his useful labours at the dyer's vat before his master made him noble."

Now it was Hugh's turn to colour, but when he understood the insult Grey Dick could contain himself no more.

"Ay, Sir Cheat and Traitor," he said in his hissing voice. "The vat in which it has been dipped was that of the life-blood of your dupe, Sir Pierre de la Roche, and of many a nobler Norman. Oh, did we not stand where we do I'd thrust it down your false throat, and with it twist out your slanderous tongue."

"Peace, peace!" cried the Doge, while those present who understood English translated Dick's wild words to their neighbours, and Cattrina laughed mockingly at the success of his sneer. "Have I not said that such words are unseemly? Ah! I thought it; well, my lord, you have brought it on yourself."

For while he spoke, the page, a mincing young man tied up with bows and ribbon like a woman, had lifted the glove. Holding it between his thumb and forefinger, he returned it to Hugh with a low, mock bow, being careful as he did so, as all might see, to tread upon Dick's foot and hustle him. Next moment two things happened. The first was that, dropping his cased bow, Grey Dick seized that young in his iron grip and hurled him into the air so that he fell heavily on the marble floor and lay there stunned, the blood running from his nose and mouth. The second was that, seizing his gauntlet, Hugh strode to where Cattrina stood, and struck him with it across the face, saying:

"Let your lips kiss what your fingers are too fine to touch."

With an oath Cattrina drew his sword and out flashed Hugh's in answer, as he cried:

"Ay, here and now if you will! Here and now!"

Then the Guard rushed in and forced them apart.

"Is this a place for brawling?" cried Dandolo in wrath, adding: "Yet I cannot blame the Englishmen overmuch, seeing that they were sore affronted, as I saw with my eyes and heard with my ears. Be silent, my lord of Cattrina. After your fashion you make trouble at my Court. And—hearken all—blood so hot had best be quickly cooled lest one or other of these knights should take a fever. Moreover, the noble Cattrina has but to-day asked my leave to ride from Venice to-morrow, having urgent business at Avignon at the Court of Pope Clement. So I decree that this combat *à outrance* shall take place in our presence on the Campo del Marte to-morrow, three hours before noon, ere the sun grows too hot. To all the details of the combat our heralds will attend forthwith. Officer, take soldiers and escort the Ambassador and the Champion of his Grace of England, together with this Captain of Archers, back to their own door. Set guards there and see that none molest them by word or deed under pain of fine and strait imprisonment. Sir Geoffrey Carleon, your requests are granted; be pleased to write it to the most puissant Edward, whom you serve, and for this time fare you well. Why, what is it, Captain Ambrosio?" he added irritably, addressing a raw-boned, lantern-jawed giant of a man clad in the splendid uniform of the Guard who stepped before his throne and saluted.

"Most Illustrious," said Ambrosio, in bad, guttural Italian, "my mother was a Swiss."

"Then congratulations to the Swiss, Ambrosio, but what of it?"

"Very Illustrious," replied the captain in his hollow voice, "the Swiss are brave and do not swallow insults. That lad whom the Englishman kicked, or smote, or tossed like a bull," and he pointed to the poor page, who, still senseless, was being carried from the hall, "is my youngest brother, who resembles our Venetian father somewhat more than I do."

"We see it, we see it. Indeed are you sure that the father was—" and the Doge checked himself. "The point, captain; we would dine."

"Illustrious, I would avenge my brother and myself on the Englishman, whom I will beat to a jelly," said the giant. "I crave leave to fight him to-morrow when the lord Cattrina fights his master," and advancing toward Grey Dick he made as though he would pull his nose.

"What is it he wants?" asked Grey Dick, staring up at the great fellow with a look in his eyes that caused Ambrosio to cease flourishing his fists.

The challenge was translated to him, and its reason. "Oh," said Dick, "tell him I am much obliged and that I will fight him with the bow or with the axe and dagger, or with all three. Then we will see whether he beats me to a jelly, or whether I cut him into *collops*, who, as I think, needs shortening."

Now the Captain Ambrosio consulted with his friends, who with much earnestness prayed him have nothing to do with arrows. They pointed out that there his bulk would put him at a disadvantage, especially in dealing with an English archer who had an eye like a snake and a face like that of death itself.

In short, one and all they recommended the battle-axe and the dagger as his most appropriate weapons—since his adversary refused swords. The battle-axe with which to knock him down, as he could easily do, being so strong, and the dagger with which to finish him.

When this was explained to Grey Dick he assented to the proposal with a kind of unholy joy that was almost alarming to those who saw it. Moreover, as neither of them had gauntlets to throw down or pick up, he stretched out his hand to seal the bargain, which, incautiously enough, the huge, half-breed Swiss accepted.

Dick's grasp, indeed, was so firm and long that presently the giant was observed first to move uneasily, secondly to begin to dance and thirdly to shout out with pain.

"What is the matter?" asked his friends.

"The matter is," he groaned, as Dick let go, "that this son of Satan has a blacksmith's vice in place of a hand," and he showed his great fingers, from beneath the nails of which the blood was oozing.

His Venetian companions of the Guard looked at them, then they looked at Grey Dick and gave him a wide berth. Also Ambrosio said something about having offered to fight a man and not a fiend. But it was too late to retract, for the Doge, taking, as was natural, no share in this small matter, had already left his throne.

Then, escorted by Sir Geoffrey and the city Guards, Hugh and Grey Dick passed through that splendid company away home to dinner, Dick carrying his bow-case in one hand and the sack of armour which de Noyon had not thought fit to claim in the other.

In the midst of dead silence, they departed, for now no one seemed to find either of them a fit subject for jest. Indeed there were some who said, as they watched the pair pass the door, that Cattrina and the giant would do well to consult a lawyer and a priest that night.

## Chapter 12

# The Man From the East

In a great, cool room of his splendid Venetian palace, Sir Edmund Acour, Seigneur of Cattrina sat in consultation with the priest Nicholas. Clearly he was ill at ease; his face and his quick, impatient movements showed it.

"You arrange badly," he said in a voice quite devoid of its ordinary melodious tones. "Everything goes wrong. How is it you did not know that this accursed Englishman and his Death's-head were coming here? What is the use of a spy who never spies? Man, they should have been met upon the road, for who can be held answerable for what brigands do? Or, at the least, I might have started for Avignon two days earlier."

"Am I omnipotent, lord, that I should be held able to read the minds of men in far countries and to follow their footsteps?" asked the aggrieved Nicholas. "Still it might have been guessed that this bulldog of a Briton would hang to your heels till you kick out his brains or he pulls you down. Bah! the sight of that archer, who cannot miss, always gives me a cold pain in the stomach, as though an arrow-point were working through my vitals. I pity yonder poor fool of a Swiss to-morrow, for what chance has he against a fish-eyed wizard?"

"Ten thousand curses on the Swiss!" said Acour. "He thrust himself into the affair and will deserve all he gets. I pity myself. You know I am no coward, as not a few have learned before to-day, but I have little luck against this Englishman. I tell you that there at Crecy I went down before him like a ninepin, and he spared my life. My God! he spared my life, being a fool like all his breed. And now the tale is known against me and that of the changed armour, too. Why could not de la Roche die without speaking, the faithless hound whom I had fed so well! So, so, regrets are vain; de Cressi is here, and must be faced or I be shamed."

"You may be killed as well as shamed," Nicholas suggested unpleasantly. "It is certain that either you or that Englishman will die to-morrow, since he's set for no fancy tilting with waving of ladies' kerchiefs and tinsel crowns of victory, and so forth. Merchant bred or not, he is a sturdy fighter, as we all learned in France. Moreover, his heart is full with wrong, and the man whose quarrel is just is always to be feared."

"A pest on you!" snarled Cattrina. "Have you the evil eye that you then croak disaster in my ears? Look you, priest, I must come through this game unharmed. Death is a companion I do not seek just yet, who have too much to live for—power and wealth and high renown, if my plans succeed; and as you should know, they are well laid. Moreover, there is that English girl, Red Eve, my wife, from whose sweet side you made me flee. I tell you, Nicholas, I burn for her and had rather taste her hate than the love of any other woman on the earth. Now, too, the Pope has summoned me to Avignon, and her also, to lay our causes before him. Being bold, mayhap she will come, for his Holiness has sent her safe-conduct under his own hand. Nor has he mentioned—for I saw a copy of the brief—that the same business will take me to Avignon about this time. Well, if she comes she will not go away again alone; the French roads are too rough for ladies to travel unescorted. And if she does not come, at least our marriage will be declared valid and I'll take her when and where I can, and her wealth with her, which will be useful."

"Only then, lord, you must not die, nor even be wounded, to-morrow. It is the Englishman who should die, for whatever the Pope may decree I think that while de Cressi lives the slumberous eyes of that Eve of yours will find a way to charm you to a sleep that has no wakening. She is not a fair-haired toy that weeps, forgets and at last grows happy in her babe. She's a woman to make men or break them. Oh, when her sense came back to her, for a flash she looked me cold yonder in that English chapel, and it seemed to me that God's curse was in her stare."

"You've caught the terror, Nicholas, like so many just now in Venice. Why, to-day I've not met a man or woman who is not afraid of something, they know not what—save the Englishman and his death's-head. I think 'tis the unwholesome air of this strange season, and all the signs and omens we hear of on every side that conjure vapours to the brain."

"Yes, I've the terror," said Nicholas with something like a groan. "Every sin I ever did—and most of them have been for you, lord—

seems to haunt my sleep. Yes, and to walk with me when I wake, preaching woe at me with fiery tongues that repentance or absolution cannot quench or still."

"Yet, Nicholas, I think that you must add one more to their count, or a share of it, which should weigh light among so many. Either I or de Cressi must pack for our last journey, and if we meet face to face to-morrow, how know I that it will be de Cressi? Better far that we should not meet."

"Lord, lord, you cannot fly! He is King Edward's champion, so proclaimed before all whose names are written in the Golden Book of Venice. He would cry your shame in every Court, and so would they. There's not a knight in Europe but would spit upon you as a dastard, or a common wench but would turn you her back! You cannot fly!"

"Nay, fool, but he can die—and before to-morrow. What makes your brain so dull, Nicholas? It is not its wont."

"Ah, I see—not flight, murder. I had forgotten; it is not a usual sauce to a banquet of honour even in Italy, and therefore, perhaps, the safer to serve. But how is it to be done? Poison? He is in Carleon's house; Carleon has faithful servants. Though perhaps a basket of rare fruits—but then he might not eat them; those Englishmen live mostly on half-raw meat. The *signora* would probably eat them, and the others."

"Nay, no more of your drugs; your skill in them is too well known. Come, these men have been watched since they set foot in Venice. Have they offended none besides myself and the Swiss?"

A look of intelligence crept into the eyes of Nicholas.

"Now that you mention it, lord, they have. There is a certain boatman and bravo called Giuseppe. With him and his mates they quarrelled about their fare and threw them into the canal in front of the ambassador's house, just because they drew a knife or two. A woman I know told me of it. He's a great villain, this Giuseppe, who would do anything for ten pieces, also revengeful and a hater of cold water."

"Send for him, Nicholas, or send this woman to him—that may be safer. Ten pieces! I'll pay him fifty."

"Ay, lord, but the Englishman may not give him a chance. Only fools would go out walking in Venice along after dark if they should happen to have enemies here, and the house is watched by the Doge's Guards. Yet one can try. Fortune loves the brave, and Englishmen are very great fools. They might stroll abroad to see the moon rise over the Adriatic."

"Try, Nicholas, try as you never tried before. Succeed, too, lest you and I should part company and you never be named abbot after all."

********

The afternoon of the day of their reception by the Doge was well filled for Hugh and Dick. Scarcely had they eaten with their host when the Marshal and his officers arrived with the articles of the Morrow's combat very fully drawn up, each of which must be considered with the help of Sir Geoffrey Carleon, lest they should hide some trick, before they confirmed them with their signatures. Not that Hugh was over-anxious about the details. As he said to Sir Geoffrey, all he sought was to come face to face with his enemy, even if he had but a club for a weapon.

At length these articles were signed and the Marshal departed with his fee, for they must be paid for as though they were a legal document. Next Hugh must try various horses from Sir Geoffrey's stable, and choose one of them as his war steed for the morrow, since the beast he had ridden to Venice was in no condition to bear a full-armed knight. In the end he selected a grey gelding, quiet of temperament and rather heavy of build, which it was reported had been used by its former owner in several tournaments and there borne itself handsomely. This done, well or ill, his armour must be seen to, and Dick's also, such as it was; his lance tested, and all their other weapons sharpened on a whetstone that Sir Geoffrey borrowed. For this was a task that Grey Dick would leave to no other hand.

At length all was prepared as well as possible in such haste, and they went to supper with Lady Carleon, who, now she understood that they were to fight for their lives on the morrow, was more mournful even than she had been on the previous night. When at last she asked what they desired as to their funerals and if they had any tokens to be sent to friends in England, Hugh, whose thoughts were already sad enough, could bear no more of it. So he rose, saying that he would seek Sir Geoffrey, who was already in his cabinet engaged upon a letter to King Edward descriptive of these events and other business. But when they were out of the room he said that he must have fresh air or he would faint, which was not strange, seeing that heat prevailed on this night in Venice of an intensity unknown there at this season of the year.

"Whither shall we go?" asked Dick, mopping his brow. "Guards stand at the door and, I doubt, will not let us pass."

"I wish to see the place where we are to fight to-morrow," answered Hugh, "so as to form my judgment of it, if only we may come there."

At this moment an English lad of Sir Geoffrey's household chanced to pass by, having come to ask as to the feeding of the horse which Hugh should ride. Dick caught him by the arm and asked whether he could get them out of the house secretly, so that the Guards would not see them, and conduct them to the spot called the Place of Arms, where they understood they were to fight.

The lad, whose name was David Day, replied somewhat doubtfully that he could do so by a back door near the kitchen, and guide them also, but that they must protect him from the anger of Sir Geoffrey. This Hugh promised to do. So presently they started, carrying their weapons, but wearing no mail because of the intense heat, although Dick reminded his master how they had been told that they should not venture forth without body armour.

"I have a sword and you have bow and axe," answered Hugh, "so we'll risk it. In leather-lined mail we should surely melt."

So they put on some light cloaks made of black silk, with hoods to them, such as the Venetians wore at their masques, for David knew where these were to be found. Slipping out quite unobserved by the kitchen door into a little courtyard, they passed into an unlighted back street through a postern gate whereof the lad had the key. At the end of the street they came to a canal, where David, who talked Italian perfectly, hailed a boat, into which they entered without exciting remark. For this sharp youth pointed to their cloaks and told the boatman that they were gallants engaged upon some amorous adventure.

On they rowed down the silent lanes of water, through the slumberous city of palaces, turning here, turning there, till soon they lost all knowledge of the direction in which they headed. At length David whispered to them that they drew near the place where they must land. Everybody seemed to speak in a whisper that heavy night, even the folk, generally so light of heart and quick of tongue, who sat on the steps or beneath the porticoes of their houses gasping for air, and the passers-by on the *rivas* or foot walks that bordered the canals. At a sign from David the boat turned inward and grated against the steps of a marble quay. He paid the boatman, who seemed to have no energy left to dispute the fare, telling him in the same low voice that if he cared to wait he might perhaps row them back within an hour or so. Then they climbed steps and entered a narrow street where there was no canal, on either side of which stood tall houses or dark frowning gateways.

Just as they stepped into the shadow of this street they heard the prow of another boat grate against the marble steps behind them and caught the faint sound of talk, apparently between their rower and others in the second boat.

"Forward, Sir Hugh," said Day a little nervously. "This part of Venice has no good name, for many wicked deeds are done here, but soon we shall be through it."

So they stepped out briskly, and when they were about half-way down the street heard other steps behind them. They turned and looked back through the gloom, whereon the sound of the following steps died away. They pushed on again, and so, unless the echo deceived them, did those quick, stealthy steps. Then, as though by common consent, though no one gave the word, they broke into a run and gained the end of the street, which they now saw led into a large open space lit by the light of the great moon, that broke suddenly through the veil of cloud or mist. Again, as though by common consent, they wheeled round, Hugh drawing his sword, and perceived emerging from the street six or seven cloaked fellows, who, on catching sight of the flash of steel, halted and melted back into the gloom.

"Who follow us so fast?" asked Hugh.

"Thieves, I think," answered David, even more nervously than before, adding, "but if so, we are safe from them here."

"Yes, sure enough," said Grey Dick, "for I can shoot by moonlight," and, drawing the black bow from its case, which he threw to the lad to carry, he strung it, after which they saw no more of their pursuers.

Having waited a while, they began to examine the spot where they found themselves, which Day told them was that Place of Arms where they must fight on the morrow. It was large and level, having been used as a drilling ground for generations. Perhaps it measured four hundred yards square, and almost in the centre of it rose a stand of painted timber roofed with canvas, and ornamented with gilded flagstaffs, from which hung banners. On this stand, David said, the Doge and nobles would take their seats to see the fray, for in front of it the charging knights must meet.

They walked up and down the course taking note of everything, and especially of how the sun would shine upon them and the foothold of the soil, which appeared to be formed of fine, trodden sand.

"I ask no better ground to fight on," said Hugh at length, "though it is strange to think," he added with a sigh, "that here within a dozen hours or so two men must bid the world farewell."

"Ay," answered Dick, who alone seemed untouched by the melancholy of that night. "Here will die the knave with three names and the big fool of a half-bred Swiss, and descend to greet their ancestors in a place that is even hotter than this Venice, with but a sorry tale to tell them. By St. George! I wish it were nine of the clock to-morrow."

"Brag not, Dick," said Hugh with a sad smile, "for war is an uncertain game, and who knows which of us will be talking with his ancestors and praying the mercy of his Maker by this time to-morrow night?"

Then, having learned all they could, they walked across the ground to the quay that bordered it on the seaward side. Here, as they guessed from the stone pillars to which ships were made fast, was one of the harbours of Venice, although as it happened none lay at that quay this night. Yet, as they looked they saw one coming in, watched curiously by groups of men gathered on the wall.

"Never knew I vessel make harbour in such a fashion," exclaimed Dick presently. "See! she sails stern first."

Hugh studied her and saw that she was a great, decked galley of many oars, such as the Venetians used in trading to the East, high-bowed and pooped. But the strange thing was that none worked these oars, which, although they were lashed, swung to and fro aimlessly, some yet whole and some with their blades broken off and their shafts bundles of jagged splinters. Certain sails were still set on the ship's mast, in tatters for the most part, though a few remained sound, and it was by these that she moved, for with the moonrise a faint wind had sprung up. Lastly, she showed no light at peak or poop, and no sound of officer's command or of boatswain's whistle came from her deck. Only slowly and yet as though of set purpose she drifted in toward the quay.

Those who watched her, sailors such as ever linger about harbours seeking their bread from the waters, though among these were mingled people from the town who had come to this open place to escape the heat, began to talk together affrightedly, but always in the dread whisper that was the voice of this fearful knight. Yes, even the hoarse-throated sailormen whispered like a dying woman.

"She's no ship," said one, "she's the wraith of a ship. When I was a lad I saw such a craft in the Indian seas, and afterward we foundered, and I and the cook's mate alone were saved."

"Pshaw!" answered another, "she's a ship right enough. Look at the weed and barnacles on her sides when she heaves. Only where in Christ's name are her crew?"

"Yes," said a third, "and how could she win through all the secret channels without a pilot?"

"What use would be a pilot," said a fourth, "if there are none to work the rudder and shift the sails? Do I not know, who am of the trade?"

"At least she is coming straight to the quay," exclaimed a fifth, "though what sends her Satan alone knows, for the tide is slack and this wind would scarce move a sponge boat. Stand by with the hawser, or she'll swing round and stave herself against the pier."

So they talked, and all the while the great galley drifted onward with a slow, majestic motion, her decks hid in shadow, for a sail cut off the light of the low moon from them. Presently, too, even this was gone, for the veil of cloud crept again over the moon's face, obscuring everything.

Then of a sudden a meteor blazed out in the sky, such a meteor as no living man had ever seen in Venice, for the size of it was that of the sun. It seemed to rise out of the ocean to the east and to travel very slowly across the whole arc of the firmament till at last it burst with a terrible noise over the city and vanished. While it shone, the light it gave was that of mid-day, only pale blue in colour, turning all it touched to a livid and unnatural white.

It showed the placid sea and fish leaping on its silver face half-a-mile or more away. It showed the distant land with every rock and house and bush. It showed the wharf and the watchers on it; among them Hugh noted a man embracing his sweetheart, as he thought under cover of the cloud. But most of all it showed that galley down to her last rope and even the lines of caulking on her deck. Oh, and now they saw the rowers, for they lay in heaps about the oars. Some of them even hung over these limply, moving to and fro as they swung, while others were stretched upon the benches as though they slept. They were dead—all dead; the wind following the meteor and blowing straight on shore told them that they were certainly all dead. Three hundred men and more upon that great ship, and all dead!

Nay, not all, for now on the high poop stood a single figure who seemed to wear a strange red head-dress, and about his shoulders a black robe. Straight and silent he stood, a very fearful figure, and in his hand a coil of rope. The sight of him sent those watchers mad. They ceased from their whisperings, they raved aloud.

"It is Satan!" they shouted, "Satan, who comes to drag the folk of Venice down to hell. Kill him ere he lands. Kill him!"

Even Grey Dick went mad like a dog when he meets a ghost. His pale hair rose upon his head, his cold, quiet eyes started. He set an arrow on the string of the black bow, drew it to his ear and loosed at the figure on the poop. But that arrow never left the string; it shattered to flinders where it was and fell tinkling to the marble floor. Only the barb of it turned and wounded Grey Dick in the chin, yes, and stuck there for a while, for his right arm was numbed so that he could not lift his hand to pull it forth.

"Truly, I have shot at the Fiend and hit that at which I did not aim," muttered Grey Dick, and sat himself down on a post of the quay to consider the matter. Only, as it seemed to him, he who stood on the poop of the ship not ten yards away smiled a little.

Unheeding of the clamour, this man upon the poop suddenly lifted the coil of rope and threw it shoreward. It was a thick and heavy rope, with a noose at its end, so heavy that none would have believed that one mortal could handle it. Yet it shot from him till it stood out stiff as an iron bar. Yes, and the noose fell over one of the stone posts on the quay, and caught there. Now the rope grew straighter still, stretching and groaning like a thing in pain as it took the weight of the great, drifting ship. She stayed; she swung round slowly and ranged herself broadside on against the quay as a berthed ship does. Then down the ladder on her side came the Man. Deliberately he set his white-sandaled feet upon the quay, advanced a few paces into the full light of the bright moon and stood still as though to suffer himself to be seen of every eye.

Truly he was worth the seeing. Hugh noted his garments first, and particularly the head-dress, which caught his glance and held it, for never had he known such a one before. It was a cap fitting tight to the skull, only running across the crown of it was a stiff raised ridge, of leather perhaps, jagged and pointed something like the comb of a cock. This comb, of brilliant red, was surmounted at its highest point by a ball of black of the size of a small apple. The cap itself was yellow, except its lowest band, which stood out from it and was also black. In the centre of this band upon the forehead glowed a stone like a ruby.

Such was the head-dress. The broad shoulders beneath were covered with a cape of long and glossy fur blacker than coal, on to either shoulder of which drooped ear-rings made of rings of green stone which afterward Hugh came to know was jade. The cape of fur, which hung down to the knees and was set over a kind of surplice of yellow silk, was open in front, revealing its wearer's naked bosom that was clothed only with row upon row of round gems of the size of a hazel nut. These like the fur were black, but shone with a strange and lustrous sheen. The man's thick arms were naked, but on his hands he wore white leather gloves made without division like a sock, as though to match the white sandals on his feet.

This was the Man's attire. Now for him who wore it. He was tall, but not taller than are many other men; he was broad, but not broader than many other men, and yet he looked stronger than all the men in the world. On his brow, which was prominent, smooth black hair parted in the middle was plastered back as that of women sometimes is, making hard lines against the yellow skin below. He had very thin eyebrows that ran upward on either side of a bow-shaped wrinkle in the centre of his forehead. The eyes beneath were small and pale—paler even than those of Grey Dick—yet their glance was like the points of thrusting swords. With those little eyes alone he seemed to smile, for the rest of his countenance did not move. The nose was long and broad at the end with wide spreading nostrils and a deep furrow on either side. The mouth was thin-lipped and turned downward at the corners, and the chin was like a piece of iron, quite hairless, and lean as that of a man long dead.

There he stood like some wild vision of a dream, smiling with those small unblinking eyes that seemed to take in all present one by one. There he stood in the moonlit silence, for the mob was quiet enough now for a little while, that yet was not silence because of a soughing noise which seemed to proceed from the air about his head.

Then suddenly the tumult broke out again with its cries of "Kill the devil! Tear the wizard to pieces! Death is behind him! He brings death! Kill, kill, kill!"

A score of knives flashed in the air, only this time Grey Dick set no arrow on his string. Their holders ran forward; then the Man lifted his hand, in which was no weapon, and they stopped.

Now he spoke in a low voice so cold that, to Hugh's excited fancy, the words seemed to tinkle like falling ice as one by one they came from his lips. He spoke in Italian—perfect Italian of Venice—and young Day, whose teeth where chattering with fear, translated his words.

"Is this your welcome to a stranger," he said, "the companions of whose voyage have unhappily met with misfortune?" Here with a faint motion of his fingerless glove he indicated the dead who lay all about the decks of that fatal ship. "Would you, men of Venice, kill a poor, unarmed stranger who has travelled to visit you from the farthest East and seen much sorrow on his way?"

"Ay, we would, sorcerer!" shouted one. "Our brothers were in that ship, which we know, and you have murdered them."

"How did you learn Italian in the farthest East?" asked another.

Then for the second time, like hounds closing in on a stag at bay, they sprang toward him with their poised knives.

Again he lifted his hand, again the semi-circle halted as though it must, and again he spoke.

"Are there none here who will befriend a stranger in a strange land? None who are ashamed to see a poor, unarmed stranger from the East done to death by these wolves who call themselves children of the white Christ of Mercy?"

Now Hugh touched Dick upon the shoulder.

"Rise and come," he said, "it is our fate"; and Dick obeyed.

Only after he had translated the Man's words, David fell down flat upon the quay and lay there.

They stepped to the yellow-capped Man and stood on each side of him, Hugh drawing his sword and Dick the battle-axe that he carried beneath his robe of silk.

"We will," said Hugh shortly, in English.

"Now there are three of us," went on the Man. "The stranger from the East has found defenders from the West. On, defenders, for I do not fight thus," and he folded his arms across his broad breast and smiled with the awful eyes.

Hugh and Dick knew no Italian, yet they both of them understood, and with a shout leaped forward toward those hungry knives. But their holders never waited for them. Some sudden panic seized them all, so that they turned and ran—ran straight across the wide Place of Arms and vanished into the network of narrow streets by which it was surrounded.

## Chapter 13

# Murgh's Arrow

Hugh and Dick came back. Something seemed to call them back, although no blow had been struck. The Man stood where they had left him, staring at nothing in particular. Apparently he was engaged in meditation.

"Thanking his gods because they have saved him from sudden death," muttered Grey Dick. "If he's got any gods!" he added doubtfully.

Now the three, or rather the four of them, for David Day had recovered, and once more stood upon his feet from time to time glancing at the stranger's costume with a frightened eye, were left alone upon the great place with no company save the shipful of dead behind them and the wild, white moon above. The silence that, save for the soughing sound for which they could not account, was intense, oppressed them, as also did the heat.

Grey Dick coughed, but the Man took no notice. Then he dropped his axe with a clatter on the marble flooring of the quay and picked it up again, but still the Man took no notice. Evidently his Eastern imperturbability was not to be disturbed by such trifles. What was worse, or so thought Dick, his master Hugh had fallen into a very similar mood. He stood there staring at the Man, while the Man stared over or through him—at nothing in particular.

Grey Dick felt aggrieved. An arrow had burst to pieces unaccountably in his bow, numbing his arm and wounding him on the chin, and now he was outpaced at his own game of cold silence. He grew angry and dug David in the ribs with his elbow.

"Tell that foreigner," he said, "that my master and I have saved his life. Those Italian cut-throats have run away, and if he is a gentleman he should say 'thank you.'"

David hesitated, whereon Dick gave him another dig, harder than the first, and asked if he heard what he said. Then David obeyed, addressing the Man as "Most Illustrious" as though he were the Doge, and ending his speech with a humble apology in case he should have interrupted his pious thanksgiving.

The Man seemed to awake. Taking no notice of Day, he addressed himself to Dick, speaking in English and using just that dialect of it to which he, Dick, had been accustomed from his childhood in the neighbourhood of Dunwich. Not even the familiar Suffolk whine was forgotten.

"You and your master have saved my life, have you?" he said. "Well, neighbour, why did you try to save my life by shooting at me with that great black bow of yours, which I see is made of Eastern woods?" He stared at the case in which it was now again hidden as though tanned leather were no obstacle to his sight; then went on: "Do not answer: I will tell you why. You shot at me because you were afraid of me, and fear is ever cruel, is it not? Only something happened to your arrow, something that has never happened to any arrow of yours before. Oh, yes, you have saved me from the Italian cut-throats, and being a gentleman I thank you very much. Only why did the arrow burst in your bow?" and he smiled with those dreadful eyes of his.

Now, feeling overwhelmed for the second time that night, Grey Dick sat himself down upon a quay post. It was clear to him that to argue with this person in a yellow cap who talked Suffolk so well was quite useless. Why, then, waste breath which was probably his last?

Everybody seemed to be falling into meditation again, when the Man, shifting his head slowly, began to consider Hugh.

"What is your name and which is your country, O my second saviour?" he asked, still speaking in English. Only now the English was of a different and more refined sort to that which he had used when he addressed Dick; such English, for instance, as came from the lips of Sir Geoffrey Carleon or from those of the lords of Edward's Court.

"I am Sir Hugh de Cressi of Dunwich, in the county of Suffolk, in England," answered Hugh slowly.

"England. I have heard of England, and Dunwich; I have heard of Dunwich. Indeed, I travel thither, having an appointment with an old friend in that town."

Now a light came into Hugh's bewildered face, but he said nothing.

"I seem to have touched some chord of recollection in your mind, O my saviour of Dunwich," said the Man. "Look at me and tell me, who am I?"

Hugh looked, and shook his head.

"I never saw you before, nor any one at all like you," he answered.

"No, no; you never saw me, though I have been very near to you once or twice. Yet, your pardon, look again."

Hugh obeyed, and this time, for a second only, perceived that the Man's head was surrounded by a multitude of doves. Two endless lines of doves, one line black and the other line white, stretched from his right shoulder and from his left shoulder, till miles away they melted into the lofty gloom of the sky that was full of the soughing sound of their wings.

Now he knew, and for the first time in his life fell upon his knees to a man, or to what bore the semblance of man.

"You are named Murgh, Gate of the Gods," he said. "Murgh, whom old Sir Andrew saw in that courtyard over which the iron dragons watch in the country called Cathay, that courtyard with the pool of water and the many doors."

"Ay," answered the Man in a new voice, a great voice that seemed to fill the air like the mutter of distant thunder. "I am Murgh, Gateway of the Gods, and since you have striven to defend Murgh, he who is the friend of all men, although they know it not, will above all be your friend and the friend of those you love."

He stretched out his long arms and laid his white-gloved hands for an instant, one of them upon Hugh's head and one on the shoulder of Grey Dick, who sat upon the pillar of stone.

Hugh muttered, "I thank you," not knowing what else to say. But in his heart he wondered what kind of friendship this mighty and awful being would show to him and his. Perhaps he might hold that the truest kindness would be to remove him and them from the miseries of a sinful world.

If Murgh read his thoughts he only answered them with that smile of his cold eyes which was more awful than the frown of any mortal man. Turning his head slowly he began to contemplate Dick sitting on his stone.

"If I had a son," he said, "by that face of yours you might be he."

"Perchance," answered Dick, "since I never knew for certain who my father was. Only I have always heard that Life begets, not Death."

"Death! You honour me with a great name. Well, life and death are one, and you and I are one with the moon and the stars above us, and many other things and beings that you cannot see. Therefore the begetter and the begotten are one in the Hand that holds them all."

"Ay," answered Dick, "and so my bow and I are one: I've often thought it. Only you nearly made me one with my own arrow, which is closer kinship than I seek," and he touched the cut upon his chin. "Since you are so wise, my father, or my son, tell me, what is this Hand that holds them all?"

"Gladly. Only if I do, first I must ask you to die, then—say in a minute or two—you shall know."

Dick peered at him doubtfully, and said:

"If that be so, I think I'll wait for the answer, which I am sure to learn soon or late."

"Ah! Many men have thought the same, and you have sent some to seek it, have you not, being so good an archer. For instance, that was a long shaft you shot before Crecy fray at the filthy fool who mocked your English host. Doubtless now he knows the answer to your riddle."

"Who told you of that?" asked Dick, springing up.

"A friend of mine who was in the battle. He said also that your name was Richard the Archer."

"A friend! I believe that you were there yourself, as, if you are Death, you may well have been."

"Perhaps you are right, Richard. Have I not just told you that we all are one; yes, even the slayer and the slain. Therefore, if my friend—did you call him Death?—was there, I was there, if you were there I was there and it was my hand that drew yonder great black bow of yours and my eye that guided the straight shaft which laid the foul-mouthed jester low. Why, did you not say as much yourself when your master here bade farewell to his father in the ship at Calais? What were the words? Oh, I remember them. You wondered how One I may not name," and he bowed his solemn head, "came to make that black bow and yours and you 'the death that draw it.'"

Now at length Grey Dick's courage gave out.

"Of no man upon earth am I afraid," he said. "But from you, O god or devil, who read the secret hearts of men and hear their secret words, my blood flows backward as it did when first my eyes fell on you. You would kill me because I dared to shoot at you. Well, kill, but do not torture. It is unworthy of a knight, even if he took his accolade in hell," and he placed his hands before his eyes and stood before him with bent head waiting for the end.

"Why give me such high names, Richard the Fatherless, when you have heard two humbler ones? Call me Murgh, as do my friends. Or call me 'The Gate,' as do those who as yet know me less well. But talk not of gods or devils, lest suddenly one of them should answer you. Nay, man, have no fear. Those who seek Death he often flees, as I think he flees from you to-night. Yet let us see if we cannot send a longer shaft, you and I, than that which we loosed on Crecy field. Give me the bow."

Dick, although he had never suffered living man to shoot with it before, handed him the black bow, and with it a war shaft, which he drew from his quiver.

"Tell me, Archer Dick, have you any enemy in this town of Venice? Because if so we might try a shot at him."

"One or two, Gate Murgh," answered Dick, "Still whatever your half of me may do, my bit of you does not love to strike down men by magic in the dark."

"Well said and better thought. Then bethink you of something that belongs to an enemy which will serve as well for a test of shooting. Ah! I thank you, well thought again. Yes, I see the mark, though 'tis far, is it not? Now set your mind on it. But stay! First, will you know this arrow again?"

"Surely," answered Dick, "I made it myself. Moreover, though two of the feathers are black, the third is white with four black spots and a little splash of brown. Look on it, Sir Hugh; it cannot be mistook."

Hugh looked and nodded; speak he could not for the life of him.

Then Murgh began to play a little with the bow, and oh! strange and dreadful was the music that came from its string beneath the touch of his gloved fingers. It sang like a harp and wailed like a woman, so fearfully indeed that the lad Day, who all this while stood by aghast, stopped his ears with his fingers, and Hugh groaned. Then this awful archer swiftly set the arrow on the string.

"Now think with your mind and shoot with your heart," he said in his cold voice, and, so saying, drew and loosed as though at a hazard.

Out toward Venice leaped the shaft with a rushing sound like to that of wings and, as it seemed to the watchers, light went with it, for it travelled like a beam of light. Far over the city it travelled, describing a mighty arc such as no arrow ever flew before, then sank down and vanished behind some palace tower.

"A very good bow," said the shooter, as he handed it back to Dick. "Never have I used a better, who have used thousands made of many a substance. Indeed, I think that I remember it. Did you chance to find it years ago by the seashore? Yes? Well, it was a gift of mine to a famous archer who died upon a ship. Nay, it is not strained; I can judge of the breaking strength of a bow. Whether or no I can judge of the flight of an arrow you will learn hereafter. But that this one flew fast and far cannot be doubted since—did you watchers note it?—its speed made it shine like fire. This is caused by the rubbing of the air when aught travels through it very quickly. This night you have seen a meteor glow in the same fashion, only because the air fretted it in its passage. In the East, whence I come, we produce fire just so. And now let us be going, for I have much to do to-night, and would look upon this fair Venice ere I sleep. I'll lead the way, having seen a map of the town which a traveller brought to the East. I studied it, and now it comes back to my mind. Stay, let that youth give me his garment," and he pointed to David Day, who wore a silk cloak like the others, "since my foreign dress might excite remark, as it did but now."

In a moment Day had stripped himself of his light silk-hooded gown, and in another moment it was on the person of Murgh, though how it got there, when they came to think of it afterward, none could remember. Still, the yellow and red head-dress, the coal-black silky furs, the yellow skirt, the gleaming pearls, all vanished beneath it. Nothing remained visible except the white fingerless gloves—why were they fingerless, and what lay beneath them? Hugh wondered—and the white shoes.

Forward they went across the Place of Arms, past the timber stand ornamented with banners, which Murgh stayed to contemplate for an instant, until they came to the mouth of the street up which men had followed them, apparently with evil intent.

"Sir Murgh," said Hugh, stepping forward, "you had best let me and my companion Grey Dick walk first down this place, lest you should come to harm. When we passed it a while ago we thought that we heard robbers behind us, and in Venice, as we are told, such men use knives."

"Thank you for your warning, Sir Hugh," and even beneath the shadow of the silk hood Hugh thought that he saw his eyes smile, and seeing, remembered all the folly of such talk.

"Yet I'll risk these robbers. Do you two and the lad keep behind me," he added in a sterner voice.

So they advanced down the narrow street, the man called Murgh going first, Hugh, Grey Dick and the lad following meekly behind him. As they entered its shadows a low whistle sounded, but nothing happened for a while. When they had traversed about half its length, however, men, five or six of them in all, darted out of the gloom of a gateway and rushed at them. The faint light showed that they were masked and gleamed upon the blue steel of the daggers in their hands. Two of these men struck at Murgh with their knives, while the others tried to pass him, doubtless to attack his companions, but failed. Why they failed Hugh and Dick never knew. All they saw was that Murgh stretched out his white-gloved hands, and they fell back.

The men who had struck at him fell back also, their daggers dropping to the ground, and fled away, followed by their companions, all except one whom Murgh had seized. Hugh noted that he was a tall, thin fellow, and that, unlike the rest, he had drawn no weapon, although it was at his signal that the other bravoes had rushed on. This man Murgh seemed to hold with one hand while with the other he ripped the mask off his face, turning him so that the light shone on him.

Hugh and Dick saw the face and knew it for that of the priest who had accompanied Acour to England. It was he who had drugged Red Eve and read the mass of marriage over her while she was drugged.

"Who are you?" asked Murgh in his light, cold voice. "By your shaven head a priest, I think—one who serves some God of love and mercy. And yet you come upon this ill errand as a captain of assassins. Why do you seek to do murder, O Priest of the God of mercy?"

Now some power seemed to drag the answer from Father Nicholas.

"Because I must," he said. "I have sold myself and must pay the price. Step leads to step, and he who runs may not stop upon them."

"No, priest Nicholas, since ever they grow more narrow and more steep. Yet at the foot of them is the dark abyss, and, Murderer Nicholas, you have reached the last of all your steps. Look at me!" and with one hand he threw back the hood.

Next instant they saw Nicholas rush staggering down the street, screaming with terror as he went. Then, as all the bravoes had gone, they continued their march, filled with reflections, till they came to the little landing-stage where they had left the boat. It was still there though the boatman had gone.

"Let us borrow this boat," said Murgh. "As from my study of the map I know these water-paths, I will be steersman and that tongue-tied lad shall row and tell me if I go wrong. First I will take you to the house where I think you said you lodged, and thence to go seek friends of my own in this city who will show me hospitality."

They glided on down the long canals in utter silence that was broken only by the soft dipping of the oars. The night was somewhat cooler now, for the bursting of the great meteor seemed to have cleared the air. Or perhaps the gentle breeze that had sprung up, blowing from the open sea, tempered its stifling heat.

So it came about that although it grew late many people were gathered on the *rivas* or on the balconies of the fine houses which they passed, for the most part doubtless discussing the travelling star that had been seen in the sky. Or perhaps they had already heard rumours of the strange visitor who had come to Venice, although, however fast such news may fly, this seemed scarcely probable. At the least there they were, men and women, talking earnestly together, and about them the three Englishmen noted a strange thing.

As their boat slipped by, some influence seemed to pass from it to the minds of all these people. Their talk died out, and was succeeded by a morne and heavy silence. They looked at it as though wondering why a sight so usual should draw their eyes. Then after a few irresolute moments the groups on the footpaths separated and went their ways without bidding each other good night. As they went many of them made the sign with their fingers that these Italians believed could avert evil, which gave them the appearance of all pointing at the boat or its occupants. Those in the balconies did the same thing and disappeared through the open window-places.

More than any of the wonderful things that he had done, perhaps, this effect of the Eastern stranger's presence struck terror and foreboding to Hugh's heart.

At length they came to the end of that little street where they had hired the boat, for, although none had told him the way, thither their dread steersman brought them without fault. The lad David laid down his oars and mounted the steps that led to the street, which was quite deserted, even the bordering houses being in darkness.

"Hugh de Cressi and Richard the Fatherless," said Murgh, "you have seen wonderful things this night and made a strange friend, as you may think by chance, although truly in all the wide universe there is no room for such a thing as chance. Now my counsel to you and your companion is that you speak no word of these matters lest you should be set upon as wizards. We part, but we shall meet again twice more, and after many years a third time, but that third meeting do not seek, for it will be when the last grains of sand are running from the glass. Also you may see me at other times, but if so, unless I speak to you, do not speak to me. Now go your ways, fearing nothing. However great may seem your peril, I say to you—fear nothing. Soon you will hear ill things spoken of me, yet"—and here a touch of human wistfulness came into his inhuman voice—"I pray you believe them not. When I am named Murgh the Fiend and Murgh the Sword, then think of me as Murgh the Helper. What I do is decreed by That which is greater than I, and if you could understand it, leads by terrible ways to a goal of good, as all things do. Richard the Archer, I will answer the riddle that you asked yourself upon the ship at Calais. The Strength which made your black bow an instrument of doom made you who loose its shafts and me who can outshoot you far. As the arrow travels whither it is sent, and there does its appointed work, so do you travel and so do I, and many another thing, seen and unseen; and therefore I told you truly that although we differ in degree, yet we are one. Yes, even Murgh the Eating Fire, Murgh the Gate, and that bent wand of yours are one in the Hand that shaped and holds us both."

Then divesting himself of the long robe which he had borrowed from the lad, he handed it to Hugh, and, taking the oars, rowed away clad in his rich, fantastic garb which now, as at first, could be seen by all. He rowed away, and for a while the three whom he had left behind heard the soughing of the innumerable wings that went ever with him, after which came silence.

Silence, but not for long, for presently from the borders of the great canal into which his skiff must enter, rose shouts of fear and rage, near by at first, then farther and farther off, till these too were lost in silence.

"Oh! Sir Hugh!" sobbed poor David Day, "who and what is that dreadful man?"

"I think his name is Death," answered Hugh solemnly, while Dick nodded his head but said nothing.

"Then we must die," went on David in his terror, "and I am not fit to die."

"I think not," said Hugh again. "Be comforted. Death has passed us by. Only be warned also and, as he bade you, say nothing of all that you have heard and seen."

"By Death himself, I'll say nothing for my life's sake," he replied faintly, for he was shaking in every limb.

Then they walked up the street to the yard door. As they went Hugh asked Dick what it was that he had in his mind as a mark for the arrow that Murgh had shot, that arrow which to his charmed sight had seemed to rush over Venice like a flake of fire.

"I'll not tell you, master," answered Dick, "lest you should think me madder than I am, which to-night would be very mad indeed. Stay, though, I'll tell David here, that he may be a witness to my folly," and he called the young man to him and spoke with him apart.

Then they unlocked the courtyard gate and entered the house by the kitchen door, as it chanced quite unobserved, for now all the servants were abed. Indeed, of that household none ever knew that they had been outside its walls this night, since no one saw them go or return, and Sir Geoffrey and his lady thought that they had retired to their chamber.

They came to the door of their room, David still with them, for the place where he slept was at the end of this same passage.

"Bide here a while," said Dick to him. "My master and I may have a word to say to you presently."

Then they lit tapers from a little Roman lamp that burned all night in the passage and entered the room. Dick walked at once to the window-place, looked and laughed a little.

"The arrow has missed," he said, "or rather," he added doubtfully, "the target is gone."

"What target?" asked Hugh wearily, for now he desired sleep more than he had ever done in all his life. Then he turned, the taper in his hand, and started back suddenly, pointing to something which hung upon his bed-post that stood opposite to the window.

"Who nails his helm upon my bed?" he said. "Is this a challenge from some knight of Venice?"

Dick stepped forward and looked.

"An omen, not a challenge, I think. Come and see for yourself," he said.

This is what Hugh saw: Fixed to the post by a shaft which pierced it and the carved olivewood from side to side, was the helm that they had stripped from the body of Sir Pierre de la Roche; the helm of Sir Edmund Acour, which Sir Pierre had worn at Crecy and Dick had tumbled out of his sack in the presence of the Doge before Cattrina's face. On his return to the house of Sir Geoffrey Carleon he had set it down in the centre of the open window-place and left it there when they went out to survey the ground where they must fight upon the morrow.

Having studied it for a moment, Dick went to the door and called to David.

"Friend," he said, standing between him and the bed, so that he could see nothing, "what was it that just now I told you was in my mind when yonder Murgh asked me at what target he should shoot with my bow on the Place of Arms?"

"A knight's helm," answered David, "which stood in the window of your room at the ambassador's house—a knight's helmet that had a swan for its crest."

"You hear?" said Dick to Hugh; "now come, both of you, and see. What is that which hangs upon the bed-post? Answer you, David, for perchance my sight is bewitched."

"A knight's helm," answered David, "bearing the crest of a floating swan and held there by an arrow which has pierced it through."

"What was the arrow like which I gave this night to one Murgh, master?" asked Dick again.

"It was a war shaft having two black feathers and the third white but chequered with four black spots and a smear of brown," answered Hugh.

"Then is that the same arrow, master, which this Murgh loosed from more than a mile away?"

Hugh examined it with care. Thrice he examined it, point and shaft and feathers. Then in a low voice he answered:

*"Yes!"*

## Chapter 14

# At the Place of Arms

Notwithstanding all that has been told, Hugh and Dick never slept more soundly than they did that night, nor was their rest broken by any dreams. At half past five in the morning—for they must be stirring early—David came to call them. He too, it seemed, had slept well. Also in the light of day the worst of his fear had left him.

"I am wondering, Sir Hugh," he said, looking at him curiously, "whether I saw certain things last night down yonder at the Place of Arms and in the boat, or whether I thought I saw them."

"Doubtless you thought you saw them, David," answered Hugh, adding with meaning, "and it is not always well to talk of things we think that we have seen."

The lad, who was sharp enough, nodded. But as he turned to hand Hugh some garment his eye fell upon the swan-crested helm that was still nailed by the long war-shaft with two black feathers and one white to the carved olivewood post of the bed.

"It must have been a mighty arm that shot this arrow, Sir Hugh," he said reflectively, "which could pierce a *casque* of Milan steel from side to side and a hardwood post beyond. Well for the owner of the helm that his head was not inside of it."

"Very well, and a very mighty arm, David. So mighty that I should say nothing about it for fear lest it should set another arrow upon another string and shoot again."

"God's truth, not I!" exclaimed David, "and for your comfort, sir, know that none saw us leave this house or re-enter it last night."

Then Hugh and Dick clothed themselves and saw to their weapons and mail, but this they did not don as yet, fearing lest the weight of it should weary them in that great heat. Although the day was so young, this heat was terrible, more oppressive indeed than any they had yet known in Venice.

When they were ready David left them to see to the horse which de Cressi would ride in his combat with Cattrina. Hugh, as became a God-fearing knight whom Sir Andrew Arnold had instructed from childhood, crossed himself, knelt down and said his prayers, which that morning were long and earnest. Indeed he would have confessed himself also if he could, only there was no priest at hand who knew his language, Sir Geoffrey's chaplain being away. After watching him a while even Grey Dick, whose prayers were few, followed his example, kneeling in front of his bow as though it were an image that he worshipped. When they had risen again, he said:

"You grieve that there is none to shrive us, master, but I hold otherwise, since when it was told what company we kept last night absolution might be lacking. This would weigh on you if not on me, who, after what I have learned of Father Nicholas and others, love but one priest, and he far away."

"Yet it is well to have the blessings of Holy Church ere such a business as ours, Dick; that is, if it can be come by."

"Mayhap, master. But for my part I am content with that of Murgh, which he gave us, you may remember, or so I understood him. Moreover, did he not teach that he and all are but ministers of Him above? Therefore I go straight to the head of the stair," and he nodded toward the sky. "I am content to skip all those steps which are called priests and altars and popes and saints and such-like folk, living or dead. If Murgh's wisdom be true, as I think, these are but garnishings to the dish which can well be spared by the hungry soul."

"That may be," Hugh answered dubiously, for his faith in such matters was that of his time. "Yet were I you, Dick, I'd not preach that philosophy too loud lest the priests and popes should have something to say to it. The saints also, for aught I know, since I have always heard that they love not to be left out of our account with heaven."

"Well, if so," answered Dick, "I'll quote St. Murgh to them, who is a very fitting patron for an archer." Then once again he glanced at the helm and the arrow with something not unlike fear in his cold eye.

Presently they went down to the eating chamber where they had been told that breakfast would be ready for them at seven of the clock. There they found Sir Geoffrey awaiting them.

"I trust that you have slept well, Sir Hugh," he said. "You were a wise knight to go to rest so early, having before you such a trial of your strength and manhood, and, so to speak, the honour of our King upon your hands."

"Very well indeed; thank you, sir," answered Hugh. "And you?"

"Oh, ill, extremely ill. I do not know what is the matter with me or Venice either, whereof the very air seems poisoned. Feel the heat and see the haze! It is most unnatural. Moreover, although in your bed doubtless you saw it not, a great ball of fire blazed and burnt over the city last night. So bright was it that even in a darkened room each of us could see the colour of the other's eyes. Later, too, as I watched at the window, there came a thin streak of flame that seemed to alight on or about this very house. Indeed I thought I heard a sound as of iron striking upon iron, but could find no cause for it."

"Wondrous happenings, sir," said Grey Dick. "Glad am I that we were not with you, lest the sight of them should have made us fearful on this morning of combat."

"Wondrous happenings indeed, friend Richard," said Sir Geoffrey excitedly, "but you have not heard the half of them. The herald, who has just been here with the final articles of your fray signed by the Doge and Cattrina, has told me much that I can scarce believe. He says that the great galley from this port which is called *Light of the East* drifted up to the quay at the Place of Arms last night on her return voyage from Cyprus, filled with dead and with no living thing aboard her save the devil himself in a yellow robe and a many-hued head-dress like a cock's-comb with a red eye. He swears that this fiend landed and that the mob set on him, whereon two, some say three, other devils clad in long black gowns appeared out of the water and drove them back. Also, it seems that this same cock's-combed Satan stole a boat and rowed about the city afterward, but now none can find him, although they have got the boat."

"Then they should be well satisfied," said Hugh, "since its owner has lost nothing but the hire, which with Satan at the oars is better than might be hoped. Perhaps he was not there after all, Sir Geoffrey."

"I know not, but at least the galley *Light of the East* is there, for ever since the dawn they have been taking the dead out of her to bury them. Of these they say things too terrible to repeat, for no doctor can tell of what sickness they died, never having seen its like. For my part I pray it may not be catching. Were I the Doge I would have towed her out to sea and scuttled her, cargo and all. Well, well, enough of these wild tales, of which God alone knows the truth. Come, eat, if you can in this heat. We must be on the Place of Arms by half-past eight. You and the captain go thither in my own boat, Sir Hugh; your horse David Day takes on presently. Now, while you breakfast, I'll explain to you these articles, one by one, for they are writ in Italian, which you cannot read. See you forget them not.

These Venetians are punctilious of such forms and ceremonies, especially when the case is that of combat to the death, which is rare among them."

********

The articles, which were lengthy, had been read, and the breakfast, or so much as they could eat of it, consumed. At last Hugh, accompanied by a Venetian squire of high birth sent by the Doge to bear his *casque* and other armour, stood in the vestibule waiting for the ambassador's barge of state. With him was Grey Dick, accompanied by no one and carrying the mail shirt in which he was to fight, like a housewife's parcel beneath his arm, although he wore bow on back, axe and dagger at side and iron cap upon his head.

Presently, while they lingered thus, out from a side-door appeared Lady Carleon, clothed in a white garment such as women wear when their dressing is half done, down which her grey hair hung dishevelled.

"I am come thus unkempt, Sir Hugh," she said, "for, not feeling well, I could not rise early, to bid you good-bye, since I am sure that we shall not meet again. However much that black-browed Doge may press it, I cannot go down yonder to see my countrymen butchered in this heat. Oh! oh!" and she pressed her hand upon her heart.

"What's the matter, madam?" asked Hugh anxiously.

"A pain in my breast, that is all, as though some one drove a dagger through me. There, there, 'tis gone."

"I thank you for your goodness, Lady Carleon," said Hugh when she was herself again; then paused, for he knew not what to add.

"Not so, Sir Hugh, not so; 'tis for your sakes in truth since you remember you never told me what you would wish done—afterward. Your possessions also—where are they to be sent? Doubtless you have money and other things of value. Be sure that they shall be sealed up. I'll see to it myself, but—how shall I dispose of them?"

"Madame, I will tell you when I return," said Hugh shortly.

"Nay, nay, Sir Hugh; pray do not return. Those who are gone had best keep gone, I think, who always have had a loathing of ghosts. Therefore, I beg you, tell me now, but do not come back shining like a saint and gibbering like a monkey at dead of night, because if you do I am sure I shall not understand, and if there is an error, who will set it straight?"

Hugh leaned against a marble pillar in the hall and looked at his hostess helplessly, while Sir Geoffrey, catching her drift at length, broke in:

"Cease such ill-omened talk, wife. Think you that it is of a kind to give brave men a stomach in a fight to the end?"

"I know not, Geoffrey, but surely 'tis better to have these matters settled, for, as you often say, death is always near us."

"Ay, madam," broke in Grey Dick, who could bear no more of it, "death is always near to all of us, and especially so in Venice just now. Therefore, I pray you tell me—in case we should live and *you* should die, you and all about you—whether you have any commands to give as to what should be done with your gold and articles of value, or any messages to leave for friends in England."

Then, having uttered this grim jest, Dick took his master by the arm and drew him through the door.

Afterward, for a reason that shall be told, he was sorry that it had ever passed his lips. Still in the boat Sir Geoffrey applauded him, saying that his lady's melancholy had grown beyond all bearing, and that she did little but prate to him about his will and what colour of marble he desired for his tomb.

After a journey that seemed long to Hugh, who wished to have this business over, they came to the Place of Arms. Their route there, however, was not the same which they had followed on the previous night. Leaving the short way through the low part of the town untraversed, they rowed from one of the canals into the harbour itself, where they were joined by many other boats which waited for them and so on to the quay. Hugh saw at once that the death ship, *Light of the East*, was gone, and incautiously said as much to Sir Geoffrey.

"Yes," he answered, "one of my rowers tells me that they have towed her to an island out at sea, since the stench from her holds was more than could be borne. But how did you know that she lay at this particular quay, Sir Hugh?"

"I thought you said so," he answered carelessly, adding, to change the subject: "Look, our fray will not lack for spectators," and he pointed to the thousands gathered upon the great tilting-ground.

"No, no, all Venice will be there, for these people love a show, especially if there be death in it."

"Mayhap they will see more of him than they wish before all is done," muttered Grey Dick, pausing from the task of whetting his axe's edge with a little stone which he carried in his pouch. Then he replaced the axe in its hanger, and, drawing Hugh's sword from its sheath, began to give some final touches to its razor edge, saying: "Father Sir Andrew Arnold blessed it, which should be enough, but Milan steel is hard and his old battle blade will bite none the worse for an extra sharpening. Go for his throat, master, go for his throat, the mail is always thinnest there."

"God above us, what a grim man!" exclaimed Sir Geoffrey, and so thought all in that boat and in those around them. At least they looked at Dick askance as he whetted and whetted, and then, plucking out one of the pale hairs from his head, drew it along the edge of the steel, which severed it in twain.

"There! That'll do," said Grey Dick cheerfully, as he returned the long sword to its sheath, "and God help this Cattrina, I say, for he comes to his last battle. That is, unless he runs away," he added after reflection.

Now they landed and were received by heralds blowing trumpets, and conducted through a great multitude of people with much pomp and ceremony to a pavilion which had been pitched for them, where they must arm and make ready.

This then they did, helped or hindered by bowing squires whose language they could not understand.

At length, when it lacked but a quarter to the hour of nine, David Day led Hugh's horse into the wide entrance of the pavilion, where they examined its armour, bridle, *selle* and trappings.

"The beast sweats already," said Hugh, "and so do I, who, to tell truth, dread this heat more than Cattrina's sword. Pray that they get to the business quickly, or I shall melt like butter on a hot plate."

Then his lance was given to him, a lance that was sharp and strong. When they had been tested by them both, Hugh mounted the grey and at the agreed signal of a single blast upon a trumpet, walked it slowly from the pavilion, Dick going at his side on foot.

At their coming a shout went up from the assembled thousands, for in truth it seemed, as Sir Geoffrey had said, as though all the folk in Venice were gathered on that place. When they had finished shouting the people began to criticise, finding much in the appearance of this pair that moved their ready wit. Indeed there was little show about them, for Hugh's plain armour, which lacked all ornament or inlay, was worn with war and travel, and his horse came along as soberly as if it were going out to plough. Nor was there anything fine about the apparel of Grey Dick, who wore a loose chain shirt much out of fashion—it was that which Sir Andrew had given to Hugh—an iron cap with ear-pieces, and leather buskins on his legs. In his hand was his axe, heavy but not over large; at his side hung a great knife, and on his back was the long black bow and a quiver of arrows.

Thus arrayed, taking no heed of the jests and chatter of the multitude, they were led to the front of the bedecked timber stand which they had seen on the previous night. In the centre of this stand, occupying a kind of tribune, sat the Doge Dandolo in state, and with him many nobles and captains, while to right and left the whole length of the course, for the stand was very long, were packed a countless number of the best-born men and women in Venice. These, however, were but a tithe of the spectators, who encircled the Place of Arms in one serried horde which was kept back by a line of soldiers.

Arriving in front of the Doge's tribune, the pair halted and saluted him, whereon he and his escort rose and saluted them in turn. Then another trumpet blew and from a second pavilion at the other end of the course appeared Cattrina, wearing a splendid suit of white armour, damascened in gold, with a silver swan upon the helm and a swan painted on his shield.

"Very fine, isn't it?" said Grey Dick to his master, "only this time I hope he's inside the steel. Ask to see his face before you fight, master."

On came Cattrina on a noble black horse, which pawed and caracoled notwithstanding the heat, while after him strode a gigantic figure also clad from top to toe in white mail, who fiercely brandished a long-handled battle-axe.

"Ambrosio!" said Dick. "Now I ought to feel as much afraid as though that fellow wore a yellow cap and fur cape and pearls like another warrior whom we met last night. Yet, to speak the truth, I believe he has the fainter heart of the two. Also if he swings that chopper about so much he'll grow tired."

To the multitude, however, the gallant appearance of this pair, whom they looked on as the champions of Venice against foreigners, appealed not a little. Amidst clapping of hands and *"evvivas!"* they advanced to the Doge's tribune and there made their salutations, which the Illustrious acknowledged as he had those of the Englishmen.

Then the heralds intervened and again all the articles of combat were read and translated, although to these, of which they were weary, Hugh and Dick listened little. Next they were asked if they had any objections to make and with one voice answered, "None." But on the same question being put to their adversaries, the Swiss, Ambrosio, said that he with whom he must fight appeared to be armed with a bow, which was against the articles. Thereon Dick handed the bow and quiver to David, bidding him guard them until he asked for them again as he would his own life. In the event of his death, however, David was to give them to Sir Hugh, or if they both should die, to his own master, Sir Geoffrey. All of these things David promised to do.

Next followed a long discussion as to whether the four of them were to fight in pairs, Cattrina and Ambrosio against Hugh and Dick simultaneously, or whether Ambrosio was to fight alone with Dick, and Cattrina with Hugh. Upon Cattrina and Ambrosio being asked their wishes, the former said that he desired to fight alone, as he feared lest the English archer, if he overcame Ambrosio, should turn on him also, or perhaps hamstring his horse.

Then the Englishmen were asked what they wished, and replied that they did not care how it was arranged, being ready to fight either together or separately, as the Doge might decree.

The end of it was that after long consultations with sundry experts in such matters, the Most Illustrious decided that the Captains Ambrosio and Richard the Archer should first engage on foot, and when that business was settled the two knights should take their place in the arena.

So the end of it was that more than half an hour after the combat should have begun, Dick and the gigantic Ambrosio found themselves standing face to face waiting for the signal to engage, the Swiss shouting threats and defiance and Grey Dick grinning and watching him out of his half-shut eyes.

At length it came in the shape of a single blast upon a trumpet. Now seeing that Dick stood quite still, not even raising his axe, the Swiss advanced and struck a mighty blow at him, which Dick avoided by stepping aside. Recovering himself, again Ambrosio struck. This blow Dick caught upon his shield, then, as though he were afraid, began to retreat, slowly at first, but afterward faster till his walk broke into a run.

At this sight all that mighty audience set up a hooting. "Coward! Dog! Pig of an Englishman!" they yelled; and the louder they yelled the more quickly did Grey Dick run, till at last even Hugh grew puzzled wondering what was in his mind and hoping that he would change it soon. So the audience hooted, and Grey Dick ran and the giant Swiss lumbered along after him, bellowing triumphantly and brandishing his battle-axe, which, it was noted, never seemed to be quite long enough to reach his flying foe.

When this had gone on for two or three minutes, Grey Dick stumbled and fell. The Swiss, who was following fast, likewise tripped and fell over him heavily, whereon the multitude shouted:

"Foul play! A dirty, foreign trick!"

In an instant Dick was up again, and had leapt upon the prostrate Swiss, as all thought, to kill him. But instead the only thing he did was to get behind him and kick him with his foot until he also rose. Thereat some laughed, but others, who had bets upon their champion, groaned.

Now the Swiss, having lost his shield in his fall, rushed at Dick, grasping his axe with both hands. As before, the Englishman avoided the blow, but for the first time he struck back, catching the giant on the shoulder though not very heavily. Then with a shout of "St. George and England!" he went in at him.

Hither and thither sprang Dick, now out of reach of the axe of the Swiss and now beneath his guard. But ever as he sprang he delivered blow upon blow, each harder than the last, till there appeared scars and rents in the fine white mail. Soon it became clear that the great Swiss was overmatched and spent. He breathed heavily, his strokes grew wild, he over-balanced, recovered himself, and at last in his turn began to fly in good earnest.

Now after him went Dick, battering at his back, but, as all might see, with the flat of his axe, not with its edge. Yes, he was beating him as a man might beat a carpet, beating him till he roared with pain.

"Fight, Ambrosio, fight! Don't fly!" shouted the crowd, and he tried to wheel round, only to be knocked prostrate by a single blow upon the head which the Englishman delivered with the hammer-like back of his axe.

Then Dick was seen to kneel upon him and cut the lashings of his helmet with his dagger, doubtless to give the *coup de grâce*, or so they thought.

"Our man is murdered!" yelled the common people, while those of the better sort remained shamed and silent.

Dick rose, and they groaned, thinking that all was done. But lo! stooping down he helped the breathless Swiss, whom he had disarmed, to his feet. Then, taking him by the nape of the neck, which was easy, as his helmet was off, with one hand, while in the other he held his bared knife, Dick thrust him before him till they reached the tribune of the Doge.

"Be pleased to tell the Illustrious," he said, to Sir Geoffrey, "that this braggart having surrendered, I spared his life and now return him to his brother the Page quite unharmed, since I did not wish to wound one who was in my power from the first. Only when he gets home I pray that he will look at his back in a glass and judge which of us it is that has been 'beaten to a pulp.' Let him return thanks also to his patron saint, who put pity in my heart, so that I did not cut him into *collops*, as I promised. For know, sir, that when I walked out yonder it was my purpose to hew off his hands and shorten him at the knees. Stay—one word more. If yonder boaster has more brothers who really wish to fight, I'll take them one by one and swear to them that this time I'll not give back a step unless I'm carried."

"Do you indeed yield and accept the Englishman's mercy?" asked the Doge in a stern voice.

The poor Ambrosio, making no answer, blundered forward among the crowd and there vanished, and this was the last that Dick ever saw or heard of him. But, although he waited there a while, feeling the edge of his axe and glaring about him, none of the captain's companions came forward to accept his challenge.

At length, with a shrug of his shoulders, Dick turned. Having taken his bow and quiver from David, who could not conceal his indecent joy at the utter humiliation of Ambrosio, whom he hated with a truly British hate, he walked slowly to where Hugh sat upon his horse.

"The jest is done, master, and now for good earnest, since 'tis your turn. The Saints save me such another cow hunt in this hell's heat. Had I killed him at once I should be cooler now, but it came into my mind to let the hound live. Indeed, to speak truth, I thought that I heard the voice of Murgh behind me, saying, 'Spare,' and knew that I must obey."

"I hope he will say nothing of the sort to me presently," answered Hugh, "if he is here, which I doubt. Why, what is it now? Those gold-coated marshals are talking again."

Talking they were, evidently at the instance of Cattrina, or his counsellors, who had raised some new objections, which Sir Geoffrey stepped forward to explain to them. But Hugh would not even hear him out.

"Tell the man and all whom it may concern," he said in an angry voice, "that I am ready to fight him as he will, on horse or on foot, with lance or sword or axe or dagger, or any or all of them, in mail or without it; or, if it pleases him, stripped to the shirt. Only let him settle swiftly, since unless the sweat runs into my eyes and dims them, it seems to me that night is coming before it is noon."

"You are right," answered Sir Geoffrey, "this gathering gloom is ominous and fearful. I think that some awesome tempest must be about to burst. Also it seems to me that Cattrina has no stomach for this fray, else he would not raise so many points of martial law and custom."

Then wiping his brow with a silken handkerchief he returned to deliver the message.

Now Hugh and Dick, watching, saw that Cattrina and those who advised him could find no further loophole for argument. They saw, moreover, that the Doge grew angry, for he rose in his seat, throwing off his velvet robe of office, of which it appeared that he could no longer bear the weight, and spoke in a hard voice to Cattrina and his squires. Next, once more the titles of the combatants were read, and their cause of combat, and while this went on Hugh bade Dick bind about his right arm a certain red ribbon that Eve had given him, saying that he wished to fight wearing his lady's favour.

Dick obeyed, muttering that he thought such humours foolish and that a knight might as well wear a woman's petticoat as her ribbon. By now, so dim had the light grown, he could scarce see to tie the knot.

Indeed, the weather was very strange.

From the dark, lowering sky above a palpable blackness sank downward as though the clouds themselves were falling of their own weight, while from the sea great rolls of vapour came sweeping in like waves. Also this sea itself had found a voice, for, although it was so calm, it moaned like a world in pain. The great multitude began to murmur, and their faces, lifted upward toward the sky, grew ghastly white. Fear, they knew not of what, had got hold of them. A voice cried shrilly:

"Let them fight and have done. We would get home ere the tempest bursts."

The first trumpet blew and the horses of the knights, which whinnied uneasily, were led to their stations. The second trumpet blew and the knights laid their lances in rest. Then ere the third trumpet could sound, suddenly the darkness of midnight swallowed all the scene.

Dick groped his way to Hugh's side. "Bide where you are," he said, "the end of the world is here; let us meet it like men and together."

"Ay," answered Hugh, and his voice rang hollow through his closed visor, "without doubt it is the end of the world, and Murgh, the Minister, has been sent to open the doors of heaven and hell. God have mercy on us all!"

So they stayed there, hearkening to the groans and prayers of the terrified multitude about them, Dick holding the bridle of the horse, which shook from head to foot, but never stirred. For some minutes they remained thus, till suddenly the sky began to lighten, but with no natural light. The colour of it, of the earth beneath and of the air between was a deep, terrible red, that caused all things to seem as though they were dyed in blood. Lighter and lighter and redder and redder it grew, the long stand and the pavilions became visible, and after them the dense, deep ring of spectators. Many of these were kneeling, while others, who could find no space to kneel, held their hands upstretched toward heaven, or beat their breasts and wept in the emotional fashion of the country.

Yet not on them were the eyes of Hugh and Grey Dick fixed, but rather on a single figure which stood quite alone in the midst of that great arena where Cattrina and his horse should have been, where they had been indeed but a little while before. The figure was clothed in a red and yellow cap shaped like a cock's-comb, in black furs, a yellow robe and white gloves and sandals. Yonder it stood, fantastic, fearful, its bare and brawny arms crossed upon its breast, its head bowed as though it contemplated the ground. There was not an eye of all the tens of thousands of those who were present that did not see it; there was not a voice that did not break into a yell of terror and hate, till the earth shook with such a sound as might reverberate through the choked abyss of hell.

"The fiend! The fiend! The fiend!" said the shout. "Kill him! Kill him! Kill him!"

The figure looked up, the red light shone upon its stony face that seemed one blotch of white amidst its glow. Then it stooped down and lifted from the sand a knight's lance such as Cattrina had held. It raised the lance and with it pointed four times, east and west and north and south, holding it finally for a while in the direction of the tribune, where sat the Doge with all his noble company, and of Venice beyond. Lastly, with a quick and easy motion, it cast the lance toward the sky, whence it fell, remaining fixed point downward in the earth. Then a tongue of mist that had crept up from the sea enveloped it, and when that mist cleared away the shape was gone.

Now the red haze thinned, and for the first time that morning the sun shone out in a sickly fashion. Although their nerves were torn by the unnatural darkness and the apparition that followed it, which all saw, yet none quite believed that they had seen, the multitude shouted for the combat to proceed.

Once more Hugh laid his lance in rest, thinking that Cattrina was there, although he could not see him.

Then the third trumpet rang out—in that silence it sounded like the blast of doom—and Hugh spurred his horse forward a little way, but halted, for he could perceive no foe advancing against him. He stared about him, and at last in a rage threw his lance to a squire, and, turning his horse, galloped to the tribune. There he pulled it to his haunches and shouted out in a great voice:

"Where is Cattrina? Am I to be fooled, who appear here as the champion of the King of England? Where is Cattrina? Produce Cattrina that I may slay him or be slain, or, Chivalry of Venice, be forever shamed!"

The Doge rose, uttering swift commands, and heralds ran here and there. Knights and captains searched the pavilions and every other place where a mounted man might hide. But they never found Cattrina, and, returning at length, confessed as much with bowed heads.

The Doge, maddened by this ignominy, seized the great gold chain upon his beast and burst it in two.

"Cattrina has fled!" he shouted. "Or Satan himself has carried him away! At the least let his name be erased from the Golden Book of Venice, and until he prove himself innocent, let no noble of Venice stretch out to him the hand of fellowship. Men of Venice, for you Cattrina and his House are dead."

"Will none take up his cause and fight for him?" asked Hugh through Sir Geoffrey, and presently, at the Doge's command, the challenge was repeated thrice by the herald. But to it no answer came. Of this afterward Hugh was glad, since it was Cattrina's life he sought, not that of any other man. Then Hugh spoke again, saying:

"I claim, O Illustrious, that I be written down as victor in this combat to the death, bloodless through no fault of mine."

"It shall be so written, noble Hugh de Cressi," said the Doge. "Let all Venice take notice thereof."

********

As the words left his lips the solid earth began to heave and rock.

At the first heave Hugh leaped from his horse, which screamed aloud and fled away, and gripped hold of Grey Dick. At the second, the multitude broke out into wild cries, prayers and blasphemies, and rushed this way and that. At the third, which came quite slowly and was the greatest of them all, the long stand of timber bent its flags toward him as though in salute, then, with a slow, grinding crash, fell over, entangling all within it beneath its ruin. Also in the city beyond, houses, whole streets of them, gabled churches and tall towers, sank to the earth, while where they had been rose up wreathed columns of dust. To the south the sea became agitated. Spouts of foam appeared upon its smooth face; it drew back from the land, revealing the slime of ages and embedded therein long-forgotten wrecks. It heaped itself up like a mountain, then, with a swift and dreadful motion, advanced again in one vast wave.

In an instant all that multitude were in full flight.

Hugh and Dick fled like the rest, and with them David, though whither they went they knew not.

All they knew was that the ground leapt and quivered beneath their feet, while behind them came the horrible, seething hiss of water on the crest of which men were tossed up and down like bits of floating wood.

## Chapter 15
# The Death at Work

Presently Hugh halted, taking shelter with his two companions behind the stone wall of a shed that the earthquake had shattered, for here they could not be trodden down by the mob of fugitives.

"The wave has spent itself," he said, pointing to the line of foam that now retreated toward the ocean, taking with it many drowned or drowning men. "Let us return and seek for Sir Geoffrey. It will be shameful if we leave him trapped yonder like a rat."

Dick nodded, and making a wide circuit to avoid the maddened crowd, they came safely to the wrecked stand where they had last seen Sir Geoffrey talking with the Doge. Every minute indeed the mob grew thinner, since the most of them had already passed, treading the life out of those who fell as they went.

From this stand more than three fourths of those who were seated there had already broken out, since it had not fallen utterly, and by good fortune was open on all sides. Some, however, tangled in the canvas roof, were still trying to escape. Other poor creatures had been crushed to death, or, broken-limbed, lay helpless, or, worse still, were held down beneath the fallen beams.

Several of these they freed, whereon those who were unharmed at once ran away without thanking them. But for a long while they could find no trace of Sir Geoffrey. Indeed, they were near to abandoning their search, for the sights and sounds were sickening even to men who were accustomed to those of battlefields, when Dick's quick ears caught the tones of an English voice calling for help. Apparently it came from the back of the Doge's tribune, where lay a heap of dead. Gaily dressed folk who had fallen in the flight and been crushed, not by the earthquake, but by the feet of their fellows. These blackened and disfigured men and women they dragged away with much toil, and at last, to their joy, beneath them all found Sir

Geoffrey Carleon. In another few minutes he must have died, for he was almost suffocated.

Indeed he would certainly have perished with the others had he not been thrown under a fixed bench, whence one leg projected, which, as they could see at once, was crushed and broken. They drew him out as gently as they could and gave him water to drink, whereof, mercifully for them all, since by now they were utterly parched with thirst, they had discovered a large silver pitcher full, standing in the corner of a little ante-chamber to the tribune. It was half hidden with fragments of fine dresses and even jewels torn from the persons of the lords and ladies.

"I thank you, friends," he said faintly. "I prayed them to keep seated, but they went mad and would not listen. Those behind trod down those in front, till that doorway was choked and I was hurled beneath the bench. Oh, it was terrible to hear them dying about me and to know that soon I must follow! This, had it not been for you, I should have done, for my leg is crushed and there was no air."

Then, having drunk and drunk until even their raging thirst was satisfied, they found a plank. Laying Sir Geoffrey on it, they departed from that human shambles, whence the piteous cries of those still imprisoned there, whom they could not reach, pursued them horribly.

Thus, slowly enough, for there were but three of them, two hampered by their mail, they bore Sir Geoffrey across the Place of Arms. Save for the dead and dying, and some ghoul-like knaves who plundered them, by this time it was almost deserted.

Indeed, a large band of these wretches, who had emerged like wolves from their lairs in the lowest quarters of the great city, catching sight of the gold chain Sir Geoffrey wore, ran up with drawn daggers to kill and rob them.

Seeing them come Grey Dick slipped the black bow from its case and sent an arrow singing through the heart of the one-eyed villain who captained them. Thereon the rest left him where he fell and ran off to steal and slay elsewhere. Then without a word Dick unstrung the bow and once more laid hold of an end of the plank.

They came to the mouth of that street where the bravoes had waylaid them on the previous night, only to find that they could not pass this way. Here most of the houses were thrown down, and from their ruins rose smoke and the hideous screams of those who perished. It was this part of Venice, the home of the poorer folk, which suffered most from the earthquake, that had scarcely touched many of the finer quarters. Still, it was reckoned afterward that in all it took a toll of nearly ten thousand lives.

Turning from this street, they made their way to the banks of a great canal that here ran into the harbour, that on which they had been rowed to the Place of Arms. Here by good luck they found a small boat floating keep uppermost, for it had been overturned by the number of people who crowded into it. This boat they righted with much toil and discovered within it a drowned lady, also an oar caught beneath the seat. After this their dreadful journey was easy, at least by comparison. For now all the gloom had rolled away, the sun shone out and a fresh and pleasant wind blew from the sea toward the land.

So, at last, passing many sad and strange scenes that need not be described, they came safely to the steps of the ambassador's beautiful house which was quite uninjured. Here they found several of his servants wringing their hands and weeping, for word had been brought to them that he was dead. Also in the hall they were met by another woe, for there on a couch lay stretched the Lady Carleon smitten with some dread sickness which caused blood to flow from her mouth and ears. A physician was bending over her, for by good fortune one had been found.

Sir Geoffrey asked him what ailed his wife. He answered that he did not know, having never seen the like till that morning, when he had been called in to attend three such cases in houses far apart, whereof one died within ten minutes of being struck.

Just then Lady Carleon's senses returned, and opening her eyes she saw Sir Geoffrey, whom they had laid down upon another couch close to her.

"Oh, they told me that you were dead, husband," she said, "crushed or swallowed in the earthquake! But I thank God they lied. Yet what ails you, sweetheart, that you do not stand upon your feet?"

"Little, dear wife, little," he answered in a cheerful voice. "My foot is somewhat crushed, that is all. Still 'tis true that had it not been for this brave knight and his squire I must have lain where I was till I perished."

Now Lady Carleon raised herself slightly and looked at Hugh and Dick, who stood together, bewildered and overwhelmed.

"Heaven's blessings be on your heads," she exclaimed, "for these Venetians would surely have left him to his doom. Ah, I thought that it was you who must die to-day, but now I know it is I, and perchance my lord. Physician," she added after a pause, "trouble not with me, for my hour has come; I feel it at my heart. Tend my lord there, who, unless this foul sickness takes him also, may yet be saved."

So they carried them both to their own large sleeping chamber on the upper floor. There the surgeon set Sir Geoffrey's broken bone skilfully enough, though when he saw the state of the crushed limb, he shook his head and said it would be best to cut it off. This, however, Sir Geoffrey would not suffer to be done.

"It will kill me, I am sure, or if not, then the pest which that ship, *Light of the East*, has brought here from Cyprus, will do its work on me. But I care nothing, for since you say that my wife must die I would die with her and be at rest."

At sunset Lady Carleon died. Ere she passed away she sent for Hugh and Dick. Her bed by her command had been moved to an open window, for she seemed to crave air. By it was placed that of Sir Geoffrey so that the two of them could hold each other's hand.

"I would die looking toward England, Sir Hugh," she said, with a faint smile, "though alas! I may not sleep in that churchyard on the Sussex downs where I had hoped that I might lie at last. Now, Sir Hugh, I pray this of your Christian charity and by the English blood which runs in us, that you will swear to me that you and your squire will not leave my lord alone among these Southern folk, but that you will bide with him and nurse him till he recovers or dies, as God may will. Also that you will see me buried by the bones of my child—they will tell you where."

"Wife," broke in Sir Geoffrey, "this knight is not of our kin. Doubtless he has business elsewhere. How can he bide with me here, mayhap for weeks?"

But Lady Carleon, who could speak no more, only looked at Hugh, who answered:

"Fear nothing. Here we will stay until he recovers—unless," he added, "we ourselves should die."

She smiled at him gratefully, then turned her face toward Sir Geoffrey and pressed his hand. So presently she passed away, the tears running from her faded eyes.

When it was over and the women had covered her, Hugh and Dick left the room, for they could bear no more.

"I have seen sad sights," said Hugh, with something like a sob, "but never before one so sad."

"Ay," answered Dick, "that of the wounded dying on Crecy field was a May Day revel compared to this, though it is but one old woman who has gone. Oh, how heavily they parted who have dwelt together these forty years! And 'twas my careless tongue this morning that foretold it as a jest!"

In the hall they met the physician, who rushed wild-eyed through the doorway to ask how his patients fared.

"Ah!" he said to them in French when he knew. "Well, *signors*, that noble lady has not gone alone. I tell you that scores of whom I know are already dead in Venice, swept off by this swift and horrible plague. Death and all his angels stalk through the city. They say that he himself appeared last night, and this morning on the tilting ground by the quay, and by God's mercy—if He has any left for us—I can well believe it. The Doge and his Council but now have issued a decree that all who perish must be buried at once. See to it, *signors*, lest the officers come and bear her away to some common grave, from which her rank will not protect her."

Then he went to visit Sir Geoffrey. Returning presently, he gave them some directions as to his treatment, and rushed out as he had rushed in. They never saw him again. Two days later they learned that he himself was dead of the pest.

That night they buried Lady Carleon in her son's grave, which Dick had helped to prepare for her, since no sexton could be bribed to do the work. Indeed these were all busy enough attending to the interment of the great ones of Venice. In that churchyard alone they saw six buryings in progress. Also after the priest had read his hurried Office, as they left the gates, whence Lady Carleon's bearers had already fled affrighted, they met more melancholy processions heralded by a torch or two whereof the light fell upon some sheeted and uncoffined form.

"'Twixt earthquake and plague Murgh the Helper is helping very well," said Grey Dick grimly, and Hugh only groaned in answer.

********

Such was the beginning of the awful plague which travelled from the East to Venice and all Europe and afterward became known by the name of the Black Death. Day by day the number of its victims increased; the hundreds of yesterday were the thousands of the morrow. Soon the graveyards were full, the plague pits, long and deep, were full, and the dead were taken out to sea by shiploads and there cast into the ocean. At length even this could not be done, since none were forthcoming who would dare the task. For it became known that those who did so themselves would surely die.

So where folk fell, there they lay. In the houses were many of them; they cumbered and poisoned the streets and the very churches. Even the animals sickened and perished, until that great city was turned into an open tomb. The reek of it tainted the air for miles around, so that even those who passed it in ships far out to sea turned faint and presently themselves sickened and died. But ere they died they bore on the fatal gift to other lands.

Moreover, starvation fell upon the place. Though the houses were full of riches, these would scarce suffice to buy bread for those who remained alive. The Doge and some of his Council passed laws to lighten the misery of the people, but soon few heeded these laws which none were left to enforce. The vagabonds and evil-minded men who began by robbing the deserted houses of jewels, money and plate, ended by searching them for food and casting aside their treasures as worthless dross. It was even said that some of them did worse things, things not to be named, since in its extremities nature knows no shame. Only if bread and meat were scarce, wine remained in plenty. In the midst of death men—yes, and women—who perhaps had deserted their wives, their husbands or their children, fearing to take the evil from them, made the nights horrible by their drunken blasphemies and revellings, as sailors sometimes do upon a sinking ship. Knowing that they must die, they wished to die merry.

********

Sir Geoffrey Carleon lived a long while after the death of his wife. When he passed away at last, ten days or so later, it was painlessly of the mortification of his broken limb, not of the pest, which went by him as though it knew that he was already doomed.

All this time Hugh, Grey Dick, and David Day nursed him without ceasing. Indeed with the exception of a woman so ancient and shrivelled that nothing seemed able to harm her any more, no one else was left in the great *palazzo*, for all the rest of the household had perished or fled away. This woman, who was the grandmother of one of the servants, now dead of the plague, cooked their food. Of such provision fortunately there was much laid up in the storerooms for use in the winter, since Lady Carleon had been a good and provident housewife.

So those three did not starve, although Sir Geoffrey would touch little of the salted stuff. He existed on a few fruits when they could get them, and after these were gone, on wine mingled with water.

At length came the end. For two days he had lain senseless. One night, however, David, who was watching in his chamber, crept into the room where Hugh slept hard by and told them that Sir Geoffrey was awake and calling them. They rose and went to him. By the light of the moon which shone in at the open window, that same window through which Lady Carleon had looked toward England ere she passed away, they saw him lying quietly, a happy smile upon his face.

"Friends," he said in a weak voice, "by the mercy of God, I go out of this hell to heaven, or so I think. But, if indeed this be not the end of the world, I hope that you who have lived so long will continue to live, and I have sent for you to bless you and to thank you both. In yonder case are certain papers that have to do with the King's business. I pray you deliver them to his Grace if you can and with them my homage and my thanks for the trust that he has reposed in me. Tell him what I have not written in the letters"—and here he smiled faintly—"that I think that few of his creditors in Venice will trouble him at present, though afterward their heirs, if they have left any, may do so. Say, too, to the Doge, who, I believe, still lives, that I send him my good wishes and respects. Also that I grieve that I have not been able to hand him my letters of recall in person, since the King who summons me sends none.

"So much for business, but there are two things more: I have no relatives living save my wife's sister. Therefore, Sir Hugh and Captain Richard, I have made you my joint heirs with her; my testament duly signed and witnessed is in that case with the other papers. My wealth is not great. Still there are certain land and manors in England, a sum of money placed with a merchant in London, whose name you will find written in the testament, my plate and gold coin here, though the former you may not be able to move. Therefore I charge you to bury it and return for it later on, if you can. It is of value, since all my life I have collected such trinkets. I beg you to make provision also for this good lad, David, should he be spared."

He paused a while, for he was growing very weak, then added:

"Another thing is that I ask you, if it be possible, to row my body out to sea and there sink it in deep water, deep, clean water, far from this place of stench and pestilence, for I would not lie in the common pit at last. Now kneel down and pray for my passing soul, since there is no priest to give me absolution, and I must seek it straight from God. Nay, thank me not. I have done with the world and its affairs. Kneel down and pray, as I pray for you, that you may be spared on earth and that we may meet again in heaven, where my wife and others await me."

They obeyed, weeping, yes, even Grey Dick wept a little. Presently when they looked up they saw that Sir Geoffrey was dead, dead without pain or sorrow. Of the first he had suffered none for days, and the second was far from him who wished to die.

Leaving the ancient woman in charge of the house, which she barred and bolted, next morning they took a boat, and the three of them rowed the body of the old knight a league out into the quiet sea.

There, after a brief prayer, they cast him into the deep, weighted with stones, so that he might never rise again.

Then they returned, not too soon, for they found thieves in the act of breaking into the house, probably in search of food. These miserable, half-starved men they spared, though they could have killed them easily enough. They even gave them a pouch full of biscuit and dried meat ere they dismissed them. This they did quickly, since one of them, as they could see, was already stricken by the plague and had not long to live. When they were gone, the old woman being out of the house, whence she had fled on hearing the robbers, they collected all Sir Geoffrey's and his lady's jewels and plate, of which there was much, for he lived in state in Venice, as became an ambassador. These they buried in three large iron boxes beneath the flagstones of the cellar, the safest place that they could find. Having thrown the excavated earth into the canal under cover of the dark, they replaced these stones and strewed dust over them.

Wondering whether it would ever be their lot to look upon these chests and their contents again, they left the cellar, to find the old woman knocking at the back door of the house, whither she had returned, frightened by the sights and sounds in the city. They bade her bring them food, which they needed much who had laboured so hard on that sorrowful day, and after they had eaten took counsel together.

"Seeing that all three of us are still in health, as if there is anything in the promises of Murgh we should remain, is it not time, master," asked Grey Dick, "that we left this accursed Venice? Now that Sir Geoffrey is gone, there is naught to keep us here."

"One thing I have to do first," answered Hugh, "and it is to learn whether Sir Edmund Acour, lord of Cattrina, is dead or living, and if living where he hides himself away. While Sir Geoffrey lay dying we could not leave him to make search, but now it is otherwise."

"Ay, master, though I think you'll find the task hard in this hive of pestilence and confusion."

"I have heard that the plague is at work in Cattrina's palace," broke in David, "but when I asked whether he were there or no, none could tell me. That is not a house where you'll be welcomed, Sir Hugh."

"Still I will make bold to knock at his doors to-morrow," answered Hugh. "Now let us seek what we all need—sleep."

So on the following morning shortly after sunrise Hugh and Grey Dick, guided by David, took boat and rowed through most fearful scenes and sounds to the Palazzo Cattrina, a splendid but somewhat dilapidated building situated in a part of the city that, like itself, had seen more prosperous times. The great doors of the place set in a marble archway stood half open. Over them were cut the cognizance of the floating swan, and beneath, in letters of faded gold, the titles of Acour, de Noyon, and Cattrina. No wonder they were open, since the porter's lodge was occupied only by a grisly corpse that lay rotting on the floor, a heavy key in its hand. The courtyard beyond was empty and so, save for a dead horse, were the stables to the right. Passing up the steps of the hall that also stood open, they entered.

Here the place was in confusion, as though those who dwelt there had left in haste. The mouldering remains of a meal lay on the broad oak table; a great dower-chest inlaid with ivory, but half filled with arms and armour, stood wide. A silver crucifix that had hung above was torn down and cast upon the floor, perchance by thieves who had found it too heavy to bear away. The earthquake had thrown over a carved cabinet and some bowls of glazed ware that stood upon it. These lay about shattered amidst shields and swords thrown from the walls, where pictures of saints or perchance of dead Cattrinas hung all awry. In short, if an army had sacked it this stately hall could scarce have seemed more ruined.

Hugh and Dick crossed it to a stairway of chestnut wood whereof every newel-post was surmounted by the crest of a swan, and searched the saloons above, where also there was wreck and ruin. Then, still mounting the stair, they came to the bed-chambers. From one of these they retreated hastily, since on entering it hundreds of flies buzzing in a corner advised them that something lay there which they did not wish to see.

"Let us be going. I grow sick," exclaimed Hugh.

But Dick, who had the ears of a fox, held up his hand and said:

"Hark! I hear a voice."

Following the sound, he led his master down two long corridors that ended in a chapel. There, lying before the altar, they found a man clad in a filthy priest's robe, a dying man who still had the strength to cry for help or mercy, although in truth he was wasted to a skeleton, since the plague which had taken him was of the most lingering sort. Indeed, little seemed to be left of him save his rolling eyes, prominent nose and high cheekbones covered with yellow parchment that had been skin, and a stubbly growth of unshaven hair.

Dick scanned him. Dick, who never forgot a face, then stepped forward and said:

"So once more we meet in a chapel, Father Nicholas. Say, how has it fared with you since you fled through the chancel door of that at Blythburgh Manor? No, I forgot, that was not the last time we met. A man in a yellow cap ripped off your mask in a by-street near the Place of Arms one night and said something which it did not please you to hear."

"Water!" moaned Nicholas. "For Christ's sake give me water!"

"Why should I give you water in payment for your midnight steel yonder in the narrow street? What kind of water was it that you gave Red Eve far away at Blythburgh town?" asked Dick in his hissing voice which sounded like that of an angry snake.

But Hugh, who could bear no more of it, ran down to the courtyard, where he had seen a pitcher standing by a well, and brought water.

"Thank God that you have come again," said the wretched priest, as he snatched at it, "for I cannot bear to die with this white-faced devil glaring at me," and he pointed to Grey Dick, who leaned against the chancel wall, his arms folded on his breast, smiling coldly.

Then he drank greedily, Hugh holding the pitcher to his lips, for his wasted arms could not bear its weight.

"Now," said Hugh, when his thirst was satisfied, "tell me, where is your master, Cattrina?"

"God or the fiend can say alone. When he found that I was smitten with the plague he left me to perish, as did the others."

"And as we shall do unless you tell me whither my enemy has gone," and Hugh made as though to leave the place.

The priest clutched at him with his filthy, claw-like hand.

"For Christ's sake do not desert me," he moaned. "Let one Christian soul be near me at the last ere the curse of that wizard with the yellow cap is fulfilled on me. For the sake of Jesus, stay! I'll tell all I know."

"Speak then, and be swift. You have no time to spare, I think."

"When the darkness fell there in the Place of Arms," began Nicholas, "while you knights were waiting for the third blast of the trumpet, Cattrina fled under cover it."

"As I thought, the accursed coward!" exclaimed Hugh bitterly.

"Nay, to be just, it was not all cowardice. The wizard in the yellow cap, he who showed himself to the people afterward and called down this Black Death on Venice, appeared to him in the darkness and said something to him that turned his heart to water. I think it was that if he stayed, within five short minutes he'd be dead, who otherwise, if he fled, had yet a breathing space of life. So he went."

"Ay. But whither, man? Whither?"

"Here to his house, where he disguised himself and bade me prepare to travel with him. Only then the sickness took me and I could not. So he went with some of his people, riding for Avignon."

"What to do at Avignon?"

"To obtain the confirmation of his marriage with the lady Eve Clavering. It has been promised to him by certain cardinals at Court who have the ear of his Holiness the Pope."

"Ah, I thought it! What more?"

"Only this: tidings reached him that the lady Clavering, with the old Templar, Sir Andrew Arnold, journeys to Avignon from England, there to obtain the dissolution of their marriage with Sir Edmund Acour, Count de Noyon, Lord of Cattrina. In Avignon, however the cause may go, Cattrina purposes to snare and make her his, which will be easy, for there he has many friends and she has none."

"Except God!" exclaimed Hugh, grinding his teeth.

"And Sir Andrew Arnold," broke in Dick, "who, like some others, is, I think, one of His ministers. Still, we had better be riding, master."

"Nay, nay," cried Nicholas in a hoarse scream. "Tarry a while and I'll tell you that which will force the Pope to void this marriage. Yes, it shall be set in writing and signed by me and witnessed ere I die. There is ink and parchment in yonder little room."

"That's a good thought," said Hugh. "Dick, fetch the tools, for if we try to move this fellow he will go farther than we can follow him."

Dick went and returned presently with an ink-horn, a roll of parchment, pens and a little table. Then Hugh sat himself down on the altar rail, placing the table in front of him and said:

"Say on. I'll write, since you cannot."

Now Nicholas, having before his glazing eyes the vision of imminent judgment, briefly but clearly told all the truth at last. He told how he had drugged Red Eve, giving the name of the bane which he mixed in the milk she drank. He told how when her mind was sleeping, though her body was awake, none knowing the wickedness that had been wrought save he and Acour, and least of all her father, they had led her to the altar like a lamb to the slaughter, and there married her to the man she hated. He told how, although he had fled from England to save his life, Acour had never ceased to desire her and to plot to get her into his power, any more than he had ceased to fear Hugh's vengeance. For this reason, he said, he had clad himself in the armour of another knight at Crecy, and in that guise accepted mercy at Hugh's hand, leaving de la Roche to die in his place beneath that same hand. For this reason also he had commanded him, Nicholas, to bring about the death of Hugh de Cressi and his squire beneath the daggers of assassins in the streets of Venice, a fate from which they had been saved only by the wizard in the yellow cap, whom no steel could harm.

"The black-hearted villain!" hissed Dick. "Well, for your comfort, holy priest, I'll tell you who that wizard is. He is Death himself, Death the Sword, Death the Fire, Death the Helper, and presently you'll meet him again."

"I knew it, I knew it," groaned the wretched man. "Oh! such is the end of sin whereof we think so little in our day of strength."

"Nay," broke in Hugh, "you'll meet, not the minister, but Him whom he serves and in His hand are mercies. Be silent, Dick, for this wretch makes confession and his time is short. Spare the tool and save your wrath for him who wielded it. Go now and fetch David Day that he may witness also."

So Dick went, and Nicholas continued his tale, throwing light into many a dark place, though there was little more that Hugh thought worthy of record.

Presently David came and started back in horror at the sight of that yellow tortured face set upon a living skeleton. Then the writing was read and Nicholas, held up by Dick, set his signature with a trembling hand to this his confession of the truth. This done they signed as witnesses, all three of them.

Now Hugh, whose pity was stirred, wished to move Nicholas and lay him on a bed in some chamber, and if they could, find someone to watch him till the end. But the priest refused this charity.

"Let me die before the altar," he said, "where I may set my eyes upon Him whom I have betrayed afresh," and he pointed to the carved ivory crucifix which hung above it. "Oh! be warned, be warned, my brethren," he went on in a wailing voice. "You are all of you still young; you may be led astray as I was by the desire for power, by the hope of wealth. You may sell yourselves to the wicked as I did, I who once was good and strove toward the right. If Satan tempts you thus, then remember Nicholas the priest, and his dreadful death, and see how he pays his servants. The plague has taken others, yet they have died at peace, but I, I die in hell before I see its fires."

"Not so," said Hugh, "you have repented, and I, against whom you have sinned perhaps more than all, forgive you, as I am sure my lady would, could she know."

"Then it is more than I do," muttered Grey Dick to himself. "Why should I forgive him because he rots alive, as many a better man has done, and goes to reap what he has sown, who if he had won his way would have sent us before him at the dagger's point? Yet who knows? Each of us sins in his own fashion, and perchance sin is born of the blood and not of the will. If ever I meet Murgh again I'll ask him. But perhaps he will not answer."

Thus reflected Dick, half to David, who feared and did not understand him, and half to himself. Ere ever he had finished with his thoughts, which were not such as Sir Andrew would have approved, Father Nicholas began to die.

It was not a pleasant sight this death of his, though of its physical part nothing shall be written. Let that be buried with other records of the great plague. Only in this case his mind triumphed for a while over the dissolution of his body. When there was little left of him save bone and sinew, still he found strength to cry out to God for mercy. Yes, and to raise himself and cast what had been arms about the ivory rood and kiss its feet with what had been lips, and in his last death struggle to drag it down and pant out his ultimate breath beneath its weight.

So there they left him, a horrible, huddled heap upon which gleamed the ivory crucifix, and went their way, gasping, into the air.

## Chapter 16

# At Avignon

Hard upon two months had gone by when at length these three, Hugh, Grey Dick, and David Day, set eyes upon the towers of stately Avignon standing red against the sunset and encircled by the blue waters of the Rhone. Terrible beyond imagination had been the journey of these men, who followed in the footsteps of Murgh. They saw him not, it is true, but always they saw his handiwork. Death, death, everywhere death, nothing but death!

One night they supped at an inn with the host, his family and servants, twelve folk in all, in seeming health. When they rose in the morning one old woman and a little child alone remained; the rest were dead or dying. One day they were surprised and taken by robbers, desperate outcasts of the mountains, who gave them twenty-four hours to "make their peace with heaven"—ere they hanged them because they had slain so many of the band before they were overpowered.

But when those twenty-four hours of grace had elapsed, it would have been easy for them to hang all who remained of those robbers themselves. So they took the best of their horses and their ill-gotten gold and rode on again, leaving the murderers murdered by a stronger power than man.

They went through desolate villages, where the crops rotted in the fields; they went through stricken towns whereof the moan and the stench rose in a foul incense to heaven; they crossed rivers where the very fish had died by thousands, poisoned of the dead that rolled seaward in their waters. The pleasant land had become a hell, and untouched, unharmed, they plodded onward through those deeps of hell. But a night or two before they had slept in a city whereof the population, or those who remained alive of them, seemed to have gone mad. In one place they danced and sang and made love in an open square. In another bands of naked creatures marched the streets singing hymns and flogging themselves till the blood ran down to their heels, while the passers-by prostrated themselves before them. These were the forerunners of the "Mad Dancers" of the following year.

In a field outside of this city they came upon even a more dreadful sight. Here forty or fifty frenzied people, most of them drunk, were engaged in burning a poor Jew, his wife and two children upon a great fire made of the staves of wine-casks, which they had plundered from some neighbouring cellars. When Hugh and his companions came upon the scene the Jew had already burned and this crowd of devils were preparing to cast his wife and children into the flames, which they had been forced to see devour their husband and father. Indeed, with yells of brutal laughter, they were thrusting the children into two great casks ere they rolled them into the heart of the fire, while the wretched mother stood by and shrieked.

"What do you, sirs?" asked Hugh, riding up to them.

"We burn wizards and their spawn, Sir Knight," answered the ringleader. "Know that these accursed Jews have poisoned the wells of our town—we have witnesses who saw them do it—and thus brought the plague upon us. Moreover, she," and he pointed to the woman—"was seen talking not fourteen days ago to the devil in a yellow cap, who appears everywhere before the Death begins. Now, roll them in, roll them in!"

Hugh drew his sword, for this sight was more than his English flesh and blood could bear. Dick also unsheathed the black bow, while young David produced a great knife which he carried.

"Free those children!" said Hugh to the man with whom he had spoken, a fat fellow, with rolling, bloodshot eyes.

"Get you to hell, stranger," he answered, "or we'll throw you on the fire also as a Jew in knight's dress."

"Free those children!" said Hugh again in a terrible voice, "or I send you before them. Be warned! I speak truth."

"Be you warned, stranger, for I speak truth also," replied the man, mimicking him. "Now friends," he added, "tuck up the devil's brats in their warm bed."

They were his last words, for Hugh thrust with his sword and down he went.

Now a furious clamour arose. The mob snatched up burning staves, bludgeons, knives or whatever they had at hand, and prepared to kill the three. Without waiting for orders, Dick began to shoot. David, a bold young man, rushed at one of the most violent and stabbed him, and Hugh, who had leapt from his horse, set himself back to back with the other two. Thrice Dick shot, and at the third deadly arrow these drunken fellows grew sober enough to understand that they wished no more of them.

Suddenly, acting on a common impulse, they fled away, every one, only leaving behind them those who had fallen beneath the arrows and the sword. But some who were so full of wine that they could not run, tumbled headlong and lay there helpless.

"Woman," said Hugh when they had departed, "your husband is lost, but you and your children are saved. Now go your ways and thank whatever God you worship for His small mercies."

"Alas! Sir Knight," the poor creature, a still young and not unhandsome Jewess, wailed in answer, "whither shall I go? If I return to that town those Christian men will surely murder me and my children as they have already murdered my husband. Kill us now by the sword or the bow—it will be a kindness—but leave us not here to be tortured by the Christian men according to their fashion with us poor Jews."

"Are you willing to go to Avignon?" asked Hugh, after thinking awhile.

"Ay, Sir Knight, or anywhere away from these Christians. Indeed, at Avignon I have a brother who perchance will protect us."

"Then mount my horse," said Hugh. "Dick and David, draw those two youngsters from the tubs and set them on your beasts; we can walk."

So the children, two comely little girls of eight and six years of age, or thereabout, were dragged out of their dreadful prisons and lifted to the saddle. The wretched widow, running to the bonfire, snatched from it her husband's burnt-off hand and hid it in the bosom of her filthy robe. Then she took some of the white ashes and threw them toward that city, muttering curses as she did so.

"What do you?" asked Hugh curiously.

"I pray, sir, to Jehovah, the God of the Jews, that for every grain of these ashes He may take a life in payment for that of my murdered husband, and I think that He will listen."

"Like enough," answered Hugh, crossing himself, "but, woman, can you wonder that we Christians hold you sorcerers when we hear such prayers from your lips?"

She turned with a tragic motion, and, pointing to the bones of her husband smouldering in the fire, answered:

"And can you wonder, sir, that we wretched creatures utter such prayers when you, our masters, do such deeds as this?"

"No," answered Hugh, "I cannot. Let us be going from this shambles."

So they went, a melancholy procession if ever there one was seen upon this earth. As the three Englishmen marched behind the horses with their weeping burdens Grey Dick reflected aloud after his fashion.

"Jew and Christian!" he said. "The Jews killed one Man who chanced to be a God, though they knew it not, and ever since the Christians have killed thousands of the Jews. Now, which is the most wicked, those Jews who killed the Man Who was a God, because He said He was a God, or those Christians who throw a man into a fire to burn before his wife's and children's eyes? A man who never said that he was a god, but who, they said, put poison into their wells, which he did not do, but which they believed he did because he was one of the race that thirteen hundred years ago killed their God? Ah, well! Jew and Christian, I think the same devil dwells in them all, but Murgh alone knows the truth of the matter. If ever we meet again, I'll ask him of it. Meanwhile, we go to Avignon in strange company, whereof all the holy priests yonder, if any of them still live, to say nothing of the people, may demand an account of us."

So spoke Dick as one who seeks an answer, but neither of his companions gave him any.

On they went through the ruined land unpursued, although they had just brought sundry men to their deaths. For now neither law nor justice was left and those killed who could and those died who must, unwept and unavenged. Only certain travellers, flying they knew not whither, flying from doom to doom, eyed them with hate and loathing because of their companions. Those who consorted with Jews must, they thought, be the enemies of every Christian soul.

Well was it for them perhaps that the early winter night was closing in when they reached the wonderful bridge of St. Bénézet, now quite unguarded, since a worse foe reigned in Avignon than any that it could fear from without. They crossed it, unnoted, for here none lingered in the gloom and rain save one poor woman, who called out to them that all she loved were dead and that she went to seek them. Then, before they could interfere, she scrambled to the parapet of the bridge and with a wild cry leapt into the foaming waters that rushed beneath.

"God forgive and rest her!" muttered Hugh, crossing himself. The others only shrugged their shoulders. Such dreadful sights fed their eyes daily till they learned to take little note of them.

In a deserted place on the farther side of the bridge they halted, and Hugh said to the Jewish widow:

"Woman, here is Avignon, where you tell us there are those who will befriend you, so now let us part. We have done what we can for you and it is not safe either for you or for us that we should be seen together in this Christian city."

"Sir, you speak well," she answered. "Be pleased ere we separate, to meet no more perchance, to tell me your names that I may remember them and hand them down among my people from generation to generation."

So he told her, and thrust onto her a gift of money and the most of such food as remained to them. Then the poor woman lifted up her arms and said:

"I, Rebecca, daughter of Onias and wife of Nathan, call down on you, Hugh de Cressi, Richard Archer and David Day, and on your children forever, the blessings of Jehovah, because you have rescued the widow and her children from the fire and avenged the murder of the husband and the father. O God of my people, as Thou didst save Lot and his house from the flames of Sodom, so save these true-hearted and merciful men! Turn from them the sword of Thy wrath when it smites the sinful cities! Cast the cloak of Thy protection about them and all they love! Prosper their handiwork in peace and in war, fulfil their desire upon their enemies, and at last let them die full of years and honour and so be gathered into Thy eternal bosom! Thus prayeth Rebecca, the daughter of Onias, and thus shall it be."

Then, leading her children, she turned and vanished into the darkness.

"Now," said Dick when she had gone, "although they were spoken by a Jew whom men call accursed because their forefathers, fulfilling prophecy, or some few of them, wrought a great crime when the world was young and thereby brought about the salvation of mankind, as we believe, those are among the most comfortable words to which my ears have listened, especially such of them as dealt with the fulfilling of our desire upon our enemies in war. Well, they are spoke, and I doubt not registered in a book which will not be lost. So, master, let us seek a lodging in this city of Avignon, which, for my part, I do with a light heart."

Hugh nodded, and his heart also was lightened by those words of blessing and good omen. Mounting their horses, they took a street that led them past the great Roches des Doms, on the crest of which stood the mighty palace of the Popes, as yet unfinished, but still one of the vastest buildings they had ever seen. Here on the battlements and in front of the gateway burned great fires, lit by order of his Holiness to purify the air and protect him and his Court from the plague.

Leaving this place on their right they rode slowly along one of the principal streets of the town, seeking an inn. Soon they found one, a large place that had a sign on which three shepherds were painted, and turned to enter its gateway. But, when they saw them, out of that gateway rushed a mob of frantic people waving swords and cudgels, and saying that they would have no strangers there to bring the Death among them.

"Let us go on," said Hugh, "for here it seems we are not welcome."

So they went and tried three other inns in turn. At two of them they met with a like greeting, but the doors of the third were closed and the place was deserted. Then, for a crowd began to gather round them, wearily enough they turned up another street at hazard. Thus they wended their way back toward the great central rock, thinking that there they might find some more hospitable tavern.

Following this new street, they reached a less crowded suburb of the town, where large dwellings stood in their own gardens. One of these, they saw by the flare of some of those fires. which burned all about the city in this time of pestilence, seemed to be a small castle. At least it had a moat round it and a drawbridge, which was down. Seeing that lamps burned in its windows, Hugh, who was worn out with their long journeyings, took a sudden resolution.

"Doubtless some knight dwells in this fine house," he said to his companions. "Let us go up and declare our names and degree and by virtue of them claim the hospitality which is our right."

"Be it so," grumbled Dick. "We cannot be worse treated there than we were at the inns, unless the owner adds arrows to the swords and cudgels."

They rode across the drawbridge to the gateway of the little castle, which was open, and finding no one there, through a small courtyard to the door, which also was open.

David dismounted and knocked on it, but none answered.

"An empty house belongs to no one," said Dick; "at any rate in these times. Let us enter."

They did so, and saw that the place was sumptuously appointed. Though ancient, it was not large, having, as they afterward discovered, been a fortification on an outer wall now demolished, which had been turned to the purposes of a dwelling. Leaving the hall out of which opened the refectory, they mounted a stone stair to the upper chambers, and entered one of them.

Here they saw a strange and piteous sight. On a bed, about which candles still burned, lay a young woman who had been very beautiful, arrayed in a bride's robe.

"Dead of the plague," said Hugh, "and deserted at her death. Well, she had better luck than many, since she was not left to die alone. Her dress and these candles show it."

"Ay," answered Dick, "but fear took the watchers at last and they are fled. Well, we will fill their place, and, if they do not return to-morrow, give her honourable burial in her own courtyard. Here be fine lodgings for us, master, so let us bide in them until the rightful owners cast us out. Come, David, and help me raise that drawbridge."

Fine lodgings these proved to be indeed, since, as they found, no house in Avignon was better furnished with all things needful. But, and this will show how dreadful were the times, during these days that they made this their home they never so much as learned the name of that poor lady arrayed in the bride's dress and laid out upon her marriage bed.

In the butteries and cellar were plentiful provisions of food. Having eaten of it with thankfulness, they chose out one of the bed-chambers and slept there quite undisturbed till the morning sun shone in at the window-places and awoke them. Then they arose, and, digging a shallow grave in the courtyard with some garden tools which they found in a shed, they bore out the poor bride, and, removing only her jewels, which were rich enough, buried her there in her wedding dress. This sad duty finished, they washed themselves with water from the well, and breakfasted. After they had eaten they consulted as to what they should do next.

"We came here to lay a certain cause before his Holiness," said Hugh. "Let us go up to the palace, declare our business and estate, and ask audience."

So, leaving David in charge of the house, which they named the Bride's Tower because of the dead lady and the little keep which rose above it, and of the horses that they had stalled in the stable, they went out and made their way to the great entrance of the Pope's palace. Here they found the gates shut and barred, with a huge fire burning behind them.

Still they knocked until some guards appeared armed with cross-bows, and asked their business. They said they desired to see his Holiness, or at least one of his secretaries, whereon the guards asked whence they came. They replied from Italy, and were told that if so they would find no entrance there, since the Death had come from Italy. Now Hugh gave his name and stated his business on hearing which the guards laughed at him.

"Annulment of a false marriage!" said their captain. "Go lay your petition before Death, who will do your business swiftly if he has not done it already. Get you gone, you English knight, with your white-faced squire. We want no English here at the best of times, and least of all if they hail from Italy."

"Come on, master," said Dick, "there are more ways into a house than by the front door—and we won't want to leave our brains to grease its hinges."

So they went away, wondering whither they should betake themselves or what they could do next. As it chanced, they had not long to wait for an answer. Presently a lantern-jawed notary in a frayed russet gown, who must have been watching their movements, approached them and asked them what had been their business at the Pope's palace. Hugh told him, whereon the lawyer, finding that he was a person of high degree, became deferential in his manner. Moreover, he announced that he was a notary named Basil of Tours and one of the legal secretaries of his Holiness, who just now was living without the gates of the palace by express command in order to attend to the affairs of suitors at the Papal Court during the Great Sickness. He added, however, that he was able to communicate with those within, and that doubtless it might be in his power to forward the cause of the noble knight, Sir Hugh de Cressi, in which already he took much interest.

"There would be a fee?" suggested Dick, looking at the man coldly.

Basil answered with a smirk that fees and legal affairs were inseparable; the latter naturally involved the former. Not that he cared for money, he remarked, especially in this time of general woe. Still, it would never do for a lawyer, however humble, to create a precedent which might be used against his craft in better days. Then he named a sum.

Hugh handed him double what he asked, whereon he began to manifest great zeal in his case. Indeed, he accompanied them to the fortified house that they had named the Bride's Tower, which he alleged, with or without truth, he had never seen before. There he wrote down all particulars of the suit.

"Sir Edmund Acour, Count de Noyon, Seigneur of Cattrina?" he said presently. "Why I think that a lord of those names had audience with his Holiness some while ago, just before the pest grew bad in Avignon and the gates of the palace were ordered to be shut. I know not what passed on the occasion, not having been retained in the cause, but I will find out and tell you to-morrow."

"Find out also, if it pleases you, learned Basil," said Hugh, "whether or no this knight with the three names is still in Avignon. If so, I have a word or two to say to him."

"I will, I will," answered the lantern-jawed notary. "Yet I think it most unlikely that any one who can buy or beg a horse to ride away on should stay in this old city just now, unless indeed, the laws of his order bind him to do so that he may minister to the afflicted. Well, if the pest spares me and you, to-morrow morning I will be back here at this hour to tell you all that I can gather."

"How did this sickness begin in Avignon?" asked Grey Dick.

"Noble Squire, none know for certain. In the autumn we had great rains, heavy mists and other things contrary to the usual course of nature, such as strange lights shining in the heavens, and so forth. Then after a day of much heat, one evening a man clad in a red and yellow cap, who wore a cloak of thick black furs and necklaces of black pearls, was seen standing in the market-place. Indeed, I saw him myself. There was something so strange and dreadful about the appearance of this man, although it is true that some say he was no more than a common mountebank arrayed thus to win pence, that the people set upon him. They hurled stones at him, they attacked him with swords and every other weapon, and thought that they had killed him, when suddenly he appeared outside the throng unhurt. Then he stretched out his white-gloved hand toward them and melted into the gloom.

"Only," added Basil nervously, "it was noted afterward that all those who had tried to injure the man were among the first to die of the pest. Thank God, I was not one of them. Indeed I did my best to hold them back, which, perhaps, is the reason why I am alive to-day."

"A strange story," said Hugh, "though I have heard something like it in other cities through which we have passed. Well, till to-morrow at this hour, friend Basil."

"We have learned two things, master," said Dick, when the lawyer had bowed himself out. "First, that Acour is, or has been, in Avignon, and secondly, that Murgh the Messenger, Murgh the Sword, has been or is in Avignon. Let us go seek for one of the other of them, since for my part I desire to meet them both."

So all that day they sought but found neither.

Next morning Basil reappeared, according to his promise, and informed them that their business was on foot. Also he said that it was likely to prove more difficult than he anticipated. Indeed, he understood that he who was named de Noyon and Cattrina, having friends among the cardinals, had already obtained some provisional ratification of his marriage with the lady Eve Clavering. This ratification it would now be costly and difficult to set aside.

Hugh answered that if only he could be granted an audience with his Holiness, he had evidence which would make the justice of his cause plain. What he sought was an audience.

The notary scratched his lantern jaws and asked how that could be brought about when every gate of the palace was shut because of the plague. Still, perhaps, it might be managed, he added, if a certain sum were forthcoming to bribe various janitors and persons in authority.

Hugh gave him the sum out of the store of gold they had taken from the robbers in the mountains, with something over for himself. So Basil departed, saying that he would return at the same hour on the morrow, if the plague spared him and them, his patrons, as he prayed the Saints that it might do.

Hugh watched him go, then turned to Dick and said:

"I mistrust me of that hungry wolf in sheep's clothing who talks so large and yet does nothing. Let us go out and search Avignon again. Perchance we may meet Acour, or at least gather some tidings of him."

So they went, leaving the Tower locked and barred, who perchance would have been wiser to follow Basil. A debased and fraudulent lawyer of no character at all, this man lived upon such fees as he could wring without authority from those who came to lay their suits before the Papal Court, playing upon their hopes and fears and pretending to a power which he did not possess. Had they done so, they might have seen him turn up a certain side street, and, when he was sure that none watched him, slip into the portal of an ancient house where visitors of rank were accustomed to lodge.

Mounting some stairs without meeting any one, for this house, like many others, seemed to be deserted in that time of pestilence, he knocked upon a door.

"Begone, whoever you are," growled a voice from within. "Here there are neither sick to be tended nor dead to be borne away."

Had they been there to hear it, Hugh and Dick might have found that voice familiar.

"Noble lord," he replied, "I am the notary, Basil, and come upon your business."

"Maybe," said the voice, "but how know I that you have not been near some case of foul sickness and will not bring it here?"

"Have no fear, lord; I have been waiting on the healthy, not on the sick—a task which I leave to others who have more taste that way."

Then the door was opened cautiously, and from the room beyond it came a pungent odour of aromatic essences. Basil passed in, shutting it quickly behind him. Before him at the further side of the table and near to a blazing fire stood Acour himself. He was clothed in a long robe and held a piece of linen that was soaked in some strong-smelling substance before his nose and mouth.

"Nay, come no nearer," he said to the clerk, "for this infection is most subtle, and—be so good as to cast off that filthy cloak of yours and leave it by the door."

Basil obeyed, revealing an undergarment that was still more foul. He was not one who wasted money on new apparel.

"Well, man," said Acour, surveying him with evident disgust and throwing a handful of dried herbs upon the fire, "what news now? Has my cause been laid before his Holiness? I trust so, for know that I grow weary of being cooped up here like a falcon in a cage with the dread of a loathsome death and a handful of frightened servants as companions who do nothing but drone out prayers all day long."

"Yes, lord, it has. I have it straight from Clement's own secretary, and the answer is that his Holiness will attend to the matter when the pest has passed away from Avignon, and not before. He adds also that when it does so, if ever, all the parties to the cause, by themselves or by their representatives, must appear before him. He will give no *ex parte* judgment upon an issue which, from letters that have reached him appears to be complicated and doubtful."

"Mother of Heaven!" exclaimed Acour, "what a fool am I to let you in to tell me such tidings. Well, if that is all you have to say the sooner I am out of this hateful city the better. I ride this afternoon, or, if need be, walk on foot."

"Indeed," said Basil. "Then you leave behind you some who are not so frightened of their health, but who bide here upon a very similar errand. Doubtless, as often happens to the bold, they will find a way to fulfil it."

"And who may these be, fellow?"

"A bold and warlike knight, a squire with hair like tow and a face that might be worn by Death himself, and a young English serving man."

Acour started up from the chair in which he had sat down.

"No need to tell me their names," he said, "but how, by hell's gate, came de Cressi and his familiar here."

"By the road, I imagine, lord, like others. At least, a few days ago they were seen travelling toward the bridge of St. Bénézet in the company of certain Jews, whom, I am informed, they had rescued from the just reward of their witchcraft. I have a note of all the facts, which include the slaying of sundry good Christians on behalf of the said Jews."

"Jews? Why, that is enough to hang them in these times. But what do they here and where do they lodge?"

"Like your lordship they strive to see the Pope. They desire that an alleged marriage between one Sir Edmund Acour, Count of Noyon and Seigneur of Cattrina, and one lady Eve Clavering, an Englishwoman, may be declared null and void. As they have been so good as to honour me with their confidence and appoint me their agent, I am able to detail the facts. Therefore I will tell you at once that the case of this knight de Cressi appears to be excellent, since it includes the written confession of a certain Father Nicholas, of whom perhaps you have heard."

"The written confession of Nicholas! Have you seen it?"

"Not as yet. So far I have been trusted with no original documents. Is it your will that I should try to possess myself of these? Because, if so, I will do my best, provided—" and he looked at the pocket of Acour's robe.

"How much?" asked Acour. The man named a great sum, half to be paid down and half on the delivery of the papers.

"I'll double it," said Acour, "if you can bring it about that these insolent Englishmen die—of the pest."

"How can I do that, lord?" asked Basil with a sour smile. "Such tricks might work backward. I might die, or you. Still these men have committed crimes, and just now there is a prejudice against Jews."

"Ay," said Acour, "the Englishmen are sorcerers. I tell you that in Venice they were seen in the company of that fiend of the yellow cap and the fur robe who appears everywhere before the pest."

"Prove it," exclaimed Basil, "and the citizens of Avignon will rid you of their troubling."

Then they debated long together and the end of it was that Basil departed, saying that he would return again on the morrow and make report as to certain matters.

## Chapter 17

# A Meeting

Hugh, Grey Dick, and David, trudged up and down through the streets of Avignon. All that long day they trudged seeking news and finding little. Again and again they asked at the inns whether a knight who bore the name of Acour, or de Noyon, or Cattrina, was or had been a guest there, but none whom they asked seemed to know anything of such a person.

They asked it of citizens, also of holy priests, good men who, careless of their own lives, followed biers or cartloads of dead destined to the plague pit or the river that they might pronounce over them the last blessings of the Church. They asked it of physicians, some few of whom still remained alive, as they hurried from house to house to administer to the sick or dying. But all of these either did not answer at all or else shrugged their shoulders and went on their melancholy business. Only one of them called back that he had no time to waste in replying to foolish questions, and that probably the knight they sought was dead long ago or had fled from the city.

Another man, an officer of customs, who seemed half dazed with misery and fear, said that he remembered the lord Cattrina entering Avignon with a good many followers, since he himself had levied the customary tolls on his company. As for how long it was ago he could not say, since his recollection failed him—so much had happened since. So he bade them farewell until they met in heaven, which, he added, doubtless would be soon.

The evening drew on. Wearily enough they had trudged round the great Roche des Doms, looking up at the huge palace of the Pope, where the fires burned night and day and the guards watched at the shut gates, that forbidden palace into which no man might enter. Leaving it, they struck down a street that was new to them, which led toward their borrowed dwelling of the Bride's Tower. This street was very empty save for a few miserable creatures, some of whom lay dead or dying in the gutters. Others lurked about in doorways or behind the pillars of gates, probably for no good purpose. They heard the footsteps of a man following them who seemed to keep in the shadow, but took no heed, since they set him down as some wretched thief who would never dare to attack three armed men. It did not occur to them that this was none other than the notary Basil, clad in a new robe, who for purposes of his own was spying upon their movements.

They came to a large, ruinous-looking house, of which the gateway attracted Grey Dick's sharp eyes.

"What does that entrance remind you of, master?" he asked.

Hugh looked at it carelessly and answered:

"Why, of the Preceptory at Dunwich. See, there are the same arms upon the stone shield. Doubtless once the Knights Templar dwelt there. Sir Andrew may have visited this place in his youth."

As the words left his lips two men came out of the gateway, one of them a physician to judge by the robe and the case of medicines which he carried; the other a very tall person wrapped in a long cloak. The physician was speaking.

"She may live or she may die," he said. "She seems strong. The pest, you say, has been on her for four days, which is longer than most endure it; she has no swellings, and has not bled from the lungs; though, on the other hand, she is now insensible, which often precedes the end. I can say no more; it is in the hands of God. Yes, I will ask you to pay me the fee now. Who knows if you will be alive to do so to-morrow? If she dies before then I recommend you to throw her into the river, which the Pope has blessed. It is cleaner burial than the plague pit. I presume she is your grand-daughter—a beautiful woman. Pity she should be wasted thus, but many others are in a like case. If she awakes give her good food, and if you cannot get that—wine, of which there is plenty. Five gold pieces—thank you," and he hurried away.

"Little have you told me, physician, that I did not know already," said the tall hooded figure, in a deep voice the sound of which thrilled Hugh to his marrow. "Yet you are right; it is in the hands of God. And to those hands I trust—not in vain, I think."

"Sir," said Hugh addressing him out of the shadow in which he stood, "be pleased to tell me, if you will, whether you have met in this town a knight of the name of Sir Edmund Acour, for of him I am in search?"

"Sir Edmund Acour?" answered the figure. "No, I have not met him in Avignon, though it is like enough that he is here. Yet I have known of this knight far away in England."

"Was it at Blythburgh, in Suffolk, perchance?" asked Hugh.

"Ay, at Blythburgh in Suffolk; but who are you that speak in English and know of Blythburgh in Suffolk?"

"Oh!" cried Hugh, "what do you here, Sir Andrew Arnold?"

The old man threw back his hood and stared at him.

"Hugh de Cressi, by Christ's holy Name!" he exclaimed. "Yes, and Richard the archer, also. The light is bad; I did not see your faces. Welcome, Hugh, thrice welcome," and he threw his arms about him and embraced him. "Come, enter my lodgings, I have much to say to you."

"One thing I desire to learn most of all, Father; the rest can wait. Who is the sick lady of whom you spoke to yonder physician—she that, he thought, was your grand-daughter?"

"Who could it be, Hugh, except Eve Clavering."

"Eve!" gasped Hugh. "Eve dying of the pest?"

"Nay, son: who said so? She is ill, not dying, who, I believe, will live for many years."

"You believe, Father, you believe! Why this foul plague scarce spares one in ten. Oh! why do you believe?"

"God teaches me to do so," answered the old knight solemnly. "I only sent for that physician because he has medicines which I lack. But it is not in him and his drugs that I put my trust. Come, let us go in and see her."

So they went up the stairs and turned down a long passage, into which the light flowed dimly through large open casements.

"Who is that?" asked Hugh suddenly. "I thought that one brushed past me, though I could see nothing."

"Ay," broke in the lad David, who was following, "and I felt a cold wind as though some one stirred the air."

Grey Dick also opened his lips to speak, then changed his mind and was silent, but Sir Andrew said impatiently:

"I saw no one, therefore there was no one to see. Enter!" and he opened the door.

Now they found themselves in a lighted room, beyond which lay another room.

"Bide you here, Richard, with your companion," said Sir Andrew. "Hugh, follow me, and let us learn whether I have trusted to God in vain."

Then very gently he opened the door, and they passed in together, closing it behind them.

This is what Hugh saw. At the far end of the room was a bed, near to which stood a lamp that showed, sitting up in the bed, a beautiful young woman, whose dark hair fell all about her. Her face was flushed but not wasted or made dreadful by the sickness, as happened to so many. There she sat staring before her with her large dark eyes and a smile upon her sweet lips, like one that muses on happy things.

"See," whispered Sir Andrew, "she is awakened from her swoon. I think I did not trust in vain, my son."

She caught the tones of his voice and spoke.

"Is that you, Father?" she asked dreamily. "Draw near, for I have such a strange story to tell you."

He obeyed, leaving Hugh in the shadow, and she went on:

"Just now I awoke from my sleep and saw a man standing by my bed."

"Yes, yes," Sir Andrew said, "the physician whom I sent for to see you."

"Do physicians in Avignon wear caps of red and yellow and robes of black fur and strings of great black pearls that, to tell truth, I coveted sorely?" she asked, laughing a little. "No, no. If this were a physician, he is of the sort that heals souls. Indeed, now that I think of it, when I asked him his name and business, he answered that the first was the Helper, and the second, to bring peace to those in trouble."

"Well, daughter, and what else did the man say?" asked Sir Andrew, soothingly.

"You think I wander," she said, interpreting the tone of his voice and not his words, "but indeed it is not so. Well, he said little; only that I had been very ill, near to death, in truth, much nearer than I thought, but that now I should recover and within a day or two be quite well and strong again. I asked him why he had come to tell me this. He replied, because he thought that I should like to know that he had met one whom I loved in the city of Venice in Italy; one who was named Hugh de Cressi. Yes, Father, he said Hugh de Cressi, who, with his squire, an archer, had befriended him there—and that this Hugh was well and would remain so, and that soon I should see him again. Also he added that he had met one whom I hated, who was named the lord of Cattrina, and that if this Cattrina threatened me I should do wisely to fly back to England, since there I should find peace and safety. Then, suddenly, just before you came in, he was gone."

"You have strange dreams, Eve," said Sir Andrew, "yet there is truth in their madness. Now be strong lest joy should kill you, as it has done by many a one before."

Then he turned to the shadow behind him and said, "Come." Next instant Hugh was kneeling at Eve's bedside and pressing his lips upon her hand.

********

Oh! they had much to say to each other, so much that the half of it remained unsaid. Still Hugh learned that she and Sir Andrew had come to Avignon upon the Pope's summons to lay this matter of her alleged marriage before him in person. When they reached the town they found it already in the grip of the great plague, and that to see his Holiness was almost impossible, since he had shut himself up in his palace and would admit no one. Yet an interview was promised through Sir Andrew's high-placed friends, only then the sickness struck Eve and she could not go, nor was Sir Andrew allowed to do so, since he was nursing one who lay ill.

Then Hugh began to tell his tale, to which Eve and Sir Andrew Arnold listened greedily. Of Murgh, for sundry reasons, he said nothing, and of the fight from which Acour had fled in Venice before the earthquake but little. He told them, however, that he had heard that this Acour had been or was in Avignon and that he had learned from a notary named Basil, whom he, Hugh, had retained, that Acour had won from the Pope a confirmation of his marriage.

"A lie!" interrupted Sir Andrew. "His Holiness caused me to be informed expressly that he would give no decision in this cause until all the case was before him."

As he said the words a disturbance arose in the outer room, and the harsh voice of Grey Dick was heard saying:

"Back, you dog! Would you thrust yourself into the chamber of the lady of Clavering? Back, or I will cast you through the window-place."

Sir Andrew went to see what was the matter, and Hugh, breaking off his tale, followed him, to find the notary, Basil, on his knees with Grey Dick gripping him by the collar of his robe.

"Sir Knight," said Basil, recognizing Hugh, "should I, your faithful agent, be treated thus by this fierce-faced squire of yours?"

"That depends on what you have done, Sir Lawyer," answered Hugh, motioning to Dick to loose the man.

"All I have done, Sir Knight, is to follow you into a house where I chanced to see you enter, in order to give you some good tidings. Then this fellow caught me by the throat and said that if I dared to break in upon the privacy of one whom he called Red Eve and Lady Clavering, he would kill me."

"He had his orders, lawyer."

"Then, Sir Knight, he might have executed them less roughly. Had he but told me that you were alone with some lady, I should have understand and withdrawn for a while, although to do so would have been to let precious moments slip," and the lean-faced knave leered horribly.

"Cease your foul talk and state your business," interrupted Sir Andrew, thrusting himself in front of Hugh, who he feared would strike the fellow.

"And pray, who may you be?" asked the lawyer, glancing up at the tall figure that towered above him.

Sir Andrew threw back his hood, revealing his aged, hawk-like countenance, his dark and flashing eyes and his snow-white hair and beard.

"If you would learn, man," he said, in his great voice, "in the world I was known as Sir Andrew Arnold, one of the priors of the Order of the Templars, which is a name that you may have heard. But now that I have laid aside all worldly pomp and greatness, I am but Father Andrew, of Dunwich, in England."

"Yes, yes, I have heard the name; who has not?" said the lawyer humbly; "also you are here as guardian to the lady Eve Clavering, are you not, to lay a certain cause before his Holiness? Oh! do not start, all these matters came to my knowledge who am concerned in every great business in Avignon as the chief agent and procurator of the Papal Court, though it is true that this tiding has reached me only within the last few minutes and from the lips of your own people. Holy Father, I pray your pardon for breaking in upon you, which I did only because the matter is very pressing. Sir Hugh de Cressi here has a cause to lay before the Pope with which you may be acquainted. Well, for two days I have striven to win him an audience, and now through my sole influence, behold! 'tis granted. See here," and he produced a parchment that purported to be signed by the Pope's secretary and countersigned by a cardinal, and read:

"'If the English knight, Sir Hugh de Cressi, and his squire, the captain Richard, will be in the chamber of audience at the palace at seven of the clock this evening' (that is, within something less than half an hour), 'his Holiness will be pleased to receive them as a most special boon, having learned that the said Sir Hugh is a knight much in favour with his Grace of England, who appointed him his champion in a combat that was lately to be fought at Venice.'"

"That's true enough, though I know not how the Pope heard of it," interrupted Hugh.

"Through me, Sir Knight, for I learn everything. None have so much power in Avignon as I, although it often pleases me to seem poor and of no account. But let that pass. Either you must take this opportunity or be content not to see his Holiness at all. Orders have been issued because of the increase of this pest in Avignon, that from to-night forward none shall be admitted to the palace upon any pretext whatsoever; no, not even a king."

"Then I had best go," said Hugh.

"Ay," answered Sir Andrew, "and return here with your tidings as soon as may be. Yet," he added in a low voice to Grey Dick, "I love not the look of this scurvy guide of yours. Could not your master have found a better attorney?"

"Perhaps," answered Dick, "that is if one is left alive in Avignon. Being in haste we took the first that came to hand, and it seems that he will serve our turn. At least, if he plays tricks, I promise it will be the worse for him," and he looked grimly at the rogue, who was talking to David Day and appeared to hear nothing.

So they went, and with them David, who had witnessed the confession of Father Nicholas. Therefore they thought it best that he should accompany them to testify to it if there were need.

"Bid my lady keep a good heart and say that I will be with her again ere long," said Hugh as they descended the stairs in haste.

Following the guidance of Basil, they turned first this way and then that, till soon in the gathering darkness they knew not where they were.

"What was the name of the street in which Sir Andrew had his lodging?" asked Hugh, halting.

"Rue St. Benezet," answered Basil. "Forward, we have no time to lose."

"Did you tell Sir Andrew where we dwelt, master?" said Dick presently, "for I did not."

"By my faith, Dick, no; it slipped my mind."

"Then it will be hard for him to find us if he has need, master, in this rabbit warren of a town. Still that can't be mended now. I wish we were clear of this business, for it seems to me that yon fellow is not leading us toward the palace. Almost am I minded—" and he looked at Basil, then checked himself.

Presently Dick wished it still more. Taking yet another turn they found themselves in an open square or garden that was surrounded by many mean houses. In this square great pest-fires burned, lighting it luridly. By the flare of them they saw that hundreds of people were gathered there listening to a mad-eyed friar who was preaching to them from the top of a wine-cart. As they drew near to the crowd through which Basil was leading them, Hugh heard the friar shouting:

"Men of Avignon, this pest which kills us is the work not of God, but of the Jew blasphemers and of the sorcerers who are in league with them. I tell you that two such sorcerers who pass as Englishmen are in your city now and have been consorting with the Jews, plotting your destruction. One looks like a young knight, but the other has the face of Death himself, and both of them wrought murders in a neighbouring town to protect the Jews. Until you kill the accursed Jews this plague will never pass. You will die, every one of you, with your wives and children if you do not kill the Jews and their familiars."

Just then the man, rolling his wild eyes about, caught sight of Hugh and Dick.

"See!" he screamed. "There are the wizards who in Venice were seen in the company of the Enemy of Mankind. That good Christian, Basil, has brought them face to face with you, as he promised me that he would."

As he heard these words Hugh drew his sword and leapt at Basil. But the rogue was watching. With a yell of fear he threw himself among the crowd and there vanished.

"Out weapons, and back to back!" cried Hugh, "for we are snared."

So the three of them ranged themselves together facing outward. In front of them gleamed Grey Dick's axe, Hugh's sword and David's great knife. In a moment the furious mob was surging round them like the sea, howling, "Down with the foreign wizards! Kill the friends of the Jews!" one solid wall of changing white faces.

A man struck at them with a halbert, but the blow fell short, for he was afraid to come too near. Grey Dick leapt forward, and in a moment was back again, leaving that man dead, smitten through from skull to chin. For a while there was silence, since this sudden death gave them pause, and in it Hugh cried out:

"Are blameless men to be murdered thus? Have we no friends in Avignon?"

"Some," answered a voice from the outer shadow, though who spoke they could not see.

"Save the protectors of the Jews!" cried the voice again.

Then came a rush and a counter-rush. Fighting began around them in which they took no share. When it had passed over them like a gust of wind, David Day was gone, killed or trodden down, as his companions thought.

"Now, master, we are alone," said Grey Dick. "Set your shoulders against mine and let us die a death that these dogs of Avignon will remember."

"Ay, ay!" answered Hugh. "But don't overreach, Dick, 'tis ever the archer's fault."

The mob closed in on them, then rolled back like water from a rock, leaving some behind. Again they closed in and again rolled back.

"Bring bows!" they cried, widening out. "Bring bows and shoot them down."

"Ah!" gasped Dick, "that is a game two can play, now that I have arm room."

Almost before the words had left his lips the great black bow he bore was out and strung. Next instant the shafts began to rush, piercing all before them, till at the third arrow those in front of him melted away, save such as would stir no more. Only now missiles began to come in answer from this side and from that, although as yet none struck them.

"Unstring your bow, Dick, and let us charge," said Hugh. "We have no other chance save flight. They'll pelt us under."

Dick did not seem to hear. At least he shot on as one who was not minded to die unavenged. An arrow whistled through Hugh's cap, lifting it from his head, and another glanced from the mail on his shoulder. He ground his teeth with rage, for now none would come within reach of his long sword.

"Good-bye, friend Dick," he said. "I die charging," and with a cry of "A Cressi! A Cressi!" he sprang forward.

One leap and Dick was at his side, who had only bided to sheath his bow. The mob in front melted away before the flash of the white sword and the gleam of the grey axe. Still they must have fallen, for their pursuers closed in behind them like hunting hounds when they view the quarry, and there were none to guard their backs. But once more the shrill voice cried:

"Help the friends of the Jews! Save those who saved Rebecca and her children!"

Then again there came a rush of dark-browed men, who hissed and whistled as they fought.

So fierce was the rush that those who followed them were cut off, and Dick, glancing back over his shoulder, saw the mad-eyed priest, their leader, go down like an ox beneath the blow of a leaded bludgeon. A score of strides and they were out of the range of the firelight; another score and they were hidden by the gloom in the mouth of one of the narrow streets.

"Which way now?" gasped Hugh, looking back at the square where in the flare of the great fires Christians and Jews, fighting furiously, looked like devils struggling in the mouth of hell.

As he spoke a shock-headed, half-clad lad darted up to them and Dick lifted his axe to cut him down.

"Friend," he said in a guttural voice, "not foe! I know where you dwell; trust and follow me, who am of the kin of Rebecca, wife of Nathan."

"Lead on then, kin of Rebecca," exclaimed Hugh, "but know that if you cheat us, you die."

"Swift, swift!" cried the lad, "lest those swine should reach your house before you," and, catching Hugh by the hand, he began to run like a hare.

Down the dark streets they went, past the great rock where the fires burned at the gates of the palace of the Pope, then along more streets and across an open place where thieves and night-birds peered at them curiously, but at the sight of their drawn steel, slunk away. At length their guide halted.

"See!" he said. "There is your dwelling. Enter now and up with the bridge. Hark! They come. Farewell."

He was gone. From down the street to their left rose shouts and the sound of many running feet, but there in front of them loomed the Tower against the black and rainy sky. They dashed across the little drawbridge that spanned the moat, and, seizing the cranks, wound furiously. Slowly, ah! how slowly it rose, for it was heavy, and they were but two tired men; also the chains and cogs were rusty with disuse. Yet it did rise, and as it came home at last, the fierce mob, thirsting for their blood and guessing where they would refuge, appeared in front of it and by the light of some torches which they bore, caught sight of them.

"Come in, friends," mocked Grey Dick as they ran up and down the edge of the moat howling with rage and disappointment. "Come in if you would sup on arrow-heads such as this," and he sent one of his deadly shafts through the breast of a red-headed fellow who waved a torch in one hand and a blacksmith's hammer in the other.

Then they drew back, taking the dead man with them, but as they went one cried:

"The Jews shall not save you again, wizards, for if we cannot come at you to kill you, we'll starve you till you die. Stay there and rot, or step forth and be torn to pieces, as it pleases you, English wizards."

Then they all slunk back and vanished, or seemed to vanish, down the mouths of the dark streets that ran into the open place in front of the dwelling which Hugh had named the Bride's Tower.

"Now," said Dick, wiping the sweat from his brow as they barred the massive door of the house, "we are safe for this night at least, and can eat and sleep in peace. See you, master, I have taken stock of this old place, which must have been built in rough times, for scarce a wall of it is less than five feet thick. The moat is deep all round. Fire cannot harm it, and it is loop-holed for arrows and not commanded by any other building, having the open place in front and below the wide fosse of the ancient wall, upon which it stands. Therefore, even with this poor garrison of two, it can be taken only by storm. This, while we have bows and arrows, will cost them something, seeing that we could hold the tower from stair to stair."

"Ay, Dick," answered Hugh sadly, "doubtless we can make a fight for it and take some with us to a quieter world, if they are foolish enough to give us a chance. But what did that fellow shout as to starving us out? How stand we for provisions?"

"Foreseeing something of the sort, I have reckoned that up, master. There's good water in the courtyard well and those who owned this tower, whoever they may have been, laid in great store, perchance for the marriage feast, or perchance when the plague began, knowing that it would bring scarcity. The cupboards and the butteries are filled with flour, dried flesh, wine, olives and oil for burning. Even if these should fail us there are the horses in the stable, which we can kill and cook, for of forage and fuel I have found enough."

"Then the Pope should not be more safe than we, Dick," said Hugh with a weary smile, "if any are safe in Avignon to-day. Well, let us go and eat of all this plenty, but oh! I wish I had told Sir Andrew where we dwelt, or could be sure in which of that maze of streets he and Red Eve are lodged. Dick, Dick, that knave Basil has fooled us finely."

"Ay, master," said Dick, setting his grim lips, "but let him pray his Saint that before all is done I do not fool him."

## Chapter 18

# The Plague Pit

Seven long days had gone by and still Hugh and Grey Dick held out in their Tower fortress. Though as yet unhurt, they were weary indeed, since they must watch all night and could only sleep by snatches in the daytime, one lying down to rest while the other kept guard.

As they had foreseen, except by direct assault, the place proved impregnable, its moat protecting it upon three sides and the sheer wall of the old city terminating in the deep fosse upon the fourth. In its little armoury, among other weapons they had found a great store of arrows and some good bows, whereof Hugh took the best and longest. Thus armed with these they placed themselves behind the loopholes of the embattled gateway, whence they could sweep the space before them. Or if danger threatened them elsewhere, there were embrasures whence they could command the bases of the walls. Lastly, also, there was the central tower, whereof they could hold each landing with the sword.

Thrice they had been attacked, since there seemed to be hundreds of folk in Avignon bent upon their destruction, but each time their bitter arrows, that rarely seemed to miss, had repulsed the foe with loss. Even when an onslaught was delivered on the main gateway at night, they had beaten their assailants by letting fall upon them through the *machicoulis* or overhanging apertures, great stones that had been piled up there, perhaps generations before, when the place was built.

Still the attacks did not slacken. Indeed the hate of the citizens of Avignon against these two bold Englishmen, whose courage and resource they attributed to help given to them by the powers of evil, seemed to grow from day to day, even as the plague grew in the streets of that sore-afflicted city. From their walls they could see friars preaching a kind of crusade against them. They pointed toward the tower with crucifixes, invoking their hearers to pull it stone from stone and slay the wizards within, the wizards who had conspired with the accursed Jews even beneath the eyes of his Holiness the Pope, to bring doom on Avignon.

The eighth morn broke at length, and its first red rays discovered Hugh and Dick kneeling side by side behind the battlements of the gateway. Each of them was making petition to heaven in his own fashion for forgiveness of his sins, since they were outworn and believed that this day would be their last.

"What did you pray for, Dick?" asked Hugh, glancing at his companion's fierce face, which in that half light looked deathlike and unearthly.

"What did I pray for? Well, for the first part let it be; that's betwixt me and whatever Power sent me out to do its business on the earth. But for the last—I'll tell you. It was that we may go hence with such a guard of dead French as never yet escorted two Englishmen from Avignon to heaven—or hell. Ay, and we will, master, for to-day, as they shouted to us, they'll storm this tower; but if our strength holds out there's many a one who'll never win its crest."

"Rather would I have died peacefully, Dick. Yet the blood of these hounds will not weigh upon my soul, seeing that they seek to murder us for no fault except that we saved a woman and two children from their cruel devilries. Oh! could I but know that Red Eve and Sir Andrew were safe away, I'd die a happy man."

"I think we shall know that and much more before to-morrow's dawn, master, or never know anything again. Look! they gather yonder. Now let us eat, for perhaps later we shall find no time."

********

The afternoon drew on toward evening and still these two lived. Of all the hundreds of missiles which were shot or hurled at them, although a few struck, not one of them had pierced their armour so as to do them hurt. The walls and battlements or some good Fate had protected them. Thrice had the French come on, and thrice they had retreated before those arrows that could not miss, and as yet bridge and doors were safe.

"Look," said Dick as he set down a cup of wine that he had drained, for his thirst was raging, "they send an embassy," and he pointed to a priest, the same mad-eyed fellow who preached in the square when the notary Basil led them into a trap, and to a man with him who bore a white cloth upon a lance. "Shall I shoot them?"

"Nay," answered Hugh; "why kill crazed folk who think that they serve God in their own fashion? We will hear what they have to say."

Presently the pair stood within speaking distance, and the priest called out:

"Hearken, you wizards. So far your master the devil has protected you, but now your hour has come. We have authority from those who rule this city and from the Church to summon you to surrender, and if you will not, then to slay you both."

"That, you shameless friar," answered Hugh, "you have been striving to do these many days. Yet it is not we who have been slain, although we stand but two men against a multitude. But if we surrender, what then?"

"Then you shall be put upon your trial, wizards, and, if found guilty, burned; if innocent, set free."

"Put upon our trial before our executioners! Why, I think those fires are alight already. Nay, nay, mad priest, go back and tell those whom you have fooled that if they want us they can come and take us, which they'll not do living."

Then the furious friar began to curse them, hurling at them the anathemas of the Church, till at length Dick called to him to begone or he would send an arrow to help him on the road.

So they went, and presently the sun sank.

"Now let us beware," said Dick. "The moon is near her full and will rise soon. They'll attack between times when we cannot see to shoot."

"Ay," answered Hugh, "moreover, now this gateway is no place for us. Of arrows there are few left, nor could we see to use them in the dark. The stones too are all spent and therefore they can bridge the moat and batter down the doors unharmed."

"What then?" asked Dick. "As we cannot fly, where shall we die?"

"On the roof of the old tower, I think, whence we can hurl ourselves at last and so perhaps escape being taken alive, and torment. Look you, Dick, that tower is mounted by three straight flights of steps. The first two of these we'll hold with such arrows as remain to us—there are three and twenty, as I think—and the last with axe and sword. Listen! They come! Take a brand from the hall hearth and let us go light the flambeaux."

So they went and set fire to the great torches of wood and tallow that were set in their iron holders to light the steps of the tower. Ere the last of them was burning they heard their enemies ravening without.

"Listen!" said Hugh as they descended to the head of the first flight of stairs. "They are across the moat."

As he spoke the massive doors crashed in beneath the blows of a baulk of timber.

"Now," said Hugh, as they strung their bows, "six arrows apiece here, if we can get off so many, and the odd eleven at our next stand. Ah, they come."

The mob rushed into the hall below, waving torches and swords and hunting it as dogs hunt a covert.

"The English wizards have hid themselves away," cried a voice. "Let us burn the place, for so we are sure to catch them."

"Nay, nay," answered another voice, that of the mad friar. "We must have them beneath the torture, that we may learn how to lift the curse from Avignon, and the names of their accomplices on earth and in hell. Search, search, search!"

"Little need to search," said Grey Dick, stepping out on to the landing. "Devil, go join your fellow-devils in that hell you talk of," and he sent an arrow through his heart.

For a moment there followed the silence of consternation while the mob stood staring at their fallen leader. Then with a yell of rage they charged the stair and that fray began which was told of in Avignon for generations. Hugh and Dick shot their arrows, nor could they miss, seeing what was their target; indeed some of those from the great black bow pinned foe to foe beneath them. But so crowded were the assailants on the narrow stair that they could not shoot back. They advanced helpless, thrust to their doom by the weight of those who pressed behind.

Now they were near, the dead, still on their feet, being borne forward by the living, to whom they served as shields. Hugh and Dick ran to the head of the second flight and thence shot off the arrows that remained.

Dick loosed the last of them, and of this fearful shaft it was said that it slew three men, piercing through the body of one, the throat of the second and burying its barb in the skull of the third on the lowest step. Now Dick unstrung his bow, and thrust it into its case on his shoulder, for he was minded that they should go together at the last.

"Shafts have sung their song," he said, with a fierce laugh; "now it is the turn of the axe and sword to make another music."

Then he gripped Sir Hugh by the hand, saying:

"Farewell, master. Oh, I hold this a merry death, such as the Saints grant to few. Ay, and so would you were you as free as I am. Well, doubtless your lady has gone before. Or at worst soon she will follow after and greet you in the Gate of Death, where Murgh sits and keeps his count of passing souls."

"Farewell, friend," answered Hugh, "be she quick or dead, thus Red Eve would wish that I should die. *A Cressi! A Cressi!*" he cried and drove his sword through the throat of a soldier who rushed at him.

********

They fought a very good fight, as doubtless the dead were telling each other while they passed from that red stair to such rest as they had won. They had fought a very good fight and it was hard to say which had done the best, Hugh's white sword or Dick's grey axe. And now, unwounded still save for a bruise or two, they stood there in the moonlight upon the stark edge of the tall tower, the foe in front and black space beneath. There they stood leaning on axe and sword and drawing their breath in great sobs, those two great harvestmen who that day had toiled so hard in the rich fields of death.

For a while the ever-gathering crowd of their assailants remained still staring at them. Then the leaders began to whisper to each other, for they scarcely seemed to dare to talk aloud.

"What shall we do?" asked one. "These are not men. No men could have fought as they have fought us for seven days and at last have slain us like sparrows in a net and themselves remained unhurt."

"No," answered another, "and no mortal archer could send his shaft through the bodies of three. Still it is finished now unless they find wings and fly away. So let us take them."

"Yes, yes," broke in Grey Dick with his hissing laugh, "come and take us, you curs of Avignon. Having our breath again, we are ready to be taken," and he lifted his axe and shook it.

"Seize them," shouted the leader of the French. "Seize them!" echoed those who poured up the stairs behind.

But there the matter ended, since none could find stomach to face that axe and sword. So at length they took another counsel.

"Bring bows and shoot them through the legs. Thus we shall bring them living to their trial," commanded the captain of the men of Avignon. He was their fourth captain on that one day, for the other three lay upon the stairs or in the hall.

Now Hugh and Dick spoke together, few words and swift, as to whether they should charge or leap from the wall and have done with it. While they spoke a little cloud floated over the face of the moon, so that until it had gone the French could not see to shoot.

"It's too risky," said Hugh. "If they capture us we must die a death to which I have no mind. Let us hurl our weapons at them, then leap."

"So be it," whispered Dick. "Do you aim at the captain on the left and I will take the other. Ready now! I think one creeps near to us."

"I think so, too," Hugh whispered back, "I felt the touch of his garments. Only he seemed to pass us from behind, which cannot be."

The cloud passed, and once again they were bathed in silver light. It showed the men of Avignon already bending their bows; it showed Hugh and Grey Dick lifting axe and sword to hurl them. But between them and their mark it showed also a figure that they knew well, a stern and terrible figure, wearing a strange cap of red and yellow and a cape of rich, black fur.

"O God of Heaven! 'tis Murgh the Helper," gasped Hugh.

"Ay, Murgh the Fire, Murgh the Sword," said Dick, adding quietly, "it is true I was wondering whether he would prove as good as his word. Look now, look! they see him also!"

See him they did, indeed, and for a moment there was silence on that crowded tower top where stood at least a score of men, while their fellows packed the hall and stair below by hundreds. All stared at Murgh, and Murgh stared back at them with his cold eyes. Then a voice screamed:

"Satan! Satan come from hell to guard his own! Death himself is with you! Fly, men of Avignon, fly!"

Small need was there for this command. Already, casting down their bows, those on the tower top were rushing to the mouth of the stair, and, since it was blocked with men, using their swords upon them to hew a road. Now those below, thinking that it was the English wizards who slew them, struck back.

Presently all that stair and the crowded hall below, black as the mouth of the pit, for such lights as still burned soon were swept away, rang with the screams and curses and stifled groans of the trodden down or dying. In the pitchy darkness brother smote brother, friend trampled out the life of friend, till the steep steps were piled high and the doorways blocked with dead. So hideous were the sounds indeed, that Hugh and Grey Dick crossed themselves, thinking that hell had come to Avignon, or Avignon sunk down to hell. But Murgh only folded his white-gloved hands upon his breast and smiled.

At length, save for the moaning of those hurt men who still lived, the dreadful tumult sank to silence. Then Murgh turned and spoke in his slow and icy voice:

"You were about to seek me in the fosse of this high tower, were you not, Hugh de Cressi and Richard Archer? A foolish thought, in truth, and a sinful, so sinful that it would have served you well if I had let you come. But your strait was sore and your faith was weak, and I had no such command. Therefore I have come to others whose names were written in my book. Ay, and being half human after all—for does not your creed tell you that I was born of Sin? I rejoice that it is given to me to protect those who would have protected *me* when *I* seemed to stand helpless in the hands of cruel men. Nay, thank me not. What need have I of your thanks, which are due to God alone! And question me not, for why should I answer your questions, even if I know those answers? Only do my bidding. This night seek whom you will in Avignon, but to-morrow ere the dawn ride away, for we three must meet again at a place appointed before this winter's snows are passed."

"O dread lord of Death, one thing, only one," began Hugh.

But Murgh held up his white-gloved hand and replied:

"Have I not said that I answer no questions? Now go forth and follow the promptings of your heart till we meet again."

Then gliding to the head of the stair he vanished in the shadow.

"Say, what shall we do?" asked Hugh in amazed voice.

"It matters little what we do or leave undone, master, seeing that we are fore-fated men whom, as I think, none can harm until a day that will not dawn to-morrow nor yet awhile. Therefore let us wash ourselves and eat and borrow new garments, if we can find any that are not soiled, and then, if the horses are still unharmed, mount and ride from this accursed Avignon for England."

"Nay, Dick, since first we must learn whether or no we leave friends behind us here."

"Ay, master, if you will. But since yonder Murgh said nothing of them, it was in my mind that they are either dead or fled."

"Not dead, I pray, Dick. Oh, I am sure, not dead, and I left living! When Red Eve and I met, Murgh had been with her and promised that she would recover and be strong," answered Hugh bravely, although there was a note of terror in his voice.

"Red Eve has other foes in Avignon besides the pest," muttered Grey Dick, adding: "still, let us have faith; it is a good friend to man. Did not yonder Helper chide us for our lack of it?"

They forced a way down the dead-cumbered tower stair, crawling through the darkness over the bodies of the fallen. They crossed the hall that also was full of dead, and of wounded whose pitiful groans echoed from the vaulted roof, and climbed another stair to their chamber in the gateway tower. Here from a spark of fire that still smouldered on the hearth, they lit the lamps of olive-oil and by the light of them washed off the stains of battle, and refreshed themselves with food and wine. These things done, Dick returned to the hall and presently brought thence two suits of armour and some cloaks which he had taken either from the walls or from off the slain. In these they disguised themselves as best they could, as de Noyon had disguised himself at Crecy.

Then, having collected a store of arrows whereof many lay about, they departed by the back entrance. The great front doorway was so choked with corpses that they could not pass it, since here had raged the last fearful struggle to escape. Going to the little stable-yard, where they found their horses unharmed in the stalls, although frightened by the tumult and stiff from lack of exercise, they fed and saddled them and led them out. So presently they looked their last upon the Bride's Tower that had sheltered them so well.

"It has served our turn," said Hugh, glancing back at it from the other side of the deserted square, "but oh, I pray heaven that we may never see that charnel-house again!"

As he spoke a figure appeared from the shadow of a doorway, and ran toward them. Thinking it was that of some foe, Dick lifted his axe to cut him down, whereon a voice cried in English:

"Hold! I am David!"

"David!" exclaimed Hugh. "Then thanks be to God, for know, we thought you dead these many days."

"Ay, sir," answered the young man, "as I thought you. The rumour reached the Jews, among whom I have been hiding while I recovered of my hurts, that the Mad Monk and his fellows had stormed the tower and killed you both. Therefore I crept out to learn for myself. Now I have found you by your voices, who never again hoped to look upon you living," and he began to sob in his relief and joy.

"Come on, lad," said Grey Dick kindly, "this is no place for greetings."

"Whither go you, sir?" asked David as he walked forward alongside of the horses.

"To seek that house where we saw Sir Andrew Arnold and the lady Eve," answered Hugh, "if by any chance it can be found."

"That is easy, sir," said David. "As it happens, I passed it not much more than an hour ago and knew it again."

"Did you see any one there?" asked Hugh eagerly.

"Nay, the windows were dark. Also the Jew guiding me said he had heard that all who dwelt in that house were dead of the plague. Still of this matter he knew nothing for certain."

Hugh groaned, but only answered:

"Forward!"

As they went David told them his story. It seemed that when he was struck down in the square where the crazy friar preached, and like to be stabbed and trampled to death, some of the Jews dragged him into the shadow and rescued him. Afterward they took him to a horrid and squalid quarter called La Juiverie, into which no Christian dare enter. Here he lay sick of his hurts and unable to get out until that very afternoon; the widow Rebecca, whom they had saved, nursing him all the while.

"Did you hear aught of us?" asked Dick.

"Ay, at first that you were holding Dead Bride's Tower bravely. So as soon as I might, I came to join you there if I could win in and you still lived. But they told me that you had fallen at last."

"Ah!" said Dick, "well, as it chances it was not we who fell, but that tale is long. Still, David, you are a brave lad who would have come to die with us, and my master will thank you when he can give his mind to such things. Say, did you hear aught else?"

"Ay, Dick; I heard two days ago that the French lord, Cattrina, whom Sir Hugh was to have fought at Venice, had left Avignon, none knew why or whither he went."

"Doubtless because of the plague and he wished to go where there was none," answered Dick.

But Hugh groaned again, thinking to himself that Acour would scarcely have left Avignon if Eve were still alive within its walls.

After this they went on in silence, meeting very few and speaking with none, for the part of the great city through which they passed seemed to be almost deserted. Indeed in this quarter the pest was so fearful that all who remained alive and could do so had fled elsewhere, leaving behind them only the sick and those who plundered houses.

"One thing I forgot to say," said David presently. "The Jews told me that they had certain information that the notary knave Basil was paid by the lord Cattrina to lead us to that square where the fires burned in order that we might be murdered there. Further, our death was to be the signal for the massacre of all the Jews, only, as it chanced, their plan went awry."

"As will Basil's neck if ever I meet him again," muttered Grey Dick beneath his breath. "Lord! what fools we were to trust that man. Well, we've paid the price and, please God, so shall he."

They turned the corner and rode down another street, till presently David said:

"Halt! yonder is the house. See the cognizance above the gateway!"

Hugh and Dick leapt from their horses, the latter bidding David lead them into the courtyard and hold them there. Then they entered the house, of which the door was ajar, and by the shine of the moon that struggled through the window-places, crept up the stairs and passages till they reached those rooms where Sir Andrew and Eve had lodged.

"Hist!" said Dick, and he pointed to a line of light that showed beneath the closed door.

Hugh pushed it gently and it opened a little. They looked through the crack, and within saw a man in a dark robe who was seated at a table counting out gold by the light of a lamp. Just then he lifted his head, having felt the draught of air from the open door. It was the notary Basil!

Without a word they entered the room, closing and bolting the door behind them. Then Dick leapt on Basil as a wolf leaps, and held him fat, while Hugh ran past him and threw wide the door of that chamber in which Eve had lain sick. It was empty. Back he came again and in a terrible voice, said:

"Now, Sir Notary, where are the lady Eve and Sir Andrew her guardian?"

"Alas, Sir Knight," began the knave in a quavering voice, "both of them are dead."

"What!" cried Hugh supporting himself against the wall, for at this terrible news his knees trembled beneath him, "have you or your patron Cattrina murdered them?"

"Murdered them, Sir Knight! I do murder? I, a Christian and a man of peace! Never! And the noble lord of Cattrina, Count de Noyon! Why, he wished to marry the lady, not to murder her. Indeed he swore that she was his wife."

"So you know all these things, do you, villain?" said Grey Dick, shaking him as a terrier shakes a rat.

"Sir Knight," went on the frightened fellow, "blame me not for the acts of God. He slew these noble persons, not I; I myself saw the lovely lady carried from this house wrapped in a red cloak."

"So you were in the house, were you?" said Grey Dick, shaking him again. "Well, whither did they carry her, thief of the night?"

"To the plague pit, good sir; where else in these times?"

Now Hugh groaned aloud, his eyes closed, and he seemed as though he were about to fall. Grey Dick, noting it, for a moment let go of the notary and turned as though to help his master. Like a flash Basil drew a dagger from under his dirty robe and struck at Dick's back. The blow was well aimed, nor could an unprotected man on whom it fell have escaped death. But although Basil did not see it because of Dick's long cloak, beneath this cloak he wore the best of mail, and on that mail the slender dagger broke, its point falling harmless to the ground. Next instant Dick had him again in his iron grip. Paying no further heed to Hugh, who had sunk to the floor a huddled heap, he began to speak into the lawyer's ear in his slow, hissing voice.

"Devil," he said, "whether or no you murdered Red Eve and Sir Andrew Arnold the saint, I cannot say for certain, though doubtless I shall learn in time. At least a while ago you who had taken our money, strove to murder both of us, or cause us to be torn in pieces upon yonder square where the fires burned. Now, too, you have striven to murder me with that bodkin of yours, not knowing, fool, that I am safe from all men. Well, say your prayers, since you too journey to the plague pit, for so the gatherers of the dead will think you died."

"Sir," gasped the terrified wretch, "spare me and I will speak—"

"More lies," hissed Dick into his ear. "Nay, go tell them to the father of lies, for I have no time to waste in hearkening to them. Take your pay, traitor!"

A few seconds later Basil lay dead upon the floor.

Grey Dick looked at him. Kneeling down, he thrust his hands into the man's pockets, and took thence the gold that he had been hiding away when they came upon him, no small sum as it chanced.

"Our own come back with interest," he said with one of his silent laughs, "and we shall need monies for our faring. Why, here's a writing also which may tell those who can read it something."

He cast it on the table, then turned to his master, who was awakening from his swoon.

Dick helped him to his feet.

"What has passed?" asked Hugh in a hollow voice.

"Murgh!" answered Dick, pointing to the dead man on the floor.

"Have you killed him, friend?"

"Ay, sure enough, as he strove to kill me," and again he pointed, this time to the broken dagger.

Hugh made no answer, only seeing the writing on the table, took it up, and began to read like one who knows not what he does. Presently his eyes brightened and he said:

"What does this mean, I wonder. Hearken."

"Rogue, you have cheated me as you cheat all men and now I follow her who has gone. Be sure, however, that you shall reap your reward in due season, de Noyon."

"I know not," said Dick, "and the interpreter is silent," and he kicked the body of Basil. "Perhaps I was a little over hasty who might have squeezed the truth out of him before the end."

"'Her who is gone,'" reflected Hugh aloud. "'Tis Red Eve who is gone and de Noyon is scarcely the man to seek her among passed souls. Moreover, the Jews swear that he rode from Avignon two days ago. Come, Dick, let that carrion lie, and to the plague pit."

********

An hour later and they stood on the edge of that dreadful place, hearing and seeing things which are best left untold. A priest came up to them, one of those good men who, caring nothing for themselves, still dared to celebrate the last rites of the Church above the poor departed.

"Friends," he said, "you seem to be in trouble. Can I help you, for Jesus' sake?"

"Perchance, holy Father," answered Hugh. "Tell us, you who watch this dreadful place, was a woman wrapped in a red cloak thrown in here two or three days gone?"

"Alas, yes," said the priest with a sigh, "for I read the Office over her and others. Nay, what are you about to do? By now she is two fathoms deep and burned away with lime so that none could know her. If you enter there the guards will not let you thence living. Moreover, it is useless. Pray to God to comfort you, poor man, as I will, who am sure it will not be denied."

Then Dick led, or rather carried, Hugh from the brink of that awesome, common grave.

## Chapter 19

# The Doom

It was the last night of February, the bitterest night perhaps of all that sad winter, when at length Hugh de Cressi, Grey Dick, and David Day rode into the town of Dunwich. Only that morning they had landed at Yarmouth after a long, long journey whereof the perils and the horrors may be guessed but need not be written. France, through which they had passed, seemed to be but one vast grave over which the wail of those who still survived went up without cease to the cold, unpitying heavens.

Here in England the tale was still the same. Thus in the great seaport of Yarmouth scarcely enough people were left alive to inter the unshriven dead, nor of these would any stay to speak with them, fearing lest they had brought a fresh curse from overseas. Even the horses that they rode they took from a stable where they whinnied hungrily, none being there to feed them, leaving in their place a writing of the debt.

Betwixt Yarmouth and Dunwich they had travelled through smitten towns and villages, where a few wandered fearfully, distraught with sorrow or seeking food. In the streets the very dogs lay dead and in the fields they saw the carcasses of cattle dragged from the smokeless and deserted steadings and half hidden in a winding-sheet of snow. For the Black Plague spared neither man nor beast.

At the little port of Lowestoft they met a sullen sailorman who stood staring at the beach whereon his fishing boat lay overturned and awash for lack of hands to drag it out of reach of the angry sea. They asked him if he knew of how it fared with Dunwich.

By way of answer he cursed them, adding:

"Must I be forever pestered as to Dunwich? This is the third time of late that I have heard of Dunwich from wandering folk. Begone thither and gather tidings for yourselves, which I hope will please you as well as they do me."

"Now, if I were not in haste I would stay a while to teach you manners, you foul-mouthed churl," muttered Grey Dick between his teeth.

"Let the fellow be," said Hugh wearily; "the men of Lowestoft have ever hated those of Dunwich, and it seems that a common woe does not soften hearts. Soon enough we shall learn the truth."

"Ay, you'll learn it soon enough," shouted the brute after them. "Dunwich boats won't steel Lowestoft herrings for many a year!"

So they rode on through Kessland, which they reached as night was closing in, through Benacre and Wrentham, also past houses in which none seemed to dwell.

"Murgh has been here before us, I think," said Dick at length.

"Then I hope that we may overtake him," answered Hugh with a smile, "for I need his tidings—or his rest. Oh! Dick, Dick," he added, "I wonder has ever man borne a heavier burden for all this weary while? If I were sure, it would not be so bad, for when earthly hope is done we may turn to other comfort. But I'm not sure; Basil may have lied. The priest by the pit could only swear to the red cloak, of which there are many, though few be buried in them. And, Dick, there are worse things than that. Perchance Acour got her after all."

"And perchance he didn't," answered Dick. "Well, fret on if you will; the thing does not trouble me who for my part am sure enough."

"Of what, man, of what?"

"Of seeing the lady Eve ere long."

"In this world or the next, Dick?"

"In this. I don't reckon of the next, mayhap there we shall be blind and not see. Besides, of what use is that world to you where it is written that they neither marry nor are given in marriage, but are as the angels? You'll make no good angel, I'm thinking, while as for the lady Eve, she's too human for it as yet."

"Why do you think we shall see her on earth?" asked Hugh, ignoring these reflections.

"Because he who is called the Helper said as much, and whatever he may be he is no liar. Do you not remember what Red Eve told you when she awoke from that dream of hers, which was no dream? And do you not remember what Sir Andrew told you as to a certain meeting in the snow—pest upon it!" and he wiped some of the driving flakes from his face—"Sir Andrew, who is a saint, and, therefore, like Murgh, can be no liar?"

"If you think thus," said Hugh in a new voice, "why did you not say so before?"

"Because I love not argument, master, and if I had, you would ever have reasoned with me from Avignon to Yarmouth town and spoilt my sleep of nights. Oh! where is your faith?"

"What is faith, Dick?"

"The gift of belief, master. A very great gift, seeing what a man believes is and will be true for him, however false it may prove for others. He who believes nothing, sows nothing, and therefore reaps nothing, good or ill."

"Who taught you these things, Dick?"

"One whom I am not likely to forget, or you, either. One who is my master at archery and whose words, like his arrows, though they be few, yet strike the heart of hidden truth. Oh, fear not, doubtless sorrow waits you yonder," and he pointed toward Dunwich. "Yet it comes to my lips that there's joy beyond the sorrows, the joy of battle and of love—for those who care for love, which I think foolishness. There stands a farm, and the farmer is a friend of mine, or used to be. Let us go thither and feed these poor beasts and ourselves, or I think we will never come to Dunwich through this cold and snow. Moreover," he added thoughtfully, "joy or sorrow or both of them are best met by full men, and I wish to look to your harness and my own, for sword and axe are rusted with the sea. Who knows but that we may need them in Dunwich, or beyond, when we meet with Murgh, as he promised that we should."

So they rode up to the house and found Dick's friend, the farmer, lying dead there in his own yard, whither his family had dragged him ere they determined to fly the place. Still, there was fodder in the stable and they lit a fire in the kitchen hearth and drank of the wine which they had brought with them from the ship, and ate of the bacon which still hung from the rafters. This done, they lay down to sleep a while. About one in the morning, however, Hugh roused Dick and David, saying that he could rest no more and that something in his heart bade him push on to Dunwich.

"Then let us follow your heart, master," said Dick, yawning. "Yet I wish it had waited till dawn to move you. Yes, let us follow your heart to good or evil. David, go you out and saddle up those nags."

For Dick had worked late at their mail and weapons, which now were bright and sharp again, and was very weary.

********

It was after three in the morning when at length, leaving the heath, they rode up to Dunwich Middlegate, expecting to find it shut against them at such an hour. But it stood open, nor did any challenge them from the guardhouse.

"They keep an ill watch in Dunwich now-a-days," grumbled Dick. "Well, perchance there is one here to whom they can trust that business."

Hugh made no answer, only pressed on down the narrow street, that was deep and dumb with snow, till at length they drew reign before the door of his father's house, in the market-place, the great house where he was born. He looked at the windows and noted that, although they were unshuttered, no friendly light shone in them. He called aloud, but echo was his only answer, echo and the moan of the bitter wind and the sullen roar of the sea.

"Doubtless all men are asleep," he said. "Why should it be otherwise at such an hour? Let us enter and waken them."

"Yes, yes," answered Dick as he dismounted and threw the reins of his horse to David. "They are like the rest of Dunwich—asleep."

So they entered and began to search the house by the dim light of the moon. First they searched the lower chambers, then those where Hugh's father and his brothers had slept, and lastly the attics. Here they found the pallets of the serving-folk upon the floor, but none at rest upon them.

"The house is deserted," said Hugh heavily.

"Yes, yes," answered Dick again, in a cheerful voice; "doubtless Master de Cressi and your brothers have moved away to escape the pest."

"Pray God they have escaped it!" muttered Hugh. "This place stifles me," he added. "Let us out."

"Whither shall we go, master?"

"To Blythburgh Manor," he answered, "for there I may win tidings. David, bide you here, and if you can learn aught follow us across the moor. The manor cannot be missed."

So once more Hugh and Dick mounted their horses and rode away through the town, stopping now and again before some house they knew and calling to its inmates. But though they called loudly none answered. Soon they grew sure that this was because there were none to answer, since of those houses many of the doors stood open. Only one living creature did they see in Dunwich. As they turned the corner near to the Blythburgh Gate they met a grey-haired man wrapped up in tattered blankets which were tied about him with haybands. He carried in his hand a beautiful flagon of silver. Doubtless he had stolen it from some church.

Seeing them, he cast this flagon into the snow and began to whimper like a dog.

"Mad Tom," said Dick, recognizing the poor fellow. "Tell us, Thomas, where are the folk of Dunwich?"

"Dead, dead; all dead!" he wailed, and fled away.

"Stay! What of Master de Cressi?" called Hugh. But the tower of the church round which he had vanished only echoed back across the snow, "What of Master de Cressi?"

Then at last Hugh understood the awful truth.

It was that, save those who had fled, the people of Dunwich were slain with the Sword of Pestilence, and all his kin among them.

********

They were on the Blythburgh Marshes, travelling thither by the shortest road. The moon was down and the darkness dense, for the snow-clouds hid the stars.

"Let us bide here a while," said Grey Dick as their horses blundered through the thick reeds. "It will soon be sunrise, and if we go on in this gloom we shall fall into some bog-hole or into the river, which I hear running on our left."

So they halted their weary horses and sat still, for in his wretchedness Hugh cared not what he did.

At length the east began to lighten, turning the sky to a smoky red. Then the rim of the sun rising out of the white-flecked ocean, threw athwart the desolate marsh a fierce ray that lay upon the snows like a sword of blood. They were standing on the crest of a little mound, and Dick, looking about him, knew the place.

"See," he said, pointing toward the river that ran near by, "it is just here that you killed young Clavering this day two years ago. Yonder also I shot the French knights, and Red Eve and you leapt into the Blythe and swam it."

"Ay," said Hugh, looking up idly, "but did you say two years, Dick? Nay, surely 'tis a score. Why," he added in a changed voice, "who may that be in the hollow?" and he pointed to a tall figure which stood beneath them at a distance, half-hidden by the dank snow-mists.

"Let us go and see," said Dick, speaking almost in a whisper, for there was that about this figure which sent the blood to his throat and cheeks.

He drove the spurs into his tired horse's sides, causing it to leap forward.

Half a minute later they had ridden down the slope of the hollow. A puff of wind that came with the sun drove away the mist. Dick uttered a choking cry and leapt from his saddle. For there, calm, terrible, mighty, clothed in his red and yellow cap and robe of ebon furs, stood he who was named Murgh the Fire, Murgh the Sword, Murgh the Helper, Murgh, Gateway of the Gods!

They knelt before him in the snow, while, screaming in their fright, the horses fled away.

"Knight and Archer," said Murgh, in his icy voice, counting with the thumb of his white-gloved right hand upon the hidden fingers of his left. "Friends, you keep your tryst, but there are more to come. Have patience, there are more to come."

Then he became quiet, nor dared they ask him any questions. Only at a motion of his arm they rose from their knees and stood before him.

A long while they stood thus in silence, till under Murgh's dreadful gaze Hugh's brain began to swim. He looked about him, seeking some natural thing to feed his eyes. Lo! yonder was that which he might watch, a hare crouching in its form not ten paces distant. See, out of the reeds crept a great red fox. The hare smelt or saw, and leaped away. The fox sprang at it, too late, for the white fangs closed emptily behind its scut. Then with a little snarl of hungry rage it turned and vanished into the brake.

The hare and the fox, the dead reeds, the rising sun, the snow—oh, who had told him of these things?

Ah! he remembered now, and that memory set the blood pulsing in his veins. For where these creatures were should be more besides Grey Dick and himself and the Man of many names.

He looked toward Murgh to see that he had bent himself and with his gloved hand was drawing lines upon the snow. Those lines when they were done enclosed the shape of a grave!

"Archer," said Murgh, "unsheathe your axe and dig."

As though he understood, Dick obeyed, and began to hollow out a grave in the soft and boggy soil.

Hugh watched him like one who dreams, wondering who was destined to fill that grave. Presently a sound behind caused him to turn his head.

Oh! certainly he was mad, for there over the rise not a dozen yards away came the beautiful ghost of Eve Clavering, clad in her red cloak. With her was another ghost, that of old Sir Andrew Arnold, blood running down the armour beneath his robe and in his hand the hilt of a broken sword.

Hugh tried to speak, but his lips were dumb, nor did these ghosts take any heed of him, for their eyes were fixed elsewhere. To Murgh they went and stood before him silent. For a while he looked at them, then asked in his cold voice:

"Who am I, Eve Clavering?"

"The Man who came to visit me in my dream at Avignon and told me that I should live," she answered slowly.

"And who say you that I am, Andrew Arnold, priest of Christ the God?"

"He whom I visited in my youth in far Cathay," answered the old knight in an awed whisper. "He who sat beside the pool behind the dragon-guarded doors and was named Gateway of the Gods. He who showed to me that we should meet again in such a place and hour as this."

"Whence come you now, priest and woman, and why?"

"We come from Avignon. We fled thence from one who would have done this maiden grievous wrong. He followed us. Not an hour gone he overtook us with his knaves. He set them on to seize this woman, hanging back himself. Old as I am I slew them both and got my death in it," and he touched the great wound in his side with the hilt of the broken sword. "Our horses were the better; we fled across the swamp for Blythburgh, he hunting us and seeking my life and her honour. Thus we found you as it was appointed."

Murgh turned his eyes. Following their glance, for the first time they saw Hugh de Cressi and near him Grey Dick labouring at the grave. Eve stretched out her arms and so stood with head thrown back, the light of the daybreak shining in her lovely eyes and on her outspread hair. Hugh opened his lips to speak but Murgh lifted his hand and pointed behind them.

They turned and there, not twenty paces from them, clad in armour and seated on a horse was Edmund Acour, Count de Noyon, Seigneur of Cattrina.

He saw, then wheeled round to fly.

"Archer, to your work!" said Murgh, "you know it."

Ere the words had left his lips the great black bow was bent and ere the echoes died away the horse, struck in its side by the keen arrow, sank dying to the ground.

Then Murgh beckoned to the rider and he came as a man who must. But, throwing down the bow, Grey Dick once more began to labour at the grave like one who takes no further heed of aught save his allotted task.

Acour stood before Murgh like a criminal before his judge.

"Man," said the awful figure addressing him, "where have you been and what have you done since last we spoke together in the midday dark at Venice?"

Now, dragged word by slow word from his unwilling lips, came the answer of the traitor's heart.

"I fled from the field at Venice because I feared this knight, and you, O Spirit of Death. I journeyed to Avignon, in France, and there strove to possess myself of yonder woman whom here in England, with the help of one Nicholas, I had wed, when she was foully drugged. I strove to possess myself of her by fraud and by violence. But some fate was against me. She and that aged priest bribed the knave whom I trusted. He caused a dead man and woman dressed in their garments to be borne from their lodging to the plague pit while they fled from Avignon disguised."

Here for a moment Grey Dick paused from his labours at the grave and looked up at Hugh. Then he fell to them again, throwing out the peaty soil with both hands.

"My enemy and his familiar, for man he can scarcely be," went on Acour, pointing first to Hugh and then to Dick, "survived all my plans to kill them and instead killed those whom I had sent after them. I learned that the woman and the priest were not dead, but fled, and followed them, and after me came my enemy and his familiar. Twice we passed each other on the road, once we slept in the same house. I knew them but they knew me not and the Fate which blinded me from them, saved them also from all my plots to bring them to their doom. The woman and the priest took ship to England, and I followed in another ship, being made mad with desire and with jealous rage, for there I knew my enemy would find and win her. In the darkness before this very dawn I overtook the woman and the priest at last and set my fellows on to kill the man. Myself I would strike no blow, fearing lest my death should come upon me, and so I should be robbed of her. But God fought with His aged servant who in his youth was the first of knights. He slew my men, then fled on with the woman, Eve of Clavering. I followed, knowing that he was sore wounded and must die, and that then the beauty which has lured me to shame and ruin would be mine, if only for an hour. I followed, and here at this place of evil omen, where first I saw my foe, I found *you*, O Incarnate Sword of Vengeance."

Murgh unfolded his bare arms and lifted his head, which was sunk upon his breast.

"Your pardon," he said gently, "my name is Hand of Fate and not Sword of Vengeance. There is no vengeance save that which men work upon themselves. What fate may be and vengeance may be I know not fully, and none will ever know until they have passed the Gateway of the Gods. Archer the grave is deep enough. Come forth now and let us learn who it is decreed shall fill it. Knights, the hour is at hand for you to finish that which you began at Crecy and at Venice."

Hugh heard and drew his sword. Acour drew his sword also, then cried out, pointing to Grey Dick:

"Here be two against one. If I conquer he will shoot me with his bow."

"Have no fear, Sir Thief and Liar," hissed Grey Dick, "for that shaft will not be needed. Slay the master if you can and go safe from the squire," and he unstrung his black bow and hid it in its case.

Now Hugh stepped to where Red Eve stood, the wounded Sir Andrew leaning on her shoulder. Bending down he kissed her on the lips, saying: "Soon, very soon, my sweet, whom I have lost and found again, you will be mine on earth, or I shall be yours in heaven. This, then, in greeting or farewell."

"In greeting, beloved, not in farewell," she answered as she kissed him back, "for if you die, know that I follow hard upon your road. Yet I say that yonder grave was not dug for you."

"Nay, not for you, son, not for you," said Sir Andrew lifting his faint head. "One fights for you whom you do not see, and against Him Satan and his servant cannot stand," and letting fall the sword hilt he stretched out his thin hand and blessed him.

Now when Acour saw that embrace his jealous fury prevailed against his fears. With a curse upon his lips he leapt at Hugh and smote, thinking to take him unawares. But Hugh was watching, and sprang back, and then the fray began, if fray it can be called.

A wild joy shining in his eyes, Hugh grasped his long sword with both hands and struck. So great was that blow that it bit through Acour's armour, beneath his right arm, deep into the flesh and sent him staggering back. Again he struck and wounded him in the shoulder; a third time and clove his helm so that the blood poured down into his eyes and blinded him.

Back reeled Acour, back to the very edge of the grave, and stood there swaying to and fro. At the sight of his helplessness Hugh's fury seemed to leave him. His lifted sword sank downward.

"Let God deal with you, knave," he said, "for I cannot."

For a while there was silence. There they stood and stared at the smitten man waiting the end, whatever it might be. They all stared save Murgh, who fixed his stony eyes upon the sky.

Presently it came. The sword, falling from Acour's hand into the grave, rested there point upward. With a last effort he drew his dagger. Dashing the blood from his eyes, he hurled it with all his dying strength, not at Hugh, but at Red Eve. Past her ear it hissed, severing a little tress of her long hair, which floated down on to the snow.

Then Acour threw his arms wide and fell backward—fell backward and vanished in the grave.

Dick ran to look. There he lay dead, pierced through back and bosom by the point of his own sword.

For one brief flash of time a black dove-shaped bird was seen hovering round the head of Murgh.

"Finished!" said Dick straightening himself. "Well, I had hoped to see a better fight, but cowards die as cowards live."

Leaning on Red Eve's shoulder Sir Andrew limped to the side of the grave. They both looked down on that which lay therein.

"Daughter," said the old man, "through many dangers it has come about as I foretold. The bond that in your drugged sleep bound you to this highborn knave is severed by God's sword of death. Christ have pity on his sinful soul. Now, Sir Hugh de Cressi, come hither and be swift, for my time is short."

Hugh obeyed, and at a sign took Eve by the hand. Then, speaking very low and as quickly as he might for all his life was draining from him through the red wound in his side, the old priest spoke the hallowed words that bound these two together till death should part them. Yes, there by the graveside, over the body of the dead Acour, there in the red light of the morning, amidst the lonely snows, was celebrated the strangest marriage the world has ever seen. In nature's church it was celebrated, with the grim, grey Archer for a clerk, and Death's own fearful minister for congregation.

It was done and with uplifted, trembling hands Sir Andrew blessed them both—them and the fruit of their bodies which was to be. He blessed them in the name of the all-seeing God he served. He bade them put aside their grief for those whom they had lost. Soon, he said, their short day done, the lost would be found again, made glorious, and with them himself, who, loving them both on earth, would love them through eternity.

Then, while their eyes grew blind with tears, and even the fierce archer turned aside his face, Sir Andrew staggered to where he stood who in the Land of Sunrise had been called Gateway of the Gods. Before him he bent his grey and ancient head.

"O thou who dwellest here below to do the will of heaven, to thee I come as once thou badest me," he said, and was silent.

Murgh let his eyes rest on him. Then stretching out his hand, he touched him very gently on the breast, and as he touched him smiled a sweet and wondrous smile.

"Good and faithful servant," he said, "thy work is done on earth. Now I, whom all men fear, though I be their friend and helper, am bidden by the Lord of life and death to call thee home. Look up and pass!"

The old priest obeyed. It seemed to those who watched that the radiance on the face of Murgh had fallen upon him also. He smiled, he stretched his arms upward as though to clasp what they might not see. Then down he sank gently, as though upon a bed, and lay white and still in the white, still snow.

********

The Helper turned to the three who remained alive.

"Farewell for a little time," he said. "I must be gone. But when we meet again, as meet we shall, then fear me not, for have you not seen that to those who love me I am gentle?"

Hugh de Cressi and Red Eve made no answer, for they knew not what to say. But Grey Dick spoke out boldly.

"Sir Lord, or Sir Spirit," he said, "save once at the beginning, when the arrow burst upon my string, I never feared you. Nor do I fear your gifts," and he pointed to the grave and to dead Sir Andrew, "which of late have been plentiful throughout the world, as we of Dunwich know. Therefore I dare to ask you one question ere we part for a while. Why do you take one and leave another? Is it because you must, or because every shaft does not hit its mark?"

Now Murgh looked him up and down with his sunken eyes, then answered: "Come hither, archer, and I will lay my hand upon your heart also and you shall learn."

"Nay," cried Grey Dick, "for now I have the answer to the riddle, since I know you cannot lie. When we die we still live and know; therefore I'm content to wait."

Again that smile swept across Murgh's awful face though that smile was cold as the winter dawn. Then he turned and slowly walked away toward the west.

They watched him go till he became but a blot of fantastic colour that soon vanished on the moorland.

********

Hugh spoke to Red Eve and said:

"Wife, let us away from this haunted place and take what joy we can. Who knows when Murgh may return again and make us as are all the others whom we love!"

"Ay, husband won at last," she answered, "who knows? Yet, after so much fear and sorrow, first I would rest a while with you."

So hand in hand they went till they, too, grew small and vanished on the snowy marsh.

********

But Grey Dick stayed there alone with the dead, and presently spoke aloud for company.

"The woman has him heart and soul," he said, "as is fitting, and where's the room between the two for an archer-churl to lodge? Mayhap, after all, I should have done well to take yonder Murgh for lord when I had the chance. Man, or god, or ghost, he's a fellow to my liking, and once he had led me through the Gates no woman would have dared to come to part us. Well, good-bye, Hugh de Cressi, till you are sick of kisses and the long shafts begin to fly again, for then you will bethink you of a certain bow and of him who alone can bend it."

Having spoken thus in his hissing voice, whereof the sound resembled that of an arrow in its flight, Grey Dick descended into the grave and trod the earth over Acour's false and handsome face, hiding it from the sight of men forever.

********

Then he lifted up the dead Sir Andrew in his strong arms and slowly bore him thence to burial.

www.ingramcontent.com/pod-product-compliance
Lightning Source LLC
LaVergne TN
LVHW050910080826
845145LV00001B/36

* 9 7 8 1 8 4 6 7 7 9 9 3 0 *